OXFORD WORLD'S CLASSICS

IRISH WRITING

THIS is an anthology of Irish writing in English from the revolutionary era of the 1790s to the early years of the Irish Free State in the 1930s. It spans 150 years of modern Irish culture, from the dawning of a powerful nationalist consciousness inspired by Wolfe Tone and the United Irish movement to the waning of the Irish Literary Revival and the last poems of W. B. Yeats. In that traumatic century and a half, the struggle for political independence found expression in songs and stories, poems and plays, as well as in essays, speeches, and memoirs. It was in these years that Ireland produced a new and distinctive national literature in which questions of origin, identity, and destiny were of paramount importance. This emerging tradition of Irish literature was all the more remarkable for being written in English at a time when the Irish language was being steadily eroded. The determination of Irish writers to forge a tradition of their own and to use the English language in new and often subversive ways produced a literature of startling imaginative vitality and stylistic experimentation. Selected authors include Edmund Burke, Maria Edgeworth, Thomas Moore, Oscar Wilde, Augusta Gregory, J. M. Synge, W. B. Yeats, James Joyce, Seán O'Casey, Elizabeth Bowen, Samuel Beckett, and Louis MacNeice.

STEPHEN REGAN is Professor of English at Durham University.

T0066584

OXFORD WORLD'S CLASSICS

*For over 100 years Oxford World's Classics have brought
readers closer to the world's great literature. Now with over 700
titles—from the 4,000-year-old myths of Mesopotamia to the
twentieth century's greatest novels—the series makes available
lesser-known as well as celebrated writing.*

*The pocket-sized hardbacks of the early years contained
introductions by Virginia Woolf, T. S. Eliot, Graham Greene,
and other literary figures which enriched the experience of reading.
Today the series is recognized for its fine scholarship and
reliability in texts that span world literature, drama and poetry,
religion, philosophy and politics. Each edition includes perceptive
commentary and essential background information to meet the
changing needs of readers.*

OXFORD WORLD'S CLASSICS

Irish Writing

An Anthology of Irish Literature in English 1789–1939

Edited with an Introduction and Notes by
STEPHEN REGAN

OXFORD
UNIVERSITY PRESS

OXFORD

UNIVERSITY PRESS

Great Clarendon Street, Oxford OX2 6DP

Oxford University Press is a department of the University of Oxford.
It furthers the University's objective of excellence in research, scholarship,
and education by publishing worldwide in

Oxford New York

Auckland Bangkok Buenos Aires Cape Town Chennai
Dar es Salaam Delhi Hong Kong Istanbul Karachi Kolkata
Kuala Lumpur Madrid Melbourne Mexico City Mumbai Nairobi
São Paulo Shanghai Singapore Taipei Tokyo Toronto

Oxford is a registered trade mark of Oxford University Press
in the UK and in certain other countries

Published in the United States
by Oxford University Press Inc., New York

British Library Cataloguing in Publication Data

Data available

Library of Congress Cataloging in Publication Data

Data available

ISBN 978-0-19-954982-5

13

Typeset in Ehrhardt
by RefineCatch Limited, Bungay, Suffolk
Printed and bound in Great Britain
by Clays Ltd, Elcograf S.p.A.

CONTENTS

IRISH WRITING

PART ONE: WRITINGS 1789–1890

1. POLITICAL WRITINGS AND SPEECHES

2. REFLECTIONS ON IRISH CULTURE

PART TWO: WRITINGS 1890–1939

1. NATIONALIST WRITINGS AND THE EASTER RISING

2. MEMOIRS AND AUTOBIOGRAPHIES

3. SHORT FICTION

INTRODUCTION

'The seas of literature are full of the wrecks of Irish anthologies.' With this cheering thought, W. B. Yeats set afloat his own anthology, *A Book of Irish Verse*, in 1895.[1] Yeats fervently believed that his book was a genuine contribution to a tradition of Irish writing in English, as well as a personal record of what he considered to be the best in Irish verse, but he also realized that the very word 'Irish' would summon critics with more ardent nationalist sentiments than his own. His concern was that the image of Ireland that his anthology conveyed would be regarded as insufficiently patriotic and that the times might demand a more heroic and more explicitly political representation of national identity. Any new anthology of Irish writing still runs the risk of censure for what its selection of material might suggest about Ireland and Irishness. Today, however, critics are wary of impassioned talk about tradition and identity. Anthologies are suspect because they are, by their very nature, part of a tradition-making process and tradition is often invoked as a way of defining and declaring identity. Anthologies can, of course, also acknowledge diversity and plurality.

Many of the writings in this anthology *are* overtly nationalist. This is hardly surprising, given the historical circumstances in which they were composed. Political speeches, songs, and memoirs are included here, along with stories, plays, and poems. Questions about national destiny and national identity are paramount in all of these works, but they do not as a body of writing constitute some monolithic notion of Ireland or promote some essentialist idea of what it is to be Irish. What these writings frequently reveal are the startling instabilities and uncertainties that accompany debates about identity and nationality, especially in times of violent political conflict and difficult social transition. Images of Ireland in the writings of Edmund Burke, Maria Edgeworth, J. M. Synge, W. B. Yeats, James Joyce, Elizabeth Bowen, and others are not necessarily flattering or positive images. One of the strongest dissenting voices towards the end of the period represented here is that of Louis MacNeice

[1] W. B. Yeats, *A Book of Irish Verse* (London: Methuen & Co., 1895), p. x.

provocatively asking, 'Why should I want to go back | To you, Ireland, my Ireland?'.

This is an anthology of Irish writing in English from the revolutionary era of the late eighteenth century to the formative years of the Irish Free State in the early decades of the twentieth century. It spans 150 years of modern European history, from the French Revolution, which impacted so powerfully on Irish nationalist aspirations, to the outbreak of the Second World War, in which the newly independent Irish Free State maintained its neutrality. In that traumatic century and a half, the struggle for political independence inspired patriotic speeches, songs, and stories, and these in turn gave fresh inspiration to new generations of nationalist writers and activists. The voices of Wolfe Tone and Robert Emmet are heard in the uproar of Easter 1916 and later. Other voices, of course, are inflected in different ways and not always in support of revolutionary change. There are voices of loyalist fervour as well as nationalist aspiration, voices of bewilderment as well as assurance, and voices of lament as well as celebration. Throughout the writings of this troubled century and a half, there is an intense preoccupation with Ireland itself: with issues of national identity, political liberty, sectarian conflict, territorial possession, and linguistic inheritance. This preoccupation is inflected in different ways in a variety of literary forms: in travel writing and Gothic fiction as much as in autobiographical essays and translations of early Irish poems.

Modern Irish literature: beginnings

In the years between 1789 and 1939, Irish writing gathers a powerful sense of momentum and direction, and it does so when complex cultural issues find appropriate form in equally complex rhetorical structures. This is not to suggest that there is a definitive canon of Irish writing with clearly marked characteristics, but simply to observe an emerging body of writing with a familiar set of conventions and concerns. There are discernible influences and lines of descent, from Maria Edgeworth to Elizabeth Bowen, for instance, or from William Carleton to James Joyce. In terms of its earliest and latest dates of publication, the anthology stretches from the early translations in Charlotte Brooke's *Reliques of Irish Poetry* to the *Last Poems* of W. B. Yeats, tracing what Yeats himself regarded as a national tradition of Irish writing in English. That Irish writers should have produced such an extensive and imposing body of writing in the English language is itself a remarkable phenomenon, and a high degree of self-consciousness about the political implications of adopting an imposed colonial language is a significant feature of some of the writings included here.

There were, of course, many notable Irish writers working in the English language prior to 1789, including Oliver Goldsmith and Jonathan Swift, but the French Revolution and the United Ireland movement focused the concerns of Irish writers in new and unprecedented ways. No writer records the impact of the French Revolution on Irish politics more acutely or more powerfully than Edmund Burke. While Burke is comprehensively committed to preserving political equanimity in Europe and throughout the Empire, he also retains a special affection, as well as a profound anxiety, for his native Ireland. Born in Dublin and raised in Cork, Burke considered Ireland to be 'the Country to which I am bound by my earliest instincts'.[2] He was brought up as a Protestant, but was also an ardent supporter of Catholic rights. He had close contact with the Catholic community through his mother's family in Cork, and his wife was also a Catholic. Burke's deep conviction was that Irish Catholics, under continuing duress and exclusion from political power, would become increasingly vulnerable to the spread of French revolutionary principles. It was a conviction that found dramatic confirmation in the Irish Rebellion of 1798.

As Seamus Deane has argued, Burke's *Reflections on the Revolution in France* (1790) is a foundational modern Irish text.[3] In the first place, it provides the crucial contrasting terms—'tradition' and 'modernity'—by which the progress of Ireland, as well as France, might be measured and understood. More generally, though, it prompts a debate about cultural identity and political destiny, about national character and civil liberty, and in doing so it establishes the terms on which future narratives of the nation might be constructed. Written so soon after the events it describes, the book has a striking immediacy of address. In Burke's opinion, the French Revolution

---

[2] R. B. McDowell (ed.), *The Writings and Speeches of Edmund Burke*, ix (Oxford: Clarendon Press, 1991), 389.

[3] Seamus Deane, *Strange Country: Modernity and Nationhood in Irish Writing since 1790* (Oxford: Clarendon Press, 1997), 1.

has had a terminal and irreversible effect on European civilization: 'the glory of Europe is extinguished for ever' and 'the old manners and opinions' of traditional society have been swept away by 'a savage and brutal humanity'. At the same time, Burke's text is an exercise in damage limitation—an impassioned attempt to counter any further swell of revolutionary ardour. The revolution gives _all_ Europe 'too close and connected a concern in what is done in France'. In the case of Ireland, Burke came to see that the rigidity of Protestant conservatives in the face of growing demands for Catholic enfranchisement would ignite a similarly violent rebellion.

Burke's fearful account of 'the atrocious spectacle of the sixth of October 1789' and his perception of tragic drama in the ordeal of Marie Antoinette ought to remind us that he was also the author of _A Philosophical Enquiry into the Origin of our Ideas of the Sublime and the Beautiful_ (1757). In Burke's political theory, revolution is equated with the sublime emotions of fear and dread, while order is consonant with what is beautiful, lovely, and serene. Accordingly, national cohesion and solidarity depend on bonds of affection and on the appreciation of loveliness: 'To make us love our country, our country ought to be lovely.' Ireland's distress undermines any secure sense of well-being that Burke envisages for the rest of Europe beyond revolutionary France. The alarming contradiction in Burke's theory is that the British civil society that he seeks to defend for its decency and nobility is the same that condones the abuse of civil rights among Catholics in Ireland.

The problem, as Burke saw it, lay in the continuing opposition to Catholic relief among the so-called Protestant 'Ascendancy' (a term that was still very new when Burke gave it his attention in the 1790s). This is the substance of the troubled, unfinished letter that he addressed to his son Richard in 1792. His son was an agent of the Catholic Committee in Dublin and later a leader of the Catholic Association of Ireland, and his father pays tribute to him as one 'engaged in the relief of an oppressed people'. In recognizing the Ascendancy as a persecuting faction, Burke emphatically makes a political as well as a religious distinction between Catholics and Protestants. Burke's writings, then, acknowledge and inform the sectarian politics that increasingly dominate discussions of national identity from the 1790s onwards.

At the same time, Burke is clearly alert to comparisons between the Ascendancy in Ireland and the East India Company in India. If he enables political discussion of Ireland's future within the immediate context of revolutionary Europe, he also acutely registers the predicament of Ireland within a long and continuing history of Empire. Even so, Ireland remains a special case, and one of the problems facing Burke and later Irish writers is how to articulate Ireland's difference from England and other constituent parts of the Empire. If, in some obvious respects, Ireland seems an extension of the British system, sharing similar values and ideals, it is also in other respects profoundly different, resistant to foreign ways, and implacably opposed to the imposition of colonial institutions and regulations.

Burke and later writers saw that 'Ireland was being treated as an irredeemably strange country', both familiar and alien, both known and unknown.[4] While Burke continued to hope that Ireland might have a peaceful and secure role in the British imperial system, he also ruefully acknowledged the injustices and inequities that made such a prospect unlikely. Burke's impact on modern Irish culture is profound. In seeking to establish the appropriate conditions for a harmonious civil society in Ireland, he gives serious consideration to questions of national identity and national character. His work provides the impulse for the Protestant Ascendancy to authenticate its political power by rooting itself in tradition, and in this respect it can be seen to anticipate the Literary Revival spearheaded by W. B. Yeats and his contemporaries a century later.[5] In equally lasting ways, however, Burke provides a model of Irish eloquence in the English language and sets a standard of linguistic opulence in those rhetorical skills for which he is justly remembered: 'his vivid vocabulary, his profusion of epithets, his ready resort to metaphor, his exuberance in praise, denunciation, and ridicule, his infusion of poetry into the exposition of political practicalities.'[6]

Burke's fears about the vulnerability of Ireland in the wake of the French Revolution were not exaggerated. He accurately predicted that Catholic demands for religious toleration and civil liberties would be joined and supported by expressions of discontent among

---

[4] Deane, *Strange Country*, 16.

[5] The point is well made by Declan Kiberd in *Irish Classics* (Cambridge, Mass.: Harvard University Press, 2000), 219.

[6] McDowell (ed.), *The Writings and Speeches of Edmund Burke*, ix. 391.

radical Protestant dissenters, including Belfast Presbyterians. This alliance on revolutionary principles between two disaffected groups provided the impulse behind the United Irish movement of 1797–8. That alliance is memorably celebrated by Wolfe Tone in 'An Argument on Behalf of the Catholics of Ireland' (1791) and proudly recalled in his autobiography: 'To unite the whole people of Ireland, to abolish the memory of all past dissentions, and to substitute the common name of Irishman in place of the denominations of Protestant, Catholic and Dissenter—these were my means.'

There are good reasons for seeing the 1790s as 'the pivotal decade in the evolution of modern Ireland'. The United Irish movement sought to transcend sectarian differences and establish a political system founded on universal ideas of equality and justice. The suppression of those aspirations by the British state was to have profound consequences, both in terms of subsequent constitutional arrangements and in terms of the direction that popular republican and loyalist sentiment would take. As Kevin Whelan and other historians of the period have argued, what has since proved elusive is 'an agreed political structure, capable of representing Irish people in all their inherited complexities'.[7] If the events of the 1790s were crucial to the evolution of modern Ireland, they also impacted in significant ways on the imaginative and artistic life of the country.

Reading Tone's autobiography in the knowledge of his certain failure in the Irish rebellion of 1798 is a poignant experience. The revolutionary excitement and promise of the 1790s, however, are given popular expression in songs and ballads of the time, including 'The Croppy Boy' and 'The Wearin' o' the Green', as well as in much later literary works, including Ethna Carbery's 'Rody McCorley' and that controversial play of the Irish Literary Revival, *Cathleen ni Houlihan* (1902). In the aftermath of rebellion, the extirpation of French revolutionary ideals was accompanied by a more pragmatic governmental attempt at pacification: the Act of Union in 1800. Direct control from Westminster did not, however, prevent a further uprising by another United Irishman of Protestant background, though Robert Emmet insisted in his 'Speech in the Dock' that he was 'no emissary' of France but the advocate of a proudly independent Ireland. Emmet and Tone together provide a

---

[7] Kevin Whelan, *Fellowship of Freedom: The United Irishmen and 1798* (Cork: Cork University Press, 1998), p. ix.

model of exemplary patriotism for the abject Yeats in his poem of mourning for a lost Romantic Ireland, 'September 1913'.

Yeats was clearly less impressed by Daniel O'Connell, whose redoubtable energies helped to mobilize Catholic opinion on a massive scale and achieve emancipation in 1829. His 'Speech at Tara' is a powerful demonstration of his skills in rhetoric, as well as a compelling example of his insistent call for the repeal of the Union. O'Connell's constitutional endeavours contrast markedly, however, with the militant republicanism of James Fintan Lalor and the emerging Fenian Brotherhood. The difference in outlook is, in part, a consequence of the Famine years, during which almost a million people died from starvation and disease and a million and a half sought emigration as an escape from desperate circumstances. Lalor articulates the uncompromising nationalism of an Ireland suffering the dire social and economic consequences of the Famine and intent on dealing with issues of land ownership and reform. If Lalor revives the republican spirit of Wolfe Tone, he also anticipates the militant politics of Patrick Pearse and the patriots of Easter 1916.

Political essays, speeches, letters, and memoirs were instrumental in the making of an Irish national literature, and so, too, were works of travel writing and cultural anthropology. There is a special sense in which Burke's *Reflections on the Revolution in France* might be regarded as a work of travel writing, and this ought to remind us that travel writing often functions as social and political critique.[8] In late eighteenth-century and early nineteenth-century Europe, there are numerous works of journeying and observation inspired by an Enlightenment curiosity in social and cultural differences. What prompts these works of travel writing is a desire to know a country and to find appropriate ways of rendering it knowable. Ireland stirs the imagination of the traveller/anthropologist in peculiar ways. Even when the traveller is an insider like John Gamble or William Carleton, Ireland is rendered phantasmagorically strange. When the traveller is an outsider, the representation is sometimes startling in its novelty.

One of the most remarkable travel books from the revolutionary 1790s is *A Frenchman's Walk Through Ireland* (1797), the work of Chevalier de la Tocnaye, a Breton officer and Royalist supporter

---

[8] Again, I am indebted to Seamus Deane's *Strange Country* (see pp. 4–6).

who fled his country in 1792 and arrived in London, not knowing English. His 'promenade dans l'Irlande' is sharply responsive to the contrasting grandeur and misery of Dublin, but it also reports from remoter places like 'the neighbourhood of Armagh' on 'the subject of the troubles, which for so long have desolated this beautiful country'. The book offers a French Royalist perspective on both sectarian grievances and United Irish solidarity in the north at a time of immense political uncertainty. In contrast, John Gamble and William Carleton, both writing in the early decades of a new century, are intent on recording the spiritual as well as the political life of the people. Both writers, in the essays included here, depict a Gaelic peasant Ireland holding stubbornly to its own rituals, customs, and superstitions. A century later, a similar kind of writing would help to lay the foundations of the Irish Literary Revival, and John Millington Synge would follow these earlier writers in converting the stuff of his observations in the Aran Islands and the Wicklow Hills into powerful creative works like *Riders to the Sea* (1904). Indeed, for Yeats and Synge and other Revivalists caught up in debates about identity and nationhood, the very act of wandering becomes not only a means of observation but a mode of self-definition and self-realization.

Irish fiction and political crisis

Gamble's *Sketches of History, Politics, and Manners, in Dublin, and the North of Ireland, in 1810* belongs to a polite genre of writing popular with English readers. The aesthetic delicacy of 'sketches' and the ostensible concern with 'manners' position the writer as a mediator between very different styles of life. The preface to the book confirms this in its declaration that the author 'endeavours to make known a very peculiar people, and a state of society, unhappily unparalleled on the civilised earth'.[9] Gamble's moving account of an Irish wake, preceded by the cry of the Banshee, is astutely observant and impeccably detailed, but it also shows his flair for telling a good tale. Like Carleton, he prepares the ground on which the Irish tale is transformed into printed literary forms, including novels.

Carleton, too, has a fondness for telling a good tale, but the title of

[9] John Gamble, *Sketches of History, Politics, and Manners, in Dublin, and the North of Ireland, in 1810*, new edn. (London: Baldwin, Cradock and Joy, 1826), p. v.

his *Traits and Stories of the Irish Peasantry* points to a particular interest in the exploration of national character. In the preface to that book (a new edition of which was published in 1843–4), Carleton presents his writings as 'works which may be said to treat exclusively of a people who form such an important and interesting portion of the empire as the Irish peasantry do'. He claims, as author, to be concerned with 'removing many absurd prejudices which have existed for time immemorial against his countrymen', though it might be argued that his account of Catholic ritual in 'A Pilgrim at Lough Derg' is itself a work of comic absurdity and one that reinforces as many prejudices as it seeks to dispel.[10]

In other respects, however, 'A Pilgrim at Lough Derg' was of crucial importance both to Carleton and his successors. It constituted his 'début in literature', but it also prompted him to forsake his vocation as a Catholic priest. It was, he says, 'the cause of changing the whole destiny of my subsequent life'. The wealth of characterization, the shrewdness of observation, and the vigorous delivery of Irish speech all point towards significant developments in the history of Irish fiction. Ironically, Carleton renders the Irish peasant knowable in print only by transforming himself: by adopting the Protestant faith and appealing to his readers through an educated English syntax and diction. Even in the passage describing his abandoned vocation, the transformation appears inevitable and complete: 'I had nothing for it now but to forget my sacerdotal prospects.'[11] Paul Muldoon has made the excellent point that as well as representing 'an extraordinary straddling of the two main religio-political traditions in Ireland', Carleton shows a powerful combination of intimacy with, and enmity towards, his subject-matter that anticipates the work of James Joyce.[12]

Over a century and a half later, Carleton comes back to inspire and instruct the pilgrim poet Seamus Heaney in *Station Island* (1984). The dialogue between them is an act of mutual confession, with Heaney telling Carleton's shade, 'Your *Lough Derg Pilgrim* | haunts me every time I cross this mountain | . . . A lot of what you wrote | I heard and did', and Carleton acknowledging his 'old fork-tongued

---

[10] William Carleton, *Traits and Stories of the Irish Peasantry*, new edn. (Dublin: William Curry & Co., 1843–4), p. i.

[11] Ibid., p. xvi.

[12] Paul Muldoon, *To Ireland, I* (Oxford: Oxford University Press, 2000), 25.

turncoat' tendencies. Carleton is 'an aggravated man | raving on
about nights spent listening for | gun butts to come cracking on the
door'. He is deeply dismayed to find that nothing has changed. He
offers a lesson to Heaney in being true to oneself: 'It is a road you
travel on your own.'[13] Heaney's marvellous encounter with Carleton
is just one instance of how the earlier writer's predicament continues
to haunt a generation of later writers.

Irish fiction, with the help of prolific practitioners like Carleton,
gained immense popularity among English readers in the nineteenth
century. As well as representing Ireland to readers unfamiliar with
its topography and culture, the fiction of the time provided an
appropriate space for imaginative explorations of national identity
and political unity. The Act of Union in 1800 prompted fresh consideration of power relations between Protestant and Catholic, and
between Anglo-Irish Ascendancy and Irish peasant society, and these
were frequently cast in fictional form. Some of the best-known
novels of the time seem to function as moral fables in which questions of leadership and government are intricately caught up with
issues of land ownership, legal rights, and family lineage. The pressing concerns of *Castle Rackrent* (1800) are still apparent in later
novels such as *The Real Charlotte* (1894) and *The Last September*
(1929), all novels by women writers who were both privileged
enough to be part of the Ascendancy ethos and yet ironically disposed towards the uses and abuses of power around them. One of the
peculiar and distinctive features of Irish fiction in the nineteenth
century is the disparity between its insistence on telling the truth or
showing things as they are and its actual instability and profound
uncertainty about its capacity for realist verisimilitude. This element
of indeterminacy is palpably evident in some of the popular Irish
novels of the time, including *Castle Rackrent*, *The Wild Irish Girl*
(1806), and *Hurrish* (1886).

Castle Rackrent was published shortly before the Act of Union was
passed in 1800, though it was probably written in the closing years of
the 1790s during a time of revolutionary disturbance. It purports,
however, to be a tale of Irish life at the beginning of the 1780s,
recounting the decline and fall of the Rackrent family in that earlier
decade. The narrator of the story, Thady Quirk, is a dutiful servant

---

[13] Seamus Heaney, *Station Island* (London: Faber and Faber, 1984), 64–6.

whose personal loyalty to the family contrasts markedly with the opportunistic attitude of his son, Jason. The novel's extended chronology helps to conceal its more immediate concern with the fate of the Protestant Ascendancy in the context of recent political rebellion and allows a retrospective view on a class that has lost its claims to leadership over Ireland's benighted peasantry. What gives complexity to the narrative is its subtle combination of ironic critique and intimate lament.

The moral and political anxieties embodied in *Castle Rackrent* can be readily identified and understood in relation to the events of the 1790s, especially in the light of Burke's similar concerns about the responsibilities of the Ascendancy. What is perhaps harder to comprehend is the curiously unstable and indeterminate nature of its narrative structure. To characterize the work as an early regional novel on the basis of its realist interest in local place and local speech is to overlook the extent to which it flagrantly displays its various fictional devices. The illiterate Thady's story, supposedly dictated to an editor, is complemented and extended by a preface, a glossary, and a series of scholarly footnotes, but in straining for an impression of editorial control and objectivity, the novel risks collapsing into incoherence.

The Wild Irish Girl likewise creates an impression of realist veracity and simultaneously undermines it. In this case, the use of epistolary conventions and polite English diction are compounded with scenes of romantic extravagance that strain credulity. Mortimer, the son of an absentee landlord, encounters the old Gaelic civilization and seeks in marriage a way of reconciling Irish tradition and English modernity. The ancestral ruins of Inismore and the wild landscape around it contribute to the novel's exploration of Irishness. The extravagant description of the Irish landscape is matched only by the elaborate description of the people who live there. An Irish Chieftain, a man 'gigantic in stature', with 'limbs of Herculean mould', wears 'a triangular mantle of bright *scarlet* cloth, embroidered and frayed round the edges' and 'fastened at the breast with a large circular golden brooch of a workmanship most curiously beautiful'. James Joyce was to seize on these exuberant descriptions of Irish nobility in his comic undermining of an idealized ancient Ireland in *Ulysses*.

Joyce also gave extended comic life to the 'broad-shouldered, loose-limbed, genial-faced giant' known as Hurrish in the 1886 novel of that title by Emily Lawless.[14] *Hurrish* opens with a powerful evocation of the wild Atlantic coast of the west of Ireland and suggests a correlation between this landscape and the wild Irish who dwell there. Hurrish's mother, the ardent patriot, Bridget O'Brien, is 'black-browed' and 'witch-like ... an elderly bird of prey ... with claws ever upon the watch to tear'. Remarkably, the book was praised for its accurate depiction of Ireland and the Irish. The London *St James Gazette* insisted on the novel's objectivity: 'At a time when the eyes of all men are turned upon Ireland, a vivid and striking picture of the Irish peasant as he really is – a description coloured by no political or partisan motive – is doubly valuable.' The *Dublin Irish Times* agreed that *Hurrish* offered 'A realistic and truthful depiction of existing conditions in Ireland', while the British Prime Minister, William Ewart Gladstone, considered the novel essential reading for anyone who wished to understand contemporary Irish politics and the raging Land Wars in the 1880s.[15]

Castle Rackrent, The Wild Irish Girl, and *Hurrish* all contain incidental details of setting and characterization that might loosely be identified as Gothic.[16] Wildness and strangeness at the level of description are often accompanied by heightened emotions of fear and terror, sporadic violence, and supernatural visitings. These are also the characteristic features of other European Gothic novels, but it might be argued that in Irish fiction they are bound up in a complex psychological way with political insecurity and the waning of colonial power. The title of 'first Irish Gothic novelist' is usually reserved for Charles Robert Maturin, whose Faustian hero Melmoth embodies a profound sense of dislocation and alienation. Sebastian Melmoth was the pseudonym adopted by Oscar Wilde as he embarked on his troubled wanderings after release from Reading

[14] See, for instance, Joyce's description of the 'longheaded deepvoiced barekneed brawnyhanded hairylegged ruddyfaced, sinewyarmed hero' in the Cyclops episode of *Ulysses*. James Joyce, *Ulysses*, ed. Jeri Johnson (Oxford: Oxford University Press, 1993), 284.

[15] Quotations from reviews included in the preliminary pages of *Hurrish: A Study*, 3rd edn. (London and Edinburgh: William Blackwood & Sons, 1887).

[16] For an excellent account of Irish Gothic, see W. J. McCormack, *Dissolute Characters: Irish Literary History through Balzac, Sheridan Le Fanu, Yeats and Bowen* (Manchester: Manchester University Press, 1993), and also his introduction to 'Irish Gothic and After 1820–1945', in *The Field Day Anthology of Irish Writing*, ed. Seamus Deane (Derry: Field Day Publications, 1991), ii. 831–45.

Gaol in 1897. In the earlier period of the 1820s, however, Melmoth
signifies the growing crisis of a Protestant Ascendancy collapsing in
ruins and increasingly alienated by the shifting balance of power.

The House by the Church-yard (1863), Sheridan Le Fanu's macabre
tale, also deserves its place in the haunted halls of Irish Gothic, even
if the more obvious sensationalist aspects of the fiction sometimes
detract from other areas of critical interest. As one of his editors
remarked, 'his gusto for lively eccentric character might have made
him an Irish Dickens if the ghosts had not dominated him'.[17] The
proliferation of Irish Gothic writing should not come as a surprise.
Edmund Burke's early writings on beauty gave aesthetic sanctioning
to the sublime emotions of terror and fear, and Wolfe Tone (as good
a name as any for a Gothic novelist) is thought to have tried his hand
at the genre. A preoccupation with psychic disturbance and the
supernatural persists in Irish writing, finding notorious expression
in Bram Stoker's *Dracula* (1897), but also featuring significantly in
the writings of Oscar Wilde, W. B. Yeats, and James Joyce. The
celebrated closing story of Joyce's *Dubliners*, 'The Dead', takes on
the lineaments of a ghost story when read within this context of Irish
supernaturalism.

Songs and poems: enshrining the nation

Irish fiction in the nineteenth century provides an imaginative space
for narratives riven with political insecurity and uncertainty. Irish
poetry and Irish song, however, seem to strive for a more buoyant
and assertive view of national identity and national destiny. The lyric
potential of poetry is put to the service of an inspiring and enduring
national spirit. Ironically, a new sense of national pride is furbished
from the fragmented remains of a disappearing Gaelic culture. What
is often regarded as antiquarianism provides a vital impulse for cultural nationalism throughout the nineteenth century. As Yeats and
Augusta Gregory were to discover at the end of the century, the
Literary Revival depended heavily on literary retrieval. One of the
principal works informing this process of cultural recovery was
Charlotte Brooke's *Reliques of Irish Poetry* (1789), which brought
together a selection of Irish poems with translations for the benefit

---

[17] Introduction to *The House by the Church-yard* (Dublin: The Parkside Press, 1945), 3.

of an English-speaking audience. Brooke, like later revivalists, sees poetry as 'the vital soul of the nation' and wishes to convey an impression of Irish bardic refinement and nobility. Her cultural project, however, is to encourage a closer union between countries: 'The British muse is not yet informed that she has an elder sister in this isle; let us then introduce them to each other! Together let them walk abroad from their bowers, sweet ambassadresses of cordial union between two countries that seem formed by nature to be joined by every bond of interest, and of amity.' Later revivalists and translators like Samuel Ferguson would seek to perpetuate the spirit of *entente cordiale*, while Patrick Pearse and others would place their knowledge of Ireland's distinctive cultural heritage in the service of an uncompromising political separatism.

The idea that the 'spirit' of Gaelic culture might be preserved and conveyed through the English language was given widespread popular expression in Thomas Moore's *Irish Melodies*, published in ten parts between 1807 and 1834. Moore knew little Irish, but his success involved a certain kind of translation in fusing simple, affecting English lyrics with melancholic Irish airs. From the outset, Moore faced accusations that he had transformed the old Gaelic culture into drawing-room songs for easy consumption by the privileged few. William Hazlitt famously remarked that Moore 'converts the wild harp of Erin into a musical snuff-box'.[18] Intriguingly, however, the political resonance and potential of the songs seem all the greater for their willingness to risk sentimentality and nostalgia. The nationalist appeal of the songs derives, in part, from their quiet insistence on secrecy and solidarity, a technique that is aptly demonstrated in the title of Moore's impassioned tribute to Robert Emmet: 'Oh! breathe not his name.' The emotional force of Moore's lamentation for Ireland's betrayed and bewildered idealists left a powerful impact on the young James Joyce and the *Melodies* are recalled in his fiction as a shaping influence on the hearts and minds of several generations of Dubliners.

A similar conviction that songs might revive and sustain the spirit of the nation was central to the Young Ireland movement of the 1840s under the guidance of Thomas Davis. With two Catholic friends, Charles Gavan Duffy and John Blake Dillon, the Protestant

---

[18] P. P. Howe (ed.), *The Complete Works of William Hazlitt*, 21 vols. (London: J. M. Dent & Sons, 1930–4), vii. 234.

Davis founded *The Nation*, a journal that received wide ecumenical support. His own songs, among which the best known are probably 'The West's Asleep' and 'A Nation Once Again', undoubtedly owe something to Moore's example, though their nationalist sentiment is more brusque and overt than the mournful patriotic spirit of the *Melodies*. Like Moore, Davis appreciated the popular educative role of song in restoring national pride, but his role as an educator extended to many other spheres of Irish culture, including history, painting, and architecture. Davis provides a powerful stimulus for the Irish Literary Revival later in the century, even though Yeats and others resisted what they saw as an overtly dogmatic style. As well as seeking an alliance between peasant Ireland and the Protestant Ascendancy in the interests of political independence, his work provides an ideal of cultural nationalism that draws a sharp distinction between Irish imagination and creativity and English commercialism and philistinism.

Among the poets encouraged by Davis and his editorship of *The Nation* was James Clarence Mangan, whose legendary strangeness has tended to inhibit a full and serious consideration of his prodigious linguistic achievements. With his green spectacles, conical hat, and battered umbrella, and with a self-destructive propensity for alcohol and opium, Mangan provided a perfect image of the *poète maudit*. It is perhaps too easy to establish a correspondence between Mangan's tormented imagination and the political turmoil of his day. Even so, there is no doubt that his struggle for artistic integrity and recognition was caught up with the peculiar circumstances of being an Irish writer working with the English language in the charged political and cultural climate of the 1830s and 1840s. Mangan's earliest critics and biographers were inclined to present him as either an unworldly aesthete or a committed nationalist, but it was precisely the uncertain relationship between these roles and possibilities that informed a good deal of Mangan's work and fascinated W. B. Yeats and James Joyce, both of whom saw Mangan as a motivating force in the history of Irish writing.

In his 1902 and 1907 lectures on Mangan, Joyce acknowledges the poet as 'the type of his race', whose work embodies 'nobly suffered misfortunes' and 'irreparable devastations of the soul', but he also regards him as the type of the outcast artist and internal exile, 'a stranger in his country, a rare and bizarre figure in the streets'.[19] This dual response to Mangan epitomizes Joyce's own divided instincts concerning the role of the writer in modern Ireland. On the one hand, Mangan appears to be the unfortunate vessel for the great traditions of his race: 'love of sorrow, desperation, high-sounding threats'; on the other hand, he is 'one of those strange aberrant spirits who believe that the artistic life should be nothing other than the continuous and true revelation of the spiritual life'. It is Mangan's struggle between national and aesthetic priorities that prompts Joyce to see him as 'a would-be herald, a prototype for a would-be nation'.[20] Like Joyce's own Stephen Dedalus in *A Portrait of the Artist as a Young Man* (1914), Mangan's role is to forge anew 'the uncreated conscience' of his race.[21] Ultimately, Joyce's essay gives unstinting and unqualified praise to Mangan as 'the most distinguished poet of the modern Celtic world and one of the most inspired poets of any country ever to make use of the lyric form'.[22]

Mangan's lyric amplitude and felicity tend to conceal the fact that many of his best-known poems, including 'Dark Rosaleen' and 'Kathaleen Ny-Houlihan', are neither original compositions nor direct translations from the Irish. They are essentially reworkings or reinventions of Irish poems presented to Mangan in literal English versions already prepared by other scholars. This realization in no way diminishes the immediate political force of a poem like 'Dark Rosaleen', published in *The Nation* in 1846, during the most desperate months of the Great Famine. Mangan embodies that strange inverse proportion in modern Irish culture between the wealth of linguistic and imaginative resources and the deprivation of social and material existence. Brian Friel gives that predicament a memorable dramatic realization in his 1980 play *Translations*, when he has a hedge-school master, Hugh O'Donnell, tell a British soldier that 'certain cultures expend on their vocabularies and syntax acquisitive energies and ostentations entirely lacking in their material lives'.[23]

Set in the 1830s at a time when the Irish language is being rapidly

---

[19] James Joyce, *Occasional, Critical, and Political Writing*, ed. Kevin Barry (Oxford: Oxford University Press, 2000), 59, 135, 131.

[20] Ibid. 136, 134.

[21] James Joyce, *A Portrait of the Artist as a Young Man* (1916), ed. Jeri Johnson (Oxford: Oxford University Press, 2000), 213.

[22] Joyce, *Occasional, Critical, and Political Writing*, 130.

[23] Brian Friel, *Translations* (London: Faber and Faber, 1981), 42.

displaced by the introduction of a national school system promoting the English language, Friel's play explores the psychic and cultural consequences of linguistic dispossession. One of his characters, a young woman called Maire, who dreams of emigrating to America, cites Daniel O'Connell's verdict that 'the old language is a barrier to modern progress'.[24] At the same time, however, the play is sensitive to what has been lost and to what the country is about to suffer in the Famine years. The Famine hastened the decline of the Irish language so rapidly that by 1851 only 23 per cent of the population spoke Irish, and of these only 5 per cent were monoglot. Many writers would then have little choice but to declare with Yeats that 'Gaelic is my national language, but it is not my mother tongue'.[25] Translation gives only a fleeting impression of those qualities that Friel acknowledges when his hedge-school master pays ironic tribute to a language 'full of the mythologies of fantasy and hope and self-deception—a syntax opulent with tomorrows'.

The Irish Literary Revival: Yeats and Joyce

The impulse that generated the Irish Literary Revival at the end of the nineteenth century came largely from Protestant idealists such as W. B. Yeats, Augusta Gregory, J. M. Synge, Douglas Hyde, and George Russell. As Catholic nationalism intensified and Home Rule for Ireland became a strong possibility, it was imperative for these writers to have their say on matters of identity and nationality; and as Protestant power began to wane, it seemed that supremacy might be retained in the realm of culture if not practical politics. The Abbey Theatre, which opened in December 1904 and included *Cathleen ni Houlihan* and *Riders to the Sea* among its first productions, was a lasting realization of the desire that Yeats and others expressed for an Irish literary theatre. Yeats had a powerful role as poet, dramatist, folklorist, essayist, and critic in articulating the idea of a distinctive national literature. He was fond of quoting his friend and mentor, John O'Leary, on this issue: 'There is no great literature without nationality, no great nationality without literature.'[26] The

[24] Ibid.

[25] W. B. Yeats, 'A General Introduction for my Work' (1937), *Essays and Introductions* (London: Macmillan, 1961), 520.

[26] W. B. Yeats, *Letters to the New Island* (London: Macmillan, 1989), 30.

emphatic nature of this declaration disguises both the profound uncertainty about what constituted nationality in late nineteenth-century Ireland and the problematic attempt by writers like Yeats to embody national characteristics in literature.

One of the obvious problems confronting Yeats and his contemporaries was how to create an Irish national literature in the English language. There was no easy consensus on this issue. Opposition came from the likes of D. P. Moran, intent on promoting 'the philosophy of Irish Ireland', and from Irish language revivalists in the Gaelic League, founded on 31 July 1893. In a lecture to the National Literary Society in November 1892, the future president of the Gaelic League, Douglas Hyde, had spoken of 'the necessity for de-Anglicising Ireland'.[27] Yeats's response was to ask, 'Can we not build up a national tradition, a national literature, which shall be none the less Irish in spirit from being English in language?'[28] The most thoroughgoing exploration of this ideal was to appear later in Thomas MacDonagh's *Literature in Ireland: Studies Irish and Anglo-Irish*, published in the year he was executed by the British as one of the leaders of the 1916 rebellion. MacDonagh, to whom Yeats pays tribute in 'Easter 1916' ('So sensitive his nature seemed, | So daring and sweet his thought'), proposes an ideal of Irish writing in English that possesses sound patterns and rhythmic qualities reminiscent of the older Gaelic culture. There was no simple return to the past in any of this, but vigorous debate and a revolutionizing of tradition.

Yeats's early poem, 'The Lake Isle of Innisfree', shows how the syllabic measures and stresses of Gaelic poetry might be reproduced in English. This hybrid quality is evident in the title (an Anglicized version of the Gaelic place name 'Inis Fraoigh'), which both roots the poem topographically in Ireland and conveniently evokes the spirit of freedom. At the same time, however, the poem is written from an implied perspective of distance and remoteness from its subject. Yeats claimed that the poem came to him while he was walking homesick through Fleet Street in London. It is, essentially, a poem of willed return. Edward Said's post-colonial reading of early

[27] See D. P. Moran, *The Philosophy of Irish Ireland* (Dublin: James Duffy & Co., 1905), and Douglas Hyde, 'The Necessity for De-Anglicising Ireland', in *The Revival of Irish Literature*, ed. C. G. Duffy, G. Sigerson, and D. Hyde (London: T. Fisher Unwin, 1894).

[28] John Kelly and Eric Domville (eds.), *The Collected Letters of W. B. Yeats*, i: *1865–1895* (Oxford: Clarendon Press, 1986), 338.

poems by Yeats identifies a strong liberationist and utopian impulse in their geographical imagination—a seeming desire to recover lost territory—but just as powerful is the Protestant insistence on duty and responsibility in the resounding echo of Luke's Gospel (15: 18) in the King James Bible: 'I will arise and go to my father.'[29] The prodigal son is just one of a number of wandering figures with whom Yeats identifies in the early writings. His nationalism is both propelled and restrained by the peculiar estrangement and displacement of the Irish Protestant class to which he belonged.

'To Ireland in the Coming Times' (1892) is a revealing instance of Yeats's complicated nationalist sentiments. The forthright address and imperative mood of the opening lines create an impression of undivided commitment and unwavering loyalty:

> *Know, that I would accounted be,*
> *True brother of a company*
> *That sang, to sweeten Ireland's wrong,*
> *Ballad and story, rann and song . . .*

The poem's relationship with Irish national culture, however, is more complex than at first appears. Each stanza of the poem involves both a declaration of allegiance to national tradition and a declaration of difference:

> *Nor may I less be counted one*
> *With Davis, Mangan, Ferguson,*
> *Because, to him who ponders well,*
> *My rhymes more than their rhyming tell*
> *Of things discovered in the deep,*
> *Where only body's laid asleep.*

The pursuit of the red rose of spiritual beauty and an occultist fascination for 'things discovered in the deep' have to be reconciled with 'thoughts of Ireland'. The ancient past provides the most obvious meeting ground. Yeats's desire to 'Sing of old Eire and the ancient ways' was to be sorely tested, even within the early years of the 1890s.[30] In September 1894 he wrote to Alice Milligan that 'My experience of Ireland, during the last three years, has changed my

---

[29] Edward Said, *Yeats and Decolonization* (Derry: Field Day, 1988). This Field Day Pamphlet is reprinted in a slightly revised form in *Culture and Imperialism* (London: Chatto and Windus, 1993).

[30] This line is from Yeats's 1892 poem 'To the Rose upon the Rood of Time'.

views very greatly'. His belief now is that the role of the Irish man of letters is 'not so much to awaken or quicken or preserve the national ideal among the mass of the people but to convert the educated classes to it' and 'to fight for moderation, dignity, & the rights of the intellect among his fellow nationalists'.[31]

Loss of faith in a popular national literature and growing disillusionment with divisive nationalist politics are defiantly registered in Yeats's later poems. Heartfelt words and goodwill gestures for 'the dim coming times' are displaced by the more strident and acerbic idiom of poems like 'To a Shade' and 'September 1913' in the aptly titled volume, *Responsibilities* (1914). Both are profoundly elegiac poems, mourning the loss of a dignified civic idealism typified by Charles Stewart Parnell and John O'Leary respectively. Modern democracy and the lure of 'the greasy till' have spoiled an earlier pristine image of nationhood: 'Romantic Ireland's dead and gone, | It's with O'Leary in the grave'. The poem's refrain suggests an irrecoverable loss, yet in other ways the poem is strangely buoyant. What rescues it from defeatist gloom is its sheer rhetorical brilliance. In a beautifully cadenced shift of mood and register, the poem recalls both a seemingly lost heroism and an attitude of reverence that it once inspired. Among 'The names that stilled your childish play' are those of Robert Emmet and Wolfe Tone.

'To a Shade' dismisses the ghost of Parnell from the streets of modern Dublin, but the assertion that the time 'has not come' keeps alive a flicker of hope. In his 1923 Nobel Prize acceptance speech, Yeats looked back on Parnell's troubled career and saw in his demise a turning from parliamentary politics to other means of persuasion and coercion:

The modern literature of Ireland, and indeed all that stir of thought which prepared for the Anglo-Irish war, began when Parnell fell from power in 1891. A disillusioned and embittered Ireland turned from parliamentary politics; an event was conceived; and the race began, as I think, to be troubled by that event's long gestation.[32]

In the curious formulation of 'all that stir of thought' Yeats would appear to be including not just the modern literature of the Revival but the extra-parliamentary, revolutionary ideas of Patrick Pearse,

---

[31] Kelly and Domville (eds.), *The Collected Letters of W. B. Yeats*, i: *1865–1895*, 399.
[32] W. B. Yeats, *Autobiographies* (London: Macmillan, 1955), 559.

James Connolly, Maud Gonne, Constance Markiewicz, and others. The event 'conceived' is the Easter 1916 rebellion and the terms in which Yeats acknowledges that event are consonant with those in his poem 'Easter 1916', in which the uprising 'troubles' the living stream of history and 'A terrible beauty is *born*'.

To read Yeats's famous poem alongside other accounts of Easter 1916, including James Stephens's meticulous day-by-day rendering of events in *The Insurrection in Dublin*, is to be reminded of how strategically and stylishly Yeats mythologizes the rebellion and gives himself a place on the stage of an unfolding tragic drama. Easter 1916 did, of course, prove Yeats wrong in the assumptions that inform 'September 1913'. Another elegy with a different roll-call had then to be devised from the names of those who had only recently occupied the same Dublin haunts and thoroughfares as the urbane speaker of the poem: 'MacDonagh and MacBride | And Connolly and Pearse'. Pearse had written of 'the terrible, beautiful voice that comes out of the heart of battles', though Sheridan Le Fanu had earlier used the phrase 'a terrible beauty'.[33] In other respects, the poem is Burkean in its response to political violence. As well as grasping the 'terrible beauty' that Burke acknowledges in his treatise on the sublime and the picturesque, it resonates with an unmistakable echo of Burke's *Reflections on the Revolution in France*: 'All changed, changed utterly.' Burke's insistence that 'now all is to be changed' provides a touchstone for Yeats in his own changing world, and it surfaces again in the autumnal reflections of that great post-revolutionary poem, 'The Wild Swans at Coole'. Yeats continued to invoke the names of Robert Emmet and Wolfe Tone in poems like 'Parnell's Funeral' (1934), but it is Edmund Burke who hovers over the ancestral houses of his later civil war poetry and provides his most 'Befitting emblems of adversity'.

Burke is also a presiding spirit in the Irish literary tradition that Joyce constructs in his 1907 Italian lectures. Surveying developments in Irish literature written in the English language during the eighteenth century, Joyce applauds 'the so-called English Demosthenes, Edmund Burke, considered even by English critics as the most profound orator ever to speak in the Chamber of Deputies, and one of the most learned men of state even among the crafty ranks of

---

[33] See John Wilson Foster, 'Yeats and the Easter Rising', *Colonial Consequences: Essays in Irish Literature and Culture* (Dublin: Lilliput Press, 1991), 140.

the politicians of blonde Albion'.[34] Joyce also shares with Yeats a deep and abiding respect for Parnell, as well as a troubled dismay at some manifestations of nationalist sentiment in the period following the demise of Irish parliamentary fortunes.

There is a tantalizing glimpse of Joyce's thoughts on literature and nationalism in the remaining fragment of his 1907 lecture on the Irish Literary Renaissance. He notes how 'the youth of Ireland, disillusioned by the moral assassination of Parnell, aligns itself increasingly with a nationalism that is broader and, at the same time, more severe'. Despite sharing some political and cultural allegiances with Yeats, Joyce harboured very different notions of Irish nationality and was sharply critical of what he described as 'a revival in another guise of the ancient civilisation of the Celt'. Joyce felt no compunction to 'Sing of old Eire and the ancient ways'. In the third of his 1907 lectures, 'Ireland: Island of Saints and Sages', he makes the point emphatically: 'Just as ancient Egypt is dead, so is ancient Ireland. Its dirge has been sung and the seal set upon its gravestone.' The alternative conception of nationality that Joyce proposes is pluralistic, flexible, and accommodating: 'Our civilization is an immense woven fabric in which very different elements are mixed ... In such a fabric, it is pointless searching for a thread that has remained pure, virgin and uninfluenced by other threads nearby.'[35]

Throughout his fiction, Joyce ironically exposes essentialist notions of Irishness and comically undermines the heroic ideal of the Celt. His method in *Dubliners* (1914) is to counter prevailing images of a romantic Ireland with a sobering naturalistic truthfulness. Urging his publisher Grant Richards to proceed with the printing of his stories, Joyce insisted that his work would function as a moral corrective to the false consciousness of the time: 'I seriously believe you will retard the course of civilisation in Ireland by preventing the Irish people from having one good look at themselves in my nicely-polished looking-glass.'[36] Joyce's collection of short stories is not only an unflattering depiction of a stagnating colonial city, it is also an intensely psychological study of defeated aims and desires in the people who live there. 'A Painful Case', for instance, is a squalid narrative of drunkenness and suicide, but it also points to hidden

---

[34] Joyce, *Occasional, Critical, and Political Writing*, 123.

[35] Ibid. 137, 125, 118.

[36] *The Letters of James Joyce*, ed. Stuart Gilbert (London: Faber, 1957; 1966), 64.

depths of repression beyond the representational capacity of language.

In *Ulysses* (1922), the 'nicely polished looking-glass' is exchanged for 'the cracked lookingglass of a servant', a more appropriate symbol of Irish art and one that is borrowed from Oscar Wilde. In the opening episode of the novel, the looking-glass is literally a servant's mirror, but it is also a fitting emblem of colonial servitude and an indication that Irish fiction must now break decisively with the stable realist modes of the English novel. What Joyce then devises is 'a narrative frame . . . flexible enough to endure vertiginous variations of style'.[37] In doing so he liberates Irish fiction from any lingering sense of colonial inferiority to the English novel and gives to Irish writers a new freedom of experimentation with the English language. Seamus Heaney spoke for many of his contemporaries when he remarked that Joyce had shown how 'the English language was no longer an imperial humiliation but a native weapon'.[38]

The opening episode of *Ulysses* also plays satirically with familiar images of ancient Ireland and Revivalist hopes for the preservation of the Irish language. The old woman who arrives at the Martello tower and respectfully takes payment for her milk is both the Athenian messenger of Greek legend and the Shan Van Vocht of Irish legend. Ironically, though, she is unable to speak any Irish and cannot distinguish between French and Irish when the Englishman Haines demonstrates his linguistic skills: 'I don't speak the language myself. I'm told it's a grand language by them that knows.' Between *Dubliners* and *Ulysses* Joyce perfects a comic, satirical mode of writing in close alliance with a sceptical apprehension of the idealized, romantic aspects of cultural nationalism in his own day. At the same time, as Andrew Gibson reminds us, Joyce was deeply influenced by 'the pervasive hostility to England within Irish political and cultural nationalism', and his laughter is often the antagonistic laughter of the ironist or trickster. From the outset, *Ulysses* 'pits Stephen against the English presence in Ireland' and shows him resisting both the patronage of Haines and the complicity of Mulligan.[39]

[37] Seamus Deane, *A Short History of Irish Literature* (London: Hutchinson, 1986; 1989), 183.

[38] Seamus Heaney, 'The Interesting Case of John Alphonsus Mulrennan', *Planet*, 41 (Jan. 1978), 40.

[39] Andrew Gibson, *Joyce's Revenge: History, Politics, and Aesthetics in Ulysses* (Oxford: Oxford University Press, 2003), 4, 23.

Disillusion and reconstruction

The glamour of ancient civilization and the bright hopes of the Revival continue to fade in Irish literature written after the mid-1920s. Joyce's influence on a new generation of writers, including Samuel Beckett and Flann O'Brien, was considerable in this respect, but the country Joyce left behind was, in any case, a profoundly different place. The momentous changes Yeats observed in the aftermath of Easter 1916 ignited the War of Independence and led to the founding of the Free State, partition of the country on sectarian grounds, and ferocious civil war. The new generation was one that felt acutely the thwarted nationalist aspirations and disappointed ideals of the time. Yeats in *The Tower* (1928) is compelled to reconsider his earlier artistic ideals as military conflict intrudes upon his dwelling place, but the violence of armed struggle in the 1920s is a subject that other writers turn to from a variety of perspectives. It is present in the short stories of Seán O'Faoláin and Liam O'Flaherty, in the plays of Seán O'Casey, in the memoirs of Earnán O'Malley, and in the fiction of Elizabeth Bowen.

A strong mood of disillusionment seeps into many of the literary works of the 1920s and 1930s as a newly independent state, severely shaken by civil war, enters a period of sober reconstruction and pragmatic reassessment. It might seem surprising, then, that this should also be a time of comic exuberance, though the comedy of Beckett, O'Brien, and O'Casey often seems to be wrung from a depressed and restrictive social milieu or else satirically aimed at the oppressive provincialism of post-revolutionary Ireland. Joyce's comic spirit continues to provide an impulse here, as does that of Oscar Wilde. If Wilde's best-known play, *The Importance of Being Earnest* (1895) partakes of a fine tradition of Irish satire directed at the English, his less well-known memoir, *De Profundis* (1905), joins an equally honourable tradition of prison journals by Irish writers. Wilde's assessment of himself and his fellow inmates evokes the spirit of Irish tragicomedy: 'We are the zanies of sorrow. We are clowns whose hearts are broken.' O'Casey catches that spirit with impressive dramatic power and colloquial vigour in *Juno and the Paycock* (1924) and the other plays in his *Dublin Trilogy*. So too, in a more reflective mode, does Elizabeth Bowen, whose 1929 novel, *The Last September*, is both a sombre elegy for the Anglo-Irish

Ascendancy in its moment of collapse and a zestful comic satire directed at the folly and complacency of that same class.

In short fiction, too, there is a comic style that tends towards ironic critique and often closes in melancholic reflection. It can be seen at work in Frank O'Connor's artfully crafted story, 'The Majesty of the Law', which gently weighs the claims of an isolated private morality against an officially sanctioned law and order, at the same time sedulously avoiding any dogmatic conclusion. O'Connor and his contemporaries look for the signs of social and moral integrity in a country that seems caught between small-town provincialism and metropolitan modernity. The title of Seán O'Faoláin's 'Lilliput' carries suggestions of Swiftian satire and points to the seemingly absurd conditions that prevail in a small town caught up in the War of Independence. The diminished revolutionary hopes of the time are evident in this early story, and the same can be said of Liam O'Flaherty's story, 'The Mountain Tavern', in which a frozen landscape seems emblematic of disappointed nationalist ideals. O'Flaherty's story both insists on a sense of continuity with the work of James Joyce and registers the profound disruption of Irish political history in the early twentieth century. The opening line of the story, 'Snow was falling', recalls the closing paragraph of 'The Dead' in Joyce's *Dubliners*, but the dead in this story are the victims of civil war and their presence persists like a black spot on the snowy landscape.

A strong anti-Revivalist impulse extends to the poetry of the 1920s and 1930s, though few writers manage to equal either the visionary brilliance or the fierce grasp of events that the work of W. B. Yeats displays in these decades. While not entirely neglecting ancient Ireland, the poetry written by Yeats's contemporaries tends to eschew romantic ideals and settle for a more modest set of images, often based on close attachment to local ways and customs, as can be seen in the poems of F. R. Higgins and Seumas O'Sullivan. It is Patrick Kavanagh, however, who best illustrates the poetic virtue of fidelity to place and time. The title of his 'Inniskeen Road: July Evening' aptly illustrates this point, but it also shows how Kavanagh takes that most prestigious of European literary forms—the sonnet—and makes it his own.

The partition of Ireland in 1921 meant that twenty-six counties now constituted the Irish Free State (not designated the Republic of

Ireland until 1949), while the six counties of Northern Ireland
remained under British rule. Kavanagh's County Monaghan, his-
torically part of Ulster, was not among the six designated counties
of Northern Ireland. Geographically, however, Kavanagh was well
positioned to influence poets both north and south of the border.
Seamus Heaney was among a later generation of poets to be moved
by 'something new, authentic and liberating' in Kavanagh's poetry.[40]
That later generation also looked to the example of John Hewitt,
whose poems seek to reconcile the national and regional imperatives
of his imagination in the Ulster landscapes of his childhood. Hewitt
was a socialist who admired the egalitarian principles of James Connolly, as well as an Ulsterman who was deeply attached to his region.
His little-known early poems are aptly represented here by a critique
of Revivalist glamour, a lyric reflection on the events of Easter 1916
and a eulogy on the Mourne Mountains.

It might be said that the Irish Literary Revival came to a final halt
with the death of W. B. Yeats in 1939. In his great elegy, 'In Memory
of W. B. Yeats', W. H. Auden famously declared of his fellow poet,
'mad Ireland hurt you into poetry'.[41] In different ways, Ireland also
hurt into poetry the dazzling imagination of Louis MacNeice.
MacNeice's *Autumn Journal*, published in 1939, is ample evidence
that the sway of the Literary Revival is at an end. In earlier poems
like 'Belfast' and 'Carrickfergus', MacNeice gives voice to the cultural distinctiveness of the north, associating it with particular historical, archaeological, and industrial images. In *Autumn Journal*,
that other Ireland of romantic myth is sharply rebuked:

> Kathaleen ni Houlihan! Why
> Must a country, like a ship or a car, be always female,
> Mother or sweetheart?

It is not just MacNeice's ironic detachment that gives his work its
special appeal. The verbal and visual excitement of poems like
'Snow' was to inspire later poets such as Michael Longley, Derek
Mahon, Paul Muldoon, and Ciaran Carson.

1939 is a year in which modern Irish literature reaches new

---

[40] Seamus Heaney, 'From Monaghan to the Grand Canal: The Poetry of Patrick
Kavanagh', in *Preoccupations: Selected Prose 1968–1978* (London: Faber and Faber,
1980), 116.

[41] *The English Auden: Poems, Essays and Dramatic Writings 1927–1939*, ed. Edward
Mendelson (London: Faber and Faber, 1977; rev. 1978), 242.

heights of achievement. As well as seeing the publication of Yeats's *Last Poems*, MacNeice's *Autumn Journal*, and O'Brien's *At Swim-Two-Birds*, it also marks the appearance of James Joyce's *Finnegans Wake*, a novel of extraordinary linguistic exuberance. One obvious sign of the growing self-confidence of Irish literature at this time is its striking capacity for dialogue with earlier literary works, repeating and revising familiar themes and stylistic gestures. Across the period from 1789 to 1939, the writings included here enter into strange and unexpected constellations with each other, challenging and renewing the various ways in which Ireland has been imagined and defined. In this respect, these writings are not so much relics of cultural antiquity as glimpses of an imagined future, always waiting to be read and always ready to be newly understood. What they leave us with is a generous conception of possibilities: not just settled reflections of Ireland as it was, but vivid imaginings of a better, more peaceful Ireland in the coming times.

NOTE ON THE ANTHOLOGY

For ease of reference, the anthology is in two parts. Part One includes works written between 1789 and 1890, and Part Two includes works written between 1890 and 1939. The mid-point of 1890 is usually associated with the emergence of the Irish Literary Revival and the beginnings of Irish modernism. W. B. Yeats and others saw the death of Parnell in 1891 as the most significant event in the decade, marking a loss of faith in parliamentary politics and a turning to a cultural nationalism that would culminate in the Easter Rising of 1916. The chronological arrangement of the anthology provides a valuable correspondence between works of literature and moments of historical crisis. There are writings that emerge from, and respond to, the revolutionary spirit of the 1790s, the aspiring Catholic nationalism of the 1820s and 1830s, the Young Ireland Movement of the 1840s, the Fenian Movement of the 1860s, and the struggle for independence in the early decades of the twentieth century. History refuses to be relegated to some subordinate role as 'background' or 'context' to the literary works included here.

The purpose of the anthology, however, is not simply to illustrate the course of Irish history, but to encourage readers to discover for themselves the strange and unexpected ways in which works of literature engage with their times. The anthology highlights the formal and linguistic complexity of Irish literature in the period 1789 to 1939 and shows how stylistic attributes correspond to certain ways of seeing and organizing the world. The works included here are diverse in form: there are letters, speeches, memoirs, and travel writings, as well as novels, stories, songs, poems, and plays. The emphasis is on 'writing' rather than 'literature' in its conventional and sometimes limiting sense. The arrangement of texts is chronological but also generic, and it is hoped that this will draw attention to significant developments of a formal, discursive kind. If these texts relate to the world in particular ways, they also relate to each other, replaying and renewing familiar rhetorical devices and stylistic resources.

The anthology concentrates, nevertheless, on fiction, poetry, and drama. There are potent connections between the novels of

1789–1890 and those of 1890–1939. From *Castle Rackrent* onwards, there is a persistent concern with Irish character, Irish landscape, and Irish speech, and also with the conventions through which these might be effectively realized in fiction. Certain preoccupations can be traced across the scope of the anthology: a curious interest in Gothic motifs and situations, for instance, or an anxious dwelling on the fate of the Protestant Ascendancy and its 'Big House' culture. Extracts from novels can give a misleading impression of an author's work and sometimes there is a limited usefulness in detaching a particular episode or sequence from a larger narrative structure. A better strategy perhaps is to introduce a novel through its opening pages, giving readers an incentive to pursue the rest of the narrative outside the anthology. Several novels are introduced in this way, including *Castle Rackrent, Melmoth the Wanderer*, and *Hurrish*. Happily, it has been possible to include the whole of the opening episode of James Joyce's *Ulysses*. The short story is a form in which Irish writers have excelled and four stories (by James Joyce, Seán O'Faoláin, Liam O'Flaherty, and Frank O'Connor) are printed in their entirety.

If there is a personal indulgence in this anthology, it is in the broad selection of poetry offered to readers. With the obvious exception of Yeats, Irish poetry has not received the critical attention it deserves. As well as situating Yeats in relation to his acknowledged predecessors—Davis, Mangan, Ferguson—the anthology also considers some less well-known influences such as William Allingham, along with a fair selection of work by some of Yeats's contemporaries, including Ethna Carbery, Seumas O'Sullivan, and Francis Ledwidge. An anthology like this cannot hope to do justice to the wealth of poetry that has been made available through translations and versions of Gaelic originals. However, some indication of that rich resource can be found in the translations and near-translations undertaken by Charlotte Brooke, Thomas Furlong, James Clarence Mangan, Samuel Ferguson, Douglas Hyde, and Augusta Gregory.

Drama, unfortunately, fares less well than poetry. There are obvious problems in trying to extract a single scene or episode from a play text and in trying to convey the dramatic potential of the larger work. In the end, it is probably better to have a small number of plays in their entirety than a large number of plays in extracted form. Three prominent plays of the Literary Revival by W. B. Yeats,

Augusta Gregory, and J. M. Synge are presented here in full, along with extracts from well-known plays by Oscar Wilde and Seán O'Casey. Inevitably, copyright restrictions impinged upon the selection of materials in the anthology and had a greater impact on fiction and drama than on poetry.

In most cases, the texts presented here are those of the earliest printing in book form. For most of the novels, including *Ulysses*, the first edition has been chosen as the copytext. *Castle Rackrent* is an important exception, as the first edition of 1800 is generally considered inferior to that which appears in the 1832 collected edition of Maria Edgeworth's works. As well as removing minor errors and making some brief amendments, the 1832 edition introduces modern conventions of punctuation. Poems and stories are generally taken from collected editions of individual authors' works. If poems and stories have previously appeared in journals, there will be an accompanying explanatory note to this effect. The dates given in brackets in the contents pages generally refer to the first book publication. Plays are dated according to their first production. The dates provided for speeches *in extremis* by Robert Emmett and Roger Casement, for Daniel O'Connell's speech at Tara, and also for Wolfe Tone's autobiography, refer to the immediate circumstances of their composition and delivery. In a few other cases, as the explanatory notes make clear, the dates given are those of composition rather than publication. It is helpful, for instance, to know that W. B. Yeats's 'Easter 1916' was written in the year of the Rising and not in 1921 when it appeared in the book titled *Michael Robartes and the Dancer*.

In selecting the materials for this anthology and in preparing the editorial notes, I have turned for guidance to a good number of books on modern Irish history and literature, all of which are listed in the Select Bibliography. Over the past few years, however, some of these books have stayed with me and have been a continuing source of information and illumination. I have returned many times to Seamus Deane's *Strange Country: Modernity and Nationhood in Irish Writing Since 1790*, which I first encountered as the Clarendon Lectures in Oxford in 1995. *The Field Day Anthology of Irish Writing* has been an immensely valuable resource as well as a pleasure to read and re-read. I have also been inspired by Declan Kiberd's lucid and stimulating criticism, most recently in his *Irish Classics*. Terry Eagleton's

Irish trilogy—*Heathcliff and the Great Hunger*, *Crazy John and the Bishop*, and *Rebels and Scholars in Nineteenth-Century Ireland*—has made a massive contribution to the study of modern Irish culture, both offering new theoretical inroads and reclaiming some forgotten figures. Two other books have been especially helpful. David Pierce's *Irish Writing in the Twentieth Century: A Reader* has provided an excellent model of editorial endeavour and Robert Welch's *Oxford Companion to Irish Literature* has more than justified its title. Without the support and guidance of Judith Luna at Oxford University Press, I might have taken Yeats to heart and thrown poor words away. As well as putting her trust in this anthology from the outset, she has gently shaped it and brought it into being.

SELECT BIBLIOGRAPHY

Reference

B. Arnold, *A Concise History of Irish Art* (London: Thames and Hudson, 1969; rev. edn. 1977).

Henry Boylan, *A Dictionary of Irish Biography*, 3rd edn. (Dublin: Gill and Macmillan, 1999).

Anne M. Brady and Brian Cleeve, *A Biographical Dictionary of Irish Writers* (Mullingar: Lilliput Press, 1985).

S. J. Connolly (ed.), *The Oxford Companion to Irish History* (Oxford: Oxford University Press, 1998).

E. E. Evans, *Irish Folkways* (London: Routledge and Kegan Paul, 1957).

Alexander G. Gonzalez (ed.), *Modern Irish Writers: A Bio-Critical Sourcebook* (London: Aldwych Press; Westport, Conn.: Greenwood Press, 1997).

Robert Hogan (ed.), *The Macmillan Dictionary of Irish Literature* (London: Macmillan, 1980).

—— (ed.), *Dictionary of Irish Literature*, 2 vols. (Westport, Conn.: Greenwood, 1996).

W. J. McCormack (ed.), *The Blackwell Companion to Modern Irish Culture* (Oxford: Blackwell, 1999).

Sean McMahon and Jo O'Donoghue, *The Mercier Companion to Irish Literature* (Cork: Mercier Press, 1998).

Victor Meally (ed.), *Encyclopaedia of Ireland* (Dublin: Allen Figgis; New York and Toronto: McGraw Hill, 1971).

G. F. Mitchell, *The Irish Landscape* (London: Collins, 1976).

Bernard O'Donoghue (ed.), *Irish Quotations* (Oxford: Oxford University Press, 1999).

Sean Sheehan (ed.), *Dictionary of Irish Quotations* (Cork: Mercier Press, 1993).

Richard Wall, *A Dictionary and Glossary for the Irish Literary Revival* (Gerrards Cross: Colin Smythe, 1995).

Robert Welch (ed.), *The Oxford Companion to Irish Literature* (Oxford: Clarendon, 1996).

Anthologies

Dermot Bolger (ed.), *The New Picador Book of Irish Fiction* (London: Picador, 2000).

Angela Bourke *et al.* (eds.), *The Field Day Anthology of Irish Writing*, iv–v (Cork: Cork University Press, 2002).

Patricia Craig (ed.), *The Oxford Book of Ireland* (Oxford: Oxford University Press, 1998).

Seamus Deane (ed.), *The Field Day Anthology of Irish Writing*, i–iii (Derry: Field Day Publications, 1991).

Noel Duffy and Theo Dorgan (eds.), *Watching the River Flow: A Century in Irish Poetry* (Dublin: Poetry Ireland, 1999).

Henry Glassie (ed.), *Irish Folk Tales* (Harmondsworth: Penguin, 1987).

David H. Greene (ed.), *An Anthology of Irish Literature* (New York: Modern Library, 1954).

John P. Harrington (ed.), *Modern Irish Drama* (New York and London: W. W. Norton, 1991).

Marie Heaney (ed.), *Over Nine Waves: A Book of Irish Legends* (London: Faber, 1994).

Brendan Kennelly (ed.), *The Penguin Book of Irish Verse* (Harmondsworth: Penguin, 1979).

Thomas Kinsella (ed.), *The New Oxford Book of Irish Verse* (Oxford and New York: Oxford University Press, 1986).

Michael Longley (ed.), *20th-Century Irish Poems* (London: Faber and Faber, 2002).

Ferdia MacAnna (ed.), *An Anthology of Irish Comic Writing* (London: Michael Joseph, 1995).

Donagh MacDonagh and Lennox Robinson (eds.), *The Oxford Book of Irish Verse, XVIIth Century-XXth Century* (Oxford: Clarendon Press, 1958).

John Montague (ed.), *The Faber Book of Irish Verse* (London: Faber and Faber, 1978).

Paul Muldoon (ed.), *The Faber Book of Contemporary Irish Poetry* (London: Faber and Faber, 1986).

Frank O'Connor (ed.), *A Book of Ireland* (London: Collins, 1959).

—— *Classic Irish Short Stories* (Oxford and New York: Oxford University Press, 1985).

Maureen O'Rourke Murphy and James MacKillop (eds.), *Irish Literature: A Reader* (Syracuse, NY: Syracuse University Press, 1987).

David Pierce (ed.), *Irish Writing in the Twentieth Century: A Reader* (Cork: Cork University Press, 2000).

Lennox Robinson (ed.), *A Golden Treasury of Irish Verse* (London: Macmillan, 1925).

Desmond Ryan (ed.), *The 1916 Poets* (Westport, Conn.: Greenwood Press, 1963).

Colm Toibin, *The Penguin Book of Irish Fiction* (London: Viking, 2000).

William Trevor (ed.), *The Oxford Book of Irish Short Stories* (Oxford and New York: Oxford University Press, 1991).

History

J. C. Beckett, *The Making of Modern Ireland 1603–1923* (London: Faber and Faber, 1966).

—— *Confrontations: Studies in Irish History* (London: Faber and Faber, 1972).

—— *The Anglo-Irish Tradition* (London: Faber and Faber, 1976).

J. B. Bell, *The Secret Army: A History of the IRA 1916–79* (London: Blond, 1970; Dublin: Academy Press, 1979).

Paul Bew, *Land and the National Question in Ireland 1858–82* (Dublin: Gill and Macmillan, 1978).

—— *Conflict and Conciliation in Ireland 1890–1910: Parnellites and Radical Agrarians* (Oxford: Clarendon Press, 1987).

—— *Ideology and the Irish Question: Ulster Unionism and Irish Nationalism 1912–1916* (Oxford: Clarendon Press, 1994).

S. Clark and J. Donnelly (eds.), *Irish Peasants: Violence and Political Unrest 1780–1914* (Manchester: Manchester University Press, 1983).

P. J. Corish, *The Irish Catholic Experience: A Historical Survey* (Dublin: Gill and Macmillan, 1985).

Ruth Dudley Edwards, *An Atlas of Irish History*, 2nd edn. (London: Methuen, 1981).

Marianne Elliott, *Partners in Revolution: The United Irishmen and France* (London and New Haven: Yale University Press, 1978).

R. F. Foster, *Modern Ireland 1600–1972* (London: Allen Lane, Penguin Books, 1988).

—— (ed.), *The Oxford Illustrated History of Modern Ireland* (London: Oxford University Press, 1989).

T. Garvin, *Nationalist Revolutionaries in Ireland 1858–1928* (Oxford: Clarendon Press, 1987).

H. Gough and D. Dickson (eds.), *Ireland and the French Revolution* (Dublin: Irish Academic Press, 1990).

Alvin Jackson, *Ireland 1798–1998* (Oxford: Blackwell, 1999).

R. Kee, *The Green Flag: A History of Irish Nationalism* (London: Weidenfeld and Nicolson, 1972).

Desmond J. Keenan, *The Catholic Church in Nineteenth-Century Ireland* (Dublin: Gill and Macmillan, 1993).

Dáire Keogh, *The French Disease: The Catholic Church and Radicalism in Ireland 1790–1800* (Dublin: Four Courts Press, 1993).

Joseph J. Lee, *The Modernisation of Irish Society 1848–1918* (Dublin: Gill and Macmillan, 1973).

—— *Ireland 1912–85: Politics and Society* (Cambridge: Cambridge University Press, 1990).

C. D. A. Leighton, *Catholicism in a Protestant Kingdom: A Study of the Irish Ancien Régime* (Dublin: Gill and Macmillan, 1994).

F. S. L. Lyons, *Ireland Since the Famine* (London: Fontana, 1973).

—— *Culture and Anarchy in Ireland 1890–1939* (Oxford: Oxford University Press, 1979).

Ian McBride (ed.), *History and Memory in Modern Ireland* (Cambridge: Cambridge University Press, 2001).

T. W. Moody (ed.), *The Fenian Movement* (Cork and Dublin: Mercier Press, 1968).

C. H. E. Philpin (ed.), *Nationalism and Popular Protest in Ireland* (Cambridge: Cambridge University Press, 1987).

T. P. Power and K. Whelan (eds.), *Endurance and Emergence: Catholics in Ireland in the Eighteenth Century* (Dublin: Irish Academic Press, 1990).

Hugh Kearney, *The British Isles: A History of Four Nations* (Cambridge: Cambridge University Press, 1989).

Kevin Whelan, *The Tree of Liberty: Radicalism, Catholicism and the Construction of Irish Identity 1760–1830* (Notre Dame, Ind.: Notre Dame University Press, 1997).

—— *Fellowship of Freedom: The United Irishmen and 1798* (Cork: Cork University Press, 1998).

Literary and Cultural Criticism

Michael Allen and Angela Wilcox (eds.), *Critical Approaches to Anglo-Irish Literature* (Gerrards Cross: Colin Smythe, 1989).

E. A. Boyd, *Ireland's Literary Renaissance* (Dublin and London: Maunsel, 1916; rev. edn., New York: Barnes and Noble, 1968).

Malcolm Brown, *The Politics of Irish Literature: From Thomas Davis to W. B. Yeats* (London: Allen and Unwin, 1972).

Terence Brown, *Ireland: A Social and Cultural History 1922–1985* (London: Fontana, 1985).

—— *Ireland's Literature: Selected Essays* (Mullingar, Co. Westmeath: The Lilliput Press; Totowa, NJ: Barnes and Noble, 1988).

James M. Cahalan, *Great Hatred, Little Room. The Irish Historical Novel* (Syracuse, NY: Syracuse University Press, 1983).

—— *The Irish Novel: A Critical History* (Dublin: Gill and Macmillan, 1988).

—— *Modern Irish Literature and Culture: A Chronology* (New York: G. K. Hall; Toronto: Maxwell Macmillan, 1993).

David Cairns and Shaun Richards, *Writing Ireland: Colonialism, Nationalism and Culture* (Manchester: Manchester University Press; New York: St Martin's Press, 1988).

Andrew Carpenter (ed.), *Place, Personality and the Irish Writer* (Gerrards Cross: Colin Smythe, 1977).

Neil Corcoran, *After Yeats and Joyce: Reading Modern Irish Literature* (Oxford and New York: Oxford University Press, 1997).

Daniel Corkery, *The Hidden Ireland: A Study of Gaelic Munster in the Eighteenth Century* (Dublin: Gill, 1925; reprinted Gill and Macmillan, 1975).

—— *Synge and Anglo-Irish Literature* (Cork: Cork University Press, 1931).

Peter Costello, *The Heart Grown Brutal: The Irish Revolution in Literature from Parnell to the Death of Yeats, 1891–1939* (Dublin: Gill and Macmillan, 1977).

John Cronin, *Irish Fiction 1900–1940* (Belfast: Appletree Press, 1992).

Michael Cronin, *Translating Ireland: Translation, Languages, Cultures* (Cork: Cork University Press, 1996).

R. Davis, *The Young Ireland Movement* (Dublin: Gill and Macmillan, 1987).

Gerald Dawe and Edna Longley (eds.), *Across a Roaring Hill: The Protestant Imagination in Modern Ireland* (Belfast: Blackstaff Press, 1985).

Seamus Deane, *Celtic Revivals: Essays in Modern Irish Literature 1880–1980* (London: Faber and Faber, 1985).

—— *A Short History of Irish Literature* (London: Hutchinson, 1986).

—— (ed.), *Nationalism, Colonialism and Literature* (Minneapolis: Field Day Company and University of Minnesota Press, 1990).

—— *Strange Country: Modernity and Nationhood in Irish Writing Since 1790* (Oxford: Clarendon Press, 1997).

Denis Donoghue, *We Irish: The Selected Essays of Denis Donoghue* (London: Harvester Press, 1986).

Terry Eagleton, *Heathcliff and the Great Hunger: Studies in Irish Culture* (London: Verso, 1995).

—— *Crazy John and the Bishop* (Cork: Cork University Press, in association with Field Day, 1998).

—— *Scholars and Rebels in Nineteenth-Century Ireland* (Oxford: Blackwell, 1999).

Una Ellis-Fermor, *The Irish Dramatic Movement* (London: Methuen, 1939; revised edition 1954).

Richard Fallis, *The Irish Renaissance* (Syracuse, NY: Syracuse University Press, 1977).

Field Day Theatre Company, *Ireland's Field Day* (London: Hutchinson, 1985; Notre Dame, Ind.: University of Notre Dame Press, 1986).

Thomas Flanagan, *The Irish Novelists 1800–1850* (New York: Columbia University Press, 1959).

John Wilson Foster, *Fictions of the Irish Revival* (Dublin: Gill and Macmillan, 1987).

—— *Colonial Consequences: Essays in Irish Literature and Culture* (Dublin: Lilliput Press, 1991).

R. F. Foster, *Paddy and Mr Punch: Connections in Irish and British History* (London: Allen Lane, 1993).

—— *The Irish Story: Telling Tales and Making it Up in Ireland* (London: Allen Lane, 2001).

Robert F. Garratt, *Modern Irish Poetry: Tradition and Community from Yeats to Heaney* (Berkeley: University of California Press, 1986).

Luke Gibbons, *Transformations in Irish Culture* (Cork: Cork University Press, 1996).

Colin Graham and Richard Kirkland (eds.), *Ireland and Cultural Theory: The Mechanics of Authenticity* (Basingstoke: Macmillan, 1999).

Colin Graham, *Deconstructing Ireland: Identity, Theory, Culture* (Edinburgh: Edinburgh University Press, 2001).

Nicholas Grene, *The Politics of Irish Drama: Plays in Context from Boucicault to Friel* (Cambridge: Cambridge University Press, 1999).

W. E. Hall, *Shadowy Heroes: Irish Literature of the 1890s* (Syracuse, NY: Syracuse University Press, 1980).

Maurice Harmon (ed.), *Image and Illusion: Anglo-Irish Literature and its Contexts* (Dublin: Wolfhound Press, 1979).

—— *The Irish Writer and the City* (Gerrards Cross: Colin Smythe; Totowa, NJ.: Barnes and Noble, 1984).

Seamus Heaney, *Preoccupations: Selected Prose 1968–1978* (London: Faber and Faber, 1980).

—— *The Government of the Tongue* (London: Faber and Faber, 1988).

—— *The Redress of Poetry* (London: Faber and Faber, 1995).

—— *Finders Keepers: Selected Prose 1971–2001* (London: Faber and Faber, 2002).

Mark Patrick Hederman and Richard Kearney (eds.), *The Crane Bag Book of Irish Studies 1977–1981* (Dublin: Blackwater Press, 1982).

—— *The Crane Bag Book of Irish Studies 1982–1985* (Dublin: Blackwater Press, 1986).

Herbert Howarth, *The Irish Writers 1880–1940: Literature Under Parnell's Star* (London: Rockliff, 1958).

Stephen Howe, *Ireland and Empire: Colonial Legacies in Irish History and Culture* (Oxford: Oxford University Press, 2000).

Hugh Hunt, *The Abbey, Ireland's National Theatre 1904–1979* (Dublin: Gill and Macmillan, 1979).

J. Hutchinson, *The Dynamics of Cultural Nationalism: The Gaelic Revival and the Creation of the Irish Nation State* (London: Allen and Unwin, 1987).

Paul Hyland and Neil Sammells (eds.), *Irish Writing: Exile and Subversion* (Basingstoke: Macmillan; New York: St Martin's Press, 1991).

C. L. Innes, *Woman and Nation in Irish Literature and Society 1880–1935* (London: Harvester Wheatsheaf, 1993).

A. N. Jeffares, *Anglo-Irish Literature* (London: Macmillan, 1982).

Dillon Johnston, *Irish Poetry After Joyce* (Notre Dame, Ind.: University of Notre Dame Press, 1985).

Hugh Kenner, *A Colder Eye: The Modern Irish Writers* (London: Allen Lane, 1983).

Ben Levitas, *The Theatre of Nation: Irish Drama and Cultural Nationalism 1890–1916* (Oxford: Oxford University Press, 2003).

Toni O'Brien Johnson and David Cairns, *Gender in Irish Writing* (Milton Keynes: Open University Press, 1991).

Richard Kearney, *Transitions: Narratives in Modern Irish Culture* (Manchester: Manchester University Press, 1988).

—— *Postnationalist Ireland: Politics, Culture, Philosophy* (London and New York: Routledge, 1997).

Michael Kenneally (ed.), *Irish Literature and Culture* (Gerrards Cross: Colin Smythe, 1992).

Declan Kiberd, *Inventing Ireland: The Literature of the Modern Nation* (London: Jonathan Cape, 1995).

—— *Irish Classics* (London: Granta; Cambridge, Mass.: Harvard University Press, 2000).

Benedict Kiely, *Modern Irish Fiction: A Critique* (Dublin: Golden Eagle Books, 1950).

—— *A Raid into Dark Corners and Other Essays* (Cork: Cork University Press, 1999).

James F. Kilroy (ed.), *The Irish Short Story: A Critical History* (Boston: Twayne, 1984).

Joep T. Leersen, *Mere Irish and Fior-Ghael: Studies in the Idea of Irish Nationality, its Development and Literary Expression Prior to the Nineteenth Century* (Amsterdam and Philadelphia: John Benjamins, 1988).

—— *Remembrance and Imagination: Patterns in the Historical and Literary Representation of Ireland in the Nineteenth Century* (Cork: Cork University Press, 1996).

David Lloyd, *Nationalism and Minor Literature: James Clarence Mangan and the Emergence of Irish Cultural Nationalism* (Berkeley: University of California Press, 1987).

—— *Irish Writing and the Post-Colonial Moment* (Dublin: Lilliput Press, 1993).

—— *Ireland After History* (Cork: Cork University Press, 1999).

Richard Loftus, *Nationalism in Modern Anglo-Irish Poetry* (Madison and Milwaukee: University of Wisconsin Press, 1969).

Edna Longley, *Poetry in the Wars* (Newcastle: Bloodaxe Books, 1986).

—— *The Living Stream: Literature and Revisionism in Ireland* (Newcastle: Bloodaxe Books, 1994).

Alan Marshall and Neil Sammells (eds.), *Irish Encounters: Poetry, Politics and Prose since 1880* (Bath: Sulis Press, 1998).

Augustine Martin, *The Genius of Irish Prose* (Dublin and Cork: Mercier Press, 1984).

W. J. McCormack, *Ascendancy and Tradition in Anglo-Irish Literature 1789–1939* (Oxford: Oxford University Press, 1985).

—— *From Burke to Beckett: Ascendancy, Tradition and Betrayal in Literary History* (Cork: Cork University Press, 1994).

Ronan McDonald, *Tragedy and Irish Literature* (Basingstoke: Palgrave, 2002).

D. E. S. Maxwell, *A Critical History of Modern Irish Drama 1891–1980* (Cambridge: Cambridge University Press, 1985).

Vivian Mercier, *The Irish Comic Tradition* (Oxford: Clarendon Press, 1962).

Julian Moynahan, *Anglo-Irish: The Literary Imagination in a Hyphenated Culture* (Princeton: Princeton University Press, 1995).

Paul Muldoon, *To Ireland, I* (Oxford: Oxford University Press, 2000).

James H. Murphy, *Catholic Fiction and Social Reality in Ireland, 1873–1922* (Westport, Conn.: Greenwood, 1997).

Christopher Murray, *Twentieth-Century Irish Drama: Mirror Up to Nature* (Manchester: Manchester University Press, 1997).

Ulick O'Connor, *Celtic Dawn: A Portrait of the Irish Literary Renaissance* (London: Hamilton, 1984).

Philip O'Leary, *The Prose Literature of the Gaelic Revival 1881–1921: Ideology and Innovation* (University Park, Pa.: Pennsylvania State University Press, 1994).

Tom Paulin, *Ireland and the English Crisis* (Newcastle: Bloodaxe Books, 1984).

—— *Writing to the Moment: Selected Critical Essays 1980–1996* (London: Faber, 1996).

Lionel Pilkington, *Theatre and State in Twentieth-Century Ireland: Cultivating the People* (London: Routledge, 2001).

Patrick Rafroidi and Terence Brown (eds.), *The Irish Short Story* (Gerrards Cross: Colin Smythe, 1979).

Shaun Richards, *The Drama of Modern Ireland: An Infinite Rehearsal* (Basingstoke: Macmillan, 2001).

Ray Ryan, *Ireland and Scotland: Literature and Culture, State and Nation, 1966–2000* (Oxford: Oxford University Press, 2000).

Gerry Smyth, *Decolonisation and Criticism: The Construction of Irish Literature* (London: Pluto, 1998).

Mark Storey, *Poetry and Ireland Since 1800: A Source Book* (London: Croom Helm, 1988).

Loreto Todd, *The Language of Irish Literature* (Basingstoke: Macmillan, 1989).

Robert Tracy, *The Unappeasable Host: Studies in Irish Identities* (Dublin: UCD Press, 1998).

William Trevor, *A Writer's Ireland: Landscape in Literature* (London: Thames and Hudson, 1984).

Norman Vance, *Irish Literature: A Social History* (Oxford: Blackwell, 1990).

—— *Irish Literature Since 1800* (Harlow: Longman, 2002).

Éibhear Walshe (ed.), *Sex, Nation and Dissent in Irish Writing* (Cork: Cork University Press, 1997).

G. J. Watson, *Irish Identity and the Literary Revival* (London: Croom Helm, 1979; 2nd edn., Washington: The Catholic University Press of America, 1994).

Robert Welch, *Irish Poetry from Moore to Yeats* (Gerrards Cross: Colin Smythe, 1980).

—— *A History of Verse Translation from the Irish 1789–1897* (Gerrards Cross: Colin Smythe, 1988).

—— *Changing States: Transformations in Modern Irish Writing* (London and New York: Routledge, 1993).

Katharine Worth, *The Irish Drama of Europe from Yeats to Beckett* (London: Athlone Press, 1978).

Studies of Individual Authors

Sue Asbee, *Flann O'Brien* (Boston: Twayne Publishers, 1991).

Derek Attridge (ed.), *The Cambridge Companion to James Joyce* (Cambridge: Cambridge University Press, 1990).

Malcolm Brown, *Sir Samuel Ferguson* (Lewisburg, Pa.: Bucknell University Press, 1973).

Terence Brown, *Louis MacNeice: Sceptical Vision* (Dublin: Gill and Macmillan, 1975).

Marilyn Butler, *Maria Edgeworth: A Literary Biography* (Oxford: Clarendon Press, 1972).

J. E. Chamberlin, *Ripe Was the Drowsy Hour: The Age of Oscar Wilde* (New York: Seabury Press, 1977).

Vincent Cheng, *Joyce, Race and Empire* (Cambridge: Cambridge University Press, 1995).

Anne Clissmann, *Flann O'Brien: A Critical Introduction to his Writings* (Dublin: Gill and Macmillan, 1975).

Elizabeth Butler Cullingford, *Yeats, Ireland and Fascism* (New York and London: New York University Press, 1981).

—— *Gender and History in Yeats's Love Poetry* (Cambridge: Cambridge University Press, 1993).

Alice Curtayne, *Francis Ledwidge: A Life of the Poet* (Dublin: New Island Books, 1998).

Peter Denman, *Samuel Ferguson: The Literary Achievement* (Gerrards Cross: Colin Smythe, 1990).

Tom Dunne, *Maria Edgeworth and the Colonial Mind* (Cork: Cork University Press, 1984).

Marianne Elliott, *Wolfe Tone: Prophet of Irish Independence* (London and New Haven: Yale University Press, 1989).

Richard Ellmann, *The Identity of Yeats* (London: Faber and Faber; New York: Oxford University Press, 1954).

—— *Eminent Domain: Yeats Among Wilde, Joyce, Pound, Eliot, and Auden* (New York: Oxford University Press, 1967).

—— *James Joyce* (1959; rev. edn. 1982; corr. New York: Oxford University Press, 1983).

—— *Yeats: The Man and the Masks* (rev. edn., New York: W. W. Norton, 1979).

—— *Oscar Wilde* (London: Hamish Hamilton, 1987).

James Fairhall, *James Joyce and the Question of History* (Cambridge: Cambridge University Press, 1993).

Richard Finneran (ed.), *Yeats Annual*, 1–2 (London: Macmillan, 1982).

R. F. Foster, *W. B. Yeats: A Life*, i: *The Apprentice Mage* (Oxford: Oxford University Press, 1997).

—— *W. B. Yeats: A Life*, ii: *The Arch-Poet* (Oxford: Oxford University Press, 2003).

Tom Furniss, *Edmund Burke's Aesthetic Ideology: Language, Gender and Political Economy in Revolution* (Cambridge: Cambridge University Press, 1993).

Andrew Gibson, *Joyce's Revenge: History, Politics, and Aesthetics in Ulysses* (Oxford: Oxford University Press, 2003).

Victoria Glendinning, *Elizabeth Bowen* (New York: Knopf, 1978).

Warwick Gould (ed.), *Yeats Annual* (London: Macmillan, 1985–   ).

Maurice Harmon, *Seán O'Faoláin: A Critical Introduction* (Notre Dame, Ind., and London: University of Notre Dame Press, 1966).

Keith Hopper, *Flann O'Brien: A Portrait of the Artist as a Young Post-modernist* (Cork: Cork University Press, 1995).

Marjorie Howes, *Yeats's Nations: Gender, Class and Irishness* (Cambridge: Cambridge University Press, 1996).

Michael Hurst, *Maria Edgeworth and the Public Scene: Intellect, Fine Feeling and Landlordism in the Age of Reform* (London: Macmillan, 1969).

A. Norman Jeffares, *A New Commentary on the Poems of W. B. Yeats* (Stanford Calif.: Stanford University Press, 1984).

Declan Kiberd, *Synge and the Irish Language* (London: Macmillan, 1979; 2nd edn. 1993).

Edward Larrissy, *Yeats the Poet: The Measures of Difference* (London: Harvester, 1994).

—— *W. B. Yeats* (Plymouth: Northcote House, 1999).

Hermione Lee, *Elizabeth Bowen: An Estimation* (Totowa, NJ: Barnes and Noble, 1981).

Edna Longley, *Louis MacNeice: A Study* (London: Faber and Faber, 1988).

Maud Gonne MacBride, *A Servant of the Queen* (1938), ed. A. N. Jeffares and Anna MacBride White (Gerrards Cross: Colin Smythe, 1994).

Colin MacCabe, *James Joyce and the Revolution of the Word* (London: Macmillan, 1978; 2nd edn., Palgrave, 2002).

—— (ed.), *James Joyce: New Perspectives* (Brighton: Harvester Press, 1982).

Jerusha McCormack (ed.), *Wilde the Irishman* (New Haven and London: Yale University Press, 1998).

W. J. McCormack, *Sheridan Le Fanu and Victorian Ireland* (Oxford: Clarendon Press, 1980).

—— *Dissolute Characters: Irish Literary History through Balzac, Sheridan Le Fanu, Yeats and Bowen* (Manchester: Manchester University Press, 1993).

—— *Fool of the Family: A Life of J. M. Synge* (London: Weidenfeld and Nicolson, 2000).

Oliver MacDonagh, *O'Connell: The Life of Daniel O'Connell 1775–1847* (London: Weidenfeld and Nicolson, 1991).

Peter McDonald, *Louis MacNeice: The Poet in his Contexts* (Oxford: Oxford University Press, 1991).

Dominic Manganiello, *Joyce's Politics* (London: Routledge and Kegan Paul, 1980).

Katherine Mullin, *James Joyce, Sexuality and Social Purity* (Cambridge: Cambridge University Press, 2003).

Sean Mythen, *Thomas Furlong: The Forgotten Wexford Poet* (Ferns, Co. Wexford: Clone Publications, 1998).

Emer Nolan, *James Joyce and Nationalism* (London and New York: Routledge, 1995).

Johann Norstedt, *Thomas MacDonagh: A Critical Biography* (Charlottesville, Va.: University of Virginia Press, 1980).

David Pierce, *James Joyce's Ireland* (New Haven and London: Yale University Press, 1992).

—— *Yeats's Worlds: Ireland, England and the Poetic Imagination* (New Haven and London: Yale University Press, 1995).

Hilary Robinson, *Somerville and Ross: A Critical Appreciation* (Dublin: Gill and Macmillan, 1980).

Ellen Shannon-Mangan, *James Clarence Mangan: A Biography* (Dublin: Irish Academic Press, 1996).

Jon Stallworthy, *Louis MacNeice* (London: Faber and Faber, 1995).

Michael Steinman, *Yeats's Heroic Figures: Wilde, Parnell, Swift, Casement* (London: Macmillan, 1983).

John Stokes, *Oscar Wilde* (London: Longman, 1978).

—— *Oscar Wilde: Myths, Miracles, and Intentions* (Cambridge: Cambridge University Press, 1996).

Mary Helen Thuente, *W. B. Yeats and Irish Folklore* (Dublin: Gill and Macmillan, 1980).

Deirdre Toomey (ed.), *Yeats and Women* (Basingstoke: Macmillan, 1997).

Joseph Valente, *James Joyce and the Problem of Justice* (Cambridge: Cambridge University Press, 1995).

Anne Varty, *A Preface to Oscar Wilde* (London: Addison-Wesley, 1998).

Katie Wales, *The Language of James Joyce* (Basingstoke: Macmillan, 1992).

Thomas R. Whitaker, *Swan and Shadow: Yeats's Dialogue with History* (Chapel Hill, NC: University of North Carolina Press, 1964).

Further Reading in Oxford World's Classics

Edmund Burke, *A Philosophical Enquiry into the Origin of our Idea of the Sublime and Beautiful*, ed. Adam Phillips.

—— *Reflections on the Revolution in France*, ed. L. G. Mitchell.

Maria Edgeworth, *The Absentee*, ed. W. J. McCormack and Kim Walker.

—— *Belinda*, ed. Kathryn Kirkpatrick.

—— *Castle Rackrent*, ed. George Watson.

Empire Writing: An Anthology of Colonial Literature 1870–1918, ed. Elleke Boehmer.

—— *Dubliners*, ed. Jeri Johnson.

James Joyce, *Occasional, Critical, and Political Writing*, ed. Kevin Barry.

James Joyce, *A Portrait of the Artist as a Young Man*, ed. Jeri Johnson.
—— *Ulysses: The 1922 Text*, ed. Jeri Johnson.
Sheridan Le Fanu, *In a Glass Darkly*, ed. Robert Tracy.
Charles Maturin, *Melmoth the Wanderer*, ed. Douglas Grant.
Sydney Owenson (Lady Morgan), *The Wild Irish Girl*, ed. Kathryn Kirkpatrick.
Bram Stoker, *Dracula*, ed. Maud Ellmann.
J. M. Synge, *The Playboy of the Western World and Other Plays*, ed. Ann Saddlemyer.
Oscar Wilde, *The Major Works*, ed. Isobel Murray.
W. B. Yeats, *The Major Works*, ed. Edward Larrissy.

CHRONOLOGY OF KEY EVENTS

1789   *Reliques of Irish Poetry* by Charlotte Brooke.

1790   *Reflections on the Revolution in France* by Edmund Burke.

1791   Wolfe Tone's *Argument on behalf of the Catholics of Ireland* and the foundation of United Irishmen. Catholic Committee petitions for civil rights.

1792   Relief Act allows Catholics to practise law. Belfast Harp Festival.

1793   Relief Act admits Catholics to parliamentary franchise. Irish Militia established.

1794   Dublin United Irishmen suppressed. Birth of William Carleton.

1795   Catholic seminary established at Maynooth. Orange Order founded.

1796   Insurrection Act and suspension of habeas corpus. French invasion attempted at Bantry Bay in support of United Irishmen.

1797   Death of Edmund Burke.

1798   Martial law imposed. Rebellion in Wexford (May). French fleet under General Humbert lands in Killala (Aug.). Wolfe Tone arrested and dies by his own hand (Nov.).

1800   Act of Union between Great Britain and Ireland receives royal assent. Ireland to be governed by Westminster. *Castle Rackrent* by Maria Edgeworth.

1801   Act of Union effective.

1803   Robert Emmet's rising, trial, and execution. Birth of James Clarence Mangan.

1806   *The Wild Irish Girl* by Sydney Owenson (Lady Morgan).

1808   Foundation of the Christian Brothers.

1810   Birth of Samuel Ferguson.

1812   *The Absentee* by Maria Edgeworth.

1814   Birth of Sheridan Le Fanu and Thomas Davis.

1820   *Melmoth the Wanderer* by Charles Maturin.

1821   Theatre Royal, Dublin, opened.

1822   Irish Constabulary Act, establishing county police forces and a salaried magistracy.

1823   Catholic Association founded, led by Daniel O'Connell.

1824   Free Trade in manufactured articles established between Britain and Ireland.

1825 Catholic Emancipation bill rejected by House of Lords.

1828 O'Connell elected for County Clare.

1829 Catholic Emancipation Act allows Catholics to sit in parliament.

1830 _Traits and Stories of the Irish Peasantry_ by William Carleton (2nd series, 1833).

1831 Introduction of national system of elementary education. Foundation of the Sisters of Mercy.

1832 Irish Reform Act passed.

1833 Irish Church Temporalities Act. _Dublin University Magazine_ founded.

1834 O'Connell introduces a parliamentary debate on repeal of the Union. First steam-powered train in Ireland. _Reliques of Father Prout_ by Francis Sylvester Mahony.

1837 Accession of Queen Victoria.

1838 Irish Poor Law enacted. Foundation of Father Mathew's temperance movement.

1840 O'Connell's Repeal Association founded. Irish Municipal Reform Act.

1841 First reliable census of the population (8,175,124 people recorded). _Cork Examiner_ founded. O'Connell elected Lord Mayor of Dublin.

1842 _The Nation_ newspaper founded by Thomas Davis.

1843 'Monster' repeal meeting held at Tara, Co. Meath. Repeal meeting at Clontarf prohibited.

1845 Colleges Act: Queen's Colleges established in Belfast, Cork, and Galway. Blight in the potato harvest. Beginning of the Great Famine (1845–9). Death of Thomas Davis.

1846 Repeal of the Corn Laws. Total failure of potato harvest. First deaths from starvation (Oct.). Posthumous publication of _Poems_ and _Literary and Historical Essays_ by Thomas Davis.

1847 Foundation of Irish Confederation. Peak of fever academic. Death of Daniel O'Connell.

1848 Foundation of the _United Irishman_ journal by John Mitchel. Rising of Young Irelanders in Ballingarry, Co. Tipperary.

1849 Encumbered Estates Act, facilitating sale of land. Opening of the Queen's Colleges. _The Poets and Poetry of Munster_ by James Clarence Mangan. Death of Mangan. Death of Maria Edgeworth.

1850 Irish Reform Act trebles county electorate and reduces borough electorate. Establishment of the Irish Tenant League.

1851 Census taken (6,552,385 people recorded).

1852 Birth of George Moore. Birth of Isabella Augusta Persse (Lady Gregory). Death of Thomas Moore.

1854 Catholic University of Ireland founded under the rectorship of John Henry Newman. Birth of Oscar Wilde.

1856 Phoenix Society (forerunner of the Fenian movement) founded in Skibbereen. Birth of George Bernard Shaw.

1858 James Stephens returns from France and establishes the Irish Republican Brotherhood.

1859 Fenian Brotherhood founded in the USA. First number of the *Irish Times*.

1860 *Collected Works* by William Carleton. Birth of Douglas Hyde.

1861 Census taken (5,798,967 people recorded).

1863 *The House by the Church-yard* by Sheridan Le Fanu.

1865 John O'Leary arrested. Birth of W. B. Yeats. *Lays of the Western Gael* by Samuel Ferguson.

1866 Archbishop Paul Cullen becomes the first Irish Cardinal.

1867 Fenian rising suppressed. Execution of the 'Manchester Martyrs'. Birth of George Russell (AE). *On the Study of Celtic Literature* by Matthew Arnold.

1868 Foundation of the Amnesty campaign for Fenian prisoners.

1869 Disestablishment of the Church of Ireland by W. E. Gladstone. Death of William Carleton. Birth of John Millington Synge.

1870 Gladstone's first Irish Land Act, acknowledging tenant rights. Foundation of the Home Rule movement by Isaac Butt.

1871 Census taken (5,412,377 people recorded).

1873 Home Rule League founded. Defeat of Gladstone's Irish University Bill. Death of Sheridan Le Fanu.

1874 UK General election: 60 Home Rulers elected. Home Rule Parliamentary Party created.

1875 Charles Stewart Parnell elected MP for County Meath.

1876 Society for the Preservation of the Irish Language established.

1877 Parnell elected president of Home Rule Confederation of Great Britain.

1878 *History of Ireland: Heroic Period* by Standish O'Grady (Vol. II in 1880). Birth of Oliver St John Gogarty.

1879 Irish National Land League founded. Beginning of land agitation at Irishtown, Co. Mayo. Birth of Patrick Pearse.

1880   Parnell elected chairman of Irish Parliamentary Party. Parnell
        visits the USA. Birth of Seán O'Casey. Birth of James Stephens.

1881   Gladstone's second Land Act. Ladies' Land League founded.
        Royal University of Ireland established. Census taken (5,174,836
        people recorded). Birth of Padraic Colum. *Poems* by Oscar Wilde.

1882   Irish National League replaces Land League. Kilmainham 'treaty'
        marks end of land war. Phoenix Park murders of Chief Secretary
        of Ireland, Lord Frederick Cavendish, and his Under-Secretary,
        T. H. Burke. Gaelic League founded. University College, Dublin,
        founded. Birth of James Joyce.

1884   Franchise extended by Representation of the People Act. Gaelic
        Athletic Association founded.

1885   Irish Loyal and Patriotic Union founded. Irish Parliamentary
        Party under Parnell wins 86 seats at Westminster.

1886   Government of Ireland (Home Rule) bill defeated in Commons.
        Death of Samuel Ferguson. *Hurrish* by Emily Lawless.

1887   National Library of Ireland established.

1888   *Confessions of a Young Man* by George Moore. *The Happy Prince
        and Other Tales* by Oscar Wilde. *Fairy and Folk Tales of the Irish
        Peasantry* by W. B. Yeats.

1889   O'Shea names Parnell as co-respondent in divorce petition. *The
        Wanderings of Oisin and Other Poems* by W. B. Yeats.

1890   Gladstone threatens to resign if Parnell remains as leader. Parnell
        denounced by own party. *Beside the Fire: A Collection of Irish
        Gaelic Folk Stories* by Douglas Hyde.

1891   Parnell's death (Oct.). Irish Literary Society founded in London
        by W. B. Yeats and others. *The Quintessence of Ibsenism* by George
        Bernard Shaw. *The Picture of Dorian Gray* by Oscar Wilde.

1892   *The Countess Kathleen and Various Legends and Lyrics* by W. B.
        Yeats. *Lady Windermere's Fan* by Oscar Wilde.

1893   Second Government of Ireland (Home Rule) bill defeated in
        Lords. Gaelic League founded, with Douglas Hyde as president.
        Love Songs of Connacht by Douglas Hyde. *The Celtic Twilight* by
        W. B. Yeats. *Salomé* by Oscar Wilde.

1894   Foundation of Irish Agricultural Organisation Society and Irish
        Trades Union Congress. *Esther Waters* by George Moore. *The Real
        Charlotte* by Edith Somerville and Martin Ross.

1895   *The Story of Early Gaelic Literature* by Douglas Hyde. *The
        Importance of Being Earnest* and *An Ideal Husband* by Oscar Wilde.
        Trial and imprisonment of Oscar Wilde.

1896   Foundation of the Irish Socialist Republican Party. Birth of Liam O'Flaherty.

1897   *Bards of the Gael and Gall* by George Sigerson. *Dracula* by Bram Stoker. *The Secret Rose* by W. B. Yeats.

1898   United Irish League founded. Local government reform applies parliamentary franchise to local elections, extending vote to some women. *The Ballad of Reading Gaol* by Oscar Wilde.

1899   *United Irishman* founded by Arthur Griffith. Irish Literary Theatre founded. *A Literary History of Ireland* by Douglas Hyde. *The Heather Field* by Edward Martyn. *Some Experiences of an Irish R. M.* by Edith Somerville and Martin Ross. *The Wind Among the Reeds* by W. B. Yeats.

1900   John Redmond elected Chairman of Irish Parliamentary Party and United Irish League. *The Leader* begun by D. P. Moran. 'The Necessity for De-Anglicising Ireland' (lecture) by Douglas Hyde. Death of Oscar Wilde. Birth of Seán O'Faoláin.

1901   Death of Queen Victoria and accession of Edward VII. Census taken (4,458,775 people recorded).

1902   Land conference brings together landlords and tenants. Maud Gonne in first performance of *Cathleen ni Houlihan* by W. B. Yeats and Lady Augusta Gregory. *Cuchulain of Muirthemne* by Lady Gregory.

1903   Land Act: comprehensive scheme of land purchase launched. Formation of Arthur Griffith's National Council and Sloan's Independent Orange Order. *Poets and Dreamers* by Lady Gregory. *The Untilled Field* by George Moore. Birth of Frank O'Connor (Michael Francis O'Donovan).

1904   Irish Reform Association founded. Abbey Theatre, Dublin, opened. Irish Folk Song Society formed. *John Bull's Other Island* by George Bernard Shaw. *Riders to the Sea* by J. M. Synge. *In the Seven Woods* by W. B. Yeats. Birth of Patrick Kavanagh. James Joyce leaves Ireland.

1905   Formation of Ulster Unionist Council and Irish Industrial Development Association. Sinn Féin established. *The Philosophy of Irish Ireland* by D. P. Moran. *In the Shadow of the Glen* and *The Well of the Saints* by J. M. Synge. *De Profundis* by Oscar Wilde.

1906   *Religious Songs of Connacht* by Douglas Hyde. Birth of Samuel Beckett.

1907   Dockers' strike and riots in Belfast. Rioting at opening performances of *The Playboy of the Western World* by J. M. Synge. *The*

Rising of the Moon by Lady Gregory. *Deirdre* by W. B. Yeats. *The Aran Isles* by J. M. Synge. Birth of Louis MacNeice.

1908   National University of Ireland established. *The Tinker's Wedding* by J. M. Synge. Irish Women's Franchise League founded by Hannah and Francis Sheehy-Skeffington.

1909   Foundation of Irish Transport and General Workers' Union by James Larkin. First compulsory powers of land purchase enacted.

1910   Edward Carson becomes leader of Ulster Unionist Party. *Deirdre of the Sorrows* by J. M. Synge. *The Green Helmet and Other Poems* by W. B. Yeats.

1911   SS *Titanic* launched by Harland and Wolff in Belfast. Census taken (4,381,951 people recorded). *Hail and Farewell* by George Moore. Birth of Flann O'Brien.

1912   Asquith's introduction of third Government of Ireland (Home Rule) bill. Irish Labour Party begun by James Connolly and James Larkin. Catholic workers expelled from Belfast shipyards. Ulster Covenants signed on 'Ulster Day' (28 Sept.) in opposition to Home Rule. *Titanic* disaster. *The Crock of Gold* by James Stephens.

1913   Formation of Ulster Volunteer Force, Irish Citizens' Army, and Irish (National) Volunteers. Dublin strikes and lock-out. Death of Emily Lawless. *Collected Poems* by AE (George Russell).

1914   Illegal importation of arms by Ulster Volunteers and Irish Volunteers. Buckingham Palace conference fails to reach agreement on exclusion of Ulster from Home Rule. Outbreak of war between Britain and Germany. Home Rule enacted but suspended. *Responsibilities* by W. B. Yeats. *Dubliners* by James Joyce.

1915   Reorganization of the Irish Republican Brotherhood. Military Council formed. Gaelic League votes to take a more overtly political line and Douglas Hyde resigns from the presidency. *Lusitania* sunk by U-boat (Sir Hugh Lane among passengers lost).

1916   Easter Rising. Irish Republic proclaimed in Dublin (24 Apr.). Martial law imposed, rebels surrender (29 Apr.) and face imprisonment and execution. Lloyd George attempts to implement Home Rule with exclusion of six counties. W. B. Yeats composes 'Easter 1916'. Sir Roger Casement hanged. *Songs of the Fields* by Francis Ledwidge. *Literature in Ireland, Studies Irish and Anglo-Irish* by Thomas MacDonagh. *A Portrait of the Artist as a Young Man* by James Joyce.

1917   Sinn Féin and Irish Volunteers reorganize under Eamon de Valera's leadership. *The Wild Swans at Coole* by W. B. Yeats.

1918 Sinn Féin success (73 seats) in general election (Dec.). *Exiles* by James Joyce.

1919 Anglo-Irish War (War of Independence), 1919–21. Formation of Dáil Éireann. De Valera seeks recognition of Irish claim through Peace Conference and embarks on tour of USA.

1920 Better Government of Ireland Act introduces partition between two Home Rule states. Riots in Derry and Belfast. Revival of Ulster Volunteers, expulsion of Catholic shipyard workers, and Republican 'Belfast Boycott'. Reorganization of police and imposition of limited martial law. Terence MacSwiney, Mayor of Cork, dies on hunger strike in Brixton Prison.

1921 Truce in Anglo-Irish War. Meetings of Lloyd George and de Valera followed by peace conference and Anglo-Irish Treaty (6 Dec.). *Michael Robartes and the Dancer* by W. B. Yeats.

1922 Formation of provisional government under Michael Collins (Jan.). Convention of anti-Treaty Irish Republican Army. Arrest of anti-Treaty leaders and outbreak of Civil War (June). National Army given emergency powers. Assassination of Michael Collins. Inauguration of Irish Free State. *Ulysses* by James Joyce.

1923 End of Civil War. Irish Free State government led by W. T. Cosgrave. Free State admitted to League of Nations. W. B. Yeats awarded Nobel Prize for poetry. *The Shadow of a Gunman* by Seán O'Casey.

1924 Reorganization of National Army. Death of Edward Martyn. *The Hidden Ireland* by Daniel Corkery. *Juno and the Paycock* by Seán O'Casey.

1925 Partition confirmed by tripartite agreement. *A Vision* by W. B. Yeats. *The Informer* by Liam O'Flaherty.

1926 De Valera founds Fianna Fáil. Radio Eireann begins broadcasting. Rioting at opening of *The Plough and the Stars* by Seán O'Casey. Census taken (2,971,992 people recorded in Irish Free State and Northern Ireland).

1927 Kevin O'Higgins, Minister of Justice, assassinated. Fianna Fáil enters Dáil. General election, Irish Free State. *Pomes Penyeach* by James Joyce.

1928 Gate Theatre, Dublin, opened. *The Tower* by W. B. Yeats.

1929 General election, Northern Ireland. Opening of the Shannon hydro-electric scheme. Proportional Representation abolished in Northern Ireland. Censorship of Publications Act. *The Last September* by Elizabeth Bowen. *The Silver Tassie* by Seán O'Casey.

1930 Irish Free State elected to the Council of the League of Nations. Irish Labour Party and Trades Union Congress separate.

1931 Banning of the IRA in Free State. *The Moon in the Yellow River* by Denis Johnston. *Guests of the Nation* by Frank O'Connor.

1932 Fianna Fáil success in general election. De Valera replaces Cosgrave as president of Executive Council. Opening of the Stormont parliament building in Northern Ireland. Death of Lady Gregory. *Midsummer Madness* by Seán O'Faoláin. *Words for Music Perhaps* by W. B. Yeats.

1933 National Guard (Blueshirts) formed. United Ireland Party (Fine Gael) formed under O'Duffy (Blueshirts leader). Death of George Moore. *A Nest of Simple Folk* by Seán O'Faoláin. *The Winding Stair and Other Poems* and *Collected Poems* by W. B. Yeats.

1934 Cosgrave reinstated as O'Duffy resigns. *Collected Plays* by W. B. Yeats.

1935 Irish Folklore Commission established. Public Dance Halls Act. Rioting in Belfast during celebrations of George V's Jubilee. Death of Edward Carson. Death of George Russell (AE). *Poems* by Louis MacNeice. *A Full Moon in March* by W. B. Yeats.

1936 Free State Senate abolished. IRA proscribed. First Aer Lingus flight from Dublin to London. *Ploughman and Other Poems* by Patrick Kavanagh. *Bird Alone* by Seán O'Faoláin.

1937 General election and constitutional referendum. Constitution of Éire replaces Free State. *Famine* by Liam O'Flaherty. *As I Was Going Down Sackville Street* by Oliver St John Gogarty.

1938 Anglo-Irish Agreement: settlement of economic war. New Irish Senate established. Douglas Hyde elected first President of Éire. *Murphy* by Samuel Beckett. *The Death of the Heart* by Elizabeth Bowen. *The Green Fool* by Patrick Kavanagh. *New Poems* by W. B. Yeats.

1939 IRA bombing campaign in Britain. Éire's declaration of neutrality implemented after outbreak of Second World War (Sept.). Death of W. B. Yeats. *Last Poems and Two Plays* by W. B. Yeats. *Finnegans Wake* by James Joyce. *Call My Brother Back* by Michael McLaverty. *Autumn Journal* by Louis MacNeice. *At Swim-Two-Birds* by Flann O'Brien.

PART ONE
WRITINGS 1789–1890

1. POLITICAL WRITINGS AND SPEECHES

EDMUND BURKE
(1729–1797)

from *Reflections on the Revolution in France* (1790)

It is now sixteen or seventeen years since I saw the queen of France, then the dauphiness, at Versailles; and surely never lighted on this orb, which she hardly seemed to touch, a more delightful vision. I saw her just above the horizon, decorating and cheering the elevated sphere she just began to move in,—glittering like the morning-star, full of life, and splendor, and joy. Oh! what a revolution! and what an heart must I have, to contemplate without emotion that elevation and that fall! Little did I dream when she added titles of veneration to those of enthusiastic, distant, respectful love, that she should ever be obliged to carry the sharp antidote against disgrace concealed in that bosom; little did I dream that I should have lived to see such disasters fallen upon her in a nation of gallant men, in a nation of men of honour and of cavaliers. I thought ten thousand swords must have leaped from their scabbards to avenge even a look that threatened her with insult.—But the age of chivalry is gone.—That of sophisters, oeconomists, and calculators, has succeeded; and the glory of Europe is extinguished for ever. Never, never more, shall we behold that generous loyalty to rank and sex, that proud submission, that dignified obedience, that subordination of the heart, which kept alive, even in servitude itself, the spirit of an exalted freedom. The unbought grace of life, the cheap defence of nations, the nurse of manly sentiment and heroic enterprize is gone! It is gone, that sensibility of principle, that chastity of honour, which felt a stain like a wound, which inspired courage whilst it mitigated ferocity, which ennobled whatever it touched, and under which vice itself lost half its evil, by losing all its grossness.

This mixed system of opinion and sentiment had its origin in the

antient chivalry; and the principle, though varied in its appearance
by the varying state of human affairs, subsisted and influenced
through a long succession of generations, even to the time we live in.
If it should ever be totally extinguished, the loss I fear will be great.
It is this which has given its character to modern Europe. It is this
which has distinguished it under all its forms of government, and
distinguished it to its advantage, from the states of Asia, and possibly
from those states which flourished in the most brilliant periods of
the antique world. It was this, which, without confounding ranks,
had produced a noble equality, and handed it down through all the
gradations of social life. It was this opinion which mitigated kings
into companions, and raised private men to be fellows with kings.
Without force, or opposition, it subdued the fierceness of pride and
power; it obliged sovereigns to submit to the soft collar of social
esteem, compelled stern authority to submit to elegance, and gave a
domination vanquisher of laws, to be subdued by manners.

But now all is to be changed. All the pleasing illusions, which
made power gentle, and obedience liberal, which harmonized the
different shades of life, and which, by a bland assimilation, incorpor-
ated into politics the sentiments which beautify and soften private
society, are to be dissolved by this new conquering empire of light
and reason. All the decent drapery of life is to be rudely torn off. All
the superadded ideas, furnished from the wardrobe of a moral
imagination, which the heart owns, and the understanding ratifies, as
necessary to cover the defects of our naked shivering nature, and to
raise it to dignity in our own estimation, are to be exploded as a
ridiculous, absurd, and antiquated fashion.

On this scheme of things, a king is but a man; a queen is but a
woman; a woman is but an animal; and an animal not of the highest
order. All homage paid to the sex in general as such, and without
distinct views, is to be regarded as romance and folly. Regicide, and
patricide, and sacrilege, are but fictions of superstition, corrupting
jurisprudence by destroying its simplicity. The murder of a king, or a
queen, or a bishop, or a father, are only common homicide; and if the
people are by any chance, or in any way gainers by it, a sort of
homicide much the most pardonable, and into which we ought not to
make too severe a scrutiny.

On the scheme of this barbarous philosophy, which is the offspring of cold hearts and muddy understandings, and which is as

void of solid wisdom, as it is destitute of all taste and elegance, laws are to be supported only by their own terrors, and by the concern, which each individual may find in them, from his own private speculations, or can spare to them from his own private interests. In the groves of *their* academy, at the end of every visto, you see nothing but the gallows. Nothing is left which engages the affections on the part of the commonwealth. On the principles of this mechanic philosophy, our institutions can never be embodied, if I may use the expression, in persons; so as to create in us love, veneration, admiration, or attachment. But that sort of reason which banishes the affections is incapable of filling their place. These public affections, combined with manners, are required sometimes as supplements, sometimes as correctives, always as aids to law. The precept given by a wise man, as well as a great critic, for the construction of poems, is equally true as to states. *Non satis est pulchra esse poemata, dulcia sunto.** There ought to be a system of manners in every nation which a well-formed mind would be disposed to relish. To make us love our country, our country ought to be lovely.

But power, of some kind or other, will survive the shock in which manners and opinions perish; and it will find other and worse means for its support. The usurpation which, in order to subvert antient institutions, has destroyed antient principles, will hold power by arts similar to those by which it has acquired it. When the old feudal and chivalrous spirit of *Fealty*, which, by freeing kings from fear, freed both kings and subjects from the precautions of tyranny, shall be extinct in the minds of men, plots and assassinations will be anticipated by preventive murder and preventive confiscation, and that long roll of grim and bloody maxims, which form the political code of all power, not standing on its own honour, and the honour of those who are to obey it. Kings will be tyrants from policy when subjects are rebels from principle.

When antient opinions and rules of life are taken away, the loss cannot possibly be estimated. From that moment we have no compass to govern us; nor can we know distinctly to what port we steer. Europe undoubtedly, taken in a mass, was in a flourishing condition the day on which your Revolution was compleated. How much of that prosperous state was owing to the spirit of our old manners and opinions is not easy to say; but as such causes cannot be indifferent in their operation, we must presume, that, on the whole, their operation was beneficial.

We are but too apt to consider things in the state in which we find them, without sufficiently adverting to the causes by which they have been produced, and possibly may be upheld. Nothing is more certain, than that our manners, our civilization, and all the good things which are connected with manners, and with civilization, have, in this European world of ours, depended for ages upon two principles; and were indeed the result of both combined; I mean the spirit of a gentleman, and the spirit of religion. The nobility and the clergy, the one by profession, the other by patronage, kept learning in existence, even in the midst of arms and confusions, and whilst governments were rather in their causes than formed. Learning paid back what it received to nobility and to priesthood; and paid it with usury, by enlarging their ideas and by furnishing their minds. Happy if they had all continued to know their indissoluble union, and their proper place! Happy if learning, not debauched by ambition, had been satisfied to continue the instructor, and not aspired to be the master! Along with its natural protectors and guardians, learning will be cast into the mire, and trodden down under the hoofs of a swinish multitude.*

If, as I suspect, modern letters owe more than they are always willing to own to antient manners, so do other interests which we value full as much as they are worth. Even commerce, and trade, and manufacture, the gods of our oeconomical politicians, are themselves perhaps but creatures; are themselves but effects, which, as first causes, we choose to worship. They certainly grew under the same shade in which learning flourished. They too may decay with their natural protecting principles. With you, for the present at least, they all threaten to disappear together. Where trade and manufactures are wanting to a people, and the spirit of nobility and religion remains, sentiment supplies, and not always ill supplies their place; but if commerce and the arts should be lost in an experiment to try how well a state may stand without these old fundamental principles, what sort of a thing must be a nation of gross, stupid, ferocious, and at the same time, poor and sordid barbarians, destitute of religion, honour, or manly pride, possessing nothing at present, and hoping for nothing hereafter?

I wish you may not be going fast, and by the shortest cut, to that horrible and disgustful situation. Already there appears a poverty of conception, a coarseness and vulgarity in all the proceedings of the assembly and of all their instructors. Their liberty is not liberal. Their science is presumptuous ignorance. Their humanity is savage and brutal.

It is not clear, whether in England we learned those grand and decorous principles, and manners, of which considerable traces yet remain, from you, or whether you took them from us. But to you, I think, we trace them best. You seem to me to be—*gentis incunabula nostrae.** France has always more or less influenced manners in England; and when your fountain is choaked up and polluted, the stream will not run long, or not run clear with us, or perhaps with any nation. This gives all Europe, in my opinion, but too close and connected a concern in what is done in France. Excuse me, therefore, if I have dwelt too long on the atrocious spectacle of the sixth of October 1789, or have given too much scope to the reflections which have arisen in my mind on occasion of the most important of all revolutions, which may be dated from that day, I mean a revolution in sentiments, manners, and moral opinions. As things now stand, with every thing respectable destroyed without us, and an attempt to destroy within us every principle of respect, one is almost forced to apologize for harbouring the common feelings of men.

from *Letter to Richard Burke* (1792)

MY DEAR SON,

We are all again assembled in Town, to finish the last, but the most laborious of the tasks which have been imposed upon me during my Parliamentary service. We are as well as, at our time of life, we can expect to be. We have indeed some moments of anxiety about you. You are engaged in an undertaking similar in its principle to mine. You are engaged in the relief of an oppressed people. In that service you must necessarily excite the same sort of passions in those who have exercised, and who wish to continue that oppression, that I have had to struggle with in this long labour. As your Father has done, you must make enemies of many of the rich, of the proud, and of the powerful. I and you began in the same way. I must confess, that if our place was of our choice, I could wish it had been your lot to begin the

Edmund Burke

career of your life with an endeavour to render some more moderate, and less invidious service to the publick. But being engaged in a great and critical work, I have not the least hesitation about your having hitherto done your duty as becomes you. If I had not an assurance not to be shaken, from the character of your mind I should be satisfied on that point, by the cry that is raised against you. If you had behaved as they call it discreetly, that is, faintly and treacherously, in the execution of your trust, you would have had for a while, the good word of all sorts of men; even of many of those whose cause you had betrayed; and whilst your favour lasted, you might have coined that false reputation into a true and solid interest to yourself. This you are well apprized of; and you do not refuse to travel that beaten road from an ignorance, but from a contempt of the objects it leads to.

When you choose an arduous and slippery path, God forbid that any weak feelings of my declining age, which calls for soothings and supports, and which can have none but from you, should make me wish that you should abandon what you are about, or should trifle with it. In this House we submit, though with troubled minds, to that order, which has connected all great duties with toils and with perils, which has conducted the road to glory through the regions of obloquy and reproach, and which will never suffer the disparaging alliance of spurious, false, and fugitive praise, with genuine and permanent reputation. We know, that the Power which has settled that order, and subjected you to it by placing you in the situation you are in, is able to bring you out of it, with credit, and with safety. His will be done. All must come right. You may open the way with pain, and under reproach. Others will pursue it with ease and with applause.

I am sorry to find that pride and passion, and that sort of zeal for religion, which never shews any wonderful heat but when it afflicts and mortifies our neighbour, will not let the ruling description perceive that the privilege for which your clients contend, is very nearly as much for the benefit of those who refuse it, as those who ask it. I am not to examine into the charges that are daily made on the Administration of Ireland. I am not qualified to say how much in them is cold truth, and how much rhetorical exaggeration. Allowing some foundation to the complaint, it is to no purpose that these people alledge that their Government is a job in its administration. I am sure it is a job in its constitution; nor is it possible, a scheme of polity which, in total exclusion of the body of the community, confines (with little or no regard to their rank or condition in life) to a certain set of favoured citizens the rights which formerly belonged to the whole, should not, by the operation of the same selfish and narrow principles, teach the persons who administer in that Government, to prefer their own particular, but well understood private interest, to the false and ill calculated private interest of the monopolizing Company they belong to. Eminent characters, to be sure, overrule places and circumstances. I have nothing to say to that virtue which shoots up in full force by the native vigour of the seminal principle, in spite of the adverse soil and climate that it grows in. But speaking of things in their ordinary course, in a Country of monopoly there *can* be no patriotism. There may be a party spirit—but public spirit there can be none. As to a spirit of liberty, still less can it exist, or any thing like it. A liberty made up of penalties! a liberty made up of incapacities! a liberty made up of exclusion and proscription, continued for ages of four-fifths, perhaps, of the inhabitants of all ranks and fortunes! In what does such liberty differ from the description of the most shocking kind of servitude?

But it will be said, in that Country, some people are free—why this is the very description of despotism. *Partial freedom is privilege and prerogative, and not liberty.* Liberty, such as deserves the name, is an honest, equitable, diffusive, and impartial principle. It is a great and enlarged virtue, and not a sordid, selfish, and illiberal vice. It is the portion of the mass of the citizens; and not the haughty licence of some potent individual, or some predominant faction.

If any thing ought to be despotick in a Country, it is its Government; because there is no cause, of constant operation, to make its yoke unequal. But the dominion of a party must continually, steadily, and by its very essence, lean upon the prostrate description. A Constitution formed so as to enable a party to overrule its very Government, and to overpower the people too, answers the purposes neither of Government nor of freedom. It compels that power, which ought, and often would be, disposed *equally* to protect the Subjects, to fail in its trust, to counteract its purposes, and to become no better than the instrument of the wrongs of a faction. Some degree of influence must exist in all Governments. But a Government, which has no interest to please the body of the people, and can neither support them, nor with safety call for their support, nor is of power to sway the domineering faction, can only exist by corruption; and taught by that monopolizing party which usurps the title and qualities of the publick, to consider the body of the people as out of the Constitution, they will consider those who are in it in the light in which they choose to consider themselves. The whole relation of Government and of freedom, will be a battle, or a traffick.

This system in its real nature, and under its proper appellations, is odious and unnatural, especially when a Constitution is admitted, which not only, as all Constitutions do profess, has a regard to the good of the multitude, but in its theory makes profession of their power also. But of late, this scheme of theirs has been new christened—*honestum nomen imponitur vitio.** A word has been lately struck in the mint of the Castle of Dublin; thence it was conveyed to the Tholsel, or City-hall, where having passed the touch of the Corporation,*—so respectably stamped and vouched, it soon became current in Parliament, and was carried back by the Speaker of the House of Commons* in great pomp, as an offering of homage from whence it came. The word is *ascendancy*. It is not absolutely new. But the sense in which I have hitherto seen it used, was to signify an influence obtained over the minds of some other person by love and reverence, or by superior management and dexterity. It had therefore, to this its promotion, no more than a moral, not a civil or political use. But I admit it is capable of being so applied; and if the Lord Mayor of Dublin,* and the Speaker of the Irish Parliament, who recommend the preservation of the Protestant ascendancy, mean to employ the word in that sense, that is, if they understand by it the preservation of the influence of that description of gentlemen over the Catholicks, by means of an authority derived from their wisdom and virtue, and from an opinion they raise in that people of a pious regard and affection for their freedom and happiness, it is impossible not to commend their adoption of so apt a term into the family of politicks. It may be truly said to enrich the language. Even if the Lord Mayor and Speaker mean to insinuate that this influence is to be obtained and held by flattering their people, by managing them by skilfully adapting themselves to the humours and passions of those whom they would govern, he must be a very untoward critick who would cavil even at this use of the word, though such cajoleries would perhaps be more prudently practised than professed. These are all meanings laudable, or at least tolerable. But when we look a little more narrowly, and compare it with the plan to which it owes its present technical application, I find it has strayed far from its original sense. It goes much further than the privilege allowed by Horace. It is more than *parce detorsum.** This Protestant ascendancy means nothing less than an influence obtained by virtue, by love, or even by artifice and seduction; full as little an influence derived from the means by which Ministers have obtained an influence, which might be called, without straining, an *ascendancy* in publick Assemblies in England, that is, by a liberal distribution of places and pensions and other graces of Government. This last is wide indeed of the signification of the word. New *ascendancy* is the old mastership. It is neither more nor less than the resolution of one set of people in Ireland, to consider themselves as the sole citizens in the commonwealth; and to keep a dominion over the rest by reducing them to absolute slavery, under a military power; and thus fortified in their power, to divide the publick estate, which is the result of general contribution, as a military booty, solely amongst themselves.

The poor word ascendancy, so soft and melodious in its sound, so lenitive and emollient in its first usage, is now employed to cover to the world, the most rigid and perhaps not the most wise of all plans of policy. The word is large enough in its comprehension. I cannot conceive what mode of oppression in civil life, or what mode of religious persecution, may not come within the methods of preserving an *ascendancy*. In plain old English, as they apply it, it signifies *pride and dominion* on the one part of the relation, and on the other *subserviency and contempt*—and it signifies nothing else. The old words are as fit to be set to musick as the new; but use has long since affixed to them their true signification, and they sound, as the other will, harshly and odiously to the moral and intelligent ears of mankind.

This ascendancy, by being a *Protestant* ascendancy, does not better it from the combination of a note or two more in this anti-harmonick scale. If Protestant ascendancy means the proscription from citizenship of by far the major part of the people of any Country, then Protestant ascendancy is a bad thing; and it ought to have no existence. But there is a deeper evil. By the use that is so frequently made of the term, and the policy which is engrafted on it, the name

Protestant becomes nothing more or better than the name of a persecuting faction, with a relation of some sort of theological hostility
to others, but without any sort of ascertained tenets of its own, upon
the ground of which it persecutes other men; for the patrons of this
Protestant ascendancy neither do nor can, by any thing positive,
define or describe what they mean by the word Protestant. . . .

A very great part of the mischiefs that vex the world, arises from
words. People soon forget the meaning, but the impression and the
passion remain. The word Protestant is the charm that locks up in
the dungeon of servitude three millions of your people. It is not
amiss to consider this spell of potency, this abracadabra that is hung
about the necks of the unhappy, not to heal, but to communicate
disease. We sometimes hear of a Protestant *Religion*, frequently of a
Protestant *interest*. We hear of the latter the most frequently, because
it has a positive meaning. The other has none. We hear of it the most
frequently, because it has a word in the phrase, which, well or ill
understood, has animated to persecution and oppression at all times
infinitely more than all the dogmas in dispute between religious
factions. These are indeed well formed to perplex and torment the
intellect; but not half so well calculated to inflame the passions and
animosities of men.

I do readily admit, that a great deal of the wars, seditions and
troubles of the world, did formerly turn upon the contention
between *interests* that went by the names of Protestant and Catholick.
But I imagined that at this time no one was weak enough to believe,
or impudent enough to pretend, that questions of Popish and Protestant opinions or interest are the things by which men are at present
menaced with crusades by foreign invasion, or with seditions which
shake the foundations of the State at home. It is long since all this
combination of things has vanished from the view of intelligent
observers. The existence of quite another system of opinions and
interests is now plain to the grossest sense. Are these the questions
that raise a flame in the minds of men at this day? If ever the Church
and the Constitution of England should fall in these Islands (and
they will fall together) it is not Presbyterian discipline, nor Popish
hierarchy, that will rise upon their ruins. It will not be the Church
of Rome, nor the Church of Scotland—not the Church of Luther,
nor the Church of Calvin. On the contrary, all these Churches are
menaced, and menaced alike. It is the new fanatical Religion, now in

the heat of its first ferment, of the Rights of Man, which rejects all Establishments, all discipline, all Ecclesiastical, and in truth all Civil order, which will triumph, and which will lay prostrate your Church; which will destroy your distinctions, and which will put all your properties to auction, and disperse you over the Earth. If the present Establishment should fall, it is this Religion which will triumph in Ireland and in England, as it has triumphed in France. This Religion, which laughs at creeds and dogmas and confessions of faith, may be fomented equally amongst all descriptions, and all sects; amongst nominal Catholicks, and amongst nominal Churchmen; and amongst those Dissenters who know little, and care less, about a Presbytery, or any of its discipline, or any of its doctrine.

Against this new, this growing, this exterminatory system, all these Churches have a common concern to defend themselves. How the enthusiasts of this rising sect rejoice to see you of the old Churches play their game, and stir and rake the cinders of animosities sunk in their ashes, in order to keep up the execution of their plan for your common ruin!

WOLFE TONE
(1763–1798)

from *The Life of Theobald Wolfe Tone* (1797)

The French Revolution had now been above a twelvemonth in its progress; at its commencement, as the first emotions are generally honest, every one was in its favour; but, after some time, the probable consequences to monarchy and aristocracy began to be foreseen, and the partisans of both to retrench considerably in their admiration.

In England, Burke had the triumph completely to decide the public; fascinated by an eloquent publication,* which flattered so many of their prejudices, and animated by their unconquerable hatred of France, which no change of circumstances could alter, the whole English nation, it may be said, retracted from their first decision in favour of the glorious and successful efforts of the French people; they sickened at the prospect of the approaching liberty and happiness of that mighty nation: they calculated, as merchants, the probable effects which the energy of regenerated France might have on their commerce; they rejoiced when they saw the combination of despots formed to restore the ancient system, and perhaps to dismember the monarchy; and they waited with impatience for an occasion, which, happily for mankind, they soon found, when they might, with some appearance of decency, engage in person in the infamous contest.

But matters were very different in Ireland, an oppressed, insulted, and plundered nation. As we well knew, experimentally, what it was to be enslaved, we sympathized most sincerely with the French people, and watched their progress to freedom with the utmost anxiety; we had not, like England, a prejudice rooted in our very nature against France. As the Revolution advanced, and as events expanded themselves, the public spirit of Ireland rose with a rapid acceleration. The fears and animosities of the aristocracy rose in the same, or a still higher proportion. In a little time the French Revolution became the test of every man's political creed, and the nation was fairly divided into two great parties, the Aristocrats and the Democrats (epithets borrowed from France), who have ever since been measuring each other's strength, and carrying on a kind of smothered war, which the course of events, it is highly probable, may soon call into energy and action.

It is needless, I believe, to say that I was a Democrat from the very commencement, and, as all the retainers of Government, including the sages and judges of the law, were, of course, on the other side, this gave the *coup de grâce** to any expectations, if any such I had, of my succeeding at the Bar, for I soon became pretty notorious; but, in fact, I had for some time renounced all hope, and, I may say, all desire, of succeeding in a profession which I alway disliked, and which the political prostitution of its members (though otherwise men of high honour and of great personal worth) had taught me sincerely to despise. I therefore seldom went near the Four Courts, nor did I adopt any one of the means, and, least of all, the study of the law, which are successfully employed by those young men whose object it is to rise in their profession.

It was pretty much about this time that my connection with the Catholic body commenced in a manner which I am about to relate. I cannot pretend to strict accuracy as to dates, for I write entirely from memory; all my papers being in America.

Russell* had, on his arrival to join his regiment at Belfast, found the people so much to his taste, and in return had rendered himself so agreeable to them, that he was speedily admitted into their confidence, and became a member of several of their clubs. This was an unusual circumstance, as British officers, it may well be supposed, were no great favourites with the Republicans of Belfast.

Russell wrote me an account of all this, and it immediately set me on thinking more seriously than I had yet done upon the state of Ireland. I soon formed my theory, and on that theory I have unvaryingly acted ever since.

To subvert the tyranny of our execrable Government, to break the connection with England, the never-failing source of all our political evils, and to assert the independence of my country—these were my objects. To unite the whole people of Ireland, to abolish the memory of all past dissentions, and to substitute the common name of Irishman in place of the denominations of Protestant, Catholic, and Dissenter—these were my means. To effectuate these great objects, I reviewed the three great sects. The Protestants I despaired of from the outset for obvious reasons. Already in possession by an unjust monopoly of the whole power and patronage of the country, it was not to be supposed they would ever concur in measures the certain tendency of which must be to lessen their influence as a party, how much soever the nation might gain. To the Catholics I thought it unnecessary to address myself, because, that as no change could make their political situation worse, I reckoned upon their support to a certainty; besides, they had already begun to manifest a strong sense of their wrongs and oppressions; and finally, I well knew that, however it might be disguised or suppressed, there existed in the breast of every Irish Catholic an inextirpable abhorrence of the English name and power. There remained only the Dissenters, whom I knew to be patriotic and enlightened; however, the recent events at Belfast had showed me that all prejudice was not yet entirely removed from their minds. I sat down accordingly, and wrote a pamphlet addressed to the Dissenters, and which I entitled, 'An Argument on behalf of the Catholics of Ireland,' the object of which was to convince them that they and the Catholics had but one common interest and one common enemy; that the depression and slavery of Ireland was produced and perpetuated by the divisions existing between them, and that, consequently, to assert the independence of their country, and their own individual liberties, it was necessary to forget all former feuds, to consolidate the entire strength of the whole nation, and to form for the future but one people. These principles I supported by the best arguments which suggested themselves to me, and particularly by demonstrating that the cause of the failure of all former efforts, and more especially of the Volunteer Convention in 1783,* was the unjust neglect of the claims of their Catholic brethren. This pamphlet which appeared in September, 1791, under the signature of A Northern Whig, had a considerable degree of success. As my pamphlet spread more and more, my acquaintance amongst the Catholics extended accordingly. My first friend in the body was John Keogh,* and through him I became acquainted with all the leaders, as Richard McCormick, John Sweetman, Edward Byrne, Thomas Braughall,—in short, the whole sub-committee, and most of the active members of the General Committee. In short, I began to grow into something like reputation, and my company was, in a manner, a requisite all that winter.

The Volunteers of Belfast, of the first or green company, were pleased, in consequence of my pamphlet, to elect me an honorary member of their corps, a favour which they were very delicate in bestowing, as I believe I was the only person, except the great Henry Flood,* who was ever honoured with that mark of their approbation. I was also invited to spend a few days in Belfast, in order to assist in framing the first club of United Irishmen, and to cultivate a personal acquaintance with those men whom, though I highly esteemed, I knew as yet but by reputation. In consequence, about the beginning of October, I went down with my friend Russell, who had, by this time, quit the army, and was in Dublin, on his private affairs. The incidents of that journey, which was by far the most agreeable and interesting one I had ever made, I recorded in a kind of diary, a practice which I then commenced, and have ever since, from time to time, continued, as circumstances of sufficient importance occurred. To that diary I refer.

ROBERT EMMET
(1778–1803)

Speech from the Dock (1803)

I am asked what I have to say why sentence of death should not be pronounced on me, according to law. I have nothing to say that can alter your pre-determination, nor that it will become me to say, with any view to the mitigation of that sentence which you are to pronounce and I must abide by. But I have that to say which interests me more than life and which you have laboured to destroy. I have much to say why my reputation should be rescued from the load of false accusation and calumny which has been cast upon it. I do not imagine that, seated where you are, your minds can be so free from prejudice as to receive the least impression from what I am going to utter. I have no hope that I can anchor my character in the breast of a court constituted and trammeled as this is.

I only wish, and that is the utmost that I can expect, that your lordships may suffer it to float down your memories untainted by the foul breath of prejudice, until it finds some more hospitable harbour to shelter it from the storms by which it is buffeted. Were I only to suffer death, after being adjudged guilty by your tribunal, I should bow in silence, and meet the fate that awaits me without a murmur; but the sentence of the law which delivers my body to the executioner will, through the ministry of the law, labour in its own vindication, to consign my character to obloquy; for there must be guilt somewhere, whether in the sentence of the court or in the catastrophe—time must determine. A man in my situation has not only to encounter the difficulties of fortune, and the force of power over minds which it has corrupted or subjugated, but the difficulties of established prejudice. The man dies, but his memory lives. That mine may not perish, that it may live in the respect of my countrymen, I seize upon this opportunity to vindicate myself from some of the charges alleged against me. When my spirit shall be wafted to a more friendly port, when my shade shall have joined the bands of those martyred heroes who have shed their blood on the scaffold and in the field in defense of their country and of virtue, this is my hope: I wish that my memory and my name may animate those who survive me, while I look down with complacency on the destruction of that perfidious government which upholds its domination by blasphemy of the Most High; which displays its power over man as over the beasts of the forest; which sets man upon his brother, and lifts his hand in the Name of God, against the throat of his fellow who believes or doubts a little more or a little less than the government standard, a government which is steeled to barbarity by the cries of the orphans and the tears of the widows it has made.

Here Lord Norbury interrupted Emmet, saying that 'the mean and wicked enthusiasts who felt as he did, were not equal to the accomplishment of their wild designs.'

I appeal to the immaculate God, I swear by the Throne of Heaven, before which I must shortly appear, by the blood of the murdered patriots who have gone before me, that my conduct has been, through all this peril, and through all my purposes, governed only by the conviction which I have uttered, and by no other view than that of the emancipation of my country from the super-inhuman oppression under which she has so long and too patiently travailed; and I confidently hope that, wild and chimerical as it may appear, there is still union and strength in Ireland to accomplish this noblest of enterprises. Of this I speak with confidence, with intimate knowledge, and with the consolation that appertains to that confidence. Think not, my lords, I say this for the petty gratification of giving you a transitory uneasiness. A man who never yet raised his voice to assert a lie will not hazard his character with posterity by asserting a falsehood on a subject so important to his country, and on an occasion like this. Yes, my lords, a man who does not wish to have his epitaph written until his country is liberated, will not leave a weapon in the power of envy, or a pretense to impeach the probity which he means to preserve, even in the grave to which tyranny consigns him.

Here he was again interrupted by Norbury.

Again I say that what I have spoken was not intended for your lordship, whose situation I commiserate rather than envy—my expressions were for my countrymen. If there is a true Irishman present, let my last words cheer him in the hour of his affliction.

Here he was again interrupted. Lord Norbury said he did not sit there to hear treason.

I have always understood it to be the duty of a judge, when a prisoner has been convicted, to pronounce the sentence of the law. I have also understood that judges sometimes think it their duty to hear with patience, and to speak with humanity; to exhort the victim of the laws, and to offer, with tender benignity, their opinions of the motives by which he was actuated in the crime of which he was adjudged guilty. That a judge has thought it his duty so to have done, I have no doubt; but where is the boasted freedom of your institutions, where is the vaunted impartiality, clemency and mildness of your courts of justice if an unfortunate prisoner, whom your policy and not justice is about to deliver into the hands of the executioner, is not suffered to explain his motives sincerely and truly, and to vindicate the principles by which he was actuated? My lord, it may be a part of the system of angry justice to bow a man's mind by humiliation to the purposed ignominy of the scaffold; but worse to me than the purposed shame of the scaffold's terrors would be the shame of such foul and unfounded imputations as have been laid against me in this court. You, my lord, are a judge; I am the supposed culprit. I am a man; you are a man also. By a revolution of power we might exchange places? Though we never could change characters. If I stand at the bar of this court and dare not vindicate my character, what a farce is your justice! If I stand at this bar and dare not vindicate my character, how dare you calumniate it? Does the sentence of death, which your unhallowed policy inflicts on my body, condemn my tongue to silence and my reputation to reproach? Your executioner may abridge the period of my existence; but while I exist I shall not forebear to vindicate my character and motives from your aspersion; and as a man to whom fame is dearer than life, I will make the last use of that life in doing justice to that reputation which is to live after me, and which is the only legacy I can leave to those I honour and love and for whom I am proud to perish. As men, my lords, we must appear on the great day at one common tribunal; and it will then remain for the Searcher of all hearts to show a collective universe, who was engaged in the most virtuous actions or swayed by the purest motives, my country's oppressor, or—

Here he was interrupted and told to listen to the sentence of the court.

My lords, will a dying man be denied the legal privilege of exculpating himself in the eyes of the community from an undeserved reproach, thrown upon him during his trial, by charging him with ambition and attempting to cast away for paltry consideration the liberties of his country? Why did your lordships insult me? Or rather, why insult justice, in demanding of me why sentence of death should not be pronounced against me? I know my lords, that form prescribes that you should ask the question, the form also presents the right of answering. This, no doubt, may be dispensed with, and so might the whole ceremony of the trial, since sentence was already pronounced at the Castle before the jury was impaneled. Your lordships are but the priests of the oracle, and I insist on the whole of the forms.

I am charged with being an emissary of France. An emissary of France! And for what end? It is alleged that I wished to sell the independence of my country. And for what end? Was this the object of my ambition? And is this the mode by which a tribunal of justice reconciles contradiction? No, I am no emissary; and my ambition was to hold a place among the deliverers of my country, not in power nor in profit, but in the glory of the achievement. Sell my country's independence to France! And for what? Was it a change of masters? No, but for my ambition. O, my country, was it a personal ambition that could influence me? Had it been the soul of my actions, could I not by my education and fortune, by the rank and consideration of my family, have placed myself amongst the proudest of your oppressors. My country was my idol. To it I sacrificed every selfish, every endearing sentiment, and for it I now offer up myself, O God! No, my lords; I acted as an Irishman, determined on delivering my country from the yoke of a foreign and unrelenting tyranny and the more galling yoke of a domestic faction, which is its joint partner and perpetrator in the patricide, from the ignominy existing with an exterior of splendour and a conscious depravity. It was the wish of my heart to extricate my country from this doubly riveted despotism; I wished to place her independence beyond the reach of any power on earth. I wished to exalt her to that proud station in the world. Connection with France was, indeed, intended, but only as far as mutual interest would sanction or require. Were the French to assume any authority inconsistent with the purest independence, it would be the signal for their destruction. We sought their aid and we sought it as we had assurance we should obtain it as auxiliaries in war and allies in peace. Were the French to come as invaders or enemies uninvited by the wishes of the people, I should oppose them to the utmost of my strength. Yes, my countrymen, I should advise you to meet them upon the beach with a sword in one hand and a torch in the other. I would meet them with all the destructive fury of war. I would animate my countrymen to immolate them in their boats, before they had contaminated the soil of my country. If they succeeded in landing, and if forced to retire before superior discipline, I would dispute every inch of the ground, burn every blade of grass, and the last entrenchment of liberty should be my grave. What I could not do myself, if I should fall, I should leave as a last charge to my countrymen to accomplish; because I should feel conscious that life, any more than death, is unprofitable when a foreign nation holds my country in subjection. But it was not as an enemy that the soldiers of France were to land. I looked, indeed, for the assistance of France; but I wished to prove to France and to the world that Irish men deserved to be assisted; that they were indignant at slavery, and ready to assert the independence and liberty of their country. I wished to procure for my country the guarantee which Washington procured for America; to procure an aid which, by its example would be as important as its valour disciplined, gallant, pregnant with science and experience, that of a people who would perceive the good and polish the rough points of our character. They would come to us as strangers and leave us as friends, after sharing in our perils and elevating our destiny. These were my objects; not to receive new task-masters, but to expel old tyrants. It was for these ends I sought aid from France; because France, even as an enemy, could not be more implacable than the enemy already in the bosom of my country.

Here he was interrupted by the court.

I have been charged with that importance in the emancipation of my country as to be considered the keystone of the combination of Irishmen; or, as your lordships expressed it, 'the life and blood of the conspiracy.' You do me honour over much; you have given to the subaltern all the credit of a superior. There are men engaged in this conspiracy who are not only superior to me, but even to your own conceptions of yourself, my lord; men before the splendour of whose genius and virtues I should bow with respectful deference and who would think themselves disgraced by shaking your blood-stained hand.

Here he was interrupted.

What! my lord, shall you tell me on the passage to the scaffold, which that tyranny (of which you are only the intermediary executioner) has erected for my murder, that I am accountable for all the blood that has been shed and will be shed in this struggle of the oppressed against the oppressor; shall thou tell me this, and must I be so very a slave as not to repel it? I do not fear to approach the Omnipotent Judge to answer for the conduct of my whole life; and am I to be appalled and falsified by a mere remnant of mortality here? By you, too, although if it were possible to collect all the innocent blood that you have shed in your unhallowed ministry in one great reservoir, your lordship might swim in it.

Here the judge interrupted.

Let no man dare, when I am dead, to charge me with dishonour; let no man taint my memory by believing that I could have engaged in any cause but that of my country's liberty and independence; or that I could have become the pliant minion of power in the oppression of my country. The Proclamation of the Provisional Government speaks for our views; no inference can be tortured from it to countenance barbarity or debasement at home, or subjection, humiliation or treachery from abroad. I would not have submitted to a foreign oppressor, for the same reason that I would resist the foreign and domestic oppressor. In the dignity of freedom I would have fought upon the threshold of my country, and its enemy would enter only by passing over the lifeless corpse. And am I who lived but for my country, and have subjected myself to the dangers of the jealous and watchful oppressor, and the bondage of the grave, only to give my countrymen their rights and my country her independence, am I to be loaded with calumny and not suffered to resent it? No; God forbid!

Here Norbury told the prisoner that his sentiments and language disgraced his family and education, but more particularly his father, Dr Robert Emmet, who was a man that would, if alive, discountenance such opinions. To which Emmet replied:

If the spirit of the illustrious dead participate in the concerns and cares of those who were dear to them in this transitory life, O, ever dear and venerated shade of my departed father, look down with scrutiny upon the conduct of your suffering son and see if I have even for a moment, deviated from those principles of morality and patriotism which it was your care to instill into my youthful mind, and for which I am now about to offer up my life! My lords, you are impatient for the sacrifice. The blood which you seek is not congealed by the artificial terrors which surround your victim; it circulates warm and unruffled through the channels which God created for noble purpose, but which you are now bent to destroy for purposes so grievous that they cry to heaven. Be yet patient! I have but a few more words to say. I am going to go to my cold and silent grave. My lamp of life is nearly extinguished. My race is run. The grave opens to receive me and I sink into its bosom. I have but one request to ask at my departure from this world. It is the charity of its silence. Let no man write my epitaph; for as no man who knows my motives dare now vindicate them, let not prejudice or ignorance asperse them. Let them and me rest in obscurity and peace; and my tomb remain uninscribed and my memory in oblivion until other times and other men can do justice to my character. When my country takes her place among the nations of the earth, then, and not till then let my epitaph be written. I have done.

DANIEL O'CONNELL
(1775–1847)

Speech at Tara (1843)

It would be the extreme of affectation in me to suggest that I have not some claims to be the leader of this majestic meeting. It would be worse than affectation—it would be drivelling folly, if I were not to feel the awful responsibility of the part I have taken in this majestic movement imposed upon me (*hear, hear.*) I feel responsibility to my country, responsibility to my Creator. Yes, I feel the tremulous nature of that responsibility—Ireland is aroused, is aroused from one end to another. Her multitudinous population have but one expression and one wish, and that is the extinction of the Union, the restoration of her nationality.

Suddenly, someone cried, 'there will be no compromise.'

Who is it that talks of compromise? I am not here for the purpose of making anything like a schoolboy's attempt at declamatory eloquence; I am not here to revive in your recollection any of those poetic imaginings respecting the spot on which we stand, and which have really become as familiar as household words; I am not here to exaggerate the historical importance of the spot on which we are congregated—but it is impossible to deny that Tara has historical recollections that give to it an importance, relatively, to other portions of the land, and deserves to be so considered by every person who comes to it for political purposes, and gives it an elevation and point of impression in the public mind that no other part of Ireland can possibly have. History may be tarnished by exaggeration, but the fact is undoubted that we are at Tara of the Kings. We are on the spot where the monarchs of Ireland were elected, and where the chieftains of Ireland bound themselves by the sacred pledge of honour and the tie of religion to stand by their native land against the Danes or any other stranger [*cheers*]. This is emphatically the spot from which emanated the social power—the legal authority—the right to dominion over the furthest extremes of the island, and the power of concentrating the force of the entire nation for the purpose of national defence. On this important spot I have an important duty to perform. I here protest in the face of my country, in the face of my Creator—in the face of Ireland and her God, I protest against the continuance of the unfounded and unjust Union. My proposition to Ireland is that the Union is not binding upon us; it is not binding, I mean, upon conscience. It is void in principle. It is void as matter of right and it is void in constitutional law. I protest everything that is sacred, without being profane, to the truth of my assertion there is really no union between the two countries.

My proposition is that there was no authority vested in any person to pass the Act of Union. I deny the authority of the Act, I deny the competency of the two legislatures to pass that Act. The English legislature had no such competency—that must be admitted by every person. The Irish legislature had no such competency; and I arraign the Union, therefore, on the ground of the incompetency of the bodies that passed it. No authority could render it binding but the authority of the Irish people, consulted individually through the counties, cities, towns, and villages; and if the people of Ireland called for the Union, then it was binding on them, but there was no other authority that could make it binding. The Irish Parliament had no such authority; they were elected to make laws and not legislatures, and it had no right to the authority which alone belonged to the people of Ireland. The trustee might as well usurp the right of the person who trusts him; the servant might as well usurp the power of the master; the Irish Parliament were elected as our trustees, we were their masters—they were but our servant and they had no right to transfer us to any other power on the face of the earth. This doctrine is manifest, and would be admitted by every person; if it were applied to England, would any person venture to assert that the Parliament of England should have the power to transfer its privileges to make laws from England to the legislative chamber of France? Would any person be so insane as to admit it, and that insanity would not be misstated even if they were allowed to send over their representatives to France? Yes, every person would admit in that case that the Union was void.

I have no higher affection for England than for France. They are both foreign authorities to me. The highest legal authority in England has declared us aliens in blood, aliens in religion, and aliens in language from the English. Let no person groan him—I thank him for the honesty of the expression. I never heard of any other act of honesty on his part, and the fact of his having committed one act of honesty ought to recommend him to your good graces. I can refer you to the principle of constitutional law, and to Locke on government, to show that the Irish Parliament had no power or authority to convey itself away. I will only detain you on that point by citing the words of Lord Chancellor Plunket. He declared in the Irish House of Commons that they had no right to transfer the power of legislation from the country. He called upon them to have his words taken down, and he defied the power of Lord Castlereagh to have him censured for the expression, limiting the authority of Parliament. He said to them that they could not transfer their authority, that the maniacal suicide might as well imagine that the blow by which he destroyed his miserable body could annihilate his immortal soul, as they to imagine they could annihilate the soul of Ireland, her constitutional right. The illustration is a happy one. I am here the representative of the Irish nation, and in the name of that great, that virtuous, that moral, temperate, brave, and religious nation, I proclaim the Union a nullity, for it is a nullity in point of right. Never was any measure carried by such iniquitous means as the Union was carried. The first thing that taints it in its origin, and makes it, even if it were a compact, utterly void, is the fraud committed in fermenting discord in the country, and encouraging the rebellion until it broke out, and in making that rebellion and the necessity for crushing it the means of taking from Ireland her constitution and her liberties. There was this second fraud committed on her, that at the time of the passing of the Act of Union Ireland had no legal protection; the habeas corpus was suspended, martial law was proclaimed, trial by jury was at an end, and the lives and liberties of all the King's subjects in Ireland were at the mercy of the courts martial. Those among you who were old enough at the time remember when the shriek from the triangle was heard from every village and town, and when the troops would march out from Trim and lay desolate the country for nine or ten miles around. The military law was established in all its horrors throughout every district of the country and the people were trampled in the dust under the feet of the yeomanry, army, and fencibles. The next fraudulent device to which England had recourse in order to carry this infamous measure, and to promote her own prosperity on the ruins of Irish nationality, was to take the most effective means in order to prevent the Irish people from meeting to remonstrate against the insult and the injury which was about to be inflicted upon them. The Union was void no less from the utter incompetency of the contracting parties to enter into any such contract than by reason of the fact, that it was carried into operation by measures most iniquitous, atrocious and illegal; the habeas corpus act was suspended, torture, flogging, pitch caps, and imprisonment were the congenial agencies whereby England endeavored to carry her infamous designs, and executions upon the gallows for no other crime than that of being suspected to be suspicious, were of daily occurrence in every part of the kingdom. Thus it was that they endeavored to crush the expression of the people's feelings, whom they resolved to plunder and degrade. The people were not permitted to assemble together for the purpose of remonstrating against the Union. Meetings convened by the officers of justice—by the high sheriffs of counties, were dispersed at the point of the bayonet. The people were not permitted to meet together for remonstrance, but they got up petitions in every direction, to testify their feelings upon the subject, and although no less than seven hundred and seven thousand signatures were signed to petitions against the Union, despite of all the corrupt influence of the Government, more than three thousand wretches could not be found to sign a petition in favour of the measure.

The next impeachment which I bring against the Union is that it was brought about not only by physical force, but by bribery the most unblushing and corruption the most profligate. One million two hundred and seventy-five thousand pounds were expended upon the purchase of rotten boroughs alone, and no less a sum than two millions of money were lavished upon peculation unparalleled, and bribery the most enormous and most palpable that ever yet disgraced the annals of humility. There was not an office, civil, military, or ecclesiastical in the county, which was not flung open to the Unionist as the pence and wages of his political depravity. Six or seven judges bought their seats upon the bench by giving in their adhesion to the Union; and having no claim to wear the ermine other than that which was to be derived from the fact of their being recreants to their country, they continued in right of this during their lives to inflict the effects of their iniquity upon the people whom they betrayed. Twelve bishops obtained their seats by voting for the Union, for the spirit of corruption spared nothing. Men were made prelates, generals, admirals, commissioners for supporting the ministry in this infamous design, and every office in the revenue and customs was placed at the disposal of those who were base enough to sell their country for a mess of pottage.* In fact, corruption was never known to have been carried before or since to such excess in any country of the world, and if such a contract, if contract it could be called, was to be binding on the Irish nation, there was no longer any use for honesty or justice in the world. But strong as was the influence of corruption on the human mind, the victory which the English ministry achieved was slow and by no means easy of accomplishment, for the intimidation to the death upon the one hand, and bribery on the other, were impotent to procure a majority for them in the Irish House of Commons in the first session, when the bill was introduced. On the contrary, when the first attempt was

made to frustrate our liberties, there was a majority of eleven against
the Union Bill. But the despoiler was not easy to be foiled, nor was
he apt to be disheartened by a single failure. The work of corruption
was set on foot with redoubled energy, and the wretches who were
not so utterly abandoned as to suffer themselves to be bribed for the
direct and positive purpose of giving their vote for the Union,
accepted bribes on the condition of withdrawing from the House
altogether, and accordingly they vacated their seats, and in their
place stepped in Englishmen and Scotchmen who knew nothing of
Ireland, and who were not impeded by any conscientious scruples
whatever from giving their unqualified sanction to any plot of the
English, how infamous so ever, to oppress and plunder the country.
By these accumulated means the Union was carried and the fate of
Ireland sealed. But the monster evil of the Union is the financial
robbery which by its means was practiced upon Ireland. A scandalous injustice thus inflicted would be in itself sufficient even in the
absence of other arguments—even if other arguments were wanting—to render the Union void and of no effect. At the passing of
that fatal act—badge of our ruin and disgrace—Ireland owed only
twenty millions, England owed four hundred and forty six millions,
and the equitable terms on which the contract was based, whereby
both countries were to be allied and identified—identified indeed!—
were these, that England was generously to undertake the liability of
one-half of her national debt, on condition that we would undertake
the responsibility of one-half of hers. This is not a befitting time nor
season to enter into minute details relative to the particulars of this
financial swindle, but I may be permitted to direct your attention to
this very obvious fact, that whereas England has only doubled her
debt since the passing of the Union, the increase of the national debt
of Ireland during the same period cannot with justice be estimated
on a different ratio, and that consequently Ireland, at the very highest calculation, cannot in reality and as of her own account, owe a
larger sum than forty millions; and I will tell you, my friends, that
never will we consent to pay one shilling more of a national debt than
that. I say it in the name and on behalf of the Irish nation. But I will
tell you this, as a secret, and you may rely upon it as a truth, that in
point of fact we do not owe one farthing more than thirty millions;
and in proof of the truth of this assertion, I beg leave to refer you to a
work published by a very near and dear relative of mine—my third

son, the member for Kilkenny*—who, by the most accurate statistical calculations, and by a process of argument intelligible to the humblest intellect, has made the fact apparent to the world, that according to the terms of honest and equitable dealing, as between both countries, Ireland's proportion of the national debt cannot be set down at a larger sum than I state, thirty millions. I am proud that there is a son of mine who, after the Repeal shall have been carried, will be able to meet the cleverest English financier of them all, foot to foot and hand to hand, and prove by arguments most incontestable how grievous and intolerable is the injustice which was inflicted upon our country in this respect by the Union. The project of robbing Ireland by joining her legislatively with England was no new scheme which entered the minds of the English for the first time about the year, 1800. It was a project which was a favourite theme of dissertation with all the English essayists for years previous to the period when it was carried into practical effect, and the policy towards Ireland, which their literary men were continually urging upon the English people for their adoption, was similar to that of the avaricious housewife who killed the goose who laid her golden eggs. Yes, such was the course they pursued towards Ireland, and you will deserve the reputation of being the lineal descendants of that goose if you be such ganders as not to declare in a voice of thunder that no longer shall this system of plunder be permitted to continue.

My next impeachment of the Union is founded upon the disastrous effects which have resulted therefrom to our commercial and manufacturing interests, as well as to our general national interests. Previous to the Union, the county Meath was filled with the seats of noblemen at Semen! What a contrast does its present state present! I, on Monday read at the Association a list of the deserted mansions which are now to be found ruined and desolate in your country. Even the spot where the Duke of Wellington—famed the world over for his detestation of his country—drew his first breath, instead of bearing a noble castle, or splendid mansion, presented the aspect of ruin and desolation, and briars and nettles adequately marked the place that produced him. The county of Meath was at one time studded thickly with manufactories in every direction, and an enormous sum was expended yearly in wages, but here, as in every other district of the country, the eye was continually shocked with sights which evidenced with but too great eloquence the lamentable decay which has been entailed upon our country by the Union. The linen trade at one period kept all Ulster in a state of affluence and prosperity. Kilkenny was for ages celebrated for its extensive blanket manufactures and Cork also—and Carrick-on-Suir, and in a thousand other localities, too numerous to mention, thousands were kept in constant and lucrative employment, at various branches of national industry, from year's end to year's end, before the passing of the Union. But this is no longer the case, and one man is not now kept in employment for a thousand who were employed before the Union. The report of the English commissioners themselves has declared this appalling fact to the world that one-third of our population are in a state of actual destitution; and yet, in the face of all this, men may be found who, claiming to themselves the character of political honesty, stand up and declare themselves in favour of the continuance of the Union. It is no bargain; it was a base swindle. Had it, indeed, been a fair bargain, the Irish would have continued faithful to it to the last, regardless of the injuries which it might have entailed upon them for the Irish people have been invariably faithful to their contracts; whereas England never yet made a promise which she did not violate, nor ever entered into a contract which she did not shamelessly and scandalously outrage. Even the Union itself, beneficial as it is to England, is but a living lie to Ireland. Everybody now admits the mischief that the Union has produced to Ireland. The very fact of its not being a compact is alone sufficient to nullify the Union, and on that ground I here proclaim, in the name of the Irish nation, that it is null and void. It is a union of legislators, but not a union of nations. Are you and I one bit more of Englishmen now than we were twenty or forty years ago? If we had a Union would not Ireland have the same parliamentary franchise that is enjoyed by England? But calling it a Union, could anything be more unjust on the part of England than to give her own people a higher and more extensive grade of franchise? And to the Irish people a more limited and an extinguishing and perishing franchise. She has given to her people an extended municipal reform, and to Ireland a wretched and miserable municipal reform. Even within the last week a plan was brought forward by Lord Elliot and the [*sneers*] Attorney-General Smith, that will have the effect of depriving one-third of those who now enjoy the franchise of its possession. No, the Union is void, but it is more peremptorily void on the ground of the ecclesiastical revenues of the counts being left to support a church of a small portion of the people. In England the ecclesiastical revenues of the country are given to the clergy that the majority of the people believe to teach the truth. In Scotland the ecclesiastical revenues are, or at least were up to a late period, paid to the clergy of the majority of the people; but the Irish people are compelled to pay the clergy of a small minority, not amounting to more than the one-tenth of the people of the entire island. The Union was effected against all constitutional principle by the most atrocious fraud—by the most violent and most iniquitous exercise of force, by the most abominable corruption and bribery, by the shifting of Irish members out of their seats, and the putting of Englishmen and Scotchmen into their places; and that was followed by the destruction of our commerce, by the annihilation of our manufactures, by the depreciation of our farmers—and you know I speak the truth when I talk of the depression of the farming interests by financial robbery, on an extensive scale to be sure, but a robbery on that very account, only the more iniquitous, fiendish, and harsh. I contend, therefore, that the Union is a nullity; but do I, on that account, advise you to turn out against it? No such thing. I advise you to act quietly and peaceably and in no other way.

Then a voice cried, 'any way you like.'

Remember that my doctrine is that 'the man who commits a crime gives strength to the enemy,' and you should not act in any manner that would strengthen the enemies of your country. You should act peaceably and quietly, but firmly and determinedly. You may be certain that your cheers here today will be conveyed to England.

The vast assemblage here commenced cheering in the most deafening and enthusiastic manner, and the distant lines of people on the limits of the assembly were seen waving their hats and handkerchiefs in response.

Yes, the overwhelming majesty of your multitude will be taken to England, and will have its effect there. The Duke of Wellington began by threatening us. He talked of civil war, but he does not say a single word of that now. He is now getting eyelet holes made in the old barracks, and only think of an old general doing such a thing, just as if we were going to break our heads against stone walls. I am glad to find that a great quantity of brandy and biscuits has been latterly imported, and I hope the poor soldiers get some of them. But the

Duke of Wellington is not now talking of attacking us, and I am glad of it; but I tell him this—I mean no disrespect to the brave, the gallant, and the good conducted soldiers that compose the Queen's army; and all of them that we have in this country are exceedingly well conducted. There is not one of you that has a single complaint to make against any of them. They are the bravest army in the world and therefore I do not mean to disparage them at all, but I feel it to be a fact, that Ireland, roused as she is at the present moment, would, if they made war upon us, furnish women enough to beat the entire of the Queen's forces. At the last fight for Ireland, when she was betrayed by having confided in England's honour, but oh! English honour will never again betray our land, for the man will deserve to be betrayed who would confide again in England. I would as soon think of confiding in the cousin-german of a certain personage having two horns and a hoof. At that last battle, the Irish soldiers, after three days fighting, being attacked by fresh troops, faltered and gave way, and 1,500 of the British army entered the breach. The Irish soldiers were fainting and retiring when the women of Limerick threw themselves between the contending forces, and actually stayed the progress of the advancing enemy. I am stating matter of history to you, and the words I use are not mine, but those of Parson Story, the chaplain of King William, who describes the siege, and who admits that the Limerick women drove back the English soldiers from fifteen to thirty paces. Several of the women were killed, when a shriek of horror resounded from the ranks of the Irish. They cried out, 'Let us rather die to the last man than that our women should be injured,' and then they threw themselves forward, and, made doubly valiant by the bravery of the women, they scattered the Saxon and the Dane before them. Yes, I have women enough in Ireland to beat them if necessary; but, my friends, it is idle to imagine that any statesman ever existed who could resist the cry that Ireland makes for justice . . .

We will break no law. See how we have accumulated the people of Ireland for this Repeal Year. When, on the 2nd of January, I ventured to call it the Repeal Year, every person laughed at me. Are they laughing now? It is our turn to laugh at present. Before twelve months more, the Parliament will be in College Green. I said the Union did not take away from the people of Ireland their legal rights. I told you that the Union did not deprive the people of that right, or take away the authority to have self-legislation. It has not lessened the prerogatives of the Crown, or taken away the rights of the Sovereign, and amongst them is the right to call her Parliament wherever the People are entitled to it, and the people of Ireland are entitled to have it in Ireland. And the Queen has only tomorrow to issue her writs and get the Chancellor to seal them, and if Sir Edward Sugden does not sign them she will soon get an Irishman that will, to revive the Irish Parliament. The towns which sold their birthright have no right to be reckoned amongst the towns sending members to Parliament. King James the First, in one day, created forty boroughs in Ireland, and the Queen has the same right as her predecessor to do so. We have a list of the towns to return members according to their population, and the Queen has only to order writs to issue, and to have honest ministers to advise her to issue those wants, and the Irish Parliament is revived by its own energy, and the force of the Sovereign's prerogative. I will only require the Queen to exercise her perogative, and the Irish people will obtain their nationality again. If, at the present moment, the Irish Parliament was in existence, even as it was in 1800, is there a coward amongst you—is there a wretch amongst you so despicable that would not die rather than allow the Union to pass?

Another voice interrupted him, 'Yes, to the last man.'

Let every man who, if we had an Irish Parliament, would rather die than allow the Union to pass lift up his hands. Yes, the Queen will call that Parliament; you may say it is the act of her ministry, if you please. To be sure it would be the act of her ministry, and the people of Ireland are entitled to have their friends appointed to the ministry. The Irish Parliament will then assemble, and I defy all the generals, old and young, and all the old women in pantaloons. Nay, I defy all the chivalry of the earth to take away that Parliament from us again. Well, my friends, may I ask you to obey me in the course of conduct I point out to you, when I dismiss you to-day; when you have heard the resolutions put, I am sure you will go home with the same tranquillity with which you came here, every man of you; and if I wanted you again, would you not come again to Tara Hill for me? Remember me, I lead you into no peril. If danger existed, it would arise from some person who would attack us, for we will attack nobody; and if that danger exists you will not find me in the rear rank. The Queen will be able to restore our Parliament to us. The absentee drains, which caused the impoverishment of the country, will be at an end—the wholesale ejectment of tenants and turning them out on the highway—the murdering of tenants by the landlords will be at an end. The rights of the landlords will be respected, but their duties shall be enforced—an equitable tenure will take the place of the cruel tyranny of the present code of laws, and the protection of the occupying tenants of Ireland be inscribed on the banner of Repeal. Carry home with you my advice. Let there be peace and quiet, law and order, and let every one of you enroll yourselves Repealers—men, women, and children. Give me three millions of Repealers, and I will soon have them. The next step is being taken, and I announce to you from this spot, that all the magistrates that have been deprived of the communion of the peace shall be appointed by the Association to settle all the disputes and differences in their neighbourhood. Keep out of the petty sessions court, and go to them on next Monday. We will submit a plan to choose persons to be arbitrators to settle the differences of the people without expense, and I call upon every man that wishes to be thought the friend of Ireland, to have his disputes settled by the arbitrators, and not again to go to the petty sessions. We shall shortly have the preservative society to arrange the means of procuring from her Majesty the exercise of her prerogative, and I believe I am able to announce to you that twelve months cannot possibly elapse without having a hurrah for our Parliament in College Green. Remember, I pronounce the Union to be null—to be obeyed, as an injustice must be obeyed, when it is supported by law until we have the royal authority to set the matter right, and substitute our own Parliament. I delight at having this day presided over such an assemblage on Tara Hill. Those shouts that burst from you were enough to recall to life the Kings and Chiefs of Ireland. I almost fancy that the spirits of the mighty dead are hovering over us, that the ancient Kings and Chiefs of Ireland are from yonder clouds listening to us. Oh, what a joyous and cheering sound is conveyed in the chirrup for Old Ireland! It is the most beautiful, the most fertile—the most abundant, the most productive country on the face of the earth. It is a lovely land, indented with noble harbours, intersected with transcendent, translucent streams divided by mighty estuaries. Its harbours are open at every hour for every tide, and are sheltered from every storm that can blow from any quarter of Heaven. Oh, yes, it is a lovely land and where is the coward that would not dare to die for it! Yes, our country exhibits the extreme of civilization, and your majestic movement is already the admiration of the civilised world. No other country could produce such an amount of physical force, coupled with so much decorum and propriety of conduct. Many thousands of persons assembled together, and, though they have force sufficient to carry any battle that ever was fought, they separate with the tranquillity of schoolboys breaking up in the afternoon. I wish you could read my heart, to see how deeply the love of Ireland is engraven upon it, and let the people of Ireland, who stood by me so long, stand by me a little longer, and Ireland shall be a nation again.

JAMES FINTAN LALOR
(1807–1849)

Letter to the Irish Felon (1848)

... Without agreement as to our objects we cannot agree on the course we should follow. It is requisite the paper should have but one object and that the public should understand what that object is. Mine is not to repeal the Union, nor restore Eighty-two. This is not the year '82; this is the year '48. For Repeal I never went into 'Agitation' and will not go into insurrection. On that question I refuse to arm, or to act in any mode—and the country refuses. O'Connell made no mistake when he pronounced it to be not worth the price of one drop of blood; and for myself, I regret it was not left in the hands of Conciliation Hall whose lawful property it was and is. Moral force, and Repeal, the means and the purpose, were just fitted to each other, *Arcades ambo*,* balmy Arcadians both. When the means were limited it was only proper and necessary to limit the purpose. When the means were enlarged, the purpose ought to have been enlarged also. Repeal in its vulgar meaning, I look on as utterly impracticable by any mode of action whatever, and the constitution of '82 as absurd, worthless, and worse than worthless. The English government will never concede or surrender to any species of moral force whatsoever; and the country-peasantry will never arm and fight for it—neither will I. If I am to stake life and fame it must assuredly be for something better and greater, more likely to last, more likely to succeed, and better worth success. And a stronger passion, a higher purpose, a nobler and more needful enterprise is fermenting in the hearts of the people. A mightier question moves Ireland today than that of merely repealing the Act of Union. Not the constitution that Tone died to abolish, but the constitution that Tone died to obtain,* independence, full and absolute independence, for this island, and for every man within this island. Into no movement that would leave an enemy's garrison in possession of all our lands, masters of our liberties, our lives and all our means of life and happiness—into no such movement will a single man of the greycoats enter with an armed band, whatever the town population may do. On a wider fighting field, with stronger positions and greater resources than are afforded by the paltry question of Repeal, must we close for our final struggle with England, or sink and surrender. Ireland her own— Ireland her own, and all therein, from the sod to the sky. The soil of Ireland for the people of Ireland, to have and to hold from God alone who gave it—to have and to hold to them and their heirs for ever, without suit or service, faith or fealty, rent or render, to any power under Heaven. From a worse bondage than the bondage of any foreign government, from a dominion more grievous and grinding than the dominion of England in its worst days—from the cruellest tyranny that ever yet laid its vulture clutch on the body and soul of a country, from the robber rights and robber rule that have turned us into slaves and beggars in the land that God gave us for ours.— Deliverance, oh Lord; Deliverance or Death—Deliverance, or this island a desert! This is the one prayer, and terrible need, and real passion of Ireland today, as it has been for ages. Now, at last it begins to shape into defined and desperate purpose; and into it all smaller and meaner purposes must settle and merge. It might have been kept in abeyance, and away from the sight of the sun—aye, till this old native race had been finally conquered out and extinguished *sub silentio*,* without noise or notice. But once propounded and pro-claimed as a principle, not in the dusk of remote country districts, but loudly and proudly, in the tribunes of the capital, it must now be accepted and declared, as the first great Article of Association in the National Covenant of organised defence and armed resistance; as the principle to take ground, and stand and fight upon. When a greater and more ennobling enterprise is on foot, every inferior and feebler project or proceeding will soon be left in the hands of old women, of dastards, impostors, swindlers, and imbeciles. All the strength and manhood of the island—all the courage, energies, and ambition—all the passions, heroism, and chivalry—all the strong men, and strong minds—all those things that make revolutions will quickly desert it, and throw themselves into the greater movement, throng into the larger and loftier undertaking and flock round the banner that flies nearest the sky. There go the young and the gallant, the gifted, and the daring, and there too go the wise. For wisdom knows that in national action *littleness* is more fatal than the wildest rashness; that greatness of object is essential to greatness of effort, strength, and success; that a revolution ought never to take its stand on low or narrow ground, but seize on the broadest and highest ground it can lay hands on; and that a petty enterprise seldom succeeds. Had America aimed or declared for less than independence she would probably have failed, and been a fettered slave today.

Not to repeal the Union, then, but to repeal the Conquest—not to disturb or dismantle the empire, but to abolish it forever—not to fall back on '82 but act up to '48—not to resume or restore an old constitution, but to found a new nation, and raise up a free people, and strong as well as free, and secure as well as strong, based on a peasantry rooted like rocks in the soil of the land—this is my object, as I hope it is yours; and this, you may be assured, is the easier, as it is the nobler and more pressing enterprise. For Repeal, all the moral means at our disposal have been used, abused, and abandoned. All the military means it can command will fail as utterly. Compare the two questions. Repeal would require a national organization; a central representative authority, formally convened, formally elected; a regular army, a regulated war of concerted action, and combined movement. When shall we have them? Where is your National Council of Three Hundred? Where is your National Guard of Three Hundred Thousand? On Repeal, Ireland, of necessity, should resolve and act *by the kingdom*, all together, linked and led; and if beaten in the kingdom there would be nothing to fall back upon. She could not possibly act by parishes. To club and arm would not be enough, or rather it would be nothing; and for Repeal alone Ireland will neither club nor arm. The towns only will do so. A Repeal-war would probably be the fight and defeat of a single field-day; or if protracted, it would be a mere game of chess—and England, be assured, would beat you in the game of chess. On the other question all circumstances differ, as I could easily show you. But I have gone into this portion of the subject prematurely and unawares, and here I stop—being reluctant besides to trespass too long on the time of her Majesty's legal and military advisers.

I would regret much to have my meaning, in any degree, misconceived. I do not desire, by any means, to depreciate the value and importance of Repeal, in the valid and vigorous sense of the term, but only in its vulgar acceptation. I do not want to make the tenure question the sole or main topic or purpose of the *Felon*, or to make Repeal only secondary and subservient. I do not wish—far from it—to consider the two questions as antagonistic or distinct. My wish is to combine and cement the two into one; and so, perfect, and reinforce, and carry both. I, too, want to bring about an alliance and 'combination of classes'—an alliance more wanted and better worth, more feasible, effective and honourable, than any treasonable alliance with the enemy's garrison, based on the surrender and sacrifice of the rights and lives of the Irish people. I want to ally the town and country. Repeal is the question of the town population; the land tenure question is that of the country peasantry; both combined, taking each in its full extent and efficacy, form the question of Ireland—her question for the battle-day.

The principle I state, and mean to stand upon, is this, that the entire ownership of Ireland, moral and material, up to the sun, and down to the centre, is vested of right in the people of Ireland; that they, and none but they, are the land-owners and law-makers of this island; that all laws are null and void not made by them; and all titles to land invalid not conferred and confirmed by them; and that this full right of ownership may and ought to be asserted and enforced by any and all means which God has put in the power of man. In other, if not plainer words, I hold and maintain that the entire soil of a country belongs of right to the people of that country, and is the rightful property not of any one class, but of the nation at large, in full effective possession, to let to whom they will on whatever tenures, terms, rents, services, and conditions they will; one condition, however, being unavoidable, and essential, the condition that the tenant shall bear full, true, and undivided fealty, and allegiance to the nation, and the laws of the nation whose lands he holds, and own no allegiance whatsoever to any other prince, power, or people, or any obligation of obedience or respect to their will, orders, or laws. I hold further, and firmly believe, that the enjoyment by the people of this right, of first ownership of the soil, is essential to the vigour and vitality of all other rights; to their validity, efficacy, and value; to their secure possession and safe exercise. For let no people deceive themselves, or be deceived by the words, and colours, and phrases, and forms, of a mock freedom, by constitutions, and charters and articles, and franchises. These things are paper and parchment, waste and worthless. Let laws and institutions say what they will, this fact will be stronger than all laws, and prevail against them—the fact that those who own your land will make your laws, and command your liberties, and your lives. But this is tyranny and slavery—tyranny in its wildest scope, and worst shape; slavery of body and soul from the cradle to the coffin—slavery, with all its horrors, and with none of its physical comforts and security; even as it is in Ireland, where the whole community is made up of tyrants, slaves, and slave-drivers. A people whose lands and lives are thus in the keeping and custody of others, instead of in their own, are not in a position of common safety. The Irish famine of '46 is example and proof. The corn crops were sufficient to feed the island. But the landlords *would* have their rents in spite of famine, and in defiance of fever. They took the whole harvest and left hunger to those who raised it. Had the people of Ireland been the landlords of Ireland, not a single human creature would have died of hunger, nor the failure of the potato been considered a matter of any consequence.

This principle, then, that the property and possession of land, as well as the powers of legislation, belong of right to people who live in the land and under the law—do you assent to it in its full integrity, and to the present necessity of enforcing it? Your *reason* may assent, yet your *feelings* refuse and revolt—or those of others at least may do so. Mercy is for the merciful; and you may think it pity to oust and abolish the present noble race of land-owners, who have ever been pitiful and compassionate themselves.

What! is your sympathy for a class so great, and your sympathy for a whole people so small? For those same land-owners are now treading out the very life and existence of an entire people, and trampling down the liberties and hopes of this island for ever. It is a mere question between a people and a class—between a people of eight

millions and a class of eight thousand. They or we must quit this
island. It is a people to be saved or lost—it is the island to be kept or
surrendered. They have served us with a general writ of ejectment.
Wherefore, I say, let them get a notice to quit at once; or we shall oust
possession under the law of nature. There are men who claim protection for them, and for all their tyrannous rights and powers, being as
'one class of the Irish people.' I deny the claim. They form no class
of the Irish people, or of any other people. Strangers they are in this
land they call theirs—strangers here and strangers everywhere, own-
ing no country and owned by none; rejecting Ireland, and rejected by
England; tyrants to this island, and slaves to another; here they stand
hating and hated—their hand ever against us, as ours against them,
an outcast and ruffianly horde, alone in the world, and alone in its
history, a class by themselves. They do not know, and never did
belong to this island. Tyrants and traitors have they ever been to us
and ours since first they set foot on our soil. Their crime it is and not
England's that Ireland stands where she does today—or rather it is
our own that have borne them so long. Were they a class of the Irish
people the Union could be repealed without a life lost. Had they
been a class of the Irish people that Union would have never been.
But for them we would now be free, prosperous and happy. Until
they be removed no people can ever take root, grow up and flourish
here. The question between them and us must sooner or later have
been brought to a deadly issue. For heaven's sake, and for Ireland's,
let us settle it now, and not leave it to our children to settle. Indeed it
must be settled now—for it is plain to any ordinary sight that they or
we are doomed. A cry has gone up to heaven for the living and the
dead—to save the living, and avenge the dead.

There are, however, many landlords perhaps, and certainly a few,
not fairly chargeable with the crimes of their order; and you may
think it hard they should lose their lands. But recollect, the principle
I assert would make Ireland *in fact* as she is of *right*, the mistress and
queen of all those lands; that she, poor lady, had ever a soft and
grateful disposition; and that she may, if she please, in reward of
allegiance, confer new titles, or confirm the old. Let us crown her a
queen; and then let her do with her lands as a queen may do.

In the case of any existing interest, of what nature soever, I feel
assured that no question but one would need to be answered. Does
the owner of that interest assent to swear allegiance to the people of

Ireland, and to hold in fee from the Irish nation? If the assent may be assured he will suffer no loss. No eventual or permanent loss, I mean; for some temporary loss he must assuredly suffer. But such loss would be incidental and inevitable to any armed insurrection whatever, no matter on what principle the right of resistance would be resorted to. If he refuse—then I say away with him—out of this land with him—himself and all his robber rights, and all the things himself and his rights have brought into our island—blood, and tears, and famine, and the fever that goes with famine. Between the relative merits and importance of the two rights, the people's right to the land, and their right to legislation, I do not mean or wish to institute any comparison. I am far indeed from desirous to put the two rights in competition, or contrast, for I consider each alike as the natural complement of the other, necessary to its theoretical completeness, and practical efficacy. But, considering them for a moment as distinct, I do mean to assert this—that the land question contains, and the legislative question does *not* contain, the materials from which victory is manufactured; and that, therefore, if we be truly in earnest and determined on success, it is on the former question, and not on the latter that we must take our stand, fling out our banner, and hurl down to England our gage of battle.* Victory follows that banner alone, that and no other. This island is ours, and have it we will, if the leaders be true to the people, and the people be true to themselves.

The rights of property may be pleaded. No one has more respect for the real rights of property than I have; but I do not class among them the robber's right by which the lands of this country are now held in fee for the British crown. I acknowledge no right of property in a small class which goes to abrogate the rights of a numerous people. I acknowledge no right of property in eight thousand persons, be they noble or ignoble, which takes away all rights of property, security, independence, and existence itself, from a population of eight millions, and stands in bar to all the political rights of the island, and all the social rights of its inhabitants. I acknowledge no right of property which takes away the food of millions, and gives them a famine—which denies to the peasant the right of a home, and concedes, in exchange, the right of a workhouse. I deny and challenge all such rights, howsoever founded or enforced. I challenge them, as founded only on the code of the brigand, and enforced only by the sanction of the hangman. Against them I assert the true and indefeasible right of property—the right of our people to live in this land and possess it—to live in it in security, comfort and independence, and to live in it by their own labour, on their own land, as God and nature intended them to do. Against them I shall array, if I can, all the forces that yet remain in this island. And against them I am determined to make war—to their destruction or my own.

These are my principles and views. I shall have other opportunities to develop and defend them. I have some few other requisitions to make, but I choose to defer them for other reasons besides want of time and space. Our first business, before we can advance a step, is to fix our own footing and make good our position. That once done, this contest must, if possible, be brought to a speedy close.

2. REFLECTIONS ON
IRISH CULTURE

CHARLOTTE BROOKE
(*c*.1740–1793)

Preface to Reliques of Irish Poetry (1789)

In a preface to a translation of ancient Irish poetry, the reader will naturally expect to see the subject elucidated and enlarged upon, with the pen of learning and antiquity. I lament that the limited circle of my knowledge does not include the power of answering so just an expectation; but my regret at this circumstance is considerably lessened, when I reflect, that had I been possessed of all the learning requisite for such an undertaking, it would only have qualified me for an unnecessary foil to the names of O'CONOR, O'HALLORAN and VALLANCEY.

My comparatively feeble hand aspires only (like the ladies of ancient Rome) to strew flowers in the paths of these laureled champions of my country. The flowers of earth, the *terrestrial* offspring of Phœbus, were scattered before the steps of victorious WAR; but, for triumphant GENIUS are reserved the *cælestial* children of his beams, the unfading flowers of the Muse. To pluck, and thus to bestow them, is mine, and I hold myself honoured in the task.

'The esteem (says Mr O'HALLORAN) which mankind conceive of nations in general, is always in proportion to the figure they have made in arts and in arms. It is on this account that all civilized countries are eager to display their heroes, legislators, poets and philosophers—and with justice, since every individual participates in the glory of his illustrious countrymen.'—But where, alas, is this thirst for national glory? when a subject of such importance is permitted to a pen like mine! Why does not some *son of Anak* in genius step forward, and boldly throw his gauntlet to Prejudice, the avowed and approved champion of his country's lovely muse?

It is impossible for imagination to conceive too highly of the pitch of excellence to which a science must have soared which was cherished with such enthusiastic regard and cultivation as that of poetry, in this country. It was absolutely, for ages, the vital soul of the nation;[1] and shall we then have no curiosity respecting the productions of genius once so celebrated, and so prized?

True it is, indeed, and much to be lamented, that few of the compositions of those ages that were famed, in Irish annals, for the *light of song*, are now to be obtained by the most diligent research. The greater number of the poetical remains of our Bards, yet extant, were written during the middle ages; periods when the genius of Ireland was in its wane,

> —— Yet still, not lost
> All its original brightness——.

On the contrary, many of the productions of those times breathe the true spirit of poetry, besides the merit they possess with the Historian and Antiquary, as so many faithful delineations of the manners and ideas of the periods in which they were composed.

With a view to throw some light on the antiquities of this country, to vindicate, in part, its history, and prove its claim to scientific as well as to military fame, I have been induced to undertake the following work. Besides the four different species of composition which it contains, (the HEROIC POEM, the ODE, the ELEGY, and the SONG) others yet remain unattempted by translation:—the ROMANCE, in particular, which unites the fire of Homer with the enchanting wildness of Ariosto. But the limits of my present plan have necessarily excluded many beautiful productions of genius, as little more can be done, within the compass of a single volume, than merely to give a few specimens, in the hope of awakening a just and useful curiosity, on the subject of our poetical compositions.

Unacquainted with the rules of translation, I know not how far those rules may censure, or acquit me. I do not profess to give a merely literal version of my originals, for that I should have found an impossible undertaking.—Besides the spirit which they breathe, and which lifts the imagination far above the tameness, let me say, the *injustice*, of such a task,—there are many complex words that could

---

[1] See the elegant and faithful O'CONOR upon this subject; (*Dissertations on the History of Ireland*, p. 66.) and he is supported by the testimonies of the most authentic of antient and modern historians.

not be translated literally, without great injury to the original,— without being 'false to its sense, and falser to its fame.'

I am aware that in the following poems there will sometimes be found a sameness, and repetition of thought, appearing but too plainly in the English version, though scarcely perceivable in the original Irish, so great is the variety as well as beauty peculiar to that language. The number of synonima[2] in which it abounds, enables it, perhaps beyond any other, to repeat the same thought, without tiring the fancy or the ear.

It is really astonishing of what various and comprehensive powers this neglected language is possessed. In the pathetic, it breathes the most beautiful and affecting simplicity; and in the bolder species of composition, it is distinguished by a force of expression, a sublime dignity, and rapid energy, which it is scarcely possible for any translation fully to convey; as it sometimes fills the mind with ideas altogether new, and which, perhaps, no modern language is entirely prepared to express. One compound epithet must often be translated by two lines of English verse, and, on such occasions, much of the beauty is necessarily lost; the force and effect of the thought being weakened by too slow an introduction on the mind; just as that light which dazzles, when flashing swiftly on the eye, will be gazed at with indifference, if let in by degrees.

But, though I am conscious of having, in many instances, failed in my attempts to do all the justice I wished to my originals, yet still, some of their beauties are, I hope, preserved; and I trust I am doing an acceptable service to my country, while I endeavour to rescue from oblivion a few of the invaluable reliques of her ancient genius; and while I put it in the power of the public to form some idea of them, by clothing the thoughts of our Irish muse in a language with which they are familiar, at the same time that I give the originals, as vouchers for the fidelity of my translation, as far as two idioms so widely different would allow.

However deficient in the powers requisite to so important a task, I may yet be permitted to point out some of the good consequences which might result from it, if it were but performed to my wishes. The productions of our Irish Bards exhibit a glow of cultivated

---

[2] There are upwards of forty names to express a *Ship* in the Irish language, and nearly an equal number for a *House*, &c.

genius,—a spirit of elevated heroism,—sentiments of pure honor,—
instances of disinterested patriotism,—and manners of a degree of
refinement, totally astonishing, at a period when the rest of Europe
was nearly sunk in barbarism: And is not all this very honorable to
our countrymen? Will they not be benefited,—will they not be grati-
fied, at the lustre reflected on them by ancestors so very different
from what modern prejudice has been studious to represent them?
But this is not all.——

As yet, we are too little known to our noble neighbour of Britain;
were we better acquainted, we should be better friends. The British
muse is not yet informed that she has an elder sister in this isle; let us
then introduce them to each other! together let them walk abroad
from their bowers, sweet ambassadresses of cordial union between
two countries that seem formed by nature to be joined by every bond
of interest, and of amity. Let them entreat of Britain to cultivate a
nearer acquaintance with her neighbouring isle. Let them conciliate
for us her esteem, and her affection will follow of course. Let them
tell her, that the portion of her blood which flows in our veins is
rather ennobled than disgraced by the mingling tides that descended
from our heroic ancestors. Let them come—but will they answer to a
voice like mine? Will they not rather depute some favoured pen, to
chide me back to the shade whence I have been allured, and where,
perhaps, I ought to have remained, in respect to the memory, and
superior genius of a Father—it avails not to say how dear!—But my
feeble efforts presume not to emulate,—and they cannot injure his
fame.

To guard against criticism I am no way prepared, nor do I suppose
I shall escape it; nay, indeed, I do not wish to escape the pen of the
candid critic: And I would willingly believe that an individual capable
of no offence, and pretending to no pre-eminence, cannot possibly
meet with any severity of criticism, but what the mistakes, or the
deficiencies of this performance, may be justly deemed to merit; and
what, indeed, could scarcely be avoided by one unskilled in composition, and now, with extreme diffidence, presenting, for the first
time, her literary face to the world.

It yet remains to say a few words relative to the TALE which is
annexed to this volume: for that I had no original; the story, however,
is not my own; it is taken from a revolution in the history of
ancient Ireland, Anno Mundi 3649. And no where will the Muse be

furnished with nobler subjects than that neglected history affords. The whole reign of CEALLACHAIN is one continued series of heroism, and high-wrought honor, that rises superior to all the flight of ROMANCE, and defies Poetic fable to surpass it. Also, the reign of BRIAN BOIROIMH, and the famous retreat of the glorious tribe of DALGAIS; besides many other instances too numerous for detail; amongst which I selected the story of MAON, as a subject more suited to my limited powers, than those which demand a 'Muse of fire,' to record them.

LE CHEVALIER DE LA TOCNAYE
(*c*.1767–?)

from *A Frenchman's Walk Through Ireland* (1797)

Dublin

Dublin is a very considerable city, about one-fourth the size of London, of which it is the image in little—even the streets bear the same names; the beauty of the buildings may dispute for precedence with those of the capital; one is astonished at their magnificence and number. The Parliament House does honour to the nation's representatives; it is an immense circular building surrounded by a magnificent colonnade.

It is worthy of remark that the place where the deputies or representatives of the greatest nation assemble is commonly an old, irregular, ugly building, for which there is such attachment or affection that nobody thinks of displacing it by a new and more commodious structure.

The Bourse or Royal Exchange is somewhat like the Mansion House in London, but smaller. The Customs House is much too fine for its work, and the new building which they call the Four Courts of Justice* gives Themis* the pleasure to see herself decently lodged, a rare thing in European countries. Her old residence was a frightful place, as much on account of the members as by reason of the lugubrious and sombre appearance of the cave where they practised. I amused myself often by walking among them, and as it was extremely unlikely that I, in my circumstances, should ever have anything to do with them, I could laugh at their big wigs, in which the face is so buried that only a long nose protrudes. They reminded me of hawks dressed to pounce on their prey, with the beaks only visible. If rumour is to be believed, attorneys here yield in nothing to their brethren of our courts; indeed, from certain stories I have heard it would seem that they are even cleverer.

The squares are large and well built, only the port seems to me to be unworthy of the city. There has just been constructed an immense dock, which will make good certain shortcomings when some houses have been built to protect it from wind. It is singular that the inhabitants have never thought of building a beautiful church here: the churches are all old and without the least decoration. Among them all there are but two miserable bell-towers, and this want prevents the city from having the fine appearance it should exhibit from a distance.

As my object is not to give a topographical description of this great city, I shall not attempt to describe the Castle and the beautiful buildings associated. The splendid carriages and the apparent wealth of the principal houses render the more displeasing the sight of the beggars, whose abject poverty is horrible. They may be seen hanging on for hours to the railings of basement stories, forcing charity by depriving those who live in these places of light and air. Some of them are insolent, seeking to get in some fashion, by force, what is not forthcoming by good-will. These disgusting scenes harden the heart little by little, and I never felt less disposed to alms-giving than after having lived some time in Dublin.

I occupied my leisure in the early days of my sojourn as I do ordinarily in such times elsewhere, by moving from one place to another, and mixing as much as possible with the crowd. I joined one which seemed, on a certain day, to be expecting something with impatience, and found myself among them in front of a large building which had something of the look of an old castle. There was a little platform at the level of a window in the second storey; two men of somewhat disagreeable look made their appearance on it, and I thought I was about to witness some peculiar ceremony. But I was promptly disabused of this idea, for one of them passed a loop of rope round the neck of the other and fastened the cord to a bar of iron above him. I turned to get away, but the crowd was too dense for movement; the poor wretch stood for a moment, alone, in view of the people, then a bolt slipped, and the little platform on which he stood fell against the wall. The Irish have, perhaps, got the better of their neighbours in the matter of hanging people with grace, but to me it appears a great cruelty to make a sort of parade of the death of a man, and in diminishing the horror of the punishment crime is increased and executions multiplied. I think I am not far wrong in assigning this as the reason why there are more people hung in Great Britain and Ireland than in all the rest of Europe.

The crowd seemed to move steadily in one direction, and I followed again—this time to be led to Phœnix Park, where there was a horse race. I really could not say which of the two—execution or race—gave the greater pleasure to the hundred-headed monster.

Although the part of the city where the well-to-do people live is perhaps as beautiful as anything similar in Europe, nothing anywhere can compare with the dirt and misery of the quarters where the lower classes vegetate. They call these quarters 'The Liberties'* of Dublin, and this made me think often of 'liberties' of France under Robespierre, than which there was nothing more disgusting in the universe. . . .

Cork

The climate of Cork is rainy in the extreme. It rains every day in life, and the temperature of the air has perhaps influenced the character of the inhabitants. It would not be incorrect to call this country 'The Land of Whim and Spleen.' There are a great number of people here who are called 'characters,' and who have all sorts of strange whims and crotchets. One will never sit down to table for fear of being suffocated by the odour of the viands, and takes his meals alone in the vestibule; another spends his income on favourite animals, or 'pets,' as they are called; a third, after having enchanted you by a beautiful voice and charming music, finishes up by boxing you. There is one with a red cap who gallops through the streets and enters shops on horseback, when he wants to buy anything. There is one who plays the bagpipes and who is willing to be disinherited from nearly two thousand pounds sterling per annum, rather than give up his pipes, which are at present his sole source of income. There is a man who believes that everybody wishes to poison him. He watches for the entry of any person into a baker's shop, follows him, and when the stranger has bought a loaf he seizes it and runs off with it, believing that the bakers are not anxious to poison anybody but himself. He acts the same way in butchers' shops. Another has constituted himself children's nurse, and washes, rubs, combs, and wipes them. I could mention many other examples of these 'characters,' but have said enough.

There is no place of shelter for the weak-minded of Cork—it is a hideous spectacle to see them in the streets. For the greater part, it is true, they are quiet, but it is so cruel and humiliating to see human nature degraded that an effort should be made to separate them from society.

Yet it must be admitted that the city of Cork has recently made great progress in commerce, in increase of houses, and of inhabitants, and, to some degree, in their amelioration. The city stands on several little marshy islands in the middle of the river, and it is from this circumstance that it takes its name, for Cork means 'muddy' in Irish, and it is passably well named. The narrow canals which separate the islands are only filled with water at high tide, and so destroy considerably the salubrity of the air.

It would seem to be absolutely necessary for the prosperity of the town that the principal magistrates, for a dozen years, should be strong and prudent men, whose judgment would not be narrowed to the dust of their offices, and who would not be so much accustomed to count halfpennies and farthings, or to think of interest at four, five or six per cent. In the whole of Great Britain, the Mayor or Provost is always elected from amongst the merchants and general traders, the inhabitants justly confiding their interests to one who has a commercial career. This arrangement works very well in towns that are much frequented, where the opinion of the merchant is enlightened by that of a large public, and of strangers who may visit the place; but in towns where the merchant can have no ideas other than his own, or where, being a foreigner, his sole aim is to gather as much money as possible, and quit the country afterwards, it must be evident that the embellishments and amelioration of the city, of which he is a principal magistrate for a year, will not interest him very much.

I believe that what I have said may explain the little progress which Cork has made in the arts and in matters of public welfare and interest. I imagine that if a man of character generally esteemed (Lord Shannon, for instance) would consent, during several years, to clean this Augean stable,* he would be actuated by a desire for the public good, instead of by self-interest, and he would not be found to retard the construction of establishments required by the mass of the inhabitants because the revenues of the city might diminish by a few shillings or pounds.

Since I have extended my remarks on this subject so much, the reader will perhaps want to know what are the ameliorations of which I speak, and what I think the public-spirited Mayor might do. I shall mention a few of the principal, and in a manner most concise. First of all, demolish the two hideous prisons which are at the end of the bridges joining this muddy island with the banks of the river and build new, outside the town, in an airy position. Clean the streets— don't permit the inhabitants to allow their pigs to roam wherever they may seek pasture, and don't let these pigs be seen after their throats have been cut. Build a grain market in a suitable position. Establish public schools and hospitals where the people may be sure that their children are instructed in the religion they wish to follow, and not in that which others wish them to follow. Build an asylum for the insane. Furnish the city with public fountains. Clear the quays of the sheds which disfigure them. Encourage, as far as possible, manufactures of all kinds, and establish a House of Industry, so as to get rid of the beggars which dishonour the streets. Have public works in which every man wanting bread may find the means to earn it, &c.

I am convinced that if these plans could be carried out during fifty years, Cork would become more important than Dublin itself, on account of the safety and fine situation of its port. The principal exportation is at present of salted meat; beasts are killed in the season by thousands, and the season over, there is nothing to do. I have known a merchant who, from what I am told, kills every year between twenty and twenty-five thousand pigs, which statement gave me occasion to say to him that he was the greatest murderer of hogs I ever knew. This digression is a little long, and may perhaps appear fastidious to some who do not take much interest in Cork, but it is more for the Irish than the foreigner that I write, and I hope that the purity of my motive will be taken as excuse. . . .

Armagh

This country is entirely occupied in the manufacture of linen, but the late troubles have made trade to languish. The mills, however, are still going, and it is hoped that a year of peace will restore order and prosperity. Military law was rigorously enforced here on the inhabitants; they were not permitted to have lights in their houses after nine o'clock, and any person found in the streets after that hour was in danger of being arrested. A fair was held during the time I stayed in this little town, and it passed over quite peacefully; the soldiers promenaded through the market-place and obliged women who wore anything green, ribbon or otherwise,* to take it off. Had one-fourth of the precaution taken here been observed in France, there would certainly have been no Revolution. I was much struck here by the thought of the different results which different characters in government may produce. It is remarkable how in France a weak government and foolish ministers have led a people entirely Royalist to slay a King they loved, and whose good qualities they respected, and to destroy a flourishing monarchy for whose prosperity they had been enthusiastic; while here, surrounded by enemies, a vigorous government in Ireland has been able to repress, and hold in the path of duty, a people discontented and seduced by the success of the French innovations.

The boldness of the United Irishmen increased each day as long as the Government did not interfere; many who had joined them had done so out of fear, and there were with them a number of weak, undecided people ready to range themselves on the winning side, and so immediately on the Government's determination to act vigorously, it was only necessary to let the soldiers appear upon the scene, and the difficulties disappeared.

The poor peasant on this occasion, as in so many others, was the dupe of rogues, who put him in the front, and were very careful themselves to stay behind the curtain. The troops went through the country, burning the houses of those who were suspected of having taken the 'Union' oath, or of having arms, and on many occasions they acted with great severity.

On the way to Armagh I passed through a superb country; there is a charming valley, and well-wooded, near Tandragee. Between this town and Armagh I met a company of Orangemen,* as they are called, wearing orange cockades, and some of them having ties of the same colour. The peasantry seemed very much afraid of them. I went into one or two cabins to rest myself, and was offered, certainly, hospitality in the ordinary way, but it did not seem to be with the same air as before, and at last, near the town, a good woman said to me, 'You seem to have come from far, my dear Sir, I hope that your umbrella or the string of it will not bring you into trouble.' I laughed at the good woman's fears, but, on reflection, I felt that since she had remarked that my umbrella was greenish, and the cord of a bright green, soldiers might make the same observation, and that in any case it would be very disagreeable to have any trouble over such a silly thing, and I cut the green cord off my umbrella.

Arriving in the town of St Patrick, I went immediately to pay my duty to his metropolitan church. The foundations of this, they say, were laid by the Saint himself on the ruins of a Druidic establishment. History relates that there was here a lively passage at arms between the Saint and the Druids in presence of the great monarch who was then King of Ulster, and the Saint, having convinced his Majesty, baptised him and all his court, and afterwards sent missionaries into the other kingdoms of Ireland. The old cathedral has been destroyed and burned several times, and has been rebuilt always on the same spot.

The city had been reduced to the miserable state of a little country town, but the last Archbishop, the Rev. —— Robertson, being a man of learning and friend of the public welfare, liberal, and without family, set himself to improve and increase it, so that at present it is really a very handsome little city. The cathedral is situated on a rocky height (as the name Ard indicates), and here, a few years ago, among some ruins was found an ancient cross of stone in one piece, with strange looking figures thereon carved, and appearing to be a representation of a man baptising converts. It has been erected in the market-place.

Primate Robertson has built at his own charges an observatory, and has furnished funds to give it an annual income of £300 sterling, which is paid to the person in charge. He has also established, at great cost, a well-furnished library, which is open to the public four hours every day. He has erected a hospital and several other edifices, and certainly merits as much gratitude from the inhabitants of the diocese as may be considered due to St Patrick himself.

The revenues of the Archbishop amount to eight or nine thousand pounds sterling per annum, but it is known that the estates belonging to the seat bring in to those who have farmed them £150,000 (3,750,000 francs). If the Archbishop had such an income, it might well excite the jealousy of the Government, as well as the discontent of the rent-farmers, who regard these estates as heritages belonging to their families, thus, prudently, the leases are renewed every year at the same price, plus a considerable *pot-de-vin*.* The demesne of the Archbishop is superb; the Palace, although very large and well built, does not seem too magnificent for the embellishments of the park surrounding. There is in it a chapel, brilliant in architecture, in which there is some very fine stained glass.

There are four Archbishops in Ireland, who all take the title of Primate. He of Armagh is called Primate of All Ireland, the Dublin Archbishop is called Primate of Ireland, that of Cashel, Primate of Munster, and that of Tuam, Primate of Connaught. This is pretty well for Primates. In England there are only two: the Archbishop of Canterbury, Primate of All England, and that of York, Primate of England. I am sorry I cannot remember how many there were in France; but perhaps the reader is pleased to be without the information.

The country in the neighbourhood of Armagh is charming, full of little hills and plains and pretty little lakes. Among the places I saw I remarked, especially, Castle Dillon and Drumilly, where I was received by Colonel Spencer, whose acquaintance I had made at Westport in the summer. Certainly there could not be a more agreeable quarter; the country is a little paradise, it is impossible to conceive anything better cultivated or more romantic. What a pity then, that the spirit of discord and fury has laid hold of the inhabitants to a point that might well make one fear to live among them. Every morning there is news of crimes committed during the night. Not a day passes without murders or the burning of houses. For the sake of a walk I accompanied one of the officers who was going to verify information by visiting a man who had been beaten. We found the man with one eye punched in, it is true, but I thought the injury might just as well have been the result of a private dispute with which politics had nothing to do. The house of one good woman had certainly been 'wrecked,' as they say, by some armed men, but that was all we were able to learn.

I think it my duty to give here a little information on the subject of the troubles, which for so long have desolated this beautiful country. The quarrel between Catholics and Protestants of this county began with a private dispute between two peasants at a fair. The one was Catholic and the other Protestant. During the fight ill-advised words passed from one side to the other, and these had the effect, as is unfortunately the custom at most fairs, of ranging the friends of the two combatants into parties who fought each other with sticks. That day the Protestants were beaten, but at another fair they took their revenge, falling, armed, on the Catholics, and a number were killed. The animosity between the parties manifested itself for a long time before the Government appeared to take any notice; in the end, however, the magistrates, although not very energetically, took certain proceedings, and put into execution a part of the law which at that time forbade Catholics to have possession of arms. It followed that, as there was no power to disarm the other side, the former were entirely at the mercy of the latter.

I have been assured that there were certain persons who thought it their duty to take the Protestant side in order not to lose their votes in the parliamentary elections. This unfortunate partisanship increased the audacity of the triumphant side, who formed a military corps, to which they gave the name of 'Orange Boys,' in memory of the Prince of Orange (King William) and of the Revolution. The other side took, correctly enough, the name of 'Defenders,' for it is true that, at first, they only thought of defence. The Orange Boys had the advantage over their adversaries, seeing that they were armed, and the others were not. Matters came to such a point that Defenders, who were obnoxious, received letters in these terms:

'Peter —— or James ——, you have —— time to sell your things and go to Connaught, or you will go to Hell.'

Some disdained to submit to these barbarous orders, and during the night their cabins would be overturned or demolished over their heads, or a dozen of shots would be sent into a bedroom. These horrors started the Defenders to commit excesses no less cruel. The atrocities were not repressed with the necessary vigour to put an end to them, in fact it seemed as if very little attention was given to them. Peaceful families of both religions, frightened at these disorders, hastened to sell their effects at loss, and retired to the province of

Connaught, where I have seen a number of them welcomed by Colonel Martin and Lord Altamont.

While, here, matters were in this distressing state, it is very singular that troubles of a totally different character appeared in the neighbouring counties. Those of Armagh really belonged to a religious war, those of the Counties of Down, Antrim, and Londonderry had, for pretext, the reform of Parliament, and the discontented affected to speak with indifference of all religions. I have known cases of men who, having practised the most barbarous cruelties on their compatriots on religious pretexts, affected, in the name of United Irishmen, to say that all religions were equal, while they appeared not to believe in any.

They assembled, appointed chiefs, announced republican opinions, and declared that they only waited the arrival of the French to join them.

It is certain that this new spirit of dissension by throwing ridicule at, and treating with contempt, the troubles of Armagh succeeded in settling these to a great extent. But the new ideas, by their immediate connection with the revolution in France, were likely to become much more dangerous than the first. It is well known to what indefensible excesses the United Irishmen proceeded. I have mentioned some of them which happened before I reached Scotland. I was convinced then, by the knowledge I had of the people of this country, that this frenzy would calm down, and that unless there were really an invasion on a large scale, there was absolutely no fear about the surety of the Government. Such was the situation of the country at the time I started for Scotland. Perhaps on my return I would have found things in the same state, if the arrival of the French Fleet in the bay of Bantry had not opened the eyes of the Government as to the dangers they ran, and convinced them of the necessity for rigorous methods in dealing with the dissatisfaction.

JOHN GAMBLE
(1770–1831)

An Irish Wake (1826)

An Irish wake has been often described, and often ridiculed; I saw nothing ridiculous in the present one: though every apartment in the house was crowded, the most perfect order and decorum prevailed; the kitchen was filled with servants and labourers, to whom tea and tobacco were liberally given; in the parlour were assembled the neighbouring farmers and shopkeepers; wine and punch were on the table; but they were taken sparingly, and several did not take them at all; these were Catholics: of late years, they are not permitted to drink at wakes: this is a regulation of their clergy,—a most laudable one, as disgusting scenes of drunkenness, doubtless, often occurred: nothing more forcibly marks the influence the Catholic clergy possess over the middle and lower classes of their own order than this circumstance; if they gave up whiskey, they would give up any thing.

Two large candles were placed on a table in the room where the corpse lay: they gave a gloomy and sepulchral kind of light, as superstition does not allow them to be snuffed: the bed was hung round with white; the body was dressed in a shroud and a cap with black riband; a plate of salt was laid on the breast, not, as has been supposed, in the expectation of its keeping the dead from corruption, but on account of its preserving the living from infection; possibly, likewise, from some fanciful analogy between corporeal and spiritual corruption.

I approached the dead body and uncovered the face: I contemplated it long: I scarcely know a more sublime object than the face of a dead man: the passions that distorted it are fled; there is no longer either joy or sorrow; all is silent as the dark mansion in which it is to be enclosed.

I have witnessed the last struggles of many dying persons: in general, I am happy to state (for in the last struggles of poor human nature we are all interested), they seemed to suffer much less than would be supposed: convulsions passed over, but seldom much distorted, the face; a smile, even, would often play upon the lips while they stood quivering on the cheeks and temples; a celestial expression would shine in their eyes, as they imitated, with their hands on the bed-clothes, the pretty movements of gathering flowers, and talked in broken and indistinct language of green fields and falling waters: who can tell but at those moments they had lofty glimpses of thought, more sublime than ever entered into the conception of a poet? who can tell but at those moments they had a bright foretaste of the happiness of Heaven in the verdant meadows, the shady bowers, and cooling streams, in which, in fancy, they were wandering?

They gradually sank down lower and lower in the bed; a slight heaving of the shoulders, and drawing up of the limbs, were almost immediately followed by their stretching themselves out to everlasting quietness. Cæsar, when he found his fate inevitable, drew his robes around him, that he might fall with dignity; in falling so, he did no more than is done by the commonest man: the attitude of death is ever a graceful one.

The company in this apartment were relations of the deceased, and mostly women; for where sorrow is, women are mostly to be found.

In England, relations generally keep away on such occasions; I suppose, because it is not accounted wise to indulge in unavailing sorrow: it *is wise* to indulge in it; for, 'by the sadness of the countenance, the heart is made better:' it is wise to contemplate, often to contemplate, what we must one day be ourselves: we may run away from our friend's funeral, we cannot run away from our own.

The conversation was carried on in an under voice, and turned on death and judgment, and ghosts and apparitions: more stories were told of these latter than I can remember: I was as forcibly struck with the look and tone of terror and affright, with which they were told and listened to, as I was with the importance they showed man is of to himself, who cannot die but that hundreds of imaginary beings are conjured up to bewail his dissolution, and give warning of it.

The Banshee (a spiritual being who foretels death by the most plaintive cries), a cousin of the deceased related, was heard wailing the live-long night of his death, and, just before it happened, vanished, clapping her hands, and crying, 'Oh, Katty Galbraith (the young man's mother)! Katty Galbraith! but you are going to get a sore heart.'

The sudden death, a short time before, of a young lady in the neighbourhood, was talked of, and lamented, as a most unexpected and unaccountable circumstance. 'Dear heart! dear heart!' said an old woman, 'I might have told of it weeks and weeks before. Didn't I see, with my own eyes, her *wraith* going up the bank of the river, behind her father's house, with a water-bottle in her hand?'

A wraith is such a shadowy representation of a living person, as a ghost is of a dead one: whenever it is seen, it is a sure sign that the person, man or woman, to whom it belongs, is shortly to die.

From death, I know not by what transition, they came to talk of marriage. In marriage, as well as in hanging, there has always been supposed a destiny, and fate was powerful in these marriages. It is an article of popular belief in Ireland, as well as in Scotland, that if certain ceremonies are performed at midnight on Allhallows eve,* the person who performs them shall see the figure of his or her future wife or husband: the beautiful poem of Halloween, by Robert Burns, contains a faithful and amusing account of these lingering superstitions of other days: to those, if there be any, who have not read it, the following will give a faint idea of them.

Two girls went out at the dark of the moon, and washed their shifts* in south running water, in the devil's name; they hung them before the fire in the room where they lay, keeping awake and silent, as the charm requires. Towards morning, two apparitions came in and turned them: the one was that of a man with a rope about his neck, the other was that of a man in a coffin. Shortly afterwards, the two girls were married to men bearing the forms in question: one of these was hanged for horse-stealing, and the other died the day after his marriage.

A comely servant maid of a neighbouring farmer went out, in a similar manner, to wash her shift in the devil's name: the apparition of her master passed; as she had left him asleep in bed, she was in a terrible fright: she came in, and told the circumstance to her mistress, who persuaded her to go out a second time, and to take with her a pair of scissors: the apparition once again slowly passed; she, unobserved, cut off a piece from the skirt of its coat, and returned with it to her mistress. 'Well!' said the good woman, 'what must be must; you will be his second wife; and be kind to my children, for I have but a short time to live.' The servant maid, however, forgot this injunction; and when married to her master, which she was about twelve months afterwards, proved a very step-mother.

At the dawn of day, the whole company, with one voice, uttered a wild and sudden shriek: this is an ancient custom, and appears to me a natural one: the first rays of new-born day break dismally on the brilliant halls of rejoicing, and give the gay figures, who glide over their figured floors, a sad and livid hue; they may well be supposed to make death more ghastly, and its apartment more sorrowful.

At eight o'clock the funeral went out: the frantic sorrow of the mother and sisters, as the coffin was removing, it would be impossible to describe; they hung round it, tore their hair, which they flung in handfuls on it, clasped it in their arms, beat on it with their hands, called on the deceased by his name, by a thousand tender, by a thousand almost reproachful names, to hear, to answer, to come forth: they called on their Saviour, who had raised Lazarus from the grave, to burst the bands of death, and bid him come forth—in his winding-sheet, in putrefaction, in corruption, to come forth: the mother flung herself across the head of the little stairs to block up the passage, and it was only by stepping over her, that the body could at length be brought down.

I felt as if the weight of a mountain were taken off my breast, when I got out of hearing (which was not for a long time) of her, and of her daughters' cries.

The priest stopped at a field near the church: the coffin was laid at his feet, and the people ranged themselves round, while he read the funeral service of the church of Rome in a solemn and impressive manner. Fondly attached to their ancient burying-places, which they regard as holy ground, the Catholics still bear their dead to them, though they are mostly now Protestant churchyards. It is almost superfluous to say, that they are not allowed to perform there the ceremonies of their religion, and that the body is laid in the clay, and that the earth falls lumbering upon it, with no solemn mass said or dirge sung. This, to the eye of reason that resides in a large town, will appear a slight evil, but to the heart of sensibility that dwells in the country it is a great one. The more, indeed, I reflect on the evils of the people of Ireland, I am the more disposed to refer a portion of them to feeling, as much as to condition, and to believe that, had they people of feeling to deal with (which statesmen rarely are), they might be got rid of.

The service was succeeded by the mournful cry of death, which continued until we reached the churchyard. To my ears—perhaps attuned to it by the lamentations they just had heard—it seemed a sadly pleasing strain, such as sorrow well might utter, and pensiveness might love to hear. Many who will not allow the Irish cry to be musical, have admitted that it is melancholy; and have thereby admitted their own want of knowledge of music. No concourse of sounds can be melancholy without being musical, nor, paradoxical as it may appear, can any, I think, be fully musical without being melancholy. Music, as well as poetry, issues from heaven, and never can reside in its perfection with noisy mirth or broad-faced laughter.

WILLIAM CARLETON
(1794–1869)

from *The Lough Derg Pilgrim* (1828)

The next morning, when I awoke, I joined with all haste the aggregate crowd that proceeded in masses towards the lake—or Purgatory*—which lies amongst the hills that extend to the north-east of Petigo.* While ascending the bleak, hideous mountain range, whose ridge commands a full view of this celebrated scene of superstition, the manner and appearance of the pilgrims were deeply interesting. Such groupings as pressed forward around me would have made fine studies either for him who wished to deplore or to ridicule the degradations and absurdities of human nature; indeed there was an intense interest in the scene. I look back at this moment with awe towards the tremulous and high-strained vibrations of my mind, as it responded to the excitement. Reader, have you ever approached the Eternal City? have you ever, from the dreary solitudes of the Campagna, seen the dome of St Peter's for the first time? and have the monuments of the greatest men and the mightiest deeds that ever the earth witnessed—have the names of the Cæsars, and the Catos, and the Scipios, excited a curiosity amounting to a sensation almost too intense to be borne? I think I can venture to measure the expansion of your mind, as it enlarged itself before the crowding visions of the past, as the dim grandeur of ages rose up and developed itself from amidst the shadows of time; and entranced amidst the magic of your own associations, you desired to stop—you were almost content to go no farther—your *own* Rome, you were in the midst of—Rome free—Rome triumphant—Rome classical. And perhaps it is well you awoke in good time from your shadowy dream, to escape from the unvaried desolation and the wasting *malaria* that brooded all around. Reader, I can fancy that such might have been your sensations when the domes and the spires of the world's capital first met your vision: and I can assure you, that while ascending the ridge that was to give me a view of Patrick's Purgatory, my sensations were as impressively, as powerfully excited. For I desire you to recollect, that the welfare of your immortal soul was not connected with your imaginings, your magnificent visions did not penetrate into the soul's doom. You were not submitted to the agency of a transcendental power. You were, in a word, a poet, but not a fanatic. What comparison, then, could there be between the exercise of your free, manly, cultivated understanding, and my feelings on this occasion, with my thick-coming visions of immortality, that almost lifted me from the mountain-path I was ascending, and brought me, as it were, into contact with the invisible world? I repeat it, then, that such were my feelings, when all the faculties which exist in the mind were aroused and concentrated upon one object. In such a case, the pilgrim stands, as it were, between life and death; and as it was superstition that placed him there, she certainly conjures up to his heated fancy those dark, fleeting, and indistinct images which are best adapted to that gloom which she has already cast over his mind. Although there could not be less than two hundred people, young and old, boys and girls, men and women, the hale and the sickly, the blind and the lame, all climbing to gain the top with as little delay as possible, yet was there scarcely a sound, certainly not a word, to be heard among them. For my part, I plainly heard the palpitations of my heart, both loud and quick. Had I been told that the veil of eternity was about to be raised before me at that moment, I could scarcely have felt more intensely. Several females were obliged to rest for some time, in order to gain both physical and moral strength—one fainted; and several old men were obliged to sit down. All were praying, every crucifix was out, every bead in requisition; and nothing broke a silence so solemn but a low, monotonous murmur of deep devotion.

As soon as we ascended the hill, the whole scene was instantly before us: a large lake, surrounded by an amphitheatre of mountains, bleak, uncomfortable, and desolate. In the lake itself, about half a

mile from the edge next us, was to be seen the 'Island,' with two or
three slated houses on it, naked and unplastered, as desolate-looking
almost as the mountains. A little range of exceeding low hovels,
which a dwarf could scarcely enter without stooping, appeared to the
left; and the eye could rest on nothing more, except a living mass of
human beings crawling slowly about. The first thing the pilgrim
does when he gets a sight of the lake, is to prostrate himself, kiss the
earth, and then on his knees *offer up* three *Paters* and *Aves*, and a
Creed* for the favour of being permitted to see this blessed place.
When this is over, he descends to the lake, and after paying tenpence
to the ferryman, is rowed over to the Purgatory.

When the whole view was presented to me, I stood for some time
to contemplate it; and I cannot better illustrate the reaction which
took place in my mind, than by saying that it resembles that awkward
inversion which a man's proper body experiences when, on going to
pull something from which he expects a marvellous resistance, it
comes with him at a touch, and the natural consequence is, that he
finds his head down and his heels up. That which dashed the whole
scene from the dark elevation in which the romance of devotion had
placed it was the appearance of slated houses, and of the smoke that
curled from the hovels and the prior's residence. This at once
brought me back to humanity; and the idea of roasting meat, boiling
pots, and dressing dinners, dispossessed every fine and fearful image
which had floated through my imagination for the last twelve hours.
In fact, allowing for the difference of situation, it nearly resembled
John's Well, or James's Fair, when beheld at a distance, turning the
slated houses into inns, and the hovels into tents. A certain idea,
slight, untraceable, and involuntary, went over my brain on that
occasion, which, though it did not *then* cost me a single effort of
reflection, I think was revived and developed at a future period of my
life, and became, perhaps to a certain extent, the means of opening a
wider range of thought to my mind, and of giving a new tone to my
existence. Still, however, nothing except my idea of its external
appearance disappointed me; I accordingly descended with the rest,
and in a short time found myself among the living mass upon the
island.

The first thing I did was to hand over my three cakes of oaten
bread which I had got made in Petigo, tied up in a handkerchief, as
well as my hat and second shirt, to the care of the owner of one of the

huts: having first, by the way, undergone a second prostration on touching the island, and greeted it with fifteen holy kisses, and another string of prayers. I then, according to the regulations, should commence the *stations*,* lacerated as my feet were after so long a journey; so that I had not a moment to rest. Think, therefore, what I must have suffered, on surrounding a large chapel, in the direction of from east to west, over a pavement of stone spikes, every one of them making its way along my nerves and muscles to my unfortunate brain. I was absolutely stupid and dizzy with the pain, the praying, the jostling, the elbowing, the scrambling and the uncomfortable penitential murmurs of the whole crowd. I knew not what I was about, but went through the forms in the same mechanical spirit which pervaded all present. As for that solemn, humble, and heart-felt sense of God's presence, which Christian prayer demands, its existence in the mind would not only be a moral but a physical impossibility in Lough Derg. I verily think that if mortification of the body, without conversion of the life or heart—if penance and not repentance *could* save the soul, no wretch who performed a pilgrim-age here could with a good grace be damned. Out of hell the place is matchless, and if there *be* a purgatory in the other world, it may very well be said there is a fair rehearsal of it in the county of Donegal in Ireland!

When I commenced my station, I started from what is called the 'Beds,' and God help St Patrick if he lay upon them: they are sharp stones placed circularly in the earth, with the spike ends of them up, one circle within another; and the manner in which the pilgrim gets as far as the innermost, resembles precisely that in which school-boys enter the 'Walls of Troy' upon their slates. I moved away from these upon the sharp stones with which the whole island is surfaced, keeping the chapel, or 'Prison,' as it is called, upon my right; then turning, I came round again, with a *circumbendibus*,* to the spot from which I set out. During this circuit, as well as I can remember, I *repeated* fifty-five *paters* and *aves*, and five creeds, or five decades; and be it known, that the fifty prayers were *offered up* to the Virgin Mary, and the odd five to God! I then commenced getting round the external beds, during which I *repeated*, I think, fifteen *paters* and *aves* more; and as the beds decreased in circumference, the prayers decreased in length, until a short circuit and three *paters* and *aves* finished the last and innermost of these blessed couches. I really forget how many times each day the prison and these beds are to be surrounded, and how many hundred prayers are to be *repeated* during the circuit, though each circuit is in fact making the grand tour of the island; but I never shall forget that I was the best part of a July day at it, when the soles of my feet were flayed, and the stones hot enough to broil a beef-steak! When the first day's station was over, is it necessary to say that a little rest would have been agreeable? But no, this would not suit the policy of the place: here it may be truly said that there is no rest for the wicked. The only luxury allowed me was the privilege of feasting upon one of my cakes (having not tasted food that blessed day until then); upon one of my cakes, I say, and a copious supply of the water of the lake, which, to render the repast more agreeable, was made lukewarm! This was to keep my spirits up after the delicate day's labour I had gone through, and to cheer me against the pleasant prospect of a hard night's praying without sleep, which lay in the back ground! But when I saw every one at this refreshing meal with a good, thick, substantial *bannock,** and then looked at the immateriality of my own, I could not help reverting to the woman who made them for me, with a degree of vivacity not altogether in unison with the charity of a Christian. The knavish creature defrauded me of one half of the oatmeal, although I had purchased it myself in Petigo for the occasion; being determined that as I was only to get two meals in the three days, they should be such as a person could fast upon. Never was there a man more bitterly disappointed; for they were not thicker than crown-pieces, and I searched for them in my mouth to no purpose—the only thing like substance I could feel there was the warm water. At last, night came; but here to describe the horrors of what I suffered I hold myself utterly inadequate. I was wedged in a shake-down bed with seven others, one of whom was a Scotch Papist—another a man with a shrunk leg, who wore a crutch—all afflicted with that disease which northern men that feed on oatmeal are liable to; and then the swarms that fell upon my poor young skin, and probed, and stung, and fed on me! it was pressure and persecution almost insupportable, and yet such was my fatigue that sleep even here began to weigh down my eyelids.

I was just on the point of enjoying a little rest, when a man ringing a large hand-bell, came round, crying out in a low, supernatural growl, which could be heard double the distance of the loudest shout—'Waken up, waken up, and come to prison!' The words were no sooner out of his mouth, than there was a sudden start, and a general scramble in the dark for our respective garments. When we got dressed, we proceeded to the waters of the lake, in which we washed our face and hands, repeating prayers during the ablution. This to me was the most impressive and agreeable part of the whole station. The night while we were in bed, or rather in torture, had become quite stormy, and the waves of the lake beat against the shore with the violence of an agitated sea. There was just sufficient moon to make the 'darkness visible,' and to show the black clouds drifting with rapid confusion, in broken masses, over our heads. This, joined to the tossing of the billows against the shore—the dark silent groups that came, like shadows, stooping for a moment over the surface of the waters, and retreating again in a manner which the severity of the night rendered necessarily quick, raising thereby in the mind the idea of gliding spirits—then the pre-conceived desolation of the surrounding scenery—the indistinct shadowy chain of dreary mountains which, faintly relieved by the lurid sky, hemmed in the lake—the silence of the forms, contrasted with the tumult of the elements about us—the loneliness of the place—its isolation and remoteness from the habitations of men—all this put together, joined to the feeling of deep devotion in which I was wrapped, had really a sublime effect upon me. Upon the generality of those who were there, blind to the natural beauty and effect of the hour and the place, and viewing it only through the medium of superstitious awe, it was indeed calculated to produce the notion of something not belonging to the circumstances and reality of human life.

From this scene we passed to one, which, though not character-ised by its dark awful beauty, was scarcely inferior to it in effect. It was called the 'Prison,' and it is necessary to observe here, that every pilgrim must pass twenty-four hours in this place, kneeling, without food or sleep, although one meal of bread and warm water, and whatever sleep he could get in Petigo with seven in a bed, were his allowance of food and sleep during the twenty-four hours previous. I must here beg the good reader's attention for a moment, with refer-ence to our penance in the 'Prison.' Let us consider now the nature of this pilgrimage: it must be performed on foot, no matter what the distance of residence (allowing for voyages)—the condition of life—the age or the sex of the pilgrim may be. Individuals, from France, from America, England, and Scotland visit it—as voluntary devotees, or to perform an act of penance for some great crime, or perhaps to atone for a bad life in general. It is performed, too, in the dead heat of summer, when labour is slack, and the lower orders have sufficient leisure to undertake it; and, I may add, when travelling on foot is most fatiguing: they arrive, therefore, without a single exception, blown and jaded almost to death. The first thing they do, notwithstanding this, is to commence the fresh rigours of the station, which occupies them several hours. This consists in what I have already described, viz. the pleasant promenade upon the stony spikes around the prison and the 'beds;' that over, they take their first and only meal for the day; after which, as in my own case just related, they must huddle themselves in clusters, on what is barefacedly called a bed, but which is nothing more nor less than a beggarman's shake-down, where the smell, the heat, the filth, and above all, the vermin, are intolerable to the very farthest stretch of the superlative degree. As soon as their eyes begin to close here, they are roused by the bellman, and summoned at the hour of twelve—first washing themselves as aforesaid, in the lake, and then adjourning to the prison, which I am about to describe. There is not on earth, with the exception of pagan rites,—and it is melancholy to be compelled to compare any institution of the Christian religion with a Juggernaut,*—there is not on earth, I say, a regulation of a religious nature, more barbarous and inhuman than this. It has destroyed thousands since its establishment—has left children without parents, and parents childless. It has made wives widows, and torn from the disconsolate husband the mother of his children; and is itself the monster which St Patrick is said to have destroyed in the place—a monster, which is a complete and significant allegory of this great and destructive superstition. But what is even worse than death, by stretching the powers of human sufferance until the mind cracks under them, it is said sometimes to return these pitiable creatures maniacs—exulting in the laugh of madness, or sunk for ever in the incurable apathy of religious melancholy. I mention this now, to exhibit the purpose for which these calamities are turned to account, and the dishonesty which is exercised over these poor, unsuspecting people, in consequence of their occurrence. The pilgrims, being thus aroused at midnight, are sent to prison; and what think you is the impression under which they enter it? one indeed, which, when we consider their bodily weakness and mental excitement, must do its work with success. It is this: that as soon as they enter the prison, a *supernatural* tendency to sleep will come over them, which, they say, is peculiar to the place; that this is an emblem of the influence of sin over the soul, and a type of their future fate; that if they resist this they will be saved; but that if they yield to it, they will not only be damned in the next world, but will go mad, or incur some immediate and dreadful calamity in this. Is it any wonder that a weak mind and exhausted body, wrought upon by these bugbears, should induce upon by itself, by its own terrors, the malady of derangement? We know that nothing acts so strongly and so fatally upon reason, as an imagination diseased by religious terrors: and I regret to say, that I had upon that night an opportunity of witnessing a fatal instance of it.

After having washed ourselves in the dark waters of the lake, we entered this famous 'prison,' which is only a naked, unplastered chapel, with an altar against one of the side-walls, and two galleries. On entering this place, a scene presented itself altogether unparalleled on the earth, and in every point of view capable to sustain the feelings raised in the mind by the midnight scenery of the lake as seen during the ablutions. The prison was full, but not crowded; for had it been crowded, we would have been happy. It was, however, just sufficiently filled to give every individual the pleasure of sustaining himself, without having it in his power to recline for a moment in an attitude of rest, or to change that most insupportable of all bodily suffering, uniformity of position. There we knelt upon a hard ground floor, and commenced praying; and again I must advert to the policy which prevails in this island. During the period of imprisonment, there are no prescribed prayers nor ceremonies whatever to be performed, and this is the more strange, as every other stage of the station has its proper devotions. But these are suspended here, lest the attention of the prisoners might be fixed on any particular object, and the supernatural character of drowsiness imputed to the place be thus doubted—they are, therefore, turned in without anything to excite them to attention, or to resist the propensity to sleep occasioned by their fatigue and want of rest. Having thus nothing to do, nothing to sustain, nothing to stimulate them, it is very natural that they should, even if unexhausted by previous lassitude, be inclined to sleep; but everything that can weigh them down is laid upon them in this heavy and oppressive superstition, that the strong delusion may be kept up.

On entering the prison, I was struck with the dim religious twilight of the place. Two candles gleamed faintly from the altar, and there was something I thought of a deadly light about them, as they burned feebly and stilly against the darkness which hung over the other part of the building. Two priests, facing the congregation, stood upon the altar in silence, with pale spectral visages, their eyes catching an unearthly glare from the sepulchral light of the slender tapers. But that which was strangest of all, and, as I said before, without parallel in this world, was the impression and effect produced by the deep, drowsy, hollow, hoarse, guttural, ceaseless, and monotonous *hum*, which proceeded from about four hundred individuals, half asleep and at prayer; for their cadences were blended and slurred into each other, as they repeated, in an awe-struck and earnest undertone, the prayers in which they were engaged. It was certainly the strangest sound I ever heard, and resembled a thousand subterraneous groans, uttered in a kind of low, deep, unvaried chant. Nothing could produce a sense of gloomy alarm in a weak superstitious mind equal to this; and it derived much of its wild and singular character, as well as of its lethargic influence, from its continuity; for it still—still rung lowly and supernaturally on my ear. Perhaps the deep, wavy prolongation of the bass of a large cathedral bell, or that low, continuous sound, which is distinct from its higher and louder intonations, would give a faint notion of it, yet only a faint one; for the body of hoarse monotony here was immense. Indeed, such a noise had something so powerfully lulling, that human nature, even excited by the terrible suggestions of superstitious fear, was scarcely able to withstand it.

Now the poor pilgrims forget, that this strong disposition to sleep arises from the weariness produced by their long journeys—by the exhausting penance of the station, performed without giving them time to rest—by the other still more natural consequence of not giving them time to sleep—by the drowsy darkness of the chapel—and by the heaviness caught from the low peculiar murmur of the pilgrims, which would of itself overcome the lightest spirit. I was here but a very short time when I began to doze, and just as my chin was sinking placidly on my breast, and the words of an *Ave Maria* dying upon my lips, I felt the charm all at once broken by a well-meant rap upon the occiput, conferred through the instrumentality of a little angry-looking squat urchin of sixty years, and a remarkably good black-thorn cudgel, with which he was engaged in thwacking the heads of such sinners as, not having the dread of insanity and the regulations of the place before their eyes, were inclined to sleep. I declare the knock I received told to such purpose on my head, that nothing occurred during the pilgrimage that vexed me so much.

After all, I really slept the better half of the night; yet so indescribably powerful was the apprehension of derangement, that my hypocritical tongue wagged aloud at the prayers, during these furtive naps. Nay, I not only slept but dreamed. I experienced also that singular state of being, in which, while the senses are accessible to the influence of surrounding objects, the process of thought is suspended, the man seems to enjoy an inverted existence, in which the soul sleeps, and the body remains awake and susceptible of external impressions. I once thought I was washing myself in the lake, and that the dashing noise of its waters rang in my ears: I also fancied myself at home in conversation with my friends; yet, in neither case, did I altogether forget where I was. Still in struggling to bring my mind back, so paramount was the dread of awaking deranged should I fall asleep, that these occasional visions—associating themselves with this terror—and this again broken in upon by the hoarse murmurs about me, throwing their dark shade on every object that passed my imagination, the force of reason being too vague at the moment; these occasional visions, I say, and this jumbling together of broken images and disjointed thoughts, had such an effect upon me, that I imagined several times that the awful penalty was exacted, and that my reason was gone for ever. I frequently started, and on seeing two dim lights upon the altar, and on hearing the ceaseless and eternal murmurs going on—going on—around me, without being immediately able to ascribe them to their proper cause, I set myself down as a lost man; for on that terror I was provokingly clear during the whole night. I more than once gave an involuntary groan or shriek, on finding myself in this singular state; so did many others, and these groans and shrieks were wildly and fearfully contrasted with the never-ending hum, which, like the ceaseless noise of a distant waterfall, went on during the night. The perspiration occasioned by this inconceivable distress, by the heat of the place, and by the unchangeableness of my position, flowed profusely from every pore. About two o'clock in the morning an unhappy young man, either in a state of lethargic indifference, or under the influence of these sudden paroxysms, threw himself, or fell from one of the galleries, and was so shattered by the fall, that he died next day at twelve o'clock,—and, what was not much to the credit of the clergyman on the island,—without the benefit of the clergy; for I saw a priest with his stole and box of chrism* finishing off his extreme unction* when he was quite dead. This is frequently done in the Church of Rome, under a hope that life may not be utterly extinct, and that consequently the final separation of the soul and body may not have taken place.

In this prison, during the night, several persons go about with rods and staves, rapping those on the head whom they see heavy; snuff-boxes also go round very freely, elbows are jogged, chins chucked, and ears twitched, for the purpose of keeping each other awake. The rods and staves are frequently changed from hand to hand, and I thought it would be a lucky job if I could get one for a little, to enable me to change my position. I accordingly asked a man who had been a long time banging in this manner, if he would allow me to take his place for some time, and he was civil enough to do so. I therefore set out on my travels through the prison, rapping about me at a great rate, and with remarkable effect; for, whatever was the cause of it, I perceived that not a soul seemed the least inclined to doze after a visit from me; on the contrary, I observed several to scratch their heads, giving me at the same time significant looks of very sincere thankfulness.

But what I am convinced was the most meritorious act of my whole pilgrimage, as it was certainly the most zealously performed, was a remembrance I gave the squat fellow, who visited me in the early part of the night. He was engaged, tooth and nail, with another man, at a *De profundis*,* and although not asleep at the time, yet on the principle that prevention is better than cure, I thought it more prudent to let him have his rap before the occasion for it might come on: he accordingly got full payment, at compound interest, for the villanous knock he had *lent* me before.

This employment stirred my blood a little, and I got much lighter. I could now pay some attention to the scene about me, and the first object that engaged it was a fellow with a hare-lip, who had completely taken the lead at prayer. The organs of speech seemed to have been transferred from his mouth to his nose, and, although Irish was his vernacular language, either some fool or knave had taught him to *say his prayers* in English: and you may take this as an observation founded on fact, that the language which a Roman Catholic of the lower class does *not* understand, is the one in which he is disposed to pray. As for him he had lots of English prayers, though he was totally ignorant of that language. The twang from the nose, the loud and rapid tone in which he spoke, and the *malapro-prian** happiness with which he travestied every prayer he uttered, would have compelled any man to smile. The priests laughed out-right before the whole congregation, particularly one of them, whom I well knew; the other turned his face towards the altar, and leaning over a silver pix, in which, according to their own tenets, the Redeemer of the world must have been at that moment, as it con-tained the consecrated wafers, gave full vent to his risibility. Now it is remarkable that no one present attached the slightest impropriety to this—I for one did not; although it certainly occurred to me with full force at a subsequent period.

When morning came, the blessed light of the sun broke the leaden charm of the prison, and infused into us a wonderful portion of fresh vigour. This day being the second from our arrival, we had our second station to perform, and consequently all the sharp spikes to re-traverse. We were not permitted at all to taste food during these twenty-four hours, so that our weakness was really very great. I beg leave, however, to return my special acknowledgements for the truly hospitable allowance of *wine* with which I, in common with every other pilgrim, was treated. This wine is made by filling a large pot with the lake water, and making it lukewarm. It is then handed round in jugs and wooden noggins—to their credit be it recorded—in the greatest possible abundance. On this alone I breakfasted, dined, and supped, during the second or prison day of my pilgrimage

At twelve o'clock that night we left prison, and made room for another squadron, who gave us their kennels. Such a luxury was sleep to me, however, that I felt not the slightest inconvenience from the vermin, though I certainly made a point to avoid the Scotchman and the cripple. On the following day, I confessed; and never was an unfortunate soul so grievously afflicted with a bad memory as I was on that occasion—the whole thing altogether, but particularly the prison scene, had knocked me up, I could not therefore remember a tithe of my sins; and the priest, poor man, had really so much to do, and was in such a hurry, that he had me clean absolved before I had got half through the preface, or knew what I was about. I then went with a fresh batch to receive the sacrament, which I did from the hands of the good-humoured gentleman who enjoyed so richly the praying talents of the hare-lipped devotee in the prison.

I cannot avoid mentioning here a practice peculiar to Roman Catholics, which consists in an exchange of one or more prayers, by a stipulation between two persons: *I offer up a pater* and *ave* for you, and you again for me. It is called *swapping* or exchanging *prayers*. After I had received the sacrament, I observed a thin, sallow little man, with a pair of beads, as long as himself, moving from knot to knot, but never remaining long in the same place. At last he glided up to me, and in a whisper asked me if I knew him. I answered in the negative. 'Oh, then, a lanna,* ye war never here before?' 'Never.' 'Oh, I see that, a cushla,* you would a-known me if you had: well then, did ye never hear of Sol Donnel, the pilgrim?'

'I never did,' I replied, 'but are we not all pilgrims while here?'

'To be sure, aroon,* but I'm a pilgrim every place else, you see, as well as here, my darlin' sweet young man.'

'Then you're a pilgrim by profession?' 'That's it, astore machree;* everybody that comes here the second time, sure, knows Sol Donnel, the blessed pilgrim.'

THOMAS DAVIS
(1814–1845)

from *Ballad Poetry of Ireland* (1845)

How slow we have all been in coming to understand the meaning of Irish Nationality!

Some, dazzled by visions of pagan splendour, and the pretensions of pedigree, and won by the passions and romance of the olden races, continued to speak in the nineteenth century of an Irish nation as they might have done in the tenth. They forgot the English Pale, the Ulster Settlement,* and the filtered colonization of men and ideas. A Celtic kingdom with the old names and the old language, without the old quarrels, was their hope; and, though they would not repeat O'Neill's comment, as he passed Barrett's castle on his march to Kinsale,* and heard it belonged to a Strongbownian,* that 'he hated the Norman churl as if he came yesterday;' yet they quietly assumed that the Norman and Saxon elements would disappear under the Gaelic genius like the tracks of cavalry under a fresh crop.

The Nationality of Swift and Grattan* was equally partial. They saw that the Government and laws of the settlers had extended to the island—that Donegal and Kerry were in the Pale; they heard the English tongue in Dublin, and London opinions in Dublin—they mistook Ireland for a colony wronged, and great enough to be a nation.

A lower form of nationhood was before the minds of those who saw in it nothing but a parliament in College Green. They had not erred in judging, for they had not tried to estimate the moral elements and tendencies of the country. They were as narrow bigots to the omnipotency of an institution as any Cockney Radical. Could they, by any accummulation of English stupidity and Irish laziness, have got possession of an Irish government, they would soon have distressed every one by their laws whom they had not provoked by their administration, or disgusted by their dulness.

Far healthier with all its defects, was the idea of those who saw in Scotland a perfect model—who longed for a literary and artistic nationality—who prized the oratory of Grattan and Curran, the novels of Griffin and Carleton, the pictures of Maclise and Burton,* the ancient music, as much as any, and far more than most, of the political nationalists, but who regarded political independence as a dangerous dream. Unknowingly they fostered it. Their writings, their patronage, their talk was of Ireland; yet it hardly occurred to them that the ideal would flow into the practical, or that they, with their dread of agitation, were forwarding a revolution.

At last we are beginning to see what we are, and what is our destiny. Our duty arises where our knowledge begins. The elements of Irish nationality are not only combining—in fact, they are growing confluent in our minds. Such nationality as merits a good man's help, and wakens a true man's ambition—such nationality as could stand against internal faction and foreign intrigue, such nationality, as would make the Irish hearth happy and the Irish name illustrious, is becoming understood. It must contain and represent the races of

Ireland. It must not be Celtic, it must not be Saxon—it must be Irish. The Brehon law, and the maxims of Westminster, the cloudy and lightning genius of the Gael, the placid strength of the Sasanach, the marshalling insight of the Norman—a literature which shall exhibit in combination the passions and idioms of all, and which shall equally express our mind in its romantic, its religious, its forensic, and its practical tendencies—finally, a native government, which shall know and rule by the might and right of all; yet yield to the arrogance of none—these are components of *such* a nationality.

But what have these things to do with the 'Ballad Poetry of Ireland?' Much every way. It is the result of the elements we have named—it is compounded of all; and never was there a book fitter to advance that perfect nationality to which Ireland begins to aspire. That a country is without national poetry proves its hopeless dulness or its utter provincialism. National poetry is the very flowering of the soul—the greatest evidence of its health, the greatest excellence of its beauty. Its melody is balsam to the senses. It is the playfellow of childhood, ripens into the companion of his manhood, consoles his age. It presents the most dramatic events, the largest characters, the most impressive scenes, and the deepest passions in the language most familiar to us. It shows us magnified, and ennobles our hearts, our intellects, our country and our countrymen—binds us to the land by its condensed and gem-like history, to the future by examples and by aspirations. It solaces us in travel, fires us in action, prompts our invention, sheds a grace beyond the power of luxury round our homes, is the recognised envoy of our minds among all mankind and to all time.

In possessing the powers and elements of a glorious nationality, we owned the sources of a national poetry. In the combination and joint development of the latter, we find a pledge and a help to that of the former.

from *The History of Ireland* (1845)

Something has been done to rescue Ireland from the reproach that she was a wailing and ignorant slave.

Brag as we like, the reproach was not undeserved, nor is it quite removed.

She is still a serf-nation, but she is struggling wisely and patiently, and is ready to struggle with all the energy her advisers think politic, for liberty. She has ceased to wail—she is beginning to make up a record of English crime and Irish suffering, in order to explain the past, to justify the present, and caution the future. She begins to study the past—not to acquire a beggar's eloquence in petition, but a hero's wrath in strife. She no longer tears and parades her wounds, to win her smiter's mercy; and now she should look upon her breast and say—'That wound makes me distrust, and this makes me guard, and they all will make me steadier to resist, or, if all else fails, fiercer to avenge.'

Thus will Ireland do naturally and honourably. Our spirit has increased—our liberty is not far off.

But to make our spirit lasting and wise as it is bold—to make our liberty an inheritance for our children, and a charter for our posterity, we must study as well as strive, and learn as well as feel.

If we attempt to govern ourselves without statesmanship—to be a nation without a knowledge of the country's history, and of the propensities to good and ill of the people—or to fight without generalship, we will fail in policy, society, and war. These—all these things—we, people of Ireland, must know if we would be a free, strong nation. A mockery of Irish independence is not what we want. The bauble of a powerless parliament does not lure us. We are not children. The office of supplying England with recruits, artizans, and corn, under the benign interpositions of an Irish Grand Jury, *shall* not be our destiny. By our deep conviction—by the power of mind over the people, we say, No!

We are true to our colour, 'the green,' and true to our watchword, 'Ireland for the Irish.' We want to win Ireland and keep it. If we win it, we will not lose it, nor give it away to a bribing, a bullying, or a flattering minister. But, to be able to keep it, and use it, and govern it, the men of Ireland must know what it is, what it was, and what it can be made. They must study her history, perfectly know her present state, physical and moral—and train themselves up by science, poetry, music, industry, skill, and by all the studies and accomplishments of peace and war.

If Ireland were in national health, her history would be familiar by books, pictures, statuary, and music to every cabin and shop in the land—her resources as an agricultural, manufacturing, and trading people, would be equally known—and every young man would be trained, and every grown man able, to defend her coast, her plains, her towns, and her hills—not with his right arm merely, but by his disciplined habits and military accomplishments. These are the pillars of independence.

Academies of art, institutes of science, colleges of literature, schools and camps of war, are a nation's means for teaching itself strength, and winning safety and honour; and when we are a nation, please God, we shall have them all. Till then, we must work for ourselves. So far as we can study music in societies, art in schools, literature in institutes, science in our colleges, or soldiership in theory, we are bound as good citizens to learn. Where these are denied by power, or unattainable by clubbing the resources of neighbours, we must try and study for ourselves. We must visit museums and antiquities, and study, and buy, and assist books of history, to know what the country and people were, how they fell, how they suffered, and how they rose again. We must read books of statistics—and let us pause to regret that there is no work on the statistics of Ireland, except the scarce lithograph of Moreau,* the papers in the second Report of the Railway Commission, and the chapters, in McCulloch's '*Statistics of the British Empire*'—the Repeal Association ought to have a handbook first, and then an elaborate and vast account of Ireland's statistics brought out.

To resume, we must read such statistics as we have, and try and get better; and we must get the best maps of the country—the Ordnance and County Index Maps, price 2*s*. 6*d*. each, and the Railway Map, price £1—into our Mechanics' Institutes, Temperance Reading-rooms, and schools. We must, in making our journeys of business and pleasure, observe and ask for the nature and amount of the agriculture, commerce, and manufactures of the place we are in, and its shape, population, scenery, antiquities, arts, music, dress, and capabilities for improvement. A large portion of our people travel a greal deal within Ireland, and often return with no knowledge, save of the inn they slept in, and the traders they dealt with.

We must give our children in schools the best knowledge of science, art, and literary elements possible. And at home they should see and hear as much of national pictures, music, poetry, and military science as possible.

And finally, we must keep our own souls, and try, by teaching and example, to lift up the souls of all our family and neighbours to that pitch of industry, courage, information, and wisdom necessary to enable an enslaved, dark, and starving people to become free, and rich, and rational.

We sat down intending to write a paragraph on 'The National History of Ireland,' and were moved by the glorious prospect which a late survey of the literary projects in hand affords, to write generally upon Irishmen's duties, as students of the past and present.

3. FICTION

MARIA EDGEWORTH
(1767–1849)

from *Castle Rackrent* (1800)

Monday morning.[G]

Having, out of friendship for the family, upon whose estate, praised
be Heaven! I and mine have lived rent-free, time out of mind, volun-
tarily undertaken to publish the MEMOIRS of the RACKRENT
FAMILY, I think it my duty to say a few words, in the first place,
concerning myself. My real name is Thady Quirk, though in the
family I have always been known by no other than '*honest Thady*',—
afterwards, in the time of Sir Murtagh, deceased, I remember to hear
them calling me '*old Thady*', and now I'm come to 'poor Thady'; for
I wear a long great coat[1] winter and summer, which is very handy, as I

---

[1] The cloak, or mantle, as described by Thady, is of high antiquity. Spencer,* in his
'View of the State of Ireland', proves that it is not, as some have imagined, peculiarly
derived from the Scythians, but that 'most nations of the world anciently used the
mantle; for the Jews used it, as you may read of Elias's mantle, &c.; the Chaldees also
used it, as you may read in Diodorus; the Egyptians likewise used it, as you may read in
Herodotus, and may be gathered by the description of Berenice, in the Greek Commentary upon Callimachus; the Greeks also used it anciently, as appeared by Venus's mantle
lined with stars, though afterwards they changed the form thereof into their cloaks,
called Pallai, as some of the Irish also use: and the ancient Latins and Romans used it, as
you may read in Virgil, who was a very great antiquary, that Evander, when Æneas came
to him at his feast, did entertain and feast him sitting on the ground, and lying on
mantles: insomuch that he useth the very word mantile for a mantle,

'—Humi mantilia sternunt':

so that it seemeth that the mantle was a general habit to most nations, and not proper to
the Scythians only.'
  Spencer knew the convenience of the said mantle, as housing, bedding, and clothing.
  '*Iren.* Because the commodity doth not countervail the discommodity; for the
inconveniences which thereby do arise are much more many; for it is a fit house for an
outlaw, a meet bed for a rebel, and an apt cloak for a thief. First, the outlaw being for his
many crimes and villanies, banished from the towns and houses of honest men, and
wandering in wastes places, far from danger of law, maketh his mantle his house, and

never put my arms into the sleeves; they are as good as new, though come Holantide* next I've had it these seven years; it holds on by a single button round my neck, cloak fashion. To look at me, you would hardly think 'poor Thady' was the father of attorney Quirk; he is a high gentleman, and never minds what poor Thady says, and having better than fifteen hundred a year, landed estate, looks down upon honest Thady; but I wash my hands of his doings, and as I have lived so will I die, true and loyal to the family. The family of the Rackrents is, I am proud to say, one of the most ancient in the kingdom. Every body knows this is not the old family name, which was O'Shaughlin, related to the kings of Ireland—but that was before my time. My grandfather was driver to the great Sir Patrick O'Shaughlin, and I heard him, when I was a boy, telling how the Castle Rackrent estate came to Sir Patrick; Sir Tallyhoo Rackrent was cousin-german* to him, and had a fine estate of his own, only never a gate upon it, it being his maxim that a car* was the best gate. Poor gentleman! he lost a fine hunter and his life, at last, by it, all in one day's hunt. But I ought to bless that day, for the estate came straight into *the* family, upon one condition, which Sir Patrick O'Shaughlin at the time took sadly to heart, they say, but thought better of it afterwards, seeing how large a stake depended upon it, that he should by act of parliament, take and bear the surname and arms of Rackrent.

Now it was that the world was to see what was *in* Sir Patrick. On coming into the estate, he gave the finest entertainment ever was heard of in the country: not a man could stand after supper but Sir Patrick himself, who could sit out the best man in Ireland, let alone the three kingdoms itself.[G]* He had his house, from one year's end to another, as full of company as ever it could hold, and fuller; for rather than be left out of the parties at Castle Rackrent, many gentlemen, and those men of the first consequence and landed estates in the country, such as the O'Neils of Ballynagrotty, and the Money-gawls of Mount Juliet's Town, and O'Shannons of New

under it covereth himself from the wrath of Heaven, from the offence of the earth, and from the sight of men. When it raineth, it is his pent-house; when it bloweth, it is his tent; when it freezeth it is his tabernacle. In summer he can wear it loose; in winter he can wrap it close; at all times he can use it; never heavy, never cumbersome. Likewise for a rebel it is as serviceable; for in this war that he maketh (if at least it deserves the name of war), when he still flieth from his foe, and lurketh in the *thick woods* (*this should be black bogs*) and straight passages waiting for advantages, it is his bed, yea, and almost his household stuff.'

Town Tullyhog, made it their choice, often and often, when there
was no room to be had for love nor money, in long winter nights, to
sleep in the chicken-house, which Sir Patrick had fitted up for the
purpose of accommodating his friends and the public in general,
who honoured him with their company unexpectedly at Castle
Rackrent; and this went on, I can't tell you how long—the whole
country rang with his praises!—Long life to him! I'm sure I love to
look upon his picture, now opposite to me; though I never saw him,
he must have been a portly gentleman—his neck something short,
and remarkable for the largest pimple on his nose, which, by his
particular desire, is still extant in his picture, said to be a striking
likeness, though taken when young. He is said also to be the inventor
of raspberry whiskey, which is very likely, as nobody has ever
appeared to dispute it with him, and as there still exists a broken
punch-bowl at Castle Rackrent, in the garret, with an inscription to
that effect—a great curiosity. A few days before his death he was
very merry; it being his honour's birth-day, he called my grandfather
in, God bless him! to drink the company's health, and filled a
bumper himself, but could not carry it to his head, on account of the
great shake in his hand; on this he cast his joke, saying 'What would
my poor father say to me if he was to pop out of the grave, and see
me now? I remember when I was a little boy, the first bumper of
claret he gave me after dinner, how he praised me for carrying it so
steady to my mouth. Here's my thanks to him—a bumper toast.'
Then he fell to singing the favourite song he learned from his
father—for the last time, poor gentleman—he sung it that night as
loud and as hearty as ever with a chorus:

'He that goes to bed, and goes to bed sober,
Falls as the leaves do, falls as the leaves do, and dies in October;
But he that goes to bed, and goes to bed mellow,
Lives as he ought to do, lives as he ought to do, and dies an
    honest fellow.'*

Sir Patrick died that night: just as the company rose to drink his
health with three cheers, he fell down in a sort of fit, and was carried
off; they sat it out, and were surprised, on inquiry, in the morning, to
find that it was all over with poor Sir Patrick. Never did any gentleman live and die more beloved in the country by rich and poor. His
funeral was such a one as was never known before or since in the

county! All the gentlemen in the three counties were at it; far and near, how they flocked: my great grandfather said, that to see all the women even in their red cloaks, you would have taken them for the army drawn out. Then such a fine whillaluh![G] you might have heard it to the farthest end of the county, and happy the man who could get but a sight of the hearse! But who'd have thought it? just as all was going on right, through his own town they were passing, when the body was seized for debt—a rescue was apprehended from the mob; but the heir who attended the funeral was against that, for fear of consequences, seeing that those villains who came to serve acted under the disguise of the law: so, to be sure, the law must take its course, and little gain had the creditors for their pains. First and foremost, they had the curses of the country: and Sir Murtagh Rackrent, the new heir, in the next place, on account of this affront to the body, refused to pay a shilling of the debts, in which he was countenanced by all the best gentlemen of property, and others of his acquaintance; Sir Murtagh alleging in all companies, that he all along meant to pay his father's debts of honour, but the moment the law was taken of him, there was an end of honour to be sure. It was whispered (but none but the enemies of the family believe it), that this was all a sham seizure to get quit of the debts, which he had bound himself to pay in honour.

It's a long time ago, there's no saying how it was, but this for certain, the new man did not take at all after the old gentleman; the cellars were never filled after his death, and no open house, or any thing as it used to be; the tenants even were sent away without their whiskey.[G] I was ashamed myself, and knew not what to say for the honour of the family; but I made the best of a bad case, and laid it all at my lady's door, for I did not like her any how, nor any body else; she was of the family of the Skinflints, and a widow; it was a strange match for Sir Murtagh; the people in the country thought he demeaned himself greatly,[G] but I said nothing: I knew how it was; Sir Murtagh was a great lawyer, and looked to the great Skinflint estate; there, however, he overshot himself; for though one of the co-heiresses, he was never the better for her, for she outlived him many's the long day—he could not see that to be sure when he married her. I must say for her, she made him the best of wives, being a very notable stirring woman, and looking close to every thing. But I always suspected she had Scotch blood in her veins; any

thing else I could have looked over in her from a regard to the
family. She was a strict observer for self and servants of Lent, and
all fast days, but not holidays. One of the maids having fainted three
times the last day of Lent, to keep soul and body together, we put a
morsel of roast beef into her mouth, which came from Sir Murtagh's dinner, who never fasted, not he; but somehow or other it
unfortunately reached my lady's ears, and the priest of the parish
had a complaint made of it the next day, and the poor girl was forced
as soon as she could walk to do penance for it, before she could get
any peace or absolution, in the house or out of it. However, my lady
was very charitable in her own way. She had a charity school for
poor children, where they were taught to read and write gratis, and
where they were kept well to spinning gratis for my lady in return;
for she had always heaps of duty yarn from the tenants, and got all
her household linen out of the estate from first to last; for after the
spinning, the weavers on the estate took it in hand for nothing,
because of the looms my lady's interest could get from the Linen
Board to distribute gratis.* Then there was a bleach-yard near us,
and the tenant dare refuse my lady nothing, for fear of a lawsuit Sir
Murtagh kept hanging over him about the water-course. With these
ways of managing, 'tis surprising how cheap my lady got things
done, and how proud she was of it. Her table the same way, kept for
next to nothing; duty fowls, and duty turkies, and duty geese,[G] came
as fast as we could eat 'em, for my lady kept a sharp look-out, and
knew to a tub of butter every thing the tenants had, all round. They
knew her way, and what with fear of driving for rent and Sir
Murtagh's lawsuits, they were kept in such good order, they never
thought of coming near Castle Rackrent without a present of something or other—nothing too much or too little for my lady—eggs,
honey, butter, meal, fish, game, grouse, and herrings, fresh or salt,
all went for something. As for their young pigs, we had them,
and the best bacon and hams they could make up, with all young
chickens in spring; but they were a set of poor wretches, and we
had nothing but misfortunes with them, always breaking and running
away. This, Sir Murtagh and my lady said, was all their former
landlord Sir Patrick's fault, who let 'em get the half year's rent into
arrear; there was something in that to be sure. But Sir Murtagh was
as much the contrary way; for let alone making English tenants[G] of
them, every soul, he was always driving and driving, and pounding

and pounding, and canting and canting,[G] and replevying and replevying,* and he made a good living of trespassing cattle; there was always some tenant's pig, or horse, or cow, or calf, or goose, trespassing, which was so great a gain to Sir Murtagh, that he did not like to hear me talk of repairing fences. Then his heriots* and duty work[G] brought him in something, his turf was cut, his potatoes set and dug, his hay brought home, and, in short, all the work about his house done for nothing; for in all our leases there were strict clauses heavy with penalties, which Sir Murtagh knew well how to enforce; so many days' duty work of man and horse, from every tenant, he was to have, and had, every year; and when a man vexed him, why the finest day he could pitch on, when the cratur was getting in his own harvest, or thatching his cabin, Sir Murtagh made it a principle to call upon him and his horse; so he taught 'em all, as he said, to know the law of landlord and tenant. As for law, I believe no man, dead or alive, ever loved it so well as Sir Murtagh. He had once sixteen suits pending at a time, and I never saw him so much himself; roads, lanes, bogs, wells, ponds, eel-wires, orchards, trees, tithes, vagrants, gravelpits, sandpits, dunghills, and nuisances, every thing upon the face of the earth furnished him good matter for a suit. He used to boast that he had a lawsuit for every letter in the alphabet. How I used to wonder to see Sir Murtagh in the midst of the papers in his office! Why he could hardly turn about for them. I made bold to shrug my shoulders once in his presence, and thanked my stars I was not born a gentleman to so much toil and trouble; but Sir Murtagh took me up short with his old proverb, 'learning is better than house or land'.* Out of forty-nine suits which he had, he never lost one but seventeen;[G] the rest he gained with costs, double costs, treble costs sometimes; but even that did not pay. He was a very learned man in the law, and had the character of it; but how it was I can't tell, these suits that he carried cost him a power of money; in the end he sold some hundreds a year of the family estate; but he was a very learned man in the law, and I know nothing of the matter, except having a great regard for the family; and I could not help grieving when he sent me to post up notices of the sale of the fee-simple* of the lands and appurtenances of Timoleague. 'I know, honest Thady,' says he, to comfort me, 'what I'm about better than you do; I'm only selling to get the ready money wanting to carry on my suit with spirit with the Nugents of Carrickashaughlin.'

He was very sanguine about that suit with the Nugents of Carrickashaughlin. He could have gained it, they say, for certain, had it pleased Heaven to have spared him to us, and it would have been at the least a plump two thousand a year in his way; but things were ordered otherwise, for the best to be sure. He dug up a fairy-mount[2G] against my advice, and had no luck afterwards. Though a learned man in the law, he was a little too incredulous in other matters. I warned him that I heard the very Banshee[3] that my grandfather heard under Sir Patrick's window a few days before his death. But Sir Murtagh thought nothing of the Banshee, nor of his cough with a spitting of blood, brought on, I understand, by catching cold in attending the courts, and overstraining his chest with making himself heard in one of his favourite causes. He was a great speaker with a powerful voice; but his last speech was not in the courts at all. He and my lady, though both of the same way of thinking in some things, and though she was as good a wife and great economist as you could see, and he the best of husbands, as to looking into his affairs, and making money for his family; yet I don't know how it was, they had a great deal of sparring and jarring between them. My lady had her privy purse—and she had her weed ashes,[G] and her sealing money[G] upon the signing of all the leases, with something to buy gloves besides; and besides again often took money from the tenants, if offered properly, to speak for them to Sir Murtagh about abatements* and renewals. Now the weed ashes and the glove money he allowed her clear perquisites; though once when he saw her in a new gown saved out of the weed ashes, he told her to my face (for he could say a sharp thing), that she should not put on her weeds before her husband's death. But in a dispute about an abatement, my lady would have the last word, and Sir Murtagh grew mad;[G] I was within hearing of the door, and now I wish I had made bold to step in. He

[2] These fairy-mounts are called ant-hills in England. They are held in high reverence by the common people in Ireland. A gentleman, who in laying out his lawn had occasion to level one of these hillocks, could not prevail upon any of his labourers to begin the ominous work. He was obliged to take a *loy** from one of their reluctant hands, and began the attack himself. The labourers agreed, that the vengeance of the fairies would fall upon the head of the presumptuous mortal, who first disturbed them in their retreat.
[3] The Banshee is a species of aristocratic fairy, who, in the shape of a little hideous old woman, has been known to appear, and heard to sing in a mournful supernatural voice under the windows of great houses, to warn the family that some of them are soon to die. In the last century every great family in Ireland had a Banshee, who attended regularly; but latterly their visits and songs have been discontinued.

spoke so loud, the whole kitchen was out on the stairs.[G] All of a
sudden he stopped and my lady too. Something has surely happened,
thought I—and so it was, for Sir Murtagh in his passion broke a
blood-vessel, and all the law in the land could do nothing in that case.
My lady sent for five physicians, but Sir Murtagh died, and was
buried. She had a fine jointure settled upon her, and took herself
away to the great joy of the tenantry. I never said any thing one way or
the other, whilst she was part of the family, but got up to see her go at
three o'clock in the morning. 'It's a fine morning, honest Thady,' said
she; 'good bye to ye,' and into the carriage she stept, without a
word more, good or bad, or even half a crown; but I made my bow,
and stood to see her safe out of sight for the sake of the family.

GLOSSARY

*Some friends, who have seen Thady's history since it has been printed,
have suggested to the Editor that many of the terms and idiomatic
phrases, with which it abounds, could not be intelligible to the English
reader without further explanation. The Editor has therefore furnished
the following Glossary.*

[Page 79] *Monday morning.*—Thady begins his memoirs of the
Rackrent Family by dating *Monday morning*, because no great undertaking can be auspiciously commenced in Ireland on any morning
but *Monday morning*. 'O, please God we live till Monday morning,
we'll set the slater to mend the roof of the house. On Monday
morning we'll fall to, and cut the turf. On Monday morning we'll see
and begin mowing. On Monday morning, please your honour, we'll
begin and dig the potatoes,' &c.

All the intermediate days, between the making of such speeches
and the ensuing Monday, are wasted: and when Monday morning
comes, it is ten to one that the business is deferred to *the next* Monday morning. The Editor knew a gentleman, who, to counteract this
prejudice, made his workmen and labourers begin all new pieces of
work upon a Saturday.

[Page 80] *Let alone the three kingdoms itself.*—*Let alone*, in this sentence, means *put out of consideration*. The phrase, *let alone*, which is
now used as the imperative of a verb, may in time become a conjunction, and may exercise the ingenuity of some future etymologist.

The celebrated Horne Tooke has proved most satisfactorily, that the conjunction *but* comes from the imperative of the Anglo-Saxon verb (*bouant*) *to be out;* also that *if* comes from *gift*, the imperative of the Anglo-Saxon verb which signifies *to give*, &c.

[Page 82] *Whillaluh.*—Ullaloo, Gol, or lamentation over the dead—

'Magnoque ululante tumultu.'—VIRGIL.

'Ululatibus omne
Implevere nemus.'—OVID.

A full account of the Irish Gol, or Ullaloo, and of the Caoinan or Irish funeral song, with its first semichorus, second semichorus, full chorus of sighs and groans, together with the Irish words and music, may be found in the fourth volume of the transactions of the Royal Irish Academy. For the advantage of *lazy* readers, who would rather read a page than walk a yard, and from compassion, not to say sympathy, with their infirmity, the Editor transcribes the following passages:

'The Irish have been always remarkable for their funeral lamentations, and this peculiarity has been noticed by almost every traveller who visited them; and it seems derived from their Celtic ancestors, the primæval inhabitants of this isle . . .

'It has been affirmed of the Irish, that to cry was more natural to them than to any other nation, and at length the Irish cry became proverbial . . .

'Cambrensis in the twelfth century says, the Irish then musically expressed their griefs; that is, they applied the musical art, in which they excelled all others, to the orderly celebration of funeral obsequies, by dividing the mourners into two bodies, each alternately singing their part, and the whole at times joining in full chorus . . . The body of the deceased, dressed in grave clothes, and ornamented with flowers, was placed on a bier, or some elevated spot. The relations and keepers (*singing mourners*) ranged themselves in two divisions, one at the head, and the other at the feet of the corpse. The bards and croteries had before prepared the funeral Caoinan. The chief bard of the head chorus began by singing the first stanza in a low, doleful tone, which was softly accompanied by the harp; at the conclusion, the foot semichorus began the lamentation, or Ullaloo, from the final note of the preceding stanza, in which they were answered by the head semichorus; then both united in one general chorus. The chorus of the first stanza being ended, the chief bard of the foot semichorus began the second Gol or lamentation, in which he was answered by that of the head; and then, as before, both united in the general full chorus. Thus alternately were the song and choruses performed during the night. The genealogy, rank, possessions, the virtues and vices of the dead were rehearsed, and a number of interrogations were addressed to the deceased; as, Why did he die? If married, whether his wife was faithful to him, his sons dutiful, or good hunters or warriors? If a woman, whether her daughters were fair or chaste? If a young man, whether he had been crossed in love; or if the blue-eyed maids of Erin treated him with scorn?'

We are told, that formerly the feet (the metrical feet) of the Caoinan were much attended to; but on the decline of the Irish bards these feet were gradually neglected, and the Caoinan fell into a sort of slipshod metre amongst women. Each province had different Caoinans, or at least different imitations of the original. There was the Munster cry, the Ulster cry, &c. It became an extempore performance, and every set of keepers varied the melody according to their own fancy.

It is curious to observe how customs and ceremonies degenerate. The present Irish cry, or howl, cannot boast of such melody, nor is the funeral procession conducted with much dignity. The crowd of people who assemble at these funerals sometimes amounts to a thousand, often to four or five hundred. They gather as the bearers of the hearse proceed on their way, and when they pass through any village, or when they come near any houses, they begin to cry—Oh! Oh! Oh! Oh! Oh! Agh! Agh! raising their notes from the first *Oh!* to the last *Agh!* in a kind of mournful howl. This gives notice to the inhabitants of the village that a *funeral is passing*, and immediately they flock out to follow it. In the province of Munster it is a common thing for the women to follow a funeral, to join in the universal cry with all their might and main for some time, and then to turn and ask—'Arrah! who is it that's dead?—who is it we're crying for?' Even the poorest people have their own burying-places, that is, spots of ground in the church-yards, where they say that their ancestors have been buried ever since the wars of Ireland; and if these burial-places are ten miles from the place where a man dies, his friends and neighbours take care to carry his corpse thither. Always one priest, often five or six priests, attend these funerals; each priest repeats a mass, for which he is paid, sometimes a shilling, sometimes half-a-crown, sometimes half-a-guinea, or a guinea, according to their circumstances, or, as they say, according to the *ability* of the deceased. After the burial of any very poor man, who has left a widow or children, the priest makes what is called a *collection* for the widow; he goes round to every person present, and each contributes sixpence or a shilling, or what they please. The reader will find in the note upon the word *Wake* ... more particulars respecting the conclusion of the Irish funerals.

Certain old women, who cry particularly loud and well, are in great request, and, as a man said to the Editor, 'Every one would wish and be proud to have such at his funeral, or at that of his friends.' The lower Irish are wonderfully eager to attend the funerals of their friends and relations, and they make their relationships branch out to a great extent. The proof that a poor man has been well beloved during his life is his having a crowded funeral. To attend a neighbour's funeral is a cheap proof of humanity, but it does not, as some imagine, cost nothing. The time spent in attending funerals may be safely valued at half a million to the Irish nation; the Editor thinks that double that sum would not be too high an esti- mate. The habits of profligacy and drunkenness, which are acquired at *wakes*, are here put out of the question. When a labourer, a car- penter, or a smith, is not at his work, which frequently happens, ask where he is gone, and ten to one the answer is—'Oh faith, please your honour, he couldn't do a stroke to-day, for he's gone to *the* funeral.'

Even beggars, when they grow old, go about begging *for their own funerals*; that is, begging for money to buy a coffin, candles, pipes and tobacco. For the use of the candles, pipes, and tobacco, see *Wake*.

Those who value customs in proportion to their antiquity, and nations in proportion to their adherence to ancient customs, will, doubtless, admire the Irish *Ullaloo*, and the Irish nation, for per- severing in this usage from time immemorial. The Editor, however, has observed some alarming symptoms, which seem to prognosticate the declining taste for the Ullaloo in Ireland. In a comic theatrical entertainment, represented not long since on the Dublin stage, a chorus of old women was introduced, who set up the Irish howl round the relics of a physician, who is supposed to have fallen under the wooden sword of Harlequin. After the old women have continued their Ullaloo for a decent time, with all the necessary accompaniments of wringing their hands, wiping or rubbing their eyes with the corners of their gowns or aprons, &c. one of the mourners suddenly suspends her lamentable cries, and, turning to her neighbour, asks, 'Arrah now, honey, who is it we're crying for?'

[Page 82] *The tenants even were sent away without their whiskey.*—It is usual with some landlords to give their inferior tenants a glass of whiskey when they pay their rents. Thady calls it *their* whiskey; not that the whiskey is actually the property of the tenants, but that it becomes their *right* after it has been often given to them. In this general mode of reasoning respecting *rights* the lower Irish are not singular, but they are peculiarly quick and tenacious in claiming these rights. 'Last year your honour gave me some straw for the roof of my house, and I *expect* your honour will be after doing the same this year.' In this manner gifts are frequently turned into tributes. The high and low are not always dissimilar in their habits. It is said, that the Sublime Ottoman Porte is very apt to claim gifts as tributes: thus it is dangerous to send the Grand Seignor a fine horse on his birthday one year, lest on his next birthday he should expect a similar present, and should proceed to demonstrate the reasonableness of his expectations.

[Page 82] *He demeaned himself greatly*—means, he lowered or disgraced himself much.

[Page 83] *Duty fowls, and duty turkies, and duty geese.*—In many leases in Ireland, tenants were *formerly* bound to supply an inordinate quantity of poultry to their landlords. The Editor knew of thirty turkies being reserved in one lease of a small farm.

[Page 83] *English tenants.*—An English tenant does not mean a tenant who is an Englishman, but a tenant who pays his rent the day that it is due. It is a common prejudice in Ireland, amongst the poorer classes of people, to believe that all tenants in England pay their rents on the very day when they become due. An Irishman, when he goes to take a farm, if he wants to prove to his landlord that he is a substantial man, offers to become an *English tenant*. If a tenant disobliges his landlord by voting against him, or against his opinion, at an election, the tenant is immediately informed by the agent, that he must become an *English tenant*. This threat does not imply that he is to change his language or his country, but that he must pay all the arrear of rent which he owes, and that he must thenceforward pay his rent on that day when it becomes due.

[Page 84] *Canting*—does not mean talking or writing hypocritical nonsense, but selling substantially by auction.

[Page 84] *Duty work.*—It was formerly common in Ireland to insert clauses in leases, binding tenants to furnish their landlords with labourers and horses for several days in the year. Much petty tyranny and oppression have resulted from this feudal custom. Whenever a poor man disobliged his landlord, the agent sent to him for his duty work, and Thady does not exaggerate when he says, that the tenants were often called from their own work to do that of their landlord. Thus the very means of earning their rent were taken from them: whilst they were getting home their landlord's harvest, their own was often ruined, and yet their rents were expected to be paid as punctually as if their time had been at their own disposal. This appears the height of absurd injustice.

In Esthonia, amongst the poor Sclavonian race of peasant slaves, they pay tributes to their lords, not under the name of duty work, duty geese, duty turkies, &c., but under the name of *righteousnesses*. The following ballad is a curious specimen of Esthonian poetry:—

> This is the cause that the country is ruined,
> And the straw of the thatch is eaten away,
> The gentry are come to live in the land—
> Chimneys between the village,
> And the proprietor upon the white floor!
> The sheep brings forth a lamb with a white forehead,
> This is paid to the lord for a *righteousness sheep*.
> The sow farrows pigs,
> They go to the spit of the lord.
> The hen lays eggs,
> They go into the lord's frying-pan.
> The cow drops a male calf,

That goes into the lord's herd as a bull.
The mare foals a horse foal,
That must be for my lord's nag.
The boor's wife has sons,
They must go to look after my lord's poultry.

[Page 84] *Out of forty-nine suits which he had, he never lost one but seventeen.*—Thady's language in this instance is a specimen of a mode of rhetoric common in Ireland. An astonishing assertion is made in the beginning of a sentence, which ceases to be in the least surprising, when you hear the qualifying explanation that follows. Thus a man who is in the last stage of staggering drunkenness will, if he can articulate, swear to you—'Upon his conscience now, and may he never stir from the spot alive if he is telling a lie, upon his conscience he has not tasted a drop of any thing, good or bad, since morning at-all-at-all, but half a pint of whiskey, please your honour.'

[Page 85] *Fairy mounts*—Barrows. It is said that these high mounts were of great service to the natives of Ireland when Ireland was invaded by the Danes. Watch was always kept on them, and upon the approach of an enemy a fire was lighted to give notice to the next watch, and thus the intelligence was quickly communicated through the country. *Some years ago*, the common people believed that these barrows were inhabited by fairies, or, as they called them, by the *good people*. 'O troth, to the best of my belief, and to the best of my judgement and opinion,' said an elderly man to the Editor, 'it was only the old people that had nothing to do, and got together, and were telling stories about them fairies, but to the best of my judgement there's nothing in it. Only this I heard myself not very many years back from a decent kind of a man, a grazier, that as he was coming just *fair and easy* (*quietly*) from the fair, with some cattle and sheep, that he had not sold, just at the church of—, at an angle of the road like, he was met by a good-looking man, who asked him where he was going? And he answered, "Oh, far enough, I must be going all night." "No that you mustn't nor won't (says the man), you'll sleep with me the night, and you'll want for nothing, nor your cattle nor sheep neither, nor your *beast* (*horse*); so come along with me." With that the grazier *lit* (*alighted*) from his horse, and it was dark night; but presently he finds himself, he does not know in the wide world how, in a fine house, and plenty of every thing to eat and drink; nothing at all wanting that he could wish for or think of. And he does not *mind* (*recollect* or *know*) how at last he falls asleep; and in the morning he finds himself lying, not in ever a bed or a house at all, but just in the angle of the road where first he met the strange man: there he finds himself lying on his back on the grass, and all his sheep feeding as quiet as ever all round about him, and his horse the same way, and the bridle of the beast over his wrist. And I asked him what he thought of it; and from first to last he could think of nothing, but for certain sure it must have been the fairies that entertained him so well. For there was no house to see any where nigh hand, or any building, or barn, or place at all, but only the church and the *mole* (*barrow*). There's another odd thing enough that they tell about this same church, that if any person's corpse, that had not a right to be buried in that church-yard, went to be burying there in it, no, not all the men, women, or childer in all Ireland could get the corpse any way into the church-yard; but as they would be trying to go into the church-yard, their feet would seem to be going backwards instead of forwards; ay, continually backwards the whole funeral would seem to go; and they would never set foot with the corpse in the church-yard. Now they say that it is the fairies do all this; but it is my opinion it is all idle talk, and people are after being wiser now.'

The country people in Ireland certainly *had* great admiration mixed with reverence, if not dread, of fairies. They believed that beneath these fairy-mounts were spacious subterraneous palaces, inhabited by *the good people*, who must not on any account be disturbed. When the wind raises a little eddy of dust upon the road, the poor people believe that it is raised by the fairies, that it is a sign that they are journeying from one of the fairies' mounts to another, and they say to the fairies, or to the dust as it passes, 'God speed ye, gentlemen; God speed ye.' This averts any evil that *the good people* might be inclined to do them. There are innumerable stories told of the friendly and unfriendly feats of these busy fairies; some of these tales are ludicrous, and some romantic enough for poetry. It is a pity that poets should lose such convenient, though diminutive machinery. By-the-bye, Parnel, who showed himself so deeply 'skilled in faerie lore', was an Irishman; and though he has presented his faeries to the world in the ancient English dress of 'Britain's isle, and Arthur's days', it is probable that his first acquaintance with them began in his native country.

Some remote origin for the most superstitious or romantic popular illusions or vulgar errors may often be discovered. In Ireland, the old churches and church-yards have been usually fixed upon as the scenes of wonders. Now the antiquarians tell us, that near the ancient churches in that kingdom caves of various constructions have from time to time been discovered, which were formerly used as granaries or magazines by the ancient inhabitants, and as places to which they retreated in time of danger. There is (p. 84 of the R.I.A. Transactions for 1789) a particular account of a number of these artificial caves at the west end of the church of Killossy, in the county of Kildare. Under a rising ground, in a dry sandy soil, these subterraneous dwellings were found: they have pediment roofs, and they communicate with each other by small apertures. In the Brehon laws these are mentioned, and there are fines inflicted by those laws upon persons who steal from the subterraneous granaries. All these things show that there was a real foundation for the stories which were told of the appearance of lights, and of the sounds of voices near these places. The persons who had property concealed there very willingly countenanced every wonderful relation that tended to make these places objects of sacred awe or superstitious terror.

[Page 85] *Weed ashes.*—By ancient usage in Ireland, all the weeds on a farm belonged to the farmer's wife, or to the wife of the squire who holds the ground in his own hands. The great demand for alkaline salts in bleaching rendered these ashes no inconsiderable perquisite.

[Page 85] *Sealing money.*—Formerly it was the custom in Ireland for tenants to give the squire's lady from two to fifty guineas as a perquisite upon the sealing of their leases. The Editor not very long since knew of a baronet's lady accepting fifty guineas as sealing money, upon closing a bargain for a considerable farm.

[Page 85] *Sir Murtagh grew mad.*—Sir Murtagh grew angry.

[Page 86] *The whole kitchen was out on the stairs*—means that all the inhabitants of the kitchen came out of the kitchen, and stood upon the stairs. These, and similar expressions, show how much the Irish are disposed to metaphor and amplification.

SYDNEY OWENSON (LADY MORGAN)
(1776–1859)

from *The Wild Irish Girl* (1806)

LETTER V

TO J. D. ESQ. M.P.

Castle of Inismore, Barony of ——

Ay, 'tis even so—point your glass, and rub your eyes, 'tis all one, here I am, and here I am likely to remain for some time. But, whether a prisoner of war, or taken up on a suspicion of espionage, or to be offered as an appeasing sacrifice to the *manes** of the old Prince of Inismore, you must for awhile suspend your patience to learn.

According to the *carte du pays** laid out for me by the fisherman, I left the shore and crossed the summit of a mountain, which, after an hour's ascension, I found sloped almost perpendicularly down to a bold and rocky coast, its base terminating in a peninsula, that advanced for near half a mile into the ocean. Towards the extreme western point of this peninsula, which was wildly romantic beyond all description, arose a vast and grotesque pile of rocks, at once forming the scite and fortifications of the noblest mass of ruins on which my eye ever rested. Grand even in desolation, and magnificent in decay—it was the Castle of Inismore! The setting sun shone brightly on its mouldering turrets, and the waves, which bathed its rocky basis, reflected on their swelling bosoms the dark outlines of its awful ruins.[1]

As I descended the mountain's brow, I observed that the little isthmus, which joined the peninsula to the main-land, had been cut away, and a curious danger-threatening bridge was rudely thrown across the intervening gulf, flung from the rocks on one side to an angle of the mountain on the other, leaving a yawning chasm of some fathoms deep beneath the foot of the wary passenger. This

---

[1] Those who have visited the Castle of Dunluce, near the Giants'-Causeway, may, perhaps, trace some of its striking features in this rude draught of the Castle of Inismore.

must have been a very perilous pass in days of civil warfare; and in
the intrepidity of my daring ancestor, I almost forgot his crime.
Amidst the interstices of the rocks which skirted the shores of this
interesting peninsula, patches of the richest vegetation were to be
seen, and the trees, which sprung wildly among its venerable ruins,
were bursting into all the vernal luxuriancy of spring. In the course
of my descent, several cabins, of a better description than I had yet
seen, appeared scattered beneath the shelter of the mountain's
innumerable projections; while, in the air and dress of their
inhabitants (whom the sound of my horse's feet brought to their
respective doors), I evidently perceived an original and primitive
something, which I had never before noticed here in this class of
persons.

They appeared to me, I know not why, to be in their holiday
garb, and their dress, though grotesque and coarse, was cleanly and
characteristic. I observed that round the heads of the elderly dames
were folded several wreaths of white or coloured linen,[2] that others
had handkerchiefs[3] lightly folded round their brows and curiously
fastened under the chin; while the young wore their hair fastened
up with wooden bodkins. They were all enveloped in large shapeless
mantles of blue frieze, and most of them had a rosary hanging on
the arm, whence I inferred they were on the point of attending
vespers at the chapel of Inismore. I alighted at the door of a cabin a
few paces distant from the Alpine bridge, and entreated a shed for
my horse, while I performed my devotions. The man to whom I
addressed myself seemed the only one of several who surrounded
me, that understood English, and appeared much edified by my
pious intention, saying, 'that God would prosper my honour's
journey, and that I was welcome to a shed for my horse, and a
night's lodging for myself into the bargain.' He then offered to
be my guide, and, as we crossed the drawbridge, he told me I was
out of luck by not coming earlier, for that high mass had been
celebrated that morning for the repose of the soul of a Prince of

---

[2] 'The women's ancient head-dress so perfectly resembles that of the Egyptian Isis,
that it cannot be doubted but that the modes of Egypt were preserved among the
Irish.'—*Walker on the Ancient Irish Dress*, p. 62.

The author's father, who lived in the early part of his life in a remote skirt of the
province of Connaught, remembers to have seen the heads of the female peasantry
encircled with folds of linen in the form of a turban.

[3] These handkerchiefs they call *Binnogues:* it is a remnant of a very ancient mode.

Inismore, who had been murdered on this very day of the month. 'And when this day comes round,' he added, 'we all attend dressed in our best; for my part, I never wear my poor old grandfather's *berrad* but on the like occasion;' taking off a curious cap of a conical form, which he twirled round his hand, and regarded with much satisfaction.[4]

By heavens! as I breathed this region of superstition, so strongly was I infected, that my usual scepticism was scarcely proof against my inclination to mount my horse and gallop off, as I shudderingly pronounced—

'I am then entering the Castle of Inismore, on the anniversary of that day on which my ancestors took the life of its venerable prince!'

You see, my good friend, how much we are the creatures of situation and circumstance, and with what pliant servility the mind resigns itself to the impressions of the senses, or the illusions of the imagination.

We had now reached the ruined cloisters of the chapel; I had paused to examine their curious but dilapidated architecture, when my guide, hurrying me on, said, 'if I did not quicken my pace, I should miss getting a good view of the Prince,' who was just entering by a door opposite to that we had passed through. Behold me, then, mingling among a group of peasantry, and, like them, straining my eyes to that magnet which fascinated every glance.

And surely, Fancy, in her boldest flight, never gave to the fairy vision of poetic dreams, a combination of images more poetically fine, more strikingly picturesque, or more impressively touching. Nearly one half of the chapel of Inismore has fallen into decay, and the ocean breeze, as it rushed through the fractured roof, wafted the torn banners of the family which hung along its dismantled walls. The red beams of the sinking sun shone on the glittering tabernacle which stood on the altar, and touched with their golden light the sacerdotal vestments of the two officiating priests, who ascended its broken steps at the moment that the prince and his family entered.

The first of this most singular and interesting group was the venerable Father John, the chaplain. Religious enthusiasm never gave to

---

[4] A few years back, Hugh Dugan, a peasant of the county of Kilkenny, who affected the ancient Irish dress, seldom appeared without his *berrad*.

the fancied form of the first of the patriarchs a countenance of more holy expression, or divine resignation; a figure more touching by its dignified simplicity, or an air more beneficently mild—more meekly good. He was dressed in his pontificals,* and, with his eyes bent to earth, his hands spread upon his breast, he joined his coadjutors.

What a contrast to this saintly being now struck my view; a form almost gigantic in stature, yet gently thrown forward by evident infirmity; limbs of Herculean mould, and a countenance rather furrowed by the inroads of vehement passions, than the deep trace of years; eyes, still emanating the ferocity of an unsubdued spirit, yet tempered by a strong trait of benevolence; which, like a glory* irradiated a broad expansive brow; a mouth, on which even yet the spirit of convivial enjoyment seemed to hover, though shaded by two large whiskers on the upper lip,[5] that still preserved their ebon hue; while time or grief had bleached the scattered hairs, which hung their snows upon the manly temple. The drapery which covered this striking figure was singularly appropriate, and as I have since been told, strictly conformable to the ancient costume of the Irish nobles.[6]

The only part of the under-garment visible, was the ancient Irish *truis*, which, closely adhering to the limbs from the waist to the ankle, includes the pantaloon and hose, and terminates in a kind of buskin, not dissimilar to the Roman *perones*. A triangular mantle of bright *scarlet* cloth, embroidered and fringed round the edges, fell from his shoulders to the ground, and was fastened at the breast with a large circular golden brooch,[7] of a workmanship most curiously

---

[5] 'I have been confidently assured that the grandfather of the present Right Hon. John O'Neil (great grandfather to the present Lord O'Neile, the elegant and accomplished owner of Shanes Castle, wore his beard after the *prohibited* Irish mode.'— Walker, p. 62.

[6] The Irish mantle, with the fringed or shagged borders sewed down the edges of it, was not always made of frieze and such coarse materials, which was the dress of the lower sort of people, but, according to the rank and quality of the wearer, was sometimes made of the finest cloth, bordered with silken fringe of scarlet, and various colours.— Ware, vol. ii. p. 75.

[7] Several of these useful ornaments (in Irish *dealg fallain*), some gold, some silver, have been found in various parts of the kingdom, and are to be seen in the cabinets of our national *virtuosi*. Joseph Cooper Walker, Esq., to whose genius, learning, and exertions, Ireland stands so deeply indebted, speaking of a broach he had seen in the possession of R. Ousley, Esq., says, 'Neither my pen or pencil can give an adequate idea of the elegant gold filigree work with which it is composed.'

beautiful; round his neck hung a golden collar, which seemed to denote the wearer of some order of knighthood, probably hereditary in his family; a dagger, called a *skiene* (for my guide explained every article of the dress to me,) was sheathed in his girdle, and was discerned by the sun-beam, that played on its brilliant haft. As he entered the chapel, he removed from his venerable head a cap, or berrad, of the same form as that I had noticed with my guide, but made of velvet, richly embroidered.

The chieftain moved with dignity—yet with difficulty—and his colossal but infirm frame appeared to claim support from a form so almost impalpably delicate, that, as it floated on the gaze, it seemed like the incarnation of some pure ethereal spirit, which a sigh too roughly breathed would dissolve into its kindred air; yet to this sylphid elegance of spheral beauty was united all that symmetrical contour which constitutes the luxury of human loveliness. This scarcely 'mortal mixture of earth's mould' was vested in a robe of vestal white, which was folded beneath the bosom with a narrow girdle embossed with precious stones.

From the shoulder fell a crimson mantle, fastened at the neck with a silver bodkin, while the finely turned head was enveloped in a veil of point-lace, bound round the brow with a band, or diadem, ornamented with the same description of jewels which encircled her arms.[8]

Such was the *figure* of the Princess of Inismore! But, oh! not once was the face turned round towards that side where I stood; and, when I shifted my position, the envious veil intercepted the ardent glance which eagerly sought the fancied charms it concealed: for, was it possible to doubt the face would not 'keep the promise which the form had made?'

The group that followed was grotesque beyond all powers of description. The ancient bard, whose long white beard

'Descending swept his aged breast'—

---

[8] This was, with little variation, the general costume of the female *noblesse* of Ireland from a very early period. In the fifteenth century the veil was very prevalent, and was termed fillag, or scarf; the Irish ladies, like those of ancient or modern Greece, seldom appearing unveiled. As the veil made no part of the Celtic costume, its origin was probably merely oriental.

The great love of ornaments betrayed by the Irish ladies of other times, 'the beauties of the heroes of old,' are thus described by a quaint and ancient author:—'Their necks are hung with chains and carkanets—their arms wreathed with many bracelets.'

the incongruous constume—half modern, half antique—of the
bare-footed domestics; the ostensible air of the steward, who closed
the procession;—and, above all, the dignified importance of the
nurse, who took the lead in it immediately after her young lady: her
air, form, countenance, and dress, were indeed so singularly fantastic
and *outré*,* that the genius of masquerade might have adopted her
figure as the finest model of grotesque caricature.

Conceive for a moment a form, whose longitude bore no degree of
proportion to her latitude, dressed in a short jacket of brown cloth,
with loose sleeves from the elbow to the wrist, made of red camlet,
striped with green, and turned up with a broad cuff—a petticoat of
scarlet frieze, covered by an apron of green serge, longitudinally
striped with scarlet tape, and sufficiently short to betray an ancle that
sanctioned all the libels ever uttered against the ancles of the Irish
fair. True national brogues set off her blue worsted stockings, and
her yellow hair, dragging over a high roll, was covered on the summit with a little coif, over which was flung a scarlet handkerchief,
fastened in a large bow under her rubicund chin.[9]

As this singular and interesting group advanced up the centre aisle
of the chapel, reverence and affection were evidently blended in the
looks of the multitude, which hung upon their steps; and, though the
Prince and his daughter seemed to lose in the meekness of true
religion all sense of temporal inequality, and promiscuously mingled
with the congregation, yet *that* distinction they humbly avoided was
reverentially forced on them by the affectionate crowd, which drew
back on either side as they advanced, until the chieftain and his child
stood alone in the centre of the ruined choir—the winds of heaven
playing freely amidst their garments—the sun's setting beam enrich-
ing their beautiful figures with its orient tints, while he, like Milton's
ruined angel,*

> 'Above the rest,
> In shape and feature proudly eminent
> Stood like a tow'r;'

[9] Such was the dress of Mary Morgan, a poor peasant in the neighbourhood of
Drogheda, in 1786.—'In the close of the last century Mrs Power, of Waterford, vulgarly
called the *Queen of Credan*, appeared constantly in this dress, with the exception of
ornaments being gold, silver, and fine Brussels lace.'—See *Walker's Essay on Ancient
Irish Dress*, p. 73.

and she, like the personified spirit of Mercy, hovered round him, or supported, more by her tenderness than her strength, him from whom she could no longer claim support.

Those grey-headed domestics too—those faithful though but nominal vassals, who offered that voluntary reverence with their looks which is repaid with fatherly affection, while the anguish of a suffering heart hung on his pensive smile, sustained by the firmness of that indignant pride which lowered on his ample brow!

What a picture!

As soon as the first flush of interest, curiosity, and amazement, had subsided, my attention was carried towards the altar; and then I thought, as I watched the impressive avocation of father John, that had I been the Prince, I would have been the *Caiphas** too.

What a religion is this! How finely does it harmonize with the weakness of our nature; how seducingly it speaks to the senses; how forcibly it works on the passions; how strongly it seizes on the imagination; how interesting its forms; how graceful its ceremonies; how awful its rites. What a captivating, what a *picturesque*, faith! Who would not become its proselyte, were it not for the stern opposition of reason—the cold suggestions of philosophy!

The concluding strain of the vesper hymn died on the air as the sun's last beam faded on the casements of the chapel; when the Prince and his daughter, to avoid the intrusion of the crowd, withdrew through a private door, which communicated by a ruinous arcade with the castle.

I was the first to leave the chapel, and followed them at a distance as they moved slowly along, their fine figures sometimes concealed behind a pillar, and again emerging from the transient shade, flushed with the deep suffusion of the crimsoned firmament.

Once they paused, as if to admire the beautiful effect of the retreating light, as it faded on the ocean's swelling bosom; and once the Princess raised her hand and pointed to the evening star, which rose brilliantly on the deep cerulean blue* of a cloudless atmosphere, and shed its fairy beams on the mossy summit of a mouldering turret.

Such were the sublime objects which seemed to engage their attention, and added their *sensible* inspiration to the fervour of those more abstracted devotions in which they were so recently engaged. At last they reached the portals of the castle, and I lost sight of them.

Yet still, spell-bound, I stood transfixed to the spot whence I had caught a last view of their receding figures.

While I felt like the victim of superstitious terror when the spectre of its distempered fancy vanishes from its strained and eager gaze, all I had lately seen revolved in my mind like some pictured story of romantic fiction. I cast my eyes around; all still seemed the vision of awakened imagination—surrounded by a scenery, grand even to the boldest majesty of nature, and wild even to desolation—the day's dying splendors awfully involving in the gloomy haze of deepening twilight—the grey mists of stealing night gathering on the still-faintly illuminated surface of the ocean, which, awfully spreading to infinitude, seemed to the limited gaze of human vision to incorporate with the heaven, whose last glow it reflected—the rocks, which on every side rose to Alpine elevation, exhibiting, amidst the soft obscurity, forms savagely bold, or grotesquely wild; and those finely interesting ruins, which spread grandly desolate in the rear, and added a moral interest to the emotions excited by this view of nature in her most awful, most touching aspect.

Thus, suddenly withdrawn from the world's busiest haunts, its hackneyed modes, its vicious pursuits, and unimportant avocations—dropt as it were amidst scenes of mysterious sublimity—alone—on the wildest shores of the greatest ocean of the universe—immersed amidst the decaying monuments of past ages—still viewing in recollection such forms, such manners, such habits, (as I had lately beheld,) which to the worldly mind may be well supposed to belong to a race long passed beyond the barrier of existence, with 'the years beyond the flood'—I felt like the being of some other sphere, newly alighted on a distant orb. While the novel train of thought which stole on my mind seemed to seize its tone from the awful tranquillity by which I was surrounded, and I remained leaning on the fragment of a rock, as the waves dashed idly against its base, until their dark heads were silvered by the rising moon, and while my eyes dwelt on her silent progress, the castle-clock struck nine. Thus warned, I arose to depart, yet not without reluctance. My soul, for the first time, had there held commune with herself: the 'lying vanities' of life no longer intoxicating my senses, appeared to me for the first time in their genuine aspect, and my heart still fondly loitered over those scenes of solemn interest, where some of its best feelings had been called into existence.

Slowly departing, I raised my eyes to the Castle of Inismore, sighed, and almost wished I had been born the lord of these beautiful ruins, the prince of this isolated little territory, the adored chieftain of these affectionate and natural people. At that moment a strain of music stole by me, as if the breeze of midnight had expired in a murmur on the Eolian lyre.* Emotion, indefinite emotion, thrilled on every nerve. I listened—I trembled. The breathless silence of the region gave me every note. Was it the illusion of my now all awakened fancy, or the professional exertions of the bard of Inismore? Oh, no! for the voice it symphonized—the low, wild, tremulous voice, which sweetly sighed its soul of melody over the harp's responsive chords, was the voice of *a woman!*

Directed by the witching strain, I approached an angle of the building whence it seemed to proceed; and, perceiving a light streaming through an open casement, I climbed, with some difficulty, the ruins of a parapet wall, which encircled this wing of the castle, and which rising immediately under the casement, gave me, when I stood on it, a perfect view of the interior of that apartment to which it belonged.

Two tapers burned on a marble slab, at the remotest extremity of this vast and gloomy chamber, and shed their dim blue light on the saintly countenance of Father John, who, with a large folio open before him, seemed wholly wrapt in studious meditation; while the Prince, reclined on an immense gothic couch, with his robe thrown over the arm that supported his head, betrayed, by the expression of his countenance, those emotions which agitated his soul, as he listened to those strains which at once spoke to the heart of the father, the patriot, and the man—breathed from the chords of his country's emblem—breathed in the pathos of his country's music—breathed from the lips of his apparently inspired daughter! The 'white rising of her hands upon the harp;' the half-drawn veil, that imperfectly discovered the countenance of a seraph; the moonlight that played round her fine form, and partially touched her drapery with its silver beam—her attitude! her air!—But how cold—how inanimate—how imperfect this description! Oh! could I but seize the touching features—could I but realize the vivid tints of this enchanting picture, as they then glowed on my fancy! You would still think the mimic copy fabulous; the 'celestial visitant' of an over-heated imagination. Yet, as if the independent witchery of the lovely minstrel was not in itself all, all-sufficient, at the back of her chair stood the grotesque figure of her antiquated nurse. O the precious contrast!—and yet it heightened, it finished the picture.

While thus entranced in breathless observation, endeavouring to support my precarious tenement, and to prolong this rich feast of the senses and the soul, the loose stones on which I tottered, gave way under my feet; and, impulsively clinging to the wood-work of the casement, it mouldered in my grasp. I fell—but, before I reached the earth, I was bereft of sense. With its return I found myself in a large apartment, stretched on a bed, and supported in the arms of the Prince of Inismore! His hand was pressed to my bleeding temple; while the priest applied a styptic to the wound it had received; and the nurse was engaged in binding up my arm, which had been dread-fully bruised and fractured a little above the wrist. Some domestics, with an air of mingled concern and curiosity, surrounded my couch; and at her father's side stood the Lady Glorvina, her looks pale and disordered, and her trembling hands busily employed in preparing bandages, for which my skilful doctress impatiently called.

While my mind almost doubted the evidence of my senses, and a physical conviction alone *painfully* proved to me the reality of all I beheld, my wandering, wondering eyes met those of the Prince of Inismore! A volume of pity and benevolence was registered in their glance; nor were mine, I suppose, inexpressive of my feelings, for he thus replied to them:—

'Be of good cheer, young stranger; you are in no danger; be com-posed, be confident; conceive yourself in the midst of friends; for you are surrounded by those who would wish to be considered as such.'

I attempted to speak, but my voice faltered, my tongue was nerve-less, my mouth dry and parched. A trembling hand presented a cordial to my lips. I quaffed the philter, and fixed my eyes on the face of my ministering angel—that angel was Glorvina!—I closed them, and sunk on the bosom of her father.

'Oh, he faints again!' cried a sweet and plaintive voice.

'On the contrary,' replied the priest, 'the weariness of acute pain, something subsided, is lulling him into a soft repose! for, see, the colour re-animates his cheek, and his pulse quickens.'

'It indeed beats most wildly,' returned the sweet physician—for the pulse, which responded to her finger's thrilling pressure, moved with no languid throb.

'Let us retire,' added the priest; 'all danger is now, thank Heaven, over; and repose and quiet are the most salutary requisites for our patient.'

At these words he arose from my bedside; and the Prince, gently withdrawing his supporting arms, laid my head upon the pillow. In a moment all was deathlike stillness, and, stealing a glance from under my half-closed eyes, I found myself alone with my skilful doctress, the nurse; who shading the taper's light from the bed, had taken her distaff, and seated herself on a little stool at some distance.

This was a golden respite to feelings wound up to that vehement excess which forbade all expression, which left my tongue powerless, while my heart overflowed with emotion the most powerful.

Good God! I, the son of Lord M——, the hereditary object of hereditary detestation, beneath the roof of my implacable enemy! Supported in his arms, relieved from anguish by his charitable attention, honoured by the solicitude of his lovely daughter, overwhelmed by the charitable exertions of his whole family, and reduced to that bodily infirmity that would of necessity oblige me to continue for some time the object of their beneficent attentions!

What a series of emotions did this conviction awaken in my heart! Emotions of a character, an energy, long unknown to my apathized feelings; while gratitude to those who had drawn them into existence, combined with the interest, the curiosity, the admiration, they had awakened, tended to confirm my irresistible desire of perpetuating the immunities I enjoyed, as the guest and patient of the Prince and his daughter. And while the touch of this Wild Irish Girl's hand thrilled on every sense—while her voice of tenderest pity murmured on my ear, and I secretly triumphed over the prejudices of her father, I would not have exchanged my broken arm and wounded temple for the strongest limb and soundest head in the kingdom; but the same chance which threw me into the supporting arms of the irascible Prince, might betray to him, in the person of his patient, the son of his hereditary enemy; it was at least probable he would make some inquiries relative to the object of his benevolence, and the singular cause which rendered him such; it was therefore a necessary policy in me to be provided against this scrutiny.

Already deep in adventure, a thousand seducing reasons were suggested by my newly-awakened heart, to proceed with the romance, and to secure for my future residence in the castle, that interest, which, if known to be the son of Lord M——, I must eventually have forfeited for the cold aversion of irreclaimable prejudice. The imposition was at least innocent, and might tend to future and mutual advantage; and, after the ideal assumption of a thousand fictitious characters, I at last fixed on that of an itinerant artist, as consonant to my most cultivated talent, and to the testimony of those witnesses which I had fortunately brought with me; namely, my drawing-book, pencils, &c. &c.—self-nominated *Henry Mortimer*, to answer the initials on my linen, the only proofs against me, for I had not even a letter with me.

I was now armed at all points for inspection; and as the Prince lived in a perfect state of isolation, and I was unknown in the country, I entertained no apprehensions of discovery, during the time I should remain at the castle; and full of hope, strong in confidence, but wearied by incessant cogitation, and something exhausted by pain, I fell into that profound slumber I did before but feign.

CHARLES ROBERT MATURIN
(1780–1824)

from *Melmoth the Wanderer* (1820)

> Alive again? Then show me where he is;
> I'll give a thousand pounds to look upon him.
>
> SHAKESPEARE*

In the autumn of 1816, John Melmoth, a student in Trinity College, Dublin, quitted it to attend a dying uncle on whom his hopes for independence chiefly rested. John was the orphan son of a younger brother, whose small property scarce could pay John's college expences; but the uncle was rich, unmarried, and old; and John, from his infancy, had been brought up to look on him with that mingled sensation of awe, and of the wish, without the means to conciliate, (that sensation at once attractive and repulsive), with which we regard a being who (as nurse, domestic, and parent have tutored us to believe) holds the very threads of our existence in his hands, and may prolong or snap them when he pleases.

On receiving this summons, John set immediately out to attend his uncle.

The beauty of the country through which he travelled (it was the county Wicklow) could not prevent his mind from dwelling on many painful thoughts, some borrowed from the past, and more from the future. His uncle's caprice and moroseness,—the strange reports concerning the cause of the secluded life he had led for many years,—his own dependent state,—fell like blows fast and heavy on his mind. He roused himself to repel them,—sat up in the mail,* in which he was a solitary passenger,—looked out on the prospect,— consulted his watch;—then he thought they receded for a moment,—but there was nothing to fill their place, and he was forced to invite them back for company. When the mind is thus active in calling over invaders, no wonder the conquest is soon completed. As the carriage drew near the Lodge, (the name of old Melmoth's seat), John's heart grew heavier every moment.

The recollection of this awful uncle from infancy,—when he was never permitted to approach him without innumerable lectures,— *not to be troublesome,*—not to go too near his uncle,—not to ask him any questions,—on no account to disturb the inviolable arrangement of his snuff-box, hand-bell, and spectacles, nor to suffer the glittering of the gold-headed cane to tempt him to the mortal sin of handling it,—and, finally, to pilot himself aright through his perilous course in and out of the apartment without striking against the piles of books, globes, old newspapers, wig-blocks,* tobacco-pipes, and snuff-cannisters, not to mention certain hidden rocks of rat-traps and mouldy books beneath the chairs,—together with the final reverential bow at the door, which was to be closed with cautious gentleness, and the stairs to be descended as if he were 'shod with felt.'*—This recollection was carried on to his school-boy years, when at Christmas and Easter, the ragged poney, the jest of the school, was dispatched to bring the reluctant visitor to the Lodge,— where his pastime was to sit vis-a-vis to his uncle, without speaking or moving, till the pair resembled Don Raymond and the ghost of Beatrice in the Monk,*—then watching him, as he picked the bones of lean mutton out of his mess of weak broth, the latter of which he handed to his nephew with a needless caution not to 'take more than he liked,'—then hurried to bed by daylight, even in winter, to save the expence of an inch of candle, where he lay awake and restless

from hunger, till his uncle's retiring at eight o'clock gave signal
to the governante of the meagre household to steal up to him with
some fragments of her own scanty meal, administering between
every mouthful a whispered caution not to tell his uncle. Then his
college life, passed in an attic in the second square, uncheered by an
invitation to the country; the gloomy summer wasted in walking
up and down the deserted streets, as his uncle would not defray
the expences of his journey;—the only intimation of his existence, received in quarterly epistles, containing, with the scanty but
punctual remittance, complaints of the expences of his education,
cautions against extravagance, and lamentations for the failure of
tenants and the fall of the value of lands. All these recollections
came over him, and along with them the remembrance of that last
scene, where his dependence on his uncle was impressed on him
by the dying lips of his father.

'John, I must leave you, my poor boy; it has pleased God to take
your father from you before he could do for you what would have
made this hour less painful to him. You must look up, John, to your
uncle for every thing. He has oddities and infirmities, but you must
learn to bear with them, and with many other things too, as you will
learn too soon. And now, my poor boy, may He who is the father of
the fatherless look on your desolate state, and give you favour in the
eyes of your uncle.' As this scene rose to John's memory, his eyes
filled fast with tears, which he hastened to wipe away as the carriage
stopt to let him out at his uncle's gate.

He alighted, and with a change of linen in a handkerchief, (his
only travelling equipment), he approached his uncle's gate. The
lodge was in ruins, and a barefooted boy from an adjacent cabin ran
to lift on its single hinge what had once been a gate, but was now a
few planks so villainously put together, that they clattered like a sign
in a high wind. The stubborn post of the gate, yielding at last to the
united strength of John and his barefooted assistant, grated heavily
through the mud and gravel stones, in which it left a deep and
sloughy furrow, and the entrance lay open. John, after searching his
pocket in vain for a trifle to reward his assistant, pursued his way,
while the lad, on his return, cleared the road at a hop step and jump,
plunging through the mud with all the dabbling and amphibious
delight of a duck, and scarce less proud of his agility than of his
'starving a gentleman.' As John slowly trod the miry road which had

once been the approach, he could discover, by the dim light of an autumnal evening, signs of increasing desolation since he had last visited the spot,—signs that penury had been aggravated and sharpened into downright misery. There was not a fence or a hedge round the domain: an uncemented wall of loose stones, whose numerous gaps were filled with furze or thorns, supplied their place. There was not a tree or shrub on the lawn; the lawn itself was turned into pasture-ground, and a few sheep were picking their scanty food amid the pebblestones, thistles, and hard mould, through which a few blades of grass made their rare and squalid appearance.

The house itself stood strongly defined even amid the darkness of the evening sky; for there were neither wings, or offices, or shrubbery, or tree, to shade or support it, and soften its strong harsh outline. John, after a melancholy gaze at the grass-grown steps and boarded windows, 'addressed himself' to knock at the door; but knocker there was none: loose stones, however, there were in plenty; and John was making vigorous application to the door with one of them, till the furious barking of a mastiff, who threatened at every bound to break his chain, and whose yell and growl, accompanied by 'eyes that glow and fangs that grin',* savoured as much of hunger as of rage, made the assailant raise the siege on the door, and betake himself to a well-known passage that led to the kitchen. A light glimmered in the window as he approached: he raised the latch with a doubtful hand; but, when he saw the party within, he advanced with the step of a man no longer doubtful of his welcome.

Round a turf-fire, whose well-replenished fuel gave testimony to the 'master's' indisposition, who would probably as soon have been placed on the fire himself as seen the whole *kish** emptied on it once, were seated the old housekeeper, two or three *followers*, (*i.e.* people who ate, drank, and lounged about in any kitchen that was open in the neighbourhood, on an occasion of grief or joy, all for his honor's sake, and for the great rispict they bore the family), and an old woman, whom John immediately recognized as the doctress of the neighbourhood,—a withered Sybil, who prolonged her squalid existence by practising on the fears, the ignorance, and the sufferings of beings as miserable as herself. Among the better sort, to whom she sometimes had access by the influence of servants, she tried the effects of some simples, her skill in which was sometimes productive of success. Among the lower orders she talked much of the effects of the 'evil eye,' against which she boasted a counter-spell, of unfailing efficacy; and while she spoke, she shook her grizzled locks with such witch-like eagerness, that she never failed to communicate to her half-terrified, half-believing audience, some portion of that enthusiasm which, amid all her consciousness of imposture, she herself probably felt a large share of; still, when the case at last became desperate, when credulity itself lost all patience, and hope and life were departing together, she urged the miserable patient to confess '*there was something about his heart*;' and when his confession was extorted from the weariness of pain and the ignorance of poverty, she nodded and muttered so mysteriously, as to convey to the bystanders, that she had had difficulties to contend with which were invincible by human power. When there was no pretext, from indisposition, for her visiting either 'his honor's' kitchen, or the cottar's hut,*—when the stubborn and persevering convalescence of the whole country threatened her with starvation,—she still had a resource:—if there were no lives to be shortened, there were fortunes to be told;—she worked 'by spells, and by such daubry as is beyond our element.'* No one twined so well* as she the mystic yarn to be dropt into the lime-kiln pit, on the edge of which stood the shivering inquirer into futurity, doubtful whether the answer to her question of 'who holds?' was to be uttered by the voice of demon or lover.

No one knew so well as she to find where the four streams met, in which, on the same portentous season, the chemise was to be immersed, and then displayed before the fire, (in the name of one whom we dare not mention to 'ears polite'*), to be turned by the figure of the destined husband before morning. No one but herself (she said) knew the hand in which the comb was to be held, while the other was employed in conveying the apple to the mouth,—while, during the joint operation, the shadow of the phantom-spouse was to pass across the mirror before which it was performed. No one was more skilful or active in removing every iron implement from the kitchen where these ceremonies were usually performed by the credulous and terrified dupes of her wizardry, lest, instead of the form of a comely youth exhibiting a ring on his white finger, an headless figure should stalk to the rack, (*Anglicè*,* dresser), take down a long spit, or, in default of that, snatch a poker from the fire-side, and mercilessly take measure with its iron length of the sleeper for a coffin. No one, in short, knew better how to torment or terrify her victims into a belief of that power which may and has reduced the strongest minds to the level of the weakest; and under the influence of which the cultivated sceptic, Lord Lyttleton;* yelled and gnashed and writhed in his last hours, like the poor girl who, in the belief of the horrible visitation of the vampire, shrieked aloud, that her grandfather was sucking her vital blood while she slept, and expired under the influence of imaginary horror. Such was the being to whom old Melmoth had committed his life, half from credulity, and (*Hibernicè* speaking) *more than half* from avarice. Among this groupe John advanced,—recognising some,—disliking more,—distrusting all. The old housekeeper received him with cordiality;—he was always her 'white-headed boy,' she said,—(*imprimis,** his hair was as black as jet), and she tried to lift her withered hand to his head with an action between a benediction and a caress, till the difficulty of the attempt forced on her the conviction that that head was fourteen inches higher than her reach since she had last patted it. The men, with the national deference of the Irish to a person of superior rank, all rose at his approach, (their stools chattering on the broken flags), and wished his honor 'a thousand years, and long life to the back of that; and would not his honour take something to keep the grief out of his heart;' and so saying, five or six red and bony hands tendered him glasses of whiskey all at once. All this time the Sybil sat silent in the ample chimney-corner, sending redoubled whiffs out of her pipe. John gently declined the offer of spirits, received the attentions of the old housekeeper cordially, looked askance at the withered crone who occupied the chimney corner, and then glanced at the table, which displayed other cheer than he had been accustomed to see in his 'honor's time.' There was a wooden dish of potatoes, which old Melmoth would have considered enough for a week's subsistence. There was the salted salmon, (a luxury unknown even in London. *Vide* Miss Edgeworth's Tales,* 'The Absentee').

There was the *slink-veal,** flanked with tripe; and, finally, there were lobsters and *fried* turbot enough to justify what the author of the tale asserts, 'suo periculo,'* that when his great grandfather, the Dean of Killala,* hired servants at the deanery, they stipulated that they should not be required to eat turbot or lobster more than twice a-week. There were also bottles of Wicklow ale, long and surreptitiously borrowed from his 'honor's' cellar, and which now made their first appearance on the kitchen hearth, and manifested their impatience of further constraint, by hissing, spitting, and bouncing in the face of the fire that provoked its animosity. But the whiskey (genuine illegitimate potsheen, smelling strongly of weed and smoke, and breathing defiance to excisemen) appeared, the 'veritable Amphitryon' of the feast;* every one praised, and drank as deeply as he praised.

John, as he looked round the circle, and thought of his dying uncle, was forcibly reminded of the scene at Don Quixote's departure, where, in spite of the grief caused by the dissolution of the worthy knight, we are informed that 'nevertheless the niece eat her victuals, the housekeeper drank to the repose of his soul, and even Sancho cherished his little carcase.'* After returning, 'as he might,' the courtesies of the party, John asked how his uncle was. 'As bad as he can be;'—'Much better, and many thanks to your honor,' was uttered in such rapid and discordant unison by the party, that John turned from one to the other, not knowing which or what to believe. 'They say his honor has had a fright,' said a fellow, upwards of six feet high, approaching by way of whispering, and then bellowing the sound six inches above John's head. 'But then his honor has had *a cool* since,' said a man who was quietly swallowing the spirits that John had refused. At these words the Sybil who sat in the chimney corner slowly drew her pipe from her mouth, and turned towards the party: The oracular movements of a Pythoness on her tripod* never excited more awe, or impressed for the moment a deeper silence. 'It's not *here*,' said she, pressing her withered finger on her wrinkled forehead, 'nor *here*,—nor *here*;' and she extended her hand to the foreheads of those who were near her, who all bowed as if they were receiving a benediction, but had immediate recourse to the spirits afterwards, as if to ensure its effects.—'It's all *here*—it's all *about the heart*;' and as she spoke she spread and pressed her fingers on her hollow bosom with a force of action that thrilled her hearers.—'It's all *here*,' she added, repeating the action, (probably excited by the effect she had produced), and then sunk on her seat, resumed her pipe, and spoke no more. At this moment of involuntary awe on the part of John, and of terrified silence on that of the rest, an unusual sound was heard in the house, and the whole company started as if a musket had been discharged among them:—it was the unwonted sound of old Melmoth's bell. His domestics were so few, and so constantly near him, that the sound of his bell startled them as much as if he had been ringing the knell for his own interment. 'He used always to *rap down* for me,' said the old housekeeper, hurrying out of the kitchen; 'he said pulling the bells wore out the ropes.'

The sound of the bell produced its full effect. The housekeeper rushed into the room, followed by a number of women, (the Irish præficæ*); all ready to prescribe for the dying or weep for the dead,— all clapping their hard hands, or wiping their dry eyes. These hags all surrounded the bed; and to witness their loud, wild, and desperate grief, their cries of 'Oh! he's going, his honor's going, his honor's going,' one would have imagined their lives were bound up in his, like those of the wives in the story of Sinbad the Sailor* who were to be interred alive with their deceased husbands.

Four of them wrung their hands and howled round the bed, while one, with all the adroitness of a Mrs Quickly, felt his honor's feet, and 'upward and upward,' and 'all was cold as any stone.'*

Old Melmoth withdrew his feet from the grasp of the hag,— counted with his keen eye (keen amid the approaching dimness of death) the number assembled round his bed,—raised himself on his sharp elbow, and pushing away the housekeeper, (who attempted to settle his nightcap, that had been shoved on one side in the struggle, and gave his haggard, dying face, a kind of grotesque fierceness), bellowed out in tones that made the company start,—'What the devil brought ye all here?' The question scattered the whole party for a moment; but rallying instantly, they communed among themselves in whispers, and frequently using the sign of the cross, muttered 'The devil,—Christ save us, the devil in his mouth the first word he spoke.' 'Aye,' roared the invalid, 'and the devil in my eye the first sight I see.' 'Where,—where?' cried the terrified housekeeper, cling-ing close to the invalid in her terror, and half-hiding herself in the blanket, which she snatched without mercy from his struggling and exposed limbs. 'There, there,' he repeated, (during the battle of the blanket), pointing to the huddled and terrified women, who stood aghast at hearing themselves arointed as the very demons they came to banish. 'Oh! Lord keep your honor's head,' said the housekeeper in a more soothing tone, when her fright was over; 'and sure your honor knows them all, is'n't *her* name,—and *her* name,—and *her* name,'—and she pointed respectively to each of them, adding their names, which we shall spare the English reader the torture of reciting, (as a proof of our lenity, adding the last only, Cotchleen

O'Mulligan), 'Ye lie, ye b——h,' growled old Melmoth; 'their name
is Legion,* for they are many,—turn them all out of the room,—
turn them all out of doors,—if they howl at my death, they shall
howl in earnest,—not for my death, for they would see me dead and
damned too with dry eyes, but for want of the whiskey that they
would have stolen if they could have got at it,' (and here old Melmoth grasped a key which lay under his pillow, and shook it in vain
triumph at the old housekeeper, who had long possessed the means
of getting at the spirits unknown to his 'honor'), 'and for want of the
victuals you have pampered them with.' '*Pampered*, oh Ch—st!'
ejaculated the housekeeper. 'Aye, and what are there so many candles
for, all *fours*, and the same below I warrant. Ah! you—you—
worthless, wasteful old devil.' 'Indeed, your honor, they are all
sixes'.* Sixes,—and what the devil are you burning sixes for, d'ye
think it's *the wake* already? Ha?' 'Oh! not yet, your honor, not yet,'
chorussed the beldams; 'but in God's good time, your honor knows,'
in a tone that spoke ill suppressed impatience for the event. 'Oh! that
your honor would think of making your soul.' 'That's the first sensible word you have said,' said the dying man, 'fetch me the prayer-
book,—you'll find it there under that old boot-jack,—blow off the
cobwebs;—it has not been opened this many a year.' It was handed to
him by the old governante, on whom he turned a reproaching eye.
'What made you burn sixes in the kitchen, you extravagant jade?
How many years have you lived in this house?' 'I don't know, your
honor.' 'Did you ever see any extravagance or waste in it?' 'Oh never,
never, your honor.' 'Was any thing but a farthing candle ever burned
in the kitchen?' 'Never, never, your honor.' 'Were not you kept as
tight as hand and head and heart could keep you, were you not?
answer me that.' 'Oh yes, sure, your honor; every *sowl* about us
knows that,—every one does your honor justice, that you kept the
closest house and closest hand in the country,—your honor was
always a good warrant for it.' 'And how dare you unlock my hold
before death has unlocked it,' said the dying miser, shaking his
meagre hand at her. 'I smelt meat in the house,—I heard voices in
the house,—I heard the key turn in the door over and over. Oh that I
was up,' he added, rolling in impatient agony in his bed, 'Oh that I
was up, to see the waste and ruin that is going on. But it would kill
me,' he continued, sinking back on the bolster, for he never allowed
himself a pillow; 'it would kill me,—the very thought of it is killing

me now.' The women, discomfited and defeated, after sundry winks
and whispers, were huddling out of the room, till recalled by the
sharp eager tones of old Melmoth.—'Where are ye trooping to now?
back to the kitchen to gormandize and guzzle? Won't one of ye stay
and listen while there's a prayer read for me? Ye may want it one day
for yourselves, ye hags.' Awed by this expostulation and menace, the
train silently returned, and placed themselves round the bed, while
the housekeeper, though a Catholic, asked if his honor would not
have a clergyman to give him *the rights*, (rites) of his church. The
eyes of the dying man sparkled with vexation at the proposal. 'What
for,—just to have him expect a scarf and hat-band at the funeral. Read
the prayers yourself, you old ——; that will save something.' The
housekeeper made the attempt, but soon declined it, alleging, as her
reason, that her eyes had been watery ever since his honor took ill.
'That's because you had always a drop in them,' said the invalid,
with a spiteful sneer, which the contraction of approaching death
stiffened into a hideous grin.—'Here,—is not there one of you that's
gnashing and howling there, that can get up a prayer to keep me
from it?' So abjured, one of the women offered her services; and of
her it might truly be said, as of the 'most desartless man of the
watch' in Dogberry's time, that 'her reading and writing came by
nature;'* for she never had been at school, and had never before seen
or opened a Protestant prayer book in her life; nevertheless, on she
went, and with more emphasis than good discretion, read nearly
through the service for the 'churching of women;'* which in our
prayer-books following that of the burial of the dead, she perhaps
imagined was someway connected with the state of the invalid.

   She read with great solemnity,—it was a pity that two interrup-
tions occurred during the performance, one from old Melmoth, who,
shortly after the commencement of the prayers, turned towards the
old housekeeper, and said, in a tone scandalously audible, 'Go down
and draw the niggers* of the kitchen fire closer, and lock the door, and
let me *hear it locked*. I can't mind any thing till that's done.' The
other was from John Melmoth gliding into the room, hearing the
inappropriate words uttered by the ignorant woman, taking quietly
as he knelt beside her the prayer-book from her hands, and reading
in a suppressed voice part of that solemn service which, by the forms
of the Church of England, is intended for the consolation of the
departing.

'That is John's voice,' said the dying man; and the little kindness he had ever shewed this unfortunate lad rushed on his hard heart at this moment, and touched it. He saw himself, too, surrounded by heartless and rapacious menials; and slight as must have been his dependence on a relative whom he had always treated as a stranger, he felt at this hour he was no stranger, and grasped at his support like a straw amid his wreck. 'John, my good boy, you are there.—I kept you far from me when living, and now you are nearest me when dying.—John, *read on*.' John, affected deeply by the situation in which he beheld this *poor man*, amid all his wealth, as well as by the solemn request to impart consolation to his dying moments, read on;—but in a short time his voice became indistinct, from the horror with which he listened to the increasing hiccup of the patient, which, however, he struggled with from time to time, to ask the housekeeper if *the niggers were closed*. John, who was a lad of feeling, rose from his knees in some degree of agitation. 'What, are you leaving me like the rest?' said old Melmoth, trying to raise himself in the bed. 'No, Sir,' said John; 'but,' observing the altered looks of the dying man, 'I think you want some refreshment, some support, Sir.' 'Aye, I do, I do, but whom can I trust to get it for me. *They*, (and his haggard eye wandered round the groupe), *they* would poison me.' 'Trust me, Sir,' said John; 'I will go to the apothecary's, or whoever you may employ.' The old man grasped his hand, drew him close to his bed, cast a threatening yet fearful eye round the party, and then whispered in a voice of agonized constraint, 'I want a glass of wine, it would keep me alive for some hours, but there is not one I can trust to get it for me,—*they'd steal a bottle, and ruin me*.' John was greatly shocked. 'Sir, for God's sake, let *me* get a glass of wine for you.' 'Do you know where?' said the old man, with an expression in his face John could not understand. 'No, Sir; you know I have been rather a stranger here, Sir.' 'Take this key,' said old Melmoth, after a violent spasm; 'take this key, there is wine in that closet,—*Madeira*. I always told them there was nothing there, but they did not believe me, or I should not have been robbed as I have been. At one time I said it was whiskey, and then I fared worse than ever, for they drank twice as much of it.'

John took the key from his uncle's hand; the dying man pressed it as he did so, and John, interpreting this as a mark of kindness, returned the pressure. He was undeceived by the whisper that followed,—'John, my lad, don't drink any of that wine while you are there.' 'Good God!' said John, indignantly throwing the key on the bed; then, recollecting that the miserable being before him was no object of resentment, he gave the promise required, and entered the closet, which no foot but that of old Melmoth had entered for nearly sixty years. He had some difficulty in finding out the wine, and indeed staid long enough to justify his uncle's suspicions,—but his mind was agitated, and his hand unsteady. He could not but remark his uncle's extraordinary look, that had the ghastliness of fear super-added to that of death, as he gave him permission to enter his closet. He could not but see the looks of horror which the women exchanged as he approached it. And, finally, when he was in it, his memory was malicious enough to suggest some faint traces of a story, too horrible for imagination, connected with it. He remembered in one moment most distinctly, that no one but his uncle had ever been known to enter it for many years.

Before he quitted it, he held up the dim light, and looked around him with a mixture of terror and curiosity. There was a great deal of decayed and useless lumber, such as might be supposed to be heaped up to rot in a miser's closet; but John's eyes were in a moment, and as if by magic, rivetted on a portrait that hung on the wall, and appeared, even to his untaught eye, far superior to the tribe of family pictures that are left to moulder on the walls of a family mansion. It represented a man of middle age. There was nothing remarkable in the costume, or in the countenance, but *the eyes*, John felt, were such as one feels they wish they had never seen, and feels they can never forget. Had he been acquainted with the poetry of Southey, he might have often exclaimed in his after-life,

> 'Only the eyes had life,
> They gleamed with demon light.'—THALABA.*

From an impulse equally resistless and painful, he approached the portrait, held the candle towards it, and could distinguish the words on the border of the painting,—Jno. Melmoth, anno 1646. John was neither timid by nature, or nervous by constitution, or superstitious from habit, yet he continued to gaze in stupid horror on this singular picture, till, aroused by his uncle's cough, he hurried into his room. The old man swallowed the wine. He appeared a little revived; it was long since he had tasted such a cordial,—his heart appeared to expand to a momentary confidence. 'John, what did you see in that room?' 'Nothing, Sir.' 'That's a lie; every one wants to cheat or to rob me.' 'Sir, I don't want to do either.' 'Well, what did you see that you—you took notice of?' 'Only a picture, Sir.' 'A picture, Sir!—the original is still alive.' John, though under the impression of his recent feelings, could not but look incredulous. 'John,' whispered his uncle;—'John, they say I am dying of this and that; and one says it is for want of nourishment, and one says it is for want of medicine,— but, John,' and his face looked hideously ghastly, 'I am dying of a fright. That man,' and he extended his meagre arm toward the closet, as if he was pointing to a living being; 'that man, I have good reason to know, is alive still.' 'How is that possible, Sir?' said John involuntarily, 'the date on the picture is 1646.' 'You have seen it,— you have noticed it,' said his uncle. 'Well,'—he rocked and nodded on his bolster for a moment, then, grasping John's hand with an unutterable look, he exclaimed, 'You will see him again, he is alive.' Then, sinking back on his bolster, he fell into a kind of sleep or stupor, his eyes still open, and fixed on John.

The house was now perfectly silent, and John had time and space for reflection. More thoughts came crowding on him than he wished to welcome, but they would not be repulsed. He thought of his uncle's habits and character, turned the matter over and over again in his mind, and he said to himself, 'The last man on earth to be superstitious. He never thought of any thing but the price of stocks, and the rate of exchange, and my college expences, that hung heavier at his heart than all; and such a man to die of a fright,—a ridiculous fright, that a man living 150 years ago is alive still, and yet—he is dying.' John paused, for facts will confute the most stubborn logician. 'With all his hardness of mind, and of heart, he is dying of a fright. I heard it in the kitchen, I have heard it from himself,—he could not be deceived. If I had ever heard he was nervous, or fanciful, or superstitious, but a character so contrary to all these impressions;—a man that, as poor Butler* says, in his Remains, of the Antiquarian, would have "sold Christ over again for the numerical piece of silver which Judas got for him,"—such a man to die of fear! Yet he *is* dying,' said John, glancing his fearful eye on the contracted nostril, the glazed eye, the dropping jaw, the whole horrible apparatus of the *facies Hippocratica** displayed, and soon to cease its display.

Old Melmoth at this moment seemed to be in a deep stupor; his eyes lost that little expression they had before, and his hands, that had convulsively been catching at the blankets, let go their short and quivering grasp, and lay extended on the bed like the claws of some bird that had died of hunger,—so meagre, so yellow, so spread. John, unaccustomed to the sight of death, believed this to be only a sign that he was going to sleep; and, urged by an impulse for which he did not attempt to account to himself, caught up the miserable light, and once more ventured into the forbidden room,—the *blue chamber* of the dwelling.* The motion roused the dying man;—he sat bolt upright in his bed. This John could not see, for he was now in the closet; but he heard the groan, or rather the choaked and guggling rattle of the throat, that announces the horrible conflict between muscular and mental convulsion. He started, turned away; but, as he turned away, he thought he saw the eyes of the portrait, on which his own was fixed, *move*, and hurried back to his uncle's bedside.

Old Melmoth died in the course of that night, and died as he had lived, in a kind of avaricious delirium. John could not have imagined a scene so horrible as his last hours presented. He cursed and blasphemed about three half-pence, missing, as he said, some weeks before, in an account of change with his groom, about hay to a starving horse that he kept. Then he grasped John's hand, and asked him to give him the sacrament. 'If I send to the clergyman, he will charge me something for it, which I cannot pay,—I cannot. They say I am rich,—look at this blanket;—but I would not mind that, if I could save my soul.' And, raving, he added, 'Indeed, Doctor, I am a very poor man. I never troubled a clergyman before, and all I want is, that you will grant me two trifling requests, very little matters in your way,—save my soul, and (whispering) make interest to get me a parish coffin,—I have not enough left to bury me. I always told every one I was poor, but the more I told them so, the less they believed me.'

John, greatly shocked, retired from the bed-side, and sat down in a distant corner of the room. The women were again in the room, which was very dark. Melmoth was silent from exhaustion, and there was a death-like pause for some time. At this moment John saw the door open, and a figure appear at it, who looked round the room, and then quietly and deliberately retired, but not before John had discovered in his face the living original of the portrait. His first impulse was to utter an exclamation of terror, but his breath felt stopped. He was then rising to pursue the figure, but a moment's reflection checked him. What could be more absurd, than to be alarmed or amazed at a resemblance between a living man and the portrait of a dead one! The likeness was doubtless strong enough to strike him even in that darkened room, but it was doubtless only a likeness; and though it might be imposing enough to terrify an old man of gloomy and retired habits, and with a broken constitution, John resolved it should not produce the same effect on him.

But while he was applauding himself for this resolution, the door opened, and the figure appeared at it, beckoning and nodding to him, with a familiarity somewhat terrifying. John now started up, determined to pursue it; but the pursuit was stopped by the weak but shrill cries of his uncle, who was struggling at once with the agonies of death and his housekeeper. The poor woman, anxious for her master's reputation and her own, was trying to put on him a clean shirt and nightcap, and Melmoth, who had just sensation enough to perceive they were taking something from him, continued exclaiming feebly, 'They are robbing me,—robbing me in my last moments,—robbing a dying man. John, won't you assist me,—I shall die a beggar; they are taking my last shirt,—I shall die a beggar.'——And the miser died.

JOSEPH SHERIDAN LE FANU
(1814–1873)

from *The House by the Church-yard* (1863)

XXXIV

IN WHICH A CERTAIN TROUBLED SPIRIT WALKS

Mr Dangerfield was at the Club that night, and was rather in spirits than otherwise, except, indeed, when poor Charles Nutter was talked of. Then he looked grave, and shrugged, and shook his head, and said—

'A bad business, sir; and where's his poor wife?'

'Spending the night with us, poor soul,' said Major O'Neill, mildly, 'and hasn't an idaya, poor thing; and indeed, I hope, she mayn't hear it.'

'Pooh! sir, she must hear it; but you know she might have heard worse sir, eh?' rejoined Dangerfield.

'True for you, sir,' said the Major, suspending the filling of his pipe to direct a quiet glance of significance at Dangerfield, and then closing his eyes with a nod.

And just at this point in came Spaight.

'Well, Spaight!'

'Well, sir.'

'You saw the body, eh?' and a dozen other interrogatories followed, as, cold and wet with melting snow, dishevelled, and storm-beaten—for it was a plaguey rough night—the young fellow, with a general greeting to the company, made his way to the fire.

' 'Tis a tremendious night, gentlemen, so by your leave I'll stir the fire—and, yes, I seen him, poor Nutter—and, paugh, an ugly sight he is, I can tell you; here, Larry, bring me a rummer-glass* of punch—his right ear's gone, and a'most all his right hand—and screeching hot, do you mind—an', phiew—altogether 'tis sickening—them fishes, you know—I'm a'most sorry I went in—you remember Dogherty's whiskey shop in Ringsend*—he lies in the back parlour, and wondherful little changed in appearance.'

And so Mr Spaight with a little round table at his elbow, and his heels over the fender, sipped his steaming punch, and thawed inwardly and outwardly, as he answered their questions and mixed in their speculations.

Up at the Mills, which had heard the awful news, first from the Widow Macan, and afterwards from Pat Moran, the maids sat over their tea in the kitchen in high excitement and thrilling chat—'The poor master;' 'oh, the poor man;' 'oh, la, what's that,' with a start and a peep over the shoulders; 'and oh, dear, and how in the world will the poor little misthress ever live over the news,' and so forth, made a principal part of their talk. There was a good accompaniment of wind outside, and a soft pelting of snow on the window panes, 'and oh, my dear life, but wasn't it dark!'

Up went Moggy, with her thick-wick'd kitchen candle, to seek repose; and Betty, resolving not to be long behind, waited only 'to wash up her plates' and slack down the fire,* having made up her mind, for she grew more nervous in solitude, to share Moggy's bed for that night.

Moggy had not been twenty minutes gone, and her task was nearly

ended, when—'Oh, blessed saints!' murmurs Betty, with staring
eyes, and dropping the sweeping-brush on the flags,* she heard, or
thought she heard, her master's step, which was peculiar, crossing
the floor overhead.

She listened, herself as pale as a corpse, and nearly as breathless;
but there was nothing now but the muffled gusts of the storm, and
the close soft beat of the snow, so she listened and listened, but
nothing came of it.

' 'Tis only the vapours,'* said Betty, drawing a long breath, and
doing her best to be cheerful; and so she finished her labours, stopping every now and then to listen, and humming tunes very loud, in
fits and starts. Then it came to her turn to take her candle and go up
stairs; she was a good half hour later than Moggy—all was quiet
within the house—only the sound of the storm—the creak and rattle
of its strain, and the hurly-burly of the gusts over the roof and
chimneys.

Over her shoulder she peered jealously this way and that, as with
flaring candle she climbed the stairs. How black the window looked
on the lobby, with its white patterns of snow flakes in perpetual
succession sliding down the panes. Who could tell what horrid face
might be looking in close to her as she passed, secure in the darkness
and that drifting white lace veil of snow? So nimbly and lightly up
the stairs climbed Betty, the cook.

If listeners seldom hear good of themselves, it is also true that
peepers sometimes see more than they like; and Betty, the cook, as
she reached the landing, glancing askance with ominous curiosity,
beheld a spectacle, the sight of which nearly bereft her of her
senses.

Crouching in the deep doorway on the right of the lobby, the
cook, I say, saw something—a figure—or a deep shadow—only a
deep shadow—or maybe a dog. She lifted the candle—she peeped
under the candlestick: 'twas no shadow, as I live, 'twas a well-defined
figure!

He was draped in black, cowering down low, with the face turned
up. It was Charles Nutter's face, fixed and stealthy. It was only while
the fascination lasted—while you might count one, two, three, deliberately—that the horrid gaze met mutually. But there was no mistake there. She saw the stern dark picture as plainly as ever she did.
The light glimmered on his white eyeballs.

Starting up, he struck at the candle with his hat. She uttered a loud scream, and flinging stick and all at the figure, with a great clang against the door behind, all was swallowed in instantaneous darkness; she whirled into the opposite bed-room she knew not how, and locked the door within, and plunged head-foremost under the bed-clothes, half mad with terror.

The squall was heard of course. Moggy heard it, but she heeded not; for Betty was known to scream at mice, and even moths. And as her door was heard to slam, as was usual in panics of the sort, and as she returned no answer, Moggy was quite sure there was nothing in it.

But Moggy's turn was to come. When spirits 'walk,' I've heard they make the most of their time, and sometimes pay a little round of visits on the same evening.

This is certain; Moggy was by no means so great a fool as Betty in respect of Hobgoblins, witches, banshees, pookas, and the world of spirits in general. She eat heartily, and slept soundly, and as yet had never seen the devil. Therefore, such terrors as she that night experienced were new to her, and I can't reasonably doubt the truth of her narrative. Awaking suddenly in the night, she saw a light in the room, and heard a quiet rustling going on in the corner, where the old white-painted press* showed its front from the wall. So Moggy popped her head through her thin curtains at the side, and—blessed hour!—there she saw the shape of a man looking into the press, the doors being wide open, and the appearance of a key in the lock, though she well knew the mistress had taken it away with her.

The shape was very like her master. The saints between us and harm! The glow was reflected back from the interior of the press, and showed the front part of the figure in profile with a sharp line of light. She said he had some sort of thick slippers over his boots, a dark coat, with the cape buttoned, and a hat flapping over his face; coat and hat, and all, sprinkled over with snow.

As if he heard the rustle of the curtain, he turned toward the bed, and with an awful ejaculation she cried, ' 'Tis you, sir!'

'Don't stir, and you'll meet no harm,' he said, and over he posts to the bedside, and he laid his cold hand on her wrist, and told her again to be quiet, and for her life to tell no one what she had seen, and with that she supposed she swooned away; for the next thing she remembered was listening in mortal fear, the room being all dark, and she heard a sound at the press again, and then steps crossing the

floor, and she gave herself up for lost; but he did not come to the
bedside any more, and the tread passed out at the door, and so, as she
thought went down stairs.

In the morning the press was locked and the door shut, and the
hall-door and back-door locked, and the keys on the hall table, where
they had left them the night before.

You may be sure these two ladies were thankful to behold the gray
light, and hear the cheerful sounds of returning day; and it would be
no easy matter to describe which of the two looked most pallid,
scared, and jaded that morning, as they drank a hysterical dish of tea
together in the kitchen, close up to the window, and with the door
shut, discoursing, and crying, and praying over their tea-pot in
miserable rivalry.

EMILY LAWLESS
(1845–1913)

from *Hurrish* (1886)

I

AN IRON LAND

Wilder regions there are few to be found, even in the wildest west of
Ireland, than that portion of north Clare known to its inhabitants as
'The Burren.' Seen from the Atlantic, which washes its western
base, it presents to the eye a succession of low hills, singularly grey in
tone,—deepening often, towards evening, into violet or dull reddish
plum colour—sometimes, after sunset, to a pale ghostly iridescence.
They are quite low these hills—not above a thousand feet at their
highest point, and for the most part considerably less. Hills of this
height, whatever their other merits, seldom attain to the distinction
of being spoken of as 'grand.' Their character is essentially 'mutton-
suggesting.' You picture them dotted over with flocks of sheep,
which nibble the short sweet grass, and frisk in their idle youth over
the little declivities. If here and there like that most unaccountable of
little animals, they, too, sprang into the waves and were lost. Little
change has taken place in the aspect of the region since those

unknown races passed away. Their great stone-duns are even still in many places the largest buildings to be seen,—the little oratories and churches which succeeded them having become in their turn, with hardly an exception, ruins like themselves, their very sites forgotten, melted into the surrounding stoniness. The Burren is not—in all probability never will be—a tourist-haunt, but for the few who know it, it has a place apart, a distinct personality—strange, remote, indescribable. Everything that the eye rests on tells us that we are on one of the last standpoints of an old world, worn out with its own profusion, and reduced here to the barest elements. Mother Earth, once young, buxom, frolicsome, is here a wrinkled woman, sitting alone in the evening of her days, and looking with melancholy eyes at the sunset.

The valley of Gortnacoppin is a sort of embodiment of the Burren. Standing in it you might fairly believe yourself in the heart of some alpine region, high above the haunts of men, where only the eagle or the marmot make their homes. All the suggestions are alpine, some of them almost arctic. The white stream cutting its way through the heaped-up drift; the water churning and frothing hither and thither in its impatience, and leaving a white deposit upon all the reeds and stones; the pallid greyish-green vegetation, with here and there a bit of dazzling red or orange; the chips and flakes of rock which lie strewn about; the larger stones and boulders toppled down from the cliff above, and lying heaped one over the other in the bed of the stream,—many of the latter, you may perceive, have not long fallen, for their edges are still unweathered. Here and there over the top and sides of the drift a little thin grass has spread itself, through which trenches have been torn, showing the earth and stones below. Truly a grim scene!—suggestive of nothing so much as one of those ugly little early German prints, where every stick and stone seems to be grimacing with unpleasant intention. Only look hard enough at any of the rocks, and you will assuredly see a gnome appear!

Towards the bottom, where it approaches the sea, this valley, however, expands, and becomes an irregular lake-like circle, mapped out into small fields, separated from one another by tottering lace-work walls. After following the downward course of the upper valley, you would have been surprised at the sudden fertility of this little space, the greenness of the grass, the promising look of the small crops of bottle-green potatoes. If something of a geologist, however, you would have suspected that the mass of detritus, borne down from the hills, and spread abroad here at their feet, had something to say to that satisfactory result.

Between five and six years ago the greater part of this little fertile oasis was rented by Horatio, or, as he was less classically called by his neighbours, Hurrish O'Brien, one of the countless O'Briens of Clare. His cabin—a rather large one, built of stone and thatched— stood upon the summit of a little ridge, conspicuous, like a small fly upon a large window-pane, in the absence of any other building; rendered still more so by a good-sized ash-tree, which stood upon the ridge beside it—a noticeable distinction in so leafless a district.

It was a warm morning late in May, and even the stony Burren had begun to feel a touch of spring, its ferns and little delicate-petalled blossoms to reach out inquiring heads over their stony prisons. Hurrish had just returned to breakfast. He had been down early to the sea, to set some fishing-lines—for, like most of the inhabitants of that amphibious part of the island, he was part farmer and part fisherman,—perhaps it would be more accurate in his case to say three-parts farmer to one-part fisherman, the latter vocation being, in fact, rather a matter of 'intertainmint' than profit.

The door of the cabin was open, and the window unshuttered (the latter for an excellent reason, there were no shutters), yet the cabin itself was lit by its fire. The light, spreading from the blazing turf, broke in red flakes upon the bare rafters of the roof, upon the roughly plastered walls, upon a quantity of highly coloured pious prints upon the walls, upon others of a less pious character pinned beside them, upon a rough white terrier, two solemn black pigs, and three children scattered over the mud floor, upon an *omnium gatherum** of tags and rags, stray fragments of furniture, tools, cloth-ing, straw, bedding, sacks, heaps of potatoes,—an indescribable and incalculable collection of long accumulated rubbish, huddled, in more or less picturesque confusion, one on top of another—the sort of picturesqueness which fastidious people prefer in its painted rather than in its actual form!

Hurrish sat upon a low 'creepy' stool,* with a huge mug of stir-about (known to the ignorant as porridge) upon his knees, which he was shovelling down his throat by the aid of a large iron spoon. A broad-shouldered, loose-limbed, genial-faced giant* was Hurrish, such as these western Irish counties occasionally breed. Irish in every feature, look, and gesture, there was yet a smack of something foreign about him, to be accounted for possibly by that oft-quoted admixture of Spanish blood, the result of bygone centuries of more or less continuous intercourse. His hair was black as a cormorant's wing, and curly under the old felt hat, half of whose brim had vanished in some distant engagement; his beard was curly too, and black, yet his eyes were grey, his skin evidently originally fair, and his expression open, good-humoured, irresolute, with a spice of native fun and jollity about it. Despite the jollity which was its prevailing expression, he did not seem to be altogether a contented giant. There were lines of perplexity and disturbance here and there discernible. Yet Hurrish O'Brien was a well-to-do man. He had a good stock of cows and calves; he held his farm on a moderate rental; his wife had brought him fifty gold sovereigns tied up in a pocket-handkerchief; his children were strong and healthy; and he was regarded by his neighbours generally as one of the 'warmest' men between Blackhead and the mouth of the Shannon.

Opposite, upon another low creepy-stool, sat his mother, Bridget O'Brien, engaged in stirring a steaming black pot—an employment which would have given a sensitive looker-on a delightful thrill, so appropriate was the operation to the operator. In Bridget O'Brien the Southern type was also strongly visible. Women like her—as gaunt, as wrinkled, as black-browed, as witch-like—may be seen seated upon thousands of doorsteps all over the Spanish peninsula. It is not a very comfortable type, one would think, for everyday domestic use; too suggestive of an elderly bird of prey—a vulture, old, yet with claws ever upon the watch to tear, and a beak which yearns to plunge itself into the still palpitating flesh. Her eyes were black—a wicked black—and bright still amid the multiplicity of wrinkles which surrounded them, as cracks a half-dried pool. Her hair, too, was dark, and hung in heavy hanks about her forehead, reaching nearly to the grizzled eyebrows, projecting like unclipped eaves over her eyes.

Bridget O'Brien was an ardent patriot! The latest tide of revolutionary sentiment had begun to spread its waves even to the heart of remotest Burren, and she was the chief recipient of it in the O'Brien household. It was she who knew when, where, how, and why the latest agrarian outrage had been committed, and was the first to raise the war-cry of triumph and exultation upon these joyful occasions. Not that the rest of the family were backward in their degree. Hurrish had called himself a Fenian almost ever since he could remember, and nothing but his distance from the seat of war had prevented him from striking a blow when that ill-starred apology for a rebellion* came to its final and melancholy close. Animosity against England was a creed with him, a sort of shibboleth— something like the middle-class English hatred of France some three-quarters of a century ago. His belief in its wickedness and atrocities was a belief that knew absolutely no misgivings. Had he been assured that, like Herod of old, an order had just been issued by its Government for all infants under two years of age to be slaughtered, I doubt if it would have struck him as at all incredible, or even out of character with what he supposed to be the normal nature of its proceedings.

Hurrish's patriotic potations, however, were mild and diluted compared with those quaffed to the very dregs by his mother. He was not a man easily roused to bitterness, and would hardly, I think, have cared to kill even an Englishman, unless some very good purpose could have been served by so doing. When Bridget brought back tales of vengeance, executed upon the latest enemies of their country he listened, but rarely found himself warmed to the point of emulation; the details of those gallant achievements being apt, in fact, to have rather a chilling and discouraging effect upon his imagination. What he enjoyed was what may be called the frivolous side of patriotism,—the mere noise, the crowd, the excitement, the waving flags, the new tin-pikes, the thrilling, delightful, inexhaustible oratory of his chosen leaders. All this was meat, drink, and clothing to him, and he would have walked thirty miles any day of his life to enjoy it. On the other hand, the detailed projects of vengeance were apt to pass over his head. He admitted their necessity, but blinked the details. When Ned Clancy, for instance, with his wife and four small children, were turned out of their cabin in the dead of a January night, because Clancy had taken Lynch's farm, contrary to well-known if unwritten local laws, Hurrish had been disposed to feel sorry for the more juvenile of the criminals. Not so his mother. 'What ailed he to be pityin' of thim? wasn't it known they wouldn't have been sarved so if they hadn't been desarvin'?' that thoroughgoing woman asked fiercely. Hideous prints, of still more hideous significance, disfigured a considerable portion of the cabin walls.

There was one cheerful design in particular, representing the roasting alive of men in swallow-tail coats, tall hats, and white neck-cloths, presumably landlords and their myrmidons.* The intention was allegorical, probably, but to Bridget it was literal enough, and it was upon such pabulum* she feasted her eyes with all the relish of a petticoated vampire.

4. POETRY

ANTOINE RAFTERY
(c. 1784–1835)

I Am Raftery (c. 1830)

I am Raftery the poet,
    Full of hope and love,
With eyes that have no light,
    With gentleness that has no misery.

Going west upon my pilgrimage
    Guided by the light of my heart,
Feeble and tired,
    To the end of my road.

Behold me now,
    And my face to a wall,
A-playing music
    Unto empty pockets.

CHARLOTTE BROOKE
(c. 1740–1793)

Elegy on the Death of Carolan (1789)

I came, with friendship's face, to glad my heart,
But sad, and sorrowful my steps depart!
In my friend's stead—a spot of earth was shown,
And on his grave my woe-struck eyes were thrown!
No more to their distracted sight remain'd,
But the cold clay that all they lov'd contain'd:

And there his last and narrow bed was made,
And the drear tomb-stone for its covering laid!

Alas!—for this my aged heart is wrung!
Grief chokes my voice, and trembles on my tongue.
Lonely and desolate, I mourn the dead,
The friend with whom my every comfort fled!
There is no anguish can with this compare!
No pains, diseases, suffering, or despair,
Like that I feel, while such a loss I mourn,
My heart's companion from its fondness torn!
Oh insupportable, distracting grief!
Woe, that through life, can never hope relief!
Sweet-singing harp!—thy melody is o'er!
Sweet friendship's voice!—I hear thy sound no more!
My bliss,—my wealth of poetry is fled.
And every joy, with him I lov'd, is dead!
Alas! what wonder, (while my heart drops blood
Upon the woes that drain its vital flood,)
If maddening grief no longer can be borne,
And frenzy fill the breast, with anguish torn!

THOMAS MOORE
(1779–1852)

*Oh! breathe not his name** (1807)

Oh! breathe not his name, let it sleep in the shade,
Where cold and unhonour'd his relics are laid:
Sad, silent, and dark, be the tears that we shed,
As the night-dew that falls on the grass o'er his head.

But the night-dew that falls, though in silence it weeps,
Shall brighten with verdure the grave where he sleeps;
And the tear that we shed, though in secret it rolls,
Shall long keep his memory green in our souls.

She is far from the land* (1811)

She is far from the land where her young hero sleeps,
   And lovers are round her, sighing:
But coldly she turns from their gaze, and weeps,
   For her heart in his grave is lying.

She sings the wild song of her dear native plains,
   Every note which he lov'd awaking;—
Ah! little they think who delight in her strains,
   How the heart of the Minstrel is breaking.

He had liv'd for his love, for his country he died,
   They were all that to life had entwin'd him;
Nor soon shall the tears of his country be dried,
   Nor long will his love stay behind him.

Oh! make her a grave where the sunbeams rest,
   When they promise a glorious morrow;
They'll shine o'er her sleep, like a smile from the West,
   From her own lov'd island of sorrow.

Dear Harp of my Country (1815)

Dear Harp of my Country! in darkness I found thee,
   The cold chain of silence had hung o'er thee long,
When proudly, my own Island Harp, I unbound thee,
   And gave all thy chords to light, freedom, and song!

The warm lay of love and the light note of gladness
   Have waken'd thy fondest, thy liveliest thrill;
But, so oft hast thou echo'd the deep sigh of sadness,
   That ev'n in thy mirth it will steal from thee still.

Dear Harp of my Country! farewell to thy numbers,
   This sweet wreath of song is the last we shall twine!
Go, sleep with the sunshine of Fame on thy slumbers,
   Till touch'd by some hand less unworthy than mine;

If the pulse of the patriot, soldier, or lover,
   Have throbb'd at our lay, 'tis thy glory alone;
I was *but* as the wind, passing heedlessly over,
   And all the wild sweetness I wak'd was thy own.

The harp that once through Tara's halls* (1807)

The harp that once through Tara's halls
   The soul of music shed,
Now hangs as mute on Tara's walls
   As if that soul were fled.
So sleeps the pride of former days,
   So glory's thrill is o'er,
And hearts, that once beat high for praise,
   Now feel that pulse no more.

No more to chiefs and ladies bright
   The harp of Tara swells;
The chord alone, that breaks at night,
   Its tale of ruin tells.
Thus freedom now so seldom wakes,
   The only throb she gives,
Is when some heart indignant breaks,
   To show that still she lives.

Oft, in the stilly night (1818)

Oft, in the stilly night,
   Ere Slumber's chain has bound me,
Fond Memory brings the light
   Of other days around me;
     The smiles, the tears
     Of boyhood's years,
   The words of love then spoken;
     The eyes that shone,
     Now dimm'd and gone,
   The cheerful hearts now broken!
Thus, in the stilly night,

Ere Slumber's chain has bound me,
Sad Memory brings the light
    Of other days around me.

When I remember all
    The friends, so link'd together,
I've seen around me fall
    Like leaves in wintry weather;
        I feel like one
        Who treads alone
Some banquet-hall deserted,
    Whose lights are fled,
    Whose garlands dead,
    And all but he departed!
Thus, in the stilly night,
    Ere Slumber's chain has bound me,
Sad Memory brings the light
    Of other days around me.

The Minstrel Boy (1813)

The Minstrel Boy to the war is gone,
    In the ranks of death you'll find him;
His father's sword he has girded on,
    And his wild harp slung behind him.—
'Land of song!' said the warrior-bard,
    'Though all the world betray thee,
One sword, at least, thy rights shall guard,
    One faithful harp shall praise thee!'

The Minstrel fell!—but the foeman's chain
    Could not bring his proud soul under;
The harp he loved ne'er spoke again,
    For he tore its cords asunder;
And said, 'No chains shall sully thee,
    Thou soul of love and bravery!
Thy songs were made for the brave and free,
    They shall never sound in slavery!'

MARY TIGHE
(1772–1810)

Written at the Eagle's Nest, Killarney (1800)

Here let us rest, while with meridan blaze
   The sun rides glorious 'mid the cloudless sky,
   While o'er the lake no cooling Zephyrs fly,
But on the liquid glass we dazzled gaze,
And fainting ask for shade: lo! where his nest
   The bird of Jove has fixed: the lofty brow,
With arbutus and fragrant wild shrubs drest,
   Impendent frowns, nor will approach allow:
Here the soft turf invites; here magic sounds
   Celestially respondent shall enchant,
While Melody from you steep wood rebounds
   In thrilling cadence sweet. Sure, life can grant
No brighter hours than this; and memory oft
Shall paint this happiest scene with pencil soft.

Written at Killarney (1800)

How soft the pause! the notes melodious cease,
   Which from each feeling could an echo call;
   Rest on your oars; that not a sound may fall
To interrupt the stillness of our peace:
The fanning west-wind breathes upon our cheeks
   Yet glowing with the sun's departed beams.
   Through the blue heavens the cloudless moon pours streams
Of pure resplendent light, in silver streaks
Reflected on the still, unruffled lake.
   The Alpine hills in solemn silence frown,
   While the dark woods night's deepest shades embrown.
And now once more that soothing strain awake!
Oh, ever to my heart, with magic power,
Shall those sweet sounds recal this rapturous hour!

On Leaving Killarney (1800)

Farewel, sweet scenes! pensive once more I turn
    Those pointed hills, and wood-fringed lakes to view
    With fond regret; while in this last adieu
A silent tear those brilliant hours shall mourn
For ever past. So from the pleasant shore,
    Borne with the struggling bark against the wind,
    The trembling pennant fluttering looks behind
With vain reluctance! 'Mid those woods no more
For me the voice of pleasure shall resound,
    Nor soft flutes warbling o'er the placid lake
    Aërial music shall for me awake,
And wrap my charmed soul in peace profound!
Though lost to me, here still may Taste delight
To dwell, nor the rude axe the trembling Dryads fright!

Address to my Harp (1811)

Oh, my loved Harp! companion dear!
    Sweet soother of my secret grief,
No more thy sounds my soul must cheer,
    No more afford a soft relief.

When anxious cares my heart oppressed,
    When doubts distracting tore my soul,
The pains which heaved my swelling breast
    Thy gentle sway could oft control.

Each well remembered, practised strain,
    The cheerful dance, the tender song,
Recalled with pensive, pleasing pain
    Some image loved and cherished long.

Where joy sat smiling o'er my fate,
    And marked each bright and happy day,
When partial friends around me sat,
    And taught my lips the simple lay;

And when by disappointment grieved
    I saw some darling hope o'erthrown,
Thou hast my secret pain relieved;
    O'er thee I wept, unseen, alone.

Oh! must I leave thee, must we part,
    Dear partner of my happiest days?
I may forget thy much-loved art,
    Unused thy melody to raise,

But ne'er can memory cease to love
    Those scenes where I thy charms have felt,
Though I no more thy power may prove,
    Which taught my softened heart to melt.

Forced to forego with thee this spot,
    Endeared by many a tender tie,
When rosy pleasure blessed my lot,
    And sparkled in my cheated eye.

Yet still thy strings, in Fancy's ear,
    With soothing melody shall play;
Thy silver sounds I oft shall hear,
    To pensive gloom a silent prey.

THOMAS FURLONG
(1794–1827)

Roisin Dubh (1831)

Oh! My sweet little rose, cease to pine for the past,
For the friends that come eastward shall see thee at last;
They bring blessings—they bring favors which the past never knew,
To pour forth in gladness on my Roisin Dubh.

Long, long with my dearest, thro' strange scenes I've gone.
O'er mountains and broad valleys I have still toil'd on;

O'er the Erne I have sail'd as the rough gales blew,
While the harp pour'd its music for my Roisin Dubh.

Tho' wearied oh! My fair one! Do not slight my song,
For my heart dearly loves thee, and hath lov'd thee long;
In sadness and in sorrow I shall still be true,
And cling with wild fondness round my Roisin Dubh.

There's no flower that e'er bloom'd can my rose excel,
There's no tongue that e'er moved half my love can tell;
Had I strength, had I skill the wide world to subdue,
Oh! The queen of that wide world should be Roisin Dubh.

Had I power, oh! My lov'd one, but to plead thy right,
I should speak out in boldness for my heart's delight;
I would tell to all around me how my fondness grew,
And bid them bless the beauty of my Roisin Dubh.

The mountains, high and misty, thro' the moors must go,
The rivers shall run backward, and the lakes overflow;
And the wild waves of old ocean wear a crimson hue,
Ere the world sees the ruin of my Roisin Dubh.

Eileen a Roon (1831)

I'll love thee evermore,
Eileen a Roon!
I'll bless thee o'er and o'er,
Eileen a Roon!
Oh! For thy sake I'll tread,
Where the plains of Mayo spread;
My hope still fondly led,
Eileen a Roon!

Oh! How may I gain thee?
Eileen a Roon!
Shall feasting entertain thee?
Eileen a Roon!
I would range the world wide,

With love alone to guide,
To win thee for my bride,
Eileen a Roon!

Then wilt thou come away?
Eileen a Roon!
Oh! Wilt thou come or stay?
Eileen a Roon!
Oh yes! oh yes! with thee
I will wander far and free,
And thy only love shall be,
Eileen a Roon!

A hundred thousand welcomes,
Eileen a Roon!
A hundred thousand welcomes,
Eileen a Roon!
Oh! Welcome evermore,
With welcomes yet in store,
Till love and life are o'er,
Eileen a Roon!

The Spirit of Irish Song (1827)

Lov'd land of the Bards, and Saints! to me
There's nought so dear as thy minstrelsy;
Bright is Nature in every dress,
Rich in unborrow'd loveliness;
Winning is every shape she wears,
Winning she is in thine own sweet airs;
What to the spirit more cheering can be
Than the lay whose ling'ring notes recall
The thoughts of the holy-the fair-the free
Belov'd in life or deplor'd in their fall?
Fling, fling the forms of art aside,
Dull is the ear that these forms enthral;
Let the simple songs of our sires be tried,
They go to the heart—and the heart is all.

Give me the full responsive sigh,
The glowing cheek and the moisten'd eye;
Let these the minstrel's might attest,
And the vain and the idle—may share the rest.

JAMES CLARENCE MANGAN
(1803–1849)

To My Native Land (1832)

Awake! arise! shake off thy dreams!
    Thou art not what thou wert of yore:
Of all those rich, those dazzling beams,
    That once illum'd thine aspect o'er
Show me a solitary one
Whose glory is not quenched and gone.

The harp remaineth where it fell,*
    With mouldering frame and broken chord;
Around the song there hangs no spell—
    No laurel wreath entwines the sword;
And startlingly the footstep falls
Along thy dim and dreary halls.

When other men in future years,
    In wonder ask, how this could be?
Then answer only by thy tears,
    That ruin fell on thine and thee,
Because thyself wouldst have it so—
Because thou welcomedst the blow!

To stamp dishonour on thy brow
    Was not within the power of earth;
And art thou agonised, when now
    The hour that lost thee all thy worth
And turned thee to the thing thou art,
Rushes upon thy bleeding heart?

Weep, weep, degraded one—the deed,
   The desperate deed was all thine own:
Thou madest more than maniac speed
   To hurl thine honours from their throne.
Thine honours fell, and when they fell
The nations rang thy funeral knell.

Well may thy sons be seared in soul,
   Their groans be deep by night and day;
Till day and night forget to roll,
   Their noblest hopes shall mourn decay—
Their freshest flowers shall die by blight—
Their brightest suns shall set in night.

The stranger, as he treads thy sod,
   And views thy universal wreck,
May execrate the foot that trod
   Triumphant on a prostrate neck;
But what is that to thee? Thy woes
May hope in vain for pause or close.

Awake! arise! shake off thy dreams!
   'Tis idle all to talk of power,
And fame and glory—these are themes
   Befitting ill so dark an hour;
Till miracles be wrought for thee,
Nor fame, nor glory, shalt thou see.

Thou art forsaken by the earth,
   Which makes a by-word of thy name:
Nations, and thrones, and powers, whose birth
   As yet is not, shall rise to fame,
Shall flourish and may fall—but thou
Shalt linger as thou lingerest now.

And till all earthly powers shall wane,
   And Time's grey pillars, groaning, fall,
Thus shall it be, and still in vain
   Thou shalt essay to burst the thrall

> Which binds, in fetters forged by fate,
> The wreck and ruin of what once was great.

The Woman of Three Cows (1840)

(*From the Irish*)

O Woman of Three Cows, agragh!* don't let your tongue thus rattle!
O, don't be saucy, don't be stiff, because you may have cattle.
I have seen—and, here's my hand to you, I only say what's true—
A many a one with twice your stock not half so proud as you.

Good luck to you, don't scorn the poor, and don't be their despiser,
For worldly wealth soon melts away, and cheats the very miser,
And Death soon strips the proudest wreath from haughty human
  brows;
Then don't be stiff, and don't be proud, good Woman of Three
  Cows!

See where Momonia's* heroes lie, proud Owen More's descendants,
'Tis they that won the glorious name, and had the grand attendants!
If *they* were forced to bow to Fate, as every mortal bows,
Can *you* be proud, can *you* be stiff, my Woman of Three Cows!

The brave sons of the Lord of Clare,* they left the land to mourning;
*Movrone!** for they were banished, with no hope of their returning—
Who knows in what abodes of want those youths were driven to
  house?
Yet *you* can give yourself these airs, O Woman of Three Cows!

O, think of Donnell of the Ships,* the Chief whom nothing
  daunted—
See how he fell in distant Spain, unchronicled, unchanted!
He sleeps, the great O'Sullivan, where thunder cannot rouse—
Then ask yourself, should *you* be proud, good Woman of Three
  Cows!

O'Ruark, Maguire, those souls of fire,* whose names are shrined in
  story—

Think how their high achievements once made Erin's highest
  glory—
Yet now their bones lie mouldering under weeds and cypress
  boughs,
And so, for all your pride, will yours, O Woman of Three Cows!

The O'Carrolls,* also, famed when Fame was only for the boldest,
Rest in forgotten sepulchres with Erin's best and oldest;
Yet who so great as they of yore in battle or carouse?
Just think of that, and hide your head, good Woman of Three
  Cows!

Your neighbour's poor, and you, it seems, are big with vain ideas,
Because, *inagh!** you've got three cows—one more, I see, than *she*
  has.
That tongue of yours wags more at times than Charity allows,
But if you're strong, be merciful, great Woman of Three Cows!

The Summing Up

Now, there you go! You still, of course, keep up your scornful
  bearing,
And I'm too poor to hinder you; but, by the cloak I'm wearing,
If I had but *four* cows myself, even though you were my spouse,
I'd thwack you well to cure your pride, my Woman of Three Cows!

Lamentation of Mac Liag for Kincora (1841)

(*From the Irish*)

Oh, where Kincora! is Brian the Great?
And where is the beauty that once was thine?
Oh, where are the princes and nobles that sate
At the feast in thy halls, and drank the red wine?
                Where, oh, Kincora?

Oh, where, Kincora! are thy valorous lords?
Oh, whither, thou Hospitable! are they gone?

Oh, where are the Dalcassians* of the Golden Swords?
And where are the warriors Brian led on?
                    Where, oh, Kincora?

And where is Morogh,* the descendant of kings—
The defeater of a hundred—the daringly brave—
Who set but slight store by jewels and rings—
Who swam down the torrent and laughed at its wave?
                    Where, oh, Kincora?

And where is Donagh,* King Brian's worthy son?
And where is Conaing,* the Beautiful Chief?
And Kian,* and Corc?* Alas! they are gone—
They have left me this night alone with my grief,
                    Left me, Kincora!

And where are the chiefs with whom Brian went forth,
The ne'er vanquished son of Erin the Brave,*
The great King of Onaght,* renowned for his worth,
And the hosts of Baskinn,* from the western wave?
                    Where, oh, Kincora?

Oh, where is Duvlann* of the swift-footed Steeds?
And where is Kian, who was son of Molloy?
And where is King Lonergan,* the fame of whose deeds
In the red battle-field no time can destroy?
                    Where, oh, Kincora?

And where is that youth of majestic height,
The faith-keeping Prince of the Scots?*—Even he,
As wide as his fame was, as great as was his might,
Was tributary, oh, Kincora, to thee!
                    Thee, oh, Kincora!

They are gone, those heroes of royal birth,
Who plundered no churches, and broke no trust,
'Tis weary for me to be living on earth
When they, oh, Kincora, lie low in the dust!
                    Low, oh, Kincora!

Oh, never again will Princes appear,
To rival the Dalcassians of the Cleaving Swords!
I can never dream of meeting afar or anear,
In the east or the west, such heroes and lords!
    Never, Kincora!

Oh, dear are the images my memory calls up
Of Brian Boru!—how he never would miss
To give me at the banquet the first bright cup!
Ah! why did he heap on me honour like this?
    Why, oh, Kincora?

I am Mac Liag, and my home is on the Lake;
Thither often, to that palace whose beauty is fled
Came Brian to ask me, and I went for his sake
Oh, my grief! that I should live, and Brian be dead!
    Dead, oh, Kincora!

Kathaleen Ny-Houlahan (1841)

(*From the Irish*)

Long they pine in weary woe, the nobles of our land,
Long they wander to and fro, proscribed, alas! and banned;
Feastless, houseless, altarless, they bear the exile's brand,
 But their hope is in the coming-to of Kathaleen Ny-Houlahan!

Think her not a ghastly hag, too hideous to be seen,
Call her not unseemly names, our matchless Kathaleen;
Young she is, and fair she is, and would be crowned a queen,
 Were the king's son at home here with Kathaleen Ny-Houlahan!

Sweet and mild would look her face, O, none so sweet and mild,
Could she crush the foes by whom her beauty is reviled;
Woollen plaids would grace herself and robes of silk her child,
 If the king's son were living here with Kathaleen Ny-Houlahan!

Sore disgrace it is to see the Arbitress of thrones,
Vassal to a *Saxoneen** of cold and sapless bones!

Bitter anguish wrings our souls—with heavy sighs and groans
   We wait the Young Deliverer* of Kathaleen Ny-Houlahan!

Let us pray to Him* who holds Life's issues in His hands—
Him who formed the mighty globe, with all its thousand lands;
Girding them with seas and mountains, rivers deep, and strands,
   To cast a look of pity upon Kathaleen Ny-Houlahan!

He, who over sands and waves led Israël along—
He, who fed, with heavenly bread, that chosen tribe and throng—
He, who stood by Moses, when his foes were fierce and strong—
   May He show forth His might in saving Kathaleen Ny-Houlahan.

Dark Rosaleen (1846)

(From the Irish)

O my Dark Rosaleen,
   Do not sigh, do not weep!
The priests are on the ocean green,
   They march along the Deep.
There's wine . . . from the royal Pope
   Upon the ocean green;
And Spanish ale shall give you hope,*
   My Dark Rosaleen!
   My own Rosaleen!
Shall glad your heart, shall give you hope,
Shall give you health, and help, and hope,
   My Dark Rosaleen.

Over hills and through dales,
   Have I roamed for your sake;
All yesterday I sailed with sails
   On river and on lake.
The Erne . . . at its highest flood*
   I dashed across unseen,
For there was lightning in my blood,
   My Dark Rosaleen!
   My own Rosaleen!

Oh! there was lightning in my blood,
Red lightning lightened through my blood,
  My Dark Rosaleen!

All day long in unrest
  To and fro do I move,
The very soul within my breast
  Is wasted for you, love!
The heart . . . in my bosom faints
  To think of you, my Queen,
My life of life, my saint of saints,
  My Dark Rosaleen!
  My own Rosaleen!
To hear your sweet and sad complaints,
My life, my love, my saint of saints,
  My Dark Rosaleen!

Woe and pain, pain and woe,
  Are my lot night and noon,
To see your bright face clouded so,
  Like to the mournful moon.
But yet . . . will I rear your throne
  Again in golden sheen;
'Tis you shall reign, shall reign alone,
  My Dark Rosaleen!
  My own Rosaleen!
'Tis you shall have the golden throne,
'Tis you shall reign, and reign alone,
  My Dark Rosaleen!

Over dews, over sands
  Will I fly for your weal;
Your holy delicate white hands
  Shall girdle me with steel.
At home . . . in your emerald bowers,
  From morning's dawn till e'en,
You'll pray for me, my flower of flowers,
  My Dark Rosaleen!
  My fond Rosaleen!

You'll think of me through daylight's hours,
My virgin flower, my flower of flowers,
    My Dark Rosaleen!

I could scale the blue air,
    I could plough the high hills,
Oh, I could kneel all night in prayer,
    To heal your many ills!
And one . . . beamy smile from you
    Would float like light between
My toils and me, my own, my true,
    My Dark Rosaleen!
    My fond Rosaleen!
Would give me life and soul anew,
A second life, a soul anew,
    My Dark Rosaleen!

O! the Erne shall run red
    With redundance of blood,
The earth shall rock beneath our tread,
    And flames wrap hill and wood,
And gun-peal, and slogan cry,
    Wake many a glen serene,
Ere you shall fade, ere you shall die,
    My Dark Rosaleen!
    My own Rosaleen!
The Judgement Hour must first be nigh,
Ere you can fade, ere you can die,
    My Dark Rosaleen!

Roisin Dubh (Black-Haired Fair Rose) (1849)

Since last night's star, afar, afar
    Heaven saw my speed,
I seem'd to fly o'er mountains high,
    On magic steed,
I dashed though Erne!* the world may learn
    The cause from Love

For, light or sun shone on me none,
　　But *Roisin Dubh*!

O, Roisin mine! droop not nor pine;
　　Look not so dull!
The Pope from Rome hath sent thee home
　　A pardon full;
The priests are near: O! never fear!
　　From Heaven above
They come to thee—they come to free
　　My *Roisin Dubh*!

Thee have I loved—for thee have roved
　　O'er land and sea:
My heart was sore—it evermore
　　Beat but for thee;
I could but weep—I could not sleep—
　　I could not move;
For, night or day, I dreamt alway
　　Of *Roisin Dubh*!

Through Munsters lands, by shores and strands,
　　Far could I roam,
If I might get my loved one yet,
　　And bring her home.
O, sweetest flower, that blooms in bower,
　　Or dell, or grove,
Thou lovest me, and I love thee,
My *Roisin Dubh*!

The sea shall burn, the earth shall mourn,
　　The skies rain blood—
The world shall rise in dread surprise
　　And warful mood—
And hill and lake in Eirè shake,
　　And hawk turn dove—
Ere you shall pine, ere you decline,
　　My *Roisin Dubh*!

The Nameless One (1849)

Ballad

Roll forth, my song, like the rushing river,
  That sweeps along to the mighty sea;
God will inspire me while I deliver
    My soul of thee!

Tell thou the world, when my bones lie whitening
  Amid the last homes of youth and eld,*
That there was once one whose veins ran lightning
    No eye beheld.

Tell how his boyhood was one drear night-hour,
  How shone for *him*, through his griefs and gloom,
No star of all heaven sends to light our
    Path to the tomb.

Roll on, my song, and to after ages
  Tell how, disdaining all earth can give,
He would have taught men, from wisdom's pages,
    The way to live.

And tell how trampled, derided, hated,
  And worn by weakness, disease, and wrong,
He fled for shelter to God, who mated
    His soul with song—

With song which alway, sublime or vapid,
  Flowed like a rill in the morning beam,
Perchance not deep, but intense and rapid—
    A mountain stream.

Tell how this Nameless, condemned for years long
  To herd with demons from hell beneath,
Saw things that made him, with groans and tears, long
    For even death.

Go on to tell how, with genius wasted,
    Betrayed in friendship, befooled in love,
With spirit shipwrecked, and young hopes blasted,
        He still, still strove.

Till, spent with toil, dreeing* death for others,
    And some whose hands should have wrought for *him*
(If children live not for sires and mothers),
        His mind grew dim.

And he fell far through that pit abysmal
    The gulf and grave of Maginn and Burns,
And pawned his soul for the devil's dismal
        Stock of returns.

But yet redeemed it in days of darkness,
    And shapes and signs of the final wrath,
When death, in hideous and ghastly starkness,
        Stood on his path.

And tell how now, amid wreck and sorrow,
    And want, and sickness, and houseless nights,
He bides in calmness the silent morrow,
        That no ray lights.

And lives he still, then? Yes! Old and hoary
    At thirty-nine, from despair and woe,
He lives enduring what future story
        Will never know.

Him grant a grave to, ye pitying noble,
    Deep in your bosoms! There let him dwell!
He, too, had tears for all souls in trouble,
        Here and in hell.

FRANCIS SYLVESTER MAHONY
(1804–1866)

The Bells of Shandon (1836)

'Sabbata pango,
Funera plango,
Solemnia clango'

Inscrip. on an old Bell*

With deep affection
And recollection
I often think of
 Those Shandon bells,
Whose sounds so wild would
In the days of childhood
Fling round my cradle
 Their magic spells.
On this I ponder
Where'er I wander,
And thus grow fonder
 Sweet Cork, of thee;
With thy bells of Shandon,
That sound so grand on
The pleasant waters
 Of the river Lee.

I've heard bells chiming
Full many a clime in,
Tolling sublime in
 Cathedral shrine,
While at a glib rate
Brass tongues would vibrate—
But all their music
 Spoke naught like thine;
For memory dwelling
On each proud swelling
Of the belfry knelling

Its bold notes free,
Made the bells of Shandon
Sound far more grand on
The pleasant waters
   Of the river Lee.

I've heard bells tolling
Old 'Adrian's Mole' in,
Their thunder rolling
   From the Vatican,
And cymbals glorious
Swinging uproarious
In the gorgeous turrets
   Of Notre Dame;
But thy sounds were sweeter
Than the dome of Peter
Flings o'er the Tiber,
   Pealing solemnly;—
O! the bells of Shandon
Sound far more grand on
The pleasant waters
   Of the river Lee.

There's a bell in Moscow,
While on tower and kiosk, O!
In Saint Sophia
   The Turkman gets,
And loud in air
Calls men to prayer
From the tapering summit
   Of tall minarets.
Such empty phantom
I freely grant them;
But there is an anthem
   More dear to me,—
'Tis the bells of Shandon
That sound so grand on
The pleasant waters
   Of the river Lee.

SAMUEL FERGUSON
(1810–1886)

Lament for the Death of Thomas Davis (1847)

I walked through Ballinderry in the springtime,
　When the bud was on the tree,
And I said, in every fresh-ploughed field beholding
　The sowers striding free,
Scattering broadcast forth the corn in golden plenty,
　On the quick, seed-clasping soil,
'Even such this day, among the fresh-stirred hearts of Erin,
　Thomas Davis, is thy toil!'

I sat by Ballyshannon in the summer,
　And saw the salmon leap,
And I said, as I beheld the gallant creatures
　Spring glittering from the deep,
Through the spray and through the prone heaps striving onward
　To the calm clear streams above,
'So seekest thou thy native founts of freedom, Thomas Davis,
　In thy brightness of strength and love!'

I stood in Derrybawn in the autumn,
　I heard the eagle call,
With a clangorous cry of wrath and lamentation
　That filled the wide mountain hall,
O'er the bare, deserted place of his plundered eyrie,
　And I said, as he screamed and soared,
'So callest thou, thou wrathful-soaring Thomas Davis,
　For a nation's rights restored.'

And Alas! to think but now that thou art lying,
　Dear Davis, dead at thy mother's knee,
And I, no mother near, on my own sick-bed,
　That face on earth shall never see;
I may lie and try to feel that I am dreaming,
　I may lie and try to say, 'Thy Will be done'—

But a hundred such as I will never comfort Erin
  For the loss of that noble son.

Young husbandman of Erin's fruitful seed-time,
  In the fresh track of danger's plough!
Who will walk the heavy, toilsome, perilous furrow,
  Girt with freedom's seed-sheets now?
Who will vanish with the wholesome crop of knowledge,
  The flaunting weed and the bitter thorn,
Now that thou thyself art but a seed for hopeful planting
  Against the resurrection morn?

Young salmon of the flood-time of freedom
  That swells round Erin's shore,
Thou wilt leap against their loud, oppressive torrent
  Of bigotry and hate no more!
Drawn downward by their prone material instinct,
  Let them thunder on their rocks, and foam;
Thou hast leaped, aspiring soul, to founts beyond their raging,
  Where troubled waters never come.

But I grieve not, eagle of the empty eyrie,
  That thy wrathful cry is still,
And that the songs alone of peaceful mourners
  Are heard to-day on Erin's hill.
Better far if brothers' war be destined for us—
  God avert that horrid day, I pray!—
That ere our hands be stained with slaughter fratricidal,
  Thy warm heart should be cold in clay.

But my trust is strong in God who made us brothers,
  That He will not suffer these right hands,
Which thou hast joined in holier rites than wedlock,
  To draw opposing brands.
O many a tuneful tongue that thou madest vocal,
  Would lie cold and silent then,
And songless long once more should often-widowed Erin
  Mourn the loss of her brave young men.

O brave young men, my love, my pride, my promise,
 'Tis on you my hopes are set,
In manliness, in kindliness, in justice,
 To make Erin a nation yet;
Self-respecting, self-relying, self-advancing,
 In union or in severance, free and strong,
And if God grant this, then, under God, to Thomas Davis,
 Let the greater praise belong!

Cashel of Munster (1867)

(*From the Irish*)

I'd wed you without herds, without money, or rich array,
And I'd wed you on a dewy morning at day-dawn grey;
My bitter woe it is, love, that we are not far away
In Cashel town, though the bare deal board were our marriage bed
 this day!

Oh, fair maid, remember the green hillside,
Remember how I hunted about the valleys wide;
Time now has worn me; my locks are turned to grey,
The year is scarce and I am poor, but send me not, love, away!

Oh, deem not my blood is of base strain, my girl,
Oh, deem not my birth was as the birth of the churl;
Marry me, and prove me, and say soon you will,
That noble blood is written on my right side still!

My purse holds no red gold, no coin of the silver white,
No herds are mine to drive through the long twilight!
But the pretty girl that would take me, all bare though I be and lone,
Oh, I'd take her with me kindly to the county Tyrone.

Oh, my girl, I can see 'tis in trouble you are,
And, oh, my girl, I see 'tis your people's reproach you bear:
'I am a girl in trouble for his sake with whom I fly,
And, oh, may no other maiden know such reproach as I!'

The Coolun (1867)

(*From the Irish*)

O had you seen the Coolun
    Walking down by the cuckoo's street,
With the dew of the meadow shining
    On her milk-white twinkling feet!
My love she is, and my coleen oge,*
    And she dwells in Bal'nagar;
And she bears the palm of beauty bright
    From the fairest that in Erin are.

In Bal'nagar is the Coolun,
    Like the berry on the bough her cheek;
Bright beauty dwells for ever
    On her fair neck and ringlets sleek;
Oh, sweeter is her mouth's soft music
    Than the lark or thrush at dawn,
Or the blackbird in the greenwood singing
    Farewell to the setting sun.

Rise up, my boy! make ready
    My horse, for I forth would ride,
To follow the modest damsel,
    Where she walks on the green hillside:
For ever since our youth were we plighted
    In faith, troth, and wedlock true—
She is sweeter to me nine times over,
    Than organ or cuckoo!

For, ever since my Childhood
    I've loved the fair and darling child;
But our people came between us,
    And with lucre our pure love defiled:
Ah, my woe it is, and my bitter pain,
    And I weep it night and day,
That the coleen bawn* of my early love
    Is torn from my heart away.

Sweetheart and faithful treasure,
　　Be constant still, and true;
Nor for want of herds and houses
　　Leave one who would ne'er leave you.
I'll pledge you the blessèd Bible,
　　Without and eke within,
That the faithful God will provide for us,
　　Without thanks to kith or kin.

Oh, love, do you remember
　　When we lay all night alone,
Beneath the ash in the winter storm,
　　When the oak wood round did groan?
No shelter then from the blast had we,
　　The bitter blast or sleet,
But your gown to wrap about our heads,
　　And my coat around our feet.

Dear Dark Head (1867)

(*From the Irish*)

Put your head, darling, darling, darling,
　　Your darling black head my heart above;
Oh, mouth of honey, with the thyme for fragrance,
　　Who, with heart in breast, could deny you love?

Oh, many and many a young girl for me is pining,
　　Letting her locks of gold to the cold wind free,
For me, the foremost of our gay young fellows;
　　But I'd leave a hundred, pure love, for thee!

Then put your head, darling, darling, darling,
　　Your darling black head my heart above;
Oh, mouth of honey, with the thyme for fragrance,
　　Who, with heart in breast, could deny you love?

THOMAS DAVIS
(1814–1845)

A Nation Once Again (1845)

When boyhood's fire was in my blood,
    I read of ancient freemen,
For Greece and Rome who bravely stood,
    Three Hundred men and Three men.
And then I prayed I yet might see
    Our fetters rent in twain,
And Ireland, long a province, be
    A Nation once again.

And, from that time, through wildest woe,
    That hope has shone, a far light;
Nor could love's brightest summer glow
    Outshine that solemn starlight:
It seemed to watch above my head
    In forum, field, and fane;
Its angel voice sang round my bed,
    'A Nation once again'.

It whispered, too, that 'freedom's ark
    And service high and holy,
Would be profaned by feelings dark,
    And passions vain or lowly;
For freedom comes from God's right hand,
    And needs a godly train;
And righteous men must make our land
    A Nation once again.'

So, as I grew from boy to man,
    I bent me to that bidding—
My spirit of each selfish plan
    And cruel passion ridding;
For, thus I hoped some day to aid—
    Oh! can such hope be vain?

When my dear country shall be made
A Nation once again.

The West's Asleep (1845)

When all beside a vigil keep,
The West's asleep, the West's asleep—
Alas! and well may Erin weep,
When Connaught lies in slumber deep.
There lake and plain smile fair and free,
'Mid rocks—their guardian chivalry—
Sing oh! let man learn liberty
From crashing wind and lashing sea.

That chainless wave and lovely land
Freedom and Nationhood demand—
Be sure, the great God never plann'd,
For slumbering slaves, a home so grand.
And, long, a brave and haughty race
Honoured and sentinelled the place—
Sing oh! not even their sons' disgrace
Can quite destroy their glory's trace.

For often, in O'Connor's van,
To triumph dash'd each Connaught clan—
And fleet as deer the Normans ran
Through Coirrslabh Pass and Ard Rathain.*
And later times saw deeds as brave;
And glory guards Clanricarde's grave—
Sing, oh! they died their land to save,
At Aughrim's slopes and Shannon's wave.*

And if, when all a vigil keep,
The West's asleep, the West's asleep—
Alas! and well may Erin weep,
That Connaught lies in slumber deep.
But—hark!—some voice like thunder spake:
'The West's awake, the West's awake'—.

Sing, oh! hurra! let England quake,
We'll watch till death for Erin's sake!

AUBREY DE VERE
(1814–1902)

The Little Black Rose (1861)

The Little Black Rose shall be red at last;
　　What made it black but the March wind dry,
And the tear of the widow that fell on it fast?
　　It shall redden the hills when June is nigh.

The Silk of the Kine* shall rest at last;
　　What drove her forth but the dragon-fly?
In the golden vale she shall feed full fast,
　　With her mild gold horn and her slow, dark eye.

The wounded wood-dove lies dead at last!
　　The pine long bleeding, it shall not die!
This song is secret. Mine ear it passed
　　In a wind o'er the plains at Athenry.*

Florence MacCarthy's Farewell to His English Love (1855)

I

England's fair child, Evangeline!
In that far-distant land of mine
　　There stands a Yew-tree among tombs!
For ages there that tree hath stood,
A black pall dash'd with drops of blood;
　　O'er all my world it breathes its glooms.

II

Evangeline! Evangeline!
Because my Yew-tree is not thine,
　　Because thy Gods on mine wage war,

Farewell! Back fall the gates of brass;
The exile to his own must pass:
  I seek the land of tombs once more.

JOHN KELLS INGRAM (1823–1907)

The Memory of the Dead (1843)

Who fears to speak of Ninety-eight?
Who blushes at the name?
When cowards mock the patriot's fate,
Who hangs his head for shame?
He's all a knave, or half a slave,
Who slights his country thus;
But a true man, like you, man,
Will fill your glass with us.

We drink the memory of the brave,
The faithful and the few;
Some lie far off beyond the wave,
Some sleep in Ireland, too;
All, all are gone; but still lives on
The fame of those who died;
All true men, like you, men,
Remember them with pride.

Some on the shores of distant lands
Their weary hearts have laid,
And by the stranger's heedless hands
Their lonely graves were made;
But though their clay be far away
Beyond the Atlantic foam,
In true men, like you, men,
Their spirit's still at home.

The dust of some is Irish earth,
Among their own they rest,
And the same land that gave them birth
Has caught them to her breast;

And we will pray that from their clay
Full many a race may start
Of true men, like you, men,
To act as brave a part.

They rose in dark and evil days
To right their native land;
They kindled here a living blaze
That nothing shall withstand.
Alas! that might can vanquish right—
They fell and passed away;
But true men, like you, men,
Are plenty here to-day.

Then here's their memory—may it be
For us a guiding light,
To cheer our strife for liberty,
And teach us to unite—
Through good and ill, be Ireland's still,
Though sad as theirs your fate,
And true men be you, men,
Like those of Ninety-eight.

WILLIAM ALLINGHAM
(1824–1889)

The Fairies (1849)

(*A Child's Song*)

Up the airy mountain,
  Down the rushy glen,
We daren't go a-hunting
  For fear of little men;
Wee folk, good folk,
  Trooping all together;
Green jacket, red cap,
  And white owl's feather!

Down along the rocky shore
    Some make their home—
They live on crispy pancakes
    Of yellow tide-foam;
Some in the reeds
    Of the black mountain lake,
With frogs for their watch-dogs,
    All night awake.

High on the hill-top
    The old King sits;
He is now so old and grey
    He's nigh lost his wits.
With a bridge of white mist
    Columbkill he crosses,
On his stately journeys
    From Slieveleague to Rosses;
Or going up with music
    On cold starry nights,
To sup with the Queen
    Of the gay Northern Lights.

They stole little Bridget
    For seven years long;
When she came down again
    Her friends were all gone.
They took her lightly back,
    Between the night and morrow;
They thought that she was fast asleep,
    But she was dead with sorrow.
They have kept her ever since
    Deep within the lake,
On a bed of flag-leaves,
    Watching till she wake.

By the craggy hill-side,
    Through the mosses bare,
They have planted thorn-trees
    For pleasure here and there.

Is any man so daring
    As dig one up in spite,
He shall find their sharpest thorns
    In his bed at night.

Up the airy mountain,
    Down the rushy glen,
We daren't go a-hunting
    For fear of little men;
Wee folk, good folk,
    Trooping all together;
Green jacket, red cap,
    And white owl's feather!

The Maids of Elfin-Mere (1850)

'Twas when the spinning-room was here.
Came Three Damsels clothed in white,
With their spindles every night;
Two and one, and Three fair Maidens,
Spinning to a pulsing cadence,
Singing songs of Elfin-Mere;
Till the eleventh hour was toll'd,
Then departed through the wold.
    Years ago, and years ago;
    And the tall reeds sigh as the wind doth blow.

Three white Lilies, calm and clear,
And they were loved by every one;
Most of all, the Pastor's Son,
Listening to their gentle singing,
Felt his heart go from him, clinging
Round these Maids of Elfin-Mere;
Sued each night to make them stay,
Sadden'd when they went away.
    Years ago, and years ago;
    And the tall reeds sigh as the wind doth blow.

Hands that shook with love and fear
Dared put back the village clock,—
Flew the spindle, turn'd the rock,
Flow'd the song with subtle rounding,
Till the false 'eleven' was sounding;
Then these Maids of Elfin-Mere
Swiftly, softly, left the room,
Like three doves on snowy plume.
    Years ago, and years ago;
    And the tall reeds sigh as the wind doth blow.

One that night who wander'd near
Heard lamentings by the shore,
Saw at dawn three stains of gore
In the waters fade and dwindle.
Nevermore with song and spindle
Saw we Maids of Elfin-Mere.
The Pastor's Son did pine and die;
Because true love should never lie.
    Years ago, and years ago;
    And the tall reeds sigh as the wind doth blow.

A Dream (1850)

I heard the dogs howl in the moonlight night;
I went to the window to see the sight;
All the Dead that ever I knew
Going one by one and two by two.

On they pass'd, and on they pass'd;
Townsfellows all, from first to last;
Born in the moonlight of the lane,
Quench'd in the heavy shadow again.

Schoolmates, marching as when we play'd
At soldiers once—but now more staid;
Those were the strangest sight to me
Who were drown'd, I knew, in the awful sea.

Straight and handsome folk; bent and weak too;
Some that I loved, and gasp'd to speak to;
Some but a day in their churchyard bed;
Some that I had not known were dead.

A long, long crowd—where each seem'd lonely,
Yet of them all there was one, one only,
Raised a head or look'd my way;
She linger'd a moment,—she might not stay.

How long since I saw that fair pale face!
Ah! Mother dear! might I only place
My head on thy breast, a moment to rest,
While thy hand on my tearful cheek were prest.

On, on a moving bridge they made
Across the moon-stream from shade to shade,
Young and old, women and men;
Many long forgot, but remember'd then.

And first there came a bitter laughter;
A sound of tears the moment after;
And then a music so lofty and gay,
That every morning, day by day,
I strive to recall it if I may.

The Winding Banks of Erne (1865)

(A Local Ballad)

Adieu to Ballyshanny! where I was bred and born;
Go where/I may, I'll think of you, as sure as night and morn,
The kindly spot, the friendly town, where every one
     is known,
And not a face in all the place but partly seems my own;
There's not a house or window, there's not a field or hill,
But, east or west, in foreign lands, I'll recollect them still.

I leave my warm heart with you, though my back I'm forced to
    turn—
So adieu to Ballyshanny, and the winding banks of Erne!

No more on pleasant evenings we'll saunter down the Mall,
When the trout is rising to the fly, the salmon to the fall.
The boat comes straining on her net, and heavily she creeps,
Cast off, cast off!—she feels the oars, and to her berth she sweeps;
Now fore and aft keep hauling, and gathering up the clew,
Till a silver wave of salmon rolls in among the crew.
Then they may sit, with pipes a-lit, and many a joke and
    'yarn';—
Adieu to Ballyshanny, and the winding banks of Erne!

The music of the waterfall, the mirror of the tide,
When all the green-hill'd harbour is full from side to side—
From Portnasun to Bulliebawns, and round the Abbey Bay,
From rocky Inis Saimer to Coolnargit sandhills gray
While far upon the southern line, to guard it like a wall,
The Leitrim mountains clothed in blue gaze calmly over all,
And watch the ship sail up or down, the red flag at her stern;—
Adieu to these, adieu to all the winding banks of Erne!

Farewell to you, Kildoney lads, and them that pull an oar,
A lug-sail set, or haul a net, from the Point to Mullaghmore;
From Killybegs to bold Slieve-League, that ocean mountain steep,
Six hundred yards in air aloft, six hundred in the deep;
From Dooran to the Fairy Bridge, and round by Tullen strand,
Level and long, and white with waves, where gull and curlew stand;
Head out to sea when on your lee the breakers you discern!—
Adieu to all the billowy coast, and winding banks of Erne!

Farewell Coolmore,—Bundoran! and your summer crowds that
    run
From inland homes to see with joy th' Atlantic-setting sun;
To breathe the buoyant salted air, and sport among the waves;
To gather shells on sandy beach, and tempt the gloomy caves;
To watch the flowing, ebbing tide, the boats, the crabs, the fish;
Young men and maids to meet and smile, and form a tender wish;

The sick and old in search of health, for all things have their turn—
And I must quit my native shore, and the winding banks of Erne!

Farewell to every white cascade from the Harbour to Belleek,
And every pool where fins may rest, and ivy-shaded creek;
The sloping fields, the lofty rocks, where ash and holly grow,
The one split yew-tree gazing on the curving flood below;
The Lough, that winds through islands under Turaw mountain
      green;
And Castle Caldwell's stretching woods, with tranquil bays between;
And Breesie Hill, and many a pond among the heath and fern,—
For I must say adieu—adieu to the winding banks of Erne!

The thrush will call through Camlin groves the live-long summer
      day;
The waters run by mossy cliff, and banks with wild flowers gay;
The girls will bring their work and sing beneath a twisted thorn,
Or stray with sweethearts down the path among the growing corn;
Along the river side they go, where I have often been,—
O, never shall I see again the days that I have seen!
A thousand chances are to one I never may return,—
Adieu to Ballyshanny, and the winding banks of Erne!

Adieu to evening dances, when merry neighbours meet,
And the fiddle says to boys and girls, 'Get up and shake your feet!'
To 'shanachus'* and wise old talk of Erin's days gone by—
Who trench'd the rath* on such a hill, and where the bones may lie
Of saint, or king, or warrior chief; with tales of fairy power,
And tender ditties sweetly sung to pass the twilight hour.
The mournful song of exile is now for me to learn—
Adieu, my dear companions on the winding banks of Erne!

Now measure from the Commons down to each end of the Purt,
Round the Abbey, Moy, and Knather,—I wish no one any hurt;
The Main Street, Back Street, College Lane, the Mall, and
      Portnasun,
If any foes of mine are there, I pardon every one.
I hope that man and womankind will do the same by me;
For my heart is sore and heavy at voyaging the sea.

My loving friends I'll bear in mind, and often fondly turn
To think of Ballyshanny, and the winding banks of Erne.

If ever I'm a money'd man, I mean, please God, to cast
My golden anchor in the place where youthful years were
     pass'd;
Though heads that now are black and brown must meanwhile gather
     gray,
New faces rise by every hearth, and old ones drop away—
Yet dearer still that Irish hill than all the world beside;
It's home, sweet home, where'er I roam, through lands and waters
     wide.
And if the Lord allows me, I surely will return
To my native Ballyshanny, and the winding banks of Erne.

from *Laurence Bloomfield in Ireland* (1864)

In early morning twilight, raw and chill,
Damp vapours brooding on the barren hill,
Through miles of mire in steady grave array
Threescore well-arm'd police pursue their way;
Each tall and bearded man a rifle swings,
And under each greatcoat a bayonet clings;
The Sheriff on his sturdy cob astride
Talks with the chief, who marches by their side,
And, creeping on behind them, Paudeen Dhu
Pretends his needful duty much to rue.
Six big-boned labourers, clad in common frieze,
Walk in the midst, the Sheriff's staunch allies;
Six crowbar men, from distant county brought,—
Orange, and glorying in their work, 'tis thought,
But wrongly,—churls of Catholics are they,
And merely hired at half-a-crown a day.

The Hamlet clustering on its hill is seen,
A score of petty homesteads, dark and mean;
Poor always, not despairing until now;
Long used, as well as poverty knows how,

With life's oppressive trifles to contend.
This day will bring its history to an end.
Moveless and grim against the cottage walls
Lean a few silent men: but someone calls
Far off; and then a child 'without a stitch'
Runs out of doors, flies back with piercing screech,
And soon from house to house is heard the cry
Of female sorrow, swelling loud and high,
Which makes the men blaspheme between their teeth.
Meanwhile, o'er fence and watery field beneath,
The little army moves through drizzling rain;
A 'Crowbar' leads the Sheriff's nag; the lane
Is enter'd, and their plashing tramp draws near:
One instant, outcry holds its breath to hear;
'Halt!'—at the doors they form in double line,
And ranks of polish'd rifles wetly shine.

The Sheriff's painful duty must be done;
He begs for quiet—and the work's begun.
The strong stand ready; now appear the rest,
Girl, matron, grandsire, baby on the breast,
And Rosy's thin face on a pallet borne;
A motley concourse, feeble and forlorn.
One old man, tears upon his wrinkled cheek,
Stands trembling on a threshold, tries to speak,
But, in defect of any word for this,
Mutely upon the doorpost prints a kiss,
Then passes out for ever. Through the crowd
The children run bewilder'd, wailing loud;
Where needed most, the men combine their aid;
And, last of all, is Oona forth convey'd,
Reclined in her accustom'd strawen chair,
Her aged eyelids closed, her thick white hair
Escaping from her cap; she feels the chill,
Looks round and murmurs, then again is still.

Now bring the remnants of each household fire.
On the wet ground the hissing coals expire;
And Paudeen Dhu, with meekly dismal face,
Receives the full possession of the place.

Whereon the Sheriff, 'We have legal hold.
Return to shelter with the sick and old.
Time shall be given; and there are carts below
If any to the workhouse choose to go.'
A young man makes him answer, grave and clear,
'We're thankful to you! but there's no one here
Goin' back into them houses: do your part.
Nor we won't trouble Pigot's horse and cart.'
At which name, rushing into th' open space,
A woman flings her hood from off her face,
Falls on her knees upon the miry ground,
Lifts hands and eyes, and voice of thrilling sound,—
'Vengeance of God Almighty fall on you,
James Pigot!—may the poor man's curse pursue,
The widow's and the orphan's curse, I pray,
Hang heavy round you at your dying day!'
Breathless and fix'd one moment stands the crowd
To hear this malediction fierce and loud.

Meanwhile (our neighbour Neal is busy there)
On steady poles be lifted Oona's chair,
Well-heap'd with borrow'd mantles; gently bear
The sick girl in her litter, bed and all;
Whilst others hug the children weak and small
In careful arms, or hoist them pick-a-back;
And, 'midst the unrelenting clink and thwack
Of iron bar on stone, let creep away
The sad procession from that hill-side grey,
Through the slow-falling rain. In three hours more
You find, where Ballytullagh stood before,
Mere shatter'd walls, and doors with useless latch,
And firesides buried under fallen thatch.

5. POPULAR SONGS AND BALLADS

Boulavogue (1898)

At Boulavogue, as the sun was setting
    O'er the green May meadows of Shelmalier,
A rebel band set the heather blazing,
    And brought the neighbours from far and near.
Then Father Murphy, of old Kilcormack,
    Spurred up the rocks with a warring cry—
'Arm! Arm!' he cried, 'for I've come to lead you—
    Now priest and people must fight or die!'

He led us on 'gainst the coming soldiers,
    And the cowardly Yeomen we put to flight;
Down at the Harrow, the Boys of Wexford
    Showed Bookey's regiment how men could fight!
Look out for hirelings, King George of England,
    Search every kingdom that breeds a slave!
For Father Murphy, of the County Wexford,
    Sweeps o'er the earth like a mighty wave!

We took Camolin and Enniscorthy,
    And Wexford storming, drove out our foes;
'Twas at Slieve Kiltha our pikes were reeking
    With the crimson stream of the beaten Yeos.
At Tubberneering and Ballyellis
    Full many a Hessian* lay in his gore!
Ah, Father Murphy, had aid come over,
    A green flag floated from shore to shore!

At Vinegar Hill, o'er the pleasant Slaney,
    Our heroes vainly stood back to back,
And the Yeos at Tullow took Father Murphy,
    And burned his body upon the rack.

God give you glory, brave Father Murphy,
  And open heaven to all your men;
The cause that called you may call tomorrow
  In another war for the Green again.

The Shan Van Vocht (1842)

Oh! the French are on the sea,
  Says the *Shan Van vocht*;
The French are on the sea,
  Says the *Shan Van vocht*;
Oh! the French are in the bay,
They'll be here without delay,
And the Orange* will decay,
  Says the *Shan Van vocht*.

Chorus

Oh! the French are in the bay,
They'll be here by break of day,
And the Orange will decay,
  Says the *Shan Van vocht*.

And where will they have their camp?
  Says the *Shan Van vocht*;
Where will they have their camp?
  Says the *Shan Van vocht*;
On the Currach of Kildare,*
The boys they will be there
With their pikes in good repair,
  Says the *Shan Van vocht*.

To the Currach of Kildare
The boys they will repair,
And Lord Edward* will be there,
  Says the *Shan Van vocht*.

Then what will the yeomen do?
  Says the *Shan Van vocht*;

What *will* the yeomen do?
　Says the *Shan Van vocht*;
What *should* the yeomen do,
But throw off the red and blue,
And swear that they'll be true
　To the *Shan Van vocht*.

What *should* the yeomen do
But throw off the red and blue,
And swear that they'll be true
　To the *Shan Van vocht*.

And what colour will they wear?
　Says the *Shan Van vocht*;
What colour will they wear?
　Says the *Shan Van vocht*;
What colour should be seen
Where our fathers' homes have been,
But their own immortal Green?
　Says the *Shan Van vocht*.

What colour should be seen
Where our fathers' homes have been,
But their own immortal Green?
　Says the *Shan Van vocht*.

And will Ireland then be free?
　Says the *Shan Van vocht*;
Will Ireland then be free?
　Says the *Shan Van vocht*;
Yes! Ireland SHALL be free,
From the centre to the sea;
Then hurra for Liberty!
　Says the *Shan Van vocht*.

Yes! Ireland SHALL be free,
From the centre to the sea;
Then hurra for Liberty!
　Says the *Shan Van vocht*.

The Wearin' o' the Green (c.1798)

Oh, Paddy dear! and did ye hear the news that's goin' round?
The shamrock is forbid by law to grow on Irish ground!
No more St Patrick's day we'll keep; his colour can't be seen,
For there's a cruel law ag'in' the Wearin' o' the Green!

I met with Napper Tandy,* and he took me by the hand,
And he said, 'How's poor ould Ireland, and how does she stand?'
'She's the most distressful country that ever yet was seen,
For they're hanging men and women for the Wearin' o' the Green.'

An' if the colour we must wear is England's cruel red,
Let it remind us of the blood that Ireland has shed;
Then pull the shamrock from your hat, and throw it on the sod,
An' never fear, 'twill take root there, though under foot 'tis trod.

When law can stop the blades of grass from growin' as they grow,
An' when the leaves in summer time their colour dare not show,
Then I will change the colour, too, I wear in my caubeen;*
But till that day, plaise God, I'll stick to the Wearin' o' the Green.

The Croppy Boy (c.1798)

It was early, early in the spring,
The birds did whistle and sweetly sing,
Changing their notes from tree to tree
And the song they sang was 'Old Ireland Free'.

It was early, early in the night,
The Yeoman cavalry gave me a fright,
The Yeoman cavalry was my downfall
And I was taken by Lord Cornwall.

It was in the coach house that I was laid
And in the parlour that I was tried.
My sentence passed and my courage low
As to Duncannon I was forced to go.

As I was going up Wexford Street
My own first cousin I chanced to meet.
My own first cousin did me betray
And for one bare guinea swore my life away.

As I was passing my father's door
My brother William stood in the door.
My aged father stood there before
And my own dear mother her hair she tore.

As I was going up Wexford Hill
Oh who would blame me to cry my fill?
I looked behind and I looked before
And my own dear mother I shall ne'er see more.

As I was standing on the scaffold high
My own dear father was standing nigh.
My own dear father did me deny
And the name he gave me was 'The Croppy Boy'.

It was in Duncannon this young man died
And in Duncannon his body was laid.
Now all good people that do pass by
O spare a tear for 'The Croppy Boy'.

The Rising of the Moon (1866)

Tell me, tell me, Shawn O'Farrell,
　　Why it is you hurry so?
Hush *ma bouchal*,* hush and listen,
　　And his cheeks were in a glow.
I bear orders from the captain,
　　Get you ready quick and soon,
For our pikes must be together
　　By the rising of the moon.

Tell me, tell me, Shawn O'Farrell,
　　Where the gathering is to be.

At the old spot by the river
    That's well known to you and me.
One word more, our signal token,
    Whistle up the marching tune,
Hurrah, my boys, for Ireland's freedom,
    By the rising of the moon.

Down by the lonely river,
    A dark mass of men were seen,
Far above the starry banner
    Hung our own immortal green.
Death to every foe and traitor,
    Forward on the marching tune,
And a million pikes were shining
    By the rising of the moon.

Out of every mud wall cabin
    Eyes were watching all the night,
Many a manly breast was throbbing
    For the blessed morning light.
Murmurs passed along the valley
    Like the banshee's lonely croon,
And a million pikes were shining
    By the rising of the moon.

Well they fought for poor old Ireland,
    And bitter was their fate,
What a feeling of pride and sorrow
    Fills the name of Ninety-Eight.
But yet we have in poor old Ireland
    Hearts that beat as firm and true,
We will follow in their footsteps
    By the rising of the moon.

Granuaile (c.1798)

All through the north as I walked forth to view the shamrock plain
I stood a while where nature smiled amid the rocks and streams

On a matron mild I fixed my eyes beneath a fertile vale
As she sang her song it was on the wrongs of poor old Granuaile.

Her head was bare and her grey hair over her eyes hung down
Her waist and neck, her hands and feet, with iron chains were bound
Her pensive strain and plaintive wail mingled with the evening gale
And the song she sung with mournful tongue was Poor Old
  Granuaile.

The gown she wore was stained with gore all by a ruffian band
Her lips so sweet that monarchs kissed are now grown pale and wan
The tears of grief fell from her eyes each tear as large as hail
None could express the deep distress of poor old Granuaile.

On her harp she leaned and thus exclaimed My royal Brian* is gone
Who in his day did drive away the tyrants every one
On Clontarf's plains against the Danes his faction did prepare
Brave Brian Boru cut their lines in two and freed old Granuaile.

But now, alas, I must confess, avengers I have none
There's no brave Lord to wave his sword in my defence—not one
My enemies just when they please with blows they do assail
The flesh they tore clean off the bones of poor old Granuaile.

Six hundred years the briny tears have flowed down from my eyes
I curse the day that Henry made of me proud Albion's prize
From that day down with chains I'm bound no wonder I look pale
The blood they drained from every vein of poor old Granuaile.

There was a lord came from the south he wore a laurel crown
Saying 'Grania dear, be of good cheer, no longer you'll be bound
I am the man they call great Dan, who never yet did fail
I have got the bill for to fulfil your wishes Granuaile.'

With blood besmeared and bathed in tears her harp she sweetly
  strung
And oh the change, her mournful air from one last chord she wrung
Her voice so clear fell on my ear, at length my strength did fail
I went away and thus did say, 'God help you, Granuaile'.

PART TWO
WRITINGS 1890–1939

1. NATIONALIST WRITINGS AND THE EASTER RISING

MAUD GONNE
(1866–1953)

The Famine Queen (1900)

'The Queen's visit to Ireland is in no way political,' proclaims the Lord Lieutenant, and the English ministers. 'The Queen's visit has no political signification, and the Irish nation must receive her Majesty with the generous hospitality for which it is celebrated,' hastens to repeat Mr John Redmond, and our servile Irish members whose nationality has been corrupted by a too lengthy sojourn in the enemy's country.

'The Queen's visit to Ireland has nothing at all to do with politics,' cries the fishmonger, Pile, whose ambitious soul is not satisfied by the position of Lord Mayor and who hankers after an English title.

'Let us to our knees, and present the keys of the city to her Most Gracious Majesty, and compose an address in her honour.'

'Nothing political! nothing political! Let us present an address to this virtuous lady,' echo 30 town councillors, who when they sought the votes of the Dublin people called themselves Irishmen and Nationalists, but who are overcome by royal glamour. Poor citizens of Dublin! your thoughtlessness in giving your votes to these miserable creatures will cost you dear. It has already cost the arrests of sixteen good and true men, and many broken heads and bruised limbs from police batons, for you have realised—if somewhat late— the responsibility of Ireland's capital, and, aghast at the sight of the men elected by you betraying and dishonouring Ireland, you have, with a courage which makes us all proud of you, raised a protest, and cried aloud, 'The visit of the Queen of England is a political action, and if we accord her a welcome we shall stand shamed before the nations. The world will no longer believe in the sincerity of our demand for National Freedom!'

And in truth, for Victoria, in the decrepitude of her eighty-one years, to have decided after an absence of half-a-century to revisit the country she hates and whose inhabitants are the victims of the criminal policy of her reign, the survivors of sixty years of organised famine, the political necessity must have been terribly strong; for after all she is a woman, and however vile and selfish and pitiless her soul may be, she must sometimes tremble as death approaches when she thinks of the countless Irish mothers who, shelterless under the cloudy Irish sky, watching their starving little ones, have cursed her before they died.

Every eviction during sixty-three years has been carried out in Victoria's name, and if there is a Justice in Heaven the shame of those poor Irish emigrant girls whose very innocence renders them an easy prey and who have been overcome in the terrible struggle for existence on a foreign shore, will fall on this woman, whose bourgeoise virtue is so boasted and in whose name their homes were destroyed. If she comes to Ireland again before her death to contemplate the ruin she has made it is surely because her ministers and advisors think that England's situation is dangerous and that her journey will have a deep political importance. England has lived for years on a prestige which has had no solid foundation. She has hypnotised the world with the falsehood of her greatness; she has made great nations and small nations alike, believe in her power. It required the dauntless courage and energy of the Boers to destroy for ever this illusion and rescue Europe from the fatal enchantment. Today no one fears the British Empire, her prestige has gone down before the rifles of a few thousand heroic peasants.

If the British Empire means to exist she will have to rely on real strength, and real strength she has not got. England is in decadence. She has sacrificed all to getting money, and money cannot create men, nor give courage to her weakly soldiers. The men who formerly made her greatness, the men from the country districts have disappeared; they have been swallowed up by the great black manufacturing cities; they have been flung into the crucible where gold is made. Today the giants of England are the giants of finance and of the Stock Exchange, who have risen to power on the backs of a struggling mass of pale, exhausted slaves. The storm approaches; the gold which the English have made out of the blood and tears of millions of human beings attracts the covetousness of the world. Who will aid the pirates to keep their spoils? In their terror they turn to Victoria, their Queen. She has succeeded in amassing more gold than any of her subjects; she has always been ready to cover with her royal mantle the crimes and turpitude of her Empire, and now, trembling on the brink of the grave, she rises once more at their call. Soldiers are needed to protect the vampires. The Queen issues an appeal in England, the struggling mass of slaves cry 'Hurrah'; but there is no blood in their veins, no strength in their arms. Soldiers must be found, so Victoria will go herself to fetch them; she will go over to Ireland—to this people who have despised gold, and who, in spite of persecutions and threats, have persisted in their dream of Freedom and idealism, and who, though reduced in numbers, have maintained all the beauty and strength and vitality of their race.

Taking the Shamrock in her withered hand she dares to ask Ireland for soldiers—for soldiers to protect the exterminators of their race! And the reply of Ireland comes sadly but proudly, not through the lips of the miserable little politicians who are touched by the English canker but through the lips of the Irish people:

'Queen, return to your own land; you will find no more Irishmen ready to wear the red shame of your livery. In the past they have done so from ignorance, and because it is hard to die of hunger when one is young and strong and the sun shines, but they shall do so no longer; see! your recruiting agents return unsuccessful and alone from my green hills and plains, because once more hope has revived, and it will be in the ranks of your enemies that my children will find employment and honour! As to those who today enter your service to help in your criminal wars, I deny them! If they die, if they live, it matters not to me, they are no longer Irishmen.'

PATRICK PEARSE
(1879–1916)

The Coming Revolution (1913)

I have come to the conclusion that the Gaelic League, as the Gaelic League, is a spent force; and I am glad of it. I do not mean that no work remains for the Gaelic League, or that the Gaelic League is no longer equal to work; I mean that the vital work to be done in the new Ireland will be done not so much by the Gaelic League itself as by men and movements that have sprung from the Gaelic League or have received from the Gaelic League a new baptism and a new life of grace. The Gaelic League was no reed shaken by the wind, no mere *vox clamantis*:* it was a prophet and more than a prophet. But it was not the Messiah. I do not know if the Messiah has yet come, and I am not sure that there will be any visible and personal Messiah in this redemption: the people itself will perhaps be its own Messiah, the people labouring, scourged, crowned with thorns, agonising and dying, to rise again immortal and impassible. For peoples are divine and are the only things that can properly be spoken of under figures drawn from the divine epos.

If we do not believe in the divinity of our people we have had no business, or very little, all these years in the Gaelic League. In fact, if we had not believed in the divinity of our people, we should in all probability not have gone into the Gaelic League at all. We should have made our peace with the devil, and perhaps might have found him a very decent sort; for he liberally rewards with attorney-generalships, bank balances, villa residences, and so forth, the great and the little who serve him well. Now, we did not turn our backs upon all these desirable things for the sake of *is* and *tá*.* We did it for the sake of Ireland. In other words, we had one and all of us (at least, I had, and I hope that all you had) an ulterior motive in joining the Gaelic League. We never meant to be Gaelic Leaguers and nothing more than Gaelic Leaguers. We meant to do something for Ireland, each in his own way. Our Gaelic League time was to be our tutelage: we had first to learn to know Ireland, to read the lineaments of her face, to understand the accents of her voice; to re-possess ourselves, disinherited as we were, of her spirit and mind, re-enter into our mystical birthright. For this we went to school to the Gaelic League. It was a good school, and we love its name and will champion its fame throughout all the days of our later fighting and striving. But we do not propose to remain schoolboys for ever.

I have often said (quoting, I think, Herbert Spencer)* that education should be a preparation for complete living; and I say now that our Gaelic League education ought to have been a preparation for our complete living as Irish Nationalists. In proportion as we have been faithful and diligent Gaelic Leaguers, our work as Irish

Nationalists (by which term I mean people who accept the ideal of, and work for, the realisation of an Irish Nation, by whatever means) will be earnest and thorough, a valiant and worthy fighting, not the mere carrying out of a ritual. As to what your work as an Irish Nationalist is to be, I cannot conjecture; I know what mine is to be, and would have you know yours and buckle yourself to it. And it may be (nay, it is) that yours and mine will lead us to a common meeting-place, and that on a certain day we shall stand together, with many more beside us, ready for a greater adventure than any of us has yet had, a trial and a triumph to be endured and achieved in common.

This is what I meant when I said that our work henceforward must be done less and less through the Gaelic League and more and more through the groups and the individuals that have arisen, or are arising, out of the Gaelic League. There will be in the Ireland of the next few years a multitudinous activity of Freedom Clubs, Young Republican Parties, Labour Organisations, Socialist Groups, and what not; bewildering enterprises undertaken by sane persons and insane persons, by good men and bad men, many of them seemingly contradictory, some mutually destructive, yet all tending towards a common objective, and that objective: the Irish Revolution.

For if there is one thing that has become plainer than another it is that when the seven men met in O'Connell Street to found the Gaelic League,* they were commencing, had there been a Liancourt* there to make the epigram, not a revolt, but a revolution. The work of the Gaelic League, its appointed work, was that: and the work is done. To every generation its deed. The deed of the generation that has now reached middle life was the Gaelic League: the beginning of the Irish Revolution. Let our generation not shirk *its* deed, which is to accomplish the revolution.

I believe that the national movement of which the Gaelic League has been the soul has reached the point which O'Connell's movement had reached at the close of the series of monster meetings. Indeed, I believe that our movement reached that point a few years ago—say, at the conclusion of the fight for Essential Irish; and I said so at the time. The moment was ripe then for a new Young Ireland Party, with a forward policy; and we have lost much by our hesitation. I propose in all seriousness that we hesitate no longer—that we push on. I propose that we leave Conciliation Hall behind us and go into the Irish Confederation.

Whenever Dr Hyde,* at a meeting at which I have had a chance of speaking after him, has produced his dove of peace, I have always been careful to produce my sword; and to tantalise him by saying that the Gaelic League has brought into Ireland 'Not Peace, but a Sword.' But this does not show any fundamental difference of outlook between my leader and me; for while he is thinking of peace between brother-Irishmen, I am thinking of the sword-point between banded Irishmen and the foreign force that occupies Ireland: and his peace is necessary to my war. It is evident that there can be no peace between the body politic and a foreign substance that has intruded itself into its system: between them war only until the foreign substance is expelled or assimilated.

Whether Home Rule means a loosening or a tightening of England's grip upon Ireland remains yet to be seen. But the coming of Home Rule, if come it does, will make no material difference in the nature of the work that lies before us: it will affect only the means we are to employ, our plan of campaign. There remains, under Home Rule as in its absence, the substantial task of achieving the Irish Nation. I do not think it is going to be achieved without stress and trial, without suffering and bloodshed; at any rate, it is not going to be achieved without *work*. Our business here and now is to get ourselves into harness for such work as has to be done.

I hold that before we can do any work, any *men's* work, we must first realise ourselves as men. Whatever comes to Ireland she needs men. And we of this generation are not in any real sense men, for we suffer things that men do not suffer, and we seek to redress grievances by means which men do not employ. We have, for instance, allowed ourselves to be disarmed; and, now that we have the chance of re-arming, we are not seizing it. Professor Eoin Mac Neill* pointed out last week that we have at this moment an opportunity of rectifying the capital error we made when we allowed ourselves to be disarmed; and such opportunities, he reminds us, do not always come back to nations.

A thing that stands demonstrable is that nationhood is not achieved otherwise than in arms: in one or two instances there may have been no actual bloodshed, but the arms were there and the ability to use them. Ireland unarmed will attain just as much freedom as it is convenient for England to give her; Ireland armed will attain ultimately just as much freedom as she wants. These are matters which may not concern the Gaelic League, as a body; but they concern every member of the Gaelic League, and every man and woman of Ireland. I urged much of this five or six years ago in addresses to the Ard-Chraobh:* but the League was too busy with resolutions to think of revolution, and the only resolution that a member of the League could not come to was the resolution to be a man. My fellow-Leaguers had not (and have not) apprehended that the thing which cannot defend itself, even though it may wear trousers, is no man.

I am glad, then, that the North has 'begun.'* I am glad that the Orangemen have armed, for it is a goodly thing to see arms in Irish hands. I should like to see the A. O. H.* armed. I should like to see the Transport Workers* armed. I should like to see any and every body of Irish citizens armed. We must accustom ourselves to the thought of arms, to the sight of arms, to the use of arms. We may make mistakes in the beginning and shoot the wrong people; but bloodshed is a cleansing and a sanctifying thing, and the nation which regards it as the final horror has lost its manhood. There are many things more horrible than bloodshed; and slavery is one of them.

JAMES CONNOLLY
(1868–1916)

The Irish Flag (1916)

The Council of the Irish Citizen Army has resolved, after grave and earnest deliberation, to hoist the green flag of Ireland over Liberty Hall, as over a fortress held for Ireland by the arms of Irishmen.

This is a momentous decision in the most serious crisis Ireland has witnessed in our day and generation. It will, we are sure, send a thrill through the hearts of every true Irish man and woman, and send the red blood coursing fiercely along the veins of every lover of the race.

It means that in the midst of and despite the treasons and back-slidings of leaders and guides, in the midst of and despite all the weaknesses, corruption and moral cowardice of a section of the people, in the midst of and despite all this there still remains in Ireland a spot where a body of true men and women are ready to hoist, gather round, and to defend the flag made sacred by all the sufferings of all the martyrs of the past.

Since this unholy war first started we have seen every symbol of Irish freedom desecrated to the purposes of the enemy, we have witnessed the prostitution of every holy Irish tradition. That the young men of Ireland might be seduced into the service of the nation that denies every national power to their country, we have seen appeals made to our love of freedom, to our religious instincts, to our sympathy for the oppressed, to our kinship with suffering.

The power that for seven hundred years has waged bitter and unrelenting war upon the freedom of Ireland, and that still declares that the rights of Ireland must forever remain subordinate to the interests of the British Empire, hypocritically appealed to our young men to enlist under her banner and shed their blood 'in the interests of freedom'.

The power whose reign in Ireland has been one long carnival of corruption and debauchery of civic virtue, and which has rioted in the debasement and degradation of everything Irish men and women hold sacred, appealed to us in the name of religion to fight for her as the champion of christendom.

The power which holds in subjection more of the world's population than any other power on the globe, and holds them in subjection as slaves without any guarantee of freedom or power of self-government, this power that sets Catholic against Protestant, the Hindu against the Mohammedan, the yellow man against the brown, and keeps them quarrelling with each other whilst she robs and murders them all—this power appeals to Ireland to send her sons to fight under England's banner for the cause of the oppressed. The power whose rule in Ireland has made of Ireland a desert, and made the history of our race read like the records of a shambles, as she plans for the annihilation of another race appeals to our manhood to fight for her because of our sympathy for the suffering, and of our hatred of oppression.

For generations the shamrock was banned as a national emblem of Ireland, but in her extremity England uses the shamrock as a means for exciting in foolish Irishmen loyalty to England. For centuries the green flag of Ireland was a thing accurst and hated by the English garrison in Ireland, as it is still in their inmost hearts. But in India, in Egypt, in Flanders, in Gallipoli, the green flag is used by our rulers to encourage Irish soldiers of England to give up their lives for the power that denies their country the right of nationhood. Green flags wave over recruiting offices in Ireland and England as a bait to lure on poor fools to dishonourable deaths in England's uniform.

The national press of Ireland, the true national press, uncorrupted and unterrified, has largely succeeded in turning back the tide of demoralization, and opening up the minds of the Irish public to a realization of the truth about the position of their country in the war. The national press of Ireland is a real flag of freedom flying for Ireland despite the enemy, but it is well that also there should fly in Dublin the green flag of this country as a rallying point of our forces and embodiment of all our hopes. Where better could that flag fly than over the unconquered citadel of the Irish working class, Liberty Hall, the fortress of the militant working class of Ireland.

We are out for Ireland for the Irish. But who are the Irish? Not the rack-renting, slum-owning landlord; not the sweating, profit-grinding capitalist; not the sleek and oily lawyer; not the prostitute pressman—the hired liars of the enemy. Not these are the Irish upon whom the future depends. Not these, but the Irish working class, the only secure foundation upon which a free nation can be reared.

The cause of labour is the cause of Ireland, the cause of Ireland is the cause of labour. They cannot be dissevered. Ireland seeks freedom. Labour seeks that an Ireland free should be the sole mistress of her own destiny, supreme owner of all material things within and upon her soil. Labour seeks to make the free Irish nation the guardian of the interests of the people of Ireland, and to secure that end would vest in that free Irish nation all property rights as against the claims of the individual, with the end in view that the individual may be enriched by the nation, and not by the spoiling of his fellows.

Having in view such a high and holy function for the nation to perform, is it not well and fitting that we of the working class should fight for the freedom of the nation from foreign rule, as the first requisite for the free development of the national powers needed for our class? It is so fitting. Therefore on Sunday, 16 April 1916, the green flag of Ireland will be solemnly hoisted over Liberty Hall as the symbol of our faith in freedom, and as a token to all the world that the working class of Dublin stands for the cause of Ireland, and the cause of Ireland is the cause of a separate and distinct nationality.

In these days of doubt, despair, and resurgent hope we fling our banner to the breeze, the flag of our fathers, the symbol of our national redemption, the sunburst shining over an Ireland re-born.

JAMES STEPHENS
(1880–1950)

from *The Insurrection in Dublin* (1916)

III
WEDNESDAY

It was three o'clock before I got to sleep last night, and during the hours machine guns and rifle firing had been continuous.

This morning the sun is shining brilliantly, and the movement in the streets possesses more of animation than it has done. The movement ends always in a knot of people, and folk go from group to group vainly seeking information, and quite content if the rumour they presently gather differs even a little from the one they have just communicated.

The first statement I heard was that the Green had been taken by the military; the second that it had been re-taken; the third that it had not been taken at all. The facts at last emerged that the Green had not been occupied by the soldiers, but that the Volunteers had retreated from it into a house which commanded it. This was found to be the College of Surgeons, and from the windows and roof of this College they were sniping. A machine gun was mounted on the roof; other machine guns, however, opposed them from the roofs of the Shelbourne Hotel, the United Service Club, and the Alexandra Club. Thus a triangular duel opened between these positions across the trees of the Park.

Through the railings of the Green some rifles and bandoliers could be seen lying on the ground, as also the deserted trenches and snipers' holes. Small boys bolted in to see these sights and bolted out again with bullets quickening their feet. Small boys do not believe that people will really kill them, but small boys were killed.

The dead horse was still lying stiff and lamentable on the footpath.

This morning a gunboat came up the Liffey and helped to bombard Liberty Hall. The Hall is breeched and useless. Rumour says that it was empty at the time, and that Connolly with his men had marched long before to the Post Office and the Green. The same source of information relates that three thousand Volunteers came from Belfast on an excursion train and that they marched into the Post Office.

On this day only one of my men came in. He said that he had gone on the roof and had been shot at, consequently that the Volunteers held some of the covering houses. I went to the roof and remained there for half an hour. There were no shots, but the firing from the direction of Sackville Street was continuous and at times exceedingly heavy.

To-day the *Irish Times* was published. It contained a new military proclamation, and a statement that the country was peaceful, and told that in Sackville Street some houses were burned to the ground.

On the outside railings a bill proclaiming Martial Law was posted.

Into the newspaper statement that peace reigned in the country one was inclined to read more of disquietude than of truth, and one said is the country so extraordinarily peaceful that it can be dismissed in three lines. There is too much peace or too much reticence, but it will be some time before we hear from outside of Dublin.

Meanwhile the sun was shining. It was a delightful day, and the streets outside and around the areas of fire were animated and even gay. In the streets of Dublin there were no morose faces to be seen. Almost everyone was smiling and attentive, and a democratic feeling was abroad, to which our City is very much a stranger; for while in private we are a sociable and talkative people we have no street manners or public ease whatever. Every person spoke to every other person, and men and women mixed and talked without constraint.

Was the City for or against the Volunteers? Was it for the Volunteers, and yet against the rising? It is considered now (writing a day or two afterwards) that Dublin was entirely against the Volunteers, but on the day of which I write no such certainty could be put forward. There was a singular reticence on the subject. Men met and talked volubly, but they said nothing that indicated a personal desire or belief. They asked for and exchanged the latest news, or, rather, rumour, and while expressions were frequent of astonishment at the suddenness and completeness of the occurrence, no expression of opinion for or against was anywhere formulated.

Sometimes a man said, 'They will be beaten of course,' and, as he prophesied, the neighbour might surmise if he did so with a sad heart or a merry one, but they knew nothing and asked nothing of his views, and themselves advanced no flag.

This was among the men.

The women were less guarded, or, perhaps, knew they had less to fear. Most of the female opinion I heard was not alone unfavourable but actively and viciously hostile to the rising. This was noticeable among the best dressed class of our population; the worst dressed, indeed the female dregs of Dublin life, expressed a like antagonism, and almost in similar language. The view expressed was—

'I hope every man of them will be shot.'

And—

'They ought to be all shot.'

Shooting, indeed, was proceeding everywhere. During daylight, at least, the sound is not sinister nor depressing, and the thought that perhaps a life had exploded with that crack is not depressing either.

In the last two years of world-war our ideas on death have undergone a change. It is not now the furtive thing that crawled into your bed and which you fought with pill-boxes and medicine bottles. It has become again a rider of the wind whom you may go coursing with through the fields and open places. All the morbidity is gone, and the sickness, and what remains to Death is now health and excitement. So Dublin laughed at the noise of its own bombardment, and made no moan about its dead—in the sunlight. Afterwards—in the rooms, when the night fell, and instead of silence that mechanical barking of the maxims and the whistle and screams of the rifles, the solemn roar of the heavier guns, and the red glare covering the sky. It is possible that in the night Dublin did not laugh, and that she was gay in the sunlight for no other reason than that the night was past.

On this day fighting was incessant at Mount Street Bridge. A party of Volunteers had seized three houses covering the bridge and converted these into forts. It is reported that military casualties at this point were very heavy. The Volunteers are said also to hold the South Dublin Union. The soldiers have seized Guinness's Brewery, while their opponents have seized another brewery in the neighbourhood, and between these two there is a continual fusilade.

Fighting is brisk about Ringsend and along the Canal. Dame Street was said to be held in many places by the Volunteers. I went down Dame Street, but saw no Volunteers, and did not observe any sniping from the houses. Further, as Dame Street is entirely commanded by the roofs and windows of Trinity College, it is unlikely that they should be here.

It was curious to observe this, at other times, so animated street, broad and deserted, with at the corners of side streets small knots of people watching. Seen from behind, Grattan's Statue in College Green seemed almost alive, and he had the air of addressing warnings and reproaches to Trinity College.

The Proclamation issued to-day warns all people to remain within doors until five o'clock in the morning, and after seven o'clock at night.

It is still early. There is no news of any kind, and the rumours begin to catch quickly on each other and to cancel one another out. Dublin is entirely cut off from England, and from the outside world. It is, just as entirely cut off from the rest of Ireland; no news of any kind filters in to us. We are land-locked and sea-locked, but, as yet, it does not much matter.

Meantime the belief grows that the Volunteers may be able to hold out much longer than had been imagined. The idea at first among the people had been that the insurrection would be ended the morning after it had begun. But to-day, the insurrection having lasted three days, people are ready to conceive that it may last for ever. There is almost a feeling of gratitude towards the Volunteers because they are holding out for a little while, for had they been beaten the first or second day the City would have been humiliated to the soul.

People say: 'Of course, they will be beaten.' The statement is almost a query, and they continue, 'but they are putting up a decent fight.' For being beaten does not greatly matter in Ireland, but not fighting does matter. 'They went forth always to the battle; and they always fell,' Indeed, the history of the Irish race is in that phrase.

The firing from the roofs of Trinity College became violent. I crossed Dame Street some distance up, struck down the Quays, and went along these until I reached the Ballast Office. Further than this it was not possible to go, for a step beyond the Ballast Office would have brought one into the unending stream of lead that was pouring from Trinity and other places. I was looking on O'Connell Bridge and Sackville Street, and the house facing me was Kelly's—a red-brick fishing tackle shop, one half of which was on the Quay and the other half in Sackville Street. This house was being bombarded.

I counted the report of six different machine guns which played on it. Rifles innumerable and from every sort of place were potting its windows, and at intervals of about half a minute the shells from a heavy gun lobbed in through its windows or thumped mightily against its walls.

For three hours that bombardment continued, and the walls stood in a cloud of red dust and smoke. Rifle and machine gun bullets pattered over every inch of it, and, unfailingly the heavy gun pounded its shells through the windows.

One's heart melted at the idea that human beings were crouching inside that volcano of death, and I said to myself, 'Not even a fly can be alive in that house.'

No head showed at any window, no rifle cracked from window or roof in reply. The house was dumb, lifeless, and I thought every one of those men are dead.

It was then, and quite suddenly, that the possibilities of street fighting flashed on me, and I knew there was no person in the house, and said to myself, 'They have smashed through the walls with a hatchet and are sitting in the next house, or they have long ago climbed out by the skylight and are on a roof half a block away.' Then the thought came to me—they have and hold the entire of Sackville Street down to the Post Office. Later on this proved to be the case, and I knew at this moment that Sackville Street was doomed.

I continued to watch the bombardment, but no longer with the anguish which had before torn me. Near by there were four men, and a few yards away, clustered in a laneway, there were a dozen others. An agitated girl was striding from the farther group to the one in which I was, and she addressed the men in the most obscene language which I have ever heard. She addressed them man by man, and she continued to speak and cry and scream at them with all that obstinate, angry patience of which only a woman is capable.

She cursed us all. She called down diseases on every human being in the world excepting only the men who were being bombarded.

She demanded of the folk in the laneway that they should march at least into the roadway and prove that they were proud men and were not afraid of bullets. She had been herself into the danger zone. Had stood herself in the track of the guns, and had there cursed her fill for half an hour, and she desired that the men should do at least what she had done.

This girl was quite young—about nineteen years of age—and was dressed in the customary shawl and apron of her class. Her face was rather pretty, or it had that pretty slenderness and softness of outline which belong to youth. But every sentence she spoke contained half a dozen indecent words. Alas, it was only that her vocabulary was not equal to her emotions, and she did not know how to be emphatic without being obscene—it is the cause of most of the meaningless swearing one hears every day. She spoke to me for a minute, and her eyes were as soft as those of a kitten and her language was as gentle as her eyes. She wanted a match to light a cigarette, but I had none, and said that I also wanted one. In a few minutes she brought me a match, and then she recommenced her tireless weaving of six vile words into hundreds of stupid sentences.

About five o'clock the guns eased off of Kelly's.

To inexperienced eyes they did not seem to have done very much damage, but afterwards one found that although the walls were standing and apparently solid there was no inside to the house. From roof to basement the building was bare as a dog kennel. There were no floors inside, there was nothing there but blank space; and on the ground within was the tumble and rubbish that had been roof and floors and furniture. Everything inside was smashed and pulverised into scrap and dust, and the only objects that had consistency and their ancient shape were the bricks that fell when the shells struck them.

Rifle shots had begun to strike the house on the further side of the street, a jewellers' shop called Hopkins & Hopkins. The impact of these balls on the bricks was louder than the sound of the shot which immediately succeeded, and each bullet that struck brought down a shower of fine red dust from the walls. Perhaps thirty or forty shots in all were fired at Hopkins', and then, except for an odd crack, firing ceased.

During all this time there had been no reply from the Volunteers, and I thought they must be husbanding their ammunition, and so must be short of it, and that it would be only a matter of a few days before the end. All this, I said to myself, will be finished in a few days, and they will be finished; life here will recommence exactly where it left off, and except for some newly-filled graves, all will be as it had been until they become a tradition and enter the imagination of their race.

I spoke to several of the people about me, and found the same willingness to exchange news that I had found elsewhere in the City, and the same reticences as regarded their private opinions. Two of them, indeed, and they were the only two I met with during the insurrection, expressed, although in measured terms, admiration for the Volunteers, and while they did not side with them they did not say anything against them. One was a labouring man, the other a gentleman. The remark of the latter was:

'I am an Irishman, and (pointing to the shells that were bursting through the windows in front of us) I hate to see that being done to other Irishmen.'

He had come from some part of the country to spend the Easter Holidays in Dublin, and was unable to leave town again.

The labouring man—he was about fifty-six years of age—spoke very quietly and collectedly about the insurrection. He was a type with whom I had come very little in contact, and I was surprised to find how simple and good his speech was, and how calm his ideas. He thought labour was in this movement to a greater extent than was imagined. I mentioned that Liberty Hall had been blown up, and that the garrison had either surrendered or been killed. He replied that a gunboat had that morning come up the river and had blown Liberty Hall into smash, but, he added, there were no men in it. All the Labour Volunteers had marched with Connolly into the Post Office.

He said the Labour Volunteers might possibly number about one thousand men, but that it would be quite safe to say eight hundred, and he held that the Labour Volunteers, or the Citizens' Army, as they called themselves, had always been careful not to reveal their numbers. They had always announced that they possessed about two hundred and fifty men, and had never paraded any more than that number at any one time. Workingmen, he continued, knew that the men who marched were always different men. The police knew it, too, but they thought that the Citizens Army was the *most deserted-from force* in the world.

The men, however, were not deserters—you don't, he said, desert a man like Connolly, and they were merely taking their turn at being drilled and disciplined. They were raised against the police who, in the big strike of two years ago, had acted towards them with unparalleled savagery, and the men had determined that the police would never again find them thus disorganised.

This man believed that every member of the Citizen Army had marched with their leader.

'The men, I know,' said he, 'would not be afraid of anything, and,' he continued, 'they are in the Post Office now.'

'What chance have they?'

'None,' he replied, 'and they never said they had, and they never thought they would have any.'

'How long do you think they'll be able to hold out?'

He nodded towards the house that had been bombarded by heavy guns.

'That will root them out of it quick enough,' was his reply.

'I'm going home,' said he then, 'the people will be wondering if I'm dead or alive,' and he walked away from that sad street, as I did myself a few minutes afterwards.

CONSTANCE MARKIEWICZ
(1868–1927)

Stephen's Green (1926)

I am afraid I can only give you a little account of those who were enrolled like me in the Irish Citizen Army, and those who were with me or whom I met during the week. Some were members of Cumann na mBan, and others just women who were ready to die for Ireland.

My activities were confined to a very limited area. I was mobilised for Liberty Hall and was sent from there via the City Hall, to Stephen's Green, where I remained.

On Easter Monday there was a great hosting of disciplined and armed men and women at Liberty Hall. Padraig Pearse and James Connolly addressed us and told us that from now on the

Volunteers and the ICA were not two forces, but two wings of the Irish Republican Army.

There were a considerable number of ICA women. These were absolutely on the same footing as the men. They took part in all marches, and even in the manoeuvres that lasted all night. Moreover, Connolly made it quite clear to us that unless we women took our share in the drudgery of training and preparing, we should not be allowed to take any share at all in the fight. You may judge how fit we were when I tell you that sixteen miles was the length of the average route march.

Connolly had appointed two staff officers—Commandant Mallin and myself. I held a commission, giving me the rank of Staff Lieutenant. I was accepted by Tom Clarke and the members of the Provisional Government as the second of Connolly's 'ghosts'. Ghosts was the name we gave to those who stood secretly behind the leaders, and who were entrusted with enough of the plans of the Rising to enable them to carry on that leader's work should anything happen to himself. Commandant Mallin was over me and next in command to Connolly. Dr Kathleen Lynn was our medical officer, holding the rank of Captain.

We watched the little bodies of men and women march off— Pearse and Connolly to the GPO, Sean Connolly to the City Hall. I went with the Doctor in her car. We carried a huge store of first aid necessities and drove off through the quiet, dusty streets and across the river, reaching the City Hall just at the very moment Commandant Sean Connolly and his little troop of men and women swung round the corner and he raised his gun and shot the policeman who barred the way. A wild excitement ensued, people running from every side to see what was up. The Doctor got out, and I remember Mrs Barrett—sister of Scan Connolly—and others helping to carry in the Doctor's bundle. I did not meet Dr Lynn again till my release, when her car met me, and she welcomed me to her house where she cared for me and fed me up and looked after me till I had recovered from the evil effects of the English prison system.

When I reported with the car to Commandant Mallin in Stephen's Green he told me that he must keep me. He said that, owing to MacNeill's call-off of the Volunteers, a lot of the men who should have been under him had had to be distributed round other posts and that few of those left him were trained to shoot, so I must stay and be ready to take up the work of a sniper. He took me round the Green and showed me how the barricading of the gates and digging trenches had begun, and left me in charge of this work while he went to superintend the erection of barricades in the street and arrange other work. About two hours later he definitely promoted me to be his second-in-command. This work was very exciting when the fighting began. I continued to go round and round the Green, reporting back if anything was wanted or tackling any sniper who was particularly objectionable.

Madeleine ffrench-Mullen was in charge of the Red Cross and the commissariat in the Green. Some of the girls had revolvers and with these they sallied forth and held up bread-vans.

This was necessary, because the first prisoner we took was a British officer, and Commandant Mallin treated him as such. He took his parole as 'an officer and a gentleman' not to escape and he left him at large in the Green before the gates were shut. This English gentleman walked around and found out all he could and then 'bunked.'

We had a couple of sick men and prisoners in the band-stand, the Red Cross flag flying to protect them. The English in the Shelbourne turned a machine-gun on to them. A big group of our girls were attending to the sick, making tea for the prisoners, or resting themselves. I never saw anything like their courage. Madeleine ffrench-Mullen brought them, with the sick and the prisoners, out and into a safer place. It was all done slowly and in perfect order. More than one girl said to me: 'What is there to be afraid of? Won't I go straight to heaven if I die for Ireland.' However it was, they came out unscathed from under a shower of shrapnel.

On Tuesday we began to be short of food. There were no bread carts on the streets. We retired into the College of Surgeons that evening and were joined by some of our men, who had been in other places, and by quite a large squad of Volunteers, and with this increase in our numbers the problem of food became very serious.

Nellie Gifford was put in charge of one large classroom with a big grate; but alas! there was nothing to cook. When we were all starving she produced a quantity of oatmeal from somewhere and made pot after potful of the most delicious porridge, which kept us going. But, all the same, on Tuesday and Wednesday we absolutely starved. There seemed to be no bread in the town.

Later on Mary Hyland was given charge of a little kitchen somewhere down through the houses, near where the Eithne Workroom now is.

We had only one woman casualty—Margaret Skinnider. She, like myself, was in uniform and carried an army rifle. She had enlisted as a private in the ICA. She was one of a party who went out to set fire to a house just behind Russell's Hotel. The English opened fire on them from the ground floor of a house just opposite. Poor Freddy Ryan was killed and Margaret was very badly wounded. She owes her life to William Partridge. He carried her away under fire and back to the College.

God rest his noble soul! Brilliant orator and labour leader, comrade and friend of Connolly's, he was content to serve as a private in the ICA. He was never strong and the privations he suffered in an English jail left him a dying man.

Margaret's only regret was her bad luck in being disabled so early in the day, though she must have suffered terribly; but the end was nearer than we thought, for it was only a few days later that we had her carried over to Vincent's Hospital, so that she would not fall wounded into the hands of the English.

The memory of Easter Week with its heroic dead is sacred to us who survived. Many of us could almost wish we had died in the moment of ecstasy when, with the Tricolour over our heads we went out and proclaimed the Irish Republic and with guns in our hands tried to establish it. We failed, but not until we had seen regiment after regiment run from our few guns. Our effort will inspire the people who come after us and will give them hope and courage. If we failed to win, so did the English. They slaughtered and imprisoned, only to rouse the nation to a passion of love and loyalty—loyalty to Ireland and hatred of foreign rule. Once they see clearly that the English rule us still, only with a new personnel of traitors and new uniforms, they will finish the work begun by the men and women of Easter Week.

ROGER CASEMENT
(1864–1916)

Speech from the Dock (1916)

I may say at once, my lord, that I protest against that jurisdiction of this court in my case on this charge and the argument that I am now going to read is addressed not to this court, but to my own countrymen. There is an objection, possibly not good in law, but surely good on moral grounds, against the application to me here of this old English statute, 565 years old, that seeks to deprive an Irishman today of life and honour, not for adhering to the king's enemies, but for adhering to his own people. When this statute was passed in 1351, what was the state of men's minds on the question of a far higher allegiance—that of a man to God and his kingdom? The law of that day did not permit a man to forsake his Church, or deny his God, save with his life. The 'heretic' then had the same doom as the 'traitor'. Today, a man may forswear God and his heavenly kingdom without fear or penalty—all earlier statutes having gone the way of Nero's edicts against the Christians; but that Constitutional phantom, 'the King', can still dig up from the dungeons and torture-chambers of the Dark Ages a law that takes a man's life and limb for an exercise of conscience.

If true religion rests on love, it is equally true that loyalty rests on love. The law I am charged under has no parentage in love, and claims the allegiance of to-day on the ignorance and blindness of the past. I am being tried, in truth, not by my peers of the live present, but by the fears of the dead past; not by the civilization of the twentieth century, but by the brutality of the fourteenth; not even by a statute framed in the language of the land that tries me, but emitted in the language of an enemy-land—so antiquated is the law that must be sought to-day to slay an Irishman, whose offence is that he puts Ireland first! Loyalty is a sentiment, not a law. It rests on love, not on restraint. The government of Ireland by England rests on restraint, and not on law; and, since it demands no love, it can evoke no loyalty.

But this statute is more absurd even than it is antiquated; and if it be potent to hang even one Irishman, it is still more potent to gibbet all Englishmen. Edward III was king, not only of the realm of England, but also of the realm of France, and he was not king of Ireland. Yet his dead hand to-day may pull the noose around the Irishman's neck, whose sovereign he was not, but it can strain no strand around the Frenchman's throat, whose sovereign he was. For centuries, the successors of Edward III claimed to be kings of France, and quartered the arms of France on their royal shield down to the Union with Ireland on January 1st, 1801. Throughout these hundreds of years, these 'kings of France' were constantly at war with their realm of France and their French subjects, who should have gone from birth to death with an obvious fear of treason before their eyes. But did they? Did the 'kings of France' resident here at Windsor or in the Tower of London hang, draw and quarter as a traitor every Frenchman for four hundred years who fell into their power with arms in his hands? On the contrary, they received embassies of these traitors, presents from these traitors, even knighthood itself at the hands of these traitors, feasted with them, tilted with them, fought with them—but did not assassinate them by law.

Judicial assassination to-day is reserved only for one race of the king's subjects—for Irishmen, for those who cannot forget their allegiance to the realm of Ireland. The kings of England as such had no rights in Ireland up to the time of Henry VIII, save such as rested on compact and mutual obligation entered into between them and certain princes, chiefs and lords of Ireland. This form of legal right, such as it was, gave no king of England lawful power to impeach an Irishman for his high treason under this statute of King Edward III of England until an Irish Act, known as Poyning's Law, the tenth of Henry VII, was passed in 1494 at Drogheda by the Parliament of the Pale in Ireland and enacted as law *in that part of Ireland*. But if by Poyning's Law an Irishman of the Pale could be indicted for high treason under this Act, he could be indicted only in one way, and before one tribunal—by the law of the realm of Ireland, and in Ireland. The very law of Poyning, which, I believe, applies this statute of Edward III to Ireland, enacted also for the Irishman's defence 'all those laws by which England claims her liberty'. And what is the fundamental charter of an Englishman's liberty? That he shall be tried by his peers. With all respect, I assert this court is to me, an Irishman, not a jury of my peers to try me in this vital issue; for it is patent to every man of conscience that I have an indefeasible right, if tried at all under this statute of high treason, to be tried in Ireland, before an Irish Court and by an Irish jury. This court, this jury, the public opinion of this country, England, cannot but be prejudiced in varying degrees against me, most of all in time of war. I did not land in England. I landed in Ireland. It was to Ireland I came; to Ireland I wanted to come; and the last place I desired to land in was England.

But, for the Attorney-General of England there is only England; there is no Ireland; there is only the law of England, no right of Ireland; the liberty of Ireland and of Irishmen is to be judged by the power of England. Yet for me, the Irish outlaw, there is a land of Ireland, a right of Ireland, and a charter for all Irishmen to appeal to, in the last resort, a charter that even the very statutes of England itself cannot deprive us of—nay more, a charter that Englishmen themselves assert as the fundamental bond of law that connects the two kingdoms. This charge of high treason involves a moral responsibility, as the very terms of the indictment against myself recite, inasmuch as I committed the acts I am charged with to 'the evil example of others in the like case'. What was the evil example I set to others in the like case, and who were these others? The 'evil example' charge is that I asserted the right of my own country, and 'the others' to whom I appealed to aid my endeavour were my own countrymen. The example was given not to Englishmen, but to Irishmen, and 'the like case' can never arise in England, but only in Ireland. To Englishmen, I set no evil example, for I make no appeal to them. I asked no Englishman to help me. I asked Irishmen to fight for their rights. The 'evil example' was only to other Irishmen, who might come after me and in 'like case' seek to do as I did. How, then, since neither my example nor my appeal was addressed to Englishmen, can I be rightly tried by them?

If I did wrong in making that appeal to Irishmen to join with me in an effort to fight for Ireland, it is by Irishmen, and by them alone, I can be rightfully judged. From this court and its jurisdiction I appeal to those I am alleged to have wronged and injured by my 'evil example' and claim that they alone are competent to decide my guilt or innocence. If they find me guilty, the statute may affix the penalty; but the statute does not override or annul my right to seek judgement at their hands. This is so fundamental a right, so natural, so obvious, that it is clear the Crown were aware of it when they brought me by force and by stealth from Ireland to this country. It was not I who landed in England, but the Crown that dragged me here, away from my own country, to which I had returned with a price upon my head; away from my own countrymen, whose loyalty is not in doubt, and safe from the judgement of my peers, whose judgement I do not shrink from. I admit no other judgement but theirs. I accept no verdict save at their hands.

I assert from this dock that I am being tried here, not because it is just, but because it is unjust. Place me before a jury of my countrymen, be it Protestant or Catholic, Unionist or Nationalist, Sinn Féineach or Orange, and I shall accept the verdict, and bow to the statute and all its penalties. But I shall accept no meaner finding against me than that of those whose loyalty I endangered by my example and to whom alone I made appeal. If they adjudge me guilty, then guilty I am. It is not I who am afraid of their verdict—it is the Crown. If this is not so, why fear the test? I fear it not. I demand it as my right. This is the condemnation of English rule, of English-made law, of English government in Ireland, that it dare not rest on the will of the Irish people, but exists in defiance of their will; that it is a rule derived not from right, but from conquest. But conquest, my lord, gives no title; and, if it exists over the body, it fails over the mind. It can exert no empire over men's reason and judgement and affections; and it is from this law of conquest that I appeal. I would add that the generous expressions of sympathy extended to me from many quarters, particularly from America, have touched me very much. In that country, as in my own, I am sure my motives are understood, and not misjudged,—for the achievement of their liberty has been an abiding inspiration to Irishmen, and to all men elsewhere, rightly struggling to be free.

Let me pass from myself and my own fate to a more pressing, as it is a far more urgent theme—not the fate of the individual Irishman who may have tried and failed, but the claims and the fate of the country that has not failed. Ireland has not failed. Ireland has outlived the failure of all her hopes—and she still hopes. Ireland has seen her sons—aye, and her daughters, too!—suffer from generation to generation, always for the same cause, meeting always the same fate, and always at the hands of the same power. Still, always a fresh generation has passed on to withstand the same oppression. For if English authority be omnipotent—a power, as Mr Gladstone phrased it, that reaches to the very ends of the earth—Irish hope exceeds the dimensions of that power, excels its authority, and renews with each generation the claims of the last. The cause that begets this indomitable persistency, the faculty of preserving through centuries of misery the remembrance of lost liberty—this surely is the noblest cause ever man strove for, ever lived for, ever died for. If this be the cause I stand here to-day indicted for and convicted of sustaining, then I stand in a goodly company and a right noble succession.

My counsel has referred to the Ulster Volunteer movement, and I will not touch at length upon that ground, save only to say this: that neither I nor any of the leaders of the Irish Volunteers, who were founded in Dublin in November 1913, had any quarrel with the Ulster Volunteers as such, who were born a year earlier. Our movement was not directed against them, but against the men who misused and misdirected the courage, the sincerity and the local patriotism of the men of the North of Ireland. On the contrary, we welcomed the coming of the Ulster Volunteers, even while we deprecated the aims and intentions of those Englishmen who sought to pervert to an English party use—to the mean purposes of their own bid for place and power in England—the armed activity of simple Irishmen. We aimed at winning the Ulster Volunteers to the cause of a United Ireland. We aimed at uniting all Irishmen in a natural and national bond of cohesion based on mutual self-respect. Our hope was a natural one and, were we left to ourselves, not hard to accomplish. If internal influences of disintegration would but leave us alone, we were sure that nature itself must bring us together. It was not we, the Irish Volunteers, who broke the law, but a British party. The Government had permitted the Ulster Volunteers to be armed by Englishmen, to threaten not merely an English party in its hold on office, but to threaten that party through the lives and blood of Irishmen.

The battle was to be fought in Ireland in order that the political 'outs' of to-day should be the 'ins' of to-morrow in Great Britain. A law designed for the benefit of Ireland was to be met, not on the floor of Parliament, where the fight had indeed been won, but on the field of battle much nearer home, where the armies would be composed of Irishmen slaying each other for some English party gain; and the British Navy would be the chartered 'transports' that were to bring to our shores a numerous assemblage of military and ex-military experts in the congenial and profitable exercise of holding down subject populations abroad. Our choice lay in submitting to foreign lawlessness or resisting it, and we did not hesitate to choose. But while the law-breakers had armed their would-be agents openly, and had been permitted to arm them openly, we were met within a few days of founding of our movement—that aimed at a United Ireland from within—by Government action from without, directed against our obtaining any arms at all.

The Manifesto of the Irish Volunteers, promulgated at a public meeting in Dublin, November 25th 1913, stated with certainty the aims of the organization, as I have outlined them. If the aims set out in that manifesto were a threat to the unity of the British Empire, then so much the worse for the Empire. An Empire that can only be held together by one section of its governing population perpetually holding down and sowing dissension among a smaller but none-the-less governing section, must have some canker at its heart, some ruin at its root. The Government that permitted the arming of those whose leaders declared that Irish national unity was a thing that should be opposed by force of arms, within nine days of the issue of our manifesto of good-will to Irishmen of every creed and class, took steps to nullify our efforts by prohibiting the import of all arms into Ireland as if it had been a hostile and blockaded coast. And this Proclamation of the 4th December 1913, known as the Arms Proclamation, was itself based on an illegal interpretation of the law, as the Chief Secretary* has now publicly confessed. The Proclamation was met by the loyalists of Great Britain with an act of still more lawless defiance—an act of widespread gun-running into Ulster, that was denounced by the Lord Chancellor of England as 'grossly illegal and utterly unconstitutional'.* How did the Irish Volunteers meet the incitements to civil war that were uttered by the party of law and order in England?

I can answer for my own acts and speeches. While one English party was responsible for preaching a doctrine of hatred, designed to bring about civil war in Ireland, the other—and that the party in power—took no active steps to restrain a propaganda that found its advocates in the Army, Navy and Privy Council—in the Houses of Parliament and in the State Church—a propaganda the methods of whose expression were so 'grossly illegal and utterly unconstitutional' that even the Lord Chancellor of England could find only words and no repressive action to apply them. Since lawlessness sat in high places in England and laughed at the law as at the custodians of the law, what wonder was it that Irishmen should refuse to accept the verbal protestations of an English Lord Chancellor as a sufficient safeguard for their liberties. I know not how all my colleagues on the Volunteer Committee in Dublin received the growing menace, but those with whom I was in closest co-operation re-doubled, in face of these threats from without, our efforts to unite all Irishmen from within. Our appeals were made to Protestant and Unionist as much almost as to Catholic and Nationalist Irishmen. We hoped that by the exhibition of affection and good-will on our part towards our political opponents in Ireland, we should yet succeed in winning them from the side of an English party, whose sole interest in our country lay in its oppression in the past, and in the present in its degradation to the mean and narrow needs of their political animosities.

It is true that they based their actions—so they averred—on 'fears for the Empire' and on a very diffuse loyalty that took in all the peoples of the Empire, save only the Irish. That blessed word *Empire*, that bears so paradoxical resemblance to charity! For if charity begins at home, *Empire* begins in other men's homes, and both may cover a multitude of sins. I, for one, was determined that Ireland was much more to me than *Empire*, and that, if charity begins at home, so must loyalty. Since arms were so necessary to make our organization a reality, and to give to the minds of Irishmen, menaced with the most outrageous threats, a sense of security, it was our bounden duty to get arms before all else. I decided, with this end in view, to go to America, with surely, a better right to appeal to Irishmen there for help in an hour of great national trial than those envoys of Empire could assert for their week-end descents on Ireland, or their appeals to Germany. If, as the right honourable gentleman, the present Attorney-General,* asserted in a speech at Manchester, Nationalists would neither fight for Home Rule nor pay for it, it was our duty to show him that *we* knew how to do both. Within a few weeks of my arrival in the United States, the fund that had been opened to secure arms for the Volunteers of Ireland amounted to many thousands of pounds. In every case the money subscribed, whether it came from the purse of the wealthy man or the still readier pocket of the poor man, was Irish gold.

Then came the war!—which, as Mr Birrell said, 'upset all calculations'. It upset mine no less than Mr Birrell's, and put an end to my
peaceful effort in America. A constitutional movement in Ireland is
never very far from a breach of the constitution, as the loyalists of
Ulster have been so eager to show us. A constitution, to be maintained intact, must be the achievement and the pride of the people
themselves, must rest on their own free will and on their own
determination to maintain it, instead of being something resident in
another land, whose chief representative is an armed force—armed
not to protect the population, but to hold it down. We had seen the
workings of 'the Irish Constitution' in the refusal of the Army of
Occupation at the Curragh to obey the orders of the Crown.* And
now that we were told the first duty of an Irishman was to enter that
army, in return for a promissory note, payable after death—a scrap
of paper that might or might not be redeemed—I felt, over there, in
America, that my first duty was to keep Irishmen at home in the only
army that could safeguard our national existence. If small nation-
alities were to be the pawns in this game of embattled giants, I saw no
reason why Ireland should shed her blood in any cause but her own,
and, if that be treason beyond the seas, I am not ashamed to avow it,
or to answer for it here with my life. And when we had the doctrine
of Unionist loyalty at last—'Mausers* and Kaisers, and any king
you like', and I have heard that at Hamburg, not far from Limburg
on the Lahn—I felt that I needed no other than that these words
conveyed, to go forth and do likewise.

The difference between us was that the Unionist champions chose
a path which they felt would lead to the woolsack, while I went a
road I knew must lead to the dock. The difference between us was
that my 'treason' was based on a ruthless sincerity that forced me to
attempt in time and season to carry out in action what I said in
words, whereas their treason lay in verbal incitements that they knew
would never be made good in their bodies. And so I am prouder to
stand here to-day, in the traitor's dock, to answer this impeachment,
than to fill the place of my right honourable accusers.

We have been told, have been asked to hope, that after this war
Ireland will get Home Rule as a reward for the life-blood shed in a
cause which, whomever else its success may benefit, can surely not
benefit Ireland. And what will Home Rule be in return for what its
vague promise has taken, and still hopes to take, from Ireland? It is

not necessary to climb the painful stairs of Irish history—to review the long list of British promises, made only to be broken; of Irish hopes, raised only to be dashed to the ground. Home Rule, when it comes, if come it does, will find an Ireland drained of all that is vital to its very existence, unless it be that unquenchable hope that we build on the graves of the dead. We are told that if Irishmen go by the thousand to die *not* for Ireland, but for Flanders, for Belgium, for a patch of sand on the deserts of Mesopotamia, or a rocky trench on the heights of Gallipoli, they are winning self-government for Ireland. But if they dare to lay down their lives on their native soil, if they dare to dream even that freedom can be won only at home by men resolved to fight for it there, then they are traitors to their country.

But history is not so recorded in other lands. In Ireland alone, in this twentieth century, is loyalty held to be a crime. If loyalty be something less than love and more than law, then we have had enough of such loyalty for Ireland or Irishmen. Self-government is our right, a thing born in us at birth, a thing no more to be doled out to us or withheld from us by another people than the right to life itself—the right to feel the sun or smell the flowers, or love our kind. It is only from the convict these things are withheld, for crime committed and proven—and Ireland, that has wronged no man, that has injured no land, that has sought no dominion over others—Ireland is being treated to-day among the nations of the world as if she were a convicted criminal. If it be treason to fight against such an unnatural fate as this, then I am proud to be a rebel, and shall cling to my 'rebellion', with the last drop of my blood. If there be no right of rebellion against this state of things that no savage tribe would endure without resistance, then I am sure that it is better for men to fight and to die without right than to live in such a state of right as this. Where all your rights have become only an accumulated wrong, where men must beg with bated breath for leave to subsist in their own land, to think their own thoughts, to sing their own songs, to garner the fruits of their own labours, and, even while they beg, to see things inexorably withdrawn from them—then, surely, it is a braver, a saner and a truer thing to be a rebel in act and deed against such circumstances than tamely to accept them as the natural lot of men.

My lord, I have done. Gentlemen of the jury, I wish to thank you for your verdict. I hope you will not take amiss what I said, or think that I made any imputation upon your truthfulness or your integrity when I spoke and said that this was not a trial by my peers. I maintain that I have a natural right to be tried in that natural jurisdiction, Ireland, my own country; and I would put it to you, how would you feel in the converse case—rather, how would all men here feel in the converse case—if an Englishman had landed here in England, and the Crown or the Government, for its own purposes, had conveyed him secretly from England to Ireland under a false name, committed him to prison under a false name, and brought him before a tribunal in Ireland under a statute which they knew involved a trial before an Irish jury? How would you feel, yourselves, as Englishmen if that Englishman was to be submitted to trial by jury in a land inflamed against him, and believing him to be a criminal, when his only crime was that he had cared for England more than for Ireland?

THOMAS MACDONAGH
(1878–1916)

from *Literature in Ireland* (1916)

In Ireland a period intervened between the last days of the Gaelic literature that mattered and the beginning of the new literature in the English tongue, between the hope and admiration that captured the imagination of the people in the days of Hugh O'Neill and Hugh O'Donnell,* then of Eoghan Ruadh O'Neill,* then of the Jacobites, and the new hope and anticipation that dawned in the last century and is widened to morning in this. The old Gaelic polity and culture having lost their force and their integrity, Gaelic literature became decadent in the time of the Penal Laws.* Whatever the fate of the Gaelic language and literature now may be—whether its long sickness end now in death without issue, or, as some of us confidently hope, in revival and vigorous life, with renewal of the same personality, a second youth, or in the birth of a new language to utter a new literature, destined to take after its Gaelic mother only in some parts, and for the rest to bear the name of bastard in its childhood and of true-born heir in its age, a well of Irish undefiled—whatever is to be in the unknown future, it would be folly to deny the sickness, the decadence, of the immediate past. And while Irish was decadent, English was not yet able either to carry on the tradition or to syllable anew for itself here. The English-speaking population in Ireland had none of the qualities—social cohesion and integrity, culture, enthusiasm, joy, high and brave emotion—to stammer and then to utter clearly the new word. That word came to the call of the country. It came in the new language and was heard in the new day. The Renaissance that stirred England to its greatest literature brought the mingling of the cosmopolitan with the national. Here the waters have been stirred by the breath of freedom: the alien language has stirred to expression on the lips of the native people.

The revival of nationalism among the Irish subject majority following the days of the Irish Volunteers, the United Irishmen, the independent Parliament; this nationalism, strengthened by O'Connell* with Catholic Emancipation and the franchise; this nationalism, hardened by the austere independence of Parnell,* by the land war and its victorious close; this, brought to full manhood by the renewed struggle for legislative freedom and the certainty of triumph and responsibility; this, free from alien hope and fear, craving no ease, hearing always the supreme song of victory on the dying lips of martyrs; this produced the unrest, the impetuous, intrepid adventure that shouts the song of joy for the sad things and for the glad things of life. The song in the new language demanded an intellectual effort that gave it a worth apart. English had to be broken and re-made to serve that song. The language that had been brought to perfection for English use, and then worn by that use, that had had the fixing of the printing press and had set the printer's word above the spoken, that language, in order to serve the different purpose of the new people, had to go back to the forge of the living speech. King Alfred, in the first days of English prose, wrote long, awkward strings of words for sentences, with little syntactical order. The modern English author writes well-balanced, well-ordered sentences. But the Saxon King expressed more truly his thought; in him the word order imaged more truly the thought order. The modern writer uses counters where he used coin. The modern writer cannot distinguish between his idea and the set phrase that does duty for its expression, though its terms have other meanings. He alludes to things. His prose is a hint, perfectly understood no doubt by others who know the code, but not for all that a true language. Almost perfectly it does duty for a true language to the people with whom it has grown; better than perfectly in its poetry, which gains in suggestiveness more than its loss in concreteness. Compare the prose of this language with the superior prose of French. Compare its poetry with the far inferior poetry of French. It was, in a word, the English language, good for the English people, redolent of English history, even of the vagaries and absurdities of the history of the English people, with practical jokes and puns and stupid grammatical blunders smelling sweet with the aroma of some splendid verse—with golden lads and girls that come to dust, as chimney sweepers, and with deeds of derring-do. This language, now a courser of ethereal race, now a hack between the shafts of commercialism, serving Shakespeare and the stenographer, used efficiently in William Blake's lyrics and in telegrams; this differed in many of the ways of linguistic difference from the language of the Gael. In it the ideas of the Gael did not find easy expression.

But I have been led on a little too far. The language that was brought face to face with Irish in the eighteenth and nineteenth centuries was not the language of English commerce. The Gaelic people had for English tutors the descendants of the old English settlers, in whose mouths the language was still the language of Shakespeare. The transplanted slip of a language does not develop as does the parent tree. By comparison it rather ceases to develop. The descendants of the earliest English colonists here were found, by a new Englishman of Elizabeth's time, using 'the dregs of the old ancient Chaucer English.' So in our day we find in the mouths of the people what such a progressive might call the dregs of the old ancient Shakespeare English. And this was the English that had to be knit into a different complication from the modern complication of the central English language. For the rest, it is not only in Ireland that the phenomenon has occurred: analogous is the use of English by the American booster and by the mystic who has to express in terms of sense and wit the things of God that are made known to him in no language. . . .

The Gaelic Renaissance means to us not only the revival of interest in this old Irish literature, the revival of interest in the civilization, the culture and the history of ancient Ireland, the enthusiasm, the adventure, the pride, the satisfaction, the emotion that are quickened by the discovery of the old monuments, but, added to these, the study of modern Irish as a language capable of literature, the interest in the fragments and traditions that have survived, the reconstruction of our new state on some of the old foundations, and so, patriotism. A recent writer has lamented that instead of the Classic there did not take place in the fourteenth century a Gaelic Renaissance. Of course, the lament and all discussion of it is futile. I listen dreamily to it. To the speakers of the Romance languages, to the readers of Romance literatures, the Classic Renaissance was such as to a strange people, who had seen only the statues of men of our race, would be the sight of the living models. The remarkable thing about the coming of the Classic Renaissance is not its coming in the fourteenth century, but its not coming earlier. The coming was inevitable. It was long prepared for. And when we use the same word, Renaissance, for the Gaelic revival, springing from the rediscovery of the ancient language and literature, and branching now into a double literature in two languages, we do not claim that it is quite the counterpart of the Classic. The old literature that was to be discovered, the ancient Irish art, were not in such consonance even with what of literature and art we still held, as were Classic literature and art with those of mediaeval Europe, with the culture that still held allegiance to Rome and had memories of ancient Greece. Still at the heart of that lament for a Gaelic Renaissance five hundred years ago is this truth, that if history had been different the ancient culture and the ancient literature of our people might have had a more powerful influence on the culture and literature of Europe. The Celtic peoples had kindred memories with ours though they had changed their speech. Of Gaelic influence in literature, in art, in music, there have always been the sure marks and the sure effects, as has been pointed out by Dr Sigerson* and others; but only during the last century has it come home and thriven.

This is not the place to attempt a history of the Revival. I propose here rapidly to survey portions of the literature of ancient Ireland and to come thence to the literature and the prospects of to-day. The poems of Old Irish are from eight to fourteen centuries old. There has been in the intervening period a steady enough stream of literature in Middle and Modern Irish; but my ignorance of all but a small amount of this and my sympathy with the way of the old time send me back to the beginning and then draw me home to the new age opening now.

The themes of Early Irish Literature are many of them the themes of modern romantic literature—in lyric poetry, nature and humanity:—nature: the joy of natural things; the joy of the earth's beauty, the woods and the birds in the woods; the delight of summer, season surpassing, grateful to dwellers in a northern land; the terror of the white winter when not a bell is heard and no crane talks, when shapes are all gone; the joy of the sea, the plain of Ler, with its witching song, the delightful home of ships, the image of Hell with its dread tempest:—humanity: men and women, love and destiny: humanity at odds with life: a king and a hermit; a girl who died for love; a warrior who kept his tryst after death; Deirdre, the pre-destined of sorrow, winning some joy from life before her fate falls; an old woman who has seen the passing away of her famous beauty, who sees the ebb tide carrying away her years, who sees the flood-wave foaming in for others. Later, after the English are settled in the land, not humanity but the nation, Kathleen ni Houlihan, is our heroic theme. The manifestations of nationality are symbolised by man and nature. The silk of the kine* goes lurking in the woods, weeping down tears, while her foe has wine on his table. The little shining rose is black. Ned of the Hill beats on the bolted door of the Nation; he is out under the snow, under the frost, under the rain, without comradeship, hunted with hail of bullets, desolate most of all at the thought that he must go east over the sea because it is there he has no kindred. No wonder that those who, lured by the felicity of gracious words, have learned to read with satisfaction in Shakespeare the easy hideous history of the English Wars of the Roses, half won to sympathy with ravening lust and barbarity, are perplexed by Gaelic Literature of the middle period. And so all Irish Literature is set down as vague, mysterious, obscure. Nothing could be more clear, more direct, more gem-like, hard and delicate and bright, than the earlier lyric poetry, nothing more surely true to nature, full of natural piety, nothing of another kind greater in suggestion, however brief in form. Not till the advent of Wordsworth comes there any-thing like this intimacy with nature into other modern literature. Not till we listen to the voice of Shelley do we hear in other lyric poetry such prophecy of song as has come down through folk poetry in Irish, a lyric poetry which, as Mr John Eglinton* said some years ago, 'has far more in common with the later developments of English poetry—with poems, for example, like Shelley's *When the Lamp is Shattered* or George Meredith's *Love in a Valley*—than anything produced by the wits of the London coffee houses.'

The themes of the old sagas have been used by many in our day as the story of the Trojan war has been used by many nations that read Greek. Deirdre is to us

'the morning star of loveliness,
Unhappy Helen of a western land.'[1]

They have not been used as successfully as the Greek models. They are not the inheritance of this alien civilization. They require different standards. To quote Mr John Eglinton again: 'These subjects, much as we may admire them and regret that we have nothing equivalent to them in the modern world, obstinately refuse to be taken up out of their old environment, and be transplanted into the world of modern sympathies. The proper mode of treating them is a secret lost with the subjects themselves.' It is possible, of course that, while I write, these *dicta* are being disproved. It would be vain, even if unluckily we wished it or could do it, to set bounds to literary genius, which is always breaking new soil, or rather always coming in a new manifestation. It is at its best and highest a new epiphany. Some in our day or after our day may make a great new literature in the tradition of this old world of Early Irish Literature. But I rather expect that the literature of to-morrow will be in terms of the life of to-morrow, and that the old world is too different, too far apart, too much wronged now, I fear, by misrepresentation, by false praise that would make it good of another kind than of its way of goodness, by false blame that would call its culture barbarism, its strength brutality or impropriety, its mysticism magic, its austere sincerity in literature a defect of power and richness, its power and richness, when it has such, exaggeration. We may admit that we cannot now feel those old emotions at first heart, so to put it. We have not reverence for the same things. We cannot pray to the old gods. We could not blaspheme the old gods. We are of a different day; a different light shines upon us. History is between us and our heroes. We cannot rid our memories of the glories and the calamities of our story, of the mighty things, of the futile things. Our thought is woven of the stuff of memory and elder thought and of a knowledge that has gained on this side and lost on that like an island in the sea. Our dreams are children dreams and parent dreams. A part of the old world lives in

---

[1] *The Three Sorrows of Story-Telling: Deirdre*, by Douglas Hyde.

us; to a large part we are alien not in speech only but in feeling, in sense, in instinct, in vision. We are true to the best of the old literature when we are true to that part of it which we inherit now in the twentieth century, when we discover in ourselves something of its good tradition, something that has remained true by the changing standards and measures. . . .

My race has survived the wiles of the foreigner here. It has refused to yield even to defeat, and emerges strong to-day, full of hope and of love, with new strength in its arms to work its new destiny, with a new song on its lips and the word of the new language, which is the ancient language, still calling from age to age. The adorable delicacy, the shrinking sensibility, the paralysing diffidence which has its root in charity, the qualities which make for temporary defeat and yet, being of their nature joined with the unwavering conviction of truth and right, for ultimate victory,—these live on. Now with them, in the same breasts with them, lives this too: its day is come. This arrogance is a sign of energy, of vitality, and so here is good. The Gaelic movement is a revival. Though, through changes of methods and modes of advance, the exhaustion of old methods and the need for new movements, it may seem to-day that the central movement has lost force, it still goes forward. Of a tide of thought, drawn by the inspiration of an ancient cause, there is no ebb. This will have a voice, a literature, tomorrow, the voice of a people new to such a way of speech, the literature of a fresh people. To be a poet one must look with fresh eyes on life; to produce poets a nation must be fresh. Ireland has already produced a great literature of old: the fragments that remain prove that. But, as we are now, we are a fresh people, fresh to literature. We have begun to produce a literature in English, a foreign tongue. This will not injure or delay the progress of Gaelic literature, which must be the work of other writers. Most of the Anglo-Irish poets—and it is almost all poetry still—have spent in attaining their knowledge and mastery of their craft all the resources of learning and acquirement in them. In the matter of technique— and this is all but supremely necessary in modern poetry—one language only will one poet master. Whether our people go forward in Anglo-Irish literature or not, some of our poets and writers of the next generation will certainly continue the production of a new literature in Irish. As I have said, we are fresh in other senses too— fresh from the natural home of man, the fields and the country. We have not all grown up in streets amid the artificialities of civilization, with traditional memories of brick and plaster. The influences of nature will be felt by us as by the true poets of all tongues. Our nature poetry will owe nothing to the botanical observations of city dwellers; it will be no sham pastoral imitation; it will be natural and spontaneous, and our own. But above all we are fresh in language, which the most city-hating English lover of nature cannot be. We are the children of a race that, through need or choice, turned from Irish to English. We have now so well mastered this language of our adoption that we use it with a freshness and power that the English of these days rarely have. But now also we have begun to turn back to the old language, not old to us. The future poets of the country will probably be the sons and daughters of a generation that learned Irish as a strange tongue; the words and phrases of Irish will have a new wonder for them; the figures of speech will have all their first poetry. Carlyle says of Imagination:* 'Metaphors are her stuff; examine language—what, if you except some primitive elements, what is it but metaphors, recognised as such or no longer recognised, still fluid and florid, or now solid-grown and colourless?' The metaphors of Irish will not be colourless to the fresh eyes of the next generation, though the language be their native idiom. Perhaps the temporary abandonment of Irish has not been an unmitigated disaster, now that its revival is assured. A language that transmits its literature mainly by oral tradition cannot, if spoken only by thousands, bequeath as much to posterity as if spoken by millions. The loss of idiom and of literature is a disaster. But, on the other hand, the abandonment has broken a tradition of pedantry and barren conventions; and sincerity gains thereby. The *aisling** is now at last dead; the simple beautiful folk-songs in which recent Irish literature is richer perhaps than any other, are more likely to serve as models than the vain word-weaving of the bards. The writers of the *dán díreach** became at last, to use a mis-translated phrase, mere 'schoolmen of condensed speech,' but their verse at worst had the high virtue of restraint. Their successors became fluent, eloquent craftsmen of skilful word-music. The poets of the next age will learn from the faults of both schools; they will make restraint a canon of their art, not a pedantry; they will know that the too facile use of the adjective is a vice, and verse-music a snare. Let us postulate continuity, but continuity in the true way.

2. MEMOIRS AND AUTOBIOGRAPHIES

JOHN O'LEARY
(1830–1907)

from *Recollections of Fenians and Fenianism* (1896)

It is with a sad heart and a somewhat doubtful mind that I set myself down, on the borders of old age, to say something of what I felt and thought and did in my early youth and mature manhood. Times have changed in Ireland greatly since then, and, no doubt, I have very greatly changed myself—but scarcely with the times. Whether this be my misfortune or my fault, or simply a necessary and inevitable result of the passage of the years, it is impossible for me to tell. I can only recognize the fact, and I feel that my readers will be but too likely to keep it well before their minds. I do not think that I have much of the *laudator temporis acti** in my nature, but I am certainly very little in love with the present, and but for my strong hope of a future other and better than the present, I should have but little pleasure in looking back upon my past or any past.

But to come to that past. Where shall I begin? There is something of a difficulty here, though perhaps not a great one. Nearly all our thoughts and acts have their roots in a past whose distance it is almost impossible to calculate. But then I am not writing of my relation to the universe, but merely of my relation to Fenianism. Here I have little difficulty myself as to where to begin, while feeling that the thing may not be at all so clear to my readers, and especially to such English ones as I may chance to find. I commence my story, then, in what my aforesaid English reader may probably consider a somewhat Irish fashion, by telling how I became a Young Irelander—for here was certainly the root of the matter to me. I have said something of this elsewhere more than once, but here I must go more fully into it.

Sometime in the year 1846, while recovering from a fever, I came across the poems and essays of Thomas Davis,* then recently dead. What Davis has been to more than a generation of Irishmen since his death is well known in his own country, and may in a measure be understood by Englishmen now, since the publication of his prose writings (edited by T. W. Rolleston, in the Camelot series), and of his life, written by his co-labourer and friend, Sir C. G. Duffy.* What he was then to me I feel as if I can only faintly shadow forth at this distance of time. Perhaps it may give some notion of the effect produced on me to say that I then went through a process analogous to what certain classes of Christians call 'conversion.' I can but vaguely remember my unregenerate state. Doubtless (from my surroundings) I was not anti-Irish or West-British:* but then I am confident I was not strongly Irish, and I am sure I was strongly ambitious, and can easily conceive that my ambition, stimulated by much reading of English literature, necessarily either directly or indirectly anti-Irish in spirit, might have led me where it has unfortunately led so many of my countrymen before and since. Now, however, everything was changed. The world was an altered world to me. I felt in quite a new sense that I was an Irishman, and that for weal or woe my fate must be linked with that of my country. I do not think that either then or since I ever had much of that spurious Irishism of Moore's song,* which associates Ireland with virtue and England with guilt; but Irish in a higher and better sense I think I may claim to have at least struggled to be, and, in so far as I have fought the good fight, to Thomas Davis more than any other, or, indeed more than to all others, is the credit due. I do not like to exaggerate, and do not think I am doing so. I do not, of course, mean in the least to convey that the largest part of my intellectual and moral training does not necessarily come from other and wider regions, but for all that is Irish in me, and, above all, for the inspiration that made me Irish, the fountain and the origin must always be sought in Davis.

But what came out of all this? Little, perhaps, at once—or at least little in the shape of action. What must have followed very soon was the close study of the leading columns, and indeed of many other columns, of the *Nation** newspaper. For what I found there I was, of course, perfectly prepared by the previous reading of Davis; and what was to be found in that paper I must leave the reader to gather from another pen than mine. Something, however, I must say even at this stage as to how the *Nation* affected me; later I shall have more to tell. In leading article, essay, and poem we read, from week to week, the story of Ireland's sufferings under English rule; and now and then we heard of other countries groaning under alien domination, and of their efforts, successful or unsuccessful, to shake it off. At first, perhaps, the teaching of the *Nation* was not directly unconstitutional, though, indirectly, it certainly was so from the beginning. From ceasing to 'fear to speak of '98'* to wishing to imitate the men of that time the transition was very easy indeed to the youthful mind. Many, if not most, of the younger amongst us were Mitchelites before Mitchel, or rather before Mitchel* had put forth his programme. We were told much about the doings of Hugh O'Neill and Owen Roe and Sarsfield,* and led to seek what more we could gather about them elsewhere. But as to the men of '98 there was no difficulty where to search and what to find. We had the fascinating 'Memoirs of Wolfe Tone,'* and the very laborious and full, if somewhat dull and chaotic, book of Madden,* and many a biography and history beside. I may perhaps be mixing up some things in my memory here; but the impression I mean to convey is certainly correct. I may be attributing to the *Nation* other things than I got from it; but that matters little, for Davis was the *Nation* and the *Nation* was Davis; and in saying this I most surely do not in the least mean to detract from the merit of the many able men who with Davis, and without him, made the *Nation*. Anyway, the feeling and sentiment upon which I acted then, and have mainly acted ever since, came from Davis; and what the *Nation* no doubt gave me, or taught me where to get, were such additional facts and fancies as my opinions sought by way of justification of the faith that was in me. . . .

And so the years passed on, leaving Ireland where she was, disgusted, disheartened, and, to all outward appearance, entirely apathetic. The period between the collapse of the Tenant League and the rise of Fenianism was the 'deadest' time in Irish politics within my memory, and perhaps within the memory of any man now living. We were not indeed without our excitements during this period; but they were none of our making, and so left us very much where we were. There was the Crimean War, for instance, which stirred England to the very depths, but which only touched the outer fringe, or, perhaps, I had better call it, the upper crust of Irish Society. The masses were interested, if not moved, but in an adverse sense from that of England. The Czar Nicholas,* who, to the prejudiced and stupid English mind of the time, was simply the incarnation of evil, was to the equally prejudiced, but by no means stupid, Irish mind not in any way a saint or hero, but a being who, whatever might be his nature, must necessarily be beneficent to Ireland in proportion as he was maleficent to England. That was rather a simple way of looking at things, but it has always been our way, is our way still—all pretence of 'union of hearts' notwithstanding—and can only cease to be our way when our relations with England cease to be what they are.

Our feelings during the Crimean War were somewhat complicated by the fact that the French were on the side of England. We did not, any of us, wish them any ill, though many of us wished no good to their scoundrel of an Emperor. But in the next difficulty of England there was no such complication of feeling. Our feelings—that is the feelings of the great mass of Irishmen—were entirely on the side of India during the mutiny. We were altogether untouched by the thrilling stories of Indian cruelty, knowing but too well, from our own history, that England was quite sure to give as good as she got; and all subsequent and authentic accounts of the suppression of the mutiny show that we were quite right in preserving our equanimity, and that England in every sense showed herself quite worthy of her ancient fame, on this occasion.

The Crimean War and the Indian Mutiny came and went, but left us quite as we were before. England's difficulty is proverbially said to be Ireland's opportunity, but opportunities may present themselves to nations, as to individuals, to little effect. Here were opportunities—especially in the case of the Indian Mutiny, when Ireland was nearly entirely denuded of troops—if only we could avail ourselves of them. But, alas! we could not. The country had not yet recovered from the physical collapse of '48, or what may be called the moral collapse of '55. She was without organization, or even the thought of organization, and so such an opportunity as we had not had for long before, have not had since, nor are likely to have soon again, passed away, leaving us no nearer freedom. If Fenianism had been then, things might have been far different now; but the idea still lay more or less dormant in the brain of James Stephens, to wake up into activity, however, very soon after.

OSCAR WILDE
(1854–1900)

from *De Profundis* (1905)

I was a man who stood in symbolic relations to the art and culture of my age. I had realised this for myself at the very dawn of my manhood, and had forced my age to realise it afterwards. Few men hold such a position in their own lifetime and have it so acknowledged. It is usually discerned, if discerned at all, by the historian, or the critic, long after both the man and his age have passed away. With me it was different. I felt it myself, and made others feel it. Byron was a symbolic figure, but his relations were to the passion of his age and its weariness of passion. Mine were to something more noble, more permanent, of more vital issue, of larger scope.

The gods had given me almost everything. I had genius, a distinguished name, high social position, brilliancy, intellectual daring: I made art a philosophy, and philosophy an art: I altered the minds of men and the colours of things: there was nothing I said or did that did not make people wonder: I took the drama, the most objective form known to art, and made it as personal a mode of expression as the lyric or the sonnet, at the same time that I widened its range and enriched its characterisation: drama, novel, poem in rhyme, poem in prose, subtle or fantastic dialogue, whatever I touched I made beautiful in a new mode of beauty: to truth itself I gave what is false no less than what is true as its rightful province, and showed that the false and the true are merely forms of intellectual existence. I treated Art as the supreme reality, and life as a mere mode of fiction: I awoke the imagination of my century so that it created myth and legend around me: I summed up all systems in a phrase, and all existence in an epigram.

Along with these things, I had things that were different. I let myself be lured into long spells of senseless and sensual ease. I amused myself with being a *flâneur*, a dandy, a man of fashion. I surrounded myself with the smaller natures and the meaner minds. I became the spendthrift of my own genius, and to waste an eternal youth gave me a curious joy. Tired of being on the heights I deliberately went to the depths in the search for new sensations. What the paradox was to me in the sphere of thought, perversity became to me in the sphere of passion. Desire, at the end, was a malady, or a madness, or both. I grew careless of the lives of others. I took pleasure where it pleased me and passed on. I forgot that every little action of the common day makes or unmakes character, and that therefore what one has done in the secret chamber one has some day to cry aloud on the housetops. I ceased to be Lord over myself. I was no longer the Captain of my Soul,* and did not know it. I allowed you to dominate me, and your father to frighten me. I ended in horrible disgrace. There is only one thing for me now, absolute Humility also. You had better come down into the dust and learn it beside me.

I have lain in prison for nearly two years. Out of my nature has come wild despair; an abandonment to grief that was piteous even to look at: terrible and impotent rage: bitterness and scorn: anguish that wept aloud: misery that could find no voice: sorrow that was dumb. I have passed through every possible mood of suffering. Better than Wordsworth* himself I know what Wordsworth meant when he said:

> Suffering is permanent, obscure, and dark
> And has the nature of Infinity.

But while there were times when I rejoiced in the idea that my sufferings were to be endless, I could not bear them to be without meaning. Now I find hidden away in my nature something that tells me that nothing in the whole world is meaningless, and suffering least of all. That something hidden away in my nature, like a treasure in a field, is Humility.

It is the last thing left in me, and the best: the ultimate discovery at which I have arrived: the starting-point for a fresh development. It has come to me right out of myself, so I know that it has come at the proper time. It could not have come before, nor later. Had anyone told me of it, I would have rejected it. Had it been brought to me, I would have refused it. As I found it, I want to keep it. I must do so. It is the one thing that has in it the elements of life, of a new life, a *Vita Nuova** for me. Of all things it is the strangest. One cannot give it away, and another may not give it to one. One cannot acquire it, except by surrendering everything that one has. It is only when one has lost all things, that one knows that one possesses it.

Now that I realise that it is in me, I see quite clearly what I have got to do, what, in fact, I must do. And when I use such a phrase as that, I need not tell you that I am not alluding to any external sanction or command. I admit none. I am far more of an individualist than I ever was. Nothing seems to me of the smallest value except what one gets out of oneself. My nature is seeking a fresh mode of self-realisation. That is all I am concerned with. And the first thing that I have got to do is to free myself from any possible bitterness of feeling against you.

I am completely penniless, and absolutely homeless. Yet there are worse things in the world than that. I am quite candid when I tell you that rather than go out from this prison with bitterness in my heart against you or against the world I would gladly and readily beg my bread from door to door. If I got nothing from the house of the rich, I would get something at the house of the poor. Those who have much are often greedy. Those who have little always share. I would not a bit mind sleeping in the cool grass in summer, and when winter came on sheltering myself by the warm close-thatched rick, or under the penthouse of a great barn, provided I had love in my heart. The external things of life seem to me now of no importance at all. You can see to what intensity of individualism I have arrived, or am arriving rather, for the journey is long, and 'where I walk there are thorns.'

Of course I know that to ask for alms on the highway is not to be my lot, and that if ever I lie in the cool grass at night-time it will be to write sonnets to the Moon. When I go out of prison, Robbie* will be waiting for me on the other side of the big iron-studded gate, and he is the symbol not merely of his own affection, but of the affection of many others besides. I believe I am to have enough to live on for about eighteen months at any rate, so that, if I may not write beautiful books, I may at least read beautiful books, and what joy can be greater? After that, I hope to be able to recreate my creative faculty. But were things different: had I not a friend left in the world: were there not a single house open to me even in pity: had I to accept the wallet and ragged cloak of sheer penury: still as long as I remained free from all resentment, hardness, and scorn, I would be able to face life with much more calm and confidence than I would were my body in purple and fine linen, and the soul within it sick with hate. And I shall really have no difficulty in forgiving you. But to make it a pleasure for me you must feel that you want it. When you really want it you will find it waiting for you.

I need not say that my task does not end there. It would be comparatively easy if it did. There is much more before me. I have hills far steeper to climb, valleys much darker to pass through. And I have to get it all out of myself. Neither Religion, Morality, nor Reason can help me at all.

Morality does not help me. I am a born antinomian. I am one of those who are made for exceptions, not for laws. But while I see that there is nothing wrong in what one does, I see that there is something wrong in what one becomes. It is well to have learned that.

Religion does not help me. The faith that others give to what is unseen, I give to what one can touch, and look at. My Gods dwell in temples made with hands, and within the circle of actual experience is my creed made perfect and complete: too complete it may be, for like many or all of those who have placed their Heaven in this earth, I have found in it not merely the beauty of Heaven, but the horror of Hell also. When I think about Religion at all, I feel as if I would like to found an order for those who cannot believe: the Confraternity of the Fatherless one might call it, where on an altar, on which no taper burned, a priest, in whose heart peace had no dwelling, might celebrate with unblessed bread and a chalice empty of wine. Everything to be true must become a religion. And agnosticism should have its ritual no less than faith. It has sown its martyrs, it should reap its saints, and praise God daily for having hidden Himself from man. But whether it be faith or agnosticism, it must be nothing external to me. Its symbols must be of my own creating. Only that is spiritual which makes its own form. If I may not find its secret within myself, I shall never find it. If I have not got it already, it will never come to me.

Reason does not help me. It tells me that the laws under which I am convicted are wrong and unjust laws, and the system under which I have suffered a wrong and unjust system. But, somehow, I have got to make both of these things just and right to me. And exactly as in Art one is only concerned with what a particular thing is at a particular moment to oneself, so it is also in the ethical evolution of one's character. I have got to make everything that has happened to me good for me. The plank-bed, the loathsome food, the hard ropes shredded into oakum till one's finger-tips grow dull with pain, the menial offices with which each day begins and finishes, the harsh orders that routine seems to necessitate, the dreadful dress that makes sorrow grotesque to look at, the silence, the solitude, the shame—each and all of these things I have to transform into a spiritual experience. There is not a single degradation of the body which I must not try and make into a spiritualising of the soul.

I want to get to the point when I shall be able to say, quite simply and without affectation, that the two great turning-points of my life were when my father sent me to Oxford, and when society sent me to prison. I will not say that it is the best thing that could have happened to me, for that phrase would savour of too great bitterness towards myself. I would sooner say, or hear it said of me, that I was so typical a child of my age that in my perversity, and for that perversity's sake, I turned the good things of my life to evil, and the evil things of my life to good. What is said, however, by myself or by others matters little. The important thing, the thing that lies before me, the thing that I have to do, or be for the brief remainder of my days one maimed, marred, and incomplete, is to absorb into my nature all that has been done to me, to make it part of me, to accept it without complaint, fear, or reluctance. The supreme vice is shallowness. Whatever is realised is right. . . .

I hope to live long enough, and to produce work of such a character, that I shall be able at the end of my days to say, 'Yes: this is just where the artistic life leads a man.' Two of the most perfect lives I have come across in my own experience are the lives of Verlaine* and of Prince Kropotkin:* both of them men who passed years in prison: the first, the one Christian poet since Dante, the other a man with the soul of that beautiful white Christ that seems coming out of Russia. And for the last seven or eight months, in spite of a succession of great troubles reaching me from the outside world almost without intermission, I have been placed in direct contact with a new spirit working in this prison through men and things, that has helped me beyond any possibility of expression in words; so that while for the first year of my imprisonment I did nothing else, and can remember doing nothing else, but wring my hands in impotent despair, and say 'What an ending! What an appalling ending!' Now I try to say to myself, and sometimes when I am not torturing myself do really and sincerely say, 'What a beginning! What a wonderful beginning!' It may really be so. It may become so. If it does, I shall owe much to this new personality that has altered every man's life in this place.

Things in themselves are of little importance, have indeed—let us for once thank Metaphysics for something that she has taught us—no real existence. The spirit alone is of importance. Punishment may be inflicted in such a way that it will heal, not make a wound, just as alms may be given in such a manner that the bread changes to a stone in the hands of the giver. What a change there is—not in the regulations, for they are fixed by iron rule, but in the spirit that uses them as its expression—you can realise when I tell you that had I been released last May, as I tried to be, I would have left this place loathing it and every official in it with a bitterness of hatred that would have poisoned my life. I have had a year longer of imprisonment, but Humanity has been in the prison along with us all, and now when I go out I shall always remember great kindnesses that I have received here from almost everybody, and on the day of my release will give my thanks to many people and ask to be remembered by them in turn.

The prison-system is absolutely and entirely wrong. I would give anything to be able to alter it when I go out. I intend to try. But there is nothing in the world so wrong but that the spirit of Humanity, which is the spirit of Love, the spirit of the Christ who is not in Churches, may make it, if not right, at least possible to be borne without too much bitterness of heart.

I know also that much is waiting for me outside that is very delightful, from what St Francis of Assisi calls '*my brother the wind*' and '*my sister the rain*,' lovely things both of them, down to the shop-windows and sunsets of great cities. If I made a list of all that still remains to me, I don't know where I should stop: for, indeed, God made the world just as much for me as for anyone else. Perhaps I may go out with something I had not got before. I need not tell you that to me Reformations in Morals are as meaningless and vulgar as Reformations in Theology. But while to propose to be a better man is a piece of unscientific cant, to have become a *deeper* man is the privilege of those who have suffered. And such I think I have become. You can judge for yourself.

If after I go out a friend of mine gave a feast, and did not invite me to it, I shouldn't mind a bit. I can be perfectly happy by myself. With freedom, books, flowers, and the moon, who could not be happy?

Besides, feasts are not for me any more. I have given too many to care about them. That side of life is over for me, very fortunately I dare say. But if, after I go out, a friend of mine had a sorrow, and refused to allow me to share it, I should feel it most bitterly. If he shut the doors of the house of mourning against me I would come back again and again and beg to be admitted, so that I might share in what I was entitled to share in. If he thought me unworthy, unfit to weep with him, I should feel it as the most poignant humiliation, as the most terrible mode in which disgrace could be inflicted on me. But that could not be. I have a right to share in Sorrow, and he who can look at the loveliness of the world, and share its sorrow, and realise something of the wonder of both, is in immediate contact with divine things, and has got as near to God's secret as anyone can get.

Perhaps there may come into my art also, no less than into my life, a still deeper note, one of greater unity of passion, and directness of impulse. Not width but intensity is the true aim of modern Art. We are no longer in Art concerned with the type. It is with the exception we have to do. I cannot put my sufferings into any form they took, I need hardly say. Art only begins where Imitation ends. But something must come into my work, of fuller harmony of words perhaps, of richer cadences, of more curious colour-effects, of simpler architectural-order, of some aesthetic quality at any rate.

When Marsyas* was 'torn from the scabbard of his limbs'—*dalla vagina delle membre sue*, to use one of Dante's most terrible, most Tacitean phrases—he had no more song, the Greeks said. Apollo had been victor. The lyre had vanquished the reed. But perhaps the Greeks were mistaken. I hear in much modern Art the cry of Marsyas. It is bitter in Baudelaire,* sweet and plaintive in Lamartine,* mystic in Verlaine. It is in the deferred resolutions of Chopin's music.* It is in the discontent that haunts the recurrent faces of Burne-Jones's women.* Even Matthew Arnold,* whose song of Callicles tells of 'the triumph of the sweet persuasive lyre,' and the 'famous final victory,' in such a clear note of lyrical beauty—even he, in the troubled undertone of doubt and distress that haunts his verse, had not a little of it. Neither Goethe nor Wordsworth could heal him, though he followed each in turn, and when he seeks to mourn for 'Thyrsis' or to sing of 'the Scholar Gipsy,' it is the reed that he has to take for the rendering of his strain. But whether or not the Phrygian Faun was silent, I cannot be. Expression is as necessary to me as leaf and blossom are to the black branches of the trees that show themselves above the prison wall and are so restless in the wind. Between my art and the world there is now a wide gulf, but between Art and myself there is none. I hope at least that there is none.

To each of us different fates have been meted out. Freedom, pleasure, amusements, a life of ease have been your lot, and you are not worthy of it. My lot has been one of public infamy, of long imprisonment, of misery, of ruin, of disgrace, and I am not worthy of it either—not yet, at any rate. I remember I used to say that I thought I could bear a real tragedy if it came to me with purple pall and a mask of noble sorrow, but that the dreadful thing about modernity was that it put Tragedy into the raiment of Comedy, so that the great realities seemed commonplace or grotesque or lacking in style. It is quite true about modernity. It has probably always been true about actual life. It is said that all martyrdoms seemed mean to the looker-on. The nineteenth century is no exception to the general rule.

Everything about my tragedy has been hideous, mean, repellent, lacking in style. Our very dress makes us grotesques. We are the zanies of sorrow. We are clowns whose hearts are broken. We are specially designed to appeal to the sense of humour. On November 13th 1895 I was brought down here from London. From two o'clock till half-past two on that day I had to stand on the centre platform of Clapham Junction in convict dress and handcuffed, for the world to look at. I had been taken out of the Hospital Ward without a moment's notice being given to me. Of all possible objects I was the most grotesque. When people saw me they laughed. Each train as it came up swelled the audience. Nothing could exceed their amusement. That was of course before they knew who I was. As soon as they had been informed, they laughed still more. For half an hour I stood there in the grey November rain surrounded by a jeering mob.

For a year after that was done to me I wept every day at the same hour and for the same space of time. That is not such a tragic thing as possibly it sounds to you. To those who are in prison, tears are a part of every day's experience. A day in prison on which one does not weep is a day on which one's heart is hard, not a day on which one's heart is happy.

Well, now I am really beginning to feel more regret for the people who laughed than for myself. Of course when they saw me I was not on my pedestal. I was in the pillory. But it is a very unimaginative nature that only cares for people on their pedestals. A pedestal may be a very unreal thing. A pillory is a terrific reality. They should have known also how to interpret sorrow better. I have said that behind Sorrow there is always Sorrow. It were still wiser to say that behind sorrow there is always a soul. And to mock at a soul in pain is a dreadful thing. Unbeautiful are their lives who do it. In the strangely simple economy of the world people only get what they give, and to those who have not enough imagination to penetrate the mere outward of things and feel pity, what pity can be given save that of scorn?

I have told you this account of the mode of my being conveyed here simply that you should realise how hard it has been for me to get anything out of my punishment but bitterness and despair. I have however to do it, and now and then I have moments of submission and acceptance. All the spring may be hidden in a single bud, and the low ground-nest of the lark may hold the joy that is to herald the feet of many rose-red dawns, and so perhaps whatever beauty of life still remains to me is contained in some moment of surrender, abasement and humiliation. I can, at any rate, merely proceed on the lines of my own development, and by accepting all that has happened to me make myself worthy of it.

J. M. SYNGE
(1871–1909)

from *The Aran Islands* (1907)

I am in Aranmor,* sitting over a turf fire, listening to a murmur of Gaelic that is rising from a little public-house under my room.

The steamer which comes to Aran sails according to the tide, and it was six o'clock this morning when we left the quay of Galway in a dense shroud of mist.

A low line of shore was visible at first on the right between the movement of the waves and fog, but when we came further it was lost sight of, and nothing could be seen but the mist curling in the rigging, and a small circle of foam.

There were few passengers; a couple of men going out with young pigs tied loosely in sacking, three or four young girls who sat in the cabin with their heads completely twisted in their shawls, and a builder, on his way to repair the pier at Kilronan, who walked up and down and talked with me.

In about three hours Aran came in sight. A dreary rock appeared at first sloping up from the sea into the fog; then as we drew nearer, a coastguard station and the village.

A little later I was wandering out along the one good roadway of the island, looking over low walls on either side into small flat fields of naked rock. I have seen nothing so desolate. Grey floods of water were sweeping everywhere upon the limestone, making at times a wild torrent of the road, which twined continually over low hills and cavities in the rock or passed between a few small fields of potatoes or grass hidden away in corners that had shelter. Whenever the cloud lifted I could see the edge of the sea below me on the right, and the naked ridge of the island above me on the other side. Occasionally I passed a lonely chapel or schoolhouse, or a line of stone pillars with crosses above them and inscriptions asking a prayer for the soul of the person they commemorated.

I met few people; but here and there a band of tall girls passed me on their way to Kilronan, and called out to me with humorous wonder, speaking English with a slight foreign intonation that differed a good deal from the brogue of Galway. The rain and cold seemed to have no influence on their vitality, and as they hurried past me with eager laughter and great talking in Gaelic, they left the wet masses of rock more desolate than before.

A little after midday when I was coming back one old half-blind man spoke to me in Gaelic, but, in general, I was surprised at the abundance and fluency of the foreign tongue.

In the afternoon the rain continued, so I sat here in the inn looking out through the mist at a few men who were unlading hookers that had come in with turf from Connemara, and at the long-legged pigs that were playing in the surf. As the fishermen came in and out of the public-house underneath my room, I could hear through the broken panes that a number of them still used the Gaelic, though it seems to be falling out of use among the younger people of this village.

The old woman of the house had promised to get me a teacher of the language, and after a while I heard a shuffling on the stairs, and the old dark man I had spoken to in the morning groped his way into the room.

I brought him over to the fire, and we talked for many hours. He told me that he had known Petrie and Sir William Wilde, and many living antiquarians, and had taught Irish to Dr Finck, and Dr Pedersen, and given stories to Mr Curtin* of America. A little after middle age he had fallen over a cliff, and since then he had had little eyesight, and a trembling of his hands and head.

As we talked he sat huddled together over the fire, shaking and blind, yet his face was indescribably pliant, lighting up with an ecstasy of humour when he told me of anything that had a point of wit or malice, and growing sombre and desolate again when he spoke of religion or the fairies.

He had great confidence in his own powers and talent, and in the superiority of his stories over all other stories in the world. When we were speaking of Mr Curtin, he told me that this gentleman had brought out a volume of his Aran stories in America, and made five hundred pounds by the sale of them.

'And what do you think he did then?' he continued; 'he wrote a book of his own stories after making that lot of money with mine. And he brought them out, and the divil a halfpenny did he get for them. Would you believe that?'

Afterwards he told me how one of his children had been taken by the fairies.

One day a neighbour was passing, and she said, when she saw it on the road, 'That's a fine child.'

Its mother tried to say 'God bless it,' but something choked the words in her throat.

A while later they found a wound on its neck, and for three nights the house was filled with noises.

'I never wear a shirt at night,' he said, 'but I got up out of bed, all naked as I was, when I heard the noises in the house, and lighted a light, but there was nothing in it.'

Then a dummy came and made signs of hammering nails in a coffin.

The next day the seed potatoes were full of blood, and the child told his mother that he was going to America.

That night it died, and 'Believe me,' said the old man, 'the fairies were in it.'

(When he went away, a little bare-footed girl was sent up with turf and the bellows to make a fire that would last for the evening.

She was shy, yet eager to talk, and told me that she had good spoken Irish, and was learning to read it in the school, and that she had been twice to Galway, though there are many grown women in the place who have never set a foot upon the mainland.)

The rain has cleared off, and I have had my first real introduction to the island and its people.

I went out through Killeany—the poorest village in Aranmor—to a long neck of sandhill that runs out into the sea towards the south-west. As I lay there on the grass the clouds lifted from the Connemara mountains and, for a moment, the green undulating foreground, backed in the distance by a mass of hills, reminded me of the country near Rome. Then the dun top-sail of a hooker swept above the edge of the sandhill and revealed the presence of the sea.

As I moved on a boy and a man came down from the next village to talk to me, and I found that here, at least, English was imperfectly understood. When I asked them if there were any trees in the island they held a hurried consultation in Gaelic, and then the man asked if 'tree' meant the same thing as 'bush', for if so there were a few in sheltered hollows to the east.

They walked on with me to the sound which separates this island from Inishmaan—the middle island of the group—and showed me the roll from the Atlantic running up between two walls of cliff.

They told me that several men had stayed on Inishmaan to learn Irish, and the boy pointed out a line of hovels where they had lodged running like a belt of straw round the middle of the island. The place looked hardly fit for habitation. There was no green to be seen, and no sign of the people except these beehive-like roofs, and the outline of a Dun that stood out above them against the edge of the sky.

(After a while my companions went away and two other boys came and walked at my heels, till I turned and made them talk to me. They spoke at first of their poverty, and then one of them said—

'I dare say you do have to pay ten shillings a week in the hotel?'

'More,' I answered.

'Twelve?'

'More.'

'Fifteen?'

'More still.'

Then he drew back and did not question me any further, either thinking that I had lied to check his curiosity, or too awed by my riches to continue.)

Repassing Killeany I was joined by a man who had spent twenty years in America, where he had lost his health and then returned, so long ago that he had forgotten English and could hardly make me understand him. He seemed hopeless, dirty, and asthmatic, and after going with me for a few hundred yards he stopped and asked for coppers. I had none left, so I gave him a fill of tobacco, and he went back to his hovel.

When he was gone, two little girls took their place behind me and I drew them in turn into conversation.

They spoke with a delicate exotic intonation that was full of charm, and told me with a sort of chant how they guide 'ladies and gintlemins' in the summer to all that is worth seeing in their neighbourhood, and sell them pampooties and maidenhair ferns, which are common among the rocks.

We were now in Kilronan, and as we parted they showed me holes in their own pampooties, or cowskin sandals, and asked me the price of new ones. I told them that my purse was empty, and then with a few quaint words of blessing they turned away from me and went down to the pier.

All this walk back had been extraordinarily fine. The intense insular clearness one sees only in Ireland, and after rain, was throwing out every ripple in the sea and sky, and every crevice in the hills beyond the bay. . . .*

I am settled at last on Inishmaan in a small cottage with a continual drone of Gaelic coming from the kitchen that opens into my room.

Early this morning the man of the house came over for me with a four-oared curagh—that is, a curagh with four rowers and four oars on either side, as each man uses two—and we set off a little before noon.

It gave me a moment of exquisite satisfaction to find myself moving away from civilisation in this rude canvas canoe of a model that has served primitive races since men first went on the sea.

We had to stop for a moment at a hulk that is anchored in the bay, to make some arrangements for the fish-curing of the middle island, and my crew called out as soon as we were within earshot that they had a man with them who had been in France a month from this day.

When we started again, a small sail was run up in the bow, and we set off across the sound with a leaping oscillation that had no resemblance to the heavy movement of a boat.

The sail is only used as an aid, so the men continued to row after it had gone up, and as they occupied the four cross seats I lay on the canvas at the stern and the frame of slender laths, which bent and quivered as the waves passed under them.

When we set off it was a brilliant morning of April, and the green, glittering waves seemed to toss the canoe among themselves, yet as we drew nearer this island a sudden thunderstorm broke out behind the rocks we were approaching, and lent a momentary tumult to this still vein of the Atlantic.

We landed at a small pier, from which a rude track leads up to the village between small fields and bare sheets of rock like those in Aranmor. The youngest son of my boatman, a boy of about seventeen, who is to be my teacher and guide, was waiting for me at the pier and guided me to his house, while the men settled the curagh and followed slowly with my baggage.

My room is at one end of the cottage, with a boarded floor and ceiling, and two windows opposite each other. Then there is the kitchen with earth floor and open rafters, and two doors opposite each other opening into the open air, but no windows. Beyond it there are two small rooms of half the width of the kitchen with one window apiece.

The kitchen itself, where I will spend most of my time, is full of beauty and distinction. The red dresses of the women who cluster round the fire on their stools give a glow of almost Eastern richness, and the walls have been toned by the turf-smoke to a soft brown that blends with the grey earth-colour of the floor. Many sorts of fishing-tackle, and the nets and oil-skins of the men, are hung upon the walls or among the open rafters; and right overhead, under the thatch, there is a whole cowskin from which they make pampooties.

Every article on these islands has an almost personal character, which gives this simple life, where all art is unknown, something of the artistic beauty of mediæval life. The curaghs and spinning-wheels, the tiny wooden barrels that are still much used in the place of earthenware, the home-made cradles, churns, and baskets, are all full of individuality, and being made from materials that are common here, yet to some extent peculiar to the island, they seem to exist as a natural link between the people and the world that is about them.

The simplicity and unity of the dress increases in another way the local air of beauty. The women wear red petticoats and jackets of the island wool stained with madder, to which they usually add a plaid shawl twisted round their chests and tied at the back. When it rains they throw another petticoat over their heads with the waistband round their faces, or, if they are young, they use a heavy shawl like those worn in Galway. Occasionally other wraps are worn, and during the thunderstorm I arrived in I saw several girls with men's waistcoats buttoned round their bodies. Their skirts do not come much below the knee and show their powerful legs in the heavy indigo stockings with which they are all provided.

The men wear three colours: the natural wool, indigo, and a grey flannel that is woven of alternate threads of indigo and the natural wool. In Aranmor many of the younger men have adopted the usual fisherman's jersey, but I have only seen one on this island.

As flannel is cheap—the women spin the yarn from the wool of their own sheep, and it is then woven by a weaver in Kilronan for fourpence a yard—the men seem to wear an indefinite number of waistcoats and woollen drawers one over the other. They are usually surprised at the lightness of my own dress, and one old man I spoke to for a minute on the pier, when I came ashore, asked me if I was not cold with 'my little clothes.'

As I sat in the kitchen to dry the spray from my coat, several men who had seen me walking up came in to talk to me, usually murmuring on the threshold, 'The blessing of God on this place,' or some similar words.

The courtesy of the old woman of the house is singularly attractive, and though I could not understand much of what she said—she has no English—I could see with how much grace she motioned each visitor to a chair, or stool, according to his age, and said a few words to him till he drifted into our English conversation.

For the moment my own arrival is the chief subject of interest, and the men who come in are eager to talk to me.

Some of them express themselves more correctly than the ordinary peasant, others use the Gaelic idioms continually and substitute 'he' or 'she' for 'it', as the neuter pronoun is not found in modern Irish.

A few of the men have a curiously full vocabulary, others know only the commonest words in English, and are driven to ingenious devices to express their meaning. Of all the subjects we can talk of war seems their favourite, and the conflict between America and Spain is causing a great deal of excitement. Nearly all the families have relations who have had to cross the Atlantic, and all eat the flour and bacon that is brought from the United States, so they have a vague fear that 'if anything happened to America,' their own island would cease to be habitable.

Foreign languages are another favourite topic, and as these men are bilingual they have a fair notion of what it means to speak and think in many different idioms. Most of the strangers they see on the islands are philological students, and the people have been led to conclude that linguistic studies, particularly Gaelic studies, are the chief occupation of the outside world.

'I have seen Frenchmen, and Danes, and Germans,' said one man, 'and there does be a power of Irish books along with them, and they reading them better than ourselves. Believe me there are few rich men now in the world who are not studying the Gaelic.'

They sometimes ask me the French for simple phrases, and when they have listened to the intonation for a moment, most of them are able to reproduce it with admirable precision.

When I was going out this morning to walk round the island with Michael, the boy who is teaching me Irish, I met an old man making his way down to the cottage. He was dressed in miserable black clothes which seemed to have come from the mainland, and was so bent with rheumatism that, at a little distance, he looked more like a spider than a human being.

Michael told me it was Pat Dirane, the story-teller old Mourteen had spoken of on the other island. I wished to turn back, as he appeared to be on his way to visit me, but Michael would not hear of it.

'He will be sitting by the fire when we come in,' he said; 'let you not be afraid, there will be time enough to be talking to him by and by.'

He was right. As I came down into the kitchen some hours later old Pat was still in the chimney-corner, blinking with the turf smoke.

GEORGE MOORE
(1852–1933)

from *Hail and Farewell* (1911)

One of Ireland's many tricks is to fade away to a little speck down on the horizon of our lives, and then to return suddenly in tremendous bulk, frightening us. My words were: In another ten years it will be time enough to think of Ireland again. But Ireland rarely stays away so long. As well as I can reckon, it was about five years after my meditation in the Temple* that W. B. Yeats, the Irish poet, came to see me in my flat in Victoria Street, followed by Edward. My surprise was great at seeing them arrive together, not knowing that they even knew each other; and while staring at them I remembered they had met in my rooms in the King's Bench Walk. But how often had Edward met my friends and liked them, in a way, yet not sufficiently to compel him to hook himself on to them by a letter or a visit? He is one of those self-sufficing men who drift easily into the solitude of a pipe or a book; yet he is cheerful, talkative, and forthcoming when one goes to see him. Our fellowship began in boyhood, and there is affection on his side as well as mine, I am sure of that; all the same he has contributed few visits to the maintenance of our friendship. It is I that go to him, and it was this knowledge of the indolence of his character that caused me to wonder at seeing him arrive with Yeats. Perhaps seeing them together stirred some fugitive jealousy in me, which passed away when the servant brought in the lamp, for, with the light behind them, my visitors appeared a twain as fantastic as anything ever seen in Japanese prints—Edward great in girth as an owl (he is nearly as neckless), blinking behind his glasses, and Yeats lank as a rook, a dream in black silhouette on the flowered wall-paper.

But rooks and owls do not roost together, nor have they a habit or an instinct in common. A mere doorstep casualty, I said, and began to prepare a conversation suitable to both, which was, however, checked by the fateful appearance they presented, sitting side by side, anxious to speak, yet afraid. They had clearly come to me on some great business! But about what, about what? I waited for the servant to leave the room, and as soon as the door was closed they broke forth, telling together that they had decided to found a Literary Theatre in Dublin; so I sat like one confounded, saying to myself: Of course they know nothing of Independent Theatres, and, in view of my own difficulties in gathering sufficient audience for two or three performances, pity began to stir in me for their forlorn project. A forlorn thing it was surely to bring literary plays to Dublin! . . . Dublin of all cities in the world!

It is Yeats, I said, who has persuaded dear Edward, and looking from one to the other, I thought how the cunning rook had enticed the profound owl from his belfry—an owl that has stayed out too late, and is nervous lest he should not be able to find his way back; perplexed, too, by other considerations, lest the Dean and Chapter, having heard of the strange company he is keeping, may have, during his absence, bricked up the entrance to his roost.

As I was thinking these things, Yeats tilted his chair in such dangerous fashion that I had to ask him to desist, and I was sorry to have to do that, so much like a rook did he seem when the chair was on its hind legs. But if ever there was a moment for seriousness, this was one, so I treated them to a full account of the Independent Theatre, begging them not to waste their plays upon Dublin.

It would give me no pleasure whatever to produce my plays in London, Edward said. I have done with London.

Martyn would prefer the applause of our own people, murmured Yeats, and he began to speak of the by-streets, and the lanes, and the alleys, and how one feels at home when one is among one's own people.

Ninety-nine is the beginning of the Celtic Renaissance, said Edward.

I am glad to hear it; the Celt wants a renaissance, and badly; he has been going down in the world for the last two thousand years.

We are thinking, said Yeats, of putting a dialogue in Irish before our play . . . Usheen and Patrick.

Irish spoken on the stage in Dublin! You are not—

Interrupting me, Edward began to blurt out that a change had come, that Dublin was no longer a city of barristers, judges, and officials pursuing a round of mean interests and trivial amusements, but the capital of the Celtic Renaissance.

With all the arts for crown—a new Florence, I said, looking at Edward incredulously, scornfully perhaps, for to give a Literary Theatre to Dublin seemed to me like giving a mule a holiday, and when he pressed me to say if I were with them, I answered with reluctance that I was not; whereupon, and without further entreaty, the twain took up their hats and staves, and they were by the open door before I could beg them not to march away like that, but to give me time to digest what they had been saying to me, and for a moment I walked to and forth, troubled by the temptation, for I am naturally propense to thrust my finger into every literary pie-dish. Something was going on in Ireland for sure, and remembering the literary tone that had crept into a certain Dublin newspaper—somebody sent me the *Express* on Saturdays—I said, I'm with you, but only platonically. You must promise not to ask me to rehearse your plays. I spoke again about the Independent Theatre, and of the misery I had escaped from when I cut the painter.*

But you'll come to Ireland to see our plays, said Edward.

Come to Ireland! and I looked at Edward suspiciously; a still more suspicious glance fell upon Yeats. Come to Ireland! Ireland and I have ever been strangers, without an idea in common. It never does an Irishman any good to return to Ireland . . . and we know it.

One of the oldest of our stories, Yeats began. Whenever he spoke these words a thrill came over me; I knew they would lead me through accounts of strange rites and prophecies, and at that time I believed that Yeats, by some power of divination, or of ancestral memory, understood the hidden meaning of the legends, and whenever he began to tell them I became impatient of interruption. But it was now myself that interrupted, for, however great the legend he was about to tell, and however subtle his interpretation, it would be impossible for me to give him my attention until I had been told how he had met Edward, and all the circumstances of the meeting, and how they had arrived at an agreement to found an Irish Literary Theatre. The story was disappointingly short and simple. When Yeats had said that he had spent the summer at Coole* with Lady Gregory I saw it all; Coole is but three miles from Tillyra: Edward is often at Coole; Lady Gregory and Yeats are often at Tillyra; Yeats and Edward had written plays—the drama brings strange fowls to roost.

So an owl and a rook have agreed to build in Dublin. A strange nest indeed they will put together, one bringing sticks, and the other—with what materials does the owl build? My thoughts hurried on, impatient to speculate on what would happen when the shells began to chip. Would the young owls cast out the young rooks, or would the young rooks cast out the young owls, and what view would the beholders take of this wondrous hatching? And what view would the Church?

So it was in Galway the nest was builded, and Lady Gregory elected to the secretaryship, I said. The introduction of Lady Gregory's name gave me pause . . . And you have come over to find actors, and rehearse your plays. Wonderful, Edward, wonderful! I admire you both, and am with you, but on my conditions. You will remember them? And now tell me, do you think you'll find an audience in Dublin capable of appreciating *The Heather Field?**

Ideas are only appreciated in Ireland, Edward answered, somewhat defiantly.

I begged them to stay to dinner, for I wanted to hear about Ireland, but they went away, speaking of an appointment with Miss Vernon—that name or some other name—a lady who was helping them to collect a cast.

As soon as they had news they would come to me again. And on this I returned to my room deliciously excited, thrilling all over at the thought of an Irish Literary Theatre, and my own participation in the Celtic Renaissance brought about by Yeats. So the drama, I muttered, was not dead but sleeping, and while the hour before dinner was going by, I recalled an evening I had spent about two years ago in the Avenue Theatre. It was there I had seen Yeats for the first time, and it amused me to remember with what eyes I had seen him first, just after the performance of his little one-act play, *The Land of Heart's Desire.** His play neither pleased nor displeased; it struck me as an inoffensive trifle, but himself had provoked in me a violent antipathy, because I judged him from his appearance, and thereby lost two years of his wonderful company. It is true that when I saw him he was on exhibition, striding to and forth at the back of the dress circle, a long black cloak drooping from his shoulders, a soft black sombrero on his head, a voluminous black silk tie flowing from his collar, loose black trousers dragging untidily over his long, heavy feet—a man of such excessive appearance that I could not do otherwise—could I?—than to mistake him for an Irish parody of the poetry that I had seen all my life strutting its rhythmic way in the alleys of the Luxembourg Gardens, preening its rhymes by the fountains, excessive in habit and gait.

As far back as the days when I was a Frenchman,* I had begun to notice that whosoever adorns himself will soon begin to adorn his verses, so robbing them of that intimate sense of life which we admire in Verlaine; his verses proclaim him to have been a man of modest appearance. Never did Hugo or Banville affect any eccentricity of dress—and there are others. But let us be content with the theory, and refrain from collecting facts to support it, for in doing so we shall come upon exceptions, and these will have to be explained away. Suffice it to say, therefore, that Yeats's appearance at the Avenue Theatre confirmed me in the belief that his art could not be anything more than a merely pretty externality, if it were as much, and I declined to allow Nettleship to introduce me to him. No, my good friend, I don't want to know him; he wouldn't interest me, not any more than the Book of Kells*—not so much; Kells has at all events the merit of being archaic, whereas—No, no; to speak to him would make me 'eave—if I may quote a girl whom I heard speaking in the street yesterday.

It was months after, when I had forgotten all about Yeats, that my fingers distractedly picked up a small volume of verse out of the litter in Nettleship's room. Yeats! And after turning over a few pages, I called to Nettleship, who, taking advantage of my liking for the verses, begged again that he might be allowed to arrange a meeting, and, seduced by the strain of genuine music that seemed to whisper through the volume, I consented.

The Cheshire Cheese* was chosen as a tryst, and we started for that tavern one summer afternoon, talking of poetry and painting by turns, stopping at the corner of the street to finish an argument or an anecdote. Oxford Street was all aglow in the sunset, and Nettleship told, as we edged our way through the crowds, how Yeats's great poem was woven out of the legends of the Fianna,* and stopped to recite verses from it so often that when we arrived the poet was seated in front of a large steak, eating abstractedly, I thought, as if he did not know what he was eating—which was indeed the case— for he did not pretend any interest in the remonstrance that I addressed to Nettleship for having failed to choose Friday to dine at the Cheshire Cheese, it being the day when steak-and-kidney pudding was on at that tavern.

In order to help us through the first awkward five minutes, Nettleship informed me that Yeats was writing a work on Blake,* and the moment Blake's name was mentioned Yeats seemed altogether to forget the food before him, and very soon we were deep in a discussion regarding the Book of Thel, which Nettleship said was Blake's most effectual essay in metre. The designs that accompanied Blake's texts were known to me, and when the waiter brought us our steaks, Blake was lost sight of in the interest of the food, and in our interest in Yeats's interpretation of Blake's teaching.

But as the dinner at the Cheshire Cheese was given so that I should make Yeats's acquaintance, Nettleship withdrew from the conversation, leaving me to continue it, expecting, no doubt, that the combat of our wits would provide him with an entertainment as exciting as that of the cock-fights which used to take place a century ago in the adjoining yard. So there was no choice for me but to engage in disputation or to sulk, and the reader will agree with me that I did well to choose the former course, though the ground was all to my disadvantage, my knowledge of Blake being but accidental. There was, however, no dread of combat in me, my adversary not inspiring much belief that he would prove a stout one, and feeling sure that without difficulty I could lay him dead before Nettleship, I rushed at him, all my feathers erect. Yeats parried a blow on which I counted, and he did this so quickly and with so much ease that he threw me on the defensive in a moment. A dialectician, I muttered, of the very first rank; one of a different kind from any I have met before; and a few moments after I began to notice that Yeats was sparring beautifully, avoiding my rushes with great ease, evidently playing to tire me, with the intention of killing me presently with a single spur stroke. In the bout that ensued I was nearly worsted, but at the last moment an answer shot into my mind. Yeats would have discovered its weakness in a moment, and I might have fared ill, so it was a relief to me to notice that he seemed willing to drop our argument about Blake and to talk about something else. He was willing to do this, perhaps because he did not care to humiliate me, or it may have been that he wearied of talking about a literature to one who was imperfectly acquainted with it, or it may have been that I made a better show in argument than I thought for.

EARNÁN O'MALLEY
(1898–1957)

from *On Another Man's Wound* (1936)

I slept out with men from Rosegreen Company at the Centre under a tent which had once been a hayrick cover; some had hammocks which they slung in the hedge from tree branches. I was working in 47 when a scout came to see me. Three men had been captured on the hillside; they were British officers, and the Rosegreen men had them in a dugout lower down. I met the two boys who had captured them. One had a rifle and two rounds of ammunition, the other an empty bandolier, when they saw the three men coming across the fields. The boy with the rifle halted them; the men began to run. He fired. One of the men was wounded slightly, the others came back and all three surrendered. Each had an automatic in his pocket and an identification card. Two were gunner officers from Fethard Artillery Barracks, five miles across the hill. I sent two boys up the hill to find out where the officers had stopped and what they had been doing. Later one came back. The officers had been searching hedges; at a house on the slope they had asked about dug-outs. They had questioned the young man of the house.

I brought them up one by one. They gave me their names, ranks, the name of their commanding officer. They had been out for a walk, they said.

'Any officers we capture in this area are to be shot until such time as you cease shooting your prisoners.'

'We have nothing to do with the shooting of prisoners,' one said.

'This is not a personal question. Our men whom your men may capture and later shoot will have nothing to do with your being shot. My mind is made up about it. You will be shot at dawn tomorrow.'

'Can't you consider the matter?' one asked.

'You will have to consult your officers,' another said; 'you can't do it without authority.'

'I happen to be in command of this area. This is my authority. It would be better to prepare your minds. I will get food ready for you.' I gave them cigarettes. A boy with a rifle lay near the entrance to the dug-out.

A scout rushed down to where I sat. Beside me were six riflemen who had been mobilized in the meantime.

'Soldiers with a machine-gun. They've just come over the brow of the hill and they're searching.'

'Easy,' I said, 'the officers will hear you.'

The scouring soldiers came from Fethard. Other sections of troops would possibly be making their way in our direction.

I blindfolded the officers so that they could not see where they were going. The covering on their eyes made them helpless; their hands were free, but tying a man's hands was not a job we liked. Men held them by the sleeves so that they could walk more easily. One of them limped. He had a slight flesh wound. I put him on a cart.

'If we are surrounded,' I said to the one whose face I liked best, 'I'll let you go. I'm not going to shoot you like dogs.' The guard of riflemen grumbled.

'But you'll shoot them tomorrow, anyhow,' said the Brigade Q.M.* 'Where's the difference?'

The Q.M. was right, but it was tough to have to turn on them suddenly when we were hard put in a fight to shoot them like injured beasts.

One of the officers said, 'We can do first-aid for your wounded if there's a fight.'

A sloe-skin dusk came slowly down on the steep western slopes of Slievenamon* and across the woods there. It blurred the valley of the Suir below the Comeraghs; hedges of tangled hawthorn with fresh leaves, in amongst the neat stems of spruce, stood out against the rise of hills. There was a strong, spicy smell carried across from the bright pink blossoms of a corner hedge of wild crab.

We halted at a gateway. A horse and trap came up. The officers got up into the seats.

A young girl came out from a house. She peered at the men in the half-light. 'Who are they?' she asked.

'English officers,' said a guard.

'Shooting's too good for them,' she said, bitterly; as she looked up at them. They looked down at her with set faces.

'Oh, leave them alone,' I said.

'God help the poor boys,' said a woman beside her, 'perhaps they'd like a sup of milk.' She came back with a large jug and three delph mugs. The officers drank. They thanked her.

We walked into the closing-in darkness, riflemen in front and behind the trap, until we were a distance from where the officers had been captured. I expected a big round-up in which the countryside would be combed by troops from Cahir and Clonmel—both strong military posts. They would probably converge in the triangular area of which Fethard was the apex. We came to a farmhouse up in the fields some way off the main Clonmel road. Sentries were posted. The girls and women of the house got ready supper; they did not ask any questions. A fire was lighted in the room where the officers were. After supper I went into the room. The blinds were drawn so that they could not look out. It was a large room. They were seated at a table. One had his head in his hands.

'Would you like to see a clergyman of your own religion?'

'No,' said one. The others shook their heads.

'Would you like a civilian, an Imperialist, to stay with you?'

'No.' They did not need anyone.

'Here's writing paper and envelopes. You can write to anyone you wish. If you give me your words of honour that you won't mention anything of military importance, you can seal the envelopes yourselves.'

Each gave me his word. There were beds for them to sleep on.

I sat in the kitchen by the fire. The women of the house had gone to bed quietly. None of us spoke for a long time. I was putting myself in the place of the men inside. My turn might come, too, and soon. It seemed easier to face one's own execution than to have to shoot others. 'It's very dark outside,' said the Quartermaster. 'I hope the boys are keeping a good lookout.' He strode into the darkness.

He was an elderly man. Freckles showed through a wintered face. There were thin folds in his neck. He had a long skillet of a jaw, he showed the wide gaps between his teeth when he smiled. His step was as deliberate as a gander's. He would have his say no matter what happened; he was accustomed to jump objections—for that was a quarter-master's offensive. He could advise about a round of ammunition as seriously as we would discuss or draw up a plan of operations. He was the oldest of us, about thirty-five years. He spoke slowly and carefully, toothing his words in a dry humour.

None of us was twenty-four; the youngest officer inside was about that age. One was tall and dark with brown eyes. He had ill-treated prisoners in Tipperary, one of the Rosegreen men said. He had been insulting when on raids. One was stout with a thick neck, his hair was a little thin. He had been more anxious to talk and to remonstrate than the others. The third was quiet and reserved. He had a sensitive face and he did not talk. I liked him best. I was worried about him because he was wounded. It was an accepted convention that a wounded man should not be shot until he was able to walk. I did not bother about the convention, only the presence of the wounded man made its own conditions. I did not see any sense in keeping him for a few days longer. It would be harder on him if his companions went first.

'I wish it were over,' I said to the Q.M. There were two other men seated on chairs making a round of the fire.

'It'll be over soon enough,' he said. He was calm enough about it. I knew that I would continue to shoot their officers. Of that, there would be no doubt, but this kind of work was hard enough. If we shot enough of them, it would make the others think a little. I don't know what we talked about. Odds and rags of conversation about men in other battalions, the relative merits of different kinds of explosives; the making of improvised Stokes guns and the history of this part of Desmond. Two men went out to relieve their comrades. I walked outside in the darkness. The night was misty, the moon shone softly through cloud veils. Sounds carried well; away through the distance came the lonely bray of an ass; it was answered in sardonic harshness nearby. Sheep coughed drily in the shelter of a hedge and a cow chewed loudly.

'It'll soon be dawn,' said the Q.M.

I knocked at the door. They were seated around the table. Their faces looked worn and drawn. None of them had slept.

'Have you written your letters?'

'Yes,' said the thin swarthy one; 'here they are.'

'If you would like to send your money or valuables to your friends or relatives, I will forward them for you.'

'We would like to send them with a note to our C.O., Major Y, in Fethard,' the quiet one said.

I found an empty Fry's chocolate box on a side table. They put their watches, money, and rings inside.

'Would you like some tea? It'll soon be dawn and we'll have to be on our way.'

'No, thanks, we don't want anything.'

We walked down the sloping fields towards the roadway. The sky was clouded with heavy grey. The light was dim, a cold dawn wind blew across the thick hedges. It ruffled the grass which was shiny with dewdrops. Men with rifles formed an extended five-pointed figure. An officer walked on each side of the Q.M. I was behind with the third.

'It's a mistake,' he said. 'It won't do any good. We could be good to prisoners.'

'None of us want to do it,' I said, 'but I must think of our men.' I could not see the ultimate implications of our proposed action. The sky lighted silvery grey, the wind dropped.

We caught up with the three in front. 'Stiff banks those for hunting,' said the tall, swarthy officer. They smiled as if they had thought of horses and the sight of a red-brown fox.

'There's not much hunting now,' I said. We had stopped hunting through the martial law area.

We reached the roadway. There was a wall in front of a church. The three officers were placed on the green grass edge of the dusty road.

'Do you mind?' I said, as I placed their handkerchiefs around their eyes. One handkerchief was of silk and claret-coloured.

'No.'

'This is good-bye,' I said.

They shook hands with the Q.M. and myself. Their hands were cold and limp. They shook hands with each other.

The six men of the firing squad stood near the other side of the road. One of the men fumbled for a while with his magazine. He could not click it into place. An officer pulled down his handkerchief and looked at us, then he put it back over his eyes. Perhaps he thought we were trying to frighten and test them and that we did not intend to shoot.

'Ram in the magazine,' I whispered to the Q.M.

'Are you ready?' asked the Q.M.

One of the officers nodded. They joined hands. 'Good-bye, old boy,' they said, inclining their heads.

'Squad' . . . 'Ready' . . . 'Fire.'

The volley crashed sharply. The three fell to the ground; their arms twitched. The Q.M. put his revolver to each of their foreheads in turn and fired. The bodies lay still on the green grass. We stood to attention. Then slowly we went up the hill across country making for the Centre. None of us spoke till we had crossed a good many fields where wind had snaked the rye grass.

3. SHORT FICTION

JAMES JOYCE
(1882–1941)

A Painful Case (1905)

Mr James Duffy* lived in Chapelizod* because he wished to live as far as possible from the city of which he was a citizen and because he found all the other suburbs of Dublin mean, modern and pretentious. He lived in an old sombre house and from his windows he could look into the disused distillery or upwards along the shallow river on which Dublin is built. The lofty walls of his uncarpeted room were free from pictures. He had himself bought every article of furniture in the room: a black iron bedstead, an iron washstand, four cane chairs, a clothes-rack, a coal-scuttle, a fender and irons and a square table on which lay a double desk.* A bookcase had been made in an alcove by means of shelves of white wood. The bed was clothed with white bed-clothes and a black and scarlet rug covered the foot. A little hand-mirror hung above the washstand and during the day a white-shaded lamp stood as the sole ornament of the mantelpiece. The books on the white wooden shelves were arranged from below upwards according to bulk. A complete Wordsworth stood at one end of the lowest shelf and a copy of the *Maynooth Catechism*,* sewn into the cloth cover of a notebook, stood at one end of the top shelf. Writing materials were always on the desk. In the desk lay a manuscript translation of Hauptmann's *Michael Kramer*,* the stage directions of which were written in purple ink, and a little sheaf of papers held together by a brass pin. In these sheets a sentence was inscribed from time to time and, in an ironical moment, the headline of an advertisement for *Bile Beans** had been pasted on to the first sheet. On lifting the lid of the desk a faint fragrance escaped—the fragrance of new cedarwood pencils or of a bottle of gum or of an over-ripe apple which might have been left there and forgotten.

Mr Duffy abhorred anything which betokened physical or mental disorder. A mediæval doctor would have called him saturnine. His face, which carried the entire tale of his years, was of the brown tint of Dublin streets. On his long and rather large head grew dry black hair and a tawny moustache did not quite cover an unamiable mouth. His cheekbones also gave his face a harsh character; but there was no harshness in the eyes which, looking at the world from under their tawny eyebrows, gave the impression of a man ever alert to greet a redeeming instinct in others but often disappointed. He lived at a little distance from his body, regarding his own acts with doubtful side-glances. He had an odd autobiographical habit which led him to compose in his mind from time to time a short sentence about himself containing a subject in the third person and a predicate in the past tense. He never gave alms to beggars and walked firmly, carrying a stout hazel.

He had been for many years cashier of a private bank in Baggot Street. Every morning he came in from Chapelizod by tram. At midday he went to Dan Burke's and took his lunch—a bottle of lager beer and a small trayful of arrowroot biscuits. At four o'clock he was set free. He dined in an eating-house in George's Street where he felt himself safe from the society of Dublin's gilded youth and where there was a certain plain honesty in the bill of fare. His evenings were spent either before his landlady's piano or roaming about the outskirts of the city. His liking for Mozart's music brought him sometimes to an opera or a concert: these were the only dissipations of his life.

He had neither companions nor friends, church nor creed. He lived his spiritual life without any communion with others, visiting his relatives at Christmas and escorting them to the cemetery when they died. He performed these two social duties for old dignity's sake but conceded nothing further to the conventions which regulate the civic life. He allowed himself to think that in certain circumstances he would rob his bank but, as these circumstances never arose, his life rolled out evenly—an adventureless tale.

One evening he found himself sitting beside two ladies in the Rotunda.* The house, thinly peopled and silent, gave distressing prophecy of failure. The lady who sat next him looked round at the deserted house once or twice and then said:

—What a pity there is such a poor house to-night! It's so hard on people to have to sing to empty benches.

He took the remark as an invitation to talk. He was surprised that she seemed so little awkward. While they talked he tried to fix her permanently in his memory. When he learned that the young girl beside her was her daughter he judged her to be a year or so younger than himself. Her face, which must have been handsome, had remained intelligent. It was an oval face with strongly marked features. The eyes were very dark blue and steady. Their gaze began with a defiant note but was confused by what seemed a deliberate swoon of the pupil into the iris, revealing for an instant a temperament of great sensibility. The pupil reasserted itself quickly, this half-disclosed nature fell again under the reign of prudence, and her astrakhan jacket, moulding a bosom of a certain fulness, struck the note of defiance more definitely.

He met her again a few weeks afterwards at a concert in Earlsfort Terrace and seized the moments when her daughter's attention was diverted to become intimate. She alluded once or twice to her husband but her tone was not such as to make the allusion a warning. Her name was Mrs Sinico. Her husband's great-great-grandfather had come from Leghorn.* Her husband was captain of a mercantile boat plying between Dublin and Holland; and they had one child.

Meeting her a third time by accident he found courage to make an appointment. She came. This was the first of many meetings; they met always in the evening and chose the most quiet quarters for their walks together. Mr Duffy, however, had a distaste for underhand ways and, finding that they were compelled to meet stealthily, he forced her to ask him to her house. Captain Sinico encouraged his visits, thinking that his daughter's hand was in question. He had dismissed his wife so sincerely from his gallery of pleasures that he did not suspect that anyone else would take an interest in her. As the husband was often away and the daughter out giving music lessons Mr Duffy had many opportunities of enjoying the lady's society. Neither he nor she had had any such adventure before and neither was conscious of any incongruity. Little by little he entangled his thoughts with hers. He lent her books, provided her with ideas, shared his intellectual life with her. She listened to all.

Sometimes in return for his theories she gave out some fact of her own life. With almost maternal solicitude she urged him to let his nature open to the full; she became his confessor. He told her that for some time he had assisted at the meetings of an Irish Socialist Party where he had felt himself a unique figure amidst a score of sober workmen in a garret lit by an inefficient oil-lamp. When the party had divided into three sections, each under its own leader and in its own garret, he had discontinued his attendances. The workmen's discussions, he said, were too timorous; the interest they took in the question of wages was inordinate. He felt that they were hard-featured realists and that they resented an exactitude which was the product of a leisure not within their reach. No social revolution, he told her, would be likely to strike Dublin for some centuries.

She asked him why did he not write out his thoughts. For what, he asked her, with careful scorn. To compete with phrasemongers, incapable of thinking consecutively for sixty seconds? To submit himself to the criticisms of an obtuse middle class which entrusted its morality to policemen and its fine arts to impresarios?

He went often to her little cottage outside Dublin; often they spent their evenings alone. Little by little, as their thoughts entangled, they spoke of subjects less remote. Her companionship was like a warm soil about an exotic. Many times she allowed the dark to fall upon them, refraining from lighting the lamp. The dark discreet room, their isolation, the music that still vibrated in their ears united them. This union exalted him, wore away the rough edges of his character, emotionalized his mental life. Sometimes he caught himself listening to the sound of his own voice. He thought that in her eyes he would ascend to an angelical stature; and, as he attached the fervent nature of his companion more and more closely to him, he heard the strange impersonal voice which he recognized as his own, insisting on the soul's incurable loneliness. We cannot give ourselves, it said: we are our own. The end of these discourses was that one night during which she had shown every sign of unusual excitement, Mrs Sinico caught up his hand passionately and pressed it to her cheek.

Mr Duffy was very much surprised. Her interpretation of his words disillusioned him. He did not visit her for a week; then he wrote to her asking her to meet him. As he did not wish their last interview to be troubled by the influence of their ruined confessional they met in a little cakeshop near the Parkgate.* It was cold autumn weather but in spite of the cold they wandered up and down the roads of the Park for nearly three hours. They agreed to break off their intercourse: every bond, he said, is a bond to sorrow. When they came out of the Park they walked in silence towards the tram; but here she began to tremble so violently that, fearing another collapse on her part, he bade her good-bye quickly and left her. A few days later he received a parcel containing his books and music.

Four years passed. Mr Duffy returned to his even way of life. His room still bore witness of the orderliness of his mind. Some new pieces of music encumbered the music-stand in the lower room and on his shelves stood two volumes by Nietzsche: *Thus Spake Zarathustra* and *The Gay Science*. He wrote seldom in the sheaf of papers which lay in his desk. One of his sentences, written two months after his last interview with Mrs Sinico, read: Love between man and man is impossible because there must not be sexual inter-course and friendship between man and woman is impossible because there must be sexual intercourse. He kept away from con-certs lest he should meet her. His father died; the junior partner of the bank retired. And still every morning he went into the city by tram and every evening walked home from the city after having dined moderately in George's Street and read the evening paper for dessert.

One evening as he was about to put a morsel of corned beef and cabbage into his mouth his hand stopped. His eyes fixed themselves on a paragraph in the evening paper which he had propped against the water-carafe. He replaced the morsel of food on his plate and read the paragraph attentively. Then he drank a glass of water, pushed his plate to one side, doubled the paper down before him between his elbows and read the paragraph over and over again. The cabbage began to deposit a cold white grease on his plate. The girl came over to him to ask was his dinner not properly cooked. He said it was very good and ate a few mouthfuls of it with difficulty. Then he paid his bill and went out.

He walked along quickly through the November twilight, his stout hazel stick striking the ground regularly, the fringe of the buff *Mail** peeping out of a side-pocket of his tight reefer overcoat. On the lonely road which leads from the Parkgate to Chapelizod he slackened his pace. His stick struck the ground less emphatically and his breath, issuing irregularly, almost with a sighing sound, con-densed in the wintry air. When he reached his house he went up at once to his bedroom and, taking the paper from his pocket, read the paragraph again by the failing light of the window. He read it not aloud, but moving his lips as a priest does when he reads the prayers *Secreto*.* This was the paragraph:

DEATH OF A LADY AT SYDNEY PARADE

A PAINFUL CASE

To-day at the City of Dublin Hospital the Deputy Coroner (in the absence of Mr Leverett) held an inquest on the body of Mrs Emily Sinico, aged forty-three years, who was killed at Sydney Parade Station yesterday evening. The evidence showed that the deceased lady, while attempting to cross the line, was knocked down by the engine of the ten o'clock slow train from Kingstown, thereby sustaining injuries of the head and right side which led to her death.

James Lennon, driver of the engine, stated that he had been in the employment of the railway company for fifteen years. On hearing the guard's whistle he set the train in motion and a second or two afterwards brought it to rest in response to loud cries. The train was going slowly.

P. Dunne, railway porter, stated that as the train was about to start he observed a woman attempting to cross the lines. He ran towards her and shouted but, before he could reach her, she was caught by the buffer of the engine and fell to the ground.

A juror—You saw the lady fall?

Witness—Yes.

Police Sergeant Croly deposed that when he arrived he found the deceased lying on the platform apparently dead. He had the body taken to the waiting-room pending the arrival of the ambulance.

Constable 57E corroborated.

Dr Halpin, assistant house surgeon of the City of Dublin Hospital, stated that the deceased had two lower ribs fractured and had sustained severe contusions of the right shoulder. The right side of the head had been injured in the fall. The injuries were not sufficient to have caused death in a normal person. Death, in his opinion, had been probably due to shock and sudden failure of the heart's action.

Mr H. B. Patterson Finlay, on behalf of the railway company, expressed his deep regret at the accident. The company had always taken every precaution to prevent people crossing the lines except by the bridges, both by placing notices in every station and by the use of patent spring gates at level crossings. The deceased had been in the habit of crossing the lines late at night from platform to platform and, in view of certain other circumstances of the case, he did not think the railway officials were to blame.

Captain Sinico, of Leoville, Sydney Parade, husband of the deceased, also gave evidence. He stated that the deceased was his wife. He was not in Dublin at the time of the accident as he had arrived only that morning from Rotterdam. They had been married for twenty-two years and had lived happily until about two years ago when his wife began to be rather intemperate in her habits.

Miss Mary Sinico said that of late her mother had been in the habit of going out at night to buy spirits. She, witness, had often tried to reason with her mother and had induced her to join a league.* She was not at home until an hour after the accident.

The jury returned a verdict in accordance with the medical evidence and exonerated Lennon from all blame.

The Deputy Coroner said it was a most painful case, and expressed great sympathy with Captain Sinico and his daughter. He urged on the railway company to take strong measures to prevent the possibility of similar accidents in the future. No blame attached to anyone.

Mr Duffy raised his eyes from the paper and gazed out of his window on the cheerless evening landscape. The river lay quiet beside the empty distillery and from time to time a light appeared in some house on the Lucan road. What an end! The whole narrative of her death revolted him and it revolted him to think that he had ever spoken to her of what he held sacred. The threadbare phrases, the inane expressions of sympathy, the cautious words of a reporter won over to conceal the details of a commonplace vulgar death attacked his stomach. Not merely had she degraded herself; she had degraded him. He saw the squalid tract of her vice, miserable and malodorous. His soul's companion! He thought of the hobbling wretches whom he had seen carrying cans and bottles to be filled by the barman. Just God, what an end! Evidently she had been unfit to live, without any strength of purpose, an easy prey to habits, one of the wrecks on which civilisation has been reared. But that she could have sunk so low! Was it possible he had deceived himself so utterly about her? He remembered her outburst of that night and interpreted it in a harsher sense than he had ever done. He had no difficulty now in approving of the course he had taken.

As the light failed and his memory began to wander he thought her hand touched his. The shock which had first attacked his stomach was now attacking his nerves. He put on his over-coat and hat quickly and went out. The cold air met him on the threshold; it crept into the sleeves of his coat. When he came to the public-house at Chapelizod Bridge he went in and ordered a hot punch.

The proprietor served him obsequiously but did not venture to talk. There were five or six working-men in the shop discussing the value of a gentleman's estate in County Kildare. They drank at intervals from their huge pint tumblers and smoked, spitting often on the floor and sometimes dragging the sawdust over their spits with their heavy boots. Mr Duffy sat on his stool and gazed at them, without seeing or hearing them. After a while they went out and he called for another punch. He sat a long time over it. The shop was very quiet. The proprietor sprawled on the counter reading the *Herald** and yawning. Now and again a tram was heard swishing along the lonely road outside.

As he sat there, living over his life with her and evoking alternately the two images in which he now conceived her, he realized that she was dead, that she had ceased to exist, that she had become a memory. He began to feel ill at ease. He asked himself what else could he have done. He could not have carried on a comedy of deception with her; he could not have lived with her openly. He had done what seemed to him best. How was he to blame? Now that she was gone he understood how lonely her life must have been, sitting night after night alone in that room. His life would be lonely too until he, too, died, ceased to exist, became a memory—if anyone remembered him.

It was after nine o'clock when he left the shop. The night was cold and gloomy. He entered the park by the first gate and walked along under the gaunt trees. He walked through the bleak alleys where they had walked four years before. She seemed to be near him in the darkness. At moments he seemed to feel her voice touch his ear, her hand touch his. He stood still to listen. Why had he withheld life from her? Why had he sentenced her to death? He felt his moral nature falling to pieces.

When he gained the crest of the Magazine Hill he halted and looked along the river towards Dublin, the lights of which burned redly and hospitably in the cold night. He looked down the slope and, at the base, in the shadow of the wall of the park, he saw some human figures lying. Those venal and furtive loves filled him with despair. He gnawed the rectitude of his life; he felt that he had been outcast from life's feast. One human being had seemed to love him and he had denied her life and happiness: he had sentenced her to ignominy, a death of shame. He knew that the prostrate creatures down by the wall were watching him and wished him gone. No one wanted him; he was outcast from life's feast. He turned his eyes to the grey gleaming river, winding along towards Dublin. Beyond the river he saw a goods train winding out of Kingsbridge Station, like a worm with a fiery head winding through the darkness, obstinately and laboriously. It passed slowly out of sight; but still he heard in his ears the laborious drone of the engine reiterating the syllables of her name.

He turned back the way he had come, the rhythm of the engine pounding in his ears. He began to doubt the reality of what memory told him. He halted under a tree and allowed the rhythm to die away. He could not feel her near him in the darkness nor her voice touch his ear. He waited for some minutes listening. He could hear nothing: the night was perfectly silent. He listened again: perfectly silent. He felt that he was alone.

SEÁN O'FAOLÁIN
(1900–1991)

Lilliput (1926)

On those nights when curfew came at ten o'clock and people were hastening within doors, locking doors, bolting doors, chaining doors at a full quarter to the hour, the poor alone were leisurely. Shandon* had therefore struck ten before the last of the apple-sellers began to drag her basket after her into the lanes, but once she was gone the bridge was as empty as a plain.

There had been a fragrance in the air as long as the apples lay there exposed but the smell of the river was about to conquer again. A light fog had crept up the valley of the Lee* from the harbour mouth and the lamps on the bridges had gathered from it a rich and reddish hue, while their dagger-like reflections trembled but slightly in the cold and glassy river-water. Farther down the quays the lovers were parting in the darker nooks, the men with one eye raised for the coming of the patrols, the women drawing their shawls closer around their lovers for the last embrace. Where the nets were drying there hung an odour of tar, and where they wash the sheep-skins the slips and pavement smelt in the night air. Already in the side-streets where there lie stables and storehouses and an occasional dwelling-house it might have been the first hours of the morning. But in one of these streets which lead from the quaysides to the centre of the city through a middle-class quarter, there stood, and had stood all the day long, a cart surmounted by a black box-like erection—a sort of miserable caravan without windows, without chimney and without an animal to support the slanting shafts. It might remind you of the little cart of the Poor Shepherd Nuns, or of a small-scale fever-cart intended to carry away the infected clothes from a condemned house. Inside were three children fast asleep. Clothes and cloths and mere rags filled this box of a house. Straw, a bucket, a board, chains—these with some huge stones at the wheels were scattered around it on the street. The cart carried no lamp. The open doorway facing the shafts was curtained by an old yellow coat, but at this hour the whole was a black mass inviting collision from the last-minute jarvey-cars* careering past with their drunken passengers clinging to the seat.

It was now several minutes past the forbidden hour, and any moment the first lorries would be heard tearing along the quays and through the principal streets. None the less you could hear in the square near-by a war of words and distinguish them if you chose to listen. A woman was answering two or three male voices, young and soft in spite of their jeering tones, and as they parted farther and farther from one another, and the steps of the woman came nearer, and the voices of the other more shrill in the distance you might have heard every swear.

'Aha! The Kerry porther* is the best porther, I can tell ye.'

They answered with a crying call such as a savage might use in battle.

'Go home to yeer mothers,' she responded, and followed with a cry as wild as theirs.

Just then the lorries began to whir in the distance and the boyish feet scampered for safety. Indifferent to them she sang herself back to her cart, sometimes muttering between the lines about her husband, and the police, and her donkey-ass. She sang out,

'O-o-oh!
Will anybody tell me where the Blarney roses grow?
Is it over in Kilmurry South, or yonder in Cloghroe?'

and tumbled into her cart, and sank at once into a profound sleep. The people of the quarter, however, sate up in their beds for an hour waiting for the patrols to come and take her, and when she was still there in the morning, they said such ungenerous things as 'The devil always looks after his own'; or, 'Look how a good person wouldn't have been so fortunate'; and went by to church with disapproving eyes.

At the first Angelus* the haze still hung over the city, but the morning broke in sunshine shortly before the second bell rang in the noon. From that onwards there were ding-dongs all over the city at intervals of hours or half-hours. Finally when all the children were returning from their usual Sunday Mass she was arisen and had made some slops of tea. The city children gathered around her in wonderment as she washed the little girls' faces in the water she had borrowed near-by. Unperturbed, she combed their hair, peering at the scalp.

She was a sturdy woman with fresh colour in her cheeks, but her dun-coloured hair hung around her in contrast to the neat little figures that watched her and her cart in wonder. She saw this herself and eventually sate down on the sloping shaft to examine their spotless muslin frocks, their white shoes, their frilly lace, and sky-blue ribbons. She began to tell them disconsolately of her husband who was in Moore's Hotel—they knew Moore's Hotel was a jail—and she spoke pityingly of her three children and of the donkey-ass whom 'Cruelty' had led away when her husband was taken. So, all the day long she sate there, only rising at intervals. Once she picked and plucked at the three children, and went off with them to the jail. But she soon returned like a huge liner with three small tenders on her flanks, and began speaking of their father to some women that had gathered around her. The 'polis' had taken him for beating the donkey-ass 'till he brayed and died.' It was a tree fell on the donkey-ass, she said. They asked her had she come far, and she said from Headford. They said she was a pity, and one of the poorest came to her with a pot of soup and vegetables and potatoes. But her eldest child knocked it over by accident, and her mother called her a jade, and sate down for a spell.

All day long there was a changing little crowd around her. Patiently she told again and again of the donkey-ass and *their* father, and Moore's Hotel. She had once lived in Blarney Street and was four years on the road. Or she had lived in Barrackah and was ten years on the road. Or she had been born on the road and didn't know what a roof-tree meant. She told all her stories with her cheek on her fist, occasionally cocking her eye at her listeners but with a bored air. Each one of her listeners said she and her three children were a pity. She told them of the blackguards who called her low names last night, and they promised to keep guard for her, even to go to the sessions with her, and she answered she must rely on the help of God and her neighbours in all things. Some of the women did not like her and asked her questions that she refused to answer, but the other women said that these things were her own business.

At tea-hour the crowd did not slacken. The children from the streets all around became more noisy and familiar and had to be hunted away by the women. She borrowed water again, and a passing man bought her the last two loaves from the nearest huckster's shop. She gave tea to her three little girls within the cart, she herself eating from the roadway like a photographer behind the curtaining yellow coat, just as if her cart were a huge black camera.

At dusk and dark the people of the district became very nervous, and wondered why the police did not come to move her away, and complained that the whole country was in a shocking state, and feared above all, saying so to one another from door to door and window to window, that she would attract the attention of the Tans* and the patrols to their quiet street and they would have no wink of sleep at all that night. At last the police came, but they had no mind to argue with her, and they merely told her to take her cart to hell out of that street even as she brought it in, and then because they knew she would begin to ask how was she to do that, they went away at once so that they should have the last word.

Then the children around began to enjoy themselves in earnest. They laid themselves under the shafts, and, shouting, began to strain and pull, or they heaved the huge stones from beneath the wheels and cried out for orders from the woman. The hoydens from the lane-ways told her to wheel her cart to this place or that, and the children chimed in that Harper's lane was not at all like this street, but was a small narrow lane, down below there. The women gathered around her again and again, or sank on their haunches before her children and returning, told the mother that they were chatting away to themselves. Amid cries the cart began to move, and the loose chains to swing and ring in the dark as the children dragged it from the kerb. But the woman hailed them, and they ordered one another to wheel it back again, and there it stayed yet another night. She lit a candle and put the little girls to bed and its light shone brightly from the interior of the cart until she drew the yellow coat across it.

It was now almost ten o'clock and the women began to scatter, talking among themselves and asking her if she would be all right there. She walked away with a few of them and the wind blew the candle out and the night moulded the cart into the blackness of the street, and the street became as quiet as early dawn. A man who asked the children who owned the cart, and where she was now, had to chase them because they pelted him with stones and called out ribald answers. Then the street settled down to the night again. But a priest walked down the street from the riverside, showing like a statue in jet under the lamps above him. Three girls clasping one another's waists cried out that he was coming and retired to a corner of the square. He looked around when he reached the cart, and down the street ahead of him, and tapped politely at the side of the cart, and looked to the right and then went home tapping his silver-headed stick on the flags. The girls ran another way to watch him and all was still again until the lorries began to whir in the distance as Shandon struck the hour and the girls raced for their homes.

The woman returned shortly after and crept into the cart on her knees. An old woman shuffled along and asked her if she were there last night also, and asked why was the poor man taken, and prayed God to help us all. The woman within spoke out to her to go away for Virgin Mary's sake and let her sleep—which the old woman did, looking back several times as she padded away on her bare feet, the woman within snoring out loud snores that might be heard by a passer-by long before he distinguished the cart from the darkness around it.

Towards midnight a patrol of military tramped slowly down the street while the wakeful householders held their breath. The patrol halted at the cart, and the officer flashed his torch into the interior. Then he murmured something to his sergeant and the sergeant ordered his men to move on.

'Blimey!' whispered the sergeant to the corporal, and he passed on the word to the men. 'Blimey, if it isn't a woman.'

'Oo is it?' asked a stupid private.

'Mary Mac* and the Holy Trinity,' said the corporal, who was an atheist; and sniggering they all tramped away—quietly and slowly as if they would not disturb her sleep.

LIAM O'FLAHERTY
(1896–1984)

The Mountain Tavern (1929)

Snow was falling.* The bare, flat, fenceless road had long since disappeared. Now the white snow fell continuously on virgin land, all level, all white, all silent, between the surrounding dim peaks of the mountains. Through the falling snow, on every side, squat humps were visible. They were the mountain peaks. And between them, the moorland was as smooth as a ploughed field. And as silent, oh, as silent as an empty church. Here, the very particles of the air entered the lungs seemingly as big as pebbles and with the sweetness of ripe fruit. An outstretched hand could almost feel the air and the silence. There was absolutely nothing, nothing at all, but falling flakes of white snow, undeflected, falling silently on fallen snow.

Up above was the sky and God perhaps, though it was hard to believe it; hard to believe that there was anything in the whole universe but a flat white stretch of virgin land between squat mountain peaks and a ceaseless shower of falling snow-flakes.

There came the smell of human breathing from the east. Then three figures appeared suddenly, dark, although they were covered with snow. They appeared silently, one by one, stooping forward. The leading man carried his overcoat like a shawl about his head, with a rifle, butt upwards, slung on his right shoulder and two cloth ammunition belts slung across his body. He wore black top boots. His grim young eyes gazed wearily into the falling snow and his boots, scarcely lifted, raked the smooth earth, scattering the fallen snow-flakes.

The second man wore a belted leather coat, of which one arm hung loose. With the other hand he gripped his chest and staggered forward, with sagging, doddering head. A pistol, pouched in a loose belt, swung back and forth with his gait. There was blood on his coat, on his hand and congealed on his black leggings, along which the melting snow ran in a muddy stream. There was a forlorn look in his eyes, but his teeth were set. Sometimes he bared them and drew in a deep breath with a hissing sound.

The third man walked erect. He wore no overcoat and his head was bare. His hair curled and among the curls the snow lay in little rows like some statue in winter. He had a proud, fearless face, bronzed, showing no emotion nor weariness. Now and again, he shook his great body and the snow fell with a rustling sound off his clothes and off the heavy pack he carried. He also had two rifles wrapped in a cape under his arm; and in his right hand he carried a small wooden box that hung from a leather strap.

They walked in each other's tracks slowly. Rapidly the falling snow filled up the imprints of their feet. And when they passed there was silence again.

The man in front halted and raised his eyes to look ahead. The second man staggered against him, groaned with pain and gripped the other about the body with his loose hand to steady himself. The third man put the wooden box on the ground and shifted his pack.

'Where are we now?' he said.

His voice rang out, hollow, in the stillness and several puffs of hot air, the words, jerked out, like steam from a starting engine.

'Can't say,' muttered the man in front. 'Steady, Commandant. We can't be far now. We're on the road anyway. It should be there in front. Can't see, though. It's in a hollow. That's why.'

'What's in a hollow, Jack?' muttered the wounded man. 'Let me lie down here. It's bleeding again.'

'Hold on, Commandant,' said the man in front. 'We'll be at the Mountain Tavern in half a minute. Christ!'

'Put him on my back,' said the big man. 'You carry the stuff.'

'Never mind. I'll walk,' said the wounded man. 'I'll get there all right. Any sign of them?'

They peered into the falling snow behind them. There was utter silence. The ghostly white shower made no sound. A falling curtain.

'Lead on then,' said the big man. 'Lean on me, Commandant.'

They moved on. The wounded man was groaning now and his feet began to drag. Shortly he began to rave in a low voice. Then they halted again. Without speaking, the big man hoisted his comrade, crosswise, on his shoulders. The other man carried the kit. They moved on again.

The peak in front became larger. It was no longer a formless mass. Gradually, through the curtain of snow, it seemed to move towards them and upwards. The air became still more thin. As from the summit of a towering cliff, the atmosphere in front became hollow; and soon, through the haze of snow, they caught a glimpse of the distant plains, between two mountain peaks. There below it lay, like the bottom of a sea, in silence. The mountain sides sank down into it, becoming darker; for it did not snow down there. There was something, after all, other than the snow. But the snowless, downland earth looked dour and unapproachable.

'It must be here,' the leading man said again. 'Why can't we see it? It's just under the shelter of that mountain. There is a little clump of pine trees and a barn with a red roof. Sure I often had a drink in it. Where the name of God is it, anyway?'

'Go on. Stop talking,' said the curly-headed man.

'Can't you be easy?' muttered the leading man, moving ahead and peering into the snow that made his eyelids blink and blink. 'Supposing this is the wrong road, after all. They say people go round and round in the snow. Sure ye could see it from the other end, four miles away in clear weather, two storey high and a slate roof with the sun shining on it. It's facing this way too, right on the top of the hill, with a black board, "Licensed to Sell." Man called Galligan owns it. I'd swear by the Cross of Christ we must be up on it.'

'Hurry on,' snapped the curly man. 'There's a gurgle in his throat. Jesus! His blood is going down my neck. Why can't you hurry on, blast it?'

'Hey, what place is that?' cried the leading man, in a frightened voice. 'D'ye see a ruin?'

They halted. A moment ago there had been nothing in front but a curtain of falling snow, beyond which, as in a child's sick dream, the darkening emptiness of the snowless lowland approached, tumbling like a scudding black cloud. Now a crazy blue heap appeared quite close. Suddenly it heaved up out of the snow. It was a ruined house. There was a smell from it too. From its base irregular tufts of smoke curled up spasmodically; dying almost as soon as they appeared and then appearing again.

The two men watched it. There was no emotion in their faces. They just looked, as if without interest. It was too strange. The *Mountain Tavern* was a smoking ruin.

'It's gone west',* murmured the leading man.

'Eh?' shouted the curly man. 'Gone did ye say?'

'Aye. Burned to the ground. See?'

'Well?'

'God knows. We're up the pole.'*

Suddenly the curly man uttered a cry of rage and staggered forward under his load. The other man opened his mouth wide, drew in an enormous breath and dropped his head wearily on his chest. Trailing his rifle in the snow behind him, he reeled forward shaking his head from side to side, with his under lip trembling. Then he began to sing foolishly under his breath. There were people around the ruined house. And as the two men, with their dying comrade, came into view, quite close, these people stopped and gaped at them. There was a woman in front of the house, on the road, sitting on an upturned barrel. She was a thin woman with a long pointed nose and thin black hair that hung in disorder on her thin neck, with hairpins sticking in it. She had a long overcoat buttoned over her dress and a man's overcoat about her shoulders. She held a hat with red feathers on it in her right hand, by the rim. Two children, wrapped in queer clothes, stood beside her, clinging to her, a boy and a girl. They also were thin and they had pointed noses like their mother. One man was pulling something out of a window of the ruined house. Another man, within the window, had his head stuck out. He had been handing out something. Another man was in the act of putting a tin trunk on a cart, to which a horse was harnessed, to the right of the house. All looked, gaping, at the newcomers.

'God save all here,' said the curly man, halting near the woman.

Nobody replied. The other man came up and staggered towards the woman, who was sitting on the upturned barrel. The two children, silent with fear, darted around their mother, away from the man. They clutched at her, muttering something inaudibly.

'Is that you, Mrs Galligan?'

'It is then,' said the woman in a stupid, cold voice. 'And who might you be?'

'We're Republican soldiers,' said the curly man. 'I have a dying man here.'

He lowered the wounded man gently to the ground. Nobody spoke or moved. The snow fell steadily.

'Mummy, mummy,' cried one of the children, 'there's blood on him. Oh! mummy.'

The two children began to howl. The dying man began to throw his hands about and mutter something. A great rush of blood flowed from him.

'In the name of the Lord God of Heaven,' yelled the curly man, 'are ye savages not to move a foot? Eh? Can't ye go for a doctor? Is there nothing in the house?'

He stooped over the dying man and clutching him in his arms, he cried hoarsely:

'Easy now, Commandant. I'm beside ye. Give us a hand with him, Jack. We'll fix the bandage.'

The two of them, almost in a state of delirium, began to fumble with the dying man. The children wept. The dying man suddenly cried out:

'Stand fast. Stand fast boys. Stand . . .'

Then he made a violent effort to sit up. He opened his mouth and did not close it again.

The woman looked on dazed, with her forehead wrinkled and her lips set tight. The three men who had been doing something among the ruin began to come up slowly. They also appeared dazed, terrified.

'He's gone,' murmured the curly man, sitting erect on his knees. 'God have mercy on him.'

He laid the corpse flat on the ground. The blood still flowed out. The other soldier took off his hat and then, just as he was going to cross himself, he burst into tears. The three men came close and looked on. Then they sheepishly took off their hats.

'Is he dead?' said one of them.

The curly man sat back on his heels.

'He's dead,' he said. 'The curse o' God on this country.'

'And what did ye say happened?'

'Ambush back there. Our column got wiped out. Haven't ye got anything in the house?'

The woman laughed shrilly. The children stopped crying.

'Is there nothing in the house, ye daylight robber?' she cried. 'Look at it, curse ye. It's a black ruin. Go in. Take what ye can find, ye robber.'

'Robbers!' cried the soldier who had been weeping. 'Come on, Curly. Stand by me. I'm no robber. God! Give me a drink. Something to eat. Christ! I'm dyin'.'

He got to his feet and took a pace forward like a drunken man. The curly-headed soldier caught him.

'Keep yer hair on, Jack,' he said.

'Look at what ye've done,' cried the woman. 'Ye've blown up the house over me head. Ye've left me homeless and penniless with yer war. Oh! God, why don't ye drop down the dome of Heaven on me?'

'Sure we didn't blow up yer house,' cried the curly soldier. 'An' we lookin' for shelter after trampin' the mountains since morning. Woman, ye might respect the dead that died for ye.'

The woman spat and hissed at him.

'Let them die. They didn't die for me,' she said. 'Amn't I ruined and wrecked for three long years with yer fightin', goin' back and forth, lootin' and turnin' the honest traveller from my door? For three long years have I kept open house for all of ye and now yer turnin' on one another like dogs after a bitch.'

'None o' that now,' cried the hysterical soldier, trying to raise his rifle.

'Hold on, man,' cried one of the other men. 'She has cause. She has cause.'

'He grew excited and waved his hands and addressed his own comrades instead of addressing the soldiers.

'The Republicans came to the house this morning,' he cried. 'So Mr Galligan told me an' he goin' down the road for McGilligan's motor. The Republicans came, he said. And then . . . then the Free Staters* came on top of them and the firing began. Women and children out, they said, under a white flag. So Galligan told me. "They damn near shot me," says he to me, "harbourin' Irregulars* under the new act." Shot at sight, or what's worse, they take ye away on the cars, God knows where. Found in a ditch. None of us, God blast my soul if there is a word of a lie in what I am sayin', none of us here have a hand or part in anything. Three miles I came up in the snow when Mr Galligan told me. Says he to me, "I'll take herself and the kids to aunt Julia's in McGilligan's motor." '

'Where did they go?' said the curly soldier.

'I was comin' to that,' said the man, spitting in the snow and turning towards the woman. 'It's with a bomb they did it, Galligan said to me. Something must have fallen in the fire. They stuck it out, he said. There were six men inside. Not a man came out without a wound. So he said. There were two dead. On a door they took 'em away. They took 'em all off in the cars. And they were goin' to take Mr Galligan too. There you are now. May the Blessed Virgin look down on here. An' many's a man 'll go thirsty from this day over the mountain road.'

'Aye,' said the woman. 'For twenty years in that house, since my father moved from the village, after buyin' it from Johnny Reilly.'

'Twenty years,' she said again.

'Can't ye give us something to eat?' cried the hysterical man, trying to break loose from the curly soldier, who still held him.

'There's nothing here,' muttered a man, 'until Mr Galligan comes in the motor. He should be well on the way now.'

'They were all taken,' said the curly soldier.

'All taken,' said the three men, all together.

'Sit down, Jack,' said the curly soldier.

He pulled his comrade down with him on to the snow. He dropped his head on his chest. The others looked at the soldiers sitting in the snow. The others had a curious, malign look in their eyes. They looked at the dazed, exhausted soldiers and at the corpse with a curious apathy. They looked with hatred. There was no pity in their eyes. They looked steadily without speech or movement, with the serene cruelty of children watching an insect being tortured. They looked patiently, as if calmly watching a monster in its death agony.

The curly-headed soldier suddenly seemed to realize that they were watching him. For he raised his head and peered at them shrewdly through the falling snow. There was utter silence everywhere, except the munching sound made by the horse's jaws as he chewed hay. The snow fell, fell now, in the fading light, mournfully, blotting out the sins of the world.

The soldier's face, that had until then shown neither fear nor weariness, suddenly filled with despair. His lips bulged out. His eyes almost closed. His forehead gathered together and he opened his nostrils wide.

'I'm done,' he said. 'It's no use. Say, men. Send word that we're here. Let them take us. I'm tired fightin'. It's no use.'

No one spoke or stirred. A sound approached. Strange to say, no one paid attention to the sound. And even when a military motor lorry appeared at the brow of the road, nobody moved or spoke. There were Free State soldiers on the lorry. They had their rifles pointed. They drew near slowly. Then, with a rush, they dismounted and came running up.

The two Republican soldiers put up their hands, but they did not rise to their feet.

'Robbers,' screamed the woman. 'I hate ye all. Robbers.'

Her husband was there with them.

'Mary, we're to go in the lorry,' he said to her. 'They're goin' to look after us they said. Fr. Considine went to the barracks.'

'The bloody robbers,' she muttered, getting off the barrel.

'Who's this?' the officer said, roughly handling the corpse.

He raised the head of the corpse.

'Ha!' he said. 'So we got him at last. Eh? Heave him into the lorry, boys. Hurry up. Chuck 'em all in.'

They took away the corpse and the prisoners. There was a big dark spot where the corpse had lain. Snow began to fall on the dark spot.

They took away everybody, including the horse and cart. Everybody went away, down the steep mountain road, into the dark lowland country, where no snow was falling. All was silent again on the flat top of the mountain.

There was nothing in the whole universe again but the black ruin and the black spot where the corpse had lain. Night fell and snow fell, fell like soft soothing white flower petals on the black ruin and on the black spot where the corpse had lain.

FRANK O'CONNOR
(1903–1966)

The Majesty of the Law (1935)

Old Dan Bride was breaking brosna* for the fire when he heard a step up the path. He paused, a bundle of saplings on his knee.

Dan had looked after his mother while the spark of life was in her, and after her death no other woman had crossed the threshold. Signs on it, his house had that look. Almost everything in it he had made with his own hands in his own way. The seats of the chairs were only slices of log, rough and round and thick as the saw had left them, and with the rings still plainly visible through the grime and polish that coarse trouser bottoms had in the course of long years imparted. Into these Dan had rammed stout knotted ash boughs which served alike for legs and back. The deal table, bought in a shop, was an inheritance from his mother, and a great pride and joy to him, though it rocked forward and back whenever he touched it. On the wall, unglazed and flyspotted, hung in mysterious isolation a Marcus Stone print* and beside the door was a calendar representing a racehorse. Over the door hung a gun, old but good and in excellent condition, and before the fire was stretched an old setter who raised his head expectantly whenever Dan rose or even stirred.

He raised it now as the steps came nearer, and when Dan, laying down the bundle of saplings, cleaned his hands thoughtfully in the seat of his trousers, he gave a loud bark, but this expressed no more than a desire to display his own watchfulness. He was half human and knew that people thought he was old and past his prime.

A man's shadow fell across the oblong of dusty light thrown over the half door before Dan looked round.

'Are you alone, Dan?' asked an apologetic voice.

'Oh, come in, come in, sergeant, come in and welcome,' exclaimed the old man, hurrying on rather uncertain feet to the door, which the tall policeman opened and pushed in. He stood there, half in sunlight, half in shadow, and seeing him so, you would have realised how dark was the interior of Dan's house. One side of his red face was turned so as to catch the light, and behind it an ash tree raised its boughs of airy green against the sky. Green fields, broken here and there by clumps of red-brown rock, flowed downhill, and beyond them, stretched all across the horizon was the sea, flooded and almost transparent with light. The sergeant's face was fat and fresh, the old man's face, emerging from the twilight of the kitchen, had the colour of wind and sun, while the features had been so shaped by the struggle with time and the elements that they might as easily have been found impressed upon the surface of a rock.

'Begor,* Dan,' said the sergeant, ' 'tis younger you're getting.'

'Middling I am, sergeant, middling,' agreed the old man in a voice which seemed to accept the remark as a compliment of which politeness would not allow him to take too much advantage. 'No complaints.'

'Faix,* and 'tis as well. No wan but a born idiot would believe them. And th' ould dog don't look a day older.'

The dog gave a low growl as though to show the sergeant that he would remember this unmannerly reference to his age, but indeed he growled every time he was mentioned, under the impression that people could have nothing but ill to say of him.

'And how's yourself, sergeant?'

'Well, now, like that in the story, Dan, neither on the pig's back or at the horse's tail. We have our own little worries, but, thanks be to God, we have our compensations.'

'And the wife and care?'

'Good, glory and praise be to God, good. They were away from me with a month, the lot of them, at the mother-in-law's place in Clare.'

'Ah, do you tell me so?'

'I had a fine, quiet time.'

The old man looked about him, and then retired to the near-by bedroom from which he emerged a moment later with an old shirt. With this he solemnly wiped the seat and back of the log-chair nearest the fire.

'Take your ease, now, take your ease. 'Tis tired you must be after the journey. How did you come?'

'Teigue Leary it was that gave me a lift. Wisha,* now Dan, don't you be putting yourself about. I won't be stopping. I promised them I'd be back inside an hour.'

'What hurry is on you?' asked the old man. 'Look now, your foot was on the path when I rose from putting kindling on the fire.'

'Now! Now! You're not making tea for me.'

'I am not then, but for myself, and very bad I'll take it if you won't join me.'

'Dan, Dan, that I mightn't stir, but 'tisn't an hour since I had a cup at the barracks.'

'Ah, *Dhe*, whisht,* now! Whisht, will you! I have something that'll put an appetite on you.'

The old man swung the heavy kettle on to the chain over the open fire, and the dog sat up, shaking his ears with an expression of the deepest interest. The policeman unbuttoned his tunic, opened his belt, took a pipe and a plug of tobacco from his breast-pocket, and crossing his legs in easy posture, began to cut the tobacco slowly and carefully with his pocket-knife. The old man went to the dresser, and took down two handsomely decorated cups, the only cups he had, which, though chipped and handleless, were used at all only on very rare occasions: for himself, he preferred tea from a basin. Happening to glance into them, he noticed that they bore the trace of disuse and had collected a substantial share of the fine white dust which was constantly circulating within the little smoky cottage. Again he thought of the shirt, and, rolling up his sleeves with a stately gesture, he wiped them inside and out till they shone. Then he bent and opened the cupboard. Inside was a quart bottle of pale liquid, obviously untouched. He removed the cork and smelt the contents, pausing for a moment in the act as though to recollect where exactly he had noticed that particular smoky odour before. Then, reassured, he rose and poured out with a liberal hand.

'Try that now, sergeant,' he said.

The sergeant, concealing whatever qualms he might have felt at the thought of imbibing illegal whiskey, looked carefully into the cup, sniffed, and glanced up at old Dan.

'It looks good,' he commented.

'It should be.'

'It tastes good, too,' he added.

'Ah, sha,'* said Dan, clearly not wishing to praise his own hospitality in his own house, 'tis of no great excellence.'

'You're a good judge, I'd say,' said the sergeant without irony.

'Ever since things became what they are,' said Dan, carefully guarding himself from a too direct reference to the peculiarities of the law administered by his guest, 'liquor is not what it used to be.'

'I have heard that remark made before now,' said the sergeant thoughtfully. 'I have often heard it said by men of wide experience that liquor used to be better in the old days.'

'Liquor,' said the old man, 'is a thing that takes time. There was never a good job done in a hurry.'

' 'Tis an art in itself.'

'Just so.'

'And an art takes time.'

'And knowledge,' added Dan with emphasis. 'Every art has its secrets, and the secrets of distilling are being lost the way the old songs were lost. When I was a boy there wasn't a man in the barony but had a hundred songs in his head, but with people running here, there and everywhere, the songs were lost. . . . Ever since things became what they are,' he repeated on the same guarded note, 'there's so much running about the secrets are lost.'

'There must have been a power of them.'

'There was. Ask any man to-day that makes liquor do he know how to make it of heather.'

'And was it made of heather?' asked the policeman.

'It was.'

'Did you ever drink it yourself?'

'I did not; but I knew men that drank it. And a purer, sweeter, wholesomer drink never tickled a man's gullet. Babies they used to give it to and growing children.'

'Musha,* Dan, I think sometimes 'twas a great mistake of the law to set its hand against it.'

Dan shook his head. His eyes answered for him, but it was not in nature that in his own house a man should criticise the occupation of his guest.

'Maybe so, maybe not,' he said in a non-committal tone.

'But sure, what else have the poor people?'

'Them that makes the laws have their own good reasons.'

'All the same, Dan, all the same, 'tis a hard law.'

The sergeant would not be outdone in generosity. Politeness required him not to yield to the old man's defence of his superiors and their mysterious ways.

'It is the secrets I would be sorry for,' said Dan, summing up. 'Men die, and men are born, and where one man drained another will plough, but a secret lost is lost for ever.'

'True,' said the sergeant mournfully. 'Lost for ever.'

Dan took the policeman's cup, rinsed it in a bucket of clear water beside the door and cleaned it anew with the aid of the shirt. Then he placed it carefully at the sergeant's elbow. From the dresser he took a jug of milk and a blue bag containing sugar: this he followed up with a slab of country butter and—a sign that his visitor was not altogether unexpected—a round cake of home-made bread, fresh and uncut. The kettle sang and spat, and the dog, shaking his ears, barked at it angrily.

'Go 'way, you brute!' growled Dan, kicking him out of his way.

He made the tea and filled the two cups. The sergeant cut himself a large slice of bread and buttered it thickly.

'It is just like medicines,' said the old man, resuming his theme with the imperturbability of age. 'Every secret there was is lost. And leave no one tell me a doctor is the measure of one that has secrets from old times.'

'How could he?' asked the sergeant with his mouth full.

'The proof of that was seen when there were doctors and wise people there together.'

'It wasn't to the doctors the people went, I'll engage.'

'It was not. And why?' . . . With a sweeping gesture the old man took in the whole world outside his cabin. 'Out there on the hillsides is the sure cure for every disease. Because it is written'—he tapped the table with his thumb—'it is written by the poets *"an galar 'san leigheas go bhfaghair le ceile"* ("wherever you find the disease you will find the cure"). But people walk up the hills and down the hills and all they see is flowers. Flowers! As if God Almighty—honour and praise to Him!—had nothing better to do with His time than be making ould flowers!'

'Things no doctor could cure the wise people cured.'

'Ah musha, 'tis I know it,' said Dan bitterly, ' 'tis I know it, not in my mind but in my own four bones.'

'Do you tell me the rheumatics do be at you always?'

'They do. . . . Ah, if you were living, Kitty O'Hara, or you, Nora Malley of the Glen, 'tisn't I would be dreading the mountain wind or the sea wind; 'tisn't I'd be creeping down with me misfortunate red ticket for the blue and pink and yellow dribble-drabble of their ignorant dispensary!'

'Why then, indeed,' said the sergeant with sudden determination, 'I'll get you a bottle for that.'

'Ah, there's no bottle ever made will cure me!'

'There is, there is. Don't talk now till you try it. My own mother's brother, it cured him when he was that bad he wanted the carpenter to cut the two legs off him with a hand-saw.'

'I'd give fifty pounds to be rid of it,' said Dan. 'I would and five hundred!'

The sergeant finished his tea in a gulp, blessed himself and struck a match which he then allowed to go out as he answered some question of the old man's. He did the same with a second and third, as though titillating his appetite with delay. At last he succeeded in getting it alight, and then the two men pulled round their chairs, placed their toes side by side in the ashes, and in deep puffs, lively bursts of conversation and long long silences, enjoyed their pipes.

'I hope I'm not keeping you,' said the sergeant, as though struck by the length of his visit.

'Erra,* what keep?'

'Tell me if I am. The last thing I'd like to do is to waste a man's time.'

'Och, I'd ask nothing better than to have you here all night.'

'I like a little talk myself,' admitted the policeman.

And again they became lost in conversation. The light grew thick and coloured, and wheeling about the kitchen before it disappeared became tinged with gold; the kitchen itself sank into a cool greyness with cold light upon the cups and the basins and plates upon the dresser. From the ash tree a thrush began to sing. The open hearth gathered brightness till its light was a warm, even splash of crimson in the twilight.

Twilight was also descending without when the sergeant rose to go. He fastened his belt and tunic and carefully brushed his clothes. Then he put on his cap, tilted a little to side and back.

'Well,' he said, 'that was a great talk.'

'It's a pleasure,' said Dan, 'a real pleasure, that's what it is.'

'And I won't forget the bottle.'

'Heavy handling from God to you!'

'Good-bye now, Dan.'

'Good-bye and good luck.'

Dan did not offer to accompany the sergeant beyond the door. Then he sat down in his old place by the fire. He took out his pipe once more, blew through it thoughtfully, and just as he leaned forward for a twig to kindle it he heard steps returning to the house. It was the sergeant. He put his head a little way over the half door.

'Oh, Dan,' he called softly.

'Ay, sergeant,' replied Dan, looking round, but with one hand still reaching for the twig. He could not see the sergeant's face, only hear his voice.

'I suppose you're not thinking of paying that little fine, Dan?'

There was a brief silence. Dan pulled out the lighted twig, rose slowly and shambled towards the door, stuffing it down into the almost empty bowl of the pipe. He leaned over the half door, while the sergeant with hands in the pockets of his trousers gazed rather in the direction of the laneway, yet taking in a considerable portion of the sea-line.

'The way it is with me, sergeant,' replied Dan unemotionally, 'I am not.'

'I was thinking that, Dan. I was thinking you wouldn't.'

There was a long silence during which the voice of the thrush grew shriller and merrier. The sunken sun lit up islands of purple cloud moored high above the wind.

'In a way,' said the sergeant, 'that was what brought me.'

'I was just thinking so, sergeant, it struck me and you going out the door.'

'If 'twas only the money, I'm sure there's many would be glad to oblige you.'

'I know that, sergeant. No, 'tisn't the money so much as giving that fellow the satisfaction of paying. Because he angered me, sergeant.'

The sergeant made no comment upon this and another long silence ensued.

'They gave me the warrant,' he said at last in a tone which dissociated him from all connection with the document.

'Ay, begod!'* said Dan, without interest.

'So whenever 'twould be convenient to you—'

'Well, now you mention it,' said Dan, by way of throwing out a suggestion for debate, 'I could go with you now.'

'Oh, tut, tut!' protested the sergeant with a wave of his hand, dismissing the idea as the tone required.

'Or I could go to-morrow,' added Dan, warming up to the issue.

'Just as you like now,' replied the sergeant, scaling up his voice accordingly.

'But as a matter of fact,' said the old man emphatically, 'the day that would be most convenient to me would be Friday after dinner, seeing that I have some messages to do in town, and I wouldn't have me jaunt for nothing.'

'Friday will do grand,' said the sergeant with relief that this delicate matter was now practically disposed of. 'You could just walk in yourself and tell them I told you.'

'I'd rather have yourself, if 'twould be no inconvenience, sergeant. As it is, I'd feel a bit shy.'

'You needn't then. There's a man from my own parish there, a warder; one Whelan. You could say you wanted him, and I'll guarantee when he knows you're a friend of mine he'll make you as comfortable as if you were at home by your own fire.'

'I'd like that fine,' said Dan with satisfaction.

'Well, good-bye again now, Dan. I'll have to hurry.'

'Wait now, wait, till I see you to the road!'

Together the two men strolled down the lane way while Dan explained how it was that he, a respectable old man, had had the grave misfortune to open the head of another old man in such a way as to necessitate his being removed to hospital, and why it was that he could not give the old man in question the satisfaction of paying in cash for an injury brought about through the victim's own unmannerly method of argument.

'You see, sergeant,' he said, 'the way it is, he's there now, and he's looking at us as sure as there's a glimmer of sight in his wake, wandering, wathery eyes, and nothing would give him more gratification than for me to pay. But I'll punish him. I'll lie on bare boards for him. I'll suffer for him, sergeant, till he won't be able to rise his head, nor any of his children after him, for the suffering he put on me.'

On the following Friday he made ready his donkey and butt* and set out. On his way he collected a number of neighbours who wished to bid him farewell. At the top of the hill he stopped to send them back. An old man, sitting in the sunlight, hastily made his way within doors, and a moment later the door of his cottage was quietly closed.

Having shaken all his friends by the hand, Dan lashed the old donkey, shouted 'hup, there!' and set out alone along the road to prison.

4. FICTION

SOMERVILLE AND ROSS
(1858–1949)   (1862–1915)

from *The Real Charlotte* (1894)

II

The east wind was crying round a small house in the outskirts of an Irish country town. At nightfall it had stolen across the grey expanse of Lough Moyle, and given its first shudder among the hollies and laurestinas that hid the lower windows of Tally Ho Lodge from the too curious passer-by, and at about two o'clock of the November night it was howling so inconsolably in the great tunnel of the kitchen chimney, that Norry the Boat,* sitting on a heap of turf by the kitchen fire, drew her shawl closer about her shoulders, and thought gruesomely of the Banshee.*

The long trails of the monthly roses tapped and scratched against the window panes, so loudly sometimes that two cats, dozing on the rusty slab of a disused hothearth, opened their eyes and stared, with the expressionless yet wholly alert scrutiny of their race. The objects in the kitchen were scarcely more than visible in the dirty light of a hanging lamp, and the smell of paraffin filled the air. High presses and a dresser lined the walls, and on the top of the dresser, close under the blackened ceiling, it was just possible to make out the ghostly sleeping form of a cockatoo. A door at the end of the kitchen opened into a scullery of the usual prosaic, not to say odorous kind, which was now a cavern of darkness, traversed by twin green stars that moved to and fro as the lights move on a river at night, and looked like anything but what they were, the eyes of cats prowling round a scullery sink.

The tall, yellow-faced clock gave the gurgle with which it was accustomed to mark the half-hour, and the old woman, as if reminded of her weariness, stretched out her arms and yawned loudly and dismally.

She put back the locks of greyish-red hair that hung over her forehead and, crouching over the fireplace, she took out of the embers a broken-nosed teapot, and proceeded to pour from it a mug of tea, black with long stewing. She had taken a few sips of it when a bell rang startlingly in the passage outside, jarring the silence of the house with its sharp outcry. Norry the Boat hastily put down her mug, and scrambled to her feet to answer its summons. She groped her way up two cramped flights of stairs that creaked under her as she went, and advanced noiselessly in her stockinged feet across a landing to where a chink of light came from under a door.

The door was opened as she came to it, and a woman's short thick figure appeared in the doorway.

'The mistress wants to see Susan,' this person said in a rough whisper; 'is he in the house?'

'I think he's below in the scullery,' returned Norry; 'but, my Law! Miss Charlotte, what does she want of him? Is it light in her head she is?'

'What's that to you? Go fetch him at once,' replied Miss Charlotte, with a sudden fierceness. She shut the door, and Norry crept downstairs again, making a kind of groaning and lamenting as she went.

Miss Charlotte walked with a heavy step to the fireplace. A lamp was burning dully on a table at the foot of an old-fashioned bed, and the high foot-board threw a shadow that made it difficult to see the occupant of the bed. It was an ordinary little shabby bedroom, the ceiling, seamed with cracks, bulged down till it nearly touched the canopy of the bed. The wall paper had a pattern of blue flowers on a yellowish background; over the chimney shelf a filmy antique mirror looked strangely refined in the company of the Christmas cards and discoloured photographs that leaned against it. There was no sign of poverty, but everything was dingy, everything was taste-less, from the worn Kidderminster carpet to the illuminated text that was pinned to the wall facing the bed.

Miss Charlotte gave the fire a frugal poke, and lit a candle in the flame provoked from the sulky coals. In doing so some ashes became imbedded in the grease, and taking a hair-pin from the ponderous mass of brown hair that was piled on the back of her head, she began to scrape the candle clean. Probably at no moment of her forty years of life had Miss Charlotte Mullen looked more startlingly plain than now, as she stood, her squat figure draped in a magenta flannel dressing-gown, and the candle light shining upon her face. The night of watching had left its traces upon even her opaque skin. The lines about her prominent mouth and chin were deeper than usual; her broad cheeks had a flabby pallor; only her eyes were bright and untired, and the thick yellow-white hand that manipulated the hair-pin was as deft as it was wont to be.

When the flame burned clearly she took the candle to the bedside, and, bending down, held it close to the face of the old woman who was lying there. The eyes opened and turned towards the overhanging face: small dim, blue eyes, full of the stupor of illness, looking out of the pathetically commonplace little old face with a far-away perplexity.

'Was that Francie that was at the door?' she said in a drowsy voice that had in it the lagging drawl of intense weakness.

Charlotte took the tiny wrist in her hand, and felt the pulse with professional attention. Her broad perceptive finger-tips gauged the forces of the little thread that was jerking in the thin network of tendons, and as she laid the hand down she said to herself, 'She'll not last out the turn of the night.'

'Why doesn't Francie come in?' murmured the old woman again in the fragmentary, uninflected voice that seems hardly spared from the unseen battle with death.

'It wasn't her you asked me for at all,' answered Charlotte. 'You said you wanted to say good-bye to Susan. Here, you'd better have a sip of this.'

The old woman swallowed some brandy and water, and the stimulant presently revived unexpected strength in her.

'Charlotte,' she said, 'it isn't cats we should be thinking of now. God knows the cats are safe with you. But little Francie, Charlotte, we ought to have done more for her. You promised me that if you got the money you'd look after her. Didn't you now, Charlotte? I wish I'd done more for her. She's a good little thing—a good little thing—' she repeated dreamily.

Few people would think it worth their while to dispute the wandering futilities of an old dying woman, but even at this eleventh hour Charlotte could not brook the revolt of a slave.

'Good little thing!' she exclaimed, pushing the brandy bottle noisily in among a crowd of glasses and medicine bottles, 'a strapping big woman of nineteen! You didn't think her so good the time you had her here, and she put Susan's father and mother in the well!'

The old lady did not seem to understand what she had said.

'Susan, Susan!' she called quaveringly, and feebly patted the crochet quilt.

As if in answer, a hand fumbled at the door and opened it softly. Norry was standing there, tall and gaunt, holding in her apron, with both hands, something that looked like an enormous football.

'Miss Charlotte!' she whispered hoarsely, 'here's Susan for ye. He was out in the ashpit, an' I was hard set to get him, he was that wild.'

Even as she spoke there was a furious struggle in the blue apron.

'God in Heaven! ye fool!' ejaculated Charlotte. 'Don't let him go!' She shut the door behind Norry. 'Now, give him to me.'

Norry opened her apron cautiously, and Miss Charlotte lifted out of it a large grey tom-cat.

'Be quiet, my heart's love,' she said, 'be quiet.'

The cat stopped kicking and writhing, and, sprawling up on to the shoulder of the magenta dressing-gown, turned a fierce grey face upon his late captor. Norry crept over to the bed, and put back the dirty chintz curtain that had been drawn forward to keep out the draught of the door. Mrs Mullen was lying very still; she had drawn her knees up in front of her, and the bedclothes hung sharply from the small point that they made. The big living old woman took the hand of the other old woman who was so nearly dead, and pressed her lips to it.

'Ma'am, d'ye know me?'

Her mistress opened her eyes.

'Norry,' she whispered, 'give Miss Francie some jam for her tea to-night, but don't tell Miss Charlotte.'

'What's that she's saying?' said Charlotte, going to the other side of the bed. 'Is she asking for me?'

'No, but for Miss Francie,' Norry answered.

'She knows as well as I do that Miss Francie's in Dublin,' said Charlotte roughly; ' 'twas Susan she was asking for last. Here, a'nt, here's Susan for you.'

She pulled the cat down from her shoulder, and put him on the bed, where he crouched with a twitching tail, prepared for flight at a moment's notice.

He was within reach of the old lady's hand, but she did not seem to know that he was there. She opened her eyes and looked vacantly round.

'Where's little Francie? You mustn't send her away, Charlotte; you promised you'd take care of her; didn't you, Charlotte?'

'Yes, yes,' said Charlotte quickly, pushing the cat towards the old lady; 'never fear, I'll see after her.'

Old Mrs Mullen's eyes, that had rested with a filmy stare on her niece's face, closed again, and her head began to move a little from one side to the other, a low monotonous moan coming from her lips with each turn. Charlotte took her right hand and laid it on the cat's brindled back. It rested there, unconscious, for some seconds, while the two women looked on in silence, and then the fingers drooped and contracted like a bird's claw, and the moaning ceased. There was at the same time a spasmodic movement of the gathered-up knees, and a sudden rigidity fell upon the small insignificant face.

Norry the Boat threw herself upon her knees with a howl, and began to pray loudly. At the sound the cat leaped to the floor, and the hand that had been placed upon him in the only farewell his mistress was to take, dropped stiffly on the bed. Miss Charlotte snatched up the candle, and held it close to her aunt's face. There was no mistaking what she saw there, and, putting down the candle again, she plucked a large silk handkerchief from her pocket, and, with some hideous preliminary heavings of her shoulders, burst into transports of noisy grief.

BRAM STOKER
(1847–1912)

from *Dracula* (1897)

When I had written my two letters I sat quiet, reading a book whilst the Count wrote several notes, referring as he wrote them to some books on his table. Then he took up my two and placed them with his own, and put by his writing materials, after which, the instant the door had closed behind him, I leaned over and looked at the letters, which were face down on the table. I felt no compunction in doing so, for under the circumstances I felt that I should protect myself in every way I could.

One of the letters was directed to Samuel F. Billington, No. 7, The Crescent, Whitby; another to Herr Leutner, Varna; the third was to Coutts & Co., London, and the fourth to Herren Klopstock & Billreuth, bankers, Buda-Pesth. The second and fourth were unsealed. I was just about to look at them when I saw the door-handle move. I sank back in my seat, having just had time to replace the letters as they had been and to resume my book before the Count, holding still another letter in his hand, entered the room. He took up the letters on the table and stamped them carefully, and then, turning to me, said:—

'I trust you will forgive me, but I have much work to do in private this evening. You will, I hope, find all things as you wish.' At the door he turned, and after a moment's pause said:—

'Let me advise you, my dear young friend—nay, let me warn you with all seriousness, that should you leave these rooms you will not by any chance go to sleep in any other part of the castle. It is old, and has many memories, and there are bad dreams for those who sleep unwisely. Be warned! Should sleep now or ever overcome you, or be like to do, then haste to your own chamber or to these rooms, for your rest will then be safe. But if you be not careful in this respect, then—' He finished his speech in a gruesome way, for he motioned with his hands as if he were washing them. I quite understand; my only doubt was as to whether any dream could be more terrible than the unnatural, horrible net of gloom and mystery which seemed closing round me.

Later.—I endorse the last words written, but this time there is no doubt in question. I shall not fear to sleep in any place where he is not. I have placed the crucifix over the head of my bed—I imagine that my rest is thus freer from dreams; and there it shall remain.

When he left me I went to my room. After a little while, not hearing any sound, I came out and went up the stone stair to where I could look out towards the south. There was some sense of freedom in the vast expanse, inaccessible though it was to me, as compared with the narrow darkness of the courtyard. Looking out on this, I felt that I was indeed in prison, and I seemed to want a breath of fresh air, though it were of the night. I am beginning to feel this nocturnal existence tell on me. It is destroying my nerve. I start at my own

shadow, and am full of all sorts of horrible imaginings. God knows
that there is ground for any terrible fear in this accursed place! I
looked out over the beautiful expanse, bathed in soft yellow moonlight till it was almost as light as day. In the soft light the distant hills
became melted, and the shadows in the valleys and gorges of velvety
blackness. The mere beauty seemed to cheer me; there was peace and
comfort in every breath I drew. As I leaned from the window my eye
was caught by something moving a story below me, and somewhat
to my left, where I imagined, from the lie of the rooms, that the
windows of the Count's own room would look out. The window
at which I stood was tall and deep, stone-mullioned, and though
weather-worn, was still complete; but it was evidently many a day
since the case had been there. I drew back behind the stonework, and
looked carefully out.

What I saw was the Count's head coming out from the window. I
did not see the face, but I knew the man by the neck and the movement of his back and arms. In any case, I could not mistake the hands
which I had had so many opportunities of studying. I was at first
interested and somewhat amused, for it is wonderful how small a
matter will interest and amuse a man when he is a prisoner. But my
very feelings changed to repulsion and terror when I saw the whole
man slowly emerge from the window and begin to crawl down the
castle wall over that dreadful abyss, *face down*, with his cloak spreading out around him like great wings. At first I could not believe my
eyes. I thought it was some trick of the moonlight, some weird effect
of shadow; but I kept looking, and it could be no delusion. I saw the
fingers and toes grasp the corners of the stones, worn clear of the
mortar by the stress of years, and by thus using every projection and
inequality move downwards with considerable speed, just as a lizard
moves along a wall.

What manner of man is this, or what manner of creature is it in
the semblance of man? I feel the dread of this horrible place over-
powering me; I am in fear—in awful fear—and there is no escape for
me; I am encompassed about with terrors that I dare not think of. . . .

15 May.—Once more have I seen the Count go out in his lizard
fashion. He moved downwards in a sidelong way, some hundred feet
down, and a good deal to the left. He vanished into some hole or
window. When his head had disappeared I leaned out to try and see
more, but without avail—the distance was too great to allow a proper

angle of sight. I knew he had left the castle now, and thought to use the opportunity to explore more than I had dared to do as yet. I went back to the room, and taking a lamp, tried all the doors. They were all locked as I had expected, and the locks were comparatively new; but I went down the stone stairs to the hall where I had entered originally. I found I could pull back the bolts easily enough and unhook the great chains; but the door was locked, and the key was gone! That key must be in the Count's room; I must watch should his door be unlocked, so that I may get it and escape. I went on to make a thorough examination of the various stairs and passages, and to try the doors that opened from them. One or two small rooms near the hall were open, but there was nothing to see in them except old furniture, dusty with age and moth-eaten. At last, however, I found one door at the top of a stairway which, though it seemed to be locked, gave a little under pressure. I tried it harder, and found it was not really locked, but that the resistance came from the fact that the hinges had fallen somewhat, and the heavy door rested on the floor. Here was an opportunity which I might not have again, so I exerted myself, and with many efforts forced it back so that I could enter. I was now in a wing of the castle further to the right than the rooms I knew and a story lower down. From the windows I could see that the suite of rooms lay along to the south of the castle, the windows of the end room looking out both west and south. On the latter side, as well as to the former, there was a great precipice. The castle was built on the corner of a great rock, so that on three sides it was quite impregnable, and great windows were placed here where sling, or bow, or culverin could not reach, and consequently light and comfort, impossible to a position which had to be guarded, were secured. To the west was a great valley, and then, rising far away, great jagged mountain fastnesses, rising peak on peak, the sheer rock studded with mountain ash and thorn, whose roots clung in cracks and crevices and crannies of the stone. This was evidently the portion of the castle occupied in bygone days, for the furniture had more air of comfort than any I had seen. The windows were curtainless, and the yellow moonlight, flooding in through the diamond panes, enabled one to see even colours, whilst it softened the wealth of dust which lay over all and disguised in some measure the ravages of time and the moth. My lamp seemed to be of little effect in the brilliant moonlight, but I was glad to have it with me, for there was a dread loneliness in the place which chilled my heart and made my nerves tremble. Still, it was better than living alone in the rooms which I had come to hate from the presence of the Count, and after trying a little to school my nerves, I found a soft quietude come over me. Here I am, sitting at a little oak table where in old times possibly some fair lady sat to pen, with much thought and many blushes, her ill-spelt love-letter, and writing in my diary in shorthand all that has happened since I closed it last. It is nineteenth century up-to-date with a vengeance. And yet, unless my senses deceive me, the old centuries had, and have powers of their own which mere 'modernity' cannot kill.

Later: the Morning of 16 May.—God preserve my sanity, for to this I am reduced. Safety and the assurance of safety are things of the past. Whilst I live on here there is but one thing to hope for: that I may not go mad, if, indeed, I be not mad already. If I be sane, then surely it is maddening to think that of all the foul things that lurk in this hateful place the Count is the least dreadful to me; that to him alone I can look for safety, even though this be only whilst I can serve his purpose. Great God! merciful God! Let me be calm, for out of that way lies madness indeed. I begin to get new lights on certain things which have puzzled me. Up to now I never quite knew what Shakespeare meant when he made Hamlet say:—

> 'My tablets! quick, my tablets!
> 'Tis meet that I put it down,' etc.,*

for now, feeling as though my own brain was unhinged or as if the shock had come which must end in its undoing, I turn to my diary for repose. The habit of entering accurately must help to soothe me.

The Count's mysterious warning frightened me at the time; it frightens me more now when I think of it, for in future he has a fearful hold upon me. I shall fear to doubt what he may say!

When I had written in my diary and had fortunately replaced the book and pen in my pocket, I felt sleepy. The Count's warning came into my mind, but I took a pleasure in disobeying it. The sense of sleep was upon me, and with it the obstinacy which sleep brings as outrider. The soft moonlight soothed, and the wide expanse without gave a sense of freedom which refreshed me. I determined not to return to-night to the gloom-haunted rooms, but to sleep here, where of old ladies had sat and sung and lived sweet lives whilst their gentle breasts were sad for their menfolk away in the midst of remorseless wars. I drew a great couch out of its place near the corner, so that, as I lay, I could look at the lovely view to east and south, and unthinking of and uncaring for the dust, composed myself for sleep.

I suppose I must have fallen asleep; I hope so, but I fear, for all that followed was startlingly real—so real that now, sitting here in the broad, full sunlight of the morning, I cannot in the least believe that it was all sleep.

I was not alone. The room was the same, unchanged in any way since I came into it; I could see along the floor, in the brilliant moonlight, my own footsteps marked where I had disturbed the long accumulation of dust. In the moonlight opposite me were three young women, ladies by their dress and manner. I thought at the time that I must be dreaming when I saw them, for, though the moonlight was behind them, they threw no shadow on the floor. They came close to me and looked at me for some time and then whispered together. Two were dark, and had high aquiline noses, like the Count's, and great dark, piercing eyes, that seemed to be almost red when contrasted with the pale yellow moon. The other was fair, as fair as can be, with great, wavy masses of golden hair and eyes like pale sapphires. I seemed somehow to know her face, and to know it in connection with some dreamy fear, but I could not recollect at the moment how or where. All three had brilliant white teeth, that shone like pearls against the ruby of their voluptuous lips. There was something about them that made me uneasy, some longing and at the same time some deadly fear. I felt in my heart a wicked, burning desire that they would kiss me with those red lips. It is not good to note this down, lest some day it should meet Mina's eyes and cause her pain; but it is the truth. They whispered together, and then they all three laughed—such a silvery, musical laugh, but as hard as though the sound never could have come through the softness of human lips. It was like the intolerable, tingling sweetness of waterglasses* when played on by a cunning hand. The fair girl shook her head coquettishly, and the other two urged her on. One said:—

'Go on! You are first, and we shall follow; yours is the right to begin.' The other added:—

'He is young and strong; there are kisses for us all.' I lay quiet, looking out under my eyelashes in an agony of delightful anticipation. The fair girl advanced and bent over me till I could feel the movement of her breath upon me. Sweet it was in one sense, honey-sweet, and sent the same tingling through the nerves as her voice, but with a bitter underlying the sweet, a bitter offensiveness, as one smells in blood.

I was afraid to raise my eyelids, but looked out and saw perfectly under the lashes. The fair girl went on her knees and bent over me, fairly gloating. There was a deliberate voluptuousness which was both thrilling and repulsive, and as she arched her neck she actually licked her lips like an animal, till I could see in the moonlight the moisture shining on the scarlet lips and on the red tongue as it lapped the white sharp teeth. Lower and lower went her head as the lips went below the range of my mouth and chin and seemed about to fasten on my throat. Then she paused, and I could hear the churning sound of her tongue as it licked her teeth and lips, and could feel the hot breath on my neck. Then the skin of my throat began to tingle as one's flesh does when the hand that is to tickle it approaches nearer—nearer. I could feel the soft, shivering touch of the lips on the supersensitive skin of my throat, and the hard dents of two sharp teeth, just touching and pausing there. I closed my eyes in a languorous ecstasy and waited—waited with beating heart.

But at that instant another sensation swept through me as quick as lightning. I was conscious of the presence of the Count, and of his being as if lapped in a storm of fury. As my eyes opened involuntarily I saw his strong hand grasp the slender neck of the fair woman and with giant's power draw it back, the blue eyes transformed with fury, the white teeth champing with rage, and the fair cheeks blazing red with passion. But the Count! Never did I imagine such wrath and fury, even in the demons of the pit. His eyes were positively blazing. The red light in them was lurid, as if the flames of hell-fire blazed behind them. His face was deathly pale, and the lines of it were hard like drawn wires; the thick eyebrows that met over the nose now seemed like a heaving bar of white-hot metal. With a fierce sweep of his arm, he hurled the woman from him, and then motioned to the others, as though he were beating them back; it was the same imperious gesture that I had seen used to the wolves. In a voice which, though low and almost a whisper, seemed to cut through the air and then ring round the room, he exclaimed:—

'How dare you touch him, any of you? How dare you cast eyes on him when I had forbidden it? Back, I tell you all! This man belongs to me! Beware how you meddle with him, or you'll have to deal with me.' The fair girl, with laugh of ribald coquetry, turned to answer him:—

'You yourself never loved; you never love!' On this the other women joined, and such a mirthless, hard, soulless laughter rang through the room that it almost made me faint to hear; it seemed like the pleasure of fiends. Then the Count turned, after looking at my face attentively, and said in a soft whisper:—

'Yes, I too can love; you yourselves can tell it from the past. Is it not so? Well, now I promise you that when I am done with him, you shall kiss him at your will. Now go! go! I must awaken him, for there is work to be done.'

'Are we to have nothing to-night?' said one of them, with a low laugh, as she pointed to the bag which he had thrown upon the floor, and which moved as though there were some living thing within it. For answer he nodded his head. One of the women jumped forward and opened it. If my ears did not deceive me there was a gasp and a low wail, as of a half-smothered child. The women closed round, whilst I was aghast with horror; but as I looked they disappeared, and with them the dreadful bag. There was no door near them, and they could not have passed me without my noticing. They simply seemed to fade into the rays of the moonlight and pass out through the window, for I could see outside the dim, shadowy forms for a moment before they entirely faded away.

Then the horror overcame me, and I sank down unconscious.

JAMES JOYCE
(1882–1941)

from *Ulysses* (1922)

Stately, plump Buck Mulligan came from the stairhead, bearing a bowl of lather on which a mirror and a razor lay crossed. A yellow dressinggown, ungirdled, was sustained gently behind him by the mild morning air. He held the bowl aloft and intoned:

—*Introibo ad altare Dei.**

Halted, he peered down the dark winding stairs and called up coarsely:

—Come up, Kinch. Come up, you fearful Jesuit.

Solemnly he came forward and mounted the round gunrest. He faced about and blessed gravely thrice the tower, the surrounding country and the awaking mountains. Then, catching sight of Stephen Dedalus, he bent towards him and made rapid crosses in the air, gurgling in his throat and shaking his head. Stephen Dedalus, displeased and sleepy, leaned his arms on the top of the staircase and looked coldly at the shaking gurgling face that blessed him, equine in its length, and at the light untonsured hair, grained and hued like pale oak.

Buck Mulligan peeped an instant under the mirror and then covered the bowl smartly.

—Back to barracks, he said sternly.

He added in a preacher's tone:

—For this, O dearly beloved, is the genuine Christine: body and soul and blood and ouns.* Slow music, please. Shut your eyes, gents. One moment. A little trouble about those white corpuscles. Silence, all.

He peered sideways up and gave a long low whistle of call then paused awhile in rapt attention, his even white teeth glistening here and there with gold points. Chrysostomos.* Two strong shrill whistles* answered through the calm.

—Thanks, old chap, he cried briskly. That will do nicely. Switch off the current, will you?

He skipped off the gunrest and looked gravely at his watcher, gathering about his legs the loose folds of his gown. The plump shadowed face and sullen oval jowl recalled a prelate, patron of arts in the middle ages. A pleasant smile broke quietly over his lips.

—The mockery of it, he said gaily. Your absurd name, an ancient Greek.*

He pointed his finger in friendly jest and went over to the parapet, laughing to himself. Stephen Dedalus stepped up, followed him wearily halfway and sat down on the edge of the gunrest, watching him still as he propped his mirror on the parapet, dipped the brush in the bowl and lathered cheeks and neck.

Buck Mulligan's gay voice went on.

—My name is absurd too: Malachi Mulligan, two dactyls. But it has a Hellenic ring, hasn't it? Tripping and sunny like the buck himself. We must go to Athens. Will you come if I can get the aunt to fork out twenty quid?

He laid the brush aside and, laughing with delight, cried:

—Will he come? The jejune jesuit.

Ceasing, he began to shave with care.

—Tell me, Mulligan, Stephen said quietly.

—Yes, my love?

—How long is Haines going to stay in this tower?

Buck Mulligan showed a shaven cheek over his right shoulder.

—God, isn't he dreadful? he said frankly. A ponderous Saxon. He thinks you're not a gentleman. God, these bloody English. Bursting with money and indigestion. Because he comes from Oxford. You know, Dedalus, you have the real Oxford manner. He can't make you out. O, my name for you is the best: Kinch, the knifeblade.

He shaved warily over his chin.

—He was raving all night about a black panther, Stephen said. Where is his guncase?

—A woful lunatic, Mulligan said. Were you in a funk?

—I was, Stephen said with energy and growing fear. Out here in the dark with a man I don't know raving and moaning to himself about shooting a black panther. You saved men from drowning. I'm not a hero, however. If he stays on here I am off.

Buck Mulligan frowned at the lather on his razor blade. He hopped down from his perch and began to search his trouser pockets hastily.

—Scutter, he cried thickly.

He came over to the gunrest and, thrusting a hand into Stephen's upper pocket, said:

—Lend us a loan of your noserag to wipe my razor.

Stephen suffered him to pull out and hold up on show by its corner a dirty crumpled handkerchief. Buck Mulligan wiped the razorblade neatly. Then, gazing over the handkerchief, he said:

—The bard's noserag. A new art colour for our Irish poets: snot-green. You can almost taste it, can't you?

He mounted to the parapet again and gazed out over Dublin bay, his fair oakpale hair stirring slightly.

—God, he said quietly. Isn't the sea what Algy* calls it: a great sweet mother? The snotgreen sea. The scrotumtightening sea. *Epi oinopa ponton.** Ah, Dedalus, the Greeks. I must teach you. You must read them in the original. *Thalatta! Thalatta!** She is our great sweet mother. Come and look.

Stephen stood up and went over to the parapet. Leaning on it he looked down on the water and on the mailboat clearing the harbour mouth of Kingstown.

—Our mighty mother, Buck Mulligan said.

He turned abruptly his great searching eyes from the sea to Stephen's face.

—The aunt thinks you killed your mother, he said. That's why she won't let me have anything to do with you.

—Someone killed her, Stephen said gloomily.

—You could have knelt down, damn it, Kinch, when your dying mother asked you, Buck Mulligan said. I'm hyperborean* as much as you. But to think of your mother begging you with her last breath to kneel down and pray for her. And you refused. There is something sinister in you . . .

He broke off and lathered again lightly his farther cheek. A tolerant smile curled his lips.

—But a lovely mummer, he murmured to himself. Kinch, the loveliest mummer of them all.

He shaved evenly and with care, in silence, seriously.

Stephen, an elbow rested on the jagged granite, leaned his palm against his brow and gazed at the fraying edge of his shiny black coatsleeve. Pain, that was not yet the pain of love, fretted his heart. Silently, in a dream she had come to him after her death, her wasted body within its loose brown graveclothes giving off an odour of wax and rosewood, her breath, that had bent upon him, mute, reproachful, a faint odour of wetted ashes. Across the threadbare cuffedge he saw the sea hailed as a great sweet mother by the wellfed voice beside him. The ring of bay and skyline held a dull green mass of liquid. A bowl of white china had stood beside her deathbed holding the green sluggish bile which she had torn up from her rotting liver by fits of loud groaning vomiting.

Buck Mulligan wiped again his razorblade.

—Ah, poor dogsbody, he said in a kind voice. I must give you a shirt and a few noserags. How are the secondhand breeks?

—They fit well enough, Stephen answered.

Buck Mulligan attacked the hollow beneath his underlip.

—The mockery of it, he said contentedly, secondleg they should be. God knows what poxy bowsy left them off. I have a lovely pair with a hair stripe, grey. You'll look spiffing in them. I'm not joking, Kinch. You look damn well when you're dressed.

—Thanks, Stephen said. I can't wear them if they are grey.

—He can't wear them, Buck Mulligan told his face in the mirror. Etiquette is etiquette. He kills his mother but he can't wear grey trousers.

He folded his razor neatly and with stroking palps of fingers felt the smooth skin.

Stephen turned his gaze from the sea and to the plump face with its smokeblue mobile eyes.

—That fellow I was with in the Ship last night said Buck Mulligan says you have g. p. i. He's up in Dottyville* with Conolly Norman. Genera paralysis of the insane.

He swept the mirror a half circle in the air to flash the tidings abroad in sunlight now radiant on the sea. His curling shaven lips laughed and the edges of his white glittering teeth. Laughter seized all his strong wellknit trunk.

—Look at yourself, he said, you dreadful bard.

Stephen bent forward and peered at the mirror held out to him, cleft by a crooked crack, hair on end. As he and others see me. Who chose this face for me? This dogsbody to rid of vermin. It asks me too.

—I pinched it out of the skivvy's room, Buck Mulligan said. It does her all right. The aunt always keeps plainlooking servants for Malachi. Lead him not into temptation. And her name is Ursula.*

Laughing again, he brought the mirror away from Stephen's peering eyes.

—The rage of Caliban* at not seeing his face in a mirror, he said. If Wilde were only alive to see you.

Drawing back and pointing, Stephen said with bitterness:

—It is a symbol of Irish art. The cracked lookingglass of a servant.*

Buck Mulligan suddenly linked his arm in Stephen's and walked with him round the tower, his razor and mirror clacking in the pocket where he had thrust them.

—It's not fair to tease you like that, Kinch, is it? he said kindly.
God knows you have more spirit than any of them.

Parried again. He fears the lancet of my art as I fear that of his.
The cold steel pen.

—Cracked lookingglass of a servant. Tell that to the oxy chap*
downstairs and touch him for a guinea. He's stinking with money
and thinks you're not a gentleman. His old fellow made his tin by
selling jalap to Zulus or some bloody swindle or other. God, Kinch,
if you and I could only work together we might do something for the
island. Hellenise it.*

Cranly's arm. His arm.

—And to think of your having to beg from these swine. I'm the
only one that knows what you are. Why don't you trust me more?
What have you up your nose against me? Is it Haines? If he makes
any noise here I'll bring down Seymour and we'll give him a ragging
worse than they gave Clive Kempthorpe.

Young shouts of moneyed voices in Clive Kempthorpe's rooms.
Palefaces: they hold their ribs with laughter, one clasping another,
O, I shall expire! Break the news to her gently, Aubrey! I shall die!
With slit ribbons of his shirt whipping the air he hops and hobbles
round the table, with trousers down at heels, chased by Ades of
Magdalen with the tailor's shears. A scared calf's face gilded with
marmalade. I don't want to be debagged! Don't you play the giddy
ox with me!

Shouts from the open window startling evening in the quadrangle.*
A deaf gardener, aproned, masked with Matthew Arnold's face,
pushes his mower on the sombre lawn watching narrowly the
dancing motes of grasshalms.

To ourselves . . . new paganism . . . omphalos.*

—Let him stay, Stephen said. There's nothing wrong with him
except at night.

—Then what is it? Buck Mulligan asked impatiently. Cough it up.
I'm quite frank with you. What have you against me now?

They halted, looking towards the blunt cape of Bray Head that lay
on the water like the snout of a sleeping whale. Stephen freed his
arm quietly.

—Do you wish me to tell you? he asked.

—Yes, what is it? Buck Mulligan answered. I don't remember
anything.

He looked in Stephen's face as he spoke. A light wind passed his brow, fanning softly his fair uncombed hair and stirring silver points of anxiety in his eyes.

Stephen, depressed by his own voice, said:

—Do you remember the first day I went to your house after my mother's death?

Buck Mulligan frowned quickly and said:

—What? Where? I can't remember anything. I remember only ideas and sensations. Why? What happened in the name of God?

—You were making tea, Stephen said, and I went across the landing to get more hot water. Your mother and some visitor came out of the drawing room. She asked you who was in your room.

—Yes? Buck Mulligan said. What did I say? I forget.

—You said, Stephen answered, *O, it's only Dedalus whose mother is beastly dead.*

A flush which made him seem younger and more engaging rose to Buck Mulligan's cheek.

—Did I say that? he asked. Well? What harm is that?

He shook his constraint from him nervously.

—And what is death, he asked, your mother's or yours or my own? You saw only your mother die. I see them pop off every day in the Mater and Richmond and cut up into tripes in the dissecting room. It's a beastly thing and nothing else. It simply doesn't matter. You wouldn't kneel down to pray for your mother on her deathbed when she asked you. Why? Because you have the cursed Jesuit strain in you, only it's injected the wrong way. To me it's all a mockery and beastly. Her cerebral lobes are not functioning. She calls the doctor Sir Peter Teazle* and picks buttercups off the quilt. Humour her till it's over. You crossed her last wish in death and yet you sulk with me because I don't whinge like some hired mute from Lalouette's.* Absurd! I suppose I did say it. I didn't mean to offend the memory of your mother.

He had spoken himself into boldness. Stephen, shielding the gaping wounds which the words had left in his heart, said very coldly:

—I am not thinking of the offence to my mother.

—Of what, then? Buck Mulligan asked.

—Of the offence to me, Stephen answered.

Buck Mulligan swung round on his heel.

—O, an impossible person! he exclaimed.

He walked off quickly round the parapet. Stephen stood at his post, gazing over the calm sea towards the headland. Sea and headland now grew dim. Pulses were beating in his eyes, veiling their sight, and he felt the fever of his cheeks.

A voice within the tower called loudly:

—Are you up there, Mulligan?

—I'm coming, Buck Mulligan answered.

He turned towards Stephen and said:

—Look at the sea. What does it care about offences? Chuck Loyola,* Kinch, and come on down. The Sassenach wants his morning rashers.

His head halted again for a moment at the top of the staircase, level with the roof:

—Don't mope over it all day, he said. I'm inconsequent. Give up the moody brooding.

His head vanished but the drone of his descending voice boomed out of the stairhead:

> *And no more turn aside and brood*
> *Upon love's bitter mystery*
> *For Fergus rules the brazen cars.**

Woodshadows floated silently by through the morning peace from the stairhead seaward where he gazed. Inshore and farther out the mirror of water whitened, spurned by lightshod hurrying feet. White breast of the dim sea. The twining stresses, two by two. A hand plucking the harpstrings merging their twining chords. Wavewhite wedded words shimmering on the dim tide.

A cloud began to cover the sun slowly, shadowing the bay in deeper green. It lay behind him, a bowl of bitter waters. Fergus' song: I sang it above in the house, holding down the long dark chords. Her door was open: she wanted to hear my music. Silent with awe and pity I went to her bedside. She was crying in her wretched bed. For those words, Stephen: love's bitter mystery.

Where now?

Her secrets: old feather fans, tassled dancecards, powdered with musk, a gaud of amber beads in her locked drawer. A birdcage hung in the sunny window of her house when she was a girl. She heard old Royce sing in the pantomine of Turko the terrible* and laughed with others when he sang:

> *I am the boy*
> *That can enjoy*
> *Invisibility.*

Phantasmal mirth, folded away: muskperfumed.

> *And no more turn aside and brood.*

Folded away in the memory of nature with her toys. Memories beset his brooding brain. Her glass of water from the kitchen tap when she had approached the sacrament. A cored apple, filled with brown sugar, roasting for her at the hob on a dark autumn evening. Her shapely fingernails reddened by the blood of squashed lice from the children's shirts.

In a dream, silently, she had come to him, her wasted body within its loose graveclothes giving off an odour of wax and rosewood, her breath bent over him with mute secret words, a faint odour of wetted ashes.

Her glazing eyes, staring out of death, to shake and bend my soul. On me alone. The ghostcandle to light her agony. Ghostly light on the tortured face. Her hoarse loud breath rattling in horror, while all prayed on their knees. Her eyes on me to strike me down. *Liliata rutilantium te confessorum turma circumdet: iubilantium te virginum chorus excipiat.**

Ghoul! Chewer of corpses!

No, mother. Let me be and let me live.

—Kinch ahoy!

Buck Mulligan's voice sang from within the tower. It came nearer up the staircase, calling again. Stephen, still trembling at his soul's cry, heard warm running sunlight and in the air behind him friendly words.

—Dedalus, come down, like a good mosey. Breakfast is ready. Haines is apologising for waking us last night. It's all right.

—I'm coming, Stephen said, turning.

—Do, for Jesus' sake, Buck Mulligan said. For my sake and for all our sakes.

His head disappeared and reappeared.

—I told him your symbol of Irish art. He says it's very clever. Touch him for a quid, will you? A guinea, I mean.

—I get paid this morning, Stephen said.

—The school kip? Buck Mulligan said. How much? Four quid? Lend us one.

—If you want it, Stephen said.

—Four shining sovereigns, Buck Mulligan cried with delight. We'll have a glorious drunk to astonish the druidy druids. Four omnipotent sovereigns.

He flung up his hands and tramped down the stone stairs, singing out of tune with a Cockney accent:

> *O, won't we have a merry time,*
> *Drinking whisky, beer and wine,*
> *On coronation*
> *Coronation day?*
> *O, won't we have a merry time*
> *On coronation day?* *

Warm sunshine merrying over the sea. The nickel shavingbowl shone, forgotten, on the parapet. Why should I bring it down? Or leave it there all day, forgotten friendship?

He went over to it, held it in his hands awhile, feeling its coolness, smelling the clammy slaver of the lather in which the brush was stuck. So I carried the boat of incense then at Clongowes.* I am another now and yet the same. A servant too. A server of a servant.*

In the gloomy domed livingroom of the tower Buck Mulligan's gowned form moved briskly about the hearth to and fro, hiding and revealing its yellow glow. Two shafts of soft daylight fell across the flagged floor from the high barbacans: and at the meeting of their rays a cloud of coalsmoke and fumes of fried grease floated, turning.

—We'll be choked, Buck Mulligan said. Haines, open that door, will you?

Stephen laid the shavingbowl on the locker. A tall figure rose from the hammock where it had been sitting, went to the doorway and pulled open the inner doors.

—Have you the key? a voice asked.

—Dedalus has it, Buck Mulligan said. Janey Mack, I'm choked.

He howled without looking up from the fire:

—Kinch!

—It's in the lock, Stephen said, coming forward.

The key scraped round harshly twice and, when the heavy door had been set ajar, welcome light and bright air entered. Haines

stood at the doorway, looking out. Stephen haled his upended val-
ise to the table and sat down to wait. Buck Mulligan tossed the fry
on to the dish beside him. Then he carried the dish and a large
teapot over to the table, set them down heavily and sighed with
relief.

—I'm melting, he said, as the candle remarked when . . . But
hush. Not a word more on that subject. Kinch, wake up. Bread,
butter, honey. Haines, come in. The grub is ready. Bless us, O Lord,
and these thy gifts. Where's the sugar? O, jay, there's no milk.

Stephen fetched the loaf and the pot of honey and the butter-
cooler from the locker. Buck Mulligan sat down in a sudden pet.

—What sort of a kip is this? he said. I told her to come after eight.

—We can drink it black, Stephen said. There's lemon in the
locker.

—O, damn you and your Paris fads, Buck Mulligan said. I want
Sandycove milk.

Haines came in from the doorway and said quietly:

—That woman is coming up with the milk.

—The blessings of God on you, Buck Mulligan cried, jumping up
from his chair. Sit down. Pour out the tea there. The sugar is in the
bag. Here, I can't go fumbling at the damned eggs. He hacked
through the fry on the dish and slapped it out on three plates, saying:

—*In nomine Patris et Filii et Spiritus Sancti.**

Haines sat down to pour out the tea.

—I'm giving you two lumps each, he said. But, I say, Mulligan,
you do make strong tea, don't you?

Buck Mulligan, hewing thick slices from the loaf said in an old
woman's wheedling voice:

—When I makes tea I makes tea, as old mother Grogan said. And
when I makes water I makes water.

—By Jove, it is tea, Haines said.

Buck Mulligan went on hewing and wheedling:

—*So I do, Mrs Cabill,* says she. *Begob, ma'am,* says Mrs Cahill,
God send you don't make them in the one pot.

He lunged towards his messmates in turn a thick slice of bread,
impaled on his knife.

—That's folk, he said very earnestly, for your book, Haines. Five
lines of text and ten pages of notes about the folk and the fishgods of
Dundrum. Printed by the weird sisters in the year of the big wind.*

He turned to Stephen and asked in a fine puzzled voice, lifting his brows:

—Can you recall, brother, is mother Grogan's tea and water pot spoken of in the Mabinogion* or is it in the Upanishads?*

—I doubt it, said Stephen gravely.

—Do you now? Buck Mulligan said in the same tone. Your reasons, pray?

—I fancy, Stephen said as he ate, it did not exist in or out of the Mabinogion. Mother Grogan was, one imagines, a kinswoman of Mary Ann.

Buck Mulligan's face smiled with delight.

—Charming, he said in a finical sweet voice, showing his white teeth and blinking his eyes pleasantly. Do you think she was? Quite charming.

Then, suddenly overclouding all his features, he growled in a hoarsened rasping voice as he hewed again vigorously at the loaf:

—*For old Mary Ann*
   She doesn't care a damn.
   But, hising up her petticoats . . .

The doorway was darkened by an entering form.

—The milk, sir.

—Come in, ma'am, Mulligan said, Kinch, get the jug.

An old woman came forward and stood by Stephen's elbow.

—That's a lovely morning, sir, she said. Glory be to God.

—To whom? Mulligan said, glancing at her. Ah, to be sure.

Stephen reached back and took the milkjug from the locker.

The islanders, Mulligan said to Haines casually, speak frequently of the collector of prepuces.*

—How much, sir? asked the old woman.

—A quart, Stephen said.

He watched her pour into the measure and thence into the jug rich white milk, not hers. Old shrunken paps. She poured again a measureful and a tilly.* Old and secret she had entered from a morning world, maybe a messenger. She praised the goodness of the milk, pouring it out. Crouching by a patient cow at daybreak in the lush field, a witch on her toadstool, her wrinkled fingers quick at the squirting dugs. They lowed about her whom they knew, dewsilky cattle. Silk of the kine and poor old woman,* names given her in old times. A wandering crone, lowly form of an immortal serving her conqueror and her gay betrayer, their common cuckquean,* a messenger from the secret morning. To serve or to upbraid, whether he could not tell: but scorned to beg her favour.

—It is indeed, ma'am, Buck Mulligan said, pouring milk into their cups.

—Taste it, sir, she said.

He drank at her bidding.

—If we could only live on good food like that, he said to her somewhat loudly, we wouldn't have the country full of rotten teeth and rotten guts. Living in a bogswamp, eating cheap food and the streets paved with dust, horsedung and consumptives' spits.

—Are you a medical student, sir? the old woman asked.

—I am, ma'am, Buck Mulligan answered.

Stephen listened in scornful silence. She bows her old head to a voice that speaks to her loudly, her bonesetter, her medicineman: me she slights. To the voice that will shrive and oil for the grave all there is of her but her woman's unclean loins, of man's flesh made not in God's likeness the serpent's prey.* And to the loud voice that now bids her be silent with wondering unsteady eyes.

—Do you understand what he says? Stephen asked her.

—Is it French you are talking, sir? the old woman said to Haines.

Haines spoke to her again a longer speech, confidently.

—Irish, Buck Mulligan said. Is there Gaelic on you?

—I thought it was Irish, she said, by the sound of it. Are you from west, sir?

—I am an Englishman, Haines answered.

—He's English, Buck Mulligan said, and he thinks we ought to speak Irish in Ireland.

—Sure we ought to, the old woman said, and I'm ashamed I don't speak the language myself. I'm told it's a grand language by them that knows.

—Grand is no name for it, said Buck Mulligan. Wonderful entirely. Fill us out some more tea, Kinch. Would you like a cup, ma'am?

—No, thank you, sir, the old woman said, slipping the ring of the milkcan on her forearm and about to go.

Hanies said to her:

—Have you your bill? We had better pay her, Mulligan, hadn't we? Stephen filled again the three cups.

—Bill, sir? she said, halting. Well, it's seven mornings a pint at two pence is seven twos is a shilling and twopence over and these three mornings a quart at fourpence is three quarts is a shilling and one and two is two and two, sir.

Buck Mulligan sighed and having filled his mouth with a crust thickly buttered on both sides, stretched forth his legs and began to search his trouser pockets.

—Pay up and look pleasant, Haines said to him smiling.

Stephen filled a third cup, a spoonful of tea colouring faintly the thick rich milk. Buck Mulligan brought up a florin, twisted it round in his fingers and cried:

—A miracle!

He passed it along the table towards the old woman, saying:

—Ask nothing more of me, sweet. All I can give you I give.*

Stephen laid the coin in her uneager hand.

—We'll owe twopence, he said.

—Time enough, sir, she said, taking the coin. Time enough. Good morning, sir.

She curtseyed and went out, followed by Buck Mulligan's tender chant:

—*Heart of my heart, were it more,*
  More would be laid at your feet.

He turned to Stephen and said:

—Seriously, Dedalus. I'm stony.* Hurry out to your school kip and bring us back some money. Today the bards must drink and junket. Ireland expects that every man this day will do his duty.*

—That reminds me, Haines said, rising, that I have to visit your national library today.

—Our swim first, Buck Mulligan said.

He turned to Stephen and asked blandly:

—Is this the day for your monthly wash, Kinch?

Then he said to Haines:

—The unclean bard makes a point of washing once a month.

—All Ireland is washed by the gulfstream, Stephen said as he let honey trickle over a slice of the loaf.

Haines from the corner where he was knotting easily a scarf about the loose collar of his tennis shirt spoke:

—I intend to make a collection of your sayings if you will let me.

Speaking to me. They wash and tub and scrub. Agenbite of inwit.* Conscience. Yet here's a spot.

—That one about the cracked lookingglass of a servant being the symbol of Irish art is deuced good.

Buck Mulligan kicked Stephen's foot under the table and said with warmth of tone:

—Wait till you hear him on Hamlet, Haines.

—Well, I mean it, Haines said, still speaking to Stephen. I was just thinking of it when that poor old creature came in.

—Would I make money by it? Stephen asked.

Haines laughed and, as he took his soft grey hat from the holdfast of the hammock, said:

—I don't know, I'm sure.

He strolled out to the doorway. Buck Mulligan bent across to Stephen and said with coarse vigour:

—You put your hoof in it now. What did you say that for?

—Well? Stephen said. The problem is to get money. From whom? From the milkwoman or from him. It's a toss up, I think.

—I blow him out about you, Buck Mulligan said, and then you come along with your lousy leer and your gloomy jesuit jibes.

—I see little hope, Stephen said, from her or from him.

Buck Mulligan sighed tragically and laid his hand on Stephen's arm.

—From me, Kinch, he said.

In a suddenly changed tone he added:

—To tell you the God's truth I think you're right. Damn all else they are good for. Why don't you play them as I do? To hell with them all. Let us get out of the kip.

He stood up, gravely ungirdled and disrobed himself of his gown, saying resignedly:

—Mulligan is stripped of his garments.*

He emptied his pockets on to the table.

—There's your snotrag, he said.

And putting on his stiff collar and rebellious tie, he spoke to them, chiding them, and to his dangling watchchain. His hands plunged and rummaged in his trunk while he called for a clean handkerchief.

Agenbite of inwit. God, we'll simply have to dress the character. I want puce gloves and green boots. Contradiction. Do I contradict myself? Very well then, I contradict myself, Mercurial Malachi.* A limp black missile flew out of his talking hands.

—And there's your Latin quarter hat,* he said.

Stephen picked it up and put it on. Haines called to them from the doorway:

—Are you coming, you fellows?

—I'm ready, Buck Mulligan answered, going towards the door. Come out, Kinch. You have eaten all we left, I suppose. Resigned he passed out with grave words and gait, saying, wellnigh with sorrow:

—And going forth he met Butterly.

Stephen, taking his ashplant from its leaningplace, followed them out and, as they went down the ladder, pulled to the slow iron door and locked it. He put the huge key in his inner pocket.

At the foot of the ladder Buck Mulligan asked:

—Did you bring the key?

—I have it, Stephen said, preceding them.

He walked on. Behind him he heard Buck Mulligan club with his heavy bathtowel the leader shoots of ferns or grasses.

—Down, sir. How dare you, sir.

Haines asked:

—Do you pay rent for this tower?

—Twelve quid, Buck Mulligan said.

—To the secretary of state for war, Stephen added over his shoulder. They halted while Haines surveyed the tower and said at last:

—Rather bleak in wintertime, I should say. Martello you call it?

—Billy Pitt had them built, Buck Mulligan said, when the French were on the sea.* But ours is the *omphalos*.

—What is your idea of Hamlet? Haines asked Stephen.

—No, no, Buck Mulligan shouted in pain. I'm not equal to Thomas Aquinas* and the fiftyfive reasons he has made to prop it up. Wait till I have a few pints in me first.

He turned to Stephen, saying as he pulled down neatly the peaks of his primrose waistcoat:

—You couldn't manage it under three pints, Kinch, could you?

—It has waited so long, Stephen said listlessly, it can wait longer.

—You pique my curiosity, Haines said aimiably. Is it some paradox?

—Pooh! Buck Mulligan said. We have grown out of Wilde and paradoxes. It's quite simple. He proves by algebra that Hamlet's grandson is Shakespeare's grandfather and that he himself is the ghost of his own father.

—What? Haines said, beginning to point at Stephen. He himself?

Buck Mulligan slung his towel stolewise round his neck and, bending in loose laughter, said to Stephen's ear:

—O, shade of Kinch the elder! Japhet in search of a father!*

—We're always tired in the morning, Stephen said to Haines. And it is rather long to tell.

Buck Mulligan, walking forward again, raised his hands.

—The sacred pint alone can unbind the tongue of Dedalus, he said.

—I mean to say, Haines explained to Stephen as they followed, this tower and these cliffs here remind me somehow of Elsinore. *That beetles o'er his base into the sea,*★ isn't it?

Buck Mulligan turned suddenly for an instant towards Stephen but did not speak. In the bright silent instant Stephen saw his own image in cheap dusty mourning between their gay attires.

—It's a wonderful tale, Haines said, bringing them to halt again.

Eyes, pale as the sea the wind had freshened, paler, firm and prudent. The seas' ruler,* he gazed southward over the bay, empty save for the smokeplume of the mailboat, vague on the bright skyline, and a sail tacking by the Muglins.

—I read a theological interpretation of it somewhere, he said bemused. The Father and the Son idea. The Son striving to be atoned with the Father.

Buck Mulligan at once put on a blithe broadly smiling face. He looked at them, his wellshaped mouth open happily, his eyes, from which he had suddenly withrawn all shrewd sense, blinking with mad gaiety. He moved a doll's head to and fro, the brims of his Panama hat quivering, and began to chant in a quiet happy foolish voice:

—*I'm the queerest young fellow that ever you heard.*
My mother's a jew, my father's a bird.
With Joseph the joiner I cannot agree,
So here's to disciples and Calvary.

He held up a forefinger of warning.

—*If anyone thinks that I amn't divine*
 He'll get no free drinks when I'm making the wine
 But have to drink water and wish it were plain
 That I make when the wine becomes water again.

He tugged swiftly at Stephen's ashplant in farewell and, running forward to a brow of the cliff, fluttered his hands at his sides like fins or wings of one about to rise in the air, and chanted:

—*Goodbye, now, goodbye. Write down all I said*
 And tell Tom, Dick and Harry I rose from the dead.
 What's bred in the bone cannot fail me to fly
 *And Olivet's breezy . . . Goodbye, now, goodbye.**

He capered before them down towards the fortyfoot hole, fluttering his winglike hands, leaping nimbly, Mercury's hat quivering in the fresh wind that bore back to them his brief birdlike cries.

Haines, who had been laughing guardedly, walked on beside Stephen and said:

—We oughtn't to laugh, I suppose. He's rather blasphemous. I'm not a believer myself, that is to say. Still his gaiety takes the harm out of it somehow, doesn't it? What did he call it? Joseph the Joiner?

—The ballad of Joking Jesus, Stephen answered.

—O, Haines said, you have heard it before?

—Three times a day, after meals, Stephen said drily.

—You're not a believer, are you? Haines asked. I mean, a believer in the narrow sense of the word. Creation from nothing and miracles and a personal God.

—There's only one sense of the word, it seems to me, Stephen said.

Haines stopped to take out a smooth silver case in which twinkled a green stone.* He sprang it open with his thumb and offered it.

—Thank you, Stephen said, taking a cigarette.

Haines helped himself and snapped the case to. He put it back in his sidepocket and took from his waistcoatpocket a nickel tinderbox, sprang it open too, and, having lit his cigarette, held the flaming spunk towards Stephen in the shell of his hands.

—Yes, of course, he said, as they went on again. Either you believe or you don't, isn't it? Personally I couldn't stomach that idea of a personal God. You don't stand for that, I suppose?

—You behold in me, Stephen said with grim displeasure, a horrible example of free thought.

He walked on, waiting to be spoken to, trailing his ashplant by his side. Its ferrule followed lightly on the path, squealing at his heels. My familiar, after me, calling Steeeeeeeeeeeeephen. A wavering line along the path. They will walk on it tonight, coming here in the dark. He wants that key. It is mine, I paid the rent. Now I eat his salt bread. Give him the key too. All. He will ask for it. That was in his eyes.

—After all, Haines began . . .

Stephen turned and saw that the cold gaze which had measured him was not all unkind.

—After all, I should think you are able to free yourself. You are your own master, it seems to me.

—I am the servant of two masters, Stephen said, an English and an Italian.

—Italian? Haines said.

A crazy queen, old and jealous. Kneel down before me.

—And a third, Stephen said, there is who wants me for odd jobs.

—Italian? Haines said again. What do you mean?

—The imperial British state, Stephen answered, his colour rising, and the holy Roman catholic and apostolic church.

Haines detached from his underlip some fibres of tobacco before he spoke.

—I can quite understand that, he said calmly. An Irishman must think like that, I daresay. We feel in England that we have treated you rather unfairly. It seems history is to blame.

The proud potent titles clanged over Stephen's memory the triumph of their brazen bells: *et unam sanctam catholicam et apostolicam ecclesiam*:* the slow growth and change of rite and dogma like his own rare thoughts, a chemistry of stars. Symbol of the apostles in the mass for pope Marcellus,* the voices blended, singing alone loud in affirmation: and behind their chant the vigilant angel* of the church militant disarmed and menaced her heresiarchs. A horde of heresies fleeing with mitres awry: Photius* and the brood of mockers of whom Mulligan was one, and Arius,* warring his life long upon the consubstantiality of the Son with the Father, and Valentine,* spurning Christ's terrene body, and the subtle African heresiarch Sabellius* who held that the Father was Himself His own Son. Words Mulligan had spoken a moment since in mockery to the stranger. Idle mockery. The void awaits surely all them that weave the wind: a menace, a disarming and a worsting from those embattled angels of the church, Michael's host, who defend her ever in the hour of conflict with their lances and their shields.

Hear, hear. Prolonged applause. *Zut! Nom de Dieu!*

—Of course I'm a Britisher, Haine's voice said, and I feel as one. I don't want to see my country fall into the hands of German jews either. That's our national problem, I'm afraid, just now.

Two men stood at the verge of the cliff, watching: businessman, boatman.

—She's making for Bullock harbour.

The boatman nodded towards the north of the bay with some disdain.

—There's five fathoms out there, he said. It'll be swept up that way when the tide comes in about one. It's nine days today.

The man that was drowned. A sail veering about the blank bay waiting for a swollen bundle to bob up, roll over to the sun a puffy face, salt white. Here I am.

They followed the winding path down to the creek. Buck Mulligan stood on a stone, in shirtsleeves, his unclipped tie rippling over his shoulder. A young man clinging to a spur of rock near him, moved slowly frogwise his green legs in the deep jelly of the water.

—Is the brother with you, Malachi?

—Down in Westmeath. With the Bannons.

—Still there? I got a card from Bannon. Says he found a sweet young thing down there. Photo girl he calls her.

—Shapshot, eh? Brief exposure.

Buck Mulligan sat down to unlace his boots. An elderly man shot up near the spur of rock a blowing red face. He scrambled up by the stones, water glistening on his pate and on its garland of grey hair, water rilling over his chest and paunch and spilling jets out of his black sagging loincloth.

Buck Mulligan made way for him to scramble past and, glancing at Haines and Stephen, crossed himself piously with his thumbnail at brow and breastbone.

—Seymour's back in town, the young man said, grasping again his spur of rock. Chucked medicine and going in for the army.

—Ah, go to God, Buck Mulligan said.

—Going over next week to stew. You know that red Carlisle girl,
Lily?

—Yes.

—Spooning with him last night on the pier. The father is rotten
with money.

—Is she up the pole?

—Better ask Seymour that.

—Seymour a bleeding officer, Buck Mulligan said.

He nodded to himself as he drew off his trousers and stood up,
saying tritely:

—Redheaded women buck like goats.

He broke off in alarm, feeling his side under his flapping shirt.

—My twelfth rib is gone, he cried. I'm the *Uebermensch*.*
Toothless Kinch and I, the supermen.

He struggled out of his shirt and flung it behind him to where his
clothes lay.

—Are you going in here, Malachi?

—Yes. Make room in the bed.

The young man shoved himself backward through the water and
reached the middle of the creek in two long clean strokes. Haines sat
down on a stone, smoking.

—Are you not coming in, Buck Mulligan asked.

—Later on, Haines said. Not on my breakfast.

Stephen turned away.

—I'm going, Mulligan, he said.

—Give us that key, Kinch, Buck Mulligan said, to keep my
chemise flat.

Stephen handed him the key. Buck Mulligan laid it across his
heaped clothes.

—And twopence, he said, for a pint. Throw it there.

Stephen threw two pennies on the soft heap. Dressing, undress-
ing. Buck Mulligan erect, with joined hands before him, said
solemnly:

—He who stealeth from the poor lendeth to the Lord.* Thus spake
Zarathustra.

His plump body plunged.

—We'll see you again, Haines said, turning as Stephen walked up
the path and smiling at wild Irish.

Horn of a bull, hoof of a horse, smile of a Saxon.*

—The Ship, Buck Mulligan cried. Half twelve.

—Good, Stephen said.

He walked along the upwardcurving path.

> *Liliata rutilantium.*
> *Turma circumdet.*
> *Jubilantium te virginum.*

The priest's grey nimbus in a niche where he dressed discreetly. I will not sleep here tonight. Home also I cannot go.

A voice, sweettoned and sustained, called to him from the sea. Turning the curve he waved his hand. It called again. A sleek brown head, a seal's, far out on the water, round.

Usurper.

ELIZABETH BOWEN
(1899–1973)

from *The Last September* (1929)

IV

Lois was sent upstairs for the shawls; it appeared that a touch of dew on the bare skin might be fatal to Lady Naylor or Mrs Montmorency.* On the stairs, her feet found their evening echoes; she dawdled, listening. When she came down everybody was on the steps—at the top, on the wide stone plateau—the parlourmaid looking for somewhere to put the coffee tray. Mrs Montmorency sat in the long chair; her husband was tucking a carriage rug round her knees. 'If you do that,' Lois could not help saying, 'she won't be able to walk about, which is the best part of sitting out.'

No one took any notice: Mr Montmorency went on tucking.

'Haven't you got a wrap for yourself?' said Lady Naylor. Lois took a cushion and sat on the top step with her arms crossed, stroking her elbows. 'I shouldn't sit there,' her aunt continued; 'at this time of night stone will strike up through anything.'

'If you don't get rheumatism now,' added Francie, 'you will be storing up rheumatism.'

'It will be my rheumatism,' said Lois as gently as possible, but added inwardly: 'After you're both dead.' A thought that fifty years hence she might well, if she wished, be sitting here on the steps,—with or without rheumatism—having penetrated thirty years deeper ahead into Time than they could, gave her a feeling of mysteriousness and destination. And she was fitted for this by being twice as complex as their generation—for she must be: double as many people having gone to the making of her.

Laurence, looking resentfully round for somewhere to sit—she had taken the only cushion—said: 'I suppose you think ants cannot run up your legs if you cannot see them?'

Mr Montmorency surprised her by offering a cigarette. He had a theory, he said, that ants did not like cigarette smoke. The air was so quiet now, the flame ran up his match without a tremble. 'The ants are asleep,' she said, 'they disappear into the cracks of the steps. They don't bite, either; but the idea is horrid.'

'Don't you want a chair?' When she said she didn't, he settled back in his own. Creaks ran through the wicker, discussing him, then all was quiet. He was not due to leave the ship in which they were all rushing out into Time till ten years after the others, though it was to the others that he belonged. Turning half round, she watched light breathe at the tips of the cigarettes; it seemed as though everybody were waiting. Night now held the trees with a toneless finality. The sky shone, whiter than glass, fainting down to the fretted leaf-line, but was being steadily drained by the dark below, to which the grey of the lawns, like smoke, as steadily mounted. The house was highest of all with toppling immanence, like a cliff.

'I don't think,' said Francie, 'I remember anything so—so quiet as evenings here.'

'Trees,' said Laurence, shifting his pipe. His shirt-front was high above them, he stood by the door with his foot on the scraper.

'This time to-morrow,' said Lady Naylor, 'we shall want to be quiet—after the tennis party.' She let out a sigh that hung in the silence, like breath in cold air.

'Oh yes, the party! The tennis party . . .'

'Francie, did I tell you who were coming?'

'You told her,' said Laurence. 'I heard you.'

'It is the people who don't play tennis who make it so tiring.'

Something about the way, the resigned way, Francie's hands lay out on the rug gave her the look of an invalid. 'It is a good thing,' said Sir Richard, 'you two never went out to Canada. I never liked the idea myself; I was very much against it at the time, if you remember.'

'I was divided about it myself,' said Hugo. 'It seemed worth trying, and yet there was so much against it. I don't know that I should have done very much good—I wonder.'

They wondered with him, with degrees of indifference. Lois stroked her dress—the feel of the stuff was like cobwebs, sticky and damp. There must be dew falling.

'Oh!' cried Francie. '*Listen!*'

She had so given herself to the silence that the birth of sound, after which the others were still straining, had shocked her nerves like a blow. They looked, from the steps, over a bay of fields, between the plantations, that gave on a sea of space. Far east, beyond the demesne: a motor, straining cautiously out of the silence. A grind, an anguish of sound as it took the hill.

'Patrols,' said Laurence.

Hugo reached out and pressed a hand on to Francie's rug. 'Patrols,' he told her, translating the information.

Sir Richard explained severely: 'Out every night—not always in this direction.'

'They're early; it's half-past nine. Now I wonder . . .'

The sound paused, for a moment a pale light showed up the sky in darkness. Then behind the screen of trees at the skyline, demesne boundary, the sound moved shakily, stoopingly, like some one running and crouching behind a hedge. The jarring echoed down the spines of the listeners. They heard with a sense of complicity.

'A furtive lorry is a sinister thing.'

'Laurence, it isn't furtive!' said Lady Naylor. 'Can't you be ordinary? If it wouldn't be taken in some absurd kind of way as a demonstration, I should ask the poor fellows in to have coffee.'

'They're careful enough,' said Hugo impatiently. It seemed that the lorry took pleasure in crawling with such a menace along the boundary, marking the scope of peace of this silly island, undermining solitude. In the still night sound had a breathlessness, as of intention.

'The roads are so rough,' said Lois: she could see the wary load lurching into the hedges. 'I wonder now,' she added, 'who is with the patrol to-night?'

'Some one you know?' cried Francie. But Sir Richard, who did not like his friends to be distracted from him by lorries any more than by introspection or headaches or the observation of nature, bore this down with one of his major chords:

'The lower tennis court, Hugo'—waving sideways into the darkness—'is not what it used to be. Some cattle got on to it after the rain and destroyed it. It's had rolling enough to level a mountain, but it won't be the same for a long time. D'you remember the fours we had on that court that summer—wasn't it nineteen-six—you and I and O'Donnell and poor John Trent?'

'I do. Now was it James O'Donnell or Peter that went to Ceylon?'

'That was a great summer; I never remember a summer like it. We had the hay in by the end of June.'

The lorry ground off east towards Ballyhinch; silence sifting down on its tracks like sand. Their world was clear of it and a pressure lightened. Once more they could have heard a leaf turn in the trees or a bird shifting along a branch. But they found it was now very dark. Francie shivered, and Lady Naylor, rising formally, said she thought they should go in. 'Poor John Trent,' she added, gathering up her cushions, 'never got over that trouble he had with the Sheehans over the Madder* fishing. It went into court, you know, and of course he lost. We always told him to keep it out of court. He was very obstinate.'

'He was indeed,' said Sir Richard. 'He made an enemy of Sheehan and it's not a good thing to have made an enemy. Though of course he's dead nowadays, so it may not matter.'

'It may to the Archie Trents. . . . Laurence, help Uncle Richard in with the long chair, and remember to bring in your own chair afterwards.'

'I never had a chair.'

'Oh, they haven't lighted the lamp in the hall. That is too bad! I am lost without Sarah—do you remember Sarah, Francie? She died, you know.'

Lois, sitting still among rising, passing and vaguely searching figures, cried: 'But it's only just beginning! You're missing the whole point. I shall walk up the avenue.'

Francie went in, groping; trailing her rug. The three men, carrying wicker chairs, converged at the door: the chairs jostled. They all put them down and apologized. Lois repeated: '*I* shall walk up the avenue.' But having arranged an order of procedure they all passed on into the house, creaking and bumping. She walked down the steps alone: she had wanted to be alone, but to be regretted.

'Mind you don't get locked out!' her uncle shouted after her. The glass doors shut with a rattle.

Lois walked alone up the avenue, where she had danced with Gerald. She thought what a happy night that had been, and how foolish Mr Montmorency now thought them. He had seemed annoyed at her being young when he wasn't. She could not hope to explain that her youth seemed to her also rather theatrical and that she was only young in that way because people expected it. She had never refused a rôle. She could not forgo that intensification, that kindling of her personality at being considered very happy and reckless, even if she were not. She could not hope to assure him she was not enjoying anything he had missed, that she was now unconvinced and anxious but intended to be quite certain, by the time she was his age, that she had once been happy. For to explain this—were explanation possible to so courteous, ironical and unfriendly a listener— would, she felt, be disloyal to herself, to Gerald, to an illusion both were called upon to maintain.

Just by the lime, in that dancing night, she had missed a step and sagged on his arm, which tightened. His hand slid up between her shoulders; then, as she steadied back to the rhythm, down again. They had set out laughing, noisy and conscious, but soon had to save their breath. Gerald's cheek, within an inch of her own, was too near to see. All the way up, he had not missed a step; he was most dependable. And remembering how the family had just now gone into the house—so flatly, so unregrettingly, slamming the glass doors—she felt *that* was what she now wanted most—his eagerness and constancy. She felt, like a steady look from him, the perfectness of their being together.

'Oh, I do want you!'

But he was very musical, he conducted a jazz band they had at the barracks: while reaching out in her thoughts she remembered, the band would be practising now. She was disappointed. To a line of tune the thought flung her, she danced on the avenue.

A shrubbery path was solid with darkness, she pressed down it. Laurels breathed coldly and close: on her bare arms the tips of leaves were timid and dank, like tongues of dead animals. Her fear of the shrubberies tugged at its chain, fear behind reason, fear before her birth; fear like the earliest germ of her life that had stirred in Laura. She went forward eagerly, daring a snap of the chain, singing; a hand to the thump of her heart, dramatic with terror. She thought of herself as forcing a pass. In her life—deprived as she saw it—there was no occasion for courage, which like an unused muscle slackened and slept.

High up a bird shrieked and stumbled down through dark, tearing the leaves. Silence healed, but kept a scar of horror. The shuttered-in drawing-room, the family sealed in lamplight, secure and bright like flowers in a paper-weight—were desirable, worth much of this to regain. Fear curled back from the carpet-border. . . . Now, on the path: grey patches worse than the dark: they slipped up her dress knee-high. The laurels deserted her groping arm. She had come to the holly, where two paths crossed.

First, she did not hear footsteps coming, and as she began to notice the displaced darkness thought what she dreaded was coming, was there within her—she was indeed clairvoyant, exposed to horror and going to see a ghost. Then steps, hard on the smooth earth; branches slipping against a trench-coat. The trench-coat rustled across the path ahead, to the swing of a steady walker. She stood by the holly immovable, blotted out in her black, and there passed within reach of her hand, with the rise and fall of a stride, a resolute profile, powerful as a thought. In gratitude for its fleshliness, she felt prompted to make some contact: not to be known seemed like a doom: extinction.

'It's a fine night,' she would have liked to observe; or, to engage his sympathies: 'Up Dublin!' or even—since it was in her uncle's demesne she was straining under a holly—boldly—'What do you want?'

It must be because of Ireland he was in such a hurry; down from the mountains, making a short cut through their demesne. Here was something else that she could not share. She could not conceive of her country emotionally: it was a way of living, an abstract of several landscapes, or an oblique frayed island, moored at the north but with an air of being detached and washed out west from the British coast.

Quite still, she let him go past in contemptuous unawareness. His intentions burnt on the dark an almost visible trail; he might well have been a murderer he seemed so inspired. The crowd of trees, straining up from the passive disputed earth, each sucking up and exhaling the country's essence—swallowed him finally. She thought: 'Has he come for the guns?'* A man in a trench-coat had passed without seeing her: that was what it amounted to.

She ran back to tell, in excitement. Below, the house waited; vast on its west side, with thin yellow lines round the downstairs shutters. It had that excluded, sad, irrelevant look outsides of houses take in the dark. Inside, they would all be drawing up closer to one another, tricked by the half-revelation of lamplight. 'Compassed about,' thought Lois, 'by so great a cloud of witnesses. . . .'* Chairs standing round dejectedly; upstairs, the confidently waiting beds; mirrors vacant and startling; books read and forgotten, contributing no more to life; dinner-table certain of its regular compulsion; the procession of elephants that throughout uncertain years had not broken file.

But as Lois went up the steps breathlessly, her adventure began to diminish. It held ground for a moment as she saw the rug dropped in the hall by Mrs Montmorency sprawl like a body across the polish. Then confidence disappeared, in a waver of shadow, among the furniture. Conceivably, she had just surprised life at a significant angle in the shrubbery. But it was impossible to speak of this. At a touch from Aunt Myra adventure became literary, to Uncle Richard it suggested an inconvenience; a glance from Mr Montmorency or Laurence would make her encounter sterile.

But what seemed most probable was that they would not listen. . . . She lighted her candle and went up to bed—uncivilly, without saying good night to anyone. Her Uncle Richard, she afterwards heard, was obliged to sit up till twelve o'clock. He had not been told she was in, so did not think it right to lock up the house.

SAMUEL BECKETT
(1906–1989)

from *Murphy* (1938)

I

The sun shone, having no alternative, on the nothing new.* Murphy sat out of it, as though he were free, in a mew in West Brompton. Here for what might have been six months he had eaten, drunk, slept, and put his clothes on and off, in a medium-sized cage of north-western aspect commanding an unbroken view of medium-sized cages of south-eastern aspect. Soon he would have to make other arrangements, for the mew had been condemned. Soon he would have to buckle to and start eating, drinking, sleeping, and putting his clothes on and off, in quite alien surroundings.

He sat naked in his rocking-chair of undressed teak, guaranteed not to crack, warp, shrink, corrode, or creak at night. It was his own, it never left him. The corner in which he sat was curtained off from the sun, the poor old sun in the Virgin* again for the billionth time. Seven scarves held him in position. Two fastened his shins to the rockers, one his thighs to the seat, two his breast and belly to the back, one his wrists to the strut behind. Only the most local movements were possible. Sweat poured off him, tightened the thongs. The breath was not perceptible. The eyes, cold and unwavering as a gull's, stared up at an iridescence splashed over the cornice moulding, shrinking and fading. Somewhere a cuckoo-clock, having struck between twenty and thirty, became the echo of a street-cry, which now entering the mew gave *Quid pro quo! Quid pro quo!* directly.

These were sights and sounds that he did not like. They detained him in the world to which they belonged, but not he, as he fondly hoped. He wondered dimly what was breaking up his sunlight, what wares were being cried. Dimly, very dimly.

He sat in his chair in this way because it gave him pleasure! First it gave his body pleasure, it appeased his body. Then it set him free in his mind. For it was not until his body was appeased that he could come alive in his mind, as described in section six. And life in his mind gave him pleasure, such pleasure that pleasure was not the word.

Murphy had lately studied under a man in Cork called Neary.* This man, at that time, could stop his heart more or less whenever he liked and keep it stopped, within reasonable limits, for as long as he liked. This rare faculty, acquired after years of application somewhere north of the Nerbudda,* he exercised frugally, reserving it for situations irksome beyond endurance, as when he wanted a drink and could not get one, or fell among Gaels and could not escape, or felt the pangs of hopeless sexual inclination.

Murphy's purpose in going to sit at Neary's feet was not to develop the Neary heart, which he thought would quickly prove fatal to a man of his temper, but simply to invest his own with a little of what Neary, at that time a Pythagorean, called the Apmonia.* For Murphy had such an irrational heart that no physician could get to the root of it. Inspected, palpated, auscultated, percussed, radiographed and cardiographed, it was all that a heart should be. Buttoned up and left to perform, it was like Petrouchka* in his box. One moment in such labour that it seemed on the point of seizing, the next in such ebullition that it seemed on the point of bursting. It was the mediation between these extremes that Neary called the Apmonia. When he got tired of calling it the Apmonia he called it the Isonomy. When he got sick of the sound of Isonomy he called it the Attunement. But he might call it what he liked, into Murphy's heart it would not enter. Neary could not blend the opposites in Murphy's heart . . .

4

In Dublin a week later, that would be September 19th, Neary minus his whiskers was recognised by a former pupil called Wylie, in the General Post Office contemplating from behind the statue of Cuchulain.* Neary had bared his head, as though the holy ground meant something to him. Suddenly he flung aside his hat, sprang forward, seized the dying hero by the thighs and began to dash his head against his buttocks, such as they are. The Civic Guard on duty in the building, roused from a tender reverie by the sound of blows, took in the situation at his leisure, disentangled his baton and advanced with measured tread, thinking he had caught a vandal in the act. Happily Wylie, whose reactions as a street bookmaker's stand were as rapid as a zebra's, had already seized Neary round the waist, torn him back from the sacrifice and smuggled him half-way to the exit.

'Howlt on there, youze,' said the C.G.

Wylie turned back, tapped his forehead and said, as one sane man to another:

'John o' God's. Hundred per cent harmless.'

'Come back in here owwathat,' said the C.G.

Wylie, a tiny man, stood at a loss. Neary, almost as large as the C.G. though not of course so nobly proportioned, rocked blissfully on the right arm of his rescuer. It was not in the C.G.'s nature to bandy words, nor had it come into any branch of his training. He resumed his steady advance.

'Stillorgan,' said Wylie. 'Not Dundrum.'

The C.G. laid his monstrous hand on Wylie's left arm and exerted a strong pull along the line he had mapped out in his mind. They all moved off in the desired direction, Neary shod with orange-peel.

'John o' God's,' said Wylie. 'As quiet as a child.'

They drew up behind the statue. A crowd gathered behind them. The C.G. leaned forward and scrutinised the pillar and draperies.

'Not a feather out of her,' said Wylie. 'No blood, no brains, nothing.'

The C.G. straightened up and let go Wylie's arm.

'Move on,' he said to the crowd, 'before yer moved on.'

The crowd obeyed, with the single diastolesystole which is all the law requires. Feeling amply repaid by this superb symbol for the trouble and risk he had taken in issuing an order, the C.G. inflected his attention to Wylie and said more kindly:

'Take my advice, mister——' He stopped. To devise words of advice was going to tax his ability to the utmost. When would he learn not to plunge into the labyrinths of an opinion when he had not the slightest idea of how he was to emerge? And before a hostile audience! His embarrassment was if possible increased by the expression of strained attention on Wylie's face, clamped there by the promise of advice.

'Yes, sergeant,' said Wylie, and held his breath.

'Run him back to Stillorgan,' said the C.G. Done it!

Wylie's face came asunder in gratification.

'Never fear, sergeant,' he said, urging Neary towards the exit, 'back to the cell, blood heat, next best thing to never being born, no heroes, no fisc, no——'

Neary had been steadily recovering all this time and now gave such a jerk to Wylie's arm that that poor little man was nearly pulled off his feet.

'Where am I?' said Neary. 'If and when.'

Wylie rushed him into the street and into a Dalkey* tram that had just come in. The crowd dispersed, the better to gather elsewhere. The C.G. dismissed the whole sordid episode from his mind, the better to brood on a theme very near to his heart.

'Is it the saloon,' said Neary, 'or the jugs and bottles?'

Wylie wet his handkerchief and applied it tenderly to the breaches of surface, a ministration immediately poleaxed by Neary, who now saw his saviour for the first time. Punctured by those sharp little features of the fury that had sustained him, he collapsed in a tempest of sobbing on that sharp little shoulder.

'Come, come,' said Wylie, patting the large heaving back. 'Needle is at hand.'

Neary checked his sobs, raised a face purged of all passion, seized Wylie by the shoulders, held him out at arm's length and exclaimed:

'Is it little Needle Wylie, my scholar that was. What will you have?'

'How do you feel?' said Wylie.

It dawned on Neary that he was not where he thought. He rose.

'What is the finest tram in Europe,' he said, 'to a man consumed with sobriety?' He made the street under his own power with Wylie close behind him.

'But by Mooney's clock,' said Wylie, 'the sad news is two-thirty-three.'

Neary leaned against the Pillar railings and cursed, first the day in which he was born, then—in a bold flash-back—the night in which he was conceived.

'There, there,' said Wylie. 'Needle knows no holy hour.'

He led the way to an underground café close by, steered Neary into an alcove and called for Cathleen. Cathleen came.

'My friend Professor Neary,' said Wylie, 'my friend Miss Cathleen na Hennessey.'*

'Pleased,' said Cathleen.

'Why the ——,' said Neary, 'is light given to a man whose way is hid.'

'Pardon,' said Cathleen.

'Two large coffees,' said Wylie. 'Three star.'

One gulp of this and Neary's way was clearer.

'Now tell us all about it,' said Wylie. 'Keep back nothing.'

'The limit of Cork endurance had been reached,' said Neary. 'That Red Branch bum* was the camel's back.'

'Drink a little more of your coffee,' said Wylie.

Neary drank a little more.

'What are you doing in this kip at all?' said Wylie. 'Why aren't you in Cork?'

'My grove on Grand Parade,' said Neary, 'is wiped as a man wipeth a plate, wiping it and turning it upside down.'

'And your whiskers?' said Wylie.

'Suppressed without pity,' said Neary, 'in discharge of a vow, never again to ventilate a virility denied discharge into its predestined channel.'

'These are dark sayings,' said Wylie.

Neary turned his cup upside down.

'Needle,' he said, 'as it is with the love of the body, so with the friendship of the mind, the full is only reached by admittance to the most retired places. Here are the pudenda of my psyche.'

FLANN O'BRIEN
(1911–1966)

from *At Swim-Two-Birds* (1939)

For seven years, to relate precisely, was Sweeny at the air travel of all Erin, returning always to his tree in charming Glen Bolcain, for that was his fortress and his haven, it was his house there in the glen. It was to this place that his foster-brother Linchehaun came for tidings concerning him, for he carried always a deep affection for Sweeny and had retrieved him three times from madness before that. Linchehaun went seeking him in the glen with shouts and found toe-tracks by the stream-mud where the madman was wont to appease himself by the eating of cresses. But track or trace of Sweeny he did not attain for that day and he sat down in an old deserted house in the glen till the labour and weariness of his pursuit brought about his sleep. And Sweeny, hearing his snore from his tree-clump in the glen, uttered this lay in the pitch darkness.

> The man by the wall snores
> a snore-sleep that's beyond me,
> for seven years from that Tuesday at Magh Rath
> I have not slept a wink.
>
> O God that I had not gone
> to the hard battle!

thereafter my name was Mad—
Mad Sweeny in the bush.

Watercress from the well at Cirb
is my lot at terce,
its colour is my mouth,
green on the mouth of Sweeny.

Chill chill is my body
when away from ivy,
the rain torrent hurts it
and the thunder.

I am in summer with the herons of Cuailgne
with wolves in winter,
at other times I am hidden in a copse—
not so the man by the wall.

And thereafter he met Linchehaun who came visiting to his tree
and they parleyed there the two of them together and the one of
them talkative and unseen in branches and prickle-briars. And
Sweeny bade Linchehaun to depart and not to pursue or annoy him
further because the curse of Ronan stopped him from putting his
trust or his mad faith in any man.

Thereafter he travelled in distant places till he came at the black
fall of a night to Ros Bearaigh and lodged himself in a hunched
huddle in the middle of the yew-tree of the church in that place. But
being besieged with nets and hog-harried by the caretaker of the
church and his false wife, he hurried nimbly to the old tree at Ros
Eareain where he remained hidden and unnoticed the length of a full
fortnight, till the time when Linchehaun came and perceived the
murk of his shadow in the sparse branches and saw the other
branches he had broken and bent in his movements and in changing
trees. And the two of them parleyed together until they had said
between them these fine words following.

Sad it is Sweeny, said Linchehaun, that your last extremity should
be thus, without food or drink or raiment like a fowl, the same man
that had cloth of silk and of satin and the foreign steed of the peer-
less bridle, also comely generous women and boys and hounds and

princely people of every refinement; hosts and tenants and men-at-arms, arms, and mugs and goblets and embellished buffalohorns for the savouring of pleasant tasted fine liquors. Sad it is to see the same man as a hapless air-fowl.

Cease now, Linchehaun, said Sweeny, and give me tidings.

Your father is dead, said Linchehaun.

That has seized me with a blind agony, said Sweeny.

Your mother is likewise dead.

Now all the pity in me is at an end.

Dead is your brother.

Gaping open is my side on account of that.

She has died too your sister.

A needle for the heart is an only sister.

Ah, dumb dead is the little son that called you pop.

Truly, said Sweeny, that is the last blow that brings a man to the ground.

When Sweeny heard the sorry word of his small son still and without life, he fell with a crap from the middle of the yew to the ground and Linchehaun hastened to his thornpacked flank with fetters and handcuffs and manacles and locks and black-iron chains and he did not achieve a resting until the lot were about the madman, and through him and above him and over him, round-wise and about. Thereafter there was a concourse of hospitallers and knights and warriors around the trunk of the yew, and after melodious talk they entrusted the mad one to the care of Linchehaun till he would take him away to a quiet place for a fortnight and a month, to the quiet of a certain room where his senses returned to him, the one after the other, with no one near him but the old mill-hag.

O hag, said Sweeny, searing are the tribulations I have suffered; many a terrible leap have I leaped from hill to hill, from fort to fort, from land to land, from valley to valley.

For the sake of God, said the hag, leap for us now a leap such as you leaped in the days of your madness.

And thereupon Sweeny gave a bound over the top of the bedrail till he reached the extremity of the bench.

My conscience indeed, said the hag, I could leap the same leap myself.

And the hag gave a like jump.

Sweeny then gathered himself together in the extremity of his jealousy and threw a leap right out through the skylight of the hostel.

I could vault that vault too, said the hag and straightway she vaulted the same vault. And the short of it is this, that Sweeny travelled the length of five cantreds of leaps until he had penetrated to Glenn na nEachtach in Fiodh Gaibhle with the hag at her hag's leaps behind him; and when Sweeny rested there in a huddle at the top of a tall ivy-branch, the hag was perched there on another tree beside him. He heard there the voice of a stag and he thereupon made a lay eulogizing aloud the trees and the stags of Erin, and he did not cease or sleep until he had achieved these staves.

> Bleating one, little antlers,
> O lamenter we like
> delightful the clamouring
> from your glen you make.
>
> O leafy-oak, clumpy-leaved,
> you are high above trees,
> O hazlet, little clumpy-branch—
> the nut-smell of hazels.
>
> O alder, O alder-friend,
> delightful your colour,
> you don't prickle me or tear
> in the place you are.
>
> O blackthorn, little thorny-one,
> O little dark sloe-tree;
> O watercress, O green-crowned,
> at the well-brink.
>
> O holly, holly-shelter,
> O door against the wind,
> O ash-tree inimical,
> you spearshaft of warrior.
>
> O birch clean and blessed,
> O melodious, O proud,

delightful the tangle
of your head-rods.

What I like least in woodlands
from none I conceal it—
stirk of a leafy-oak,
as its swaying.

O faun, little long-legs,
I caught you with grips,
I rode you upon your back
from peak to peak.

Glen Bolcain my home ever,
it was my haven,
many a night have I tried
a race against the peak.

I beg your pardon for interrupting, said Shanahan, but you're after reminding me of something, brought the thing into my head in a rush.

He swallowed a draught of vesper-milk, restoring the cloudy glass swiftly to his knee and collecting little belated flavourings from the corners of his mouth.

That thing you were saying reminds me of something bloody good. I beg your pardon for interrupting, Mr Storybook.

In the yesterday, said Finn, the man who mixed his utterance with the honeywords of Finn was the first day put naked into the tree of Coill Boirche with nothing to his bare hand but a stick of hazel. On the morning of the second day thereafter. . . .

Now listen for a minute till I tell you something, said Shanahan, did any man here ever hear of the poet Casey?

Who did you say? said Furriskey.

Casey. Jem Casey.

On the morning of the second day thereafter, he was taken and bound and rammed as regards his head into a black hole so that his white body was upside down and upright in Erin for the gazing thereon of man and beast.

Now give us a chance, Mister Storybook, yourself and your black hole, said Shanahan fingering his tie-knot with a long memory-frown

across his brow. Come here for a minute. Come here till I tell you
about Casey. Do you mean to tell me you never heard of the poet
Casey, Mr Furriskey?

Never heard of him, said Furriskey in a solicitous manner.

I can't say, said Lamont, that I ever heard of him either.

He was a poet of the people, said Shanahan.

I see, said Furriskey.

Now do you understand, said Shanahan. A plain upstanding
labouring man, Mr Furriskey, the same as you or me. A black hat or a
bloody ribbon, no by God, not on Jem Casey. A hard-working well-
made block of a working man, Mr. Lamont, with the handle of a pick
in his hand like the rest of us. Now say there was a crowd of men
with a ganger all working there laying a length of gas-pipe on the
road. All right. The men pull off their coats and start shovelling and
working there for further orders. Here at one end of the hole you
have your men crowded up together in a lump and them working
away and smoking their butts and talking about the horses and one
thing and another. Now do you understand what I'm telling you. Do
you follow me?

I see that.

But take a look at the other end of the hole and here is my brave
Casey digging away there on his own. Do you understand what I
mean, Mr Furriskey?

Oh I see it all right, said Furriskey.

Right. None of your horses or your bloody blather for him. Not a
bit of it. Here is my nabs saying nothing to nobody but working away
at a pome in his head with a pick in his hand and the sweat pouring
down off his face from the force of his work and his bloody exertions.
That's a quare one!

Do you mind that now, said Lamont.

It's a quare one and one that takes a lot of beating. Not a word to
nobody, not a look to left or right but the brain-box going there all
the time. Just Jem Casey, a poor ignorant labouring man but head
and shoulders above the whole bloody lot of them, not a man in the
whole country to beat him when it comes to getting together a
bloody pome—not a poet in the whole world that could hold a candle
to Jem Casey, not a man of them fit to stand beside him. By God I'd
back him to win by a canter against the whole bloody lot of them give
him his due.

Is that a fact, Mr Shanahan, said Lamont. It's not every day in the week you come across a man like that.

Do you know what I'm going to tell you, Mr Lamont, he was a man that could give the lot of them a good start, pickaxe and all. He was a man that could meet them . . . and meet the best . . . and beat them at their own game, now I'm telling you.

I suppose he could, said Furriskey.

Now I know what I'm talking about. Give a man his due. If a man's station is high or low he is all the same to the God I know. Take the bloody black hats off the whole bunch of them and where are you?

That's the way to look at it, of course, said Furriskey.

Give them a bloody pick, I mean, Mr Furriskey, give them the shaft of a shovel into their hand and tell them to dig a hole and have the length of a page of poetry off by heart in their heads before the five o'clock whistle. What will you get? By God you could take off your hat to what you'd get at five o'clock from that crowd and that's a sure sharkey.

You'd be wasting your time if you waited till five o'clock if you ask me, said Furriskey with a nod of complete agreement.

You're right there, said Shanahan, you'd be waiting around for bloody nothing. Oh I know them and I know my hard Casey too. By Janey he'd be up at the whistle with a pome a yard long, a bloody lovely thing that would send my nice men home in a hurry, home with their bloody tails between their legs. Yes, I've seen his pomes and read them and . . . do you know what I'm going to tell you, I have loved them. I'm not ashamed to sit here and say it, Mr Furriskey. I've known the man and I've known his pomes and by God I have loved the two of them and loved them well, too. Do you understand what I'm saying, Mr Lamont? You, Mr Furriskey?

Oh that's right.

Do you know what it is, I've met the others, the whole lot of them. I've met them all and know them all. I have seen them and I have read their pomes. I have heard them recited by men that know how to use their tongues, men that couldn't be beaten at their own game. I have seen whole books filled up with their stuff, books as thick as that table there and I'm telling you no lie. But by God, at the heel of the hunt, there was only one poet for me.

On the morning of the third day thereafter, said Finn, he was flogged until he bled water.

Only the one, Mr Shanahan? said Lamont.

Only the one. And that one poet was a man . . . by the name . . . of Jem Casey. No 'Sir', no 'Mister', no nothing. Jem Casey, Poet of the Pick, that's all. A labouring man, Mr Lamont, but as sweet a singer in his own way as you'll find in the bloody trees there of a spring day, and that's a fact. Jem Casey, an ignorant God-fearing upstanding labouring man, a bloody navvy. Do you know what I'm going to tell you, I don't believe he ever lifted the latch of a school door. Would you believe that now?

I'd believe it of Casey, said Furriskey, and

I'd believe plenty more of the same man, said Lamont. You haven't any of his pomes on you, have you, Mr Shanahan?

Now take that stuff your man was giving us a while ago, said Shanahan without heed, about the green hills and the bloody swords and the bird giving out the pay from the top of the tree. Now that's good stuff, it's bloody nice. Do you know what it is, I liked it and liked it well. I enjoyed that certainly.

It wasn't bad at all, said Furriskey, I have heard worse, by God, often. It was all right now.

Do you see what I'm getting at, do you understand me, said Shanahan. It's good, very good. But by Christopher it's not every man could see it, I'm bloody sure of that, one in a thousand.

Oh that's right too, said Lamont.

You can't beat it, of course, said Shanahan with a reddening of the features, the real old stuff of the native land, you know, stuff that brought scholars to our shore when your men on the other side were on the flat of their bellies before the calf of gold with a sheepskin around their man. It's the stuff that put our country where she stands to-day, Mr Furriskey, and I'd have my tongue out of my head by the bloody roots before I'd be heard saying a word against it. But the man in the street, where does he come in? By God he doesn't come in at all as far as I can see.

What do my brave men in the black hats care whether he's in or out, asked Furriskey. What do they care? It's a short jump for the man in the street, I'm thinking, if he's waiting for that crowd to do anything for him. They're a nice crowd, now, I'm telling you.

Oh that's the truth, said Lamont.

Another thing, said Shanahan, you can get too much of that stuff. Feed yourself up with that tack once and you won't want more for a long time.

There's no doubt about it, said Furriskey.

Try it once, said Shanahan, and you won't want it a second time.

Do you know what it is, said Lamont, there are people who read that . . . and keep reading it . . . and read damn the bloody thing else. Now that's a mistake.

A big mistake, said Furriskey.

But there's one man, said Shanahan, there's one man that can write pomes that you can read all day and all night and keep reading them to your heart's content, stuff you'd never tire of. Pomes written by a man that is one of ourselves and written down for ourselves to read. The name of that man . . .

Now that's what you want, said Furriskey.

The name of that man, said Shanahan, is a name that could be christianed on you or me, a name that won't shame us. And that name, said Shanahan, is Jem Casey.

And a very good man, said Lamont.

Jem Casey, said Furriskey.

Do you understand what I mean, said Shanahan.

You haven't any of his pomes on you, have you, said Lamont. If there's one thing I'd like. . . .

I haven't one *on* me if that's what you mean, Mr Lamont, said Shanahan, but I could give one out as quick as I'd say my prayers. By God it's not for nothing that I call myself a pal of Jem Casey.

I'm glad to hear it, said Lamont.

Stand up there and recite it man, said Furriskey, don't keep us waiting. What's the name of it now?

The name or title of the pome I am about to recite, gentlemen, said Shanahan with leisure priest-like in character, is a pome by the name of the 'Workman's Friend'. By God you can't beat it. I've heard it praised by the highest. It's a pome about a thing that's known to all of us. It's about a drink of porter.

Porter!

Porter.

Up on your legs man, said Furriskey. Mr Lamont and myself are waiting and listening. Up you get now.

Come on, off you go, said Lamont.

Now listen, said Shanahan clearing the way with small coughs.
Listen now.

He arose holding out his hand and bending his knee beneath him
on the chair.

> When things go wrong and will not come right,
> Though you do the best you can,
> When life looks black as the hour of night—
> A PINT OF PLAIN IS YOUR ONLY MAN.

By God there's a lilt in that, said Lamont.

Very good indeed, said Furriskey. Very nice.

I'm telling you it's the business, said Shanahan. Listen now.

> When money's tight and is hard to get
> And your horse has also ran,
> When all you have is a heap of debt—
> A PINT OF PLAIN IS YOUR ONLY MAN.

> When health is bad and your heart feels strange,
> And your face is pale and wan,
> When doctors say that you need a change,
> A PINT OF PLAIN IS YOUR ONLY MAN.

There are things in that pome that make for what you call
permanence. Do you know what I mean, Mr Furriskey?

There's no doubt about it, it's a grand thing, said Furriskey. Come
on, Mr Shanahan, give us another verse. Don't tell me that is the end
of it.

Can't you listen? said Shanahan.

> When food is scarce and your larder bare
> And no rashers grease your pan,
> When hunger grows as your meals are rare—
> A PINT OF PLAIN IS YOUR ONLY MAN.

What do you think of that now?

It's a pome that'll live, called Lamont, a pome that'll be heard and
clapped when plenty more . . .

But wait till you hear the last verse, man, the last polish-off, said
Shanahan. He frowned and waved his hand.

Oh it's good, it's good, said Furriskey.

> In time of trouble and lousy strife,
> You have still got a darlint plan,
> You still can turn to a brighter life—
> A PINT OF PLAIN IS YOUR ONLY MAN!

Did you ever hear anything like it in your life, said Furriskey. A pint of plain, by God, what! Oh I'm telling you, Casey was a man in twenty thousand, there's no doubt about that. He knew what he was at, too true he did. If he knew nothing else, he knew how to write a pome. A pint of plain is your only man.

Didn't I tell you he was good? said Shanahan. Oh by Gorrah you can't cod me.

There's one thing in that pome, *permanence*, if you know what I mean. That pome, I mean to say, is a pome that'll be heard wherever the Irish race is wont to gather, it'll live as long as there's a hard root of an Irishman left by the Almighty on this planet, mark my words. What do you think, Mr Shanahan?

It'll live, Mr Lamont, it'll live.

I'm bloody sure it will, said Lamont.

A pint of plain, by God, eh? said Furriskey.

5. POETRY

AUGUSTA GREGORY
(1852–1932)

Grief of a Girl's Heart (1901)

(From the Irish)

O Donal Oge, if you go across the sea,
Bring myself with you and do not forget it;
And you will have a sweetheart for fair days and market days,
And the daughter of the King of Greece beside you at night.

It is late last night the dog was speaking of you;
The snipe was speaking of you in her deep marsh.
It is you are the lonely bird through the woods;
And that you may be without a mate until you find me.

You promised me, and you said a lie to me,
That you would be before me where the sheep are flocked;
I gave a whistle and three hundred cries to you,
And I found nothing there but a bleating lamb.

You promised me a thing that was hard for you,
A ship of gold under a silver mast;
Twelve towns with a market in all of them,
And a fine white court by the side of the sea.

You promised me a thing that is not possible,
That you would give me gloves of the skin of a fish;
That you would give me shoes of the skin of a bird;
And a suit of the dearest silk in Ireland.

O Donal Oge, it is I would be better to you
Than a high, proud, spendthrift lady:

I would milk the cow; I would bring help to you;
And if you were hard pressed, I would strike a blow for you.

O, ochone,* and it's not with hunger
Or with wanting food, or drink, or sleep,
That I am growing thin, and my life is shortened;
But it is the love of a young man has withered me away.

It is early in the morning that I saw him coming,
Going along the road on the back of a horse;
He did not come to me; he made nothing of me;
And it is on my way home that I cried my fill.

When I go by myself to the Well of Loneliness,
I sit down and I go through my trouble;
When I see the world and do not see my boy,
He that has an amber shade in his hair.

It was on that Sunday I gave my love to you;
The Sunday that is last before Easter Sunday.
And myself on my knees reading the Passion;
And my two eyes giving love to you for ever.

O, aya!* my mother, give myself to him;
And give him all that you have in the world;
Get out yourself to ask for alms,
And do not come back and forward looking for me.

My mother said to me not to be talking with you, to-day,
Or to-morrow, or on Sunday;
It was a bad time she took for telling me that;
It was shutting the door after the house was robbed.

My heart is as black as the blackness of the sloe,
Or as the black coal that is on the smith's forge;
Or as the sole of a shoe left in white halls;
It was you put that darkness over my life.

You have taken the east from me; you have taken the west from me,
You have taken what is before me and what is behind me;

You have taken the moon, you have taken the sun from me,
And my fear is great that you have taken God from me!

OSCAR WILDE
(1854–1900)

Requiescat (1881)

Tread lightly, she is near
    Under the snow,
Speak gently, she can hear
    The daisies grow.

All her bright golden hair
    Tarnished with rust,
She that was young and fair
    Fallen to dust.

Lily-like, white as snow,
    She hardly knew
She was a woman, so
    Sweetly she grew.

Coffin-board, heavy stone,
    Lie on her breast,
I vex my heart alone,
    She is at rest.

Peace, Peace, she cannot hear
    Lyre or sonnet,
All my life's buried here,
    Heap earth upon it.

Avignon.

Impression du Matin (1881)

The Thames nocturne of blue and gold
   Changed to a Harmony in grey:
   A barge with ochre-coloured hay
Dropt from the wharf: and chill and cold

The yellow fog came creeping down
   The bridges, till the houses' walls
   Seemed changed to shadows, and S. Paul's
Loomed like a bubble o'er the town.

Then suddenly arose the clang
   Of waking life; the streets were stirred
   With country waggons: and a bird
Flew to the glistening roofs and sang.

But one pale woman all alone,
   The daylight kissing her wan hair,
   Loitered beneath the gas lamps' flare,
With lips of flame and heart of stone.

Helas! (1881)

To drift with every passion till my soul
Is a stringed lute on which all winds can play,*
Is it for this that I have given away
Mine ancient wisdom, and austere control?
Methinks my life is a twice-written scroll
Scrawled over on some boyish holiday
With idle songs for pipe and virelay,*
Which do but mar the secret of the whole.
Surely there was a time I might have trod
The sunlit heights, and from life's dissonance
Struck one clear chord to reach the ears of God:
Is that time dead? lo! with a little rod*
I did but touch the honey of romance—
And must I lose a soul's inheritance?

The Harlot's House (1885)

We caught the tread of dancing feet,
We loitered down the moonlit street,
And stopped beneath the Harlot's house.

Inside, above the din and fray,
We heard the loud musicians play
The 'Treues Liebes Herz'* of Strauss.

Like strange mechanical grotesques,
Making fantastic arabesques,
The shadows raced across the blind.

We watched the ghostly dancers spin
To sound of horn and violin,
Like black leaves wheeling in the wind.

Like wire-pulled automatons,
Slim silhouetted skeletons
Went sidling through the slow quadrille,*

Then took each other by the hand,
And danced a stately saraband;
Their laughter echoed thin and shrill.

Sometimes a clock-work puppet pressed
A phantom lover to her breast,
Sometimes they seemed to try and sing,

Sometimes a horrible Marionette
Came out, and smoked its cigarette
Upon the steps like a live thing.

Then turning to my love I said,
'The dead are dancing with the dead,
The dust is whirling with the dust.'

But she, she heard the violin,
And left my side, and entered in;
Love passed into the house of Lust.

Then suddenly the tune went false,
The dancers wearied of the waltz,
The shadows ceased to wheel and whirl,

And down the long and silent street,
The dawn with silver-sandalled feet,
Crept like a frightened girl.

Sonnet. On the Sale by Auction of Keats' Love Letters (1885)

These are the letters which Endymion* wrote
To one he loved in secret, and apart.
And now the brawlers of the auction mart
Bargain and bid for each poor blotted note,
Ay! for each separate pulse of passion quote
The merchant's price: I think they love not Art
Who break the crystal of a poet's heart
That small and sickly eyes may glare and gloat.

Is it not said that many years ago,
In a far Eastern town, some soldiers ran
With torches through the midnight, and began
To wrangle for mean raiment, and to throw
Dice for the garments of a wretched man,
Not knowing the God's wonder, or his woe?

Symphony in Yellow (1889)

An omnibus across the bridge
Crawls like a yellow butterfly,
And, here and there, a passer-by
Shows like a little restless midge.

Big barges full of yellow hay
Are moored against the shadowy wharf,

And, like a yellow silken scarf,
The thick fog hangs along the quay.

The yellow leaves begin to fade
   And flutter from the Temple* elms,
   And at my feet the pale green Thames
Lies like a rod of rippled jade.

DOUGLAS HYDE
(1860–1949)

My Grief on the Sea (1893)

(*From the Irish*)

My grief on the sea,
   How the waves of it roll!
For they heave between me
And the love of my soul!

Abandoned, forsaken,
   To grief and to care,
Will the sea ever waken
Relief from despair?

My grief, and my trouble!
   Would he and I were
In the province of Leinster,
Or county of Clare.

Were I and my darling—
   Oh, heart-bitter wound!—
On board of the ship
For America bound.

On a green bed of rushes
   All last night I lay,
And I flung it abroad
With the heat of the day.

And my love came behind me—
He came from the south;
His breast to my bosom,
His mouth to my mouth.

W. B. YEATS
(1865–1939)

The Lake Isle of Innisfree (1888)

I will arise and go now, and go to Innisfree,
And a small cabin build there, of clay and wattles made:
Nine bean-rows will I have there, a hive for the honey-bee,
And live alone in the bee-loud glade.

And I shall have some peace there, for peace comes dropping slow,
Dropping from the veils of the morning to where the cricket sings;
There midnight's all a glimmer, and noon a purple glow,
And evening full of the linnet's wings.

I will arise and go now, for always night and day
I hear lake water lapping with low sounds by the shore;
While I stand on the roadway, or on the pavements grey,
I hear it in the deep heart's core.

To Ireland in the Coming Times (1892)

Know, that I would accounted be
True brother of a company
That sang, to sweeten Ireland's wrong,
Ballad and story, rann* and song;
Nor be I any less of them,
Because the red-rose-bordered hem*
Of her, whose history began
Before God made the angelic clan,
Trails all about the written page.
When Time began to rant and rage

The measure of her flying feet
Made Ireland's heart begin to beat;
And Time bade all his candles flare
To light a measure here and there;
And may the thoughts of Ireland brood
Upon a measured quietude.

Nor may I less be counted one
With Davis, Mangan, Ferguson,*
Because, to him who ponders well,
My rhymes more than their rhyming tell
Of things discovered in the deep,
Where only body's laid asleep.
For the elemental creatures go
About my table to and fro,
That hurry from unmeasured mind
To rant and rage in flood and wind;
Yet he who treads in measured ways
May surely barter gaze for gaze.
Man ever journeys on with them
After the red-rose-bordered hem.
Ah, faeries, dancing under the moon,
A Druid land, a Druid tune!

While still I may, I write for you
The love I lived, the dream I knew.
From our birthday, until we die,
Is but the winking of an eye;
And we, our singing and our love,
What measurer Time has lit above,
And all benighted things that go
About my table to and fro,
Are passing on to where may be,
In truth's consuming ecstasy,
No place for love and dream at all;
For God goes by with white footfall.
I cast my heart into my rhymes,
That you, in the dim coming times,
May know how my heart went with them
After the red-rose-bordered hem.

The Song of Wandering Aengus (1897)

I went out to the hazel wood,
Because a fire was in my head,
And cut and peeled a hazel wand,*
And hooked a berry to a thread;
And when white moths were on the wing,
And moth-like stars were flickering out,
I dropped the berry in a stream
And caught a little silver trout.

When I had laid it on the floor
I went to blow the fire aflame,
But something rustled on the floor,
And some one called me by my name:
It had become a glimmering girl
With apple blossom in her hair
Who called me by my name and ran
And faded through the brightening air.

Though I am old with wandering
Through hollow lands and hilly lands,
I will find out where she has gone,
And kiss her lips and take her hands;
And walk among long dappled grass,
And pluck till time and times are done
The silver apples of the moon,
The golden apples of the sun.

To a Shade (1913)

If you have revisited the town, thin Shade,
Whether to look upon your monument
(I wonder if the builder has been paid)
Or happier-thoughted when the day is spent
To drink of that salt breath out of the sea
When grey gulls flit about instead of men,
And the gaunt houses put on majesty:

Let these content you and be gone again;
For they are at their old tricks yet.
                              A man*
Of your own passionate serving kind who had brought
In his full hands what, had they only known,
Had given their children's children loftier thought,
Sweeter emotion, working in their veins
Like gentle blood, has been driven from the place,
And insult heaped upon him for his pains,
And for his open-handedness, disgrace;
Your enemy, an old foul mouth,* had set
The pack upon him.
                    Go, unquiet wanderer,
And gather the Glasnevin coverlet*
About your head till the dust stops your ear,
The time for you to taste of that salt breath
And listen at the corners has not come;
You had enough of sorrow before death—
Away, away! You are safer in the tomb.

September 29, 1913

September 1913 (1913)

What need you, being come to sense,
But fumble in a greasy till
And add the halfpence to the pence
And prayer to shivering prayer, until
You have dried the marrow from the bone;
For men were born to pray and save:
Romantic Ireland's dead and gone,
It's with O'Leary* in the grave.

Yet they were of a different kind,
The names that stilled your childish play,
They have gone about the world like wind,
But little time had they to pray
For whom the hangman's rope was spun,

And what, God help us, could they save?
Romantic Ireland's dead and gone,
It's with O'Leary in the grave.

Was it for this the wild geese* spread
The grey wing upon every tide;
For this that all that blood was shed,
For this Edward Fitzgerald* died,
And Robert Emmet and Wolfe Tone,
All that delirium of the brave?
Romantic Ireland's dead and gone,
It's with O'Leary in the grave.

Yet could we turn the years again,
And call those exiles as they were
In all their loneliness and pain,
You'd cry, 'Some woman's yellow hair
Has maddened every mother's son':*
They weighed so lightly what they gave.
But let them be, they're dead and gone,
They're with O'Leary in the grave.

Easter 1916 (1916)

I have met them at close of day
Coming with vivid faces
From counter or desk among grey
Eighteenth-century houses.
I have passed with a nod of the head
Or polite meaningless words,
Or have lingered awhile and said
Polite meaningless words,
And thought before I had done
Of a mocking tale or a gibe
To please a companion
Around the fire at the club,
Being certain that they and I
But lived where motley is worn:
All changed, changed utterly:
A terrible beauty is born.

That woman's days* were spent
In ignorant good-will,
Her nights in argument
Until her voice grew shrill.
What voice more sweet than hers
When, young and beautiful,
She rode to harriers?
This man had kept a school
And rode our wingèd horse;*
This other* his helper and friend
Was coming into his force;
He might have won fame in the end,
So sensitive his nature seemed,
So daring and sweet his thought.
This other man* I had dreamed
A drunken, vainglorious lout.
He had done most bitter wrong
To some who are near my heart,
Yet I number him in the song;
He, too, has resigned his part
In the casual comedy;
He, too, has been changed in his turn,
Transformed utterly:
A terrible beauty is born.

Hearts with one purpose alone
Through summer and winter seem
Enchanted to a stone
To trouble the living stream.
The horse that comes from the road,
The rider, the birds that range
From cloud to tumbling cloud,
Minute by minute they change;
A shadow of cloud on the stream
Changes minute by minute;
A horse-hoof slides on the brim,
And a horse plashes within it;
The long-legged moor-hens dive,
And hens to moor-cocks call;

Minute by minute they live:
The stone's in the midst of all.

Too long a sacrifice
Can make a stone of the heart.
O when may it suffice?
That is Heaven's part, our part
To murmur name upon name,
As a mother names her child
When sleep at last has come
On limbs that had run wild.
What is it but nightfall?
No, no, not night but death;
Was it needless death after all?
For England may keep faith*
For all that is done and said.
We know their dream; enough
To know they dreamed and are dead;
And what if excess of love
Bewildered them till they died?
I write it out in a verse—
MacDonagh and MacBride
And Connolly* and Pearse
Now and in time to be,
Wherever green is worn,
Are changed, changed utterly:
A terrible beauty is born.

September 25, 1916

The Wild Swans at Coole (1916)

The trees are in their autumn beauty,
The woodland paths are dry,
Under the October twilight the water
Mirrors a still sky;
Upon the brimming water among the stones
Are nine-and-fifty swans.

The nineteenth autumn has come upon me
Since I first made my count;
I saw, before I had well finished,
All suddenly mount
And scatter wheeling in great broken rings
Upon their clamorous wings.

I have looked upon those brilliant creatures,
And now my heart is sore.
All's changed since I, hearing at twilight,
The first time on this shore,
The bell-beat of their wings above my head,
Trod with a lighter tread.

Unwearied still, lover by lover,
They paddle in the cold
Companionable streams or climb the air;
Their hearts have not grown old;
Passion or conquest, wander where they will,
Attend upon them still.

But now they drift on the still water,
Mysterious, beautiful;
Among what rushes will they build,
By what lake's edge or pool
Delight men's eyes when I awake some day
To find they have flown away?

Meditations in Time of Civil War (1921–1923)

I

Ancestral Houses

Surely among a rich man's flowering lawns,
Amid the rustle of his planted hills,
Life overflows without ambitious pains;
And rains down life until the basin spills,
And mounts more dizzy high the more it rains

As though to choose whatever shape it wills
And never stoop to a mechanical
Or servile shape, at others' beck and call.

Mere dreams, mere dreams! Yet Homer had not sung
Had he not found it certain beyond dreams
That out of life's own self-delight had sprung
The abounding glittering jet; though now it seems
As if some marvellous empty sea-shell flung
Out of the obscure dark of the rich streams,
And not a fountain, were the symbol which
Shadows the inherited glory of the rich.

Some violent bitter man, some powerful man
Called architect and artist in, that they,
Bitter and violent men, might rear in stone
The sweetness that all longed for night and day,
The gentleness none there had ever known;
But when the master's buried mice can play,
And maybe the great-grandson of that house,
For all its bronze and marble, 's but a mouse.

O what if gardens where the peacock strays
With delicate feet upon old terraces,
Or else all Juno* from an urn displays
Before the indifferent garden deities;
O what if levelled lawns and gravelled ways
Where slippered Contemplation finds his ease
And Childhood a delight for every sense,
But take our greatness with our violence?

What if the glory of escutcheoned doors,
And buildings that a haughtier age designed,
The pacing to and fro on polished floors
Amid great chambers and long galleries, lined
With famous portraits of our ancestors;
What if those things the greatest of mankind
Consider most to magnify, or to bless,
But take our greatness with our bitterness?

II

My House

An ancient bridge, and a more ancient tower,
A farmhouse that is sheltered by its wall,
An acre of stony ground,
Where the symbolic rose can break in flower,
Old ragged elms, old thorns innumerable,
The sound of the rain or sound
Of every wind that blows;
The stilted water-hen
Crossing stream again
Scared by the splashing of a dozen cows;

A winding stair, a chamber arched with stone,
A grey stone fireplace with an open hearth,
A candle and written page.
Il Penseroso's Platonist* toiled on
In some like chamber, shadowing forth
How the daemonic rage
Imagined everything.
Benighted travellers
From markets and from fairs
Have seen his midnight candle glimmering.

Two men have founded here. A man-at-arms
Gathered a score of horse and spent his days
In this tumultuous spot,
Where through long wars and sudden night alarms
His dwindling score and he seemed castaways
Forgetting and forgot;
And I, that after me
My bodily heirs may find,
To exalt a lonely mind,
Befitting emblems of adversity.

III

My Table

Two heavy trestles, and a board
Where Sato's gift, a changeless sword,*

By pen and paper lies,
That it may moralise
My days out of their aimlessness.
A bit of an embroidered dress
Covers its wooden sheath.
Chaucer had not drawn breath
When it was forged. In Sato's house,
Curved like new moon, moon-luminous,
It lay five hundred years.
Yet if no change appears
No moon; only an aching heart
Conceives a changeless work of art.
Our learned men have urged
That when and where 'twas forged
A marvellous accomplishment,
In painting or in pottery, went
From father unto son
And through the centuries ran
And seemed unchanging like the sword.
Soul's beauty being most adored,
Men and their business took
The soul's unchanging look;
For the most rich inheritor,
Knowing that none could pass Heaven's door
That loved inferior art,
Had such an aching heart
That he, although a country's talk
For silken clothes and stately walk,
Had waking wits; it seemed
Juno's peacock screamed.

IV

My Descendants

Having inherited a vigorous mind
From my old fathers, I must nourish dreams
And leave a woman and a man behind
As vigorous of mind, and yet it seems
Life scarce can cast a fragrance on the wind,
Scarce spread a glory to the morning beams,

But the torn petals strew the garden plot;
And there's but common greenness after that.

And what if my descendants lose the flower
Through natural declension of the soul,
Through too much business with the passing hour,
Through too much play, or marriage with a fool?
May this laborious stair and this stark tower
Become a roofless ruin that the owl
May build in the cracked masonry and cry
Her desolation to the desolate sky.

The Primum Mobile* that fashioned us
Has made the very owls in circles move;
And I, that count myself most prosperous,
Seeing that love and friendship are enough,
For an old neighbour's friendship chose the house
And decked and altered it for a girl's love,
And know whatever flourish and decline
These stones remain their monument and mine.

v

The Road at my Door

An affable Irregular,*
A heavily-built Falstaffian man,*
Comes cracking jokes of civil war
As though to die by gunshot were
The finest play under the sun.

A brown Lieutenant and his men,
Half dressed in national uniform,*
Stand at my door, and I complain
Of the foul weather, hail and rain,
A pear tree broken by the storm.

I count those feathered balls of soot
The moor-hen guides upon the stream,
To silence the envy in my thought;
And turn towards my chamber, caught
In the cold snows of a dream.

VI

The Stare's Nest by my Window

The bees build in the crevices
Of loosening masonry, and there
The mother birds bring grubs and flies.
My wall is loosening; honey-bees,
Come build in the empty house of the stare.*

We are closed in, and the key is turned
On our uncertainty; somewhere
A man is killed, or a house burned,
Yet no clear fact to be discerned:
Come build in the empty house of the stare.

A barricade of stone or of wood;
Some fourteen days of civil war;
Last night they trundled down the road
That dead young soldier in his blood:
Come build in the empty house of the stare.

We had fed the heart on fantasies,
The heart's grown brutal from the fare;
More substance in our enmities
Than in our love; O honey-bees,
Come build in the empty house of the stare.

VII

I see Phantoms of Hatred and of the Heart's Fullness and of the Coming Emptiness

I climb to the tower-top and lean upon broken stone,
A mist that is like blown snow is sweeping over all,
Valley, river, and elms, under the light of a moon
That seems unlike itself, that seems unchangeable,
A glittering sword out of the east. A puff of wind
And those white glimmering fragments of the mist sweep by.
Frenzies bewilder, reveries perturb the mind;
Monstrous familiar images swim to the mind's eye.

'Vengeance upon the murderers,' the cry goes up,
'Vengeance for Jacques Molay.'* In cloud-pale rags, or in lace,
The rage-driven, rage-tormented, and rage-hungry troop,
Trooper belabouring trooper, biting at arm or at face,
Plunges towards nothing, arms and fingers spreading wide
For the embrace of nothing; and I, my wits-astray
Because of all that senseless tumult, all but cried
For vengeance on the murderers of Jacques Molay.

Their legs long, delicate and slender, aquamarine their eyes,
Magical unicorns bear ladies on their backs.
The ladies close their musing eyes. No prophecies,
Remembered out of Babylonian almanacs,*
Have closed the ladies' eyes, their minds are but a pool
Where even longing drowns under its own excess;
Nothing but stillness can remain when hearts are full
Of their own sweetness, bodies of their loveliness.

The cloud-pale unicorns, the eyes of aquamarine,
The quivering half-closed eyelids, the rags of cloud or of lace,
Or eyes that rage has brightened, arms it has made lean,
Give place to an indifferent multitude, give place
To brazen hawks. Nor self-delighting reverie,
Nor hate of what's to come, nor pity for what's gone,
Nothing but grip of claw, and the eye's complacency,
The innumerable clanging wings that have put out the moon.

I turn away and shut the door, and on the stair
Wonder how many times I could have proved my worth
In something that all others understand or share;
But O! ambitious heart, had such a proof drawn forth
A company of friends, a conscience set at ease,
It had but made us pine the more. The abstract joy,
The half-read wisdom of daemonic images,
Suffice the ageing man as once the growing boy.

1923

The Tower (1925)

I

What shall I do with this absurdity—
O heart, O troubled heart—this caricature,
Decrepit age that has been tied to me
As to a dog's tail?
                              Never had I more
Excited, passionate, fantastical
Imagination, nor an ear and eye
That more expected the impossible—
No, not in boyhood when with rod and fly,
Or the humbler worm, I climbed Ben Bulben's back*
And had the livelong summer day to spend.
It seems that I must bid the Muse go pack,
Choose Plato and Plotinus* for a friend
Until imagination, ear and eye,
Can be content with argument and deal
In abstract things; or be derided by
A sort of battered kettle at the heel.

II

I pace upon the battlements and stare
On the foundations of a house, or where
Tree, like a sooty finger, starts from the earth;
And send imagination forth
Under the day's declining beam, and call
Images and memories
From ruin or from ancient trees,
For I would ask a question of them all.

Beyond that ridge lived Mrs French, and once
When every silver candlestick or sconce
Lit up the dark mahogany and the wine,
A serving-man, that could divine
That most respected lady's every wish,
Ran and with the garden shears
Clipped an insolent farmer's ears
And brought them in a little covered dish.

Some few remembered still when I was young
A peasant girl commended by a song,
Who'd lived somewhere upon that rocky place,
And praised the colour of her face,
And had the greater joy in praising her,
Remembering that, if walked she there,
Farmers jostled at the fair
So great a glory did the song confer.

And certain men, being maddened by those rhymes,
Or else by toasting her a score of times,
Rose from the table and declared it right
To test their fancy by their sight;
But they mistook the brightness of the moon
For the prosaic light of day—
Music had driven their wits astray—
And one was drowned in the great bog of Cloone.*

Strange, but the man who made the song was blind;*
Yet, now I have considered it, I find
That nothing strange; the tragedy began
With Homer that was a blind man,
And Helen has all living hearts betrayed.*
O may the moon and sunlight seem
One inextricable beam,
For if I triumph I must make men mad.

And I myself created Hanrahan*
And drove him drunk or sober through the dawn
From somewhere in the neighbouring cottages.
Caught by an old man's juggleries
He stumbled, tumbled, fumbled to and fro
And had but broken knees for hire
And horrible splendour of desire;
I thought it all out twenty years ago:

Good fellows shuffled cards in an old bawn;
And when that ancient ruffian's turn was on
He so bewitched the cards under his thumb

That all but the one card became
A pack of hounds and not a pack of cards,
And that he changed into a hare.
Hanrahan rose in frenzy there
And followed up those baying creatures towards—

O towards I have forgotten what—enough!
I must recall a man that neither love
Nor music nor an enemy's clipped ear
Could, he was so harried, cheer;
A figure that has grown so fabulous
There's not a neighbour left to say
When he finished his dog's day:
An ancient bankrupt master of this house.

Before that ruin came, for centuries,
Rough men-at-arms, cross-gartered to the knees
Or shod in iron, climbed the narrow stairs,
And certain men-at-arms there were
Whose images, in the Great Memory* stored,
Come with loud cry and panting breast
To break upon a sleeper's rest
While their great wooden dice beat on the board.

As I would question all, come all who can;
Come old, necessitous, half-mounted man;
And bring beauty's blind rambling celebrant;
The red man the juggler sent
Through God-forsaken meadows; Mrs French,
Gifted with so fine an ear;
The man drowned in a bog's mire,
When mocking muses chose the country wench.

Did all old men and women, rich and poor,
Who trod upon these rocks or passed this door,
Whether in public or in secret rage
As I do now against old age?
But I have found an answer in those eyes
That are impatient to be gone;

Go therefore; but leave Hanrahan,
For I need all his mighty memories.

Old lecher with a love on every wind,
Bring up out of that deep considering mind
All that you have discovered in the grave,
For it is certain that you have
Reckoned up every unforeknown, unseeing
Plunge, lured by a softening eye,
Or by a touch or a sigh,
Into the labyrinth of another's being;

Does the imagination dwell the most
Upon a woman won or woman lost?
If on the lost, admit you turned aside
From a great labyrinth out of pride,
Cowardice, some silly over-subtle thought
Or anything called conscience once;
And that if memory recur, the sun's
Under eclipse and the day blotted out.

III

It is time that I wrote my will;
I choose upstanding men
That climb the streams until
The fountain leap, and at dawn
Drop their cast at the side
Of dripping stone; I declare
They shall inherit my pride,
The pride of people that were
Bound neither to Cause nor to State,
Neither to slaves that were spat on,
Nor to the tyrants that spat,
The people of Burke and of Grattan*
That gave, though free to refuse—
Pride, like that of the morn,
When the headlong light is loose,
Or that of the fabulous horn,*
Or that of the sudden shower

When all streams are dry,
Or that of the hour
When the swan must fix his eye
Upon a fading gleam,
Float out upon a long
Last reach of glittering stream
And there sing his last song.
And I declare my faith:
I mock Plotinus' thought
And cry in Plato's teeth,
Death and life were not
Till man made up the whole,
Made lock, stock and barrel
Out of his bitter soul,
Aye, sun and moon and star, all,
And further add to that
That, being dead, we rise,
Dream and so create
Translunar Paradise.
I have prepared my peace
With learned Italian things
And the proud stones of Greece,
Poet's imaginings
And memories of love,
Memories of the words of women,
All those things whereof
Man makes a superhuman
Mirror-resembling dream.

As at the loophole there
The daws* chatter and scream,
And drop twigs layer upon layer.
When they have mounted up,
The mother bird will rest
On their hollow top,
And so warm her wild nest.

I leave both faith and pride
To young upstanding men

Climbing the mountain side,
That under bursting dawn
They may drop a fly;
Being of that metal made
Till it was broken by
This sedentary trade.

Now shall I make my soul,
Compelling it to study
In a learned school
Till the wreck of body,
Slow decay of blood,
Testy delirium
Or dull decrepitude,
Or what worse evil come—
The death of friends, or death
Of every brilliant eye
That made a catch in the breath—
Seem but the clouds of the sky
When the horizon fades;
Or a bird's sleepy cry
Among the deepening shades.

Sailing to Byzantium (1926)

I

That is no country* for old men. The young
In one another's arms, birds in the trees,
—Those dying generations—at their song,
The salmon-falls, the mackerel-crowded seas,
Fish, flesh, or fowl, commend all summer long
Whatever is begotten, born, and dies.
Caught in that sensual music all neglect
Monuments of unageing intellect.

II

An aged man is but a paltry thing,
A tattered coat upon a stick, unless

Soul clap its hands and sing, and louder sing
For every tatter in its mortal dress,
Nor is there singing school but studying
Monuments of its own magnificence;
And therefore I have sailed the seas and come
To the holy city of Byzantium.

III

O sages standing in God's holy fire
As in the gold mosaic of a wall,*
Come from the holy fire, perne in a gyre,*
And be the singing-masters of my soul.
Consume my heart away; sick with desire
And fastened to a dying animal
It knows not what it is; and gather me
Into the artifice of eternity.

IV

Once out of nature I shall never take
My bodily form from any natural thing,
But such a form as Grecian goldsmiths make
Of hammered gold and gold enamelling
To keep a drowsy Emperor awake;
Or set upon a golden bough* to sing
To lords and ladies of Byzantium
Of what is past, or passing, or to come.

The Circus Animals' Desertion (1937–1938)

I

I sought a theme and sought for it in vain,
I sought it daily for six weeks or so.
Maybe at last being but a broken man
I must be satisfied with my heart, although
Winter and summer till old age began
My circus animals were all on show,
Those stilted boys, that burnished chariot,
Lion and woman and the Lord knows what.

II

What can I but enumerate old themes,
First that sea-rider Oisin led by the nose
Through three enchanted islands, allegorical dreams,
Vain gaiety, vain battle, vain repose,
Themes of the embittered heart, or so it seems,
That might adorn old songs or courtly shows;
But what cared I that set him on to ride,
I, starved for the bosom of his fairy bride.*

And then a counter-truth filled out its play,
'The Countess Cathleen'* was the name I gave it,
She, pity-crazed, had given her soul away
But masterful Heaven had intervened to save it.
I thought my dear* must her own soul destroy
So did fanaticism and hate enslave it,
And this brought forth a dream and soon enough
This dream itself had all my thought and love.

And when the Fool and Blind Man stole the bread
Cuchulain fought the ungovernable sea;*
Heart mysteries there, and yet when all is said
It was the dream itself enchanted me:
Character isolated by a deed
To engross the present and dominate memory.
Players and painted stage took all my love
And not those things that they were emblems of.

III

Those masterful images because complete
Grew in pure mind but out of what began?
A mound of refuse or the sweepings of a street,
Old kettles, old bottles, and a broken can,
Old iron, old bones, old rags, that raving slut
Who keeps the till. Now that my ladder's gone
I must lie down where all the ladders start
In the foul rag and bone shop of the heart.

ETHNA CARBERY
(1866–1902)

The Love-Talker (1902)

I met the Love-Talker one eve in the glen,
He was handsomer than any of our handsome young men,
His eyes were blacker than the sloe, his voice sweeter far
Than the crooning of old Kevin's pipes beyond in Coolnagar.

I was bound for the milking with a heart fair and free—
My grief! my grief! that bitter hour drained the life from me;
I thought him human lover, though his lips on mine were cold,
And the breath of death blew keen on me within his hold.

I know not what way he came, no shadow fell behind,
But all the sighing rushes swayed beneath a fairy wind;
The thrush ceased its singing, a mist crept about,
We two clung together—with the world shut out.

Beyond the ghostly mist I could hear my cattle low,
The little cow from Ballina, clean as driven snow,
The dun cow from Kerry, the roan from Inisheer,
Oh, pitiful their calling—and his whispers in my ear!

His eyes were a fire; his words were a snare;
I cried my mother's name, but no help was there;
I made the blessed Sign: then he gave a dreary moan,
A wisp of cloud went floating by, and I stood alone.

Running ever thro' my head is an old-time rune—
'Who meets the Love-Talker must weave her shroud soon.'
My mother's face is furrowed with the salt tears that fall,
But the kind eyes of my father are the saddest sight of all.

I have spun the fleecy lint and now my wheel is still,
The linen length is woven for my shroud fine and chill,

I shall stretch me on the bed where a happy maid I lay—
Pray for the soul of Máire Óg at dawning of the day!

The Brown Wind of Connaught (1902)

The brown wind of Connaught—
  Across the bogland blown,
(*The brown wind of Connaught*),
  Turns my heart to a stone;
For it cries my name at twilight,
  And cries it at the noon—
O, Mairgread Bán! O, Mairgread Bán!
  Just like a fairy tune.

The brown wind of Connaught,
  When Dermot came to woo,
(*The brown wind of Connaught*),
  It heard his whispers too;
And while my wheel goes whirring,
  It taps on my window-pane,
Till I open wide to the Dead outside,
  And the sea-salt misty rain.

The brown wind of Connaught
  With women wailed one day
(*The brown wind of Connaught*),
  For a wreck in Galway Bay;
And many the dark-faced fishers
  That gathered their nets in fear,
But one sank straight to the Ghostly Gate—
  And he was my Dermot Dear.

The brown wind of Connaught
  Still keening in the dawn,
(*The brown wind of Connaught*),
  For my true love long gone.

Oh, cold green wave of danger,
   Drift him a restful sleep
O'er his young black head on its lowly bed,
   While his weary wake I keep.

Rody McCorley (1902)

Ho! see the fleet-foot hosts of men
Who speed with faces wan,
From farmstead and from fisher's cot
Upon the banks of Bann!*
They come with vengeance in their eyes—
Too late, too late are they—
For Rody McCorley goes to die
On the Bridge of Toome to-day.

Oh Ireland, Mother Ireland,
You love them still the best,
The fearless brave who fighting fall
Upon your hapless breast;
But never a one of all your dead
More bravely fell in fray,
Than he who marches to his fate
On the Bridge of Toome to-day.

Up the narrow street he stepped,
Smiling and proud and young;
About the hemp-rope on his neck
The golden ringlets clung.
There's never a tear in the blue, blue eyes,
Both glad and bright are they—
As Rody McCorley goes to die
On the Bridge of Toome to-day.

Ah! When he last stepped up that street,
His shining pike in hand,
Behind him marched in grim array
A stalwart earnest band!

For Antrim town! for Antrim town!
He led them to the fray—
And Rody McCorley goes to die
On the Bridge of Toome to-day.

The gray coat and its sash of green*
Were brave and stainless then;
A banner flashed beneath the sun
Over the marching men—
The coat hath many a rent this noon,
The sash is torn away,
And Rody McCorley goes to die
On the Bridge of Toome to-day.

Oh, how his pike flashed to the sun!
Then found a foeman's heart!
Through furious fight, and heavy odds,
He bore a true man's part;
And many a red-coat bit the dust
Before his keen pike-play—
But Rody McCorley goes to die
On the Bridge of Toome to-day.

Because he loved the Motherland,
Because he loved the Green,
He goes to meet the martyr's fate
With proud and joyous mien,
True to the last, true to the last,
He treads the upward way—
Young Rody McCorley goes to die
On the Bridge of Toome to-day.

The Passing of the Gael (1902)

They are going, going, going from the valleys and the hills,
They are leaving far behind them heathery moor and mountain rills,
All the wealth of hawthorn hedges where the brown thrush sways
    and trills.

They are going, shy-eyed colleens and lads so straight and tall,
From the purple peaks of Kerry, from the crags of wild Imaal,
From the greening plains of Mayo and the glens of Donegal.

They are leaving pleasant places, shores with snowy sands
    outspread;
Blue and lonely lakes a-stirring when the wind stirs overhead;
Tender living hearts that love them, and the graves of kindred dead.

They shall carry to the distant land a tear-drop in the eye
And some shall go uncomforted—their days an endless sigh
For Kathaleen Ní Houlihan's sad face, until they die.

Oh, Kathaleen Ní Houlihan, your road's a thorny way,
And 'tis a faithful soul would walk the flints with you for aye,
Would walk the sharp and cruel flints until his locks grew gray.

So some must wander to the East, and some must wander West;
Some seek the white wastes of the North, and some a Southern
    nest;
Yet never shall they sleep so sweet as on your mother breast.

The whip of hunger scourged them from the glens and quiet
    moors,
But there's a hunger of the heart that plenty never cures;
And they shall pine to walk again the rough road that is yours.

Within the city streets, hot, hurried, full of care,
A sudden dream shall bring them a whiff of Irish air—
A cool air, faintly-scented, blown soft from otherwhere.

Oh, the cabins long-deserted!—Olden memories awake—
Oh, the pleasant, pleasant places!—Hush! the blackbird in the brake!
Oh, the dear and kindly voices!—Now their hearts are fain to ache.

They may win a golden store—sure the whins were golden too;
And no foreign skies hold beauty like the rainy skies they knew;
Nor any night-wind cool the brow as did the foggy dew.

They are going, going, going, and we cannot bid them stay;
The fields are now the strangers' where the strangers' cattle stray.
Oh! Kathaleen Ní Houlihan, your way's a thorny way!

Beannacht Leat (1902)

Beannacht leat!

      I hold your hand in mine, I say
      The parting words this parting day—
      And if a sob be stifled, Dear,
      I pray you turn aside, nor hear—
      I would be brave, and yet, and yet,
      Can we two sunder without regret?

Beannacht leat!

      May every vagrant wind a-stir
      Between us be a messenger,
      Each falling wild-rose petal blow
      A haunting perfume where you go,
      And all the brown birds in the blue
      Sing memories of me to you.

Beannacht leat!

      Thank God! 'tis not a long good-bye
      We give each other, you and I—
      Sure in my heart the hope is fain
      To whisper, You will come again
      With the kind eyes, the same kind smile—
      Then for a little lonely while,
                         Beannacht leat!

LIONEL JOHNSON
(1867–1902)

By the Statue of King Charles at Charing Cross (1889)

Sombre and rich, the skies;
Great glooms, and starry plains.
Gently the night wind sighs;
Else a vast silence reigns.

The splendid silence clings
Around me: and around
The saddest of all kings
Crowned, and again discrowned.

Comely and calm, he rides
Hard by his own Whitehall:
Only the night wind glides:
No crowds, nor rebels, brawl.

Gone, too, his Court: and yet,
The stars his courtiers are:
Stars in their stations set;
And every wandering star.

Alone he rides, alone,
The fair and fatal king:
Dark night is all his own,
That strange and solemn thing.

Which are more full of fate:
The stars; or those sad eyes?
Which are more still and great:
Those brows; or the dark skies?

Although his whole heart yearn
In passionate tragedy:

Never was face so stern
With sweet austerity.

Vanquished in life, his death
By beauty made amends:
The passing of his breath
Won his defeated ends.

Brief life, and hapless? Nay:
Through death, life grew sublime.
Speak after sentence? Yea:*
And to the end of time.

Armoured he rides, his head
Bare to the stars of doom:
He triumphs now, the dead,
Beholding London's gloom.

Our wearier spirit faints,
Vexed in the world's employ:
His soul was of the saints;
And art to him was joy.

King, tired in fires of woe!
Men hunger for thy grace:
And through the night I go,
Loving thy mournful face.

Yet, when the city sleeps;
When all the cries are still:
The stars and heavenly deeps
Work out a perfect will.

Mystic and Cavalier (1889)

Go from me: I am one of those, who fall.
What! hath no cold wind swept your heart at all,
In my sad company? Before the end,
    Go from me, dear my friend!

Yours are the victories of light: your feet
Rest from good toil, where rest is brave and sweet.
But after warfare in a mourning gloom,
    I rest in clouds of doom.

Have you not read so, looking in these eyes?
Is it the common light of the pure skies,
Lights up their shadowy depths? The end is set:
    Though the end be not yet.

When gracious music stirs, and all is bright,
And beauty triumphs through a courtly night;
When I too joy, a man like other men:
    Yet, am I like them, then?

And in the battle, when the horsemen sweep
Against a thousand deaths, and fall on sleep:
Who ever sought that sudden calm, if I
    Sought not? Yet, could not die.

Seek with thine eyes to pierce this crystal sphere:
Canst read a fate there, prosperous and clear?
Only the mists, only the weeping clouds:
    Dimness, and airy shrouds.

Beneath, what angels are at work? What powers
Prepare the secret of the fatal hours?
See! the mists tremble, and the clouds are stirred:
    When comes the calling word?

The clouds are breaking from the crystal ball,
Breaking and clearing: and I look to fall.
When the cold winds and airs of portent sweep,
    My spirit may have sleep.

O rich and sounding voices of the air!
Interpreters and prophets of despair:
Priests of a fearful sacrament! I come,
    To make with you mine home.

The Dark Angel (1893)

Dark Angel, with thine aching lust
To rid the world of penitence:
Malicious Angel, who still dost
My soul such subtile violence!

Because of thee, no thought, no thing,
Abides for me undesecrate:
Dark Angel, ever on the wing,
Who never reachest me too late!

When music sounds, then changest thou
Its silvery to a sultry fire:
Nor will thine envious heart allow
Delight untortured by desire.

Through thee, the gracious Muses turn
To Furies,* O mine Enemy!
And all the things of beauty burn
With flames of evil ecstasy.

Because of thee, the land of dreams
Becomes a gathering place of fears:
Until tormented slumber seems
One vehemence of useless tears.

When sunlight glows upon the flowers,
Or ripples down the dancing sea:
Thou, with thy troop of passionate powers,
Beleaguerest, bewilderest, me.

Within the breath of autumn woods,
Within the winter silences:
Thy venomous spirit stirs and broods,
O Master of impieties!

The ardour of red flame is thine,
And thine the steely soul of ice:

Thou poisonest the fair design
Of nature, with unfair device.

Apples of ashes,* golden bright;
Waters of bitterness, how sweet!
O banquet of a foul delight,
Prepared by thee, dark Paraclete!*

Thou art the whisper in the gloom,
The hinting tone, the haunting laugh:
Thou art the adorner of my tomb,
The minstrel of mine epitaph.

I fight thee, in the Holy Name!
Yet, what thou dost, is what God saith:
Temper! should I escape thy flame,
Thou wilt have helped my soul from Death:

The second Death, that never dies,
That cannot die, when time is dead:
Live Death, wherein the lost soul cries,
Eternally uncomforted.

Dark Angel, with thine aching lust!
Of two defeats, of two despairs:
Less dread, a change to drifting dust,
Than thine eternity of cares.

Do what thou wilt, thou shalt not so,
Dark Angel! triumph over me:
Lonely, unto the Lone I go;
Divine, to the Divinity.

Ninety-Eight (1893)

Who fears to speak of ninety-eight?
He, who despairs of Ireland still:

Whose paltry soul finds nothing great
In honest failure: he, whose will,
Feeble and faint in days of gloom,
Takes old defeat for final doom.

Who fears to speak of ninety-eight?
The man, who fears to speak of death:
Who clings and clasps the knees of fate,
And whimpers with his latest breath:
Who hugs his comfort to his heart,
And dares not play a Christian's part.

Who fears to speak of ninety-eight?
The renegade, who sells his trust:
Whose love has rottened into hate,
Whose hopes have withered into dust:
He, who denies, and deems it mad,
The faith his nobler boyhood had.

Who fears to speak of ninety-eight?
The enemy of Ireland fears!
For Ireland undegenerate
Keeps yet the spirit of old years:
He sees, in visions of the night,
A nation arming for the right.

Who fears to speak of ninety-eight?
Not he, who hates a poisonous peace:
For, while the days of triumph wait,
And till the days of sorrow cease,
He, with the Lord of Hosts his friend,
Will fight for Ireland to the end.

Let sword cross sword, or thought meet thought:
One fire of battle thrills them both.
Deliverance only can be wrought
By warfare without stay or sloth:
And by your prayers at Heaven's high gate.
True hearts, that beat in Ninety-Eight.

Parnell (1893)

The wail of Irish winds,
The cry of Irish seas:
Eternal sorrow finds
Eternal voice in these.

I cannot praise our dead,
Whom Ireland weeps so well:
Her morning light, that fled;
Her morning star, that fell.

She of the mournful eyes
Waits, and no dark clouds break:
Waits, and her strong son lies
Dead, for her holy sake.

Her heart is sorrow's home,
And hath been from of old:
An host of griefs hath come,
To make that heart their fold.

Ah, the sad autumn day,
When the last sad troop came
Swift down the ancient way,
Keening a chieftain's name!

Gray hope was there, and dread;
Anger, and love in tears:
They mourned the dear and dead,
Dirge of the ruined years.

Home to her heart she drew
The mourning company:
Old sorrows met the new,
In sad fraternity.

A mother, and forget!
Nay! all her children's fate
Ireland remembers yet,
With love insatiate.

She hears the heavy bells:
Hears, and with passionate breath
Eternally she tells
A rosary of death.

Faithful and true is she,
The mother of us all:
Faithful and true! may we
Fail her not, though we fall.

Her son, our brother, lies
Dead, for her holy sake:
But from the dead arise
Voices, that bid us wake.

Not his, to hail the dawn:
His but the herald's part.
Be ours to see withdrawn
Night from our mother's heart.

GEORGE RUSSELL (AE)
(1867–1935)

Carrowmore (1913)

It's a lonely road through bogland to the lake at
        Carrowmore,
And a sleeper there lies dreaming where the water laps
        the shore;
Though the moth-wings of the twilight in their purples are
        unfurled,
Yet his sleep is filled with music by the masters of the world.

There's a hand as white as silver that is fondling with his hair.
There are glimmering feet of sunshine that are dancing by him
    there:
And half-open lips of faery that were dyed a faery red
In their revels where the Hazel Tree its holy clusters shed.

'Come away,' the red lips whisper, 'all the world is weary now;
'Tis the twilight of the ages and it's time to quit the plough.
Oh, the very sunlight's weary ere it lightens up the dew,
And its gold is changed and faded before it falls to you.

'Though your colleen's* heart be tender, a tenderer heart is near.
What's the starlight in her glances when the stars are shining clear?
Who would kiss the fading shadow when the flower-face glows
    above?
'Tis the beauty of all Beauty that is calling for your love.'

Oh, the great gates of the mountain have opened once again,
And the sound of song and dancing falls upon the ears of men,
And the Land of Youth lies gleaming, flushed with rainbow light and
    mirth,
And the old enchantment lingers in the honey-heart of earth.

EVA GORE-BOOTH
(1870–1926)

The Little Waves of Breffny (1904)

The grand road from the mountain goes shining to the sea,
And there is traffic in it and many a horse and cart,
But the little roads of Cloonagh are dearer far to me,
And the little roads of Cloonagh go rambling through my heart.

A great storm from the ocean goes shouting o'er the hill,
And there is glory in it and terror on the wind,
But the haunted air of twilight is very strange and still,
And the little winds of twilight are dearer to my mind.

The great waves of the Atlantic sweep storming on their way,
Shining green and silver with the hidden herring shoal,
But the Little Waves of Breffny have drenched my heart
    in spray,
And the Little Waves of Breffny go stumbling through
    my soul.

The Land to a Landlord (1904)

You hug to your soul a handful of dust,
And you think the round world your sacred trust—
But the sun shines, and the wind blows,
And nobody cares and nobody knows.

O the bracken waves and the foxgloves flame,
And none of them ever has heard your name—
Near and dear is the curlew's cry,
You are merely a stranger* passing by.

Sheer up through the shadows the mountain towers
And dreams wander free in this world of ours,—
Though you may turn the grass to gold,
The twilight has left you out in the cold.

Though you are king of the rose and the wheat,
Not for you, not for you is the bog-myrtle sweet,
Though you are lord of the long grass,
The hemlock bows not her head as you pass.

The poppies would flutter amongst the corn
Even if you had never been born,
With your will or without your will
The ragweed can wander over the hill.

Down there in the bog where the plovers call
You are but an outcast after all,
Over your head the sky gleams blue—
Not a cloud or a star belongs to you.

Women's Rights (1906)

Down by Glencar* Waterfall
There's no winter left at all.

Every little flower that blows
Cold and darkness overthrows.

Every little thrush that sings
Quells the wild air with brave wings.

Every little stream that runs
Holds the light of brighter suns.

But where men in office sit
Winter holds the human wit.

In the dark and dreary town
Summer's green is trampled down.

Frozen, frozen everywhere
Are the springs of thought and prayer.

Rise with us and let us go
To where the living waters flow.

Oh, whatever men may say
Ours is the wide and open way.

Oh, whatever men may dream
We have the blue air and the stream.

Men have got their towers and walls,
We have cliffs and waterfalls.

Oh, whatever men may do
Ours is the gold air and the blue.

Men have got their pomp and pride—
All the green world is on our side.

J. M. SYNGE
(1871–1909)

Prelude (1909)

Still south I went and west and south again,
Through Wicklow* from the morning till the night,
And far from cities, and the sites of men,
Lived with the sunshine and the moon's delight.

I knew the stars, the flowers, and the birds,
The grey and wintry sides of many glens,
And did but half remember human words,
In converse with the mountains, moors, and fens.

Beg-Innish (1909)

Bring Kateen-Beag and Maurya Jude
To dance in Beg-Innish,
And when the lads (they're in Dunquin)
Have sold their crabs and fish,
Wave fawney shawls and call them in,
And call the little girls who spin,
And seven weavers from Dunquin,
To dance in Beg-Innish.

I'll play you jigs, and Maurice Kean,
Where nets are laid to dry,
I've silken strings would draw a dance
From girls are lame or shy;
Four strings I've brought from Spain and France
To make your long men skip and prance,
Till stars look out to see the dance
Where nets are laid to dry.

We'll have no priest or peeler* in
To dance at Beg-Innish;
But we'll have drink from M'riarty Jim
Rowed round while gannets fish,
A keg with porter* to the brim,
That every lad may have his whim,
Till we up with sails with M'riarty Jim
And sail from Beg-Innish.

To the Oaks of Glencree (1909)

My arms are round you, and I lean
Against you, while the lark
Sings over us, and golden lights and green
Shadows are on your bark.

There'll come a season when you'll stretch
Black boards to cover me;
Then in Mount Jerome I'll lie, poor wretch,
With worms eternally.

A Question (1909)

I asked if I got sick and died, would you
With my black funeral go walking too,
If you'd stand close to hear them talk or pray
While I'm let down in that steep bank of clay.

And, No, you said, for if you saw a crew
Of living idiots pressing round that new
Oak coffin—they alive, I dead beneath
That board—you'd rave and rend them with your teeth.

In Glencullen (1909)

Thrush, linnet, stare, and wren,
Brown lark beside the sun,
Take thought of kestrel, sparrow-hawk,
Birdlime and roving gun.

You great-great-grandchildren
Of birds I've listened to,
I think I robbed your ancestors
When I was young as you.

OLIVER ST JOHN GOGARTY
(1878–1957)

To the Liffey with the Swans (1923)

Keep you these calm and lovely things,
    And float them on your clearest water;
For one would not disgrace a King's
    Transformed beloved and buoyant daughter.

And with her goes this sprightly swan,
    A bird of more than royal feather,
With alban* beauty clothed upon:
    O keep them fair and well together!

As fair as was that doubled Bird,*
    By love of Leda so besotten,
That she was all with wonder stirred,
    And the Twin Sportsmen* were begotten!

THOMAS MACDONAGH
(1878–1916)

John-John (1910)

I dreamt last night of you, John-John,
    And thought you called to me;
And when I woke this morning, John,
    Yourself I hoped to see;

But I was all alone, John-John,
  Though still I heard your call:
I put my boots and bonnet on,
  And took my Sunday shawl,
And went, full sure to find you, John,
                To Nenagh fair.

The fair was just the same as then,
  Five years ago to-day,
When first you left the thimble men
  And came with me away;
For there again were thimble men
  And shooting galleries,
And card-trick men and Maggie men
  Of all sorts and degrees—
But not a sight of you, John-John,
                Was anywhere.

I turned my face to home again,
  And called myself a fool
To think you'd leave the thimble men
  And live again by rule,
And go to Mass and keep the fast
  And till the little patch:
My wish to have you home was past
  Before I raised the latch
And pushed the door and saw you, John,
                Sitting down there.

How cool you came in here, begad,
  As if you owned the place!
But rest yourself there now, my lad,
  'Tis good to see your face;
My dream is out, and now by it
  I think I know my mind:
At six o'clock this house you'll quit,
  And leave no grief behind;—

But until six o'clock, John-John,
    My bit you'll share.

The neighbours' shame of me began
    When first I brought you in:
To wed and keep a tinker man
    They thought a kind of sin;
But now this three year since you're gone
    'Tis pity me they do,
And that I'd rather have, John-John,
    Than that they'd pity you.
Pity for me and you, John-John,
              I could not bear.

Oh, you're my husband right enough,
    But what's the good of that?
You know you never were the stuff
    To be the cottage cat,
To watch the fire and hear me lock
    The door and put out Shep—
But there now, it is six o'clock
    And time for you to step.
God bless and keep you far, John-John!
         And that's my prayer.

Of a Poet Patriot (1913)

His songs were a little phrase
    Of eternal song,
Drowned in the harping of lays
    More loud and long.

His deed was a single word,
    Called out alone
In a night when no echo stirred
    To laughter or moan.

But his songs new souls shall thrill,
    The loud harps dumb,

And his deed the echoes fill
When the dawn is come.

The Yellow Bittern (1913)

(From the Irish)

The yellow bittern that never broke out
  In a drinking bout, might as well have drunk;
His bones are thrown on a naked stone
  Where he lived alone like a hermit monk.
O yellow bittern! I pity your lot,
  Though they say that a sot like myself is curst—
I was sober a while, but I'll drink and be wise
  For I fear I should die in the end of thirst.

It's not for the common birds that I'd mourn,
  The black-bird, the corn-crake, or the crane,
But for the bittern that's shy and apart
  And drinks in the marsh from the lone bog-drain.
Oh! if I had known you were near your death,
  While my breath held out I'd have run to you,
Till a splash from the Lake of the Son of the Bird
  Your soul would have stirred and waked anew.

My darling told me to drink no more
  Or my life would be o'er in a little short while;
But I told her 'tis drink gives me health and strength
  And will lengthen my road by many a mile.
You see how the bird of the long smooth neck
  Could get his death from the thirst at last—
Come, son of my soul, and drain your cup,
  You'll get no sup when your life is past.

In a wintering island by Constantine's halls*
  A bittern calls from a wineless place,
And tells me that hither he cannot come
  Till the summer is here and the sunny days.

When he crosses the stream there and wings o'er the sea
   Then a fear comes to me he may fail in his flight—
Well, the milk and the ale are drunk every drop,
   And a dram won't stop our thirst this night.

The Night Hunt (1913)

In the morning, in the dark,
When the stars begin to blunt,
By the wall of Barna Park
Dogs I heard and saw them hunt.
All the parish dogs were there,
All the dogs for miles around,
Teeming up behind a hare,
In the dark, without a sound.

How I heard I scarce can tell—
'Twas a patter in the grass—
And I did not see them well
Come across the dark and pass;
Yet I saw them and I knew
Spearman's dog and Spellman's dog
And, beside my own dog too,
Leamy's from the Island Bog.

In the morning when the sun
Burnished all the green to gorse,
I went out to take a run
Round the bog upon my horse;
And my dog that had been sleeping
In the heat beside the door
Left his yawning and went leaping
On a hundred yards before.

Through the village street we passed—
Not a dog there raised a snout—
Through the street and out at last
On the white bog road and out

Over Barna Park full pace,
Over to the Silver Stream,
Horse and dog in happy race,
Rider between thought and dream.

By the stream at Leamy's house,
Lay a dog—my pace I curbed—
But our coming did not rouse
Him from drowsing undisturbed;
And my dog, as unaware
Of the other, dropped beside
And went running by me there
With my horse's slackened stride.

Yet by something, by a twitch
Of the sleeper's eye, a look
From the runner, something which
Little chords of feeling shook,
I was conscious that a thought
Shuddered through the silent deep
Of a secret—I had caught
Something I had known in sleep.

JOSEPH CAMPBELL
(1879–1944)

My Lagan Love (1904)

Where Lagan stream sings lullaby,
There blows a lily fair;
The twilight gleam is in her eye,
The night is on her hair.
But like a love-sick leanannsidhe,*
She has my heart in thrall.
No life I own nor liberty,
For love is lord of all.

And often when the beetle's horn
Has lulled the eve to sleep;
I steal up to her sheiling lorn
And through the dooring peep;
There by the cricket's singing-stone*
She spares* the bogwood fire,
And sings in sad sweet undertone,
The song of heart's desire.

SEUMAS O'SULLIVAN
(1879–1958)

The Lamplighter (1929)

Here to the leisured side of life,
Remote from traffic, free from strife,
A cul-de-sac, a sanctuary
Where old quaint customs creep to die
And only ancient memories stir,
At evening comes the lamplighter;
With measured steps, without a sound,
He treads the unalterable round,
Soundlessly touching one by one
The waiting posts that stand to take
The faint blue bubbles in his wake;
And when the night begins to wane
He comes to take them back again,
Before the chilly dawn can blight
The delicate frail buds of light.

Geese (1939)

My blessing on the gentle geese,
My blessing, and a lasting peace,
For on a day in fierce July
When not a cloud was in the sky,

Upon a day without a breeze
They looked like snow beneath the trees.

PATRICK PEARSE
(1879–1916)

A Rann I Made (1917)

A rann I made within my heart
To the rider, to the high king,
A rann I made to my love,
To the king of kings, ancient death.

Brighter to me than light of day
The dark of thy house, tho' black clay;
Sweeter to me than the music of trumpets
The quiet of thy house and its eternal silence.

I am Ireland (1917)

I am Ireland:
I am older than the Old Woman of Beare.

Great my glory:
I that bore Cuchulainn* the valiant.

Great my shame:
My own children that sold their mother.

I am Ireland:
I am lonelier than the Old Woman of Beare.

On the Strand of Howth (1917)

On the strand of Howth
Breaks a sounding wave;

A lone sea-gull screams
Above the bay.

In the middle of the meadow
Beside Glasnevin
The corncrake speaks
All night long.

There is minstrelsy of birds
In Glenasmole,
The blackbird and thrush
Chanting music.

There is shining of sun
On the side of Slieverua,
And the wind blowing
Down over its brow.

On the harbour of Dunleary
Are boat and ship
With sails set
Ploughing the waves.

Here in Ireland,
Am I, my brother,
And you far from me
In gallant Paris,

I beholding
Hill and harbour,
The strand of Howth
And Slieverua's side,

And you victorious
In mighty Paris
Of the limewhite palaces
And the surging hosts;

And what I ask
Of you, beloved,

Far away
Is to think at times

Of the corncrake's tune
Beside Glasnevin
In the middle of the meadow,
Speaking in the night;

Of the voice of the birds
In Glenasmole
Happily, with melody,
Chanting music;

Of the strand of Howth
Where a wave breaks,
And the harbour of Dunleary,
Where a ship rocks;

On the sun that shines
On the side of Slieverua,
And the wind that blows
Down over its brow.

The Mother (1915)

I do not grudge them: Lord, I do not grudge
My two strong sons that I have seen go out
To break their strength and die, they and a few,
In bloody protest for a glorious thing,
They shall be spoken of among their people,
The generations shall remember them,
And call them blessed;
But I will speak their names to my own heart
In the long nights;
The little names that were familiar once
Round my dead hearth.
Lord, thou art hard on mothers:
We suffer in their coming and their going;

And tho' I grudge them not, I weary, weary
Of the long sorrow—And yet I have my joy:
My sons were faithful, and they fought.

Christmas 1915 (1915)

O King that was born
To set bondsmen free,
In the coming battle,
Help the Gael!

The Wayfarer (1916)

The beauty of the world hath made me sad,
This beauty that will pass;
Sometimes my heart hath shaken with great joy
To see a leaping squirrel in a tree,
Or a red lady-bird upon a stalk,
Or little rabbits in a field at evening,
Lit by a slanting sun,
Or some green hill where shadows drifted by
Some quiet hill where mountainy man hath sown
And soon would reap; near to the gate of Heaven;
Or children with bare feet upon the sands
Of some ebbed sea, or playing on the streets
Of little towns in Connacht,
Things young and happy.
And then my heart hath told me:
These will pass,
Will pass and change, will die and be no more,
Things bright and green, things young and happy;
And I have gone upon my way
Sorrowful.

PADRAIC COLUM
(1881–1972)

She Moved Through the Fair (1916)

My young love said to me, 'My brothers won't mind,
And my parents won't slight you for your lack of kind.'
Then she stepped away from me, and this she did say,
'It will not be long, love, till our wedding day.'

She stepped away from me and she moved through the fair,
And fondly I watched her go here and go there,
Then she went her way homeward with one star awake,
As the swan in the evening moves over the lake.

The people were saying no two were e'er wed
But one had a sorrow that never was said,
And I smiled as she passed with her goods and her gear,
And that was the last that I saw of my dear.

I dreamt it last night that my young love came in,
So softly she entered, her feet made no din;
She came close beside me, and this she did say,
'It will not be long, love, till our wedding day.'

FRANCIS LEDWIDGE
(1891–1917)

A Twilight in Middle March (1914)

Within the oak a throb of pigeon wings
Fell silent, and grey twilight hushed the fold,
And spiders' hammocks swung on half-oped things
That shook like foreigners upon our cold.
A gipsy lit a fire and made a sound
Of moving tins, and from an oblong moon

The river seemed to gush across the ground
To the cracked metre of a marching tune.

And then three syllables of melody
Dropped from a blackbird's flute, and died apart
Far in the dewy dark. No more but three,
Yet sweeter music never touched a heart
Neath the blue domes of London. Flute and reed
Suggesting feelings of the solitude
When will was all the Delphi* I would heed,
Lost like a wind within a summer wood
From little knowledge where great sorrows brood.

June (1914)

Broom out the floor now, lay the fender by,
And plant this bee-sucked bough of woodbine there,
And let the window down. The butterfly
Floats in upon the sunbeam, and the fair
Tanned face of June, the nomad gipsy, laughs
Above her widespread wares, the while she tells
The farmers' fortunes in the fields, and quaffs
The water from the spider-peopled wells.

The hedges are all drowned in green grass seas,
And bobbing poppies flare like Elmo's light,*
While siren-like the pollen-stainèd bees
Drone in the clover depths. And up the height
The cuckoo's voice is hoarse and broke with joy.
And on the lowland crops the crows make raid,
Nor fear the clappers of the farmer's boy,
Who sleeps, like drunken Noah,* in the shade.

And loop this red rose in that hazel ring
That snares your little ear, for June is short
And we must joy in it and dance and sing,
And from her bounty draw her rosy worth.
Ay! soon the swallows will be flying south,
The wind wheel north to gather in the snow,

Even the roses spilt on youth's red mouth
Will soon blow down the road all roses go.

August (1914)

She'll come at dusky first of day,
White over yellow harvest's song.
Upon her dewy rainbow way
She shall be beautiful and strong.
The lidless eye of noon shall spray
Tan on her ankles in the hay,
Shall kiss her brown the whole day long.

I'll know her in the windrows, tall
Above the crickets of the hay.
I'll know her when her odd eyes fall,
One May-blue, one November-grey.
I'll watch her from the red barn wall
Take down her rusty scythe, and call,
And I will follow her away.

Thomas MacDonagh (1916)

He shall not hear the bittern cry
In the wild sky, where he is lain,
Nor voices of the sweeter birds
Above the wailing of the rain.

Nor shall he know when loud March blows
Through slanting snows her fanfare shrill,
Blowing to flame the golden cup
Of many an upset daffodil.

But when the Dark Cow leaves the moor,
And pastures poor with greedy weeds,
Perhaps he'll hear her low at morn
Lifting her horn in pleasant meads.

The Wedding Morning (1916)

Spread the feast, and let there be
Such music heard as best beseems
A king's son coming from the sea
To wed a maiden of the streams.

Poets, pale for long ago,
Bring sweet sounds from rock and flood,
You by echo's accent know
Where the water is and wood.

Harpers whom the moths of Time
Bent and wrinkled dusty brown,
Her chains are falling with a chime,
Sweet as bells in Heaven town.

But, harpers, leave your harps aside,
And, poets, leave awhile your dreams.
The storm has come upon the tide
And Cathleen weeps among her streams.

The Blackbirds (1916)

I heard the Poor Old Woman say:
'At break of day the fowler came,
And took my blackbirds from their songs
Who loved me well thro' shame and blame.

No more from lovely distances
Their songs shall bless me mile by mile,
Nor to white Ashbourne call me down
To wear my crown another while.

With bended flowers the angels mark
For the skylark the place they lie,
From there its little family
Shall dip their wings first in the sky.

And when the first surprise of flight
Sweet songs excite, from the far dawn
Shall there come blackbirds loud with love,
Sweet echoes of the singers gone.

But in the lonely hush of eve
Weeping I grieve the silent bills.'
I heard the Poor Old Woman say
In Derry of the little hills.

The Herons (1916)

As I was climbing Ardán Mór
From the shore of Sheelin lake
I met the herons coming down
Before the water's wake.

And they were talking in their flight
Of dreamy ways the herons go
When all the hills are withered up
Nor any waters flow.

F. R. HIGGINS
(1896–1941)

Father and Son (1923)

Only last week, walking the hushed fields
Of our most lovely Meath, now thinned by November,
I came to where the road from Laracor leads
To the Boyne river—that seemed more lake than river,
Stretched in uneasy light and stript of reeds.

And walking longside an old weir
Of my people's, where nothing stirs—only the shadowed
Leaden flight of a heron up the lean air—

I went unmanly with grief, knowing how my father,
Happy though captive in years, walked last with me there.

Yes, happy in Meath with me for a day
He walked, taking stock of herds hid in their own breathing;
And naming colts, gusty as wind, once steered by his hand,
Lightnings winked in the eyes that were half shy in greeting
Old friends—the wild blades, when he gallivanted the land.

For that proud, wayward man now my heart breaks—
Breaks for that man whose mind was a secret eyrie,
Whose kind hand was sole signet of his race,
Who curbed me, scorned my green ways, yet increasingly loved me
Till Death drew its grey blind down his face.

And yet I am pleased that even my reckless ways
Are living shades of his rich calms and passions—
Witnesses for him and for those faint namesakes
With whom now he is one, under yew branches,
Yes, one in a graven silence no bird breaks.

To My Blackthorn Stick (1923)

When sap ebbed low and your green days were over—
Hedging a gap to rugged land,
Bare skinned and straight you were; and there I broke you
To champion my right hand.

Well shod in bronze and lithe with hillside breeding,
Yet, like a snarl, you dogged my side,
Mailed in your tridents and flaunting out the fierceness
That bristled through your hide.

So armed as one, have we not shared each journey
On noiseless path or road of stone;
O exiled brother of the flowering sloe tree,
Your past ways are my own.

Lonesome, like me, and song-bred on Mount Nephin,
You, also, found that in your might
You broke in bloom before the time of leafing
And shocked a world with light.

But you grew shy,—eyed through by glowering twilights—
Sharing the still of night's grey brew,
Secret and shy, while things unseen were sighing
Their grass tunes under you.

Manured with earth's own sweat you stretched in saplings;
Seasoned, you cored your fruit with stone;
Then stript in fight, your strength came out of wrestling
All winds by winter blown.

I took that strength: my axe blow was your trumpet,
You rose from earth, god-cleaned and strong;
And here, as in green days you were the perch,
You're now the prop of song.

PATRICK KAVANAGH
(1904–1967)

To a Blackbird (1930)

O pagan poet you
And I are one
In this—we lose our god
At set of sun.

And we are kindred when
The hill wind shakes
Sweet song like blossoms on
The calm green lakes.

We dream while Earth's sad children
Go slowly by

Pleading for our conversion
With the Most High.

Shancoduff (1934)

My black hills have never seen the sun rising,
Eternally they look north towards Armagh.
Lot's wife would not be salt if she had been
Incurious as my black hills that are happy
When dawn whitens Glassdrummond chapel.

My hills hoard the bright shillings of March
While the sun searches in every pocket.
They are my Alps and I have climbed the Matterhorn
With a sheaf of hay for three perishing calves
In the field under the Big Forth of Rocksavage.

The sleety winds fondle the rushy beards of Shancoduff
While the cattle-drovers sheltering in the Featherna Bush
Look up and say: 'Who owns them hungry hills
That the water-hen and snipe must have forsaken?
A poet? Then by heavens he must be poor.'
I hear and is my heart not badly shaken?

Monaghan 1934

Inniskeen Road: July Evening (1935)

The bicycles go by in twos and threes—
There's a dance in Billy Brennan's* barn tonight,
And there's the half-talk code of mysteries
And the wink-and-elbow language of delight.
Half-past eight and there is not a spot
Upon a mile of road, no shadow thrown
That might turn out a man or woman, not
A footfall tapping secrecies of stone.

I have what every poet hates in spite
Of all the solemn talk of contemplation.
Oh, Alexander Selkirk* knew the plight
Of being king and government and nation.
A road, a mile of kingdom, I am king
Of banks and stones and every blooming thing.

JOHN HEWITT
(1907–1987)

To a Modern Irish Poet (1927)

You drowsed my senses by your misty kings,
   dream-drunken ladies languid as the noon,
until I deemed no other songbird sings,
   save nightingale in twilight to the moon.

You came with your strange, wistful, trembling verse,
   beguiled me for a while in quaint deceit;
and I forgot th'oppressor's blow and curse,
   the muffled tread of workless in the street.

A silver trumpet, or a golden thong,
   these are the harmonies loved of thy muse.
'Tis better done to beat from bitter wrong
   a flaming slogan's challenge, fit for use!

Easter Tuesday (1931)

I carefully let Easter pass this year
   Without a thought of Calvary's bare hill,
   being intent on bird and daffodil,
and April skies with one cold star and clear,
I watched the red-tipped daisies peep and peer
   out of the fresh thick grass, and skylarks fill
   the air with fluttered chorusing until
I felt myself a similar sonneteer.

But yesterday a man went up the street
   singing a rebel song of Easter Week.
      and the old unquiet woke within my head.
I saw again the blood bedabbled feet,
   and all the horror that I dared not speak,
      and knew that Christ and Connolly were dead.

Mourne Mountains (1937)

But these are not my hills, they are too high:
they have not been, since ice ground slowly over,
abased to any force beneath the sky;
they are too harsh for me to be their lover.
The broad stone winking with the flattened stream,
the sheer cliff barren and the timeless peak:
not even sharp against the sun's last gleam
can I find comfort in them I may speak:
for they are from a world beyond my reach,
not the warm human world of broken earth,
the hand-chipped flints along the gravel beach,
the tilted dolmen and the baked clay hearth.
I do not fear a bare land but a high:
the curlew-whistling moors have no affright:
the bog-brown trout stream twisting hurriedly
can flash no terror in the failing light.
But the cold summit harried by the rain,
smothered in cloud or bannered far with snow,
has all the high sublimities of pain
I leave for braver hearts than mine to know.

LOUIS MACNEICE
(1907–1963)

Belfast (1931)

The hard cold fire of the northerner
Frozen into his blood from the fire in his basalt*
Glares from behind the mica* of his eyes
And the salt carrion water* brings him wealth.

Down there at the end of the melancholy lough
Against the lurid sky over the stained water
Where hammers clang murderously on the girders
Like crucifixes the gantries stand.

And in the marble stores rubber gloves like polyps
Cluster; celluloid, painted ware, glaring
Metal patents, parchment lampshades, harsh
Attempts at buyable beauty.

In the porch of the chapel before the garish Virgin
A shawled factory-woman as if shipwrecked there
Lies a bunch of limbs glimpsed in the cave of gloom
By us who walk in the street so buoyantly and glib.

Over which country of cowled and haunted faces
The sun goes down with a banging of Orange drums*
While the male kind murders each its woman
To whose prayer for oblivion answers no Madonna.

Snow (1935)

The room was suddenly rich and the great bay-window was
Spawning snow and pink roses against it
Soundlessly collateral and incompatible:
World is suddener than we fancy it.

World is crazier and more of it than we think,
Incorrigibly plural. I peel and portion
A tangerine and spit the pips and feel
The drunkenness of things being various.

And the fire flames with a bubbling sound for world
Is more spiteful and gay than one supposes—
On the tongue on the eyes on the ears in the palms of
    one's hands—
There is more than glass between the snow and the huge roses.

Carrickfergus (1937)

I was born in Belfast between the mountain and the gantries
    To the hooting of lost sirens and the clang of trams:
Thence to Smoky Carrick in County Antrim
    Where the bottle-neck harbour collects the mud which jams

The little boats beneath the Norman castle,
    The pier shining with lumps of crystal salt;
The Scotch Quarter was a line of residential houses
    But the Irish Quarter was a slum for the blind and halt.

The brook ran yellow from the factory stinking of chlorine,
    The yarn-mill called its funeral cry at noon;
Our lights looked over the lough to the lights of Bangor
    Under the peacock aura of a drowning moon.

The Norman walled this town against the country
    To stop his ears to the yelping of his slave
And built a church in the form of a cross but denoting
    The list of Christ on the cross* in the angle of the nave.

I was the rector's son, born to the anglican order,
    Banned for ever from the candles of the Irish poor;
The Chichesters knelt in marble* at the end of a transept
    With ruffs about their necks, their portion sure.

The war came and a huge camp of soldiers
 Grew from the ground in sight of our house with long
Dummies hanging from gibbets for bayonet practice
 And the sentry's challenge echoing all day long;

A Yorkshire terrier ran in and out by the gate-lodge
 Barred to civilians, yapping as if taking affront:
Marching at ease and singing 'Who Killed Cock Robin?'
 The troops* went out by the lodge and off to the Front.

The steamer was camouflaged that took me to England—
 Sweat and khaki in the Carlisle train;
I thought that the war would last for ever and sugar
 Be always rationed and that never again

Would the weekly papers not have photos of sandbags
 And my governess not make bandages from moss
And people not have maps above the fireplace
 With flags on pins moving across and across—

Across the hawthorn hedge the noise of bugles,
 Flares across the night,
Somewhere on the lough was a prison ship for Germans,
 A cage across their sight.

I went to school in Dorset,* the world of parents
 Contracted into a puppet world of sons
Far from the mill girls, the smell of porter, the salt-mines
 And the soldiers with their guns.

Autumn Journal (1939)

XVI

Nightmare leaves fatigue:
 We envy men of action
Who sleep and wake, murder and intrigue

Without being doubtful, without being haunted.
And I envy the intransigence of my own
    Countrymen who shoot to kill and never
See the victim's face become their own
    Or find his motive sabotage their motives.
So reading the memoirs of Maud Gonne,*
    Daughter of an English mother and a soldier father,
I note how a single purpose can be founded on
    A jumble of opposites:
Dublin Castle, the vice-regal ball,
    The embassies of Europe,
Hatred scribbled on a wall,
    Gaols and revolvers.
And I remember, when I was little, the fear
    Bandied among the servants
That Casement* would land at the pier
    With a sword and a horde of rebels;
And how we used to expect, at a later date,
    When the wind blew from the west, the noise of shooting
Starting in the evening at eight
    In Belfast in the York Street district;
And the voodoo of the Orange bands*
    Drawing an iron net through darkest Ulster,
Flailing the limbo lands—
    The linen mills, the long wet grass, the ragged hawthorn.
And one read black where the other read white, his hope
    The other man's damnation:
Up the Rebels, To Hell with the Pope,
    And God Save—as you prefer—the King or Ireland.
The land of scholars and saints:
    Scholars and saints my eye, the land of ambush,
Purblind manifestoes, never-ending complaints,
    The born martyr and the gallant ninny;
The grocer drunk with the drum,
    The land-owner shot in his bed, the angry voices
Piercing the broken fanlight in the slum,
    The shawled woman weeping at the garish altar.
Kathaleen ni Houlihan!* Why
    Must a country, like a ship or a car, be always female,

Mother or sweetheart? A woman passing by,
   We did but see her passing.
Passing like a patch of sun on the rainy hill
   And yet we love her for ever and hate our neighbour
And each one in his will
   Binds his heirs to continuance of hatred.
Drums on the haycock, drums on the harvest, black
   Drums in the night shaking the windows:
King William is riding his white horse back
   To the Boyne* on a banner.
Thousands of banners, thousands of white
   Horses, thousands of Williams
Waving thousands of swords and ready to fight
   Till the blue sea turns to orange.
Such was my country and I thought I was well
   Out of it, educated and domiciled in England,
Though yet her name keeps ringing like a bell
   In an under-water belfry.
Why do we like being Irish? Partly because
   It gives us a hold on the sentimental English
As members of a world that never was,
   Baptised with fairy water;
And partly because Ireland is small enough
   To be still thought of with a family feeling,
And because the waves are rough
   That split her from a more commercial culture;
And because one feels that here at least one can
   Do local work which is not at the world's mercy
And that on this tiny stage with luck a man
   Might see the end of one particular action.
It is self-deception of course;
   There is no immunity in this island either;
A cart that is drawn by somebody else's horse
   And carrying goods to somebody else's market.
The bombs in the turnip sack, the sniper from the roof,
   Griffith, Connolly, Collins,* where have they brought us?
Ourselves alone!* Let the round tower stand aloof
   In a world of bursting mortar!
Let the school-children fumble their sums

In a half-dead language;
Let the censor be busy on the books; pull down the Georgian slums;
    Let the games be played in Gaelic.
Let them grow beet-sugar; let them build
    A factory in every hamlet;
Let them pigeon-hole the souls of the killed
    Into sheep and goats, patriots and traitors.
And the North, where I was a boy,
    Is still the North, veneered with the grime of Glasgow,
Thousands of men whom nobody will employ
    Standing at the corners, coughing.
And the street-children play on the wet
    Pavement—hopscotch or marbles;
And each rich family boasts a sagging tennis-net
    On a spongy lawn beside a dripping shrubbery.
The smoking chimneys hint
    At prosperity round the corner
But they make their Ulster linen from foreign lint
    And the money that comes in goes out to make more money.
A city built upon mud;
    A culture built upon profit;
Free speech nipped in the bud,
    The minority always guilty.
Why should I want to go back
    To you, Ireland, my Ireland*
The blots on the page are so black
    That they cannot be covered with shamrock.
I hate your grandiose airs,
    Your sob-stuff, your laugh and your swagger,
Your assumption that everyone cares
    Who is the king of your castle.
Castles are out of date,
    The tide flows round the children's sandy fancy;
Put up what flag you like, it is too late
    To save your soul with bunting.
*Odi atque amo:**
    Shall we cut this name on trees with a rusty dagger?
Her mountains are still blue, her rivers flow
    Bubbling over the boulders.

She is both a bore and a bitch;
    Better close the horizon,
Send her no more fantasy, no more longings which
    Are under a fatal tariff.
For common sense is the vogue
    And she gives her children neither sense nor money
Who slouch around the world with a gesture and a brogue
    And a faggot of useless memories.

6. DRAMA

OSCAR WILDE
(1854–1900)

from *The Importance of Being Earnest* (1895)

FIRST ACT

SCENE: *Morning-room in* ALGERNON'*s flat in Half Moon Street. The room is luxuriously and artistically furnished. The sound of a piano is heard in the adjoining room.*

LANE *is arranging afternoon tea on the table, and after the music has ceased,* ALGERNON *enters.*

Algernon. Did you hear what I was playing, Lane?

Lane. I didn't think it polite to listen, sir.

Algernon. I'm sorry for that, for your sake. I don't play accurately—anyone can play accurately—but I play with wonderful expression. As far as the piano is concerned, sentiment is my forte. I keep science for Life.

Lane. Yes, sir.

Algernon. And, speaking of the science of Life, have you got the cucumber sandwiches cut for Lady Bracknell?

Lane. Yes, sir. (*Hands them on a salver.*)

Algernon (*inspects them, takes two, and sits down on the sofa*). Oh! . . . by the way, Lane, I see from your book that on Thursday night, when Lord Shoreham and Mr Worthing were dining with me, eight bottles of champagne are entered as having been consumed.

Lane. Yes, sir; eight bottles and a pint.

Algernon. Why is it that at a bachelor's establishment the servants invariably drink the champagne? I ask merely for information.

Lane. I attribute it to the superior quality of the wine, sir. I have often observed that in married households the champagne is rarely of a first-rate brand.

Algernon. Good Heavens! Is marriage so demoralizing as that?

Lane. I believe it *is* a very pleasant state, sir. I have had very little experience of it myself up to the present. I have only been married once. That was in consequence of a misunderstanding between myself and a young person.

Algernon (*languidly*). I don't know that I am much interested in your family life, Lane.

Lane. No, sir; it is not a very interesting subject. I never think of it myself.

Algernon. Very natural, I am sure. That will do, Lane, thank you.

Lane. Thank you, sir.

[LANE *goes out.*

Algernon. Lane's views on marriage seem somewhat lax. Really, if the lower orders don't set us a good example, what on earth is the use of them? They seem, as a class, to have absolutely no sense of moral responsibility.

Enter LANE.

Lane. Mr Ernest Worthing.

Enter JACK.

[LANE *goes out.*

Algernon. How are you, my dear Ernest? What brings you up to town?

Jack. Oh, pleasure, pleasure! What else should bring one anywhere? Eating as usual, I see, Algy!

Algernon (*stiffly*). I believe it is customary in good society to take some slight refreshment at five o'clock. Where have you been since last Thursday?

Jack (*sitting down on the sofa*). In the country.

Algernon. What on earth do you do there?

Jack (*pulling off his gloves*). When one is in town one amuses oneself. When one is in the country one amuses other people. It is excessively boring.

Algernon. And who are the people you amuse?

Jack (airily). Oh, neighbours, neighbours.

Algernon. Got nice neighbours in your part of Shropshire?

Jack. Perfectly horrid! Never speak to one of them.

Algernon. How immensely you must amuse them! (*Goes over and takes sandwich.*) By the way, Shropshire is your county, is it not?

Jack. Eh? Shropshire? Yes, of course. Hallo! Why all these cups? Why cucumber sandwiches? Why such reckless extravagance in one so young? Who is coming to tea?

Algernon. Oh! merely Aunt Augusta and Gwendolen.

Jack. How perfectly delightful!

Algernon. Yes, that is all very well; but I am afraid Aunt Augusta won't quite approve of your being here.

Jack. May I ask why?

Algernon. My dear fellow, the way you flirt with Gwendolen is perfectly disgraceful. It is almost as bad as the way Gwendolen flirts with you.

Jack. I am in love with Gwendolen. I have come up to town expressly to propose to her.

Algernon. I thought you had come up for pleasure? . . . I call that business.

Jack. How utterly unromantic you are!

Algernon. I really don't see anything romantic in proposing. It is very romantic to be in love. But there is nothing romantic about a definite proposal. Why, one may be accepted. One usually is, I believe. Then the excitement is all over. The very essence of romance is uncertainty. If ever I get married, I'll certainly try to forget the fact.

Jack. I have no doubt about that, dear Algy. The Divorce Court* was specially invented for people whose memories are so curiously constituted.

Algernon. Oh! there is no use speculating on that subject. Divorces are made in Heaven—(JACK *puts out his hand to take a sandwich.* ALGERNON *at once interferes.*) Please don't touch the cucumber sandwiches. They are ordered specially for Aunt Augusta. (*Takes one and eats it.*)

Jack. Well, you have been eating them all the time.

Algernon. That is quite a different matter. She is my aunt. (*Takes plate from below.*) Have some bread and butter. The bread and butter is for Gwendolen. Gwendolen is devoted to bread and butter.

Jack (*advancing to table and helping himself*). And very good bread and butter it is too.

Algernon. Well, my dear fellow, you need not eat as if you were going to eat it all. You behave as if you were married to her already. You are not married to her already, and I don't think you ever will be.

Jack. Why on earth do you say that?

Algernon. Well, in the first place girls never marry the men they flirt with. Girls don't think it right.

Jack. Oh, that is nonsense!

Algernon. It isn't. It is a great truth. It accounts for the extraordinary number of bachelors that one sees all over the place. In the second place, I don't give my consent.

Jack. Your consent!

Algernon. My dear fellow, Gwendolen is my first cousin. And before I allow you to marry her, you will have to clear up the whole question of Cecily. (*Rings bell.*)

Jack. Cecily! What on earth do you mean? What do you mean, Algy, by Cecily? I don't know anyone of the name of Cecily.

Enter LANE.

Algernon. Bring me that cigarette case Mr Worthing left in the smoking-room the last time he dined here.

Lane. Yes, sir.

[LANE *goes out.*

Jack. Do you mean to say you have had my cigarette case all this time? I wish to goodness you had let me know. I have been writing frantic letters to Scotland Yard* about it. I was very nearly offering a large reward.

Algernon. Well, I wish you would offer one. I happen to be more than usually hard up.

Jack. There is no good offering a large reward now that the thing is found.

Enter LANE *with the cigarette case on a salver.* ALGERNON *takes it at once.* LANE *goes out.*

Algernon. I think that is rather mean of you, Ernest, I must say. (*Opens case and examines it.*) However, it makes no matter, for, now that I look at the inscription inside, I find that the thing isn't yours after all.

Jack. Of course it's mine. (*Moving to him.*) You have seen me with it a hundred times, and you have no right whatsoever to read what is written inside. It is a very ungentlemanly thing to read a private cigarette case.

Algernon. Oh! it is absurd to have a hard-and-fast rule about what one should read and what one shouldn't. More than half of modern culture depends on what one shouldn't read.

Jack. I am quite aware of the fact, and I don't propose to discuss modern culture. It isn't the sort of thing one should talk of in private. I simply want my cigarette case back.

Algernon. Yes; but this isn't your cigarette case. This cigarette case is a present from someone of the name of Cecily, and you said you didn't know anyone of that name.

Jack. Well, if you want to know, Cecily happens to be my aunt.

Algernon. Your aunt!

Jack. Yes. Charming old lady she is, too. Lives at Tunbridge Wells. Just give it back to me, Algy.

Algernon (*retreating to back of sofa*). But why does she call herself little Cecily if she is your aunt and lives at Tunbridge Wells? (*Reading.*) 'From little Cecily with her fondest love'.

Jack (*moving to sofa and kneeling upon it*). My dear fellow, what on earth is there in that? Some aunts are tall, some aunts are not tall. That is a matter that surely an aunt may be allowed to decide for herself. You seem to think that every aunt should be exactly like your aunt! That is absurd! For Heaven's sake give me back my cigarette case. (*Follows* ALGERNON *round the room.*)

Algernon. Yes. But why does your aunt call you her uncle? 'From little Cecily, with her fondest love to her dear Uncle Jack.' There is no objection, I admit, to an aunt being a small aunt, but why an aunt, no matter what her size may be, should call her own nephew her uncle, I can't quite make out. Besides, your name isn't Jack at all; it is Ernest.

Jack. It isn't Ernest; it's Jack.

Algernon. You have always told me it was Ernest. I have introduced you to everyone as Ernest. You answer to the name of Ernest. You look as if your name was Ernest. You are the most earnest looking person I ever saw in my life. It is perfectly absurd your saying that your name isn't Ernest. It's on your cards. Here is one of them. (*Taking it from case*.) 'Mr Ernest Worthing, B. 4, The Albany.' I'll keep this as a proof that your name is Ernest if ever you attempt to deny it to me, or to Gwendolen, or to anyone else. (*Puts the card in his pocket*.)

Jack. Well, my name is Ernest in town and Jack in the country, and the cigarette case was given to me in the country.

Algernon. Yes, but that does not account for the fact that your small Aunt Cecily, who lives at Tunbridge Wells, calls you her dear uncle. Come, old boy, you had much better have the thing out at once.

Jack. My dear Algy, you talk exactly as if you were a dentist. It is very vulgar to talk like a dentist when one isn't a dentist. It produces a false impression.

Algernon. Well, that is exactly what dentists always do. Now, go on! Tell me the whole thing. I may mention that I have always suspected you of being a confirmed and secret Bunburyist, and I am quite sure of it now.

Jack. Bunburyist? What on earth do you mean by a Bunburyist?

Algernon. I'll reveal to you the meaning of that incomparable expression as soon as you are kind enough to inform me why you are Ernest in town and Jack in the country.

Jack. Well, produce my cigarette case first.

Algernon. Here it is. (*Hands cigarette case*.) Now produce your explanation, and pray make it improbable. (*Sits on sofa*.)

Jack. My dear fellow, there is nothing improbable about my explanation at all. In fact it's perfectly ordinary. Old Mr Thomas Cardew, who adopted me when I was a little boy, made me in his will guardian to his grand-daughter, Miss Cecily Cardew. Cecily who addresses me as her uncle from motives of respect that you could not possibly appreciate, lives at my place in the country under the charge of her admirable governess, Miss Prism.

Algernon. Where is that place in the country, by the way?

Jack. That is nothing to you, dear boy. You are not going to be invited.... I may tell you candidly that the place is not in Shropshire.

Algernon. I suspected that, my dear fellow! I have Bunburyed all over Shropshire on two separate occasions. Now, go on. Why are you Ernest in town and Jack in the country?

Jack. My dear Algy, I don't know whether you will be able to understand my real motives. You are hardly serious enough. When one is placed in the position of guardian, one has to adopt a very high moral tone on all subjects. It's one's duty to do so. And as a high moral tone can hardly be said to conduce very much to either one's health or one's happiness, in order to get up to town I have always pretended to have a younger brother of the name of Ernest, who lives in the Albany, and gets into the most dreadful scrapes. That, my dear Algy, is the whole truth pure and simple.

Algernon. The truth is rarely pure and never simple. Modern life would be very tedious if it were either, and modern literature a complete impossibility!

Jack. That wouldn't be at all a bad thing.

Algernon. Literary criticism is not your forte, my dear fellow. Don't try it. You should leave that to people who haven't been at a University. They do it so well in the daily papers. What you really are is a Bunburyist. I was quite right in saying you were a Bunburyist. You are one of the most advanced Bunburyists I know.

Jack. What on earth do you mean?

Algernon. You have invented a very useful younger brother called Ernest, in order that you may be able to come up to town as often as you like. I have invented an invaluable permanent invalid called Bunbury, in order that I may be able to go down into the country whenever I choose. Bunbury is perfectly invaluable. If it wasn't for Bunbury's extraordinary bad health, for instance, I wouldn't be able to dine with you at Willis's* tonight, for I have been really engaged to Aunt Augusta for more than a week.

Jack. I haven't asked you to dine with me anywhere tonight.

Algernon. I know. You are absurdly careless about sending out invitations. It is very foolish of you. Nothing annoys people so much as not receiving invitations.

Jack. You had much better dine with your Aunt Augusta.

Algernon. I haven't the smallest intention of doing anything of the kind. To begin with, I dined there on Monday, and once a week is quite enough to dine with one's own relations. In the second place, whenever I do dine there I am always treated as a member of the family, and sent down* with either no woman at all, or two. In the third place, I know perfectly well whom she will place me next to, tonight. She will place me next Mary Farquhar, who always flirts with her own husband across the dinner-table. That is not very pleasant. Indeed, it is not even decent . . . and that sort of thing is enormously on the increase. The amount of women in London who flirt with their own husbands is perfectly scandalous. It looks so bad. It is simply washing one's clean linen in public. Besides, now that I know you to be a confirmed Bunburyist I naturally want to talk to you about Bunburying. I want to tell you the rules.

Jack. I'm not a Bunburyist at all. If Gwendolen accepts me, I am going to kill my brother, indeed I think I'll kill him in any case. Cecily is a little too much interested in him. It is rather a bore. So I am going to get rid of Ernest. And I strongly advise you to do the same with Mr . . . with your invalid friend who has the absurd name.

Algernon. Nothing will induce me to part with Bunbury, and if you ever get married, which seems to me extremely problematic, you will be very glad to know Bunbury. A man who marries without knowing Bunbury has a very tedious time of it.

Jack. That is nonsense. If I marry a charming girl like Gwendolen, and she is the only girl I ever saw in my life that I would marry, I certainly won't want to know Bunbury.

Algernon. Then your wife will. You don't seem to realize, that in married life three is company and two is none.

Jack (sententiously). That, my dear young friend, is the theory that the corrupt French Drama has been propounding for the last fifty years.

Algernon. Yes; and that the happy English home has proved in half the time.

Jack. For heaven's sake, don't try to be cynical. It's perfectly easy to be cynical.

Algernon. My dear fellow, it isn't easy to be anything nowadays. There's such a lot of beastly competition about. (*The sound of an electric bell is heard.*) Ah! that must be Aunt Augusta. Only relatives, or creditors, ever ring in that Wagnerian manner.* Now, if I get her out of the way for ten minutes, so that you can have an opportunity for proposing to Gwendolen, may I dine with you tonight at Willis's?

Jack. I suppose so, if you want to.

Algernon. Yes, but you must be serious about it. I hate people who are not serious about meals. It is so shallow of them.

Enter LANE.

Lane. Lady Bracknell and Miss Fairfax.

ALGERNON *goes forward to meet them. Enter* LADY BRACKNELL *and* GWENDOLEN.

Lady Bracknell. Good afternoon, dear Algernon, I hope you are behaving very well.

Algernon. I'm feeling very well, Aunt Augusta.

Lady Bracknell. That's not quite the same thing. In fact the two things rarely go together. (*Sees* JACK *and bows to him with icy coldness.*)

Algernon (*to* GWENDOLEN). Dear me, you are smart!

Gwendolen. I am always smart! Aren't I, Mr Worthing?

Jack. You're quite perfect, Miss Fairfax.

Gwendolen. Oh! I hope I am not that. It would leave no room for developments, and I intend to develop in many directions. (GWENDOLEN *and* JACK *sit down together in the corner.*)

Lady Bracknell. I'm sorry if we are a little late, Algernon, but I was obliged to call on dear Lady Harbury. I hadn't been there since her poor husband's death. I never saw a woman so altered; she looks quite twenty years younger. And now I'll have a cup of tea, and one of those nice cucumber sandwiches you promised me.

Algernon. Certainly, Aunt Augusta. (*Goes over to tea-table.*)

Lady Bracknell. Won't you come and sit here, Gwendolen?

Gwendolen. Thanks, mamma, I'm quite comfortable where I am.

Algernon (*picking up empty plate in horror*). Good heavens! Lane! Why are there no cucumber sandwiches? I ordered them specially.

Lane (*gravely*). There were no cucumbers in the market this morning, sir. I went down twice.

Algernon. No cucumbers!

Lane. No, sir. Not even for ready money.

Algernon. That will do, Lane, thank you.

Lane. Thank you, sir.

[*Goes out.*

W. B. YEATS AND AUGUSTA GREGORY
(1865–1939) (1852–1932)

Cathleen ni Houlihan (1902)

PERSONS IN THE PLAY

Peter Gillane	Bridget Gillane, Peter's wife
Michael Gillane, his son, going to be married	Delia Cahel, engaged to Michael
	The Poor Old Woman
Patrick Gillane, a lad of twelve, Michael's brother	Neighbours

Interior of a cottage close to Killala, in 1798. BRIDGET *is standing at a table undoing a parcel.* PETER *is sitting at one side of the fire,* PATRICK *at the other.*

Peter. What is that sound I hear?

Patrick. I don't hear anything. (*He listens.*) I hear it now. It's like cheering. (*He goes to the window and looks out.*) I wonder what they are cheering about. I don't see anybody.

Peter. It might be a hurling.*

Patrick. There's no hurling to-day. It must be down in the town the cheering is.

Bridget. I suppose the boys must be having some sport of their own. Come over here, Peter, and look at Michael's wedding clothes.

Peter (*shifts his chair to table*). Those are grand clothes, indeed.

Bridget. You hadn't clothes like that when you married me, and no coat to put on of a Sunday more than any other day.

Peter. That is true, indeed. We never thought a son of our own would be wearing a suit of that sort for his wedding, or have so good a place to bring a wife to.

Patrick (*who is still at the window*). There's an old woman coming down the road. I don't know is it here she is coming.

Bridget. It will be a neighbour coming to hear about Michael's wedding. Can you see who it is?

Patrick. I think it is a stranger, but she's not coming to the house. She's turned into the gap that goes down where Maurteen and his sons are shearing sheep. (*He turns towards* BRIDGET.) Do you re-member what Winny of the Cross Roads was saying the other night about the strange woman that goes through the country whatever time there's war or trouble coming?

Bridget. Don't be bothering us about Winny's talk, but go and open the door for your brother. I hear him coming up the path.

Peter. I hope he has brought Delia's fortune with him safe, for fear the people might go back on the bargain and I after making it. Trouble enough I had making it.

PATRICK *opens the door and* MICHAEL *comes in.*

Bridget. What kept you, Michael? We were looking out for you this long time.

Michael. I went round by the priest's house to bid him be ready to marry us to-morrow.

Bridget. Did he say anything?

Michael. He said it was a very nice match, and that he was never better pleased to marry any two in his parish than myself and Delia Cahel.

Peter. Have you got the fortune, Michael?

Michael. Here it is.

MICHAEL *puts bag on table and goes over and leans against chimney-jamb.* BRIDGET, *who has been all this time examining the clothes, pulling the seams and trying the lining of the pockets, etc., puts the clothes on the dresser.*

Peter (getting up and taking the bag in his hand and turning out the money). Yes, I made the bargain well for you, Michael. Old John Cahel would sooner have kept a share of this a while longer. 'Let me keep the half of it until the first boy is born,' says he. 'You will not,' says I. 'Whether there is or is not a boy, the whole hundred pounds must be in Michael's hands before he brings your daughter to the house.' The wife spoke to him then, and he gave in at the end.

Bridget. You seem well pleased to be handling the money, Peter.

Peter. Indeed, I wish I had had the luck to get a hundred pounds, or twenty pounds itself, with the wife I married.

Bridget. Well, if I didn't bring much I didn't get much. What had you the day I married you but a flock of hens and you feeding them, and a few lambs and you driving them to the market at Ballina?* (*She is vexed and bangs a jug on the dresser.*) If I brought no fortune I worked it out in my bones, laying down the baby, Michael that is standing there now, on a stook of straw, while I dug the potatoes, and never asking big dresses or anything but to be working.

Peter. That is true, indeed.

[*He pats her arm.*

Bridget. Leave me alone now till I ready the house for the woman that is to come into it.

Peter. You are the best woman in Ireland, but money is good, too. (*He begins handling the money again and sits down.*) I never thought to see so much money within my four walls. We can do great things now we have it. We can take the ten acres of land we have the chance of since Jamsie Dempsey died, and stock it. We will go to the fair at Ballina to buy the stock. Did Delia ask any of the money for her own use, Michael?

Michael. She did not, indeed. She did not seem to take much notice of it, or to look at it at all.

Bridget. That's no wonder. Why would she look at it when she had yourself to look at, a fine, strong young man? It is proud she must be to get you; a good steady boy that will make use of the money, and not be running through it or spending it on drink like another.

Peter. It's likely Michael himself was not thinking much of the fortune either, but of what sort the girl was to look at.

Michael (coming over towards the table). Well, you would like a nice comely girl to be beside you, and to go walking with you. The fortune only lasts for a while, but the woman will be there always.

Patrick (turning round from the window). They are cheering again down in the town. Maybe they are landing horses from Enniscrone.* They do be cheering when the horses take the water well.

Michael. There are no horses in it. Where would they be going and no fair at hand? Go down to the town, Patrick, and see what is going on.

Patrick (opens the door to go out, but stops for a moment on the threshold). Will Delia remember, do you think, to bring the grey-hound pup she promised me when she would be coming to the house?

Michael. She will surely.

[PATRICK *goes out, leaving the door open.*

Peter. It will be Patrick's turn next to be looking for a fortune, but he won't find it so easy to get it and he with no place of his own.

Bridget. I do be thinking sometimes, now things are going so well with us, and the Cahels such a good back to us in the district, and Delia's own uncle a priest, we might be put in the way of making Patrick a priest some day, and he so good at his books.

Peter. Time enough, time enough. You have always your head full of plans, Bridget.

Bridget. We will be well able to give him learning, and not to send him tramping the country like a poor scholar that lives on charity.

Michael. They're not done cheering yet.

He goes over to the door and stands there for a moment, putting up his hand to shade his eyes.

Bridget. Do you see anything?

Michael. I see an old woman coming up the path.

Bridget. Who is it, I wonder? It must be the strange woman Patrick saw a while ago.

Michael. I don't think it's one of the neighbours anyway, but she has her cloak over her face.

Bridget. It might be some poor woman heard we were making ready for the wedding and came to look for her share.

Peter. I may as well put the money out of sight. There is no use leaving it out for every stranger to look at.

He goes over to a large box in the corner, opens it and puts the bag in and fumbles at the lock.

Michael. There she is, father! (*An* OLD WOMAN *passes the window slowly. She looks at* MICHAEL *as she passes.*) I'd sooner a stranger not to come to the house the night before my wedding.

Bridget. Open the door, Michael; don't keep the poor woman waiting.

The OLD WOMAN *comes in.* MICHAEL *stands aside to make way for her.*

Old Woman. God save all here!

Peter. God save you kindly!

Old Woman. You have good shelter here.

Peter. You are welcome to whatever shelter we have.

Bridget. Sit down there by the fire and welcome.

Old Woman (*warming her hands*). There is a hard wind outside.

MICHAEL *watches her curiously from the door.* PETER *comes over to the table.*

Peter. Have you travelled far to-day?

Old Woman. I have travelled far, very far; there are few have travelled so far as myself, and there's many a one that doesn't make me welcome. There was one that had strong sons I thought were friends of mine, but they were shearing their sheep, and they wouldn't listen to me.

Peter. It's a pity indeed for any person to have no place of their own.

Old Woman. That's true for you indeed, and it's long I'm on the roads since I first went wandering.

Bridget. It is a wonder you are not worn out with so much wandering.

Old Woman. Sometimes my feet are tired and my hands are quiet, but there is no quiet in my heart. When the people see me quiet, they think old age has come on me and that all the stir has gone out of me. But when the trouble is on me I must be talking to my friends.

Bridget. What was it put you wandering?

Old Woman. Too many strangers in the house.*

Bridget. Indeed you look as if you'd had your share of trouble.

Old Woman. I have had trouble indeed.

Bridget. What was it put the trouble on you?

Old Woman. My land that was taken from me.

Peter. Was it much land they took from you?

Old Woman. My four beautiful green fields.*

Peter (*aside to* BRIDGET). Do you think could she be the widow Casey that was put out of her holding at Kilglass* a while ago?

Bridget. She is not. I saw the widow Casey one time at the market in Ballina, a stout fresh woman.

Peter (*to* OLD WOMAN). Did you hear a noise of cheering, and you coming up the hill?

Old Woman. I thought I heard the noise I used to hear when my friends came to visit me.

She begins singing half to herself.

> I will go cry with the woman,
> For yellow-haired Donough is dead,*
> With a hempen rope for a neckcloth,
> And a white cloth on his head,——

Michael (*coming from the door*). What is it that you are singing, ma'am?

Old Woman. Singing I am about a man I knew one time, yellow-haired Donough that was hanged in Galway.

> *She goes on singing, much louder.*

> I am come to cry with you, woman,
> My hair is unwound and unbound;
> I remember him ploughing his field,
> Turning up the red side of the ground,
> And building his barn on the hill
> With the good mortared stone;
> O! we'd have pulled down the gallows
> Had it happened in Enniscrone!

Michael. What was it brought him to his death?

Old Woman. He died for love of me: many a man has died for love of me.

Peter (*aside to* BRIDGET). Her trouble has put her wits astray.

Michael. Is it long since that song was made? Is it long since he got his death?

Old Woman. Not long, not long. But there were others that died for love of me a long time ago.

Michael. Were they neighbours of your own, ma'am?

Old Woman. Come here beside me and I'll tell you about them. (MICHAEL *sits down beside her on the hearth.*) There was a red man of the O'Donnells from the north, and a man of the O'Sullivans from the south, and there was one Brian that lost his life at Clontarf* by the sea, and there were a great many in the west, some that died hundreds of years ago, and there are some that will die to-morrow.

Michael. Is it in the west that men will die to-morrow?

Old Woman. Come nearer, nearer to me.

Bridget. Is she right, do you think? Or is she a woman from beyond the world?

Peter. She doesn't know well what she's talking about, with the want and the trouble she has gone through.

Bridget. The poor thing, we should treat her well.

Peter. Give her a drink of milk and a bit of the oaten cake.

Bridget. Maybe we should give her something along with that, to bring her on her way. A few pence or a shilling itself, and we with so much money in the house.

Peter. Indeed I'd not begrudge it to her if we had it to spare, but if we go running through what we have, we'll soon have to break the hundred pounds, and that would be a pity.

Bridget. Shame on you, Peter. Give her the shilling and your blessing with it, or our own luck will go from us.

PETER *goes to the box and takes out a shilling.*

Bridget (*to the* OLD WOMAN). Will you have a drink of milk, ma'am?

Old Woman. It is not food or drink that I want.

Peter (*offering the shilling*). Here is something for you.

Old Woman. This is not what I want. It is not silver I want.

Peter. What is it you would be asking for?

Old Woman. If anyone would give me help he must give me himself, he must give me all.

PETER *goes over to the table staring at the shilling in his hand in a bewildered way, and stands whispering to* BRIDGET.

Michael. Have you no one to care you in your age, ma'am?

Old Woman. I have not. With all the lovers that brought me their love I never set out the bed for any.

Michael. Are you lonely going the roads, ma'am?

Old Woman. I have my thoughts and I have my hopes.

Michael. What hopes have you to hold to?

Old Woman. The hope of getting my beautiful fields back again; the hope of putting the strangers out of my house.

Michael. What way will you do that, ma'am?

Old Woman. I have good friends that will help me. They are gathering to help me now. I am not afraid. If they are put down to-day they will get the upper hand to-morrow. (*She gets up.*) I must be going to meet my friends. They are coming to help me and I must be there to welcome them. I must call the neighbours together to welcome them.

Michael. I will go with you.

Bridget. It is not her friends you have to go and welcome, Michael; it is the girl coming into the house you have to welcome. You have plenty to do; it is food and drink you have to bring to the house. The woman that is coming home is not coming with empty hands; you would not have an empty house before her. (*To the* OLD WOMAN.) Maybe you don't know, ma'am that my son is going to be married to-morrow.

Old Woman. It is not a man going to his marriage that I look to for help.

Peter (*to* BRIDGET). Who is she, do you think, at all?

Bridget. You did not tell us your name yet, ma'am.

Old Woman. Some call me the Poor Old Woman, and there are some that call me Cathleen, the daughter of Houlihan.*

Peter. I think I knew some one of that name, once. Who was it, I wonder? It must have been some one I knew when I was a boy. No, no; I remember, I heard it in a song.

Old Woman (*who is standing in the doorway*). They are wondering that there were songs made for me; there have been many songs made for me, I heard one on the wind this morning.

Sings

> Do not make a great keening*
> When the graves have been dug to-morrow.
> Do not call the white-scarfed riders*
> To the burying that shall be to-morrow.
>
> Do not spread food to call strangers
> To the wakes that shall be to-morrow;
> Do not give money for prayers
> For the dead that shall die to-morrow . . .

They will have no need of prayers, they will have no need of prayers.

Michael. I do not know what that song means, but tell me something I can do for you.

Peter. Come over to me, Michael.

Michael. Hush, father, listen to her.

Old Woman. It is a hard service they take that help me. Many that are red-cheeked now will be pale-cheeked; many that have been free to walk the hills and the bogs and the rushes will be sent to walk hard streets in far countries; many a good plan will be broken; many that have gathered money will not stay to spend it; many a child will be born and there will be no father at its christening to give it a name. They that have red cheeks will have pale cheeks for my sake, and for all that, they will think they are well paid.

[*She goes out; her voice is heard outside singing.*

They shall be remembered for ever,
They shall be alive for ever,
They shall be speaking for ever,
The people shall hear them for ever.

Bridget (*to* PETER). Look at him, Peter; he has the look of a man that has got the touch.* (*Raising her voice.*) Look here, Michael, at the wedding clothes. Such grand clothes as these are! You have a right to fit them on now; it would be a pity to-morrow if they did not fit. The boys would be laughing at you. Take them, Michael, and go into the room and fit them on.

She puts them on his arm.

Michael. What wedding are you talking of? What clothes will I be wearing to-morrow?

Bridget. These are the clothes you are going to wear when you marry Delia Cahel to-morrow.

Michael. I had forgotten that.

He looks at the clothes and turns towards the inner room, but stops at the sound of cheering outside.

Peter. There is the shouting come to our own door. What is it has happened?

Neighbours come crowding in, PATRICK *and* DELIA *with them.*

Patrick. There are ships in the Bay; the French are landing at Killala!

PETER *takes his pipe from his mouth and his hat off, and stands up. The clothes slip from* MICHAEL's *arm.*

Delia. Michael! (*He takes no notice.*) Michael! (*He turns towards her.*) Why do you look at me like a stranger?

> *She drops his arm.* BRIDGET *goes over towards her.*

Patrick. The boys are all hurrying down the hillside to join the French.

Delia. Michael won't be going to join the French.

Bridget (*to* PETER). Tell him not to go, Peter.

Peter. It's no use. He doesn't hear a word we're saying.

Bridget. Try and coax him over to the fire.

Delia. Michael, Michael! You won't leave me! You won't join the French, and we going to be married!

> *She puts her arms about him, he turns towards her as if about to yield.*
> OLD WOMAN'*s voice outside.*

They shall be speaking for ever,
The people shall hear them for ever.

> MICHAEL *breaks away from* DELIA, *stands for a second at the door, then rushes out, following the* OLD WOMAN'*s voice.* BRIDGET *takes* DELIA, *who is crying silently, into her arms.*

Peter (*to* PATRICK, *laying a hand on his arm*). Did you see an old woman going down the path?

Patrick. I did not, but I saw a young girl, and she had the walk of a queen.

THE END

AUGUSTA GREGORY
(1852–1932)

The Rising of the Moon (1907)

PERSONS

Sergeant   *Policeman B*
Policeman X   *A Ragged Man*

SCENE: *Side of a quay in a seaport town. Some posts and chains. A large barrel. Enter three policemen. Moonlight.*

SERGEANT, *who is older than the others, crosses the stage to right and looks down steps. The others put down a pastepot and unroll a bundle of placards.*

Policeman B. I think this would be a good place to put up a notice.

[*He points to barrel.*

Policeman X. Better ask him. (*Calls to* SERGEANT.) Will this be a good place for a placard?   [*No answer.*

Policeman B. Will we put up a notice here on the barrel?

[*No answer.*

Sergeant. There's a flight of steps here that leads to the water. This is a place that should be minded well. If he got down here, his friends might have a boat to meet him; they might send it in here from outside.

Policeman B. Would the barrel be a good place to put a notice up?

Sergeant. It might; you can put it there. [*They paste the notice up.*

Sergeant (*reading it*). Dark hair—dark eyes, smooth face, height five feet five—there's not much to take hold of in that—It's a pity I had no chance of seeing him before he broke out of gaol. They say he's a wonder, that it's he makes all the plans for the whole organisa-tion. There isn't another man in Ireland would have broken gaol the way he did. He must have some friends among the gaolers.

Policeman B. A hundred pounds is little enough for the Government to offer for him. You may be sure any man in the force that takes him will get promotion.

Sergeant. I'll mind this place myself. I wouldn't wonder at all if he came this way. He might come slipping along there (*points to side of quay*), and his friends might be waiting for him there (*points down steps*), and once he got away it's little chance we'd have of finding him; it's maybe under a load of kelp he'd be in a fishing boat, and not one to help a married man that wants it to the reward.

Policeman X. And if we get him itself, nothing but abuse on our heads for it from the people, and maybe from our own relations.

Sergeant. Well, we have to do our duty in the force. Haven't we the whole country depending on us to keep law and order? It's those that are down would be up and those that are up would be down, if it wasn't for us. Well, hurry on, you have plenty of other places to placard yet, and come back here then to me. You can take the lantern. Don't be too long now. It's very lonesome here with nothing but the moon.

Policeman B. It's a pity we can't stop with you. The Government should have brought more police into the town, with *him* in gaol, and at assize time too.* Well, good luck to your watch.   [*They go out.*

Sergeant (*walks up and down once or twice and looks at placard*). A hundred pounds and promotion sure. There must be a great deal of spending in a hundred pounds. It's a pity some honest man not to be the better of that.

A ragged MAN *appears at left and tries to slip past.* SERGEANT *suddenly turns.*

Sergeant. Where are you going?

Man. I'm a poor ballad-singer, your honour. I thought to sell some of these (*holds out bundle of ballads*) to the sailors.   [*He goes on.*

Sergeant. Stop! Didn't I tell you to stop? You can't go on there.

Man. Oh, very well. It's a hard thing to be poor. All the world's against the poor.

Sergeant. Who are you?

Man. You'd be as wise as myself if I told you, but I don't mind. I'm one Jimmy Walsh, a ballad-singer.

Sergeant. Jimmy Walsh? I don't know that name.

Man. Ah, sure, they know it well enough in Ennis. Were you ever in Ennis, sergeant?

Sergeant. What brought you here?

Man. Sure, it's to the assizes I came, thinking I might make a few shillings here or there. It's in the one train with the judges I came.

Sergeant. Well, if you came so far, you may as well go farther, for you'll walk out of this.

Man. I will, I will; I'll just go on where I was going.

[*Goes towards steps.*

Sergeant. Come back from those steps; no one has leave to pass down them to-night.

Man. I'll just sit on the top of the steps till I see will some sailor buy a ballad off me that would give me my supper. They do be late going back to the ship. It's often I saw them in Cork carried down the quay in a hand-cart.

Sergeant. Move on, I tell you. I won't have anyone lingering about the quay to-night.

Man. Well, I'll go. It's the poor have the hard life! Maybe yourself might like one, sergeant. Here's a good sheet now. (*Turns one over.*) 'Content and a pipe'—that's not much. 'The Peeler and the goat'—you wouldn't like that. 'Johnny Hart'—that's a lovely song.

Sergeant. Move on.

Man. Ah, wait till you hear it. (*Sings*)—

There was a rich farmer's daughter lived near the town of Ross;
She courted a Highland soldier, his name was Johnny Hart;
Says the mother to her daughter, 'I'll go distracted mad
If you marry that Highland soldier dressed up in Highland plaid.'

Sergeant. Stop that noise.

MAN *wraps up his ballads and shuffles towards the steps.*

Sergeant. Where are you going?

Man. Sure you told me to be going, and I am going.

Sergeant. Don't be a fool. I didn't tell you to go that way; I told you to go back to the town.

Man. Back to the town, is it?

Sergeant (taking him by the shoulder and shoving him before him). Here, I'll show you the way. Be off with you. What are you stopping for?

Man (who has been keeping his eye on the notice, points to it). I think I know what you're waiting for, sergeant.

Sergeant. What's that to you?

Man. And I know well the man you're waiting for—I know him well—I'll be going.

[*He shuffles on.*

Sergeant. You know him? Come back here. What sort is he?

Man. Come back is it, sergeant? Do you want to have me killed?

Sergeant. Why do you say that?

Man. Never mind. I'm going. I wouldn't be in your shoes if the reward was ten times as much. (*Goes on off stage to left.*) Not if it was ten times as much.

Sergeant (rushing after him). Come back here, come back. (*Drags him back.*) What sort is he? Where did you see him?

Man. I saw him in my own place, in the County Clare. I tell you you wouldn't like to be looking at him. You'd be afraid to be in the one place with him. There isn't a weapon he doesn't know the use of, and as to strength, his muscles are as hard as that board (*slaps barrel*).

Sergeant. Is he as bad as that?

Man. He is then.

Sergeant. Do you tell me so?

Man. There was a poor man in our place, a sergeant from Bally-vaughan.—It was with a lump of stone he did it.

Sergeant. I never heard of that.

Man. And you wouldn't, sergeant. It's not everything that happens gets into the papers. And there was a policeman in plain clothes, too . . . It is in Limerick he was. . . . It was after the time of the attack on the police barrack at Kilmallock. . . . Moonlight . . . just like this . . . waterside . . . Nothing was known for certain.

Sergeant. Do you say so? It's a terrible county to belong to.

Man. That's so, indeed! You might be standing there, looking out that way, thinking you saw him coming up this side of the quay (*points*), and he might be coming up this other side (*points*), and he'd be on you before you knew where you were.

Sergeant. It's a whole troop of police they ought to put here to stop a man like that.

Man. But if you'd like me to stop with you, I could be looking down this side. I could be sitting up here on this barrel.

Sergeant. And you know him well, too?

Man. I'd know him a mile off, sergeant.

Sergeant. But you wouldn't want to share the reward?

Man. Is it a poor man like me, that has to be going the roads and singing in fairs, to have the name on him that he took a reward? But you don't want me. I'll be safer in the town.

Sergeant. Well, you can stop.

Man (*getting up on barrel*). All right, sergeant. I wonder, now, you're not tired out, sergeant, walking up and down the way you are.

Sergeant. If I'm tired I'm used to it.

Man. You might have hard work before you to-night yet. Take it easy while you can. There's plenty of room up here on the barrel, and you see farther when you're higher up.

Sergeant. Maybe so. (*Gets up beside him on barrel, facing right. They sit back to back, looking different ways.*) You made me feel a bit queer with the way you talked.

Man. Give me a match, sergeant (*he gives it, and Man lights pipe*); take a draw yourself? It'll quiet you. Wait now till I give you a light, but you needn't turn round. Don't take your eye off the quay for the life of you.

Sergeant. Never fear, I won't. (*Lights pipe. They both smoke.*) Indeed it's a hard thing to be in the force, out at night and no thanks for it, for all the danger we're in. And it's little we get but abuse from the people, and no choice but to obey our orders, and never asked when a man is sent into danger, if you are a married man with a family.

Man (*sings*)—

As through the hills I walked to view the hills and shamrock plain,

I stood awhile where nature smiles to view the rocks and streams,
On a matron fair I fixed my eyes beneath a fertile vale,
As she sang her song it was on the wrong of poor old Granuaile.*

Sergeant. Stop that; that's no song to be singing in these times.

Man. Ah, sergeant, I was only singing to keep my heart up. It sinks when I think of him. To think of us two sitting here, and he creeping up the quay, maybe, to get to us.

Sergeant. Are you keeping a good lookout?

Man. I am; and for no reward too. Amn't I the foolish man? But when I saw a man in trouble, I never could help trying to get him out of it. What's that? Did something hit me?   [*Rubs his heart.*

Sergeant (*patting him on the shoulder*). You will get your reward in heaven.

Man. I know that, I know that, sergeant, but life is precious.

Sergeant. Well, you can sing if it gives you more courage.

Man (*sings*)—

Her head was bare, her hands and feet with iron bands were
    bound,
Her pensive strain and plaintive wail mingles with the evening gale,
And the song she sang with mournful air, I am old Granuaile.
Her lips so sweet that monarchs kissed . . .

Sergeant. That's not it. . . . 'Her gown she wore was stained with gore.' . . . That's it—you missed that.

Man. You're right, sergeant, so it is; I missed it. (*Repeats line.*) But to think of a man like you knowing a song like that.

Sergeant. There's many a thing a man might know and might not have any wish for.

Man. Now, I daresay, sergeant, in your youth, you used to be sitting up on a wall, the way you are sitting up on this barrel now, and the other lads beside you, and you singing 'Granuaile'? . . .

Sergeant. I did then.

Man. And the 'Shan Bhean Bhocht'? . . . *

Sergeant. I did then.

Man. And the 'Green on the Cape'?*

Sergeant. That was one of them.

Man. And maybe the man you are watching for to-night used to be sitting on the wall, when he was young, and singing those same songs. . . . It's a queer world. . . .

Sergeant. Whisht! . . . I think I see something coming. . . . It's only a dog.

Man. And isn't it a queer world? . . . Maybe it's one of the boys you used to be singing with that time you will be arresting to-day or to-morrow, and sending into the dock. . . .

Sergeant. That's true indeed.

Man. And maybe one night, after you had been singing, if the other boys had told you some plan they had, some plan to free the country, you might have joined with them. . . . and maybe it is you might be in trouble now.

Sergeant. Well, who knows but I might? I had a great spirit in those days.

Man. It's a queer world, sergeant, and it's little any mother knows when she sees her child creeping on the floor what might happen to it before it has gone through its life, or who will be who in the end.

Sergeant. That's a queer thought now, and a true thought. Wait now till I think it out . . . If it wasn't for the sense I have, and for my wife and family, and for me joining the force the time I did, it might be myself now would be after breaking gaol and hiding in the dark, and it might be him that's hiding in the dark and that got out of gaol would be sitting up where I am on this barrel. . . . And it might be myself would be creeping up trying to make my escape from himself, and it might be himself would be keeping the law, and myself would be breaking it, and myself would be trying maybe to put a bullet in his head, or to take up a lump of a stone the way you said he did . . . no, that myself did . . . Oh! (*Gasps. After a pause.*) What's that? (*Grasps* MAN's *arm.*)

Man (*jumps off barrel and listens, looking out over water.*) It's nothing, sergeant.

Sergeant. I thought it might be a boat. I had a notion there might be friends of his coming about the quays with a boat.

Man. Sergeant, I am thinking it was with the people you were, and not with the law you were when you were a young man.

Sergeant. Well, if I was foolish then, that time's gone.

Man. Maybe, sergeant, it comes into your head sometimes, in spite of your belt and your tunic, that it might have been as well for you to have followed Granuaile.

Sergeant. It's no business of yours what I think.

Man. Maybe, sergeant, you'll be on the side of the country yet.

Sergeant (*gets off barrel*). Don't talk to me like that. I have my duties and I know them. (*Looks round.*) That was a boat; I hear the oars.

> [*Goes to the steps and looks down.*

Man (*sings*)—

> O, then, tell me, Shawn O'Farrell,
> Where the gathering is to be.
> In the old spot by the river
> Right well known to you and me!

Sergeant. Stop that! Stop that, I tell you!

Man (*sings louder*).

> One word more, for signal token,
> Whistle up the marching tune,
> With your pike upon your shoulder,
> At the Rising of the Moon.*

Sergeant. If you don't stop that, I'll arrest you.

A whistle from below answers, repeating the air.

Sergeant. That's a signal (*stands between him and steps.*) You must not pass this way . . . Step farther back . . . Who are you? You are no ballad-singer.

Man. You needn't ask who I am; that placard will tell you (*points to placard.*)

Sergeant. You are the man I am looking for.

Man (*takes off hat and wig.* SERGEANT *seizes them.*) I am. There's a hundred pounds on my head. There is a friend of mine below in a boat. He knows a safe place to bring me to.

Sergeant (*looking still at hat and wig*). It's a pity! it's a pity. You deceived me. You deceived me well.

Man. I am a friend of Granuaile. There is a hundred pounds on my head.

Sergeant. It's a pity, it's a pity!

Man. Will you let me pass, or must I make you let me?

Sergeant. I am in the force. I will not let you pass.

Man. I thought to do it with my tongue (*puts hand in breast*). What is that?

(*Voice of* POLICEMAN X *outside*.) Here, this is where we left him.

Sergeant. It's my comrades coming.

Man. You won't betray me ... the friend of Granuaile (*slips behind barrel*).

(*Voice of* POLICEMAN B.) That was the last of the placards.

Policeman X (*as they come in*). If he makes his escape it won't be unknown he'll make it.

SERGEANT *puts hat and wig behind his back.*

Policeman B. Did anyone come this way?

Sergeant (*after a pause*). No one.

Policeman B. No one at all?

Sergeant. No one at all.

Policeman B. We had no orders to go back to the station; we can stop along with you.

Sergeant. I don't want you. There is nothing for you to do here.

Policeman B. You bade us to come back here and keep watch with you.

Sergeant. I'd sooner be alone. Would any man come this way and you making all that talk? It is better the place to be quiet.

Policeman B. Well, we'll leave you the lantern anyhow.

[*Hands it to him.*

Sergeant. I don't want it. Bring it with you.

Policeman B. You might want it. There are clouds coming up and you have the darkness of the night before you yet. I'll leave it over here on the barrel.

> [*Goes to barrel.*

Sergeant. Bring it with you I tell you. No more talk.

Policeman B. Well, I thought it might be a comfort to you. I often think when I have it in my hand and can be flashing it about into every dark corner (*doing so*) that it's the same as being beside the fire at home, and the bits of bog-wood blazing up now and again.

> *Flashes it about, now on the barrel, now on* SERGEANT.

Sergeant (*furious*). Be off the two of you, yourselves and your lantern!

> *They go out.* MAN *comes from behind barrel. He and* SERGEANT *stand looking at one another.*

Sergeant. What are you waiting for?

Man. For my hat, of course, and my wig. You wouldn't wish me to get my death of cold?

> [SERGEANT *gives them.*

Man (*going towards steps*). Well, good-night, comrade, and thank you. You did me a good turn to-night, and I'm obliged to you. Maybe I'll be able to do as much for you when the small rise up and the big fall down . . . when we all change places at the Rising (*waves his hand and disappears*) of the Moon.

Sergeant (*turning his back to audience and reading placard*). A hundred pounds reward! A hundred pounds! (*Turns towards audience.*) I wonder now, am I as great a fool as I think I am?

> *Curtain.*

J. M. SYNGE
(1871–1909)

Riders to the Sea (1904)

PERSONS

> Maurya, an old woman
> Bartley, her son
> Cathleen, her daughter
> Nora, a younger daughter
> Men and Women

SCENE

An Island off the West of Ireland

FIRST PRODUCTION
(Dublin, 25 February 1904)

Cottage kitchen, with nets, oil-skins, spinning wheel, some new boards standing by the wall, etc. CATHLEEN, *a girl of about twenty, finishes kneading cake, and puts it down in the pot-oven* by the fire; then wipes her hands, and begins to spin at the wheel.* NORA, *a young girl, puts her head in at the door.*

Nora (in a low voice). Where is she?

Cathleen. She's lying down, God help her, and maybe sleeping, if she's able.

NORA *comes in softly, and takes a bundle from under her shawl.*

Cathleen (spinning the wheel rapidly). What is it you have?

Nora. The young priest is after bringing them. It's a shirt and a plain stocking were got off a drowned man in Donegal.

CATHLEEN *stops her wheel with a sudden movement, and leans out to listen.*

Nora. We're to find out if it's Michael's they are, some time herself will be down looking by the sea.

Cathleen. How would they be Michael's, Nora. How would he go the length of that way to the far north?

Nora. The young priest says he's known the like of it. 'If it's Michael's they are,' says he, 'you can tell herself he's got a clean burial by the grace of God, and if they're not his, let no one say a word about them, for she'll be getting her death,' says he, 'with crying and lamenting.'

The door which NORA *half closed behind her is blown open by a gust of wind.*

Cathleen (*looking out anxiously*). Did you ask him would he stop Bartley going this day with the horses to the Galway fair?

Nora. 'I won't stop him,' says he, 'but let you not be afraid. Herself does be saying prayers half through the night, and the Almighty God won't leave her destitute,' says he, 'with no son living.'

Cathleen. Is the sea bad by the white rocks, Nora?

Nora. Middling bad, God help us. There's a great roaring in the west, and it's worse it'll be getting when the tide's turned to the wind. (*She goes over to the table with the bundle.*) Shall I open it now?

Cathleen. Maybe she'd wake up on us, and come in before we'd done (*coming to the table*). It's a long time we'll be, and the two of us crying.

Nora (*goes to the inner door and listens*). She's moving about on the bed. She'll be coming in a minute.

Cathleen. Give me the ladder, and I'll put them up in the turf-loft,* the way she won't know of them at all, and maybe when the tide turns she'll be going down to see would he be floating from the east.

They put the ladder against the gable of the chimney; CATHLEEN *goes up a few steps and hides the bundle in the turf-loft.* MAURYA *comes from the inner room.*

Maurya (*looking up at* CATHLEEN *and speaking querulously*). Isn't it turf enough you have for this day and evening?

Cathleen. There's a cake baking at the fire for a short space (*throwing down the turf*), and Bartley will want it when the tide turns if he goes to Connemara.

NORA *picks up the turf and puts it round the pot-oven.*

Maurya (*sitting down on a stool at the fire*). He won't go this day
with the wind rising from the south and west. He won't go this day,
for the young priest will stop him surely.

Nora. He'll not stop him, mother, and I heard Eamon Simon and
Stephen Pheety and Colum Shawn saying he would go.

Maurya. Where is he itself?

Nora. He went down to see would there be another boat sailing in
the week, and I'm thinking it won't be long till he's here now, for the
tide's turning at the green head,* and the hooker's tacking from the
east.*

Cathleen. I hear some one passing the big stones.

Nora (*looking out*). He's coming now, and he in a hurry.

Bartley (*comes in and looks round the room; speaking sadly and
quietly*). Where is the bit of new rope, Cathleen, was bought in
Connemara?

Cathleen (*coming down*). Give it to him, Nora; it's on a nail by the
white boards. I hung it up this morning, for the pig with the black
feet* was eating it.

Nora (*giving him a rope*). Is that it, Bartley?

Maurya (*as before*). You'd do right to leave that rope, Bartley,
hanging by the boards. (BARTLEY *takes the rope.*) It will be wanting in
this place, I'm telling you, if Michael is washed up tomorrow morning, or the next morning, or any morning in the week, for it's a deep
grave we'll make him by the grace of God.

Bartley (*beginning to work with the rope*). I've no halter the way I
can ride down on the mare, and I must go now quickly. This is the
one boat going for two weeks or beyond it, and the fair will be a good
fair for horses I heard them saying below.

Maurya. It's a hard thing they'll be saying below if the body is
washed up and there's no man in it to make the coffin, and I after
giving a big price for the finest white boards you'd find in Connemara. (*She looks round at the boards.*)

Bartley. How would it be washed up, and we after looking each
day for nine days, and a strong wind blowing a while back from the
west and south?

Maurya. If it isn't found itself, that wind is raising the sea, and there was a star up against the moon, and it rising in the night. If it was a hundred horses, or a thousand horses you had itself, what is the price of a thousand horses against a son where there is one son only?

Bartley (*working at the halter, to* CATHLEEN). Let you go down each day, and see the sheep aren't jumping in on the rye, and if the jobber* comes you can sell the pig with the black feet if there is a good price going.

Maurya. How would the like of her get a good price for a pig?

Bartley (*to* CATHLEEN). If the west wind holds with the last bit of the moon let you and Nora get up weed enough for another cock for the kelp.* It's hard set we'll be from this day with no one in it but one man to work.

Maurya. It's hard set we'll be surely the day you're drown'd with the rest. What way will I live and the girls with me, and I an old woman looking for the grave?

BARTLEY *lays down the halter, takes off his old coat, and puts on a newer one of the same flannel.*

Bartley (*to* NORA). Is she coming to the pier?

Nora (*looking out*). She's passing the green head and letting fall her sails.

Bartley (*getting his purse and tobacco*). I'll have half an hour to go down, and you'll see me coming again in two days, or in three days, or maybe in four days if the wind is bad.

Maurya (*turning round to the fire, and putting her shawl over her head*). Isn't it a hard and cruel man won't hear a word from an old woman, and she holding him from the sea?

Cathleen. It's the life of a young man to be going on the sea, and who would listen to an old woman with one thing and she saying it over?

Bartley (*taking the halter*). I must go now quickly. I'll ride down on the red mare, and the grey pony'll run behind me. . . . The blessing of God on you.

[*He goes out.*

Maurya (crying out as he is in the door way). He's gone now, God spare us, and we'll not see him again. He's gone now, and when the black night is falling I'll have no son left me in the world.

Cathleen. Why wouldn't you give him your blessing and he looking round in the door? Isn't it sorrow enough is on every one in this house without your sending him out with an unlucky word behind him, and a hard word in his ear?

MAURYA *takes up the tongs and begins raking the fire aimlessly without looking round.*

Nora (turning towards her). You're taking away the turf from the cake.

Cathleen (crying out). The Son of God forgive us, Nora, we're after forgetting his bit of bread.

She comes over to the fire.

Nora. And it's destroyed* he'll be going till dark night, and he after eating nothing since the sun went up.

Cathleen (turning the cake out of the oven). It's destroyed he'll be, surely. There's no sense left on any person in a house where an old woman will be talking forever.

MAURYA *sways herself on her stool.*

Cathleen (cutting off some of the bread and rolling it in a cloth, to MAURYA). Let you go down now to the spring well and give him this and he passing. You'll see him then and the dark word will be broken, and you can say 'God speed you', the way he'll be easy in his mind.

Maurya (taking the bread). Will I be in it as soon as himself?

Cathleen. If you go now quickly.

Maurya (standing up unsteadily). It's hard set I am to walk.

Cathleen (looking at her anxiously). Give her the stick, Nora, or maybe she'll slip on the big stones.

Nora. What stick?

Cathleen. The stick Michael brought from Connemara.

Maurya (taking a stick NORA *gives her).* In the big world the old people do be leaving things after them for their sons and children,

but in this place it is the young men do be leaving things behind for
them that do be old.

[*She goes out slowly.*

NORA *goes over to the ladder.*

Cathleen. Wait, Nora, maybe she'd turn back quickly. She's that
sorry, God help her, you wouldn't know the thing she'd do.

Nora. Is she gone round by the bush?

Cathleen (*looking out*). She's gone now. Throw it down quickly,
for the Lord knows when she'll be out of it again.

Nora (*getting the bundle from the loft*). The young priest said he'd
be passing tomorrow, and we might go down and speak to him below
if it's Michael's they are surely.

Cathleen (*taking the bundle from* NORA). Did he say what way they
were found?

Nora (*coming down*). 'There were two men,' says he, 'and they
rowing round with poteen* before the cocks crowed, and the oar of
one of them caught the body, and they passing the black cliffs of the
north.'

Cathleen (*trying to open the bundle*). Give me a knife, Nora, the
string's perished with the salt water, and there's a black knot on it*
you wouldn't loosen in a week.

Nora (*giving her a knife*). I've heard tell it was a long way to
Donegal.

Cathleen (*cutting the string*). It is surely. There was a man in here a
while ago—the man sold us that knife—and he said if you set off
walking from the rocks beyond, it would be in seven days you'd be in
Donegal.

Nora. And what time would a man take, and he floating?

CATHLEEN *opens the bundle and takes out a bit of a shirt and a
stocking. They look at them eagerly.*

Cathleen (*in a low voice*). The Lord spare us, Nora! Isn't it a
queer hard thing to say if it's his they are surely?

Nora. I'll get his shirt off the hook the way we can put the one
flannel on the other. (*She looks through some clothes hanging in the
corner.*) It's not with them, Cathleen, and where will it be?

Cathleen. I'm thinking Bartley put it on him in the morning, for his own shirt was heavy with the salt in it. (*Pointing to the corner.*) There's a bit of a sleeve was of the same stuff. Give me that and it will do.

NORA *brings it to her and they compare the flannel.*

Cathleen. It's the same stuff, Nora; but if it is itself aren't there great rolls of it in the shops of Galway, and isn't it many another man may have a shirt of it as well as Michael himself?

Nora (*who has taken up the stocking and counted the stitches, crying out*). It's Michael, Cathleen, it's Michael; God spare his soul, and what will herself say when she hears this story, and Bartley on the sea?

Cathleen (*taking the stocking*). It's a plain stocking.

Nora. It's the second one of the third pair I knitted, and I put up three score stitches, and I dropped four of them.

Cathleen (*counts the stitches*). It's that number is in it. (*Crying out.*) Ah, Nora, isn't it a bitter thing to think of him floating that way to the far north, and no one to keen him but the black hags* that do be flying on the sea?

Nora (*swinging herself round and throwing out her arms on the clothes*). And isn't it a pitiful thing when there is nothing left of a man who was a great rower and fisher, but a bit of an old shirt and a plain stocking?

Cathleen (*after an instant*). Tell me is herself coming, Nora? I hear a little sound on the path.

Nora (*looking out*). She is, Cathleen. She's coming up to the door.

Cathleen. Put these things away before she'll come in. Maybe it's easier she'll be after giving her blessing to Bartley, and we won't let on we've heard anything the time he's on the sea.

Nora (*helping* CATHLEEN *to close the bundle*). We'll put them here in the corner.

They put them into a hole in the chimney corner. CATHLEEN *goes back to the spinning-wheel.*

Nora. Will she see it was crying I was?

Cathleen. Keep your back to the door the way the light'll not be on you.

NORA *sits down at the chimney corner, with her back to the door.*
MAURYA *comes in very slowly, without looking at the girls, and goes over to her stool at the other side of the fire. The cloth with the bread is still in her hand. The girls look at each other, and* NORA *points to the bundle of bread.*

Cathleen (after spinning for a moment). You didn't give him his bit of bread?

MAURYA *begins to keen softly, without turning round.*

Cathleen. Did you see him riding down?

MAURYA *goes on keening.*

Cathleen (a little impatiently). God forgive you; isn't it a better thing to raise your voice and tell what you seen, than to be making lamentation for a thing that's done? Did you see Bartley, I'm saying to you.

Maurya (with a weak voice). My heart's broken from this day.

Cathleen (as before). Did you see Bartley?

Maurya. I seen the fearfullest thing.

Cathleen (leaves her wheel and looks out). God forgive you; he's riding the mare now over the green head, and the grey pony behind him.

Maurya (starts, so that her shawl falls back from her head and shows her white tossed hair. With a frightened voice). The grey pony behind him . . .

Cathleen (coming to the fire). What is it ails you, at all?

Maurya (speaking very slowly). I've seen the fearfullest thing any person has seen, since the day Bride Dara seen the dead man with the child in his arms.

Cathleen and Nora. Uah.

They crouch down in front of the old woman at the fire.

Nora. Tell us what it is you seen.

Maurya. I went down to the spring well, and I stood there saying a prayer to myself. Then Bartley came along, and he riding on the red mare with the grey pony behind him (*she puts up her hands, as if to hide something from her eyes*). The Son of God spare us, Nora!

Cathleen. What is it you seen?

Maurya. I seen Michael himself.

Cathleen (*speaking softly*). You did not, mother; it wasn't Michael you seen, for his body is after being found in the far north, and he's got a clean burial by the grace of God.

Maurya (*a little defiantly*). I'm after seeing him this day, and he riding and galloping. Bartley came first on the red mare; and I tried to say 'God speed you,' but something choked the words in my throat. He went by quickly; and 'the blessing of God on you,' says he, and I could say nothing. I looked up then, and I crying, at the grey pony, and there was Michael upon it—with fine clothes on him, and new shoes on his feet.

Cathleen (*begins to keen*). It's destroyed we are from this day. It's destroyed, surely.

Nora. Didn't the young priest say the Almighty God won't leave her destitute with no son living?

Maurya (*in a low voice, but clearly*). It's little the like of him knows of the sea. . . . Bartley will be lost now, and let you call in Eamon and make me a good coffin out of the white boards, for I won't live after them. I've had a husband, and a husband's father, and six sons in this house—six fine men, though it was a hard birth I had with every one of them and they coming to the world—and some of them were found and some of them were not found, but they're gone now the lot of them. . . . There were Stephen, and Shawn, were lost in the great wind, and found after in the Bay of Gregory of the Golden Mouth,* and carried up the two of them on one plank, and in by that door.

She pauses for a moment; the girls start as if they heard something through the door that is half open behind them.

Nora (*in a whisper*). Did you hear that, Cathleen? Did you hear a noise in the north-east?

Cathleen (*in a whisper*). There's some one after crying out by the seashore.

Maurya (*continues without hearing anything*). There was Sheamus and his father, and his own father again, were lost in a dark night, and not a stick or sign was seen of them when the sun went up. There was Patch after was drowned out of a curagh* that turned over. I was sitting here with Bartley, and he a baby, lying on my two knees, and I seen two women, and three women, and four women coming in, and they crossing themselves, and not saying a word. I looked out then, and there were men coming after them, and they holding a thing in the half of a red sail, and water dripping out of it—it was a dry day, Nora—and leaving a track to the door.

*She pauses again with her hand stretched out towards the door. It opens softly and old women begin to come in, crossing themselves on the threshold, and kneeling down in front of the stage with red petticoats over their heads.**

Maurya (*half in a dream, to* CATHLEEN). Is it Patch, or Michael, or what is it at all?

Cathleen. Michael is after being found in the far north, and when he is found there how could he be here in this place?

Maurya. There does be a power of young men floating round in the sea, and what way would they know if it was Michael they had, or another man like him, for when a man is nine days in the sea, and the wind blowing, it's hard set his own mother would be to say what man was in it.

Cathleen. It's Michael, God spare him, for they're after sending us a bit of his clothes from the far north.

She reaches out and hands MAURYA *the clothes that belonged to* MICHAEL. MAURYA *stands up slowly, and takes them in her hands.* NORA *looks out.*

Nora. They're carrying a thing among them and there's water dripping out of it and leaving a track by the big stones.

Cathleen (*in a whisper to the women who have come in*). Is it Bartley it is?

One of the women. It is surely, God rest his soul.

Two younger women come in and pull out the table. Then men carry in the body of BARTLEY, *laid on a plank, with a bit of a sail over it, and lay it on the table.*

Cathleen (*to the women, as they are doing so*). What way was he drowned?

One of the women. The grey pony knocked him over into the sea, and he was washed out where there is a great surf on the white rocks.

MAURYA *has gone over and knelt down at the head of the table. The women are keening softly and swaying themselves with a slow movement.* CATHLEEN *and* NORA *kneel at the other end of the table. The men kneel near the door.*

Maurya (*raising her head and speaking as if she did not see the people around her*). They're all gone now, and there isn't anything more the sea can do to me. . . . I'll have no call now to be up crying and praying when the wind breaks from the south, and you can hear the surf is in the east, and the surf is in the west, making a great stir with the two noises, and they hitting one on the other. I'll have no call now to be going down and getting Holy Water in the dark nights after Samhain,* and I won't care what way the sea is when the other women will be keening. (*To* NORA.) Give me the Holy Water, Nora, there's a small sup still on the dresser. (NORA *gives it to her.* MAURYA *drops* MICHAEL's *clothes across* BARTLEY's *feet, and sprinkles the Holy Water over him.*) . . . It isn't that I haven't prayed for you, Bartley, to the Almighty God. It isn't that I haven't said prayers in the dark night till you wouldn't know what I'd be saying; but it's a great rest I'll have now, and it's time surely. It's a great rest I'll have now, and great sleeping in the long nights after Samhain, if it's only a bit of wet flour we do have to eat, and maybe a fish that would be stinking. (*She kneels down again, crossing herself, and saying prayers under her breath.*)

Cathleen (*to an old man kneeling near her*). Maybe yourself and Eamon would make a coffin when the sun rises. We have fine white boards herself bought, God help her, thinking Michael would be found, and I have a new cake you can eat while you'll be working.

The old man (*looking at the boards*). Are there nails with them?

Cathleen. There are not, Colum; we didn't think of the nails.

Another man. It's a great wonder she wouldn't think of the nails, and all the coffins she's seen made already.

Cathleen. It's getting old she is, and broken.

MAURYA *stands up again very slowly and spreads out the pieces of* MICHAEL's *clothes beside the body, sprinkling them with the last of the Holy Water.*

Nora (in a whisper to CATHLEEN). She's quiet now and easy; but the day Michael was drowned you could hear her crying out from this to the spring well. It's fonder she was of Michael, and would any one have thought that?

Cathleen (slowly and clearly). An old woman will soon be tired with anything she will do, and isn't it nine days herself is after crying, and keening, and making great sorrow in the house?

Maurya (puts the empty cup mouth downwards on the table, and lays her hands together on BARTLEY's *feet).* They're all together this time, and the end is come. May the Almighty God have mercy on Bartley's soul, and on Michael's soul, and on the souls of Sheamus and Patch, and Stephen and Shawn (*bending her head*) . . . and may He have mercy on my soul, Nora, and on the soul of everyone is left living in the world. (*She pauses, and the keen rises a little more loudly from the women, then sinks away. Continuing.*) Michael has a clean burial in the far north, by the grace of the Almighty God. Bartley will have a fine coffin out of the white boards, and a deep grave surely. . . . What more can we want than that? . . . No man at all can be living for ever, and we must be satisfied.

She kneels down again and the curtain falls slowly.

THE END

SEÁN O'CASEY
(1880–1964)

from *Juno and the Paycock* (1924)

ACT I

The living room of a two-room tenancy occupied by the BOYLE *family in
a tenement house in Dublin. Left, a door leading to another part of the
house; left of door a window looking into the street; at back a dresser;
farther to right at back, a window looking into the back of the house.
Between the window and the dresser is a picture of the Virgin; below the
picture, on a bracket, is a crimson bowl in which a floating votive light is
burning. Farther to the right is a small bed partly concealed by cretonne
hangings strung on a twine. To the right is the fireplace; near the fireplace
is a door leading to the other room. Beside the fireplace is a box containing
coal. On the mantelshelf is an alarm clock lying on its face. In a corner
near the window looking into the back is a galvanized bath. A table and
some chairs. On the table are breakfast things for one. A teapot is on the
hob and a frying-pan stands inside the fender. There are a few books on
the dresser and one on the table. Leaning against the dresser is a long-
handled shovel—the kind invariably used by labourers when turning
concrete or mixing mortar.* JOHNNY BOYLE *is sitting crouched beside the
fire.* MARY *with her jumper off—it is lying on the back of a chair—is
arranging her hair before a tiny mirror perched on the table. Beside the
mirror is stretched out the morning paper which she looks at when she isn't
gazing into the mirror. She is a well-made and good-looking girl of
twenty-two. Two forces are working in her mind—one, through the
circumstances of her life, pulling her back; the other, through the
influence of books she has read, pushing her forward. The opposing forces
are apparent in her speech and her manners, both of which are degraded
by her environment, and improved by her acquaintance—slight though it
be—with literature. The time is early forenoon.*

Mary (looking at the paper). On a little bye-road, out beyant
Finglas, he was found.

MRS BOYLE *enters by door on right; she has been shopping and carries a
small parcel in her hand. She is forty-five years of age, and twenty years*

ago she must have been a pretty woman; but her face has now assumed that look which ultimately settles down upon the faces of the women of the working-class; a look of listless monotony and harassed anxiety, blending with an expression of mechanical resistance. Were circumstances favourable, she would probably be a handsome, active and clever woman.

Mrs Boyle. Isn't he come in yet?

Mary. No, mother.

Mrs Boyle. Oh, he'll come in when he likes; struttin' about the town like a paycock with Joxer, I suppose. I hear all about Mrs Tancred's son is in this mornin's paper.

Mary. The full details are in it this mornin'; seven wounds he had—one entherin' the neck, with an exit wound beneath the left shoulder-blade; another in the left breast penethratin' the heart, an' . . .

Johnny (*springing up from the fire*). Oh, quit that readin', for God's sake! Are yous losin' all your feelins? It'll soon be that none of yous'll read anythin' that's not about butcherin'!

[*He goes quickly into the room on left.*

Mary. He's gettin' very sensitive, all of a sudden!

Mrs Boyle. I'll read it myself, Mary, by an' by, when I come home. Everybody's sayin' that he was a Die-hard*—thanks be to God that Johnny had nothin' to do with him this long time. . . . (*Opening the parcel and taking out some sausages, which she places on a plate.*) Ah, then, if that father o' yours doesn't come in soon for his breakfast, he may go without any; I'll not wait much longer for him.

Mary. Can't you let him get it himself when he comes in?

Mrs Boyle. Yes, an' let him bring in Joxer Daly along with him? Ay, that's what he'd like, an' that's what he's waitin' for—till he thinks I'm gone to work, an' then sail in with the boul' Joxer, to burn all the coal an' dhrink all the tea in the place, to show them what a good Samaritan he is! But I'll stop here till he comes in, if I have to wait till to-morrow mornin'.

Voice of Johnny inside. Mother!

Mrs. Boyle. Yis?

Voice of Johnny. Bring us in a dhrink o' wather.

Mrs Boyle. Bring in that fella a dhrink o' wather, for God's sake, Mary.

Mary. Isn't he big an' able enough to come out an' get it himself?

Mrs Boyle. If you weren't well yourself you'd like somebody to bring you in a dhrink o' wather.

[*She brings in drink and returns.*

Mrs Boyle. Isn't it terrible to have to be waitin' this way! You'd think he was bringin' twenty pouns a week into the house the way he's going on. He wore out the Health Insurance long ago, he's afther wearin' out the unemployment dole, an', now, he's thryin' to wear out me! An' constantly singin', no less, when he ought always to be on his knees offerin' up a Novena for a job!

Mary (*tying a ribbon, fillet wise around her head*). I don't like this ribbon, ma; I think I'll wear the green—it looks betther than the blue.

Mrs Boyle. Ah, wear whatever ribbon you like, girl, only don't be botherin' me. I don't know what a girl on strike wants to be wearin' a ribbon round her head for or silk stockins on her legs either; its wearin' them things that make the employers think they're givin' yous too much money.

Mary. The hour is past now when we'll ask the employers' permission to wear what we like.

Mrs Boyle. I don't know why you wanted to walk out for Jennie Claffey; up to this you never had a good word for her.

Mary. What's the use of belongin' to a Trades Union if you won't stand up for your principles? Why did they sack her? It was a clear case of victimization. We couldn't let her walk the streets, could we?

Mrs Boyle. No, of course yous couldn't—yous wanted to keep her company. Wan victim wasn't enough. When the employers sacrifice wan victim, the Trades Unions go wan betther be sacrificin' a hundred.

Mary. It doesn't matther what you say, ma—a principle's a principle.

Mrs Boyle. Yis; an' when I go into oul' Murphy's to-morrow, an' he gets to know that, instead o' payin' all, I'm goin' to borry more, what'll he say when I tell him a principle's a principle? What'll we do if he refuses to give us any more on tick?

Mary. He daren't refuse—if he does, can't you tell him he's paid?

Mrs Boyle. It's lookin' as if he was paid, whether he refuses or no.

JOHNNY *appears at the door on left. He can be plainly seen now; he is a thin delicate fellow, something younger than* MARY. *He has evidently gone through a rough time. His face is pale and drawn; there is a tremulous look of indefinite fear in his eyes. The left sleeve of his coat is empty, and he walks with a slight halt.*

Johnny. I was lyin' down; I thought yous were gone. Oul' Simon Mackay is thrampin' about like a horse over me head, an' I can't sleep with him—they're like thunder-claps in me brain! The curse o'—God forgive me for goin' to curse!

Mrs Boyle. There, now; go back an' lie down agen, an' I'll bring you in a nice cup o' tay.

Johnny. Tay, tay, tay! You're always thinkin' o' tay. If a man was dyin', you'd thry to make him swally a cup o' tay!

[*He goes back.*

Mrs Boyle. I don't know what's goin' to be done with him. The bullet he got in the hip in Easter Week was bad enough, but the bomb that shatthered his arm in the fight in O'Connell Street put the finishin' touch on him. I knew he was makin' a fool of himself. God knows I went down on me bended knees to him not to go agen the Free State.*

Mary. He stuck to his principles, an', no matther how you may argue, ma, a principle's a principle.

Voice of Johnny. Is Mary goin' to stay here?

Mary. No, I'm not goin' to stay here; you can't expect me to be always at your beck an' call, can you?

Voice of Johnny. I won't stop here be meself!

Mrs Boyle. Amn't I nicely handicapped with the whole o' yous! I don't know what any o' yous ud do without your ma. (*To* JOHNNY.) Your father'll be here in a minute, an' if you want anythin', he'll get it for you.

Johnny. I hate assin' him for anythin'. . . . He hates to be assed to stir. . . . Is the light lightin' before the picture o' the Virgin?

Mrs Boyle. Yis, yis! The wan inside to St Anthony isn't enough, but he must have another wan to the Virgin here!

JERRY DEVINE *enters hastily. He is about twenty-five, well set, active and earnest. He is a type, becoming very common now in the Labour Movement, of a mind knowing enough to make the mass of his associates, who know less, a power, and too little to broaden that power for the benefit of all.* MARY *seizes her jumper and runs hastily into room left.*

Jerry (breathless). Where's the Captain, Mrs Boyle, where's the Captain?

Mrs Boyle. You may well ass a body that: he's wherever Joxer Daly is—dhrinkin' in some snug* or another.

Jerry. Father Farrell is just afther stoppin' to tell me to run up an' get him to go to the new job that's goin' on in Rathmines; his cousin is foreman o' the job, an' Father Farrell was speakin' to him about poor Johnny an' his father bein' idle so long, an' the foreman told Father Farrell to send the Captain up an' he'd give him a start— I wondher where I'd find him?

Mrs Boyle. You'll find he's ayther in Ryan's or Foley's.

Jerry. I'll run round to Ryan's—I know it's a great house o' Joxer's.

[*He rushes out.*

Mrs Boyle (piteously). There now, he'll miss that job, or I know for what! If he gets win' o' the word, he'll not come back till evenin', so that it'll be too late. There'll never be any good got out o' him so long as he goes with that shouldher-shruggin' Joxer. I killin' meself workin', an' he sthruttin' about from mornin' till night like a paycock!

The steps of two persons are heard coming up a flight of stairs. They are the footsteps of CAPTAIN BOYLE *and* JOXER. CAPTAIN BOYLE *is singing in a deep, sonorous, self-honouring voice.*

The Captain. Sweet Spirit, hear me prayer! Hear . . . oh . . . hear . . . me prayer . . . hear, oh, hear . . . Oh, he . . . ar . . . oh, he . . . ar . . . me . . . pray . . . er!

Joxer (outside). Ah, that's a darlin' song, a daaarlin' song!

Mrs Boyle (viciously). Sweet spirit hear his prayer! Ah, then, I'll take me solemn affeydavey,* it's not for a job he's prayin'!

She sits down on the bed so that the cretonne hangings hide her from the view of those entering.

THE CAPTAIN *comes slowly in. He is a man of about sixty; stout, grey-haired and stocky. His neck is short, and his head looks like a stone ball that one sometimes sees on top of a gate-post. His cheeks, reddish-purple, are puffed out, as if he were always repressing an almost irrepressible ejaculation. On his upper lip is a crisp, tightly cropped moustache; he carries himself with the upper part of his body slightly thrown back, and his stomach slightly thrust forward. His walk is a slow, consequential strut. His clothes are dingy, and he wears a faded seaman's cap with a glazed peak.*

Boyle (to JOXER, *who is still outside).* Come on, come on in, Joxer; she's gone out long ago, man. If there's nothing else to be got, we'll furrage out a cup o' tay, anyway. It's the only bit I get in comfort when she's away. 'Tisn't Juno should be her pet name at all, but Deirdre of the Sorras,* for she's always grousin'.

JOXER *steps cautiously into the room. He may be younger than* THE CAPTAIN *but he looks a lot older. His face is like a bundle of crinkled paper; his eyes have a cunning twinkle; he is spare and loosely built; he has a habit of constantly shrugging his shoulders with a peculiar twitching movement, meant to be ingratiating. His face is invariably ornamented with a grin.*

Joxer. It's a terrible thing to be tied to a woman that's always grousin'. I don't know how you stick it—it ud put years on me. It's a good job she has to be so ofen away, for (*with a shrug*) when the cat's away, the mice can play!

Boyle (with a commanding and complacent gesture). Pull over to the fire, Joxer, an' we'll have a cup o' tay in a minute.

Joxer. Ah, a cup o' tay's a darlin' thing, a daaarlin' thing—the cup that cheers but doesn't . . .

JOXER's *rhapsody is cut short by the sight of* JUNO *coming forward and confronting the two cronies. Both are stupefied.*

Mrs Boyle (*with sweet irony—poking the fire, and turning her head to glare at* JOXER). Pull over to the fire, Joxer Daly, an' we'll have a cup o' tay in a minute! Are you sure, now, you wouldn't like an egg?

Joxer. I can't stop, Mrs Boyle; I'm in a desperate hurry, a desperate hurry.

Mrs Boyle. Pull over to the fire, Joxer Daly; people is always far more comfortabler here than they are in their own place.

JOXER *makes hastily for the door.* BOYLE *stirs to follow him; thinks of something to relieve the situation—stops, and says suddenly*

Joxer!

Joxer (*at door ready to bolt*). Yis?

Boyle. You know the foreman o' that job that's goin' on down in Killesther, don't you, Joxer?

Joxer (*puzzled*). Foreman—Killesther?

Boyle (*with a meaning look*). He's a butty o' yours, isn't he?

Joxer (*the truth dawning on him*). The foreman at Killesther—oh yis, yis. He's an oul' butty o' mine—oh, he's a darlin' man, a daarlin' man.

Boyle. Oh, then, it's a sure thing. It's a pity we didn't go down at breakfast first thing this mornin'—we might ha' been working now; but you didn't know it then.

Joxer (*with a shrug*). It's betther late than never.

Boyle. It's nearly time we got a start, anyhow; I'm fed up knockin' round, doin' nothin'. He promised you—gave you the straight tip?

Joxer. Yis. 'Come down on the blow o' dinner,' says he, 'an' I'll start you, an' any friend you like to brin' with you.' Ah, says I, you're a darlin' man, a daaarlin' man.

Boyle. Well, it couldn't come at a betther time—we're a long time waitin' for it.

Joxer. Indeed we were; but it's a long lane that has no turnin'.

Boyle. The blow up for dinner is at one—wait till I see what time it 'tis.

He goes over to the mantelpiece, and gingerly lifts the clock.

Mrs Boyle. Min' now, how you go on fiddlin' with that clock—
you know the least little thing sets it asthray.

Boyle. The job couldn't come at a betther time; I'm feelin' in
great fettle, Joxer. I'd hardly believe I ever had a pain in me legs, an'
last week I was nearly crippled with them.

Joxer. That's betther an' betther; ah, God never shut wan door
but he opened another!

Boyle. It's only eleven o'clock; we've lashins o' time. I'll slip on
me oul' moleskins afther breakfast, an' we can saunther down at our
ayse. (*Putting his hand on the shovel.*) I think, Joxer, we'd betther
bring our shovels?

Joxer. Yis, Captain, yis; it's betther to go fully prepared an' ready
for all eventualities. You bring your long-tailed shovel, an' I'll bring
me navvy. We mighten' want them, an', then agen, we might: for
want of a nail the shoe was lost, for want of a shoe the horse was lost,
an' for want of a horse the man was lost—aw, that's a darlin' proverb,
a daarlin' . . .

As JOXER *is finishing his sentence,* MRS BOYLE *approaches the door
and* JOXER *retreats hurriedly. She shuts the door with a bang.*

Boyle (*suggestively*). We won't be long pullin' ourselves together
agen when I'm working for a few weeks.

MRS BOYLE *takes no notice.*

Boyle. The foreman on the job is an oul butty o' Joxer's; I have an
idea that I know him meself. (*Silence*) . . . There's a button off the
back o' me moleskin trousers. . . . If you leave out a needle an' thread
I'll sew it on meself . . . Thanks be to God, the pains in me legs is
gone, anyhow!

Mrs Boyle (*with a burst*). Look here, Mr Jacky Boyle, them yarns
won't go down with Juno. I know you an' Joxer Daly of an oul' date,
an', if you think you're able to come it over me with them fairy tales,
you're in the wrong shop.

Boyle (*coughing subduedly to relieve the tenseness of the situation*).
U-u-u-ugh!

Mrs Boyle. Butty o' Joxer's! Oh, you'll do a lot o' good as long as
you continue to be a butty o' Joxer's!

Boyle. U-u-u-ugh!

Mrs Boyle. Shovel! Ah, then, me boyo, you'd do far more work with a knife an' fork than ever you'll do with a shovel! If there was e'er a genuine job goin' you'd be dh'other way about—not able to lift your arms with the pains in your legs! Your poor wife slavin' to keep the bit in your mouth, an' you gallivantin' about all the day like a paycock!

Boyle. It ud be betther for a man to be dead, betther for a man to be dead.

Mrs Boyle (*ignoring the interruption*). Everybody callin' you 'Captain', an' you only wanst on the wather, in an oul' collier from here to Liverpool, when anybody, to listen or look at you, ud take you for a second Christo For Columbus!

Boyle. Are you never goin' to give us a rest?

Mrs Boyle. Oh, you're never tired o' lookin' for a rest.

Boyle. D'ye want to dhrive me out o' the house?

Mrs Boyle. It ud be easier to dhrive you out o' the house than to dhrive you into a job. Here, sit down an' take your breakfast—it may be the last you'll get, for I don't know where the next is goin' to come from.

Boyle. If I get this job we'll be all right.

Mrs Boyle. Did ye see Jerry Devine?

Boyle (*testily*). No, I didn't see him.

Mrs Boyle. No, but you seen Joxer. Well, he was here lookin' for you.

Boyle. Well, let him look!

Mrs Boyle. Oh, indeed, he may well look, for it ud be hard for him to see you, an' you stuck in Ryan's snug.

Boyle. I wasn't in Ryan's snug—I don't go into Ryan's.

Mrs Boyle. Oh, is there a mad dog there? Well, if you weren't in Ryan's you were in Foley's.

Boyle. I'm telling you for the last three weeks I haven't tasted a dhrop of intoxicatin' liquor. I wasn't in ayther wan snug or dh'other—I could swear that on a prayer-book—I'm as innocent as the child unborn!

Mrs Boyle. Well, if you'd been in for your breakfast you'd ha' seen him.

Boyle (*suspiciously*). What does he want me for?

Mrs Boyle. He'll be back any minute an' then you'll soon know.

Boyle. I'll dhrop out an' see if I can meet him.

Mrs Boyle. You'll sit down an' take your breakfast, an' let me go to me work, for I'm an hour late already waitin' for you.

Boyle. You needn't ha' waited, for I'll take no breakfast—I've a little spirit left in me still!

Mrs Boyle. Are you goin' to have your breakfast—yes or no?

Boyle (*too proud to yield*). I'll have no breakfast—yous can keep your breakfast. (*Plaintively*) I'll knock out a bit somewhere, never fear.

Mrs Boyle. Nobody's goin' to coax you—don't think that.

She vigorously replaces the pan and the sausages in the press.

Boyle. I've a little spirit left in me still.

JERRY DEVINE *enters hastily.*

Jerry. Oh, here you are at last! I've been searchin' for you everywhere. The foreman in Foley's told me you hadn't left the snug with Joxer ten minutes before I went in.

Mrs Boyle. An' he swearin' on the holy prayer-book that he wasn't in no snug!

Boyle (*to* JERRY). What business is it o' yours whether I was in a snug or no? What do you want to be gallopin' about afther me for? Is a man not to be allowed to leave his house for a minute without havin' a pack o' spies, pimps an' informers cantherin' at his heels?

Jerry. Oh, you're takin' a wrong view of it, Mr Boyle; I simply was anxious to do you a good turn. I have a message for you from Father Farrell: he says that if you go to the job that's on in Rathmines, an' ask for Foreman Mangan, you'll get a start.

Boyle. That's all right, but I don't want the motions of me body to be watched the way an asthronomer ud watch a star. If you're folleyin' Mary aself, you've no pereeogative to be folleyin' me. (*Suddenly catching his thigh.*) U-ugh, I'm afther gettin' a terrible twinge in me right leg!

Mrs Boyle. Oh, it won't be very long now till it travels into your left wan. It's miraculous that whenever he scents a job in front of him, his legs begin to fail him! Then, me bucko, if you lose this chance, you may go an' furrage for yourself!

Jerry. This job'll last for some time too, Captain, an' as soon as the foundations are in, it'll be cushy enough.

Boyle. Won't it be a climbin' job? How d'ye expect me to be able to go up a ladder with these legs? An', if I get up aself, how am I goin' to get down agen?

Mrs Boyle (*viciously*). Get wan o' the labourers to carry you down in a hod! You can't climb a laddher, but you can skip like a goat into a snug!

Jerry. I wouldn't let meself be let down that easy, Mr Boyle; a little exercise, now, might do you all the good in the world.

Boyle. It's a docthor you should have been, Devine—maybe you know more about the pains in me legs than meself that has them?

Jerry (*irritated*). Oh, I know nothin' about the pains in your legs; I've brought the message that Father Farrell gave me, an' that's all I can do.

Mrs Boyle. Here, sit down an' take your breakfast, an' go an' get ready; an' don't be actin' as if you couldn't pull a wing out of a dead bee.

Boyle. I want no breakfast, I tell you; it ud choke me afther all that's been said. I've a little spirit left in me still.

Mrs Boyle. Well, let's see your spirit, then, an' go in at wanst an' put on your moleskin trousers!

Boyle (*moving towards the door on left*). It ud be betther for a man to be dead! U-ugh! There's another twinge in me other leg! Nobody but meself knows the sufferin' I'm goin' through with the pains in these legs o' mine!

He goes into the room on left as MARY *comes out with her hat in her hand.*

Mrs Boyle. I'll have to push off now, for I'm terrible late already, but I was determined to stay an' hunt that Joxer this time.

[*She goes off.*

Jerry. Are you going out, Mary?

Mary. It looks like it when I'm putting on my hat, doesn't it?

Jerry. The bitther word agen, Mary.

Mary. You won't allow me to be friendly with you; if I thry, you deliberately misundherstand it.

Jerry. I didn't always misundherstand it; you were ofen delighted to have the arms of Jerry around you.

Mary. If you go on talkin' like this, Jerry Devine, you'll make me hate you!

Jerry. Well, let it be either a weddin' or a wake! Listen, Mary, I'm standin' for the Secretaryship of our Union. There's only one opposin' me; I'm popular with all the men, an' a good speaker—all are sayin' that I'll get elected.

Mary. Well?

Jerry. The job's worth three hundred an' fifty pounds a year, Mary. You an' I could live nice an' cosily on that; it would lift you out o' this place an' . . .

Mary. I haven't time to listen to you now—I have to go.

She is going out when JERRY *bars the way.*

Jerry (*appealingly*). Mary, what's come over you with me for the last few weeks? You hardly speak to me, an' then only a word with a face o' bittherness on it. Have you forgotten, Mary, all the happy evenins that were as sweet as the scented hawthorn that sheltered the sides o' the road as we saunthered through the country?

Mary. That's all over now. When you get your new job, Jerry, you won't be long findin' a girl far betther than I am for your sweetheart.

Jerry. Never, never, Mary! No matther what happens, you'll always be the same to me.

Mary. I must be off; please let me go, Jerry.

Jerry. I'll go a bit o' the way with you.

Mary. You needn't, thanks; I want to be by meself.

Jerry (*catching her arm*). You're goin' to meet another fella; you've clicked with some one else, me lady!

Mary. That's no concern o' yours, Jerry Devine; let me go!

Jerry. I saw yous comin' out o' the Cornflower Dance Class, an' you hangin' on his arm—a thin, lanky strip of a Micky Dazzler, with a walkin'-stick an' gloves!

Voice of Johnny (*loudly*). What are you doin' there—pullin' about everything!

Voice of Boyle (*loudly and viciously*). I'm puttin' on me moleskin trousers!

Mary. You're hurtin' me arm! Let me go, or I'll scream, an' then you'll have the oul' fella out on top of us!

Jerry. Don't be so hard on a fella, Mary, don't be so hard.

Boyle (*appearing at the door*). What's the meanin' of all this hillabaloo?

Mary. Let me go, let me go!

Boyle. D'ye hear me—what's all this hillabaloo about?

Jerry (*plaintively*). Will you not give us one kind word, one kind word, Mary?

Boyle. D'ye hear me talkin' to yous? What's all this hillabaloo for?

Jerry. Let me kiss your hand, your little, tiny, white hand!

Boyle. Your little, tiny, white hand—are you takin' leave o' your senses, man?

[MARY *breaks away and rushes out.*

Boyle. This is nice goins on in front of her father!

Jerry. Ah, dhry up, for God's sake!

[*He follows* MARY.

Boyle. Chiselurs* don't care a damn now about their parents, they're bringin' their fathers' grey hairs down with sorra to the grave, an' laughin' at it, laughin' at it. Ah, I suppose it's just the same everywhere—the whole worl's in a state o' chassis!* (*He sits by the fire.*) Breakfast! Well, they can keep their breakfast for me. Not if they went down on their bended knees would I take it—I'll show them I've a little spirit left in me still! (*He goes over to the press, takes out a plate and looks at it.*) Sassige! Well, let her keep her sassige. (*He returns to the fire, takes up the teapot and gives it a gentle shake.*) The tea's wet right enough.

*A pause; he rises, goes to the press, takes out the sausage, puts it
on the pan, and puts both on the fire. He attends the sausage with
a fork.*

Boyle (*singing*):

When the robins nest agen,
And the flowers are in bloom,
When the Springtime's sunny smile seems to banish all sorrow an'
    gloom;
Then me bonny blue-ey'd lad, if me heart be true till then—
He's promised he'll come back to me,
When the robins nest agen!

He lifts his head at the high note, and then drops his eyes to the pan.

Boyle (*singing*):

            When the . . .

*Steps are heard approaching; he whips the pan off the fire and puts it
under the bed, then sits down at the fire. The door opens and a bearded
man looking in says:*

You don't happen to want a sewin' machine?

Boyle (*furiously*). No, I don't want e'er a sewin' machine!

He returns the pan to the fire, and commences to sing again.

Boyle (*singing*):

        When the robins nest agen,
        And the flowers they are in bloom,
        He's . . .

A thundering knock is heard at the street door.

Boyle. There's a terrible tatheraraa—that's a stranger—that's
nobody belongin' to the house.

        Another loud knock.

Joxer (*sticking his head in at the door*). Did ye hear them
tatherarahs?

Boyle. Well, Joxer, I'm not deaf.

Johnny (*appearing in his shirt and trousers at the door on left; his face
is anxious and his voice is tremulous*). Who's that at the door; who's

that at the door? Who gave that knock—d'ye yous hear me—are yous deaf or dhrunk or what?

Boyle (*to* JOHNNY). How the hell do I know who 'tis? Joxer, stick your head out o' the window an' see.

Joxer. An' mebbe get a bullet in the kisser? Ah, none o' them thricks for Joxer! It's betther to be a coward than a corpse!

Boyle (*looking cautiously out of the window*). It's a fella in a thrench coat.

Johnny. Holy Mary, Mother o' God, I . . .

Boyle. He's goin' away—he must ha' got tired knockin'.

[JOHNNY *returns to the room on left.*

Boyle. Sit down an' have a cup o' tay, Joxer.

Joxer. I'm afraid the missus ud pop in on us agen before we'd know where we are. Somethins tellin' me to go at wanst.

Boyle. Don't be superstitious, man; we're Dublin men, an' not boyos that's only afther comin' up from the bog o' Allen*—though if she did come in, right enough, we'd be caught like rats in a thrap.

Joxer. An' you know the sort she is—she wouldn't listen to reason—an' wanse bitten twice shy.

Boyle (*going over to the window at back*). If the worst came to the worst, you could dart out here, Joxer; it's only a dhrop of a few feet to the roof of the return room,* an' the first minute she goes into dh'other room, I'll give you the bend, an' you can slip in an' away.

Joxer (*yielding to the temptation*). Ah, I won't stop very long anyhow. (*Picking up a book from the table.*) Who's is the buk?

Boyle. Aw, one o' Mary's; she's always readin' lately—nothin' but thrash, too. There's one I was lookin' at dh' other day: three stories, The Doll's House, Ghosts, an' The Wild Duck*—buks only fit for chiselurs!

Joxer. Didja ever rade *Elizabeth, or Th' Exile o' Sibayria* . . . ah, it's a darlin' story, a daarlin' story!

Boyle. You eat your sassige, an' never min' *Th' Exile o' Sibayria*.

Both sit down; BOYLE *fills out tea, pours gravy on* JOXER's *plate, and keeps the sausage for himself.*

Joxer. What are you wearin' your moleskin trousers for?

Boyle. I have to go to a job, Joxer. Just afther you'd gone, Devine kem runnin' in to tell us that Father Farrell said if I went down to the job that's goin' on in Rathmines I'd get a start.

Joxer. Be the holy, that's good news!

Boyle. How is it good news? I wondher if you were in my condition, would you call it good news?

Joxer. I thought . . .

Boyle. You thought! You think too sudden sometimes, Joxer. D'ye know, I'm hardly able to crawl with the pains in me legs!

Joxer. Yis, yis; I forgot the pains in your legs. I know you can do nothin' while they're at you.

Boyle. You forgot; I don't think any of yous realize the state I'm in with the pains in me legs. Whut ud happen if I had to carry a bag o' cement?

Joxer. Ah, any man havin' the like of them pains id be down an' out, down an' out.

Boyle. I wouldn't mind if he had said it to meself; but, no, oh no, he rushes in an' shouts it out in front o' Juno, an' you know what Juno is, Joxer. We all know Devine knows a little more than the rest of us, but he doesn't act as if he did; he's a good boy, sober, able to talk an' all that, but still . . .

Joxer. Oh ay; able to argufy, but still . . .

Boyle. If he's runnin' afther Mary, aself, he's not goin' to be runnin' afther me. Captain Boyle's able to take care of himself. Afther all, I'm not gettin' brought up on Virol.* I never heard him usin' a curse; I don't believe he was ever dhrunk in his life—sure he's not like a Christian at all!

Joxer. You're afther takin' the word out o' me mouth—afther all, a Christian's natural, but he's unnatural.

Boyle. His oul' fella was just the same—a Wicklow man.

Joxer. A Wicklow man! That explains the whole thing. I've met many a Wicklow man in me time, but I never met wan that was any good.

Boyle. 'Father Farrell,' says he, 'sent me down to tell you.' Father Farrell! . . . D'ye know, Joxer, I never like to be beholden to any o' the clergy.

Joxer. It's dangerous, right enough.

Boyle. If they do anything for you, they'd want you to be livin' in the Chapel. . . . I'm goin' to tell you somethin', Joxer, that I wouldn't tell to anybody else—the clergy always had too much power over the people in this unfortunate country.

Joxer. You could sing that if you had an air to it!

Boyle (*becoming enthusiastic*). Didn't they prevent the people in ''47' from seizin' the corn, an' they starvin'; didn't they down Parnell; didn't they say that hell wasn't hot enough nor eternity long enough to punish the Fenians?* We don't forget, we don't forget them things, Joxer. If they've taken everything else from us, Joxer, they've left us our memory.

Joxer (*emotionally*). For mem'ry's the only friend that grief can call its own, that grief . . . can . . . call . . . its own!

Boyle. Father Farrell's beginnin' to take a great intherest in Captain Boyle; because of what Johnny did for his country, says he to me wan day. It's a curious way to reward Johnny be makin' his poor oul' father work. But, that's what the clergy want, Joxer—work, work, work for me an' you; havin' us mulin' from mornin' till night, so that they may be in betther fettle when they come hoppin' round for their dues! Job! Well, let him give his job to wan of his hymn-singin', prayer-spoutin', craw-thumpin' Confraternity men!*

The voice of a COAL-BLOCK VENDOR *is heard chanting in the street.*

Voice of coal vendor. Blocks . . . coal-blocks! Blocks . . . coal-blocks!

Joxer. God be with the young days when you were steppin' the deck of a manly ship, with the win' blowin' a hurricane through the masts, an' the only sound you'd hear was, 'Port your helm!' an' the only answer, 'Port it is, sir!'

Boyle. Them was days, Joxer, them was days. Nothin' was too hot or too heavy for me then. Sailin' from the Gulf o' Mexico to the Antanartic Ocean. I seen things, I seen things, Joxer, that no mortal man should speak about that knows his Catechism. Ofen, an' ofen, when I was fixed to the wheel with a marlinspike, an' the wins blowin' fierce an' the waves lashin' an' lashin', till you'd think every minute was goin' to be your last, an' it blowed, an' blowed—blew is the right word, Joxer, but blowed is what the sailors use . . .

Joxer. Aw, it's a darlin' word, a daarlin' word.

Boyle. An', as it blowed an' blowed, I ofen looked up at the sky an' assed meself the question—what is the stars, what is the stars?

Voice of coal vendor. Any blocks, coal-blocks; blocks, coal-blocks!

Joxer. Ah, that's the question, that's the question—what is the stars?

Boyle. An' then, I'd have another look, an' I'd ass meself—what is the moon?

Joxer. Ah, that's the question—what is the moon, what is the moon?

EXPLANATORY NOTES

EDMUND BURKE

From *Reflections on the Revolution in France* (1790). In this celebrated passage, Burke prefaces his defence of ancient principle with an exalted tribute to Marie Antoinette. His eulogistic account of the Queen provoked his opponents, who accused him of romantic indulgence. Thomas Jefferson was among those who claimed that Burke had painted the Queen of France as an angel, while overlooking her considerable vices.

5 *Non satis est pulchra esse poemata, dulcia sunto*: it is not enough for poems to be beautiful; they must also be sweet (Horace, *Ars Poetica*, 99–100).

6 *swinish multitude*: Burke's critics seized upon this phrase and turned it to advantage. There were numerous ripostes such as Thomas Spence's *Pig's Meat, or Lessons for the Swinish Multitude* (1793–5) and J. Parkinson's *An Address to Edmund Burke from the Swinish Multitude* (1793).

7 *gentis incunabula nostrae*: the cradle of our people (Virgil, *Aeneid*, iii. 105).

From Letter to Richard Burke. On 19 Feb. 1792, Burke informed his son Richard, then in Dublin, that he was writing a long letter to him, but the letter was never finished. The letter considers the grievances of Irish Catholics and dwells on the significance of the term 'Protestant Ascendancy'.

10 *honestum nomen imponitur vitio*: an honourable name is given to a vice.

the touch of the Corporation: on 20 Jan. 1792, the Corporation of Dublin approved an address to the King, pleading for the preservation of the Protestant ascendancy in Ireland.

the Speaker of the House of Commons: John Foster (1740–1828).

the Lord Mayor of Dublin: Henry Gore Sankey (d. 1821).

11 *parce detorsum*: sparingly altered (Horace, *Ars Poetica*, 53).

THEOBALD WOLFE TONE

From *The Life of Theobald Wolfe Tone* (1826). Tone's journals were collected and edited by his son, William, and published under the above title in Washington in 1826, with later editions in Paris, Dublin, and London. The passage reprinted here was purportedly written in 1797.

13 *an eloquent publication*: Burke's *Reflections on the Revolution in France* (1790).

14 *coup de grâce*: a stroke of grace (i.e. a finishing blow to put someone out of misery).

15 *Russell*: Thomas Russell, political radical who assisted Tone and Henry Joy McCracken in establishing the Society of United Irishmen in 1791.

16 *the Volunteer Convention in 1783*: companies of volunteers, uniformed and partly armed, were established in the 1770s, initially to defend the coasts of Ireland against any invader while British regiments were engaged in America. Their presence, however, strengthened nationalist sentiment and helped to bring about legislative independence in 1782.

John Keogh: John Keogh (1740–1817), Catholic leader who was largely responsible for the Catholic Convention of 1792, leading to the Relief Act of 1793.

Henry Flood: Henry Flood (1732–91), statesman and orator. MP for Kilkenny and advocate of an independent Irish legislature. He lost his place as leader of the opposition to Henry Grattan (1746–1820).

ROBERT EMMET

'Speech from the Dock', from *Report of the Proceedings in Cases of High Treason* [by William Ridgeway, Barrister at Law] (Dublin: John Exshaw, 1803). See biographical entry for details of the circumstances relating to Emmet's arrest and trial.

DANIEL O'CONNELL

In 1843, O'Connell addressed a series of vast public meetings throughout Ireland, calling for the repeal of the Act of Union (1800) and the establishment of an Irish Parliament. One of the largest of these meetings was held at Tara, Co. Meath, the seat of the high kings of Ireland until the sixth century.

27 *a mess of pottage*: literally, stuff in a pot, but also a reference to the biblical instance of Esau selling the everlasting inheritance of heaven for a mess of pottage (Genesis 25: 29–34).

29 *my third son, the member for Kilkenny*: John O'Connell (1810–58), elected MP for Youghal, 1832, and later representing Athlone, Kilkenny, Limerick, and Clonmel.

JAMES FINTAN LALOR

From the *Irish Felon*, 24 June 1848. The newspaper was founded by John Martin (1812–75) to replace John Mitchell's *United Irishman*. Mitchell, his brother-in-law, had been transported to Van Diemen's Land and the paper had been suppressed. Lalor helped to edit the *Irish Felon* and in the first number reasserted the revolutionary spirit of Wolfe Tone and advocated immediate insurrection. His letter marks a militant break with the limited constitutional independence achieved in 1782 and proposes a more radical programme of political change than Daniel O'Connell's attempt to repeal the Act of Union. Lalor was arrested in the rising of 1848, just a month later.

35 *Arcades ambo*: balmy Arcadians (the suggestion is that the ideals of

Repeal are not in keeping with the needs of the real world; Arcadia, the legendary haunt of the Greeks, also implies rural simplicity).

36 *the constitution that Tone died to obtain*: see the extract above from the autobiography of Theobald Wolfe Tone (1763–98) and also the biographical entry on Tone at the end of this volume.

   sub silentio: in silence, without remark being made.

41 *our gage of battle*: a pledge (traditionally, a glove thrown down) to signal readiness to fight.

CHARLOTTE BROOKE

This modest Preface to *Reliques of Irish Poetry* (1789) presents the book as 'a translation of ancient Irish poetry', comprising four species of composition: the Heroic Poem, the Ode, the Elegy, and the Song. An Irish typeface was designed for the printing of the originals, which appear at the end of the 1789 volume.

LE CHEVALIER DE LA TOCNAYE

From *A Frenchman's Walk Through Ireland (1796–7)* [*Promenade d'un Français dans l'Irelande*], translated by John Stevenson (Dublin: Hodges, Figgis & Co., 1914).

47 *the Four Courts of Justice*: one of Dublin's finest buildings, designed by James Gandon (1742–1823).

   Themis: the name of the ancient Greek goddess of law and justice.

49 *'The Liberties'*: a district formerly outside the walls of the medieval city of Dublin, run by local courts and free of the city regulations on trade. From the eighteenth century onwards, it was a vibrant slum area, renowned for its rebelliousness.

51 *this Augean stable*: like the abominably filthy stable of Augeas, King of Elis, which Hercules cleansed by diverting the river Alpheus through it.

52 *anything green, ribbon or otherwise*: a display of Irish nationalist sentiment (the green ribbon was the emblem of the United Irishmen).

   a company of Orangemen: members of the Orange Order, a Protestant Society founded in Co. Armagh in 1795, commemorating the victory of King William III, Prince of Orange, at the Battle of the Boyne in 1690.

54 *pot-de-vin*: literally, a pot of wine, but figuratively referring to additional benefits accrued from the lease of land.

JOHN GAMBLE

From *Sketches of History, Politics, and Manners, in Dublin, and the North of Ireland, in 1810*, new edn. (London: Baldwick, Cradock, and Joy, 1826).

59 *Allhallows eve*: the eve of All Hallows or All Saints, popularly known as Hallowe'en (31 Oct.). In the old Celtic calendar, the last night of October was 'old year's night', the night of all witches, but this was transformed by the Church into the Eve of All Saints.

   shifts: underclothes (derived from a shift or change of clothing).

WILLIAM CARLETON

From *Traits and Stories of the Irish Peasantry. A New Edition* (Dublin: William Curry & Co., 1843–4). This was Carleton's first published work. Originally titled 'A Pilgrimage to Patrick's Purgatory' and printed in the *Christian Examiner* (1828), it appeared with its new title as an accompaniment to the novella, *Father Butler* (1829), and was then revised for *Traits and Stories of the Irish Peasantry*.

61 *Purgatory*: a place of suffering and expiation. Lough Derg is referred to as Purgatory because of the penance undertaken there by St Patrick. Carleton uses the name for both the lake and the lake isle, later known as Station Island.

   Petigo: Pettigo, a village on the pilgrim route to Lough Derg in Co. Donegal.

63 *three Paters and Aves, and a Creed*: prayers of gratitude said by the Christian pilgrims arriving at Lough Derg (specifically, 'Our Father', 'Hail Mary', and 'I believe').

64 *stations*: holy places or designated sites for prayer, visited by pilgrims in fixed succession. The Stations of the Cross represent the incidents of Christ's Passion.

   circumbendibus: a roundabout process or method; a twist.

65 *bannock*: a round, flat cake, usually made from barley-meal.

67 *Juggernaut*: in Hindu myth, the image of Krishna, annually dragged in procession on a mighty car, under the wheels of which his devotees would throw themselves to be crushed; figuratively speaking, the term refers to anything to which people blindly devote themselves or are ruthlessly sacrificed.

71 *his stole and box of chrism*: the priest's vestment (usually a narrow strip of silk or linen worn over the shoulders) and the consecrated oil and balm used in the administration of certain sacraments.

   extreme unction: the sacrament in which those in extreme conditions (the sick and the dying) are anointed by a priest.

   De profundis: a prayer based on Psalm 130, 'Out of the depths have I cried to thee, O Lord'; a cry from the depths of sorrow.

72 *malaproprian*: given to the ludicrous misuse of words.

73 *lanna*: from the Irish *leanbh* (young person; child).

   a cushla: Irish term of endearment (my dear one).

73 *aroon*: another term of endearment, from the Irish *a rún* (loved one).

astore machree: yet another term of endearment, from the Irish *a stór* (treasure) and *mo chroí* (my heart).

THOMAS DAVIS

'Ballad Poetry of Ireland' first appeared in *The Nation*, 2 Aug. 1845, as a review of the book of that title edited by Charles Gavan Duffy. 'The History of Ireland' was also a book review in *The Nation*. Both essays are reprinted from *Essays Literary and Historical By Thomas Davis*, ed. D. J. O'Donoghue (Dundalk: Dundalgan Press, 1914).

   the English Pale, the Ulster Settlement: from the late fifteenth century onwards, the term 'Pale' (a defended area with clearly defined boundaries) was applied to the English parts of the four counties around Dublin which were subject to direct royal government. The Ulster Settlement refers to the seizure and reallocation of land in Ulster, following the wars between Elizabeth I and the supporters of Hugh O'Neill, 1594–1603. The process of transferring land from Catholic to Protestant ownership continued throughout the seventeenth century, with a large influx of Scots settlers in the 1630s.

74 *on his march to Kinsale*: Hugh O'Neill, Earl of Tyrone (1550–1616), led his Irish soldiers to Kinsale to assist the Spanish expeditionary force that had landed there in 1601; encountering strong opposition from Lord Mountjoy and his allies, he was forced to retreat.

   Strongbownian: a follower of Richard de Clare, Earl of Pembroke, known as 'Strongbow', who had landed in Ireland with Norman knights in 1170 prior to the arrival of Henry II.

   Swift and Grattan: Jonathan Swift (1667–1745), Dublin-born writer, author of *Gulliver's Travels* (1726) and several essays on Irish social and political concerns; Henry Grattan (1746–1820), Dublin-born politician and architect of Irish legislative independence in 1782. Davis sees their ideas of Irish nationality as limited and offers a more comprehensive ideal of national culture.

   Grattan and Curran . . . Griffin and Carleton . . . Maclise and Burton: John Philpott Curran (1750–1817), orator and MP in the Irish Parliament, and an eloquent spokesman in favour of Catholic Emancipation; Gerald Griffin (1803–40), author of *The Collegians* (1829) and other novels; William Carleton, see biographical entry in this volume; Daniel Maclise (1806–70), painter and book illustrator; Frederick William Burton (1816–1900), Dublin-based painter of miniatures and watercolour portraits, appointed Director of the National Gallery in London in 1874.

77 *the scarce lithograph of Moreau*: Caesar Moreau (1791–1861) published his valuable and scarce *Past and Present Statistical State of Ireland* in 1827, printed in a copperplate style.

MARIA EDGEWORTH

From *Castle Rackrent* (1800). The title of the novel is an acknowledgement of extortionate rents which often stretched impoverished tenants beyond their means. Thady Quirk, a steward, tells of the declining fortunes of three generations of the landowning Rackrent family. In the extract printed here (from the beginning of the novel), he recalls the dissolute behaviour of Sir Patrick Rackrent, who drinks himself to death; Sir Murtagh, an obsessive litigant; and Sir Kit, who is brought home in a wheelbarrow, fatally injured in a duel.

The notes printed at the foot of each page are the author's. Words and phrases accompanied with a superscript ^G are explained in the author's glossary at the end of the extract.

129 *Spencer*: Sir Edmund Spenser (1552–99), whose *View of the Present State of Ireland* (1596) Edgeworth proceeds to quote.

80 *Holantide*: Hallowe'en.

cousin-german: first cousin.

car: cart.

the three kingdoms itself: England, Scotland, and Ireland.

81 *He that goes to bed . . . honest fellow*: a traditional song, popular as early as the mid-seventeenth century.

83 *the Linen Board to distribute gratis*: the Linen Board was based in Dublin and encouraged the production of linen (from locally grown flax) throughout Ireland. It was only in parts of Ulster, however, that it flourished.

84 *replevying*: recovering cattle or other goods taken from him, having provided security for the case to be tried in a court of justice.

heriots: payments, often consisting of the best livestock, made to the landlord on the death of a tenant.

'learning is better than house or land': a proverb, as the novel suggests, but a possible written source is David Garrick's prologue to Oliver Goldsmith's comedy, *She Stoops to Conquer* (1733): 'When ign'rance enters, folly is at hand; | Learning is better far than house and land'.

fee-simple: feudal tenure or fief.

85 *abatements*: reductions in value.

loy: a narrow spade.

SYDNEY OWENSON (LADY MORGAN)

From *The Wild Irish Girl* (1806). The novel is set in Tireragh, Co. Sligo, where it was written. The extract reprinted here combines a vivid delight in Gothic scenery and mystery with an intense curiosity towards ancient Irish customs and manners.

95 *manes*: the shade of a departed person, seeking expiation through violent sacrifice.

   carte du pays: a chart of the land.

98 *pontificals*: the appropriate vestments of a priest.

   glory: a circle of light.

100 *outré*: out of the way; beyond the bounds of what is proper or usual.

   Milton's ruined angel: Milton's description of Satan (of which this is a slight misquotation) appears in Book 1 of *Paradise Lost*, lines 589–91.

101 *Caiphas*: Caiaphas, the high priest who interrogates Jesus after his arrest (Matthew 26: 57).

   cerulean blue: azure, the clear blue of the unclouded sky.

103 *the Eolian lyre*: the Eolian or Æolian lyre or harp (from Æolus, god of the winds) is a stringed instrument that produces musical sounds from a current of air. It was a popular symbol of inspiration for the Romantic poets.

CHARLES MATURIN

From *Melmoth the Wanderer* (1820), Maturin's celebrated Gothic novel. The extract reprinted here (chapter 1) is set in early nineteenth-century Dublin and introduces us to a student, John Melmoth, but the novel ranges far and wide as it traces the wanderings of an earlier Melmoth who, in a Faustian pact, exchanged his soul for worldly power and knowledge.

106 *Shakespeare*: the quotation is from *Henry VI*, III. iii.

107 *the mail*: the mail coach.

   wig-blocks: for supporting wigs.

   'shod with felt': 'To shoe a troop of horse with felt', Shakespeare, *King Lear*, IV. vi.

   the ghost of Beatrice in the Monk: the Gothic novel *The Monk* (1796), which earned its author, Matthew Gregory Lewis (1775–1818), the nickname of 'Monk' Lewis.

109 *'eyes that glow and fangs that grin'*: unidentified by Maturin's editors, though it possibly derives from the Gothic fiction of the time.

   kish: a large wicker basket for carrying turf.

110 *cottar's hut*: a peasant cottage.

   'as is beyond our element': Shakespeare, *The Merry Wives of Windsor*, IV. ii.

   No one twined so well: Maturin is here describing various spells (practised in peasant Ireland) for discovering the identity of a future husband.

   'ears polite': from Pope's *Epistle to Burlington*, ii. 149–50.

   Anglicè: in standard English, as distinct from *Hibernicè* (in Hiberno-English).

111 *Lord Lyttleton*: Thomas Lyttleton (1744–79) was supposed to have foreseen his own death in a dream three days earlier.

imprimis: in the first place (used here to emphasize the fact that John has black hair: the housekeeper's expression, 'white-headed boy', is just a term of endearment).

Miss Edgeworth's Tales: Maria Edgeworth (1767–1849), whose novel *The Absentee* (1812) was part of a series of 'Tales of Fashionable Life'.

slink-veal: the flesh of a premature calf.

'suo periculo': at his own risk (Latin).

the Dean of Killala: the author's great-grandfather, Peter Maturin, was Dean of Killala, Co. Mayo, from 1724 to 1741.

112 *'veritable Amphitryon' of the feast*: Amphitryon, King of Thebes, was impersonated by Zeus; Maturin is recalling Molière's dramatization of the story: 'Le veritable Amphitryon est l'Amphitryon ou l'on dine'.

'even Sancho cherished his little carcase': from the final chapter of *Don Quixote*.

a Pythoness on her tripod: one of the Priestesses of Apollo at Delphi, who conducted her prophecies from a three-legged seat.

113 *the Irish præficæ*: Irish weepers, likened to the mourners in classical literature.

the story of Sinbad the Sailor: from *The Thousand and One Nights*.

'all was cold as any stone': Shakespeare, *Henry V*, II. iii.

114 *their name is Legion*: a reference to the New Testament story of a man possessed by many devils, hence the name Legion (Luke 9: 30).

sixes: candles bought in batches of six (presumably six to the pound).

115 *'her reading and writing came by nature'*: Shakespeare, *Much Ado About Nothing*, III. iii.

'churching of women': the thanksgiving of women after childbirth.

niggers: niggards, used to reduce the size of the grate and so cut down on fuel.

117 *THALABA*: Robert Southey, *Thalaba the Destroyer* (1801), Book II, verse 5, lines 10–11.

118 *poor Butler*: Samuel Butler (1612–80), who became destitute in later years. Maturin is quoting inaccurately from the second volume of Butler's *Genuine Remains* (1759).

facies Hippocratica: the look of the face just before death (as described by Hippocrates).

119 *the blue chamber of the dwelling*: possibly adopted from the story of Bluebeard, in which entry to a particular chamber is forbidden.

SHERIDAN LE FANU

From *The House by the Church-yard*, 3 vols. (London: Tinsley, Brothers, 1863), volume II, chapter XXXIV. The novel was first serialized in the *Dublin University Magazine*. It is narrated by Charles Cresseron and set in Chapelizod, near Dublin, in the eighteenth century. The extract in this volume follows the murder of an army doctor, Sturk, by a mysterious assailant. One of the chief suspects is Charles Nutter, whose body has reportedly been discovered by fishermen.

121 *rummer-glass*: a large drinking glass (from the Dutch *roemer*).

Ringsend: area of south-east Dublin, close to the River Liffey and Dublin Bay.

slack down the fire: dampen the flames.

122 *flags*: stone slabs or flagstones.

vapours: an exhalation rising from the ground or some damp place; mist or fog.

123 *press*: a large cupboard for holding clothes and other possessions.

EMILY LAWLESS

From *Hurrish: A Study* (1886). This first novel by Emily Lawless is set in Co. Clare during the time of the Land War waged in response to agricultural depression and exploitative landlord–tenant relations. The Land League was formed in 1879 and managed to win concessions by 1882, but there was sporadic violence along the way. The violence in this case affects Horatio (Hurrish) O'Brien, an innocent smallholder who finds himself in a tragic dispute with a resentful neighbour and distant relative. The extract is from chapter 1 of the novel.

126 *omnium gatherum*: quasi Latin for a gathering of all sorts of things.

'creepy' stool: a low stool, close to the ground.

A broad-shouldered, loose-limbed, genial-faced giant: James Joyce parodies this extravagant description of the hero in the Cyclops episode of *Ulysses*.

128 *that ill-starred apology for a rebellion*: the abortive Fenian rising of 1867.

myrmidons: unscrupulous supporters or hirelings.

pabulum: fodder.

ANTOINE RAFTERY

'I am Raftery' has been translated from the Irish ('Mise Raifteri') many times, and Raftery has become an emblematic figure of Irish poetic endeavour, not just for writers of the literary revival who were rediscovering the Gaelic culture of the west, but for later writers, like Derek Mahon, contemplating the seemingly bleak poetic prospects of the contemporary north. The version here is from Douglas Hyde's *Songs of Connacht* (1903).

CHARLOTTE BROOKE

'Elegy on the Death of Carolan', from *Reliques of Irish Poetry* (1789). See note above. Turlough Carolan (Toirdhealbhach Ó Cearbhalláin, 1670–1738), Irish harper, composer, and poet, was celebrated by his contemporaries (Oliver Goldsmith wrote a notable essay about him) and his music continues to be revered today. The poem is a translation from the Irish of M'Cabe.

THOMAS MOORE

Five of the songs are from *Irish Melodies* (1807–34). 'Oft, in the stilly night' is from *National Airs* (1818).

131 *'Oh! breathe not his name'*: the title echoes the sentiments of Robert Emmet's closing words in his famous speech from the dock at his trial for high treason in Sept. 1803 (see above). Emmet had asked for the charity of silence: 'When my country takes her place among the nations of the earth, *then, and not till then,* let my epitaph be written.'

132 *'She is far from the land'*: the 'she' of the title is Sarah Curran (1780–1808), who was secretly engaged to Robert Emmet at the time of his execution in 1803. She escaped her father's anger at discovering her attachment to Emmet by staying with friends in Cork. She later married a Captain Sturgeon in Cork in 1805. She died in England shortly after.

133 *'The harp that once through Tara's halls'*: Tara, Co. Meath, was the seat of the high kings of Ireland.

MARY TIGHE

The three poems written at Killarney in 1800 are all sonnets. 'Address to my Harp' should be compared with Charlotte Brooke's 'Elegy on the Death of Carolan' and Thomas Moore's 'The harp that once through Tara's halls', in which the harp is both a national emblem and a source of comfort. All four poems are from *Psyche, with Other Poems* (London: Longman, Hurst, Rees, Orme and Brown, 1811).

THOMAS FURLONG

'Roisin Dubh', from *Irish Minstrelsy*, ed. James Hardiman (1831), is an Irish poem which, according to Hardiman, was composed in the reign of Elizabeth I to celebrate the Irish hero, Hugh Ruadh O'Donnell of Tirconnell. A love song opens out into a political allegory of Ireland's struggle for liberty. 'Roisin Dubh' (meaning 'little black rose') has been translated many times (by Samuel Ferguson and Aubrey de Vere and James Clarence Mangan, among others).

'Eileen a Roon', from *Irish Minstrelsy*, ed. James Hardiman (1831). 'A Roon' is a term of endearment, from the Irish *a rún* (loved one).

'The Spirit of Irish Song' is thought to be the last work Furlong composed.

JAMES CLARENCE MANGAN

'To My Native Land' was published in the *Comet*, 15 July 1832. It is generally considered to be Mangan's earliest nationalist poem.

140 *The harp remaineth where it fell*: the harp, a potent image of Irish national culture, lies broken, signifying the country's defeat and ruin.

'The Woman of Three Cows' was first published in the *Irish Penny Journal*, 29 Aug. 1840. It is based on an anonymous Irish poem, probably given to Mangan in a literal translation by Eugene O'Curry.

142 *agragh*: from the Irish *a ghrá* (love, as in 'my love').

Momonia: Munster, the home of the legendary Owen More (Eoghan Mór).

brave sons of the Lord of Clare: the Lord of Clare was Domhnall Ó Briain (Daniel O'Brien), the 3rd Viscount of Clare, who provided military support for James II in 1689. His elder son, Domhnall, commanded 'Clare's dragoons', and his younger son, Cormac, commanded the infantry. Both died in exile after the Treaty of Limerick.

Movrone: from the Irish *mo Bhrón* (my sorrow).

Donnell of the Ships: Donal O'Sullivan Beare (1560–1618), Gaelic chief from West Cork, who left Ireland for Spain in 1602 after the destruction of the family stronghold, Dunboy Castle. He was later assassinated in Madrid by an Anglo-Irishman, John Bathe.

O'Ruark, Maguire, those souls of fire: Brian Óg Ó Ruairc, who offered shelter to Donal O'Sullivan Beare at Leitrim Castle, and Brian Maguidhir of Fermanagh, another supporter.

143 *the O'Carrolls*: probably the prominent O'Carroll family of Éile (Ely) in Co. Tipperary.

inagh: from the Irish *an ea* (is it?), but Mangan's own note suggests 'forsooth'.

'Lamentation of Mac Liag for Kincora' was first published in the *Irish Penny Journal*, 9 Jan. 1841. MacLiag's existence seems doubtful, but the mid-seventeenth-century Irish original on which this poem is based takes its bearings from stories of Brian Boru and his victory at Clontarf in 1014. Kincora was where Brian Boru had his palace, on the banks of the River Shannon, near Killaloe, Co. Clare.

144 *Dalcassians*: the sept or tribe of which Brian Boru was chief.

Morogh: Brian's eldest son, Murchadh, killed at Clontarf.

Donagh: Brian's surviving son and successor, Donnchadh.

Conaing: his nephew, slain at Clontarf.

Kian: the son of Maolmhuaidh, an ally at Clontarf.

Corc: a Dalcassian ancestral hero.

son of Erin the Brave: Domhnall, son of Eimhin.

great King of Onaght: Scannlán, King of the Eoghanacht sept, killed at Clontarf.

hosts of Baskinn: a tribe from south-west Clare.

Duvlann: possibly Dúnlaing, King of Life (Liffey).

Lonergan: the nephew of Brian Boru.

Prince of the Scots: Domhnall, son of Eimhin.

'Kathaleen Ny-Houlahan' was first published in the *Irish Penny Journal*, 16 Jan. 1841. Kathaleen Ny-Houlahan (or Cathleen Ní Houlihan), like Roisin Dubh, is one of the names given to Ireland personified as the poet's beloved. The earliest version is thought to be by the eighteenth-century Jacobite poet, Liam Dall Ó hIfearnáin, and appears in a 'translation' by Mangan, under the title 'Caitlin Ni Uallachain' in *Poets and Poetry of Munster: A Selection of Irish Songs* (Dublin: John O'Daly, 1849).

145 *Saxoneen*: a little Saxon.

146 *the Young Deliverer*: the Stuart Pretender.

Let us pray to Him: in the final two stanzas, the poem draws on Christian exhortation based on Genesis and Exodus.

'Dark Rosaleen' was first published in *The Nation*, 30 May 1846. Mangan's version is probably based on Samuel Ferguson's literal translation of the original (thought to be by a Father Costello of Co. Cork). Mangan infuses the poem with the nationalist spirit of the 1840s and produces a powerful political lyric.

And Spanish ale shall give you hope: this, like the wine from the Pope in line 5, suggests support for Ireland from sympathetic Catholic countries.

The Erne . . . at its highest flood: the name of both the river and the lake in Co. Fermanagh.

'Black-Haired Fair Rose' is a version of 'Roisin Dubh' (see note on Thomas Furlong above). It appeared posthumously in *The Poets and Poetry of Munster* (1849).

148 *Erne*: see note on 'Dark Rosaleen'.

'The Nameless One' was published in the *Irishman*, 27 Oct. 1849, but probably composed in the autumn of 1848. The references to William Maginn (1793–1842) and Robert Burns (1759–96), both victims of alcoholism, hint at one of the sources of the poem's deep misery.

150 *eld*: old age.

151 *dreeing*: enduring.

FRANCIS SYLVESTER MAHONY

'The Bells of Shandon' was included in *The Reliques of Father Prout* (1836) in an essay titled 'The Rogueries of Thomas Moore', in which Moore is jestingly accused of borrowing heavily from sources in a variety of languages. Father Prout, the fictitious author of the book, claims that he had written 'The Bells of Shandon' while a student at the Irish College in Rome, and that Moore had plagiarized it for his 'Evening Bells: A Petersburg Air'. The eight bells are in the handsome bell-tower of St Anne's Church, just off Shandon St. in Cork.

152 *Inscrip. on an old Bell*: spurious Latin: 'I mark the Sabbath, I sob at funerals, I clang on solemn occasions.'

SAMUEL FERGUSON

'Lament for the Death of Thomas Davis', from the *Dublin University Magazine* (1847). 'Cashel of Munster', from *Lays of the Western Gael* (1865). 'The Coolun' ('Maiden of the flowing locks'), from *Lays of the Western Gael* (1865).

157 *coleen oge*: from the Irish *cailín óg* (young girl).

coleen bawn: from the Irish *cailín bán* (fair girl).

'Dear Dark Head', from *Lays of the Western Gael* (1865). The title in Irish was 'Ceann Dubh Deelish'.

THOMAS DAVIS

Both poems are reprinted from *The Poems of Thomas Davis* (Dublin: James Duffy, 1846). 'A Nation Once Again' was first published in *The Nation*. The title became an oft-quoted phrase among members of the nationalist Young Ireland movement.

'The West's Asleep' was first published in *The Nation* and then reprinted in the booklet edited by Charles Gavan Duffy, *The Spirit of the Nation*, which went through several editions. An expanded edition appeared in 1845, with musical accompaniments. 'The West's Asleep' is given the old tune, 'Brink of the White Rocks'.

160 *Coirrslabh Pass and Ard Rathain*: Coirrslabh (Coirrshliabh) Pass is in the Curlew Hills, near Boyle, Co. Roscommon. A battle between Irish and Norman forces was fought there in 1230. Ardrathan, Co. Galway, was the site of another battle in 1225.

Aughrim's slopes and Shannon's wave: the Clanricarde family fought against the English at Aughrim, Co. Galway, in 1691.

AUBREY DE VERE

'The Little Black Rose' is a version of 'Roisin Dubh' (see the note on Thomas

Furlong above). It was published in *The Sisters, Inisfail, and Other Poems* (1861).

161 *The Silk of the Kine*: the silken heifer, one of the many emblems of Ireland in early poems and songs. It continued to be used by later writers such as Thomas MacDonagh and James Joyce.

Athenry: village (now a small town) in Co. Galway.

'Florence MacCarthy's Farewell to His English Love' was first published in *Poems* (1855). A longer version appears in *The Sisters, Inisfail, and Other Poems* (1861). De Vere offers a note on the poem, explaining that Florence MacCarthy was detained in England for many years, sometimes in prison, sometimes on parole. In 1601 he was arrested, while supposedly under the Queen's protection, and imprisoned in the Tower of London. The poem is a song of exile in which the yew tree becomes a prominent symbol of a dying Ireland.

JOHN KELLS INGRAM

'The Memory of the Dead' (often referred to by its opening line, 'Who fears to speak of Ninety-eight?') was published anonymously in *The Nation* in Apr. 1843. In extolling the patriotism and heroism of the 1798 rebellion, the ballad seeks to establish continuity between the nationalist politics of the United Irishmen and the Young Ireland spirit of its own time.

WILLIAM ALLINGHAM

'The Fairies' was written in 1849 and reprinted many times, both in Allingham's volumes of poetry and in popular anthologies. It first appeared in book form in *Poems* (1850).

'The Maids of Elfin-Mere' was originally titled 'The Maidens of the Mere' and appears in Allingham's *Poems* (1850) as such. This version is taken from *Irish Songs and Poems* (1901). Mere can mean 'lake or pond', but also 'marsh or fen'.

'A Dream', from *Poems* (1850).

'The Winding Banks of Erne' is reprinted from Allingham's *Irish Songs and Poems* (1901), though earlier versions exist. In his *Fifty Modern Poems* (1865), the subtitle was 'the Emigrant's Adieu to Ballyshannon, a local ballad', and the first line began 'Adieu to Ballyshannon'. It became 'Adieu to Ballyshanny' in 1877. Allingham explains in his notes that 'The important river Erne rises in Lough Gowna, not very far from the middle of Ireland, and, after a course of some seventy miles through a chain of islanded lakes, pours its foaming waters over the Fall of Asaroe into Balyshannon Harbour on Donegal Bay.' He goes on to explain that the name of Ballyshannon is a corrupt derivation from the Irish *Bel-atha-Seanaigh* (*Bel-atha* meaning 'mouth of the ford') and *Seanaigh* possibly suggesting old (*sean*), but more likely someone's name. He claims that Ballyshanny (not Ballyshannon) is the correct vernacular.

169 *'shanachus'*: old lore. Allingham glosses this as 'old stories, histories, genealogies', but the more usual spelling would be seanchas.

rath: an earth enclosure, usually providing a fortification on a hillside.

Laurence Bloomfield in Ireland (subtitled 'A Modern Poem') is a verse novel in twelve chapters. The extract here is from chapter VII. Laurence Bloomfield is an idealistic landlord, 'Irish born and English bred', who returns to his estate at Lisnamoy during a time of agrarian conflict. He intervenes in a dispute involving a young tenant farmer, Neil Doran, who joins the outlawed secret society of Ribbonmen, and the local landlords led by their agent, Pigot. The poem is a meditation on the land question and a plea for liberal landlordism.

POPULAR SONGS AND BALLADS

The six ballads included here were inspired by the French invasion of 1796 and the rebellion of 1798. All of them have been set to music and are still frequently sung and recorded.

'Boulavogue' appeared in the *Irish Weekly Independent*, 18 June 1898 (the centenary year of the rebellion), under the title 'Father Murphy of the County Wexford'. Father John Murphy (about whom other ballads were written) was the parish priest of Kilcormack near Boulavogue in Co. Wexford. He led his parishioners in successful campaigns against the British militia in May 1798 and was eventually killed in battle by the British yeomanry. The author of the ballad was P. J. McCall (1861–1919), a founder member (with W. B. Yeats) of the Irish National Literary Society, but his ballad has now thoroughly entered the public domain. There have been many recordings of 'Boulavogue' by the Dubliners and other musicians.

173 *Hessian*: a name given to a German mercenary in the British army (from Hesse, a grand duchy of Germany).

'The Shan Van Vocht' belongs to the late 1790s, though the first printed version was in *The Nation*, 29 Oct. 1842. The Shan Van Vocht (Sean Bhean Bhoct) is the Poor Old Woman who heralds revolutionary change in Irish writing and song.

174 *the Orange*: the Orange Order, a Protestant organization, was founded in 1795 in commemoration of the victory of King William III, Prince of Orange, at the Battle of the Boyne, 1690.

Currach of Kildare: the Curragh, a plain of over 5,000 acres in Co. Kildare. A massacre of captive rebels took place here during the 1798 rebellion.

Lord Edward: Lord Edward Fitzgerald (1763–98), a leading member of the United Irishmen involved in preparations for the French invasion. He died of wounds received while resisting arrest. See W. B. Yeats's poem, 'September 1913'.

'The Wearin' o' the Green' also belongs to the late 1790s and appeared in several versions in the nineteenth century. The version printed here is shorter and more colloquial than the song that appears in Dion Boucicault's play, *Arrah-na-Pogue* (1864). Green was the colour of national pride and revolutionary aspiration, and was frequently invoked in songs of the time, such as 'The Green Cockade'. In *A Book of Ireland* (1959), Frank O'Connor refers to 'The Wearin' o' the Green' as 'the Irish Marseillaise'.

176 *Napper Tandy*: James Napper Tandy (1740–1803). In 1791 he assisted Wolfe Tone in founding the Society of United Irishmen. For much of the 1790s he was in flight from the authorities, fleeing to America in 1793, visiting Paris to gain support from the French, and trying to avoid execution. He died in Bordeaux.

caubeen: from the Irish *cáibín* (a hat).

'The Croppy Boy' has its origins in the 1798 rebellion in Wexford. The term 'croppy' refers to the rebels who cropped their hair in the French revolutionary style. There are numerous versions of the song.

'The Rising of the Moon' was written by John Keegan Casey (1846–70) shortly before its publication in *A Wreath of Shamrocks: Ballads, Songs and Legends* (1866). It had a massive circulation in broadsheet form. Casey was arrested for his Fenian activities in 1867 and imprisoned in Mountjoy Jail. An estimated 50,000 people followed his funeral. The version printed here differs slightly from the song Casey includes in his 1866 book. 'The Rising of the Moon' acquired even greater popularity after Lady Gregory used it in her play of that title in 1907.

177 *ma bouchal*: term of endearment, from the Irish *mo bhuachaill* (my boy).

'Granuaile' recounts the heroic adventures of Grace O'Malley (Gráinne Mhaol), thought to have lived as a pirate between 1530 and 1600. At her meeting with Queen Elizabeth I in London, she is said to have claimed royal prerogatives as Queen of Ireland. Legends of Granuaile were revived in the 1790s, along with those of the Shan Van Vocht, in the context of revolutionary political ambitions. The ballad singer who sings 'The Rising of the Moon' in Lady Gregory's play also sings 'Granuaile'.

179 *My royal Brian*: Brian Bóroime, better known as Brian Boru (941–1014), King of Ireland. He fought in the battle of Clontarf and was killed shortly afterwards by fleeing Vikings.

MAUD GONNE

'The Famine Queen' was first published as 'La Reine de la disette' in the Paris journal, *L'Irlande Libre*, founded by Maud Gonne in 1897 to commemorate the centenary of the 1798 rebellion. It was reprinted in the *United Irishman* on 6 Apr. 1900, but the paper was suppressed. The occasion was the visit to Ireland of Queen Victoria, then in her final years, to boost recruitment for the Boer War. See Maud Gonne MacBride, *A Servant of the Queen*, ed. A. N. Jeffares and Anna MacBride White (Gerrards Cross: Colin Smythe, 1994) and *The Gonne Yeats Letters, 1893–1938*, by the same editors (London: Hutchinson, 1992).

PATRICK PEARSE

'The Coming Revolution' was published in Nov. 1913 in the journal of the Gaelic League, *An Claidheamh* (*The Sword of Light*). It was reprinted many times after Pearse's death in 1916 and was included in *The Collected Works of Padraic H. Pearse: Political Writings and Speeches* (Dublin and London: Maunsel and Roberts Ltd., 1922). The essay marks a decisive break with the cultural ideals of the Gaelic League, in which Pearse had been active since 1896, and shows an unwavering commitment to armed insurrection.

186 *vox clamantis*: clamorous voice.

is and tá: two forms of the Gaelic verb *to be* (Pearse is talking about the rudiments of learning Irish).

Herbert Spencer: Herbert Spencer (1820–1903), founder of evolutionary philosophy and author of numerous books on sociology, ethics, education, and psychology, the most influential of which was probably *Education: Intellectual, Moral and Physical* (1861).

187 *the Gaelic League*: the Gaelic League was founded on 31 July 1893.

Liancourt: Roger du Plessis, duc de Liancourt (1598–1674).

188 *Dr Hyde*: Douglas Hyde (1860–1949). See biographical entry.

Eoin Mac Neill: Eoin MacNeill (1867–1945), a founder of the Gaelic League and first Professor of Early Irish History at University College, Dublin.

189 *Ard-Chraobh*: the governing council of the Gaelic League.

the North has 'begun': Eoin MacNeill's article 'The North Began' helped to precipitate the founding of the Irish Volunteers in the same month that Pearse's article appeared (Nov. 1913). The article was a response to the arming of loyalists in the north.

A. O. H.: Ancient Order of Hibernians, a Catholic nationalist organization.

the Transport Workers: the Irish Transport and General Workers Union (ITGWU).

JAMES CONNOLLY

'The Irish Flag' was published in the *Worker's Republic*, 8 Apr. 1916, two weeks before the Easter Rising. Connolly's passionate commitment to Irish nationalism and international socialism is encapsulated in this essay, in what has become one of his most frequently quoted statements: 'The cause of labour is the cause of Ireland, the cause of Ireland is the cause of labour. They cannot be dissevered.'

JAMES STEPHENS

From *The Insurrection in Dublin* (1916). Stephens's account of the Easter Rising is unusual because of the startling immediacy of its present-tense, first-person narrative, conveyed through the day-by-day impressions of a diary.

CONSTANCE MARKIEWICZ

'Stephen's Green', from *Cumann na mBan*, 2: 10 (1926). Constance Markiewicz describes the involvement in the Easter Rising of women members of the Irish Citizen Army and Cumann na mBan (The Irishwomen's Council), founded in Dublin in Nov. 1913 and later to become the women's division of the Irish Volunteers.

ROGER CASEMENT

For circumstances relating to his speech from the dock, see the biographical entry on Casement.

208 *the Chief Secretary*: Augustine Birrell (1850–1933).

'grossly illegal and utterly unconstitutional': Casement is referring to so-called 'gun running', and in particular to the landing of arms and ammunition at Larne, Co. Antrim, by the Ulster Volunteer Force in Apr. 1914. Despite the Lord Chancellor's denunciation, there was no police or military intervention.

209 *the present Attorney-General*: F. E. Smith (1872–1930), who led the prosecution against Casement.

210 *the refusal of the Army of Occupation at the Curragh to obey the orders of the Crown*: in Mar. 1914, officers at the Curragh military camp in Co. Kildare threatened resignation rather than take action against the Ulster opponents to Home Rule.

Mausers: the Mauser was a rifle named after its German inventor.

THOMAS MACDONAGH

From *Literature in Ireland: Studies Irish and Anglo-Irish* (1916), published posthumously after MacDonagh's execution by the British for his part in the Easter Rising. At the time of his death, as W. B. Yeats recalled, 'he was coming into his force; | He might have won fame in the end'. MacDonagh's extensive knowledge of poetry, especially his appreciation of the Elizabethan English lyric, informs his view of the possibilities of an Irish literature written in English. Departing from the ultra-nationalist ideal of an Irish Ireland, MacDonagh both welcomes the Gaelic Renaissance of his own time *and* asserts that Irish writers have begun to make the English language their own.

212   *Hugh O'Neill and Hugh O'Donnell*: Hugh O'Neill (1550–1616), Earl of
Tyrone, and Hugh O'Donnell (1571–1602), his son-in-law.

     Eoghan Ruadh O'Neill: Owen Roe O'Neill (1584–1649), a nephew of
Hugh O'Neill and commander of Irish forces in the 1640s.

     the Penal Laws: anti-Catholic legislation enacted from the 1690s onwards
and not fully removed until Catholic Emancipation in 1829.

213   *O'Connell*: Daniel O'Connell (1775–1847). See biographical entry.

     Parnell: Charles Stewart Parnell (1846–91), leader of the Irish Parlia-
mentary Party from 1880 to 1891.

215   *Dr Sigerson*: George Sigerson (1836–1925), translator and editor of *Bards
of the Gael and Gall* (1897). MacDonagh dedicated *Literature in Ireland*
to Sigerson.

216   *the silk of the kine*: the silken heifer, the strong and lustrous cow of Irish
mythology (see the note for Aubrey De Vere above).

     John Eglinton: John Eglinton (1868–1961), from *Bards and Saints* (Dub-
lin: Maunsel & Co., 1906), 48.

219   *Carlyle says of Imagination*: Thomas Carlyle (1795–1881) in *Sartor
Resartus* (1836), book 1, chapter IX.

     aisling: Irish literary genre based on a vision or dream.

     dán díreach: classical syllabic verse in Irish.

JOHN O'LEARY

From *Recollections of Fenians and Fenianism* (1896). The extract here is from
the opening chapter of O'Leary's memoir, in which he describes his early
youth and the impact of Thomas Davis's poems and essays on his feelings
about Ireland.

220   *laudator temporis acti*: one who praises the deeds of time.

221   *poems and essays of Thomas Davis*: see the writings of Davis in this
volume.

     T. W. Rolleston . . . Duffy: T. W. Rolleston edited *Prose Writings of Thomas
Davis* in 1890 and Charles Gavan Duffy wrote *Thomas Davis: The Memoirs of an Irish Patriot* in 1892.

     West-British: having British attitudes and sympathies (as if Ireland were
merely a western segment of Britain).

     Moore's song: 'The Song of O'Ruark, Prince of Breffni': 'On *our* side is
Virtue and Erin! | On *theirs* is the Saxon and Guilt.'

     the Nation: the weekly cultural and political journal founded by Thomas
Davis with John Blake Dillon and Charles Gavan Duffy on 15 Oct. 1842.
It promoted the nationalist ideals of the Young Ireland Movement.

222   *'fear to speak of '98'*: an allusion to the opening line of 'The Memory of
the Dead' by John Kells Ingram. See note above.

Mitchel: John Mitchel (1815–75), Fenian organizer and revolutionary; editor of the *United Irishman*. His *Jail Journal* (1854) became a celebrated text of Irish nationalism.

Hugh O'Neill and Owen Roe and Sarsfield: for Hugh O'Neill and Owen Roe, see the notes above for Thomas MacDonagh. Patrick Sarsfield (1655–93) was a commander in the army of James II during the Williamite War (1689–91).

'*Memoirs of Wolfe Tone*': see extract in this volume and note above.

Madden: R. R. Madden, *The United Irishmen: Their Lives and Times*, published in 4 vols. in Dublin, 1842–6.

The Czar Nicholas: Nicholas I (1796–1855), emperor of Russia. His expansionist ambitions, opposed by Britain and France, brought on the Crimean War.

OSCAR WILDE

From *De Profundis*, a letter to Lord Alfred Douglas from Reading Prison, written in 1897 and first published in an extracted version in 1905. Wilde's letter, adopting as its title the prayer based on Psalm 130 ('Out of the depths have I cried to thee, O Lord'), is one of the great works of nineteenth-century autobiography. In a style characteristic of modern Irish literature, it sees tragedy in the raiment of comedy: 'We are the zanies of sorrow. We are clowns whose hearts are broken.'

225 *the Captain of my Soul*: 'I am the master of my fate, | I am the captain of my soul', from William Ernest Henley's poem, 'Invictus' (1875).

Wordsworth: the lines that follow are from Act 3, Scene 5 of William Wordsworth's play *The Borderers* (1796–7).

Vita Nuova: New Life, the title of a principal early work by Dante Alighieri (1265–1321).

226 *Robbie*: Robert Ross, Wilde's close friend and the editor of his *Collected Works* (1908).

228 *Verlaine*: Paul Verlaine (1844–96), French poet.

Prince Kropotkin: Prince Peter Kropotkin (1842–1921), anarchist author of *Mutual Aid* (1897).

230 *Marsyas*: in Greek mythology, a celebrated player on the pipe, who challenged Apollo to a musical contest and was flayed alive after suffering defeat. His song is the song of sorrow.

Baudelaire: Charles Baudelaire (1821–67), French poet, best known for *Les Fleurs du Mal* (1857).

Lamartine: Alphonse de Lamartine (1790–1869), French poet, best known for his *Méditations Poétiques* (1820).

Chopin's music: the music of the Polish composer Frederic Chopin (1809–49) was immensely popular among the aesthetes of Wilde's generation.

Wilde alludes to Chopin's compositions, especially the nocturnes, in his poetry, essays, and fiction.

230 *Burne-Jones's women*: Edward Burne-Jones (1833–98), Pre-Raphaelite painter, whose idealized women have a distinctive androgynous quality.

Matthew Arnold: Victorian poet and critic (1822–88). Wilde is referring to his early poem *Empedocles on Etna* (1852).

J. M. SYNGE

From *The Aran Islands* (1907). Part of this opening section was originally published as an article, 'An Impression of Aran', in the *Manchester Guardian* on 24 Jan. 1905. Part autobiography, part travel writing, the book describes Synge's growing familiarity with the life and customs of Inishmore and Inishmaan. The stories and songs he translated provided an impulse for the vigorous colloquial idiom of his plays and typified the Gaelic culture of the west of Ireland that so inspired the Literary Revival.

232 *Aranmor*: the largest of the Aran Islands, better known as Inishmore.

234 *Petrie and Sir William Wilde . . . Mr Curtin*: all of them antiquarians and collectors of folk lore. Sir George Petrie (1790–1866) established the monastic origin of the round towers of Ireland and wrote extensively on Irish architecture and music. Sir William Wilde (1815–76), the father of Oscar Wilde, wrote a number of topographical and ethnological works. Jeremiah Curtin (1838–1906) was born in Detroit to Irish parents and was the author of *Myths and Folklore of Ireland* (1890) and *Tales of the Fairies and Ghost World* (1893).

236 *beyond the bay*: this was the closing sentence of the article, 'An Impression of Aran'.

GEORGE MOORE

Hail and Farewell, Moore's memoir of literary culture in the first decade of the twentieth century, was published in three volumes: *Ave* (1911), *Salve* (1912), and *Vale* (1914). Swaying between a detached chronicle and an obsessive monologue, the book provides some brilliant cameos of personalities and events, especially those associated with the Literary Revival. The extract reprinted here is from *Ave* and recalls a meeting with W. B. Yeats and Edward Martyn, when the idea of an Irish literary theatre was in the air. It is entirely characteristic of Moore's comic perspective and his deep appreciation of the visual arts that he should recall how, in the lamplight, his visitors appeared 'as fantastic as anything ever seen in Japanese prints'.

240 *the Temple*: the Inns of Court, just off Fleet Street, London.

242 *when I cut the painter*: after training as a painter, Moore came to realize that he was better suited to being a writer, hence his wariness about wrong starts and misdirections.

the summer at Coole: Coole Park, Co. Galway, was the home of Lady Gregory, and both Yeats and Martyn were visitors there.

243 *The Heather Field*: Martyn's play was produced in 1899, one of the first plays to be associated with the Irish Literary Theatre.

The Land of Heart's Desire: Yeats's play of this name was first performed in London on 29 March 1894. It was the first of his plays to be given regular production in London.

244 *the days when I was a Frenchman*: Moore lived in Paris between 1873 and 1879, nurturing his aspirations as a painter and then as a writer.

the Book of Kells: one of the finest early medieval illuminated manuscripts, from the eighth or ninth century, possibly from a monastery in Kells, Co. Meath. It is preserved and exhibited in Trinity College, Dublin.

the Cheshire Cheese: Ye Old Cheshire Cheese (a pub at 145 Fleet St., London), well known to Samuel Johnson and a popular meeting place for the poets of the Rhymers' Club, with whom Yeats was associated in the 1890s.

the legends of the Fianna: the Fionn or Ossianic cycle of stories centred on the exploits of the mythical hero Fionn mac Cumhaill (Finn Macool), his son Oisín (Ossian), and the Fianna warriors.

245 *a work on Blake*: as well as editing a 3-vol. edition of Blake's poems with Edwin J. Ellis (1893), Yeats also wrote about this time an essay titled 'William Blake and the Imagination' (1897).

EARNÁN O'MALLEY

From *On Another Man's Wound* (1936). O'Malley commanded the Second Southern Division of the IRA in Munster during the closing months of the War of Independence (1919–21). In this episode of his memoir, from May–July 1921, he describes the execution of three British officers in Co. Tipperary.

247 *the Brigade Q.M.*: the IRA Quartermaster.

Slievenamon: (mountain of the fairy women) a conical mountain north of Clonmel and a county landmark in Tipperary.

JAMES JOYCE

'A Painful Case', from *Dubliners* (1914). The story was written in 1905 (the original title was 'A Painful Incident'), but publication was delayed because of publishers' fears over libel actions against *Dubliners*. The story effectively illustrates Joyce's repeated suggestion that Dublin is a centre of paralysis by showing us Mr James Duffy's cold and loveless treatment of the musical Mrs Sinico. It also demonstrates what Joyce in his letters described as a style of 'scrupulous meanness', being both attentive to detail and unflinching in its depiction of what might be considered low and sordid. While being strongly naturalistic in style, however, the story also contains symbolic elements. The ending of the story is puzzling. Some readers sense the presence of a Joycean 'epiphany' and argue that Mr Duffy experiences enlightenment and renewal, while others find his egotism and hypocrisy unrelieved.

252 *Duffy*: from the Irish 'dubh' (black or dark).

Chapelizod: a village about three miles west of Dublin city centre, also the setting for *The House by the Church-yard* by Sheridan Le Fanu. It is used again by Joyce in *Finnegans Wake*. The name derives from the French 'Chapel d'Iseult' and is associated with the unhappy love of Tristan and Iseult in Celtic legend.

double desk: a small desk which functions both as a storage space and as a writing surface.

Maynooth Catechism: the standard text for religious instruction in Catholic schools in Ireland, issued by the National Synod at the Royal College of St Patrick in Maynooth in 1883.

Michael Kramer: a play written by the German author Gerhart Hauptmann in 1900 and translated by Joyce in 1901. It ends with the suicide of Kramer's son, Arnold.

Bile Beans: a popular cure for bilious ailments.

253 *Rotunda*: a group of buildings on the south-east corner of Rutland Square, housing a theatre, a concert hall, and assembly rooms.

254 *Leghorn*: the English name for the Italian city of Livorno in Tuscany.

255 *Parkgate*: the main entrance to Phoenix Park in north-west Dublin.

256 *Mail*: presumably the *Dublin Evening Mail*, a Unionist daily newspaper, printed on light brown paper.

257 *Secreto*: silently or quietly.

258 *a league*: a temperance league.

259 *Herald*: presumably the *Evening Herald*, a nationalist daily newspaper.

SEÁN O'FAOLÁIN

'Lilliput', from *Midsummer Night Madness and Other Stories* (1932). In *Vive Moi! An Autobiography* (1963), O'Faoláin refers to 'Lilliput' as the 'very first story that is recognisably mine'. It was first published in the *Irish Statesman* on 6 Feb. 1926, with the title 'In Lilliput'. The story is set in O'Faoláin's birthplace, the city of Cork, at the beginning of the 1920s. During this phase of the War of Independence, curfews were in force and military patrols were on the streets. The title comes from the opening book of Jonathan Swift's *Gulliver's Travels* (1726). O'Faoláin writes in a realist mode, quite unlike Swift's satirical fantasy, but he shares Swift's acute sense of observation and unusual shifts of perspective, and he shows us a place in which people's lives appear diminished. The woman traveller, however, takes on heroic proportions: O'Faoláin presents her as a female Gulliver observed by 'a changing little crowd'.

260 *Shandon*: the handsome Tower of Shandon on St Anne's Church, Shandon Street, Cork. The peal of the eight bells of Shandon is celebrated in the poem by Francis Sylvester Mahony (Father Prout) reprinted here: ' 'Tis the bells of Shandon | That sounds so grand on | The pleasant waters of the River Lee.'

the valley of the Lee: the River Lee in Cork.

261 *jarvey-cars*: small horse-pulled traps, popular in parts of rural Ireland.

porther: porter (a dark beer also known as stout).

262 *the first Angelus*: Roman Catholic devotional prayer commemorating the Incarnation ('The Angel of the Lord said unto Mary . . .'). Traditionally, as here, it was said three times a day: morning, noon, and sunset.

263 *the Tans*: the Black-and-Tans were non-Irish members of the Royal Irish Constabulary who fought against the IRA between March 1920 and July 1921 during the War of Independence. Due to shortages, they wore mixed police and army uniforms. The name was derived from a well-known pack of hounds belonging to the Skarteen Hunt in Co. Limerick and came to be applied to any irregular forces used by the British in Ireland. They were renowned for their brutality.

265 *Mary Mac*: as well as irreverently likening the sleeping woman to Mary, the Corporal also offers a jibe in the common Celtic prefix 'Mac'.

LIAM O'FLAHERTY

'The Mountain Tavern', from *The Mountain Tavern and Other Stories* (1929). O'Flaherty's story is set during the Civil War of 1922–3. It gives a specifically political dimension to the idea of 'the dead' and to the symbolism of the snow in James Joyce's story, 'The Dead'.

Snow was falling: the snow falling silently at the opening of O'Flaherty's story recalls the snow falling faintly at the end of Joyce's story.

268 *It's gone west*: euphemism for death and destruction, especially among soldiers.

We're up the pole: in a state of desperation.

270 *Free Staters*: the army of the new Irish State, after the 1921 Treaty ending the War of Independence.

Irregulars: Republican soldiers opposed to the Treaty.

FRANK O'CONNOR

'The Majesty of the Law', from *Bones of Contention* (1936). The story was first published in the *Fortnightly Review* in Aug. 1935.

273 *brosna*: a bundle of sticks for fire-wood.

Marcus Stone print: Marcus Stone (1840–1921), Victorian painter, popular for historical genre pictures and book illustrations. He was a political radical and a friend of Charles Dickens.

274 *Begor*: (begorra) by god.

  Faix: faith.

  Wisha: Well, indeed.

275 *Dhe, whisht*: be quiet, hold your tongue.

  Ah, sha: see Wisha.

276 *Musha*: see Wisha.

278 *Erra*: (arrah) But, now, really.

279 *begod*: by god.

280 *butt*: a small cart.

SOMERVILLE AND ROSS

From *The Real Charlotte* (1894). In this, their most popular novel, Edith Somerville and Violet Martin ('Martin Ross') dramatized the uncertain fortunes of the Protestant Ascendancy in a compelling narrative of desire for land and love. The heroine of the novel plots against her young cousin, Francie Fitzpatrick, and contrives to cheat her out of her inheritance. The novel is set in the West Cork village of Lismoyle. In this extract from chapter 2, the rivalry between the two women is introduced in the context of a farcical deathbed scene involving Charlotte's elderly aunt, Mrs Mullen.

282 *Norry the Boat*: a household servant.

  the Banshee: from the Irish *bean sí* (woman of the sídh or 'host of the air'). The banshee is a mythological figure whose cry of lamentation portends a family death.

BRAM STOKER

From *Dracula* (1897). The novel opens with Jonathan Harker's record of a journey undertaken to Transylvania on behalf of his law firm to meet the mysterious Count Dracula. The passage included here has fascinated generations of readers with its suggestive eroticism, but the relationship between vampire and victim has also been read in terms of colonizer and colonized.

290 *'My tablets . . . put it down,'* etc.: a mistaken recollection of Shakespeare's lines in *Hamlet*, I. v: 'My tables—meet it is I set it down | That one may smile and smile and be a villain.'

291 *water-glasses*: glasses filled with different levels of water to produce musical notes.

JAMES JOYCE

From *Ulysses* (1922). Episode 1: Telemachus. The opening of the novel recalls the first two books of Homer's *Odyssey*, in which Odysseus' son Telemachus is urged by the goddess Athena to seek his father. The novel opens at 8 a.m. on

Thursday, 16 June 1904. The setting is the Martello tower, Sandycove (Dublin Bay), in which Stephen Dedalus, newly returned from Paris, is living with his friend Malachi ('Buck') Mulligan and an English admirer of Irish culture by the name of Haines. Stephen is a lonely son, likened to both Telemachus and Hamlet, but he is also caught in a tense political and cultural relationship with Haines (a colonial Englishman) and Mulligan (an Irish collaborator). Mulligan irreverently mocks the communion rites of the mass, the first of many parodies and inauthentic experiences in the novel. Later, the milkwoman is presented as a parodic version of the legendary Old Woman of Ireland, the Shan Van Vocht.

294 *Introibo ad altare Dei*: I will go unto the altar of God (from the opening of the Latin mass).

blood and ouns: blood and wounds: Mulligan is mocking Stephen's Catholicism, parodying the form of the mass and the priest's consecration of bread and wine as the body and blood of Christ.

Chrysostomos: 'golden-mouthed', from the Greek orator Dion Chrysostomos (*c.*50–*c.*117), a reference to Mulligan's gold fillings and also his eloquence.

Two strong shrill whistles: the mailboat is leaving Ireland.

an ancient Greek: Daedalus, the father of Icarus, who fashioned wings for himself and his son to fly.

295 *Algy*: Algernon Charles Swinburne (1837–1909), Victorian poet, whose poem 'The Triumph of Time' (1866) contains the line Mulligan quotes: 'the great sweet mother . . . the sea'.

296 *Epi oinopa ponton*: 'over the wine-dark sea' (from Homer's *Odyssey*).

Thalatta! Thalatta!: The sea! The sea!, the cry of the Ten Thousand Greek mercenary soldiers when they reach the sea in Xenophon's *Anabasis*, IV. vii. 24.

hyperborean: a term used by Friedrich Nietzsche to describe those who, like the superman (Übermensch), were 'above the crowd' (*The Will to Dominate*, 1896).

297 *Dottyville*: the lunatic asylum.

Ursula: St Ursula, renowned for her chastity.

The rage of Caliban: Oscar Wilde, in his preface to *The Picture of Dorian Gray* (1891): 'The nineteenth-century dislike of Realism is the rage of Caliban seeing his own face in the glass. The nineteenth century dislike of Romanticism is the rage of Caliban not seeing his own face in the glass.'

The cracked lookingglass of a servant: the idea of art as a cracked looking-glass occurs in Wilde's essay, 'The Decay of Lying' (1889). Stephen, who is bitterly conscious of Ireland's oppression, finds it appropriate that the looking-glass Mulligan hands him should belong to a servant.

298 *oxy chap*: Haines is from Oxford, but there are also suggestions of foolish behaviour (behaving like an ox).

298 *Hellenise it*: Matthew Arnold, in *Culture and Anarchy* (1869), identifies two prominent cultural tendencies: the Hebraic (founded on the stern recognition of law and duty) and the Hellenic (founded on the love of beauty and sensuous pleasure). Wilde was to characterize aestheticism as 'the New Hellenism'.

evening in the quadrangle: Stephen conjures up a picture of Oxford.

new paganism ... omphalos: new paganism is another epithet for the return to Greek (Hellenic) ways. Omphalos is Greek for navel and is associated with Delphi, the centre of the earth in Ancient Greek culture.

299 *Sir Peter Teazle*: character in Richard Brinsley Sheridan's play *The School for Scandal* (1777).

some hired mute from Lalouette's: hired mourner from the Dublin undertaker of that name.

300 *Loyola*: St Ignatius Loyola (1491–1556), founder of the Society of Jesus (the Jesuit order) in 1534.

For Fergus rules the brazen cars: from the lyric 'Who Goes with Fergus', originally part of W. B. Yeats's 1892 play *The Countess Cathleen*.

Turko the terrible: a pantomime in which Edward Royce, a member of the Gaiety Theatre Company in London, took part. Joyce saw it in Dublin as a child.

301 *Liliata ... excipiat*: Catholic prayer for the dying: 'May the lilied throng of radiant confessors encompass thee; may the choir of rejoicing angels welcome thee.'

302 *On coronation day*: 'De Golden Wedding', a song by the African-American songwriter James A. Bland (1854–1911).

Clongowes: Clongowes Wood College, the Jesuit school where Joyce was a pupil.

A server of a servant: the altar boy serving the Priest, who is servant of God, but also the Irishman serving the Englishman, who is servant of the Empire.

303 *In nominee ... Sancti*: in the name of the father, and of the son, and of the Holy Ghost'.

the year of the big wind: a humorous dig at the folklore and occultist interests in Yeats's book, *In the Seven Woods* (1903), published by the Dun Emer Press in Dundrum in 1903, with the assistance of Elizabeth and Lily Yeats. The two sisters are likened to the witches ('the weird sisters') in Shakespeare's *Macbeth*.

304 *Mabinogion*: a group of eleven medieval Welsh tales.

Upanishads: ancient Hindu scriptures, studied by Yeats.

prepuces: foreskins.

a tilly: from the Irish *tuile* (a drop more).

Silk of the kine and poor old woman: traditional names for Ireland. For silk of the kine see notes above on Aubrey De Vere and Thomas MacDonagh.

For the poor old woman (*Sean Bhean Bhocht*) see the note for the song of that title above.

305 *cuckquean*: female cuckold.

the serpent's prey: Old Testament descriptions of woman.

306 *All I can give you I give*: this and the 'tender chant' that follows are from Swinburne's poem, 'The Oblation', from *Songs Before Sunrise* (1871).

stony: stony-broke (Mulligan, who is short of money, expects Stephen to bring some money from his teaching job).

Ireland expects . . . his duty: Mulligan mimics Lord Nelson's famous declaration at the Battle of Trafalgar (1805): 'England expects that every man this day will do his duty.'

307 *Agenbite of inwit*: remorse of conscience (Middle English).

stripped of his garments: a parody of the tenth Station of the Cross, in which Christ is stripped of his garments.

308 *Mercurial Malachi*: Stephen's view of his friend Mulligan, from a combination of the Greek and Hebrew words for 'messenger'.

Latin quarter hat: a reference to Stephen's visit to the Latin Quarter in Paris.

when the French were on the sea: an allusion to the Irish ballad, 'The Shan Van Vocht', recalling the support given to the United Irish movement by the French in the 1790s. William Pitt the Younger (1759–1806) was Prime Minister when the Martello towers were built in the early 1800s as fortifications against the French during the Napoleonic Wars.

Thomas Aquinas: St Thomas Aquinas (1225–74), Dominican theologian and scholastic philosopher, whose *Summa Theologiae* (1266–73) includes the famous 'five ways' or proofs of the existence of God.

309 *Japhet in search of a father*: the title of a novel (published in 1836) by Captain Frederick Marryat.

That beetles o'er his base into the sea: from *Hamlet*, I. iv. 71.

The seas' ruler: England (or Britannia), represented here by Haines.

310 *Goodbye, now, goodbye*: based on verses written by Oliver St John Gogarty.

a green stone: an emblem of Ireland, but the stone is held in a silver case by the Englishman Haines, suggesting colonial possession.

311 *et unam sanctam catholicam et apostolicam ecclesiam*: and in one holy, catholic and apostolic church (from the Nicene Creed).

pope Marcellus: a mass was written for Pope Marcellus II (1501–55) by Palestrina.

the vigilant angel: the Archangel Michael (depicted here as the guardian of the Catholic Church against Protestant heresy in the sixteenth century).

311 *Photius*: patriarch of Constantinople (*c.*815–97), whose appointment in 857 went against the wishes of Pope Nicholas I and resulted in the schism between the Eastern Orthodox and Roman Catholic Churches.

Arius: heretic (*c.*256–336), who refused to conform with established belief regarding the Father and the Son.

Valentine: Egyptian Gnostic who challenged established belief on Christ's humanity and suffering.

Sabellius: heretic who questioned orthodox beliefs regarding the Trinity.

313 *Uebermensch*: superman (German), as used by Friedrich Nietzsche in *Thus Spake Zarathustra* (1883).

lendeth to the Lord: parody of the biblical proverb: 'He that hath pity upon the poor lendeth unto the Lord!'

Horn of a bull, hoof of a horse, smile of a Saxon: three things the Irish should be wary of.

ELIZABETH BOWEN

From *The Last September* (1929). In one of the classic 'Big House' novels recounting the fortunes of the embattled Anglo-Irish ascendancy, Elizabeth Bowen sets a young woman's sexual awakening against the traumatic politics of the War of Independence (1919–21). The setting of the novel is Danielstown, the home of the Naylor family in Co. Tipperary. In this extract (from chapter 4), Lois Farquhar, the lonely niece of Sir Richard and Lady Naylor, tries to make sense of her own hyphenated Anglo-Irish identity.

314 *Mrs Montmorency*: Hugo and Francie Montmorency are cousins of the Naylors, visiting Danielstown. Hugo had been in love with Lois's mother.

317 *Madder*: a local river.

320 *'Has he come for the guns?'*: the suspicion is that the IRA has hidden weapons in the woods.

'by so great a cloud of witnesses': St Paul's Epistle to the Hebrews 12: 1.

SAMUEL BECKETT

From *Murphy* (1938). The two passages (from chapter 1 and chapter 4) are set in London and Dublin. The novel engages with the philosophical dilemmas that were to become a hallmark of Beckett's later work (Murphy seeks release from the Cartesian mind–body distinction), but it also has a distinctively Irish, post-Literary Revival dimension. The episode in the Dublin General Post Office, in which Wylie dashes his head against the buttocks of Cuchulain, is an irreverent response to what Beckett called the 'Cuchulainoid clichés' of the Revival. James Joyce saw the novel as neatly complementing Flann O'Brien's novel *At Swim-Two-Birds*, published the following year, and referred to Beckett and O'Brien as *Jean-qui-pleure* and *Jean-qui-rit*.

The sun shone . . . on the nothing new: 'there is nothing new under the sun' (Ecclesiastes).

321 *the poor old sun in the Virgin*: the sun enters the constellation Virgo at the end of August.

Neary: thought to be based on the Trinity College philosopher, H. S. Macran, who liked to drink in Neary's pub in Dublin.

the Nerbudda: a river in India.

322 *Apmonia*: a joke word, coined from the Greek for 'harmony', as employed by Pythagoras.

Petrouchka: the persecuted puppet in Stravinsky's 1911 ballet of that title.

the statue of Cuchulain: the statue placed in the General Post Office to commemorate the heroism of Easter 1916, designed by Oliver Sheppard (1865–1941).

323 *Dalkey*: Dalkey village, a few miles south of Dublin.

324 *Cathleen na Hennessey*: a joke at the expense of Cathleen ni Houlihan (Hennessy is an Irish brandy).

that Red Branch bum: reference to the earlier episode involving Cuchulain, who belongs to the Ulster Red Branch cycle of tales.

FLANN O'BRIEN

From *At Swim-Two-Birds* (1939). O'Brien's scintillating modernist medley makes extensive use of parody and pastiche. Clearly influenced by Joyce and (like Beckett's *Murphy*) mildly contemptuous in its attitude to the pieties of the Literary Revival, the novel grafts layer upon layer of narrative, swerving from modern Dublin to the mythological realm of Finn MacCool and the mad King Sweeney. The passage included here is a playful and skilful adaptation of the twelfth-century Irish text, *Buile Shuibne* (translated by Seamus Heaney as *Sweeney Astray*). After being cursed by the cleric Rónán, Sweeney goes mad with the din of battle and takes to wandering through Ireland, living in naked destitution, dwelling in tree tops and celebrating his close attachment to nature. Much of the comedy in the novel is generated by its dramatic shift from one parodic mode to another, in this case from the medieval Irish text to the knockabout vernacular of Shanahan, Furriskey, Lamont, and the indomitable poet of the working class, Jem Casey.

AUGUSTA GREGORY

'Grief of a Girl's Heart', from the essay 'West Irish Ballads' (1901), reprinted in *Poets and Dreamers: Studies and Translations from the Irish* (1903) and also in *The Kiltartan Poetry Book: Prose Translations from the Irish* (1918). The stanzaic arrangement of the poem printed here is taken from the *Oxford Book of Irish Verse*, ed. Donagh MacDonagh and Lennox Robinson (Oxford:

Clarendon Press, 1958). The name Donal Oge is a version of the Irish *donal Óg* (Young Donal). A recital of this poem was added to the script of *The Dead* in John Huston's 1987 film of James Joyce's short story.

337   *ochone*: cry of lamentation.

   O, aya!: expression of sorrow.

OSCAR WILDE

'Requiescat' ('May She Rest') mourns the death of Wilde's sister, Isola, who died on 23 Feb. 1867, aged 9. It was probably written when Wilde was a student at Oxford in the 1870s. He may have visited Avignon on his way to Italy in 1875, though his use of the place name is no guarantee that the poem was written there. It was first published in *Poems* (1881).

'Impression du Matin' ('Impression of the Morning') was first published in *The World: A Journal for Men and Women* (2 Mar. 1881) and was included in Wilde's *Poems* (1881). As well as showing the influence of French impressionist painting on Wilde's artistic ideals, the poem also draws on the example of the American painter, James McNeill Whistler. 'Nocturne in Blue and Gold' and 'Harmony in Grey' are titles of paintings by Whistler.

'Helas!' ('Alas!') was printed as the introductory sonnet to Wilde's *Poems* (1881).

339   *stringed lute on which all winds can play*: the Æolian harp, a common image in Romantic poetry.

   virelay: an old French lyric form.

   with a little rod: the final three lines allude to an Old Testament quotation (I Samuel 14: 43): 'I did but taste a little honey with the end of the rod that was in mine hand, and, lo, I must die'.

'The Harlot's House' was first published in the *Dramatic Review* (11 Apr. 1885) and included in Wilde's *Poems* (1908).

340   *'Treues Liebes Herz'*: 'Faithful Dear Heart'.

   quadrille: a square dance (also referred to in James Joyce's story, 'The Dead').

'Sonnet. On The Sale by Auction of Keats' Love Letters' was written in 1885 and published in the *Dramatic Review* (23 Jan. 1886). It was later included in Wilde's *Poems* (1908). The sonnet was prompted by Sotheby's auction of the letters Keats had written to Fanny Brawne. Wilde attended the sale on 2 Mar. 1885.

341   *Endymion*: Wilde gives to his fellow poet the name of the mythological hero who inspired Keats's epic poem *Endymion* (1818).

'Symphony in Yellow' was first published in the *Centennial Magazine: An Australasian Monthly Illustrated* (5 Feb. 1889) and later included in Wilde's *Poems* (1908). The title recalls the musical titles of paintings by Whistler (see note on 'Impression du Matin' above).

342 *the Temple*: the Inns of Court, just off Fleet Street, London. The bridge
in line 1 is presumably Blackfriars Bridge.

DOUGLAS HYDE

'My Grief on the Sea' is one of the translations from the Irish which Hyde
printed with a prose commentary in his *Love Songs of Connacht* (1893).

W. B. YEATS

'The Lake Isle of Innisfree', from *The Countess Kathleen and Various Legends
and Lyrics* (1892). Innisfree, from the Irish *Inis Fraoigh* (Island of Heather), is
a small island on Lough Gill, Co. Sligo. The meaning of the name helps to
explain the 'purple glow' in line 7 (the colour of heather reflected in the
water).

'To Ireland in the Coming Times', from *The Countess Kathleen and Various
Legends and Lyrics* (1892). The original title was 'Apologia addressed to Ireland in the coming days'. The version given here is that which appears in the
section of poems Yeats titled *The Rose* (1893) in later editions of his work.

343 *rann*: verse or stanza.

the red-rose bordered hem: a fleeting vision of the rose of ideal beauty, here
acknowledged as pre-Christian in origin.

344 *Davis, Mangan, Ferguson*: see biographical entries in this volume.

'The Song of Wandering Aengus', originally titled 'A Mad Song', from *The
Wind Among the Reeds* (1899). Yeats saw Aengus as the Celtic god of youth,
beauty, and poetry. In the mythological cycle of tales in medieval Irish, he falls
ill after longing for a woman seen in his dreams.

345 *hazel wand*: an instrument with magical powers of divination and
transformation.

'To a Shade', from *Responsibilities* (1914), written in memory of Charles
Stewart Parnell (1846–91), discredited as leader of the Irish Parliamentary
Party after the exposure of his affair with a married woman, Katherine O'Shea.

346 *A man*: Sir Hugh Lane (1874–1915), who offered to donate his collection
of French impressionist paintings to the Dublin Municipal Gallery on
condition that the Dublin Corporation would build a new gallery. His
offer was rebuked.

Your enemy, an old foul mouth: probably William Martin Murphy (1844–
1914), who owned two newspapers opposed to Parnell; he also objected
to Hugh Lane's proposal.

the Glasnevin coverlet: Glasnevin Cemetery, Dublin, where Parnell is
buried.

'September 1913', from *Responsibilities* (1914). Yeats contrasts the commercial ethic of modern, democratic Ireland ('the greasy till') with the inspiring heroism of an earlier generation of Irish patriots.

346 *O'Leary*: see the biographical entry on John O'Leary and the extract from his *Recollections of Fenians and Fenianism*.

347 *the wild geese*: Irish soldiers serving in Europe after the evacuation of the Irish army to France under the terms of the Treaty of Limerick, 1691. The term was also applied to later recruits to Irish brigades in continental and American armies.

Edward Fitzgerald: Lord Edward Fitzgerald (1763–98), one of the leaders of the 1798 rebellion, who died while resisting arrest.

every mother's son: the modern age would fail to comprehend the passionate commitment and sacrifice of the earlier generation and attribute it to lovesickness.

'Easter 1916', from *Michael Robartes and the Dancer* (1921). The poem was inspired by the execution of fifteen leaders of the Easter Rising of 24 Apr. 1916, when Irish Republican forces occupied the centre of Dublin and came under fierce opposition from the British army (see the accounts by James Stephens and Constance Markiewicz in this volume).

348 *That woman's days*: Constance Markiewicz (see biographical entry).

This man . . . wingèd horse: Patrick Pearse (see biographical entry). The wingèd horse is Pegasus (emblematic of poetic inspiration).

This other: Thomas MacDonagh (see biographical entry).

This other man: Major John MacBride (1865–1916), estranged husband of Maud Gonne.

349 *For England may keep faith*: the Home Rule Bill, granting Ireland a measure of independence, had been passed in the British Parliament but then suspended for the duration of the First World War.

Connolly: see biographical entry on James Connolly.

'The Wild Swans at Coole', from *The Wild Swans at Coole* (1919). Yeats first visited Coole Park, Lady Gregory's home in Co. Galway, in 1897.

'Meditations in Time of Civil War', from *The Tower* (1928). The poem was written in 1922 during the fierce and bitter conflict between the newly formed government of the Irish Free State and those Republicans opposed to the partition of Ireland required by the Anglo-Irish Treaty of 1922. The poem is in seven parts.

351 *Juno*: Queen of the Roman gods and wife of Jupiter; the peacock is sacred to Juno and later in the poem its cry heralds a new era.

352 *Il Penseroso's Platonist*: a reference to John Milton's poem, 'Il Penseroso' ('The Thinker').

Sato's . . . sword: the ceremonial Japanese sword was a gift to Yeats from Junzo Sato, an admirer of his poetry, whom he met when visiting Portland, Oregon.

354 *Primum Mobile*: First Moving: a reference to the outermost revolving sphere in medieval theories of the cosmos.

Irregular: Anti-Treaty Republican, opposed to the new Free State government.

Falstaffian man: like the robust, jocular character in Shakespeare's *Henry IV*.

national uniform: soldiers of the Free State army.

355 *stare*: a starling.

356 *Jacques Molay*: Jacques de Molay (1244–1314), Grand Master of the Order of Knights Templar, burned at the stake for heresy. Yeats associates the cry for revenge with mob rule and the perpetuation of violence.

Babylonian almanacs: books containing astrological predictions.

'The Tower', from *The Tower* (1928). The tower is Thoor Ballylee, an ancient Norman tower in Co. Galway that Yeats bought in 1917. As well as providing Yeats and his wife with a home, it also provided a wealth of symbols, being both the artist's lonely tower and a storehouse of local myths and memories. In section II of the poem, Yeats dwells on local stories of people who lived in the vicinity, including Mrs French, an eighteenth-century grandee, and Mary Hynes, a peasant girl celebrated in the poetry of Antoine Raftery.

357 *Ben Bulben's back*: Ben Bulben is a mountain in Co. Sligo, not far from where Yeats is buried.

Choose Plato and Plotinus: turn to ancient philosophy and 'abstract things' instead of poetry.

358 *the great bog of Cloone*: in Co. Galway, near Gort.

the man who made the song was blind: Antoine Raftery (see biographical entry).

Helen has all living hearts betrayed: the powerful image of Helen of Troy, from Homer's epic poem *The Iliad*.

Hanrahan: Red Hanrahan is a character who appears in stories and poems by Yeats, including 'Red Hanrahan's Song about Ireland'.

359 *the Great Memory*: the *Anima Mundi*; the collective unconscious.

360 *the people of Burke and of Grattan*: both Protestant statesmen committed to political reform in Ireland (see biographical entry for Burke and note on Grattan above, p. 476).

fabulous horn: horn of plenty: in Greek mythology, a horn forever full of fruit, possessed by Zeus.

361 *daws*: jackdaws.

'Sailing to Byzantium', from *The Tower* (1928). The poem takes the form of an imagined journey, a spiritual quest, to the holy city of Byzantium, later Constantinople, at the time of its greatest artistic splendour (*c*. AD 560).

362 *That is no country*: Ireland (and perhaps the Celtic paradise, *Tír na nÓg*, the country of the young).

363   *the gold mosaic of a wall*: Yeats had seen the mosaic procession of martyrs in the church of S. Apollinaire Nuova in Ravenna, which he visited in 1907, and knew of other examples of Byzantine art.

    perne in a gyre: spin in the spirals of time.

    set upon a golden bough: the image of a golden bird on a golden bough has been attributed to both Hans Christian Anderson's story 'The Nightingale' and Sir Walter Scott's novel *Count Robert of Paris*.

'The Circus Animals' Desertion', from *Last Poems* (1939). Yeats considered a number of titles for this late poem, including 'Tragic Toys', 'Despair', and 'On the lack of a theme'.

364   *Oisin . . . his fairy bride*: Yeats's poem *The Wanderings of Oisin* (1889) tells of how Oisin was enchanted by Niamh, one of the fairy host or Sidhe, and taken to distant realms.

    'The Countess Cathleen': in Yeats's 1899 play, the Countess sells her soul to save the people from starvation, but she is saved at the end. Maud Gonne played Countess Cathleen in the first production.

    my dear: Maud Gonne (see biographical entry).

    Cuchulain fought the ungovernable sea: Cuchulain, the legendary warrior, having unknowingly killed his own son, battles with the waves in grief and pain.

ETHNA CARBERY

Five poems from *Four Winds of Eirinn* (1902). A later edition of the book with a memoir by the poet's husband, Seumas MacManus, was published in 1918. The intense patriotism of poems like 'Rody McCorley' and 'The Passing of the Gael' is in keeping with the nationalist politics that informed her editorship of the journal *Shan Van Vocht*.

'Rody McCorley' commemorates the hanging of the young rebel, Rody McCorley, in the 1798 rising. It has become a well-known song.

367   *the banks of Bann*: the River Bann separates Co. Antrim and Co. Derry and flows through Toomebridge, Co. Antrim.

368   *sash of green*: the green sash was a popular declaration of nationalist politics in the 1790s. See the popular song, 'The Wearin' o' the Green'.

'The Passing of the Gael' became a favourite recitation piece in the early years of the twentieth century. Seán O'Casey has the hypocritical Seumas Shields recite the line 'Kathaleen Ní Houlihan, your road's a thorny way' in his 1923 play, *The Shadow of a Gunman*.

'Beannacht Leat': the title and refrain are versions of 'Beannacht libh' (a farewell greeting akin to 'Bless you'). See Miss Ivors's farewell in James Joyce's story, 'The Dead'.

LIONEL JOHNSON

'By the Statue of King Charles at Charing Cross', from *Poems* (1895). The equestrian statue of Charles I (1600–49) stands on the south side of Trafalgar Square. It was designed by Hubert Sueur and cast in 1633, but disposed of as scrap metal when the Civil War broke out. After the Restoration, it was recovered and eventually erected in 1675. It looks towards Whitehall, where Charles I was executed. Like Andrew Marvell, in his 'Horatian Ode', Johnson commemorates the King's noble death, but also recruits him as an exemplar of the ideals of art and beauty upheld by many of the poets of the 1890s.

372 *Speak after sentence?*: Charles was not allowed to speak during his trial.

'Mystic and Cavalier', from *Poems* (1895). 'The Dark Angel', from *Poems* (1895).

374 *Furies*: the avenging spirits of the underworld.

375 *Apples of ashes*: temptation that proves disappointing; very likely a reference to the biblical story of the apples of Sodom that turn to ashes when picked.

   dark Paraclete: the Paraclete is the Holy Ghost; the dark Paraclete suggests Lucifer.

'Ninety-Eight', from *Ireland, and Other Poems* (1897). Although written as early as 1893, the poem was published just one year before the centenary of the 1798 rebellion by the United Irishmen. Johnson is obviously recalling the famous ballad by John Kells Ingram, 'The Memory of the Dead' (p. 162).

'Parnell', from *Ireland, and Other Poems* (1897). First published in the journal *United Ireland*, 7 Oct. 1893, to mark the second anniversary of Parnell's death. The closing lines anticipate W. B. Yeats's 'Easter 1916': 'our part | To murmur name upon name, | As a mother names her child | When sleep at last has come'.

GEORGE RUSSELL (AE)

'Carrowmore', from *Collected Poems* (1913).

379 *colleen*: from the Irish *cailín* (girl, young woman).

EVA GORE-BOOTH

'The Little Waves of Breffny', from *The One and the Many* (1904). 'The Land to a Landlord', from *The One and the Many* (1904).

380 *merely a stranger*: 'the stranger' is often a euphemistic reference to the British or to the Anglo-Irish landowning class in Ireland. See *Cathleen ni Houlihan* (p. 426).

'Women's Rights', from *The Egyptian Pillar* (1906).

381 *Glencar* is a lake in Co. Sligo; see W. B. Yeats, 'The Stolen Child'.

JOHN MILLINGTON SYNGE

The poems included here are all from the posthumously published *Poems and Translations* (1909).

382 *Wicklow*: Synge had a deep attachment to Co. Wicklow from his child-hood onwards. Some of his walks through Wicklow in later life were recorded in a collection of his travel writing titled *In Wicklow and West Kerry* (1911).

383 *peeler*: policeman.

porter: a dark beer also known as stout.

OLIVER ST JOHN GOGARTY

'To the Liffey with the Swans', from *An Offering of Swans* (1923). Both titles refer to an event that took place during the Civil War of 1922–3. Gogarty was a Senator in the Free State and a target for dissident Republicans. He was abducted in Dublin one evening, but managed to escape by diving into the River Liffey. In gratitude, he presented the river with two swans.

384 *alban*: pure white.

that doubled Bird: Zeus in the form of a swan.

Twin Sportsmen: Love and War. From the union of Leda and the swan came two pairs of children: Pollux and Clytemnestra, and Castor and Helen (of Troy).

THOMAS MACDONAGH

'John-John', from *Songs of Myself* (1910). 'Of a Poet Patriot', from *Lyrical Poems* (1913). 'The Yellow Bittern', from *Lyrical Poems* (1913). The poem is a translation of the famous Irish poem 'An Bonnán Buí', by Cathal Buí Mac Giolla Gunna (*c.*1680–1756).

387 *Constantine's halls*: Constantine the Great, Roman emperor (*c.* AD 288–337), granted Christians freedom of worship after the Edict of Milan in 313 and embarked upon an ambitious building project, constructing new halls of worship or basilicas. He later made Byzantium (Constantinople) his capital. The island in the poem is presumably somewhere in the Mediterranean.

'The Night Hunt', from *Lyrical Poems* (1913).

JOSEPH CAMPBELL

'My Lagan Love', from *Songs of Uladh* (1904). Now a well-known song, 'My Lagan Love' was heard by Campbell in Fanad, Co. Donegal, in 1903–4, accompanied by fiddle. When he first wrote it down, it had five stanzas, but the version printed here is the most popular.

389 *leanannsidhe*: from the Irish *leanann sidhe* (fairy mistress).

390 *the cricket's singing-stone*: where the cricket or grasshopper sings (presumably the stone hearth).

spares: in renditions of the song this is usually 'stirs'.

SEUMAS O'SULLIVAN

'The Lamplighter', from *The Lamplighter and Other Poems* (1929). 'The Geese', probably written shortly before the publication of O'Sullivan's *Collected Poems* (1940), in which it appears in a section of 'later poems'.

PATRICK PEARSE

The six poems are all from *Collected Works of Padraic H. Pearse: Plays, Poems and Stories* (1917), published the year after his execution at Kilmainham Jail for his role in the Easter Rising.

'A Rann I Made': a rann is a verse or stanza. The term is also used by W. B. Yeats in his early poem 'To Ireland in the Coming Times'.

'I Am Ireland' is Pearse's own translation of an old Irish poem.

391 *Cuchulainn*: see the note for W. B. Yeats, 'The Circus Animals' Desertion'.

'On the Strand of Howth': Howth (from the Danish *hoved*, meaning 'head') is the northern end of Dublin Bay; it was once Dublin's main harbour. 'The Mother' was probably written in the autumn of 1915. 'Christmas 1915': these four lines are a characteristic embodiment of Pearse's religious and political fervour. 'The Wayfarer' is reputed to have been written by Pearse on the night before his execution (3 May 1916).

PADRAIC COLUM

'She Moved Through the Fair', from *Wild Earth and Other Poems* (1916). The poem has been so successfully adapted to the Irish folk repertoire that it is now regarded as a popular song and has been recorded numerous times (by Van Morrison, Sinead O'Connor, and others).

FRANCIS LEDWIDGE

'A Twilight in Middle March', from *Songs of The Fields* (1916). Composed 16 Mar. 1914.

396 *Delphi*: home of the Delphic oracle (source of wisdom and inspiration) in Greek mythology.

'June', from *Songs of the Fields* (1916). Probably composed in 1914.

Elmo's light: a luminous discharge caused by electricity in the atmosphere (sometimes seen around church spires and the masts of ships).

like drunken Noah: inactive and surrounded by animals.

'August', from *Songs of the Fields* (1916). Composed Aug. 1914.

'Thomas MacDonagh', from *Songs of Peace* (1917). Composed in Manchester, May 1916. See the biographical entry on Thomas MacDonagh and also the poetry and prose included in this volume. The opening line of Ledwidge's lament recalls MacDonagh's version of 'The Yellow Bittern'. This and the two poems that follow are clearly inspired by the Easter Rising of 1916.

'The Wedding Morning', from *Songs of Peace* (1917). Composed in Derry in 1916, commemorating the wedding of fellow poet Joseph Mary Plunkett and Grace Gifford in Kilmainham Jail on the eve of Plunkett's execution for his part in the Easter Rebellion.

'The Blackbirds', from *Songs of Peace* (1917). Composed in Derry in July 1916. The blackbird had been a nationalist emblem since Jacobite times. Charles Stewart Parnell was commemorated in song and verse as 'The Blackbird of Avondale'.

'The Herons', from *Songs of Peace* (1917). Composed in Derry in 1916. Ledwidge is possibly remembering Fr. Edward Smyth, one of his early supporters, who drowned in Lough Sheelin.

F. R. HIGGINS

'Father and Son' and 'To My Blackthorn Stick', from *Arable Holdings* (1923).

PATRICK KAVANAGH

All poems from *Patrick Kavanagh: Collected Poems* (London: MacGibbon and Kee, 1964). Individual dates of composition are given in the contents pages.

402 *Billy Brennan*: a likely name for a local farmer.

403 *Alexander Selkirk*: the fugitive sailor on whom Daniel Defoe based Robinson Crusoe.

JOHN HEWITT

All poems from Frank Ormsby (ed.), *Collected Poems* (1992). Individual dates of composition are given in the contents pages.

LOUIS MACNEICE

All poems from *Collected Poems 1925–1948* (1949). Individual dates of composition are given in the contents pages.

405 *basalt*: part of the geology of the north of Ireland; volcanic activity produced basalt lavas which then cooled, producing strange formations like
the Giant's Causeway.

mica: mineral deposits in granite and other rocks.

carrion water: suggesting (like 'stained water') unclean or putrid, but
water has been a source of wealth, both in the linen trade and in
shipbuilding.

banging of Orange drums: Protestant ritual commemorating the victory of
the Battle of the Boyne (1690) by King William III, Prince of Orange.

406 *the list of Christ on the cross*: the skewed alignment of the aisle is one of the
unusual features of St Nicholas's church.

the Chichesters knelt in marble: a large Elizabethan monument to the
powerful Chichester family.

407 *The troops*: a hundred men of the Yorkshire Light Infantry were deployed
in Carrickfergus at a time of increased sectarian tension accompanying
the Home Rule debate. At the outbreak of the First World War, many of
them went off to fight in France.

school in Dorset: Acreman House Preparatory School in Sherborne,
Dorset.

408 *Maud Gonne*: see biographical entry.

Casement: see biographical entry.

Orange bands: see note above.

Kathaleen ni Houlihan: see notes on James Clarence Mangan's poem of
that title above and also the play of that title by W. B. Yeats and Lady
Gregory.

409 *King William . . . To the Boyne*: King William III, Protestant victor of the
Battle of the Boyne in 1690.

Griffith, Connolly, Collins: Arthur Griffith (1871–1922), James Connolly
(1868–1916), Michael Collins (1890–1922), all prominent nationalist
leaders.

Ourselves alone: common mistranslation of *Sinn Féin* (We ourselves).

410 *Ireland, my Ireland*: an ironic echo of William Ernest Henley's patriotic
poem, 'England, My England' (1892), later retitled 'Pro Rege Nostro'
(For Our Kingdom): 'What have I done for you, | England, my
England'.

Odi atque amo: I hate and love (Catullus, *Carmina*, lxxxv).

OSCAR WILDE

From *The Importance of Being Earnest*, first performed at St James's Theatre,
London, 14 Feb. 1895, and published in 1899.

414 *The Divorce Court*: established in England in 1857.

415 *Scotland Yard*: headquarters of the London Metropolitan Police.

418 *Willis's*: popular restaurant in the 1890s, close to St James's Theatre.

419 *sent down*: asked to escort a guest to dinner.

420 *Wagnerian manner*: loud and disturbing, as some Victorians thought Wagner's operas were.

W. B. YEATS AND AUGUSTA GREGORY

Cathleen ni Houlihan was composed by Yeats and Lady Gregory between Sept. and Nov. 1901 and first produced by the Irish National Dramatic Company in Dublin on 2 Apr. 1902. Maud Gonne played the title role. Yeats explained in a letter to Lady Gregory that he had dreamed of an old woman in a long cloak: 'She was Ireland herself, that Kathleen ni Houlihan for whom so many songs have been sung and for whose sake so many have gone to their death.' The play is set in Killala, a village on the western shore of Killala Bay, Co. Mayo, at the time of the French landing in support of the 1798 rebellion. After some initial successes against British government forces, the Irish rebels and their supporters were defeated.

421 *hurling*: Gaelic sport, similar to hockey.

423 *Ballina*: town in Co. Mayo.

424 *Enniscrone*: Inishcrone, a coastal town in Co. Sligo, across the bay from Killala.

426 *Too many strangers in the house*: a covert allusion to the colonial history of Ireland and the loss of land to English and Scottish settlers.

     My four beautiful green fields: the four ancient provinces of Ireland: Ulster, Munster, Leinster, and Connaught.

     Kilglass: village close to Killala.

     yellow-haired Donough is dead: the song is based on an Irish poem that became well known at the time of the Literary Revival. It was translated by Patrick Pearse, among others.

427 *red man of the O'Donnells ... Clontarf*: Red Hugh O'Donnell (1571–1602), Gaelic chief from Donegal, who fought the English at the Battle of Kinsale; Donal O'Sullivan Beare (1560–1618), Gaelic chief from West Cork, who left Ireland for Spain in 1602 after the destruction of the family stronghold, Dunboy Castle; Brian Boru (926–1014), high king of Ireland, who helped to defeat the Danes at the Battle of Clontarf (1014), but was killed at the end of the battle.

429 *the Poor Old Woman ... Cathleen, the daughter of Houlihan*: the legendary Sean Bhean Bhoct; see the song 'The Shan Van Vocht', in which the Poor Old Woman heralds the arrival of the French in Ireland. See also the poem 'Kathaleen Ny-Houlahan' by James Clarence Mangan.

     keening: from the Irish *caoine* (funeral cry).

     the white-scarfed riders: possibly priests with white stoles.

430 *the touch*: affected by a supernatural visitation; troubled mentally; as if in a trance.

AUGUSTA GREGORY

The Rising of the Moon was first performed at the Abbey Theatre in Mar. 1907. The play is set at the time of the Fenian rising of 1867 and takes its title from a popular nationalist ballad in which the rising of the moon is equated with the political rising of Fenian rebels (see song and notes above).

433 *assize time too*: periodic legal proceedings.

437 *Granuaile*: see the version of the song reprinted in this volume.

'*Shan Bhean Bhocht*': see the version of the song printed in this volume.

'*Green on the Cape*': one of a number of songs to do with the wearing of the nationalist colour green (see the song 'The Wearin' o' the Green' in this volume).

439 *the Rising of the Moon*: see the version of the song reprinted in this volume.

J. M. SYNGE

Riders to the Sea was written in the summer of 1902, published in 1903, and first performed in Dublin (by the Irish National Theatre Society) in Feb. 1904. It is based on Synge's experiences on Inishmaan, one of the Aran Islands (see the extract from *The Aran Islands* printed in this volume).

442 *pot-oven*: the cake is traditional Irish soda bread, baked in a clay pot on the turf (peat) fire.

443 *turf-loft*: an upper room or platform for storing turf and keeping it dry.

444 *the green head*: grassy headland overlooking the sea.

the hooker's tacking from the east: small sailing boat running a course against the wind.

the pig with the black feet: perhaps an omen.

445 *the jobber*: travelling salesman or tradesman.

another cock for the kelp: kelp (seaweed) was dried in conical heaps (cocks) and used as fertilizer.

446 *destroyed*: with hunger, but the word anticipates the tragic events of the play.

447 *poteen*: illicitly distilled whiskey.

there's a black knot on it: another omen.

448 *no one to keen him but the black hags*: keen is from the Irish *caoine* (funeral cry); the black hags are cormorants flying close to the water.

450 *Bay of Gregory of the Golden Mouth*: Gregory Sound, separating Inishmore and Inishmaan.

451 *curagh*: small traditional rowing boat.

red petticoats over their heads: the women have used their petticoats as shawls, though the colour of the garments strangely reflects the torn red sail in Maurya's speech. Synge comments on the prominence of red garments in *The Aran Islands*.

452 *Samhain*: Celtic Feast of the Dead, coinciding with All Souls' Day (1 November), when the spirits of the dead were thought to move among the living.

SEÁN O'CASEY

From Act I of *Juno and the Paycock*. Seán O'Casey's play was first produced at the Abbey Theatre in 1924. Set in a Dublin tenement during the Civil War of 1922–3, when Republican opinion split over the Anglo-Irish Treaty, the play charts the fortunes and misfortunes of the Boyle family. Juno, according to her husband, 'The Captain', takes her name from a felicitous series of events: she was born in June, they met in June, and their son Johnny was born in June. However, as with other O'Casey plays, there is a comic deflation of heroic myth: for the goddess Juno in classical mythology, the peacock was a sacred bird; for the Juno of the Dublin tenements, the only 'paycock' is her strutting, idle husband.

455 *Die-hard*: a Republican 'Irregular' opposed to the Anglo-Irish Treaty of 1921 and the creation of the Irish Free State.

457 *the Free State*: the Anglo-Irish Treaty of 1921 created an Irish Free State of twenty-six counties, leaving six northern counties loyal to the Crown and so institutionalizing the partition of the island. Continuing disagreements over the government of Ireland led to the Civil War of 1922–3.

458 *snug*: a small, comfortable side-room in a public house.

459 *affeydavey*: affidavit or sworn statement (one of numerous comic malapropisms in the play).

Deirdre of the Sorras: *Deirdre of the Sorrows* (1910) was a play by J. M. Synge, based on the tragic love story of Derdriu in the Ulster cycle of tales. There were numerous accounts of Deirdre in works by Yeats and others.

466 *Chiselurs*: children.

a state o' chassis: a state of chaos (another malapropism).

468 *the bog o' Allen*: large area of turf bog to the south-west of Ireland, associated by Boyle with rural backwardness. It is also a prominent image at the end of James Joyce's story, 'The Dead'.

return room: an outbuilding or extension to the house.

The Doll's House, Ghosts, an' The Wild Duck: all naturalist plays by Henrik Ibsen (1828–1906).

469 *Virol*: a food supplement for children.

470 *the people in '47'... the Fenians*: Boyle accuses the clergy of interfering in the struggles of the people in three historical events: the Famine of 1845–8; the Home Rule campaign led by Charles Stewart Parnell in the 1880s; the political uprisings of the Fenian rebels in the late nineteenth century.

Confraternity men: the Confraternity of the Sacred Heart (a Catholic organization).

BIOGRAPHIES

William ALLINGHAM (1824–89), poet and editor, is known mainly through a small group of poems that regularly appear in anthologies of Irish verse. These include 'The Maids of Elfin-Mere', 'The Fairies', and 'The Winding Banks of Erne'. In his own day, however, Allingham was well known to poets such as Robert Browning, Dante Gabriel Rossetti, and Alfred Tennyson, and his work inspired later Irish poets, including W. B. Yeats and John Hewitt. He was born in Ballyshannon, Co. Donegal, and his first job was in the local bank, where his father was manager. In 1846, he took a post with the national excise service and spent the next twenty-four years working as a customs officer. He first visited England in 1843 and eventually settled there in 1863. He befriended the influential poet, critic, and editor, Leigh Hunt, to whom he dedicated his first book of poems in 1850. Among his later publications were *Day and Night Songs* (1854), *Fifty Modern Poems* (1865), *Songs, Ballads and Stories* (1877), *Irish Songs and Poems* (1887), and *Flower Pieces and Other Poems* (1888). His most ambitious work was the verse novel, *Laurence Bloomfield in Ireland* (1864), in which he tried to promote reform of land ownership and tenants' rights.

Samuel BECKETT (1906–89), novelist, playwright, and poet, was born in Dublin, and educated at Portora Royal School, Enniskillen, and Trinity College, Dublin. He taught French at Campbell College, Belfast, before working as a lecteur d'anglais at the École Normale Supérieure in Paris (1928–30). While in Paris, he met James Joyce, and one of his earliest published works was 'Dante . . . Bruno. Vico . . Joyce', which he contributed to a collection of essays on *Finnegans Wake* in 1929. His early poem *Whoroscope* (1930) initiated a profound interest in Descartes and in problems of self and identity. The same year, he returned to Dublin and taught French at Trinity College, but resigned the post at the end of 1931, his mental and emotional health in a state of deterioration. Between 1932 and 1937, he moved between France, Germany, England, and Ireland. During this time he worked on his collection of Dublin short stories, *More Pricks than Kicks* (1934) and the unfinished novel, *Dream of Fair to Middling Women*, which remained unpublished until 1992. Unimpressed by post-Independence Ireland (as his 1938 novel *Murphy* suggests), Beckett eventually settled in Paris. He was living in Paris at the time of the Occupation and joined the French Resistance, but later escaped to Roussilon in south-east France, where he wrote *Watt* (not published until 1953), much of it in hiding. He received the Croix de Guerre in 1945. After the war, he chose to write in French as well as English, often producing his own translations. His major work of fiction was the trilogy consisting of *Molloy* (1955), *Malone Dies* (1958), and *The Unnamable* (1959), originally written in French between 1951 and 1953. Increasingly, Beckett was to combine a harrowing exploration of the conditions of knowledge and social being with an often caustic humour. This was also evident in the plays, especially *Waiting for Godot* (1955) and *Endgame* (1956), in which the influence of popular culture, especially the slapstick routines of the music hall and the comic pathos of Charlie Chaplin and Laurel and Hardy, is clearly evident. Beckett continued to experiment with language and dramatic form, composing radio plays like *All that Fall* (1957), television plays like *Eh Joe* (1966), and a single film, simply titled *Film* (1965). He also continued to explore the possibilities of narrative in a flourish of prose works written in the 1970s and 1980s. He was awarded the Nobel Prize in 1969.

Elizabeth BOWEN (1899–1973), novelist and short story writer, was born in Dublin into an Anglo-Irish family that had settled in Cork in the seventeenth century. Her childhood years, which are vividly recounted in her memoir, *Seven Winters* (1942), were divided between Dublin and Bowen's Court, the ancestral house in Co. Cork. At the age of 7, she moved with her family to southern England, but frequently returned to Cork, especially after inheriting Bowen's Court in 1930. Her history of the house and her family, from Cromwellian times to the early twentieth century, is recorded in *Bowen's Court* (1942). In 1923, she published her first collection of short stories, *Encounters*, and married Alan Cameron. Two further collections of stories appeared in the 1920s—*Ann Lee's* (1926) and *Joining Charles* (1929)—and others were to follow in the next two decades. Her final collection of stories, *A Day in the Dark*, was published in 1965. Her first two novels were *The Hotel* (1927) and *The Last September* (1929), the latter set in Ireland in the closing months of the War of Independence. Bowen lived in London during the Second World War, working as an air-raid warden, but she also visited Ireland on numerous occasions, reporting back to the Ministry of Information. Her anxious wartime experience is captured in the short stories of *The Demon Lover* (1945) and the novel *The Heat of the Day* (1949). Among her other novels are *The House in Paris* (1935), *The Death of the Heart* (1938), and *A World of Love* (1955).

Charlotte BROOKE (*c.*1740–93) was born in Rantavan, Co. Cavan, and brought up in Co. Kildare. She was the daughter of Henry Brooke (poet, playwright, and novelist), who educated her and encouraged her to study the Irish language. She contributed translations from the Irish to *Historical Memoirs of the Irish Bards* (1786), compiled by Joseph Cooper Walker, but she is best known for the translations which appear in her *Reliques of Irish Poetry* (1789), modelled on *Reliques of Ancient English Poetry* (1765) by Bishop Thomas Percy. In the preface to the book, she pays tribute to her father, whom she cared for until his death in 1783. She edited a selection of her father's work for publication in 1792, and also produced a moral instruction book for children, *The School for Christians* (1791).

Edmund BURKE (1729–97) was born in Dublin to a father who had abandoned his Catholicism for the Established Church, and a mother who retained her Catholic faith. He was educated at the Quaker School in Ballitore, Co. Kildare, and at Trinity College, Dublin. In 1750 he began to study law in London, but he soon developed an interest in politics and a political career.

His first book, *A Vindication of Natural Society* (1756), sought to defend the established social order and expose what he saw as fraudulent reformist policies. In 1757, the year he married Jane Nugent, he published his highly influential work on aesthetics, *A Philosophical Enquiry Into the Origin of our Ideas of the Sublime and the Beautiful*. In 1758, he began to edit the *Annual Register*, a compendium of topical political, historical, and cultural issues. After briefly serving as private secretary to Lord Rockingham, the Prime Minister, he was elected as MP for Wendover. His insights as a parliamentarian are evident in his *Thoughts on the Cause of the Present Discontents* (1770), and in numerous letters, pamphlets, and speeches. In 1774, the year he became MP for Bristol, he delivered his controversial *Speech on American Taxation*, and the following year he argued once again for cautious, sympathetic policies in his *Speech on Conciliation with America*. He took a strong interest in Indian affairs, condemning the mismanagement of the East India Company and denouncing Warren Hastings, Governor-General of Bengal, for cruel and corrupt behaviour. In the wake of political events in 1789, he began writing his celebrated defence of custom and tradition in *Reflections on the Revolution in France* (1790). Afraid that revolutionary discontent would ignite Catholic grievances in Ireland, Burke supported the efforts of the Catholic Committee in Dublin in campaigning for further social and political reform. His letters to Sir Hercules Langrishe in 1792 and 1795 reveal his acute concern over the plight of Catholics and his frustration over the failure of the Protestant ascendancy to adopt a more enlightened and responsible attitude to government. Burke continues to be widely regarded as an influential exponent of conservative political thought. His views on Ireland had considerable impact on Matthew Arnold, who edited his writings and speeches on Irish affairs (1881), and also on W. B. Yeats.

Joseph CAMPBELL (1879–1944), poet and playwright, was born in Belfast and educated at St Malachy's College. He was drawn to the Ulster Literary Theatre, for which he wrote a play, *The Little Cowherd of Slaigne* (1905). He also composed lyrics for traditional tunes collected by the composer Herbert Hughes. These were published as *Songs of Uladh* (1904), with illustrations by his brother John. One of the songs, 'My Lagan Love', was to gain immense popularity. He moved to Dublin for a brief spell, then lived in London for a number of years. Several volumes of poetry appeared in quick succession, including *The Rushlight* (1906), *The Gilly of Christ* (1907), and *The Mountainy Singer* (1908). He settled in Lackendarragh, Co. Wicklow, with his wife, Agnes Maude, in 1912. That year, he composed another play, *Judgement*, which was produced at the Abbey Theatre. An organizer for the Irish Volunteers, he acted as a rescue worker during the Easter Rising. Having opposed the Anglo-Irish Treaty, he was held captive for eighteen months during the Civil War. After the Rising, he published another volume of poetry, *Earth of Cualann* (1917), illustrated with his own line drawings. After the Civil War he emigrated to the United States and founded the School of Irish Studies in New York in 1925. He also lectured in Anglo-Irish literature at Fordham University for ten years. He returned to Ireland in 1939 and resettled in Co. Wicklow.

Austin Clarke's edition of his work, *Poems of Joseph Campbell*, was published in Dublin in 1963.

Ethna CARBERY (1866–1902) was the pen-name of poet and short story writer, Anna MacManus, née Anna Isabel Johnston, who was born in Ballymena, Co. Antrim. She was a frequent contributor to nationalist papers such as *The Nation* and *United Ireland*, and with Alice Milligan she founded the journal *Shan Van Vocht* in 1896. Her patriotic poetry, published in *The Four Winds of Eirinn* (1902), included the ballad 'Rody McCorley' and 'The Passing of the Gael' (recited by Seumas Shields in Seán O'Casey's play, *The Shadow of a Gunman*). Her fiction was collected in *The Passionate Hearts* (1903), with a preface by her husband, the Donegal short story writer and playwright, Seumas MacManus. Another collection of stories, *In the Celtic Past*, appeared the following year. A memoir by Seumas MacManus appears in the revised 1918 edition of *The Four Winds of Eirinn*.

William CARLETON (1794–1869), novelist and short story writer, was the youngest of fourteen children born to an Irish-speaking family in Prillisk, Co. Tyrone. His early upbringing provided much of the detail for his later written accounts of hedge schools, weddings, wakes, and dances. In his early twenties, he left Tyrone and sought work as a teacher in various parts of Ireland before reaching Dublin. He claims in his *Traits and Stories of the Irish Peasantry* (1830) that the experience of a pilgrimage to Lough Derg destroyed his hopes of becoming a priest, but his encounter in 1828 with the Reverend Caesar Otway, a fierce anti-Catholic proselytizer, undoubtedly contributed to his turning from Catholicism and eventual acceptance of the Church of Ireland. His earliest writings, including the serialized novella, *Father Butler*, appeared in Otway's *Christian Examiner*, and Carleton began to acquire a reputation as a satirist of Catholic ritual and superstition. His first novel, *Fardorougha the Miser*, was published serially in the *Dublin University Magazine* in 1837–8. The 1840s were prolific years, with four novels appearing in 1845: *Valentine M'Clutchy*, *Art Maguire*, *Rody the Rover*, and *Para Sastha*. Three of his best-known novels were written in the aftermath of the Famine: *The Black Prophet* (1847), *The Emigrants of Ahadarra* (1848), and *The Tithe Proctor* (1849). The later writings, including *The Squanders of Castle Squander* (1852), struggle to accommodate a tension inherent in Carleton's attitude to the rural Irish poor, who are both endearingly depicted in all their quaint eccentricity and increasingly castigated for their unenlightened ways. Carleton's popularity, however, continued to flourish. *Willy Reilly and his Dear Colleen Bawn* (1855) ran to thirty editions. His *Autobiography* was never finished, but was published as *The Life of William Carleton* (ed. D. J. O'Donoghue) in 1896.

Roger CASEMENT (1864–1916) was born in Sandycove, Co. Dublin, and educated at Ballymena Academy. In 1892 he joined the British consular service in Africa. He became known as a human rights activist after he exposed the corruption and brutality of the colonial regime in the Belgian Congo. He was later appointed as consul-general in Rio de Janeiro and investigated conditions in the Peruvian rubber plantations and elsewhere. He was knighted in

1911 for his public services and retired from the colonial services the following year. He joined the Irish Volunteers in 1913, having already shown a strong commitment to nationalist politics through his involvement with the Gaelic League in Ulster as early as 1903. At the outset of the First World War, he sought German help in winning Irish independence, and travelled to Berlin in November 1914. After the dispatch of a German ship carrying arms to support the Easter Rising was intercepted in April 1916, Casement was arrested and taken to England to stand trial. He was found guilty of high treason and sentenced to be hanged. Pleas for leniency were made by George Bernard Shaw and others, but Casement was effectively discredited by the circulation of diaries revealing his homosexual relationships. The diaries, released by the British government, were thought by many to be forgeries. Casement was hanged in Pentonville Prison, London, on 3 August 1916. His remains were returned to Ireland and re-interred in Glasnevin Cemetery after a state funeral on 1 March 1965.

Padraic COLUM (1881–1972), poet, novelist, and dramatist, was born in Longford and educated at University College, Dublin. He began to write for the theatre in 1903, when *Broken Soil* (later *The Fiddler's House*) was produced by the Irish National Theatre Society, the forerunner of the Abbey Theatre, followed by *The Land* (1905) and *Thomas Muskerry* (1910). Two of his best-known lyrics, 'She Moved Through The Fair' and 'A Cradle Song', belong to these early years. His first collection of poems, *Wild Earth*, was published in 1907, and his first novel, *Castle Conquer*, in 1923. With James Stephens and Thomas MacDonagh, he founded the *Irish Review*. In 1912 he married Mary Maguire, and in 1914 they moved to America, where they both became literature teachers at Columbia University, New York. Together, they collaborated on *Our Friend James Joyce* (1958). Colum also wrote memoirs, travel books, short fiction, including stories for children, and a late novel, *The Flying Swans* (1957). He made frequent visits to Ireland from America and was President of the United Arts Club, Dublin, for many years.

James CONNOLLY (1868–1916), founder of the Irish Labour Party, was born of Irish immigrant parents in Edinburgh. He enlisted with the British army at the age of 14, and was briefly based in Dublin. He married an Irish woman, Lillie Reynolds, in 1890. Back in Edinburgh, he became involved in socialist politics and trade union organization. He returned to Dublin in 1896 as an organizer of the Dublin Socialist Club and founded the *Workers' Republic*, the first Irish socialist newspaper. He also founded the Irish Socialist Republican Party in 1898. Between 1903 and 1910 he worked in America for Daniel DeLeon's Socialist Labour Party and the Industrial Workers of the World. On his return to Dublin in 1910, he organized the Socialist Party of Ireland, and in 1911 he was appointed as Belfast agent to the Irish Transport and General Workers' Union, later succeeding James Larkin as leader of the ITGWU. In 1913 he established the Citizen Army to protect workers' rights during the Dublin lock-out strike. In 1916 he was appointed military commander of the Republican forces in Dublin. He was in command of the

General Post Office during Easter week and was badly wounded. One of the seven signatories of the Proclamation of the Irish Republic, he was shot by firing squad in Kilmainham Jail, 12 May 1916. Connolly's writings on labour issues and international socialism have been reprinted numerous times. *Labour in Irish History* (1910) was probably his most influential work, though he also wrote poetry and a play titled *Under Which Flag?*, now lost but allegedly performed at Liberty Hall in March 1916.

Thomas DAVIS (1814–45) was born in Mallow, Co. Cork, the son of a British army surgeon. He was educated at Trinity College, Dublin, and called to the bar in 1838. His 1839 address to the Trinity College Historical Society, 'The Young Irishman of the Middle Classes', instructed young educated Protestants to help in the regeneration of Ireland and was instrumental in establishing the so-called 'Young Ireland Movement'. He joined the Repeal Association and became the leader of a younger generation of Irish patriots impatient with O'Connell's constitutional methods. With Charles Gavan Duffy and John Blake Dillon, he founded *The Nation* in 1842. His writings on Irish history and culture in *The Nation* inspired his contemporaries, while his ballads, including 'A Nation Once Again', were to influence a later generation of nationalist writers, including W. B. Yeats.

Aubrey DE VERE (1814–1902), poet, was born at Curragh Chase, Co. Limerick, the son of Sir Aubrey de Vere (1788–1846). During visits to England, he made the acquaintance of William Wordsworth, Thomas Carlyle, and Alfred Tennyson. Through John Henry Newman, he came under the influence of the Tractarian Movement in Oxford. During the Famine he assisted his elder brother, Sir Stephen de Vere, in relief activities and later wrote *English Misrule and Irish Misdeeds* (1848). In 1851 he was accepted into the Catholic Church, and much of his subsequent poetry, including *May Carols or Ancilla Domini* (1857), was devoted to the Virgin Mary and the saints. In 1856, he was invited by Newman to give a series of lectures on literature at the Catholic University in Dublin, and two of these were published in his *Essays Literary and Ethical* (1889). His best-known poetic work is *Inisfail* (1861), though he also gained recognition for *The Foray of Queen Maeve* (1882), based on the heroic legends of *Táin Bó Cualinge*.

Maria EDGEWORTH (1767–1849), novelist, was born at Black Bourton, Oxfordshire, England, but in 1782 she moved to the family estate in Ireland, Edgeworthstown, Co. Longford. She assisted her father, Richard Lovell Edgeworth, in running the property and caring for her brothers and sisters. Her first publication was *Letters to Literary Ladies* (1795), closely followed by *The Parent's Assistant* (1796), a collection of stories for children. With her father, she wrote a two-volume work titled *Practical Education* (1798). Her first novel, *Castle Rackrent* (1800), was praised by Sir Walter Scott and came to be regarded as the first regional novel in English. Her second novel, *Belinda*, was published in 1801. *Essays on Irish Bulls* (written with her father) appeared in 1802, and two further works of her own, *Popular Tales* and *The Modern Griselda*, were written over the next three years. With her father, she visited

Brussels and Paris in 1802. During her travels she refused an offer of marriage from the Swedish diplomat, Chevalier Edelcrantz, for whom she wrote *Leonora* (1806). *Tales of Fashionable Life* appeared in six volumes between 1809 and 1812, and included one of her best-known works, *The Absentee* (1812). In 1813 she visited London with her father and was warmly received by admirers of her work. *Ormond* was speedily written for her father's seventy-third birthday in 1817, but she wrote relatively little after his death that year. She edited and completed his *Memoirs* in 1820. She made further visits to London and also to Abbotsford, where Scott was her host. A late novel, *Helen*, was published in 1834. Her later years were preoccupied with the management of the Edgeworthstown estate and the relief of victims of the Famine.

Robert EMMET (1778–1803) was born at St Stephen's Green, Dublin. He was a prominent member of the Historical Society at Trinity College, and a youthful member of the United Irishmen. After the United Irishmen's rebellion of 1798, a warrant was issued for his arrest, but not enforced. In France he planned another rising with his brother, Thomas Addis Emmett, hoping for French support. After returning to Dublin, he began preparations for an armed rebellion to coincide with the expected Napoleonic invasion of England in August 1803. The explosion of an arms depot led to a premature and ineffective rising on 23 May 1803. En route to Dublin Castle, Emmet's followers murdered Lord Kilwarden, the Chief Justice, and his nephew, who were travelling in a coach. Emmet went into hiding but was arrested by Major Henry Sirr, tried for treason, and found guilty. He was hanged and beheaded outside St Catherine's Church on Thomas Street, Dublin, on 20 September 1803.

Samuel FERGUSON (1810–86) was born in Belfast and educated at Belfast Academical Institution, Lincoln's Inn, London, and Trinity College, Dublin. He was called to the bar in 1838. From an early age, he showed a strong interest in literary journalism, poetry, and translation. He became a regular contributor to *Blackwood's Magazine* and the *Dublin University Magazine*, in which he published a controversial four-part review of James Hardiman's *Irish Minstrelsy* in 1834, condemning some of the translations of early Irish poems in the volume and offering his own versions, which sought to recover some of the narrative vigour and emotional power of the originals. His later work was to have a considerable impact on the Literary Revival, especially on the early writings of W. B. Yeats. Many of his best-known versions of Irish stories and legends appeared in *Lays of the Western Gael and Other Poems* (1864). Although a liberal unionist by temperament, Ferguson was a founding member of the Protestant Repeal Association in 1848 and was friends with Thomas Davis, for whom he wrote an impassioned elegy in 1845, expressing sympathy for the ideals of the Young Ireland Movement. In 1848 he married Mary Catherine Guinness, of the well-known Dublin brewing family. He continued to combine an active career in the legal profession with an enthusiastic interest in Irish archaeology and antiquities. He became QC in 1859 and Deputy Keeper of the Public Records of Ireland in 1867. He was knighted in 1878, and in 1881 was elected president of the Royal Irish Academy.

Thomas FURLONG (1794–1827) was born to a family of tenant farmers in Scarawalsh, in the township of Ballylough, between Enniscorthy and Fens in Co. Wexford. When he was 9 years old, the family moved to Clovass and his father began to expand his business interests by providing public transport to Dublin. A trip to Dublin with his father led to Furlong being apprenticed to a Dublin grocer, for whom he later wrote an elegy, 'The Burial'. The publication of the poem brought him to the attention of the famous Jameson whiskey distilling family and he was offered patronage (probably by John Jameson). Although he wrote extensively for magazines such as the *Dublin and London Magazine* and also established and edited *The New Irish Magazine and Monthly National Advocate*, only two small volumes of his poetry appeared in his lifetime. He was himself responsible for the publication of *The Misanthrope* in London in 1819. His satirical work *The Plagues of Ireland* was published in Dublin in 1824. A strong and outspoken supporter of Catholic Emancipation, he won the trust and friendship of Daniel O'Connell. Despite the support of Thomas Moore, Lady Morgan, and others, his work did not receive a great deal of acclaim. However, he was asked by James Hardiman to versify the literal translations of Irish poems that Hardiman was preparing for his two-volume *Irish Minstrelsy* (1831), and Furlong obliged with some striking and memorable versions of poems such as 'Roisin Dubh' and 'Eileen a Roon'. The first volume of *Irish Minstrelsy* contains a memoir of Furlong, who never lived to see the work in print. In addition to the translations he worked on with Hardiman, he also worked devotedly on translating the songs of the great Irish harpist, Turlogh Carolan. His long Gothic poem *The Doom of Derenzie* was published posthumously in London in 1829, the year of Catholic Emancipation. An excellent collection of Furlong's work with valuable commentary has been produced by Sean Mythen: *Thomas Furlong: The Forgotten Wexford Poet* (Co. Wexford: Clone Publications, 1998).

John GAMBLE (1770–1831), army surgeon and author, was born in Strabane, Co. Tyrone, and educated in Edinburgh. After an eye infection ended his career in the army, he began a literary career, touring Ireland for material he might use in both fictional and non-fictional works. His political sympathies were with the Protestant radical wing of the United Irishmen. His fiction includes *Sarsfield* (1814), *Howard* (1815), *Northern Irish Tales* (1818), and *Charlton* (1827). His *Sketches of History, Politics, and Manners, in Dublin, and the North of Ireland, in 1810* was published in 1812 and appeared in a new edition in 1826. Gamble claims in his preface that 'the History of Ireland is a melancholy history' and that in his book he 'endeavours to make known a very peculiar people, and a state of society, unhappily unparalleled on the civilized earth'.

Oliver St John GOGARTY (1878–1957), surgeon and writer, was born in Dublin and studied medicine at Trinity College. As a student, he showed a great flair for poetry and went to Oxford for a term in 1904, hoping to emulate Oscar Wilde's success in winning the Newdigate Prize. He was unsuccessful in his aims, but while in Oxford met R. S. Chenevix Trench, with whom he later shared the Martello tower he had rented near Dublin.

James Joyce made up the trio of intellectuals in the tower, and Gogarty, Trench, and Joyce became the models for Mulligan, Haines, and Dedalus in *Ulysses*. Gogarty married Martha Duane in 1906 and went to Vienna the following year for postgraduate research in otolaryngology. On returning to Dublin, he established a flourishing medical practice, but also pursued his interests in a literary career. He wrote a number of plays about Dublin poverty, including *Blight: The Tragedy of Dublin* (1917), which was staged at the Abbey Theatre. A supporter of the Free State, he escaped Republican kidnappers by swimming down the River Liffey. In gratitude, he presented two swans to the river, an event recounted in his first major collection of poetry, *An Offering of Swans* (1923). W. B. Yeats was to include a generous selection of Gogarty's poems in *The Oxford Book of Modern Verse* (1936). He served as a Senator from 1922 to 1926. Gogarty greatly disliked de Valera and became increasingly disillusioned with the new Ireland of the 1930s. After losing a libel action arising from the publication of his memoir, *As I was Going Down Sackville Street* (1937), he moved to London and then to America, finally abandoning his medical work. In addition to further volumes of autobiographical writings, he wrote the novels *Going Native* (1940), *Mad Grandeur* (1941), and *Mr Petunia* (1945). His *Collected Poems* appeared in 1951.

Maud GONNE (1866–1953), revolutionary and women's rights campaigner, was born in Aldershot, the daughter of a British army officer of Irish descent. She was educated by a governess in France after her mother's early death and moved to Ireland when her father was posted to Dublin in 1882. While in the south of France, recovering from a tubercular haemorrhage, she met Lucien Millevoye, who proposed that they work together for Irish freedom and the recovery of Alsace and Lorraine from German dominion. On returning to Ireland, she led protests against evictions in Donegal and helped to secure the release of Irish political prisoners. In 1890 she returned to France and resumed her friendship with Millevoye. Their daughter, Iseult, was born in 1895, but the relationship came to an end four years later. Throughout the 1890s she travelled widely in Ireland, France, and America, addressing political meetings and raising funds for nationalist causes. She met W. B. Yeats in 1889, the beginning of a passionate and impossible devotion on the part of the poet. Yeats proposed to her for the first time in 1891 and wrote *The Countess Cathleen* for her in 1892. In 1902 she played the leading role in *Cathleen ni Houlihan*. In Paris, in 1903, she married John MacBride, the former commander of the Irish Brigade in the Boer War, and their son Seán was born the following year. The marriage was not successful; she was living in France when MacBride was executed for his part in the Easter Rising in Dublin in 1916. She rejected the Anglo-Irish Treaty in 1922, and continued to work for the Republican cause, assisting prisoners and their families. In 1938 she published a memoir of her early life, *A Servant of the Queen*.

Eva GORE-BOOTH (1870–1926), poet, and sister of Countess Markiewicz, was born at Lissadell, Co. Sligo. After moving to Manchester at the age of 22, she became active in radical politics, campaigning on behalf of feminist and socialist causes. She edited *Women's Labour News* and wrote numerous essays and pamphlets on women's parliamentary representation and right to work. Her strong interest in mysticism is evident in her early books of poetry. Her collected poems were edited with a biographical introduction by Esther Roper in 1929. She wrote five verse plays, though only one was performed in her lifetime. The letters exchanged with her sister, while Constance Markiewicz was in prison, were published in 1934 with a preface by Eamon de Valera.

Augusta (Lady) GREGORY (1852–1932), dramatist, folklorist, and translator, was born in Roxburgh, Co. Galway, and privately educated. In 1880 she married Sir William Gregory of Coole Park, a former MP and Governor of Ceylon. Her husband, who was 63 years old when they married, died in 1892. Their only child, Robert, was killed in the First World War and elegized in a number of poems by W. B. Yeats, including 'An Irish Airman Foresees His Death'. Lady Gregory first met Yeats in 1894, and from 1897 onwards the poet was a frequent visitor to Coole Park, sharing her enthusiasm for Irish literature, mythology, and folklore. In 1897 she collaborated with Yeats and Edward Martyn in founding an Irish national theatre that would eventually become the Abbey Theatre, Dublin. During the 1890s and early 1900s she was intensely active in collecting local stories and translating Gaelic poems and tales. In 1901 she edited *Literary Ideals in Ireland*, a collection of essays typifying the cultural nationalism of the Literary Revival. With Yeats, she wrote *Cathleen ni Houlihan* (first performed in 1902), and in the same year she finished her translation of tales from the Ulster cycle, published as *Cuchulain of Muirthemne*. Further collections of local folklore, poetry, and myth appeared in *Poets and Dreamers* (1903), *Gods and Fighting Men* (1904), and *A Book of Saints and Wonders* (1906). The first play to be released under her own name was *Twenty Five*, which was produced by the Irish National Theatre Society in Dublin on the same night as Yeats's play *The Hour-Glass* (14 March 1903). *Spreading the News* was staged with Yeats's *On Baile's Strand* on the opening night of the Abbey Theatre (27 December 1904). She was to become a prolific playwright and energetic organizer. Among her best-known plays are *Kincora* (1905), *The White Cockade* (1905), *The Canavans* (1906), *Dervorgilla* (1907), *The Rising of the Moon* (1907), *The Deliverer* (1911), and *Grania* (1911). Her extensive field work on Irish folklore culminated in her two-volume *Visions and Beliefs in the West of Ireland* (1920). She also recorded her views of the Abbey Theatre in *Our Irish Theatre* (1913) and the history of her family home in *Coole* (1931).

John HEWITT (1907–87) was born in Belfast and educated at the Methodist College and Queen's University. He worked at the Belfast Museum and Art Gallery throughout the 1930s and 1940s, eventually leaving for a more senior appointment as Director of the Herbert Art Gallery in Coventry, where he remained for twenty years (1952–72). He was writer in residence at Queen's from 1976 to 1979. From an early age he developed a strong interest in radical politics and religious dissent, and this was later combined with a passionate commitment to Ulster regionalism and local dialect. His early poems pay tribute to James Connolly for his unswerving dedication to both Irish nationalism and international socialism, though his later work becomes more acutely concerned with the complexities of Ulster identity. Fourteen volumes of his poetry were published over the space of forty years, ranging from *Conacre* (1943) to *Freehold* (1986). His *Collected Poems* appeared posthumously in 1992. He was also a prolific critic of literature and painting, and his *Art in Ulster 1557–1957* (1977) is an illuminating guide.

Frederick Robert HIGGINS (1896–1941) was born in Foxford, Co. Mayo, but grew up in Co. Meath. At the age of 14 he began work as a clerk in a building firm, later becoming a trade union activist. In 1915 he befriended Austin Clarke, with whom he shared an interest in Gaelic civilization as well as an enthusiasm for writing poetry. His first two books of poems, *Island Blood* (1925) and *The Dark Breed* (1927), share some of the ideals of the Literary Revival, but also show his skill in metrical innovation. His later books, *Arable Holdings* (1933) and *The Gap of Brightness* (1940), are more boldly rhetorical, perhaps influenced by the later work of W. B. Yeats. He was joint editor with Yeats of a series of broadsheets published by the Cuala Press in 1935. His one-act play *A Deuce o' Jacks* was produced by the Abbey Theatre in 1935. He became a director of the Abbey and managed the company during its 1937 American tour, later becoming its business manager.

Douglas HYDE (1860–1949), cultural historian and translator, was born in Frenchpark, Co. Roscommon, where he first heard Irish and learned to speak the language. As a student at Trinity College, Dublin, he joined the Society for the Preservation of the Irish Language and also the Young Ireland Society, where he met W. B. Yeats. He began to publish poems in Irish and also became a collector of Irish books and manuscripts. He preserved and translated poems and stories that were part of the oral tradition, and contributed three folk tales to Yeats's collection of *Fairy and Folk Tales of the Irish Peasantry* (1888). His own collection of tales in *Beside the Fire* (1890) made a great impact on Irish folklore studies and demonstrated the creative potential of Hiberno-English speech. In 1891 *The Nation* began to print his series of 'The Songs of Connacht', with commentaries and translations, an initiative that was to result in the publication of his *Love Songs of Connacht* (1893). After teaching at the University of New Brunswick, Canada, for a year, he became President of the National Literary Society, and presented his inaugural address, 'On the Necessity for De-Anglicising Ireland', on 25 November 1892. He resigned the office to become President of the Gaelic League after its foundation in July 1893. He was a pioneering scholar of Irish literature, producing *The Story of Early Gaelic Literature* (1895) and *A Literary History of Ireland* (1899), and becoming first Professor of Modern Irish at University College, Dublin, in 1905. He served as an Irish Free State Senator (1925–6), and was later appointed first President of Ireland, a position he held from 1938 to 1945.

John Kells INGRAM (1823–1907) was born at the Rectory, Temple Carne, Co. Donegal, and educated at Dr Lyons's School, Newry, and Trinity College, Dublin. He became Professor of Oratory, Professor of Greek, College Librarian, and finally Vice-Provost at TCD, before retiring in 1899. He helped to found the Dublin Statistical Society in 1847. In 1873 he founded and edited *Hermathena*, a series of occasional papers on science, philosophy and literature. His *History of Political Economy* (1888) was translated into ten languages. The authorship of his famous ballad was not formally acknowledged until the publication of his *Sonnets and Other Poems* in 1900.

Lionel JOHNSON (1867–1902), poet, was born in Broadstairs, Kent, the son of an Irish army officer. He was educated at Winchester and New College, Oxford. Along with W. B. Yeats, Ernest Dowson, and others, he joined the Rhymers' Club, which met at the Old Cheshire Cheese pub on Fleet Street, London, and acquired a reputation as one of the decadent poets of the 1890s. Yeats offers a vivid portrait of Johnson in 'The Tragic Generation' (in *Autobiographies*). In 1891 he converted to Catholicism and also developed a strong interest in Irish cultural nationalism. He visited Dublin in 1893, and the following year published two books: *Poems* and *Ireland and Other Poems*. Yeats's selection of *Twenty One Poems* by Johnson was published in 1904. Johnson's austere style was greatly admired by Ezra Pound.

James JOYCE (1882–1941) was born in Rathgar, Dublin, the eldest of ten children in a middle-class Catholic family that fell from prosperity into poverty. He was educated by the Jesuits at Clongowes Wood School and Belvedere College, and then studied languages at University College, Dublin. In his student years, he published an article on Henrik Ibsen in the *Fortnightly Review* (April 1900), which came to the attention of the Norwegian dramatist. In 1902, he went to Paris with the intention of studying medicine, but his interests became increasingly preoccupied with art and literature. His mother's fatal illness in April 1903 brought him back to Dublin. In the summer of 1904 he met Nora Barnacle, who came from Galway but was then working as a chambermaid in Dublin. He persuaded her to go abroad with him, initially to Paris for a teaching post that failed to materialize. After a few months in Pola (now in Croatia), they moved to Trieste, which was to become their home until June 1915. They had two children, a son and a daughter. Despite the struggle he faced in getting his work published, Joyce persisted with his vocation as a writer. *Chamber Music*, a collection of his poems, was published in 1907, and *Dubliners* (a collection of stories he had first tried to publish in 1905) eventually appeared in 1914. His semi-autobiographical novel, *A Portrait of the Artist as a Young Man*, was published in 1916 and *Exiles*, his only play, in 1918. In July 1915, as Italy became entangled in the First World War, Joyce and his family moved to Zurich, where they stayed until 1919, briefly returning to Trieste, then settling in Paris at Ezra Pound's advice. By 1915, Joyce was already at work on *Ulysses*, which after partial publication in the *Little Review* was suppressed. The novel was eventually published in Paris on his fortieth birthday and quickly established him as one of the most inventive European modernist authors. The same year, he began work on *Finnegans Wake*, which was to occupy him for another sixteen years. It was published in 1939. During the Second World War, the family went to live in unoccupied France, eventually returning to Zurich in December 1940. Joyce died just a few weeks later, on 13 January 1941.

Patrick KAVANAGH (1904–67) was born in the parish of Inniskeen, Co. Monaghan. He assisted his father, the village shoemaker, and also helped to work his father's few acres of land. He began to 'dabble in verse' at an early age and his work came to the attention of George Russell (AE), who published three of his poems in the *Irish Statesman* in 1929–30. His first book, *Ploughman and Other Poems*, was published in London in 1936, and was followed by his autobiographical work, *The Green Fool*, in 1938. In 1939 Kavanagh moved to Dublin, hoping for regular employment, but had to scrape a living as a freelance journalist and was often penniless and in poor health. Through his acquaintance with John Betjeman, then British press attaché in Dublin, he manged to obtain some work with the BBC. Like his Dublin associates, Seán O'Faoláin and Frank O'Connor, he became a fierce critic of post-Independence Ireland. His anti-pastoral vision in *The Great Hunger* (1942) provided a critique of the idealized rural Ireland promoted by both the Literary Revival and the Free State government of Éamon de Valera. The same year, he produced his narrative poem, *Lough Derg*, though it was not published until 1971. A second collection of poems, *Soul for Sale*, was published in 1947, and an autobiographical novel, *Tarry Flynn*, appeared the following year. A new collection of poems, *Come Dance With Kitty Stobling*, was published in 1960. Kavanagh's *Collected Poems* appeared in 1964 and his *Collected Prose* in 1967. His haunting love lyric, 'Raglan Road' (sung to the air of 'The Dawning of the Day'), was written in 1946 and has been recorded many times. The definitive version was made by Luke Kelly of the Dubliners.

James Fintan LALOR (1807–49) was born in Tenakill, Co. Laois, the son of a wealthy farmer and Repeal MP. He was educated at home and at Carlow College. He was to become one of the most vociferous and radical members of the Young Ireland movement and a powerful advocate of land reform. In 1845 he founded the Tenant League with Michael Doheny and campaigned on behalf of rent refusal in Co. Tipperary. He wrote a series of letters to *The Nation*, proposing rent strikes and resistance to eviction. After the arrest of John Mitchel, the editor of the *United Irishman*, he moved to Dublin and helped to edit the *Irish Felon*, in which he openly called for armed insurrection rather than gradual measures such as the repeal of the act of union. He was arrested after the rising of July 1848. His health suffered badly during his imprisonment and he died a month after his release. His courage and conviction inspired a later generation of writers and thinkers, including James Connolly and Patrick Pearse.

Emily LAWLESS (1845–1913), novelist and poet, was born at Lyons Castle, Co. Kildare, the daughter of the 3rd Lord Cloncurry. A good part of her youth was spent with her mother's people in Co. Galway. Her first novel, *Hurrish* (1882), was admired by Gladstone for its analysis of the land question. Despite her family's history of support for the United Irishmen and Catholic Emancipation, she remained a loyalist in her politics, although sympathetically responsive to the work of the Land League at the end of the nineteenth century. Her later novels included *Grania* (1892), and *Maelcho* (1894). She also wrote a fictionalized diary, *With Essex in Ireland* (1890), and a book on

Maria Edgeworth (1904). A collection of poems, *With the Wild Geese*, appeared in 1902. On medical advice she moved to England in later life and died in Surrey.

Francis LEDWIDGE (1887–1917), poet, was born in Slane, Co. Meath, where he worked in mining and road-building before taking a job as a shop assistant in Dublin. From an early age he was interested in the activities of the Literary Revival and the Gaelic League. His first poems were published in the *Drogheda Independent*. In 1912 he made the acquaintance of Lord Dunsany, who arranged the publication of his first collection of poems, *Songs of the Field* (1916). He was an Irish Volunteers organizer and a supporter of Sinn Féin, but in October 1914 he joined the Royal Inniskilling Fusiliers (Dunsany's regiment), to fight 'neither for a principle nor a people nor a law, but for the fields along the Boyne, for the birds and the blue skies over them'. He served as a corporal, survived Gallipoli, and was killed by a shell at Ypres on 31 July 1917. He was deeply moved by the events of Easter 1916 and by the execution of his friend and fellow poet, Thomas MacDonagh. Some of his best-known poems, including his elegy for MacDonagh, were written in 1916 and published in *Songs of Peace* (1917). *Last Songs* appeared posthumously in 1918 and Dunsany edited the *Complete Poems* in 1919.

Joseph Sheridan LE FANU (1814–73), novelist, was born in Dublin. He studied classics at Trinity College and later trained as a barrister. His legal profession was soon overshadowed by his interests in literature and the press. He was proprietor and editor of several Dublin publications. From 1861 to 1869 he was editor of the *Dublin University Magazine*. He began to write fiction in the 1830s (his first published story was 'The Ghost and the Bone-Setter', 1838). His earliest novels included *The Cock and Anchor* (1845) and *The Fortunes of Colonel Torlogh O'Brien* (1847), but he became best known for *The House by the Church-yard* (1863) and *Uncle Silas* (1864), and also for the chilling collection of mystery stories, *In a Glass Darkly* (1872). He also wrote poems, including the popular ballad, 'Shamus O'Brien'.

Thomas MACDONAGH (1878–1916), poet, playwright and revolutionary, was born in Cloughjordan, Co. Tipperary, and educated at Rockwell College, Cashel. He contemplated taking orders, before abandoning ideas of a religious vocation in 1901. He taught in schools in Kilkenny and Fermoy until 1908, the year in which he met Patrick Pearse in Aran. He moved to Dublin to work with Pearse as 'his helper and his friend' at St Enda's School, becoming the first teacher on the staff. He studied part-time at University College, Dublin (1909–11), and wrote an MA thesis on Thomas Campion and the English lyric. He was subsequently appointed lecturer in English at UCD, and in the same year founded *The Irish Review* with Padraic Colum, James Stephens, and Mary Maguire. His essays on Irish writing were published posthumously in *Literature in Ireland* (1916). His books of poetry include *April and May and Other Verses* (1903), *Through the Ivory Gate* (1903), *The Golden Joy* (1906), and *Songs of Myself* (1910). He also wrote a number of plays, including *When the Dawn is Come* (1908), *Metempsychosis* (1912), and *Pagans* (1915). His passionate nationalist sentiments were evident at an early age. He joined the Gaelic League in 1902, but by 1909 became disillusioned with its activities and later joined the Irish Volunteers (1913), for which he was Director of Training. In 1915 he was co-opted on to the military council of the Irish Republican Brotherhood, and in April 1916 he was one of the signatories of the Proclamation of the Irish Republic. He took part in the Easter Rising in Dublin and was executed by firing squad on 3 May 1916. He was remembered by Yeats in 'Easter 1916' as one who 'might have won fame in the end, | So sensitive his nature seemed, | So daring and sweet his thought'.

Louis MACNEICE (1907–63), poet, playwright, and critic, was born in Belfast, son of a Church of Ireland clergyman who later became a bishop. His childhood was spent in Carrickfergus, which is vividly recalled in his poem of that title. He was educated at Sherbourne, Marlborough, and Oxford. He lectured in classics at Birmingham University from 1929 to 1936 and in Greek at Bedford College, University of London, from 1936 to 1940. His strong interest in the classics continued to pervade his poetry and was evident, too, in his acclaimed translation, *The Agamemnon of Aeschylus* (1936). In 1941 he joined the BBC as a feature writer and producer, a post he held for over twenty years. During the Second World War he served as a fire warden. His first volume of poems, *Blind Fireworks*, was published in 1929, while he was still a student. In the 1930s he was associated with a group of poets that included W. H. Auden, Stephen Spender, and Cecil Day-Lewis. His increasing rapprochement with the politically committed writing of the 1930s is evident in his *Poems* of 1935, in *The Earth Compels* (1938), and especially in his *Autumn Journal* of 1939, prompted by the Munich Crisis, the Spanish Civil War, and events in pre-war London. Towards the end of his career, he experienced a fresh burst of creative energy, evident in his last three volumes of poetry, *Visitations* (1957), *Solstices* (1961), and *The Burning Perch* (1963). He also wrote a number of radio plays, including *The Dark Tower* (1946), a critical study of the poetry of W. B. Yeats (1941), and an unfinished autobiography, *The Strings Are False* (published posthumously in 1965). He is buried in Carrowdore churchyard in Co. Down.

Francis Sylvester MAHONY (1804–66), the humorist and journalist known as 'Father Prout', was born in Cork and educated at Clongowes Wood College. He hoped to become a Jesuit and, after studying in Amiens, Paris, and Rome, he returned to Clongowes as a teacher. He was forced to resign after allegedly taking the boys on a late-night drinking spree. He left for Italy, entered the Irish College in Rome, and was ordained a priest in Lucca in 1832. He was assigned to a parish in Cork, where he assisted with relief work during a cholera epidemic, but he left for London in 1834 after a disagreement with his bishop. He became a contributor to *Fraser's Magzine*, adopting as his pseudonym the title of a real Father Prout who had died in Cork in 1830. His *Reliques of Father Prout*, a collection of his witty sketches, verses, and parodies, was published in 1837. He contributed verse to *Bentley's Miscellany*, founded by Charles Dickens, and in 1846 became Rome correspondent for the *Daily News*. In 1848 he settled in Paris, where he became correspondent for the

Globe (1858–66). He is buried in the vault of St Nicholas's church on Shandon St., Cork, beneath his own famous 'Bells of Shandon'.

James Clarence MANGAN (1803–49), poet and translator, was born in Dublin and showed an early flair and facility with European languages. His first job was as a copy clerk, but from the late 1820s he tried to establish himself as a writer with occasional employment in the Ordnance Survey Office (1833–9) and Trinity College library (1841–6). In the 1830s he was a frequent contributor to the *Comet* and the *Dublin Penny Journal*. A number of scholars, including John O'Donovan and Eugene O'Curry, provided him with literal translations of old Irish poems, which he would then re-work in an effort to preserve something of Gaelic antiquity. He wrote autobiographical sketches that bordered on the fantastic, and regularly contributed translations of modern German poetry to the *Dublin University Magazine* (these were reprinted in an anthology in 1845). He was fond of using pseudonyms such as 'Clarence' (adopted from Shakespeare's *Richard III*) and 'The Man in the Cloak'. In addition to reading contemporary German literature, Mangan also had a wide-ranging appreciation of French, Spanish, Persian, Hungarian, and Icelandic poetry. He contributed an inaugural poem to the first number of *The Nation* in 1842, and submitted some of his best-known work to the journal, including 'Dark Rosaleen'. A revolutionary fervour informs a good deal of the work he produced in the Famine years. His lurid autobiography first appeared in *The Irish Monthly* in 1882 and helped to promote the image of Mangan as an eccentric and dissolute genius. Weakened by malnutrition and alcohol abuse, he fell victim to the cholera epidemic of 1849. Both Yeats and Joyce were to acknowledge his vital contribution to Irish literary tradition.

Constance MARKIEWICZ, née Gore-Booth (1868–1927), was born at Buckingham Gate, London, and educated at the family estate at Lissadell, Co. Sligo. An aspiring artist, she studied painting at the Slade art school in London in 1893, and then in Paris from 1898 to 1900. In Paris she met Count Casimir Dunin-Markiewicz, a painter descended from a landed Polish family settled in Ukraine. They were married in London in September 1900 and had one child, Maeve Alys, who was born in Lissadell in November 1901. After brief spells in Paris and Ukraine, they settled in Dublin, and Constance was soon drawn to the work of the Gaelic League and the Abbey Theatre. Wishing to contribute to the nationalist cause, she joined Sinn Féin and Inghinidhe na hÉireann (Daughters of Ireland) in 1908, and in the following year she founded Fianna Éireann, a Republican youth organization. During the lockout of Dublin workers in 1913 she ran a soup kitchen in Liberty Hall. In the 1916 Rising she served as an officer and was based at the College of Surgeons on St Stephen's Green. Although condemned to death, she had her sentence commuted to life imprisonment. She was briefly imprisoned in Aylesbury Jail, but released under the General Amnesty of June 1917. In the general election of December 1918 she was returned for St Patrick's division of Dublin, the first woman to be elected to the British Parliament, but in accordance with Sinn Féin policy she refused to take her seat. She opposed the Anglo-Irish Treaty of 1921, and continued to hold Republican views, but joined Fianna

Fáil when it was founded by de Valera in 1926. As well as being one of the prominent figures acknowledged by W. B. Yeats in 'Easter 1916', she is also the subject of two other poems: 'On a Political Prisoner' and 'In Memory of Eva Gore-Booth and Con Markiewicz'.

Charles Robert MATURIN (1780–1824), novelist and playwright, was born in Dublin of a Huguenot family, and educated at Trinity College. He was ordained in 1803 and served as an Anglican curate at Loughrea, Co. Galway. He married Henrietta Kingsbury the following year. In 1805 he became curate of St Peter's church, Aungier Street, Dublin. His first novel, *Fatal Revenge* (1807) was based on the Gothic style of Ann Radcliffe, and was reviewed by Sir Walter Scott in the *Quarterly Review*, while *The Wild Irish Boy* (1808) and *The Milesian Chief* (1812) showed the influence of Sydney Owenson (Lady Morgan). His tragic drama, *Bertram* (1816), a success on the London stage, was followed by three other less successful plays: *Manuel, Fredolfo,* and *Osmyn the Renegade*. He is best known for his Gothic, Faustian novel, *Melmoth the Wanderer* (1820), a work greatly admired by Baudelaire and Balzac. Oscar Wilde, a distant relation of Maturin, chose the name 'Melmoth the Wanderer' on his release from Reading Gaol.

George MOORE (1852–1933), novelist and memoirist, was born into a well-established land-owning family at Moore Hall, Ballyglass, Co. Mayo. He was educated at Oscott College, Birmingham, and originally planned to become a painter. In London and Paris, he came under the influence of French naturalism and impressionism. In the early 1870s he met a number of the French painters he most admired, including Manet, Degas, Pissarro, and Renoir. His fiction was to adopt a naturalistic style in the manner of Zola, as with *A Mummer's Wife* (1885) and the better known *Esther Waters* (1894). In 1887 he published *Parnell and his Ireland*, a series of acerbic social commentaries on contemporary Irish life. In *The Confessions of a Young Man* (1888) he struck the pose of a bohemian aesthete, recalling his days in the vicinity of Montmartre. During the late 1880s and early 1890s, he was prolific in writing critical essays on art and literature, and these were gathered in *Impressions and Opinions* (1889) and *Modern Painting* (1893). His cousin Edward Martyn introduced him to W. B. Yeats in 1897 and he was briefly involved in the plans for an Irish national theatre that would eventually become the Abbey. His dealings with W. B. Yeats, Lady Gregory, Edward Martyn, and others is memorably captured in his three-part memoir, *Hail and Farewell* (1911–14). As a short story writer, he was to make a considerable impact with *The Untilled Field* in 1903. After 1911, he was based primarily in London and concentrated on the writing of historical romances such as *The Brook Kerith* (1916) and *Heloise and Abelard* (1921).

Thomas MOORE (1779–1852), poet, was born in Dublin and educated at Samuel Whyte's academy on Grafton Street and Trinity College. In 1799 he entered the Middle Temple in London, but his love of verse and music took precedence over a career in law. In 1800 he published his *Odes of Anacreon*, a series of translations from the works of the Greek poet, and his less successful

Poetical Works of the Late Thomas Little, Esq. appeared the following year. In 1803 he was appointed registrar to the Admiralty Prize Court in Bermuda, but the seclusion of the islands was not to his liking, and he returned via the United States and Canada, gathering material for his *Odes and Epistles* (1806). The following year he prepared the first instalment of his *Irish Melodies*, with music arranged by Sir John Stevenson from popular Irish tunes. The remainder of the *Irish Melodies* appeared at irregular intervals over the next twenty-seven years and earned Moore both public esteem and considerable financial income. He was offered £3,000 by Longmans to compose an oriental romance, the result of which was *Lalla Rookh* (1817). His later publications include satirical works such as *The Fudge Family in Paris* (1818) and *The Loves of the Angels* (1823). Moore had become a friend of Lord Byron in 1811 and was entrusted with the poet's memoirs, but at the behest of Byron's widow and half-sister, the papers were burned. Moore did, however, produce the two-volume *Letters and Journals of Lord Byron, with Notices of his Life* in 1830.

Lady MORGAN, née Sydney Owenson (1776–1859), was allegedly born at sea, though she claimed Dublin as her birthplace. Her father, Robert Owenson, an Irish Catholic patriot, was an unsuccessful actor-manager, with whom she toured Ireland. Her mother, Jane Hill, was an English Protestant who died at an early age. Owenson was sent to boarding school with her younger sister, Olivia. A talented musician and singer, she wrote a series of English lyrics to accompany Irish tunes, and the resulting *Twelve Original Hibernian Melodies* (1805) anticipated the similar endeavours of Thomas Moore. Two early novels, *St Clair, or the Heiress of Desmond* (1803) and *The Novice of Dominick* (1805), met with little success. *The Wild Irish Girl* (1806) was hugely popular, however, and brought her great acclaim. The Marchioness of Abercorn invited her to become her companion, and in 1812 she married Sir Charles Morgan, the family surgeon. Despite adverse criticism, she continued to attract a wide readership for her novels, including *O'Donnel* (1814), *Florence Macarthy* (1818), and *The O'Briens and the O'Flahertys* (1827). She travelled widely, writing books on French and Italian society. She also produced an essay on absentee landlordism and a collection of autobiographical sketches. In 1837 she became the first female recipient of a literary pension from the British government. She settled in London the same year.

Flann O'BRIEN was the pseudonym of Brian Ó Nualláin (1911–66), novelist and columnist, who also wrote as Myles na gCopaleen. He was born in Strabane, Co. Tyrone, but his family moved to Dublin in 1923. He was taught by the Christian Brothers, then by the Holy Ghost fathers at Blackrock College, before attending University College, Dublin. His talent for comedy found expression in student magazines, including his own publication, *Blather*, which promoted itself as a 'publication of the Gutter'. In 1935 he joined the Civil Service, eventually becoming principal officer for town planning. His first novel, *At Swim-Two-Birds* (1939), was well received, but *The Third Policeman* failed to find a publisher in 1940 and appeared posthumously in 1967. From 1940 onwards, he contributed his humorous column, 'Cruiskeen Lawn' ('Full Jug'), to the *Irish Times*, under the name of Myles na gCopaleen. The column was written in Irish at the outset, but then adopted English and gained huge popularity for its colourful mix of fantasy and satirical invective. A satirical novel in Irish, *An Béal Bocht*, made little impact when it was published in 1941, but the English version, *The Poor Mouth*, fared better in 1964. O'Brien's plays had a disappointing reception: *Faustus Kelly* ran for only two weeks at the Abbey Theatre in 1943 and *The Insect Play* for less than a week at the Gate. After leaving the Civil Service in 1953, he made a productive new start on fiction writing, producing *The Hard Life* in 1961 and *The Dalkey Archive* in 1964. An unfinished novel, *Slattery's Sago Saga*, was included in *Stories and Plays* (1974), and selections from 'Cruiskeen Lawn' were reprinted in *The Best of Myles* (1985).

Seán O'CASEY (1880–1964), playwright, was born in Dublin of working-class Protestant parents and christened John Casey. His father's death in 1886 plunged a large family into desperate poverty. He left school at 14 and worked as a labourer until 1926. He continued to educate himself and read widely, despite an eye complaint that persisted all his life. He joined the Gaelic League and the IRB, learned Irish, and was active in James Larkin's Irish Transport and General Workers' Union, becoming secretary of its political wing, the Irish Citizen Army. He took part in the lock-out strike in 1913, but left the Citizen Army the following year when it came under the revolutionary influence of James Connolly and Patrick Pearse. Encouraged by Lady Gregory, he began to submit plays to the Abbey Theatre. His first notable success was *The Shadow of a Gunman* (1923), followed by the other plays in his Dublin Trilogy: *Juno and the Paycock* (1924) and *The Plough and the Stars* (1926). His next play, *The Silver Tassie* (1928), a more experimental work dealing with the impact of the First World War, was rejected by the Abbey, and had only a lukewarm reception when it was staged in London. Disillusioned with the ethos of post-Treaty Ireland, O'Casey eventually settled in England. In 1927 he married Eileen Carey, an actress who had started her career with the D'Oyly Carte opera company. They settled in Devon in 1940. In 1939 he published *I Knock at the Door*, the first part of a six-volume autobiography. O'Casey's socialist ideals continued to inform the plays that followed, including *The Star Turns Red* (1940), *Red Roses for Me* (1942), and *The Purple Dust* (1945), but these later plays seemed to lack the vitality and vigour of the Dublin Trilogy. Among his later experimental and allegorical plays are *Cock-a-Doodle Dandy* (1949), *The Bishop's Bonfire* (1955), and *The Drums of Father Ned* (1959). His theatrical criticism is collected in two volumes: *Feathers from the Green Crow* (1956) and *Under a Coloured Cap* (1963).

Daniel O'CONNELL (1775–1847) was born at Cahirciveen, Co. Kerry, the eldest of ten children. He was brought up by his uncle Maurice at Derrynane House and was educated in France and England, before embarking on a legal career in Dublin in 1798. He quickly established himself as a brilliant advocate and outstanding orator. He protested against the Act of Union in 1800 and became increasingly involved in the struggle for Catholic Emancipation. With the foundation of the Catholic Association in 1823, he effectively became head of a nationwide movement that achieved Emancipation in 1829. He was elected MP for County Clare in 1826, being the first Catholic to stand for Parliament since the seventeenth century. He created the first Irish parliamentary party in Westminster during the 1830s and supported a wide range of reforms, including the Reform Act of 1832. After co-operating with the Whig government in the late 1830s, he founded the Repeal Association (1840) and initiated a new campaign against the Act of Union. He was persuaded to cancel one of his 'monster' meetings at Clontarf in October 1843, under threat from the Peel government. Nevertheless, he was prosecuted and tried for seditious conspiracy in May 1844. His sentence of one year's imprisonment was quashed by the House of Lords in September that year. His career was then effectively at an end: clashes with the spirited Young Ireland movement, impatient with gradual reforms, led to a split in the Repeal Association in July 1846. Before embarking on a pilgrimage to Rome at the beginning of 1847, he appealed to the House of Commons to alleviate the sufferings of a famine-stricken Ireland. He died in Genoa before he reached his destination.

Frank O'CONNOR was the pseudonym of Michael O'Donovan (1903–66), short-story writer, novelist, and translator. O'Connor was the maiden name of his mother, Minnie, affectionately recalled in his autobiography, *An Only Child* (1961). He was born in Cork and educated at St Patrick's National School, where Daniel Corkery encouraged his literary interests. He fought in the War of Independence, and took the Republican side in the Civil War, being interned in Gormanstown in 1923. His experience of the bitter struggle for independence shaped two of his earliest works: his first collection of short stories, *Guests of the Nation* (1931) and a biography of Michael Collins, *The Big Fellow* (1937). After his release, he became a librarian, moving from Wicklow to Cork to Dublin, where he made the acquaintance of George Russell and W. B. Yeats. He wrote a novel, *The Saint and Mary Kate* (1932); a volume of translations from the Irish, *The Wild Bird's Nest* (1932); and two plays for the Abbey Theatre, *In the Train* (1937) and *Moses' Rock* (1938). He was a director of the Abbey, 1935–9. In 1936 he produced another collection of short stories, *Bones of Contention*, and a collection of poems, *Three Old Brothers*. His novel *Dutch Interior* was banned in 1941, but he persisted with short story writing, despite the constraints of censorship, and later collections included *Crab Apple Jelly* (1944), *The Common Chord* (1947), and *Traveller's Samples* (1951), the latter reprinted from the *New Yorker*. His teaching in American colleges towards the end of his career led to the publication of three books of literary criticism: *The Mirror in the Roadway*, a study of the novel (1956); *The Lonely Voice*, a study of the short story (1962); and *The Backward Look*, a study of Irish literary history (1967). With David Greene, he edited *A Golden Treasury of Irish Poetry 600–1200* (1959).

Seán O'FAOLÁIN (1900–91), short story writer, novelist, and biographer, was born in Cork (christened John Whelan) and educated at the Presentation Brothers' school and University College, Cork. In his early student days, he joined the Irish Volunteers and later fought with the Republicans in the Civil War, becoming director of propaganda. He resumed his studies after the war, and took an MA in English literature at Harvard on a Commonwealth scholarship. In Boston, in 1928, he married Eileen Gould, another Cork graduate and teacher. He was teaching at St Mary's College, Strawberry Hill, Twickenham, when his first collection of short stories, *Midsummer Night Madness*, was published in 1932. He returned to Ireland soon after and produced a series of novels, including *A Nest of Simple Folk* (1934), *Bird Alone* (1936), and *Come Back to Erin* (1940). Also in the 1930s, he began the first of several biographies, including studies of Eamon de Valera, Constance Markiewicz, and Daniel O'Connell. His second volume of stories, *A Purse of Coppers*, appeared in 1937, and he was to develop the short story form with increasing assurance in subsequent collections such as *I Remember, I Remember* (1948), *The Heat of the Sun* (1966), *The Talking Trees* (1971), and *Foreign Affairs* (1976). His *Collected Stories* appeared in three volumes (1980–2). In 1940 he founded the literary journal, *The Bell*, which encouraged the work of young writers and gave a voice to liberal, progressive opinion during a sometimes stifling era of religious and cultural traditionalism. He published two travel works, *Summer in Italy* (1949) and *South to Sicily* (1953), an autobiography, *Vive Moi* (1964), and a late novel, *And Again* (1979).

Liam O'FLAHERTY (1896–1984), novelist and short story writer, was born in Gort na gCapall on Inishmore in the Aran Islands. He was educated at Oatquarter National School, Inishmore, and at Rockwell College, Co. Tipperary, encouraged by the Holy Ghost Fathers. Abandoning his vocation in 1915, he went to fight for the Irish Guards Regiment in the First World War. He was wounded in September 1917 and discharged with shellshock. He travelled aimlessly through Canada, the United States, and Latin America, finding casual work as he went. On his return to Ireland in the immediate post-Treaty years, he joined the Communist Party and in January 1922 staged an occupation of the Rotunda Rooms for several days. His first novel, *Thy Neighbour's Wife*, was published in 1923 and was quickly followed by *The Black Soul* (1924) and *The Informer* (1925), which became a powerful film in the hands of John Ford a decade later. His later novels included *The Assassin* (1928), *The House of Gold* (1929), *The Martyr* (1935), and *Skerrett* (1932). His trilogy— *Famine* (1937), *Land* (1946), and *Insurrection* (1950)—charts the rise of nationalist politics in modern Ireland. He also wrote several volumes of autobiography, including *Two Years* (1930) and *A Tourist's Guide to Ireland* (1929), an acerbic commentary on the social and political values of the time. O'Flaherty excels in his short fiction and continues to receive acclaim for the stories in volumes such as *Spring Sowing* (1924), *The Tent* (1926), and *The Mountain Tavern and Other Stories* (1929).

John O'LEARY (1830–1907) was born in Tipperary, where he inherited a small amount of property. He was educated at Erasmus Smith School and Trinity College, Dublin. He abandoned studies in law after refusing to take an oath of allegiance to the British crown, and turned instead to medicine, attending the Queen's Colleges in Cork and Galway, but failing to qualify. In 1848 he spent several weeks in Clonmel Jail after clashes with local police. He was strongly associated with the Fenian movement, although never a sworn member. In 1863, with Charles Kickham, he founded the *Irish People*, an anti-clerical nationalist newspaper, for which he was imprisoned and later exiled. On his return to Dublin in 1885, he promoted Irish culture and nationalist ideals, giving lectures and publishing his *Recollections of Fenians and Fenianism* (1896). He helped to establish the Irish National Literary Society in 1892, and the following year formed the Celtic Literary Society, a forerunner of Sinn Féin, with William Rooney, Arthur Griffith, and others. Yeats mourned the loss of all he stood for in his elegy, 'September 1913': 'Romantic Ireland's dead and gone, | It's with O'Leary in the grave'.

Earnán O'MALLEY (1898–1957) was born in Castlebar, Co. Mayo, and raised in Dublin. He was a medical student at Trinity College in 1916 and fought in the Easter Rising. He served with the IRA during the War of Independence, being highly valued for his skills in intelligence. He was arrested in December 1920 and interrogated in Dublin Castle. After his escape in February 1921, he took over the command of the newly formed Second Southern Division of the IRA in Munster. He opposed the Treaty in 1922 and took part in fierce fighting around the Four Courts in Dublin during the Civil War. During his arrest at a 'safe house' in Dublin he received multiple bullet wounds, but nevertheless took part in a Republican hunger strike during his imprisonment in Kilmainham Jail. While in prison he was elected to Dáil Éireann, but after his release he left Ireland for nearly ten years. He travelled in the United States, where he married Helen Hooker Roelofs. He later wrote articles and features for Irish and foreign journals and for broadcast on Radio Éireann and the BBC. His memoir, *On Another Man's Wound* (1936), is one of the most candid and powerful accounts of Ireland's struggle for political freedom. A sequel, *The Singing Flame*, was published posthumously in 1978. O'Malley's journalistic writings are collected in *Raids and Rallies* (1982) and his Civil War letters have been edited by Richard English and Cormac O'Malley (1991).

Seumas O'SULLIVAN was the pseudonym of the poet James Sullivan Starkey (1879–1958). He was born in Dublin and educated mainly at home. He was a pupil at Wesley College for two years and also attended the Catholic University Medical School before becoming an apprentice in his father's pharmacy. He took a strong interest in the activities of the Literary Revival, playing the Blind Man in W. B. Yeats's play, *On Baile's Strand*, on the opening night of the Abbey Theatre, 27 December 1904. The following year he published a volume of poems, *The Twilight People*, followed by *Verses Sacred and Profane* (1908), *The Earth Lover* (1909), *Requiem and Other Poems* (1917), *Personal Talk* (1936), and *Collected Poems* (1940). He was a supporter of Sinn Féin and a friend of Arthur Griffith, Oliver St John Gogarty, and James Joyce. He founded the *Dublin Magazine* (1923–58), one of the important channels of creative expression and cultural debate in the early Free State years. In 1926 he married the Dublin painter Estella Francis Solomons. His prose works include *Essays and Recollections* (1944) and *The Rose and the Bottle* (1946).

Patrick PEARSE (1879–1916) was born in Dublin at 27 Great Brunswick Street (now Pearse Street), the son of an English stonemason father and an

Irish mother. He was educated at the Christian Brothers' school in Westland Row and at the Royal University, Dublin. While at school and university, he developed a deep interest in the Irish language. He joined the Gaelic League in 1896, becoming editor of its journal, *An Claidheamh Soluis*, in 1903. His abiding belief was that educational reform was the necessary accompaniment to political self-determination. He founded St Enda's School in 1908, with the purpose of offering a progressive bilingual education, informed by a desire for 'freedom and inspiration'. In 1910 the school moved from the Dublin suburbs of Rathmines to The Hermitage, Rathfarnham. In 1913 Pearse helped to found the Irish Volunteers and was recruited into the Irish Republican Brotherhood. In 1916 he was appointed commandant-general of the Republican forces and president of the Provisional Government. The Easter Rising commenced with Pearse's reading of the Proclamation of the Irish Republic outside the General Post Office in Dublin on 24 April 1916. Five days later he agreed to an unconditional surrender. Following a court-martial, he was executed by a firing squad in Kilmainham Jail on 3 May 1916. His brother was also executed. His writings included a good number of educational and political essays, some of which were collected in *From a Hermitage* (1915). Numerous political pamphlets appeared in 1916. His play *The Singer* (1915) embodies his belief in the redemption of the nation through blood sacrifice. He wrote poems in English and Irish, and published two collections of short stories in Irish. His *Collected Works* appeared in five volumes in 1917.

Antoine RAFTERY (1779–1835) was born at Killedan, Co. Mayo, the son of a weaver from Co. Sligo. He was blinded by smallpox in childhood and he became a travelling musician and poet, spending most of his life in the Gort-Loughrea area of Co. Galway. His poems and songs are topical, dealing with such events as Daniel O'Connell's victory in the Clare election of 1828. 'Eanach Dhúin' commemorates a boating accident on Lough Corrib in September 1828. His love songs for Máire ní Eidhin (Mary Hynes) were popular many years after, as W. B. Yeats and Lady Gregory discovered when gathering stories in Co. Galway. Raftery was celebrated by the writers associated with the Literary Revival and was recalled by Yeats in his 1926 volume, *The Tower*. Douglas Hyde translated his poems and Lady Gregory wrote a play about him (*An Pósadh*), in which Hyde played Raftery in the first performance in Galway in 1902.

George RUSSELL (AE) (1867–1935) was born in Lurgan, Co. Armagh. His family moved to Dublin and he was educated at Rathmines School. From the age of 12 he studied at the Metropolitan School of Art, where he met W. B. Yeats. After working as a clerk, he joined the Irish Agricultural Organization Society. He spent much of his time encouraging agricultural co-operation in Ireland. Writing under the anonym 'AE' (from the Greek Æon), he edited the *Irish Homestead* from 1906 to 1923 and the *Irish Statesman* from 1923 to 1930. His early literary ideals overlapped with those of the Literary Revival, and he was briefly vice-president of the Irish National Theatre Society when Yeats was president. His version of *Deirdre* (1902) was performed in Dublin with Constance Markiewicz in the title role. His first book of poems was

Homeward: Songs by the Way (1894), and this was followed by *The Earth Breath and Other Poems* (1897) and *The Divine Vision and Other Poems* (1904). Two editions of his *Collected Poems* appeared in 1913 and 1926, and new books were to appear in the 1930s, including *Enchantment and Other Poems* (1930) and *The House of the Titans and Other Poems* (1934). He was deeply interested in mysticism and joined the Theosophical Society in 1886. In 1898 he founded the Hermetic Society, dedicated to pursuing the work of Madame Blavatsky and in 1918 he published *The Candle of Vision*, a collection of short essays describing his mystical experiences. In 1932 he went to live in England, settling in London and then in Bournemouth.

SOMERVILLE AND ROSS was the joint pseudonym of cousins Edith Somerville (1858–1949) and Violet Martin (1862–1915). They met for the first time at Castletownshend in 1886, and their first joint novel was *An Irish Cousin* (1889). They were to find their distinctive subject-matter in the decline of the Anglo-Irish landed gentry. By the time Violet Martin died in 1915, they had also written *Naboth's Vineyard* (1891), *The Real Charlotte* (1894), *The Silver Fox* (1898), and *Dan Russel the Fox* (1911). In 1899 they achieved widespread recognition through their stories in *Some Experiences of an Irish R.M.* (Resident Magistrate) and in two later volumes, *Further Experiences of an Irish R.M.* (1908) and *In Mr Knox's Country* (1915). They travelled together in Ireland and abroad, in Wales, France, and Denmark, recording their experiences in travel books such as *Through Connemara in a Governess Cart* (1892), *In the Vine Country* (1893), and *Beggars on Horseback* (1895). Edith Somerville continued to write and publish as Somerville and Ross and gave her account of the literary partnership in *Irish Writing* (1946). *Irish Memories* appeared in 1917, followed by other books of reminiscence, and a further five novels were published between 1919 and 1938, including *The Big House at Inver* (1925).

James STEPHENS (1880–1950) was born in Dublin. His father died and when his mother remarried he was sent to an orphanage. He ran away and eventually found work as a solicitor's clerk. In 1907 he began contributing poems, stories, and essays to Arthur Griffith's newspaper, *Sinn Féin*, and in the same year he befriended George Russell, who introduced him to W. B. Yeats and Lady Gregory. His first volume of poems was *Insurrections* (1909) and his first novel was *The Charwoman's Daughter* (1912). His next book, *The Crock of Gold* (1912), established him as a highly original and distinctive writer of fiction, by turns philosophical and fantastic. Another collection of poems, *The Hill of Vision*, also appeared in 1912, and a collection of short stories, *Here Are Ladies*, was published the following year. He went to Paris in 1912 and returned to Dublin in 1915, taking the post of registrar at the National Gallery. His experiences of the Easter Rising in 1916 are vividly recorded in *The Insurrection in Dublin*. A new collection of poems, *Green Branches*, also appeared in 1916, and a volume of poems based on Irish originals, *Reincarnations*, was published in 1918. He married Cynthia Kavanagh in 1919. In 1925 he settled in London and over the next ten years he gave lecture tours in the United States. Between 1937 and 1950 he gave numerous talks for the BBC. Three further collections of poetry appeared in the 1930s—*Theme and*

Variations (1930), *Strict Joy* (1931), and *Kings and the Moon* (1938)—and an autobiography was commissioned, though only part of it was written (it was published as 'A Rhineroceros, Some Ladies and a Horse' in 1946).

Bram [Abraham] STOKER (1847–1912) was born in Dublin and educated at Trinity College. Like his father, he became a civil servant, and his first book was *Duties of the Clerks of Petty Sessions in Ireland* (1878). As drama critic for the *Dublin Evening Mail*, he befriended the celebrated actor Henry Irving. After his marriage to Florence Balcombe, he moved to London and acted as Irving's manager. His *Personal Reminiscences of Henry Irving* appeared in 1906, a year after Irving's death. He published a collection of short stories, *Under the Sunset*, in 1882, and a novel, *The Snake's Pass*, set in Co. Mayo, in 1891. The success of *Dracula* in 1897 prompted a steady outpouring of romantic and occultist novels, including *Miss Betty* (1898), *The Mystery of the Sea* (1902), and *The Jewel of Seven Stars* (1903). His last novel was *The Lair of the White Worm* (1911).

John Millington SYNGE (1871–1909) was born into an ecclesiastical family (descendants of Bishop Edward Synge) at Newtown Little, Rathfarnham, Co. Dublin. His father died when he was only a year old, and he was greatly influenced by his fervently evangelical mother. His interest in natural history and his reading of Darwin came into sharp conflict with his mother's religious teachings. His nationalist ideals were in some ways a substitute religion: he later claimed that he gave up the kingdom of God for the kingdom of Ireland. He took a pass degree at Trinity College, but learned Irish as a student in the School of Divinity. He also studied piano, flute, and violin at the Royal Irish Academy of Music, and travelled to Germany in 1893, hoping to train as a professional musician. In 1895, however, he settled in Paris, attending lectures at the Sorbonne and deepening his knowledge of Celtic civilization. In May 1898 he visited both Inishmore and Inishmaan. He spent the next four summers (1899–1902) in the Aran Islands, gathering material that would eventually appear in *The Aran Islands* (1907). His other travel writings, written mainly for the *Manchester Guardian*, were illustrated by Jack B. Yeats, and collected as *In Wicklow and West Kerry* (1911). His growing interest in the possibilities of Hiberno-English speech as a language for modern drama, combined with stories he had heard on his travels, led to the production of two plays for the newly founded Irish National Theatre: *In the Shadow of the Glen* (1903) and *Riders to the Sea* (1904). When the Abbey Theatre opened at the end of 1904, Synge became literary adviser and later co-director with Yeats and Lady Gregory. *The Well of the Saints* (1905) was one of the first plays to be produced at the Abbey, and *The Playboy of the Western World* (1907) provoked a riot. Two of Synge's plays were not produced in his lifetime: *The Tinker's Wedding* (1909) because of its alleged anti-clericalism, and *Deirdre of the Sorrows* (1910), which was never finished. Synge's poetry was published in *Poems and Translations* (1911).

Mary TIGHE (1772–1810) was born in Dublin, the daughter of Reverend William Blachford, who died in her infancy, and Theodosia Blachford, who brought her up in the Methodist faith and provided her early education. Her mother founded the Dublin House of Refuge for Unprotected Female Servants. In 1793 she married her cousin, Henry Tighe, and moved to London. She wrote poetry in her childhood, and probably composed her Spenserian allegory, *Psyche, or the Legend of Love*, in 1795. The poem was published privately in 1805, and then commercially. A popular third edition appeared posthumously with other poems in 1811. Her sensuous imagery was sometimes compared with that of John Keats, and like Keats she suffered from consumption. Her journal entries for 1787–1802 reveal that she also suffered from acute depression and occasional suicidal tendencies. She spent her later years in Rosanna, Co. Wicklow.

Le Chevalier de la TOCNAYE (*c.*1767–?), Jacques Louis de Bougrenet, was a French royalist and military officer from an aristocratic family in Brittany. Having fled the French Revolution, he arrived in London on 29 December 1792, not knowing English. After travelling through various parts of England and Scotland, he wrote an account of his journey titled *Promenade dans la Grande Bretagne*, which was published in Edinburgh in 1797. He visited Ireland in 1796–7 and toured the country mainly on foot, seeing both city conditions (including Dublin, Cork, and Belfast) and rural environs. His *Promenade d'un Français dans l'Irlande* was published in Dublin in 1797 and reveals its author's fears of revolutionary tendencies in Ireland prior to the 1798 rebellion. John Stevenson's translation, *A Frenchman's Walk through Ireland (1796–7)*, was published in Dublin in 1914.

Theobald Wolfe TONE (1763–98) was born into a Church of Ireland family in Dublin and educated at Trinity College. He was called to the bar in 1789 and briefly practised law, but he discovered a more pressing vocation in the radical politics of the time. His *Review of the Conduct of the Administration* (1790) was followed by his *Argument on Behalf of the Catholics of Ireland* (1791), which led to his involvement as a paid agent with the Catholic Committee, pressing for political rights among Irish Catholics. Influenced by French revolutionary theory, he helped to found a Dublin branch of the Society of United Irishmen and argued for a non-sectarian Republic that would break the connection with England and 'substitute the common name of Irishman in the place of the denominations of Protestant, Catholic and Dissenter'. After his complicity in a planned French invasion of Ireland was discovered in 1795, he left for America, but received encouragement from the French minister in Philadelphia. He travelled to Paris in 1796 and assisted General Hoche in the organization of two expeditions to Ireland, neither of which was successful. The third attempt in September 1797 ended in defeat by the English navy in Lough Swilly. Tone was court-martialled in Dublin, convicted of treason, and sentenced to hang. After his request for execution by firing squad was refused, he took his own life by cutting his throat.

Oscar WILDE (1854–1900) was born in Dublin, the second son of Sir William Wilde, a renowned surgeon and antiquary, and Jane Francesca Agnes Elgee, otherwise known as the Irish nationalist poet 'Speranza'. He was educated at Portora Royal School, Enniskillen, and Trinity College, Dublin. He then studied at Magdalen College, Oxford, where he came under the influence of Walter Pater and established himself as the leading proponent of the Aesthetic Movement. In 1878 he won the coveted Newdigate Prize for his poem 'Ravenna'. His first book, simply titled *Poems*, was published in 1881. The following year he was invited to the United States and Canada, a visit timed to coincide with a tour of the Gilbert and Sullivan opera *Patience* (satirizing the Aesthetic Movement), and lectured throughout North America on the decorative arts and other topics. He married Constance Lloyd in 1884, and their two sons, Cyril and Vyvyan, were born in 1885 and 1886. Wilde made a controversial impact as a critic, with essays like 'The Decay of Lying', 'The Critic as Artist', and 'The Soul of Man Under Socialism' appearing in leading journals in the later 1880s and early 1890s. His novel *The Picture of Dorian Gray* was equally controversial when it appeared in 1891. His skills as a storyteller were evident in collections of tales such as *Lord Arthur Savile's Crime and Other Stories* (1891) and *A House of Pomegranates* (1892). Wilde's artistic reputation, however, rests heavily on his work as a dramatist, especially on the sparkling social comedies which appeared in quick succession in the closing decade of the nineteenth century: *Lady Windermere's Fan* (1892), *A Woman of No Importance* (1893), *An Ideal Husband* (1895), and *The Importance of Being Earnest* (1895). His erotic play *Salome* was refused a licence by the Lord Chamberlain in 1892, being published in French and only later in English. By this time, he had met Lord Alfred Douglas, a much younger man and an aspiring poet, who became his lover. In 1895, following an unsuccessful libel action against the Marquess of Queensbury (the father of Lord Alfred Douglas), he was sentenced to two years' imprisonment with hard labour on charges of gross indecency. The great comedian was to turn to the tragic mode in two of his most memorable and moving works, *The Ballad of Reading Gaol* (1898) and *De Profundis* (written in 1897, but published posthumously in 1905). After his release from prison in 1897, Wilde left England and travelled through France and Italy, homeless and bankrupt. He died in the Hotel d'Alsace in Paris, and is buried in Père Lachaise cemetery beneath an imposing sphinx monument by Jacob Epstein.

William Butler YEATS (1865–1939) was born at Sandymount Avenue, Dublin, the eldest child of John Butler Yeats and Susan Pollexfen. Much of his early life, until his middle teens, was spent in London, with return trips to Ireland, mainly to visit his mother's family in Co. Sligo. From 1881 to 1887, he lived in Dublin, enrolling as a student at the Metropolitan School of Art in Dublin, developing his interests in poetry, and exploring the attractions of mysticism and the occult. He helped to found the Dublin Hermetic Society in 1885 and joined the Hermetic Order of the Golden Dawn in 1890. From 1887 onwards, he worked in both London and Dublin, energetically committing himself to the ideal of a distinctive Irish literary movement. His meeting with the Fenian John O'Leary in 1885 was instrumental in turning his attention to an existing Irish tradition of poetry, songs, and stories, and in giving a strongly nationalist dimension to his early work. His involvement in nationalist politics was intensified through his meeting in 1889 with the revolutionary Maud Gonne, to whom he unsuccessfully proposed on numerous occasions throughout his life. In the same year he published *The Wanderings of Oisin and Other Poems*. Yeats saw theatre as having a powerful role to play in the emergence of a unified culture, and with Lady Gregory, Edward Martyn, and George Moore he founded the Irish National Dramatic Society out of which the Abbey Theatre was born. Maud Gonne was to play the title role in one of his earliest plays, *The Countess Cathleen*, in 1899, though the play had already been published with a selection of poems (*The Countess Kathleen and Various Legends and Lyrics*) in 1892. His influential collection of Irish folklore, *The Celtic Twilight*, was published in 1893. His later books of poems included *The Wind Among the Reeds* (1899), *Responsibilities* (1914), and *The Wild Swans at Coole* (1919). After the execution of Maud Gonne's husband, John MacBride, following the Easter Rising of 1916, Yeats once more proposed to Maud Gonne and also to her daughter Iseult, but was refused by both. In 1917 he married George Hyde-Lees, and two children (Anne and Michael) were born in 1919 and 1921. Also in 1917 he purchased the Norman tower in Ballylee, Co. Galway, which was to become their home during the difficult years of the War of Independence and the Civil War, and which provided the inspiration for some of his major poems in *The Tower* (1928) and *The Winding Stair and Other Poems* (1933). After the establishment of the Irish Free State in 1922, he became a Senator. He won the Nobel Prize for literature in 1923. Yeats remained intensely active in his later years, editing *The Oxford Book of Modern Verse* in 1936, publishing *New Poems* in 1938, and preparing his play *Purgatory* for its production at the Abbey Theatre, also in 1938. He died at Roquebrune, France, and in September 1948 was reburied in accordance with his own wishes in Drumcliff Churchyard, Co. Sligo.

PUBLISHER'S ACKNOWLEDGEMENTS

The editor and publisher gratefully acknowledge permission to reprint the following copyright material:

Samuel Beckett: extracts from *Murphy* (Routledge, 1938), copyright © 1938 by Samuel Beckett, reprinted by permission of Calder Publications Ltd. and Grove/Atlantic, Inc.

Elizabeth Bowen: extract from *The Last September* (Constable, 1929), copyright © Elizabeth Bowen 1929, reprinted by permission of Curtis Brown Group Ltd., London, on behalf of the Estate of Elizabeth Bowen.

Joseph Campbell: 'My Lagan Love' from *Songs of Uladh* (Maunsel, 1904), reprinted by permission of Simon Campbell.

Padraic Colum: 'She Moved Through the Fair' from *Wild Earth and Other Poems* (Maunsel & Co., 1916), reprinted by permission of Máire Colum O'Sullivan.

Oliver St John Gogarty: 'To the Liffey with the Swans' from *Wild Apples* (The Cuala Press, 1928), reprinted by permission of Colin Smythe Ltd. on behalf of Veronica Jane O'Mara.

Maud Gonne: 'The Famine Queen' ('La Reine de la disette') as published in *United Irishman*, 7 April 1900, first published in French in *L'Irlande Libre*, *numéro exceptionnel* (Paris, 1 April 1900), reprinted by permission of Anna McBride White.

John Hewitt: 'To a Modern Irish Poet', 'Easter Tuesday', and 'Mourne Mountains' from *The Collected Poems of John Hewitt*, edited by Frank Ormsby (Blackstaff Press, 1991), reprinted by permission of the publisher.

F. R. Higgins: 'Father and Son' and 'To My Blackthorn Stick' from *Arable Holdings: Poems* (Cuala Press, 1933); copyright holder not traced.

Douglas Hyde: 'My Grief on the Sea' from *Love Songs of Connaught* (Gill, 1893), reprinted by permission of Douglas Sealy.

James Joyce: Episode 1 from *Ulysses* and 'A Painful Case' from *Dubliners*, copyright © the Estate of James Joyce, reprinted by permission of the Estate.

Patrick Kavanagh: 'To A Blackbird', 'Inniskeen Road: July Evening', and 'Shancoduff' from *Collected Poems* (McGibbon and Kee, 1964), reprinted by permission of the Trustees of the Estate of the late Katherine B. Kavanagh, through the Jonathan Williams Literary Agency.

Louis MacNeice: 'Belfast', 'Snow', 'Carrickfergus', and 'Autumn Journal XVI' from *Collected Poems* (Faber & Faber, 1949), reprinted by permission of David Higham Associates Ltd.

George Moore: extract from *Hail and Farewell* (Wm. Heinemann, 1911–14), reprinted by permission of Colin Smythe Ltd. on behalf of the literary heirs of Charles Douglas Medley.

Flann O'Brien: extract from *At Swim-Two-Birds* (Longmans & Co., 1939), copyright © The Estate of the late Brian O'Nolan, reprinted by permission of A. M. Heath & Company Ltd., on behalf of the Estate.

Seán O'Casey: extract from *Juno and the Paycock* (1924) in *Two Plays by Sean O'Casey* (Macmillan, 1927), reprinted by permission of Macnaughton Lord 2000 Ltd., representatives of the Estate of Seán O'Casey.

Frank O'Connor: 'The Majesty of the Law' from *Bones of Contention and Other Stories* (Macmillan, 1936), copyright © Frank O'Connor 1936, reprinted by permission of PFD on behalf of the author.

Seán O'Faoláin: 'Lilliput' from *Midsummer Night Madness and Other Stories* (Jonathan Cape, 1932), copyright © Seán O'Faoláin 1932, reprinted by permission of Rogers, Coleridge & White Ltd., 20 Powis Mews, London WII IJN.

Liam O'Flaherty: 'The Mountain Tavern' from *The Mountain Tavern and Other Stories* (Jonathan Cape, 1929), copyright © Liam O'Flaherty 1929, reprinted by permission of PFD on behalf of the author.

Earnán O'Malley: extract from *On Another Man's Wound* (London and Dublin, 1936, Anvil Books, 1979), reprinted by permission of Anvil Books Ltd.

Seumas O'Sullivan: 'The Lamplighter' and 'The Geese' from *Seumas O'Sullivan: Collected Poems* (The Orwell Press, 1940), reprinted by permission of Frances Sommerville.

George Russell (AE): 'Carrowmore' from *Collected Poems* (Macmillan, 1913), reprinted by permission of Colin Smythe Ltd. on behalf of Estate of Diarmuid Russell.

Somerville and Ross: extract from *The Real Charlotte* (Ward & Downey, 1894), copyright © Somerville & Ross 1894, reprinted by permission of Curtis Brown Group Ltd., London, on behalf of the Estate of Somerville & Ross.

James Stephens: extract from *The Insurrection in Dublin* (Maunsel & Co., 1916), reprinted by permission of the Society of Authors as the Literary Representative of the Estate of James Stephens.

W. B. Yeats: 'The Lake Isle of Innisfree', 'To Ireland in the Coming Times', 'The Song of Wandering Aengus', 'September 1913', 'To a Shade', 'The Wild Swans at Coole', 'Easter 1916', copyright © 1924 by the Macmillan Company; copyright © renewed 1952 by Bertha Georgie Yeats; 'Sailing to Byzantium', 'The Tower', 'Meditations in Time of Civil War', copyright © 1928 by the Macmillan Company, copyright © renewed 1956 by Georgie Yeats; 'The Circus Animals' Desertion', copyright © 1940 by Georgie Yeats, copyright © renewed 1968 by Bertha Georgie Yeats, Michael Butler Yeats, and Anne Yeats; all poems reprinted from *The Collected Works of W. B. Yeats*, volume 1: *The Poems*, revised, edited by Richard J. Finneran (Scribner, 1997) by permission of Scribner, an imprint of Simon & Schuster Adult Publishing Group, and from *W. B. Yeats* edited by Edward

Larrissy (OUP, 1997), by permission of A. P. Watt Ltd. on behalf of Michael B. Yeats.

W. B. Yeats and Augusta Gregory: *Cathleen ni Houlihan*, reprinted by permission of A. P. Watt Ltd. on behalf of Michael B. Yeats.

INDEX OF NAMES

Page numbers of works by Irish writers included in the anthology are given in bold.

American Literature

British and Irish Literature

Children's Literature

Classics and Ancient Literature

Colonial Literature

Eastern Literature

European Literature

Gothic Literature

History

Medieval Literature

Oxford English Drama

Poetry

Philosophy

Politics

Religion

The Oxford Shakespeare

A complete list of Oxford World's Classics, including Authors in Context, Oxford English Drama, and the Oxford Shakespeare, is available in the UK from the Marketing Services Department, Oxford University Press, Great Clarendon Street, Oxford OX2 6DP, or visit the website at www.oup.com/uk/worldsclassics.

In the USA, visit www.oup.com/us/owc for a complete title list.

Oxford World's Classics are available from all good bookshops. In case of difficulty, customers in the UK should contact Oxford University Press Bookshop, 116 High Street, Oxford OX1 4BR.

	Six French Poets of the Nineteenth Century
HONORÉ DE BALZAC	**Cousin Bette** **Eugénie Grandet** **Père Goriot**
CHARLES BAUDELAIRE	**The Flowers of Evil** **The Prose Poems** and **Fanfarlo**
BENJAMIN CONSTANT	**Adolphe**
DENIS DIDEROT	**Jacques the Fatalist** **The Nun**
ALEXANDRE DUMAS (PÈRE)	**The Black Tulip** **The Count of Monte Cristo** **Louise de la Vallière** **The Man in the Iron Mask** **La Reine Margot** **The Three Musketeers** **Twenty Years After** **The Vicomte de Bragelonne**
ALEXANDRE DUMAS (FILS)	**La Dame aux Camélias**
GUSTAVE FLAUBERT	**Madame Bovary** **A Sentimental Education** **Three Tales**
VICTOR HUGO	**The Essential Victor Hugo** **Notre-Dame de Paris**
J.-K. HUYSMANS	**Against Nature**
PIERRE CHODERLOS DE LACLOS	**Les Liaisons dangereuses**
MME DE LAFAYETTE	**The Princesse de Clèves**
GUILLAUME DU LORRIS and JEAN DE MEUN	**The Romance of the Rose**

ÉMILE ZOLA

L'Assommoir
The Attack on the Mill
La Bête humaine
La Débâcle
Germinal
The Kill
The Ladies' Paradise
The Masterpiece
Nana
Pot Luck
Thérèse Raquin